BESHADOWED

SELINA A. FENECH

COMPLETE

SERIES OMNIBUS

Published by Fairies and Fantasy Pty Ltd 2022
ISBN: 978-1-922390-54-7 (paperback)
ISBN: 978-1-922390-55-4 (hardcover)

BESHADOWED

SELINA A. FENECH

COMPLETE

SERIES OMNIBUS

1

BESHADOWED

DARKNESS UNKNOWN

1

The white noise hum of anxiety grew in Everly as the man on the phone said, "I regret to inform you that your mother has passed away."

She'd missed his name. He'd introduced himself over the patchy line as the administrator of Janey Boderleth's estate and her brain jolted like touching a hot wire, blanking out the next part.

She fumbled with wet hands to get a better grip on her phone, turning away from the leaky pipe she was unscrewing. Her heart raced. The wrench in her hands dropped, clattering on the concrete floor.

The echoing clang made Harper squeak from across the basement. "Are you trying to scare a girl to death?"

Everly mouthed an apology and bent to retrieve the tool.

Am I going to have to pay for the funeral?

Maybe that shouldn't have been her first reaction to the news of her mother's death, but she couldn't handle any more expenses right now. She was already drowning. Horror struck at the thought her mother may have left her debts.

That's what she wanted to ask, but when she opened her mouth it formed the word, "How?"

The sound of papers shuffling came over the staticky line. "She was found in an alley behind the main street, but no foul play is suspected. All signs indicate it was due to substance abuse. Janey Boderleth had a number of legal and illegal drugs in her system."

No surprises there. And considering Shroudhaven's high unexplained death count, at least her mother kept things simple.

The man breathed heavily over the line. "Ms. Boderleth? Are you still there? I understand this must be very upsetting. I can call back later to discuss the details if you'd like."

"No, it's fine. I'm here." Everly's fingers trembled—a warning sign. She ran through a grounding exercise to make sure her over-enthusiastic adrenal system didn't get set off by the news.

Five things she could see: the bare red-brick walls of the basement, the water-stained

concrete floor, her pale, distorted reflection in the chrome of her wrench, the harsh glow of Harper's LED ring light, and her friend, setting up another shot across the room.

"We haven't been able to find any record of a will. It seems your mother never made one."

Lucky, or I'm sure I would have been written out of it.

Four things she could touch: the cold metal pipe, the water wetting her hands, the callous on her finger where the wrench rubbed, and the worn fabric of her red jacket's cuffs.

"And it seems as though you are the only surviving next of kin."

Acutely aware, thanks.

Three things she could hear: the man's sandpaper breaths through her phone, the hum of the water heater, and the click of Harper's camera.

"Making you sole inheritor. Although ... there are no savings."

Shocker.

Two things she could smell: ancient deposits of oil and grime, Harper's vanilla perfume.

"There are also no debts."

Everly released a long sigh of relief and completed the grounding exercise.

One thing she could taste: the blood of her bitten lip.

A bitter pain burned Everly's throat, and her voice came out child-like. "She's really dead?"

"I'm sorry, *what? Dead*?" Harper froze mid pose change.

Her lacy pink dressing gown was hanging off her shoulders and she flicked it back up, but it did little to cover the rose-gold corset and hotpants beneath that contrasted against her pained expression.

She rushed over on tappy stilettos. Her ankle turned on the broken concrete floor, and she tumbled.

Everly thrust her arms out, catching her. "Careful."

"Sorry. Thank you. *Who's dead?*"

Everly let go of her friend then lifted the wrench and one finger to shush her. Harper's lips pressed into a thin line and she stilled, waiting, as the administrator rattled off a bunch of legal terms.

He ended with, "The only asset to be dispensed with is the house."

Air rushed out of Everly's lungs. The house.

A surge of old memories from that place and her life there made Everly's heart rattle against her ribs. She thought she'd left it all behind.

Everly leaned against the wall as a wave of wooziness hit her. "Actually, I will call you back later if that's okay? I'm in the middle of something."

The moment the phone was tucked away in Everly's pocket, Harper raised the shutter remote in her hand and thrust it at Everly as though they were dueling. "Did someone *die*?"

"Yeah. My mom."

"Oh no. Oh Ev, I'm so sorry!" Harper pulled Everly into an embrace of flawless brown skin and silky black curls.

"It's okay, really."

There was pain. Everly could identify it, sitting heavy behind her eyes and beneath the curves of her chest. But it was an old pain, a familiar pain. It had been with her since the end of her and her mother's toxic relationship when she'd been kicked out of home four years ago.

She had mourned the loss of her mother since the day she left home, despite the damage the woman had done to Everly. Damage she was still working through.

"How can it be okay? I know you two had problems—"

"Understatement of the century."

"And they were *her* problems, not yours. I'm sorry. But still, your mother!" Harper brushed loose strands of Everly's silver hair away from her face and rubbed a thumb across her cheek as though wiping a tear that wasn't there.

"Honestly, I've been expecting that call forever. I'm surprised she lasted this long, considering her lifestyle."

It was a small mercy that she hadn't died in the house. That place was haunted enough already.

"She was still young, though, wasn't she?" Harper pouted, as though the greater tragedy was the lost potential of a late-in-life mother-daughter reconciliation.

Everly held onto no such hopes. "Early forties. Although the life expectancy in Shroudhaven isn't great even for the healthiest townsfolk."

"Sounds like a charming place."

"The charmingest. Gloomy weather, overabundance of deadly mishaps, conspiracy theorists aplenty ... It's a wonder I left."

Everly tried to turn back to the leaking pipe and continue her work, but Harper snatched the wrench from her hand and dropped it roughly into the canvas bag at their feet. Everly winced at the mistreatment of her beloved tools.

Taking both of Everly's hands into hers, Harper said, "What about your dragon? How is it taking the news? Not going to overreact?"

"My anxiety is fine. A little tiffed about having to speak on the phone with a stranger, but no panic attack looming." Everly gave Harper a grateful smile for the check-in.

They'd been roommates long enough now that Harper was used to Everly's anxiety and her codeword for it. The nasty dragon that plagued her emotions and flared up

when she least needed it.

"Come on. No more work for the day. Let's go treat ourselves." Harper dropped Everly's hands and started packing up her camera, tripod, and light stands.

"I have to get this finished. It's still leaking, and it's only going to get worse if I don't fix it." Everly picked up some plumber's tape and her wrench again and worked on the connection.

"These old pipes are always leaking! You're always down here patching them up."

"Kinda my job?" Everly tilted her head to the building superintendent badge clipped over her bomber jacket.

A job I can't risk losing. Not many bosses would overlook my complete lack of qualifications and fake ID. No matter how big of a sleaze-ball the landlord is, and the pocket change he pays.

Harper unclicked a lens from her camera that probably cost a year of Everly's wage. "Let it be someone else's problem. We'll be out of here soon anyway, right?"

"Sure. Soon" Not really a lie.

Everly wanted to get her and Harper out of that building ASAP too.

She knew it could be a matter of life or death. But that didn't help her to have the funds she needed to move. She didn't want Harper, everything-together-Harper, to know, to pity her, to offer to pay her share.

She'd been trying to save but her balance only kept going down. But maybe, maybe her new inheritance could change that. The house could change that. Her thoughts jangled between anxiety and hope and re-awakened trauma as she continued to work on the pipes.

Harper put her hands on her hips. "The landlord should just replace this old water system with something new and be done with it."

"We don't need a replacement. Sometimes broken things just need a little bit of care ..." Everly wiped her work clean and turned the water back on. No leaks. "And ta-da, all fixed."

"Only because you have the magic touch." Harper made kissy lips at Everly.

When it comes to objects, at least.

People? That was something Everly struggled with.

Everly zipped up her tool bag and hefted it up onto her shoulder.

Harper threw on a substantially less see-through robe for the trip back upstairs. "Thanks for letting me tag along and get some good use out of the grungy backdrop. The photos I was getting are fire."

Clicking off her LED, she juggled the mess of tripods and stands in her arms.

"Can I help carry your gear?" Everly asked.

"All good, I'm sure these don't weigh half what you're lugging around."

"Just what kind of baggage are we talking about here?" Everly tried to throw the

words out like a joke, but they made Harper give her puppy dog eyes that would put a Basset Hound to shame.

"Whatever you need today, you've got it, okay? I know, I know! You're fine! But you just lost your mom and regardless of your relationship and history, that's huge. It can't be easy having lost both parents."

Everly tried to ignore the tight knot of pain in her sternum as she locked the basement door behind them and they made their way up the dingy stairwell to the lobby.

"I'm not saying it's easy. I'm just saying I did all my boohooing about it years ago. I was barely a toddler when Dad passed, and really, I lost Mom as well at the same time."

Everly didn't know if they'd ever been a happy family. She'd been too young at the point it all fell apart. But there was a time when it had been the three of them, without her mother's substance abuse, hoarding, and addiction to never-ending streams of toxic lovers.

That had all started when Janey Boderleth's husband died, leaving her a young widow and mother to a child she was convinced was the source of all her hardship.

"I am going to hug you *so hard* again once I put down all this junk!" Harper rattled the tripods in her arms.

The lobby was brightly lit with a stream of afternoon sunlight and Everly's work boots squeaked on the tiles. She pushed the elevator button for the top floor—Harper's apartment—so she could drop off her camera gear and get changed.

Despite them living together, they still kept two apartments. There wasn't enough storage in Everly's smaller rooms for them both, and no way enough room for Harper's wardrobe.

But they both slept at Everly's, for safety.

The elevator dinged and the doors opened to reveal a man inside.

The cheerful gym-bro from floor three. Harper tensed and stepped back. Everly moved closer, standing in front of her friend as she offered the man a polite smile. He seemed to look right through her, giving Harper a long look as he walked away.

Everly was used to it. Silver-haired and plus-sized, she was practically invisible when she was beside the immaculate Harper Bells, or 'Bellsy' to her millions of social media fans. It was hard not to be in awe of someone who looked like they had a beauty filter running on them in real life.

But the kind of attention Harper had attracted recently was nothing to be envied.

A little positive attention in my direction would be appreciated though. Everly was ready for a relationship. Anything to help her get over her unrequited feelings for someone she could never have.

Harper's face scrunched as she stomped into the elevator. "I hate this. I hate jumping at every shadow. We have to get out of here."

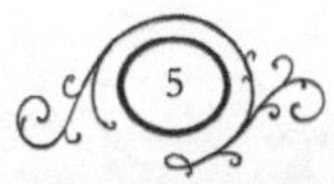

Seeing her friend feeling so powerless and being unable to help hurt Everly more than the news of her mother's death. "I'm sorry."

The elevator rattled closed and lifted them to their destination.

"Babe, it's not your fault! Sorry, I'm just venting. I'm not making today about me." Shaking off her frown, Harper's expression returned to one of picture-perfect sympathy. "What needs to be done about your mother? You know, legally?"

Sighing, Everly picked up the end of her long braid and flicked the nearly white hair between her fingers. She wished she could regulate her own emotions so well.

"I'm guessing there will have to be some kind of funeral. And apparently, I now own a house."

A toothy grin split through Harper's sympathy. "Wait, wait, wait. There's a house? Like, are we talking cute little cottage or spooky huge mansion?"

"A bit of both, with a built-in antiques store. It, plus its many riches of whatever my hoarder mother trashed the place with, are all mine. I'll call the administrator back for the details in a minute. I'm sure there's a bunch of paperwork to do to make it all official."

The elevator came to a stop and Everly noticed thinly concealed hesitation and fear on Harper's face as she stepped out.

She glanced up and down the hall twice before unlocking her door. "That's kind of exciting, right? You own a whole, real house! It could be a holiday home!"

"It wasn't in a good state when I still lived there and tried to keep it all together. Who knows how bad it is now. Maybe I can pay someone to burn it down and sell the razed earth."

If only I had enough savings to hire an arsonist.

Everly put her tool bag down and remained near the front door, careful not to touch anything. The living room of Harper's apartment was too white for Everly to move around in comfortably, especially after working. Visions of grease stains on snowy suede made her shudder.

A sickening feeling swelled inside her. Her hands tingled and her pulse thrummed in her ears. Suddenly unsteady, she leaned on the wall and hoped she wasn't smudging dirt on it. Everly counted out her breaths, trying to stay grounded.

Harper disappeared into what was once her bedroom and now all wardrobe storage. "You have to at least go back and visit first."

"Do I though?" *In for seven, hold for four, out for seven.*

Harper called back through the opened door, "For closure. And a trip back home could be good in other ways too. You might run into that boy you've been crushing over your whole life. Things might happen! I'm all for things happening for you!"

Rylan. Everly winced as she fought to force down her panic. "Even if I went back—"

"Which you are!"

"Which I'm not, I can tell you for a fact that nothing romantic is going to happen between me and Rylan. And also, he's not a boy, he's a man. At least he would be by now."

Harper gasped melodramatically. "Look at you defending his honor."

"I'm just being factual about the flow of time and aging." Everly's cheeks heated, and her heartbeat reached an overwhelming pace.

Just breathe, breathe.

Her vision darkened and blurred. She slumped against the wall and fell.

2

Everly swore as she landed on the ground. Her whole body shook with her rampant pulse. She focused on pulling herself back together, keeping her dragon contained.

Fluttering back out into the room in a new outfit of lace T-shirt and hot-pink overalls, Harper caught sight of Everly and rushed over to kneel beside her.

She pulled Everly up in a tight hug. "Panic attack?"

"Yeah. It caught up to me after all."

"I'm sorry if this is because I brought up Rylan, on top of everything. It's just that I know you still care about him, boy or not."

Pressed in her friend's embrace, the tangle of pain in Everly's chest seemed to release, spreading out through her body, heating her eyes. She blinked back tears.

Home. Her parents. Shroudhaven. Rylan. Every pain, everything there she'd left behind seemed to come crashing down onto her like an avalanche of emotional bricks.

But what could she do? The past was the tremendously screwed-up past, and Everly wasn't equipped to revisit it.

"Maybe I do care. But it doesn't matter. I get to see him all the time in my dreams, and the real Rylan has made it clear he never wants to see me again."

"Then you're better off without him. We're both better off without men and what they've put us through." Harper squeezed just a little harder.

Everly's broken heart was nothing compared to what Harper's ex had done. The danger he'd caused. The reason they had to move.

Everly needed money. And to get it, she was going to have to go back home.

Before Everly knew it, she was back in Shroudhaven. She didn't even know how she got there, out on the familiar main street in the gusting wind, staring at Pimey's Diner with its faded red-and-white awnings and candy-cane

façade, watching through the window as a monster perched on the counter like a grotesque table ornament.

"Oh, of course." Everly pressed her hands to the glass, and it rippled beneath her fingers. "This is a dream."

Those words grounded her, making her consciousness fully present.

As haunted by nightmares as Everly was, she'd done a lot of work toward controlling her sleeping mind. Lucid dreaming was the goal she and her therapist spent many sessions working toward, and once she'd cracked it, Everly considered it her small superpower.

She worked to get her bearings and decide whether this was a dream she was willing to partake in or not.

The setting didn't worry her. She was often reeled back to Shroudhaven in her dreamscapes. The next thing she checked for were threats, what challenge her mind would throw at her.

Inside the diner, a few patrons sat in booths, chewing slowly over burgers and fries too yellow to be real. Waitresses in frilly retro aprons slid up and down the room on unmoving feet, too many plates balanced in each hand.

And amid it all, the monster shifted and shivered. It was huge, almost the entire length of the vintage counter that spanned one half of the diner, across from the cozy booths down the other side.

Nobody else appeared to notice it.

Everly squinted at the creature, unafraid. It was a mess of darkness and bad feelings with no real discernable features. Her dreaming brain was really skimping on the detail tonight. All it did was label the void-like blob a *monster* and so Everly knew it was.

The way it was slowly and methodically consuming the body of a waitress was another indicator.

"Well, that's gross." Everly winced away from the view, turning to look for Rylan.

He should be showing up soon.

He always did.

A sparkling brightness caught Everly's eye as her dragon flew past, turning laps in the street behind her. Much like the monster, it was as much feeling as it was form. A creature of light and hunger that shook up Everly's insides just by setting her eyes upon it. A visible manifestation of her anxiety.

She turned her back on it. It was better to ignore the thing.

Down the cobblestone pavement, another group of monsters approached. These four were more clearly drawn than the gurgling shadow in the diner.

They moved together with purpose—humanoid, pale-skinned, with midnight eyes and fangs bared. Vampiric.

"Yawn. Can't we do something a bit fresher?" Everly called out, as though there

was anyone else in control of the reoccurring situation than herself.

Not that it was terrible seeing Rylan being all tough and vampy. As one of the four striding down the street toward her, he took the lead ahead of his three other vampire followers, face stern and wide shoulders set.

They all wore black soldierlike pants and tank tops, except for the other man in the group who wore a cardigan.

The moon bobbed full and bright behind Rylan in the starry sky, glittering over his short-cropped hair and bare arms, outlining the muscles there.

He was *bigger* than she ever remembered him being, the cords and curves of his arms and chest wrought vividly on marble-toned flesh.

Everly sighed. It was undeniably hot.

This is some cruel and unusual torture. Seeing him like this, every night, out of reach even in her dreams.

The group of four vampires—Rylan, the cardigan guy, a pointy-faced woman with a sharp blond bob, and a redheaded teen with freckles like a galaxy set bright against her deathly pallor—arrived beside Everly.

"Hey, how's it been?" she asked, expecting no reply. Dream Rylan was as unresponsive as real-life Rylan. "Busy? Yeah, me too. Have lots going on. Exciting stuff too."

Everly wasn't quite sure why she felt the need to lie to this figment of her imagination. Especially when he rarely acknowledged her presence anyway. But whenever she saw him, walls went up.

He stared through the diner window toward the monster inside, speaking in tongues to the others, a stream of fragmented English and indecipherable syllables.

When Everly focused very hard, she could hear comprehensible speech, but it was like trying to read in dreams. None of it made sense even when the words came through with clarity.

"Be careful of all the mouths."

"It's not close to fully beshadowed."

"The vasmire mist has the blivs out."

So much confusing nonsense.

Because this was just a dream. And none of it mattered. Except for how it made Everly feel. And it made her feel a lot.

Especially after the day she'd had, getting the news of her mother's death and working through what that meant for her. Regardless of how she felt about her mother as a person, her death made Everly butt up against deeper questions of mortality and existence. Which made an impetuous audacity flare within her.

She took a deep breath and stood in front of Rylan and said with her full chest, "My mother died. And I miss you. A lot."

Hovering in the sky above her, her dragon shivered, scales scintillating like a tide of stars.

Rylan's brow dropped low over his eyes that didn't look at her but over her head. He placed one hand at his sternum as though easing a pain there and then lifted it again, pointing with two fingers toward the waitress-eating beast.

Everly reached out but didn't touch Rylan. She knew he would feel solid, as solid as anything else in the ever-shifting fluidity of her dream, but it seemed wrong to put her hands on him when he was ignoring her so fully.

"Do you ever think about me? Did I ever matter to you?"

Rylan laughed and cuffed the pretty-freckled vamp on the shoulder like one of the boys. He once used to do that to Everly.

Everly blinked slow, wet eyes, and when she opened them, the four vampires were gone from the street. They were inside the diner now, circling the shadowy monster within. The creature had expanded to fill the space and lashed Rylan's group with tentacles made of darkness.

A mist swirled down the counter and crept across the floor, as though pouring out of the monster itself. Fry cooks worked the grills with blank faces as they overlooked the battle.

"Okay, we're doing this. Fine." Everly stepped up to the diner window and then stepped right through it, taking a seat in a red-and-white vinyl booth.

The squeaky bench seemed both infinitely long and too cramped, and Everly had to keep readjusting her sitting position to account for dream-physics.

With a great strength of will, Everly manifested a tub of popcorn on the table in front of her and dug in, eyes on the show.

A film grain sputtered over the blur of fighting bodies, all black and white like an old-fashioned movie.

Everly crunched on tasteless clouds as vampire Rylan grappled long tangles of inky shadow. He moved with a vicious, precise elegance, tearing clawlike hands into the living darkness.

A chunk of smoky gore spattered against the jukebox which played the haunting melody of a man singing about his beloved mermaid.

Between Everly's blinks, the scene would jump and change.

The other vampires worked in unison, grasping and pinning the monster.

Waitresses circled with stone-faced smiles, a creepy merry-go-round of aprons and clattering plates.

The creature lurched from the counter, overwhelming the redhead and cardigan guy.

Then they were all back on the counter again, rolling in a mass of limbs and swirling shadows.

The floor of the diner turned red as blood oozed out between the booths, flooding over the checkerboard tiles, vivid against the otherwise black-and-white world.

Everly lifted her feet up onto the bench and wondered whether she should wake herself up. The dream was taking a dark turn, and as much as she knew it couldn't hurt her physically, the emotional toll of her nightmares could shake her up for days when they became too intense.

Normally that meant the ones where she watched Rylan get hurt. Ones that felt too real, as though she was going to receive a call the next day much like the one she'd received about her mother.

Tonight's dream was especially vivid, and the edge of danger and death loomed over everything.

Maybe I'm more shaken up by Mom's death than I want to admit.

She watched for a moment longer, and it seemed as though dream-Rylan and his vampire buddies were getting things under control.

There was a time when Rylan's younger brother made up one of the four monsters she regularly dreamed of, but a while ago, for some unknown reason, her mind had replaced him with the redhead. Much like how at some point it had decided to change Rylan's haircut.

The cardigan guy was often around, but neither Everly nor her therapist had any idea of the significance of this dream personality always wearing a cardigan.

It wasn't something her dad did, or any other man who had been through her life— or woman, for that matter. It was waved off as some symbol of comfort or respectability.

The fact that Rylan almost always appeared in her dreams as a monster was something her therapist had *a lot* to say about.

"This person from your past caused you great emotional harm, so your psyche is presenting him in monstrous forms as a visible indicator of his capacity to cause harm and your fear of confronting the harm he caused."

Everly had tried to argue that Rylan hadn't hurt her, not on purpose or not in a way that was his fault. All he'd done was end their friendship. Fully and finally and for a reason.

Everly sometimes wondered if she appeared as a monster in his dreams as well.

"If you went back, you could ask him in person." Harper's voice intruded into the chaotic battle, crackling into the music from the jukebox.

"That's assuming I actually want to hear the answer," Everly replied.

"You could ask him in person," the disembodied voice echoed again and then again and again, growing louder.

The sound reverberated throughout the diner, rattling milkshake glasses and shaking color back into the dream with a pop so loud every face turned to stare at Everly.

Including Rylan. His features shifted—vampire, human, vampire—and his eyes flickered from galaxy black to warm green and they were on her, seeing her, in a way this dream form of him never normally managed.

Everly's mouth opened to spill the silent words clogging it but a scream cut her off. The monstrous void of lashing gloom threw the redhead across the room, then reared up behind Rylan and consumed him whole.

3

B reaths panting in frantic bursts, Everly fought the sheet tangling her body. She thrust it off, eyes snapping open into the darkness of her room. Her phone lay on the bedside, glowing numbers informing her it was two in the morning.

Rolling to her side, Everly grasped for the phone and held it to her chest for a long moment as she breathed through her nose and worked through redefining what was real and what was dream.

Rylan is fine. He's fine. There are no monsters.

Still, she unlocked her phone and scrolled down through her contacts to *R* and stared and stared with sleep-bleary eyes at his number. A deep, harrowing hollow had opened up within her, desperate to know that he really was fine.

She knew he wouldn't answer, even if she did call. Maybe she could text.

What would she write?

Hey, just wanted to know that you're still alive?

Wow, that's one awesome way to come across as a passive-aggressive stalker.

If something did happen to Rylan, or had happened to Rylan, anytime in the years since she'd seen him, would anyone even think to inform her? Would his mother or brother reach out to her?

Did they know about what had happened to Everly's mother? It was a small town. They must. But no messages of condolence had reached her.

Were any of them still there? Did any of them still think of her?

If you went back, you could ask him in person.

All her questions. All the worries and hurt and truths hanging unspoken between them. Maybe she could speak them. Maybe she could get closure.

All she had to do was return to the place where all her nightmares first began.

Rylan pulled a wad of napkins from the dispenser on the counter and wiped the viscous black blood that had splattered on his jaw and neck. It smeared slickly over his skin, refusing to absorb into the thin tissue.

This hunt was an utter mess, in more ways than one.

Annabeth was still sprawled on the floor beside one of the booths. Chunks of oozy flesh hung in her red hair.

"Sorry, I thought I had it under control." She rubbed the back of her head.

"Sorry means nothing to a dead shadyr," Vonny snarled in reply.

She marched around the counter, platinum hair swinging like the blade of a guillotine, and kicked at something that squelched. "Which we almost were thanks to you."

Jasper remained silent, lips thin as he inspected a pinpoint splatter of black on his knitted cardigan.

Even with Annabeth's skin stonelike and pale, Rylan saw the flush that colored her freckled cheeks. The girl was fresh, only part of his brace for the last six months. Rylan wasn't sure she was ready for it, but they needed a fourth when Callan up and deserted them.

Even if she hadn't been ready, six months on the job should have had her up to speed by now.

Callan only took two months from when he got brace duty to being as good as they got. But that was Callan. His brother was always trying to keep up with Rylan and more. The competitive streak between them was strong.

Damn, I miss hunting with him.

It wasn't that Annabeth was incapable. She just wasn't exceptional. And plenty of Darkfreys found their way to a grisly death from being anything less.

Rylan strode over through the swirling mist and offered her a hand. Tough love was Vonny's way, and for years it had been Rylan's way too, but Callan's decision to abandon this life, and his brother, left Rylan questioning everything.

"You did fine. You're holding form much better. And I think we all got a bit distracted there."

She took his hand, pulling up to her feet, and her blush grew. "Yeah, did you feel that weird pressure in the air?"

Rylan nodded. "Blew my ears out."

"It's no excuse. What do you expect? Beshadowings get weird. You're supposed to expect the unexpected and deal with it." There was more muttering under Vonny's breath, and Rylan could guess how she cursed this team she'd ended up with.

As the oldest of their brace by around two decades, she must feel beset by young people.

"We achieved our objectives and without casualties, so we've met the base criteria for a successful mission." Jasper straightened his cardigan, acting as though he were a few decades older than his young years too.

Not a silky-black hair slicked back on his head was out of place and barely a smudge on his warm-bronze skin.

Rylan glanced around the diner. No casualties except for the one waitress, but she was already gone before they arrived. Two other blivs lay awkwardly, toppled over and unconscious in the mist. At least Rylan's brace arrived in time to save them. It was about as successful as they got.

"Oh, technicalities, how I love thee," Annabeth crooned softly.

She smirked conspiratorially at Rylan, but when he didn't return any hint of humor, she pulled her expression back to soldierly stoic.

"Come on, let's get out of here. Our shift is done." Rylan pulled the door open to the jingling of a bell and held it as his team left the messed-up diner and remains of their hunt, bleeding out over the counter.

Dealing with the cleanup and getting the survivors out was someone else's job.

Annabeth went out first, eyes averted from his and jaw set.

Rylan hadn't rebuffed her to be mean. He had seen her subtle glances and the way she was gravitating to him more and more lately. And Rylan had no interest in pursuing a relationship with her. Or anyone, really.

What he was, what he did ... it wasn't a safe space to bring love into. And he'd already sealed and sent away that part of him long ago. And did his best not to think about it. Not more than once a day. Maybe twice.

It was a good day if he didn't think about Everly at all.

But that history had been stirred up recently, muddying his thoughts like silt churned up from below clear waters. Because Janey Boderleth was found dead.

Her death was looked into by the Darkfreys and turned out to have been as natural as they come in Shroudhaven. Not beshadowing related. Not death by any of the horrors what go bump in the night.

But every protective instinct within Rylan went on full, siren-blasting alert. Death is what happened in Shroudhaven. That could have been Everly. She had to stay away.

Does she know yet?

He tried not to imagine her receiving the news.

The brisk wind out on the street hurried Rylan and his brace into the unmarked Darkfrey van. Rylan took the driver's seat, and the two women climbed into the back. The LED clock shone an eerie cyan over the dash. Not much past two. An early night for them.

Jasper tucked away his phone that he'd been tapping on, then leaned toward

Rylan stiffly. "Would you mind detouring by the Crow's Nest so I might disembark there? I ... um ..."

"Sure, no problem." Rylan didn't wait for Jasper to attempt to conjure an excuse.

Lying was so far out of the tightly wound shadyr's league it was embarrassing to even be close to.

Exactly what Jasper was lying about, Rylan only guessed. But he had a pretty good idea. He turned and gave Jasper a long, knowing look, trying to convey solidarity.

Jasper nodded slowly, eyes on Rylan in return as though gauging just how much Rylan might know or what he might do with that knowledge. It was a look filled with suspicion and terror.

Rylan turned back to the empty nighttime street, leaving the rest unsaid. It was none of his business anyway.

There were far bigger secrets that he was trying to uncover.

After delivering Jasper to the shadyr bar, the rest of them arrived back at Darkfrey Estate, pulling the van into the garage at the same time a cleaning crew was piling into their truck.

"Heading to Pimey's Diner?" Rylan asked as he hopped down from his seat, boots thudding on the concrete.

A black woman taller than Rylan and almost as wide-shouldered pulled the zipper up on her maroon coveralls. "Yup. You lot didn't mess it up too much for us, did you?"

Vonny slammed the sliding door of the van closed behind her. "Watch your tone and know your place, *Cleaner.*"

A sparkle crossed the statuesque woman's starry gaze, and she smirked, sucking air through her teeth. "Don't pretend my place has anything to do with who is the better shadyr here. Unless you want to test it."

"I'll report you to Mordan," Vonny hissed.

Rylan casually took a step in front of Vonny, as though simply moving in that direction. "The diner is fine. Just a smallish vasmire. Shouldn't take long."

Three other shadyrs moved in behind the woman who was clearly the boss. She looked over Rylan and his abandoned attempts to remove the splashes of black blood covering his face and sniffed, unconvinced.

"If we're lucky, there won't be a body there to deal with by the time we arrive anyway, the way things have been lately." She slapped the side of the truck and yelled at her hovering team, "Come on, losers, move it! I want to be done and showered before sunrise."

Rylan watched the truck peel off into the night, and Annabeth sighed.

"A shower sounds great right now." She nodded farewell and trudged up the brightly lit pathway to the dorms.

"She's far too soft for this," Vonny muttered to Rylan once the younger woman was out of earshot.

"She's getting better. And she's still a kid. Not even eighteen yet."

Vonny raised an eyebrow at him as though she didn't think he was either.

"You know Mordan put her with us because he trusts your experience."

"Not as much as he trusts your skills, *brace leader*." Vonny shot him a sharp side-eye filled with indignation.

Rylan knew he could pull rank and discipline Vonny for her tone alone, but he honestly agreed that she was right to be annoyed in being overlooked for the role.

"Anyway, Annabeth will learn. Kids can make dumb mistakes sometimes. Which is all good as long as they make it through the mistakes alive."

The color fled from Vonny's face, and Rylan wanted to swallow his words.

"Shit. Sorry, I didn't mean ..."

Vonny looked him square in the eyes, didn't say a word, and it hit harder than if she'd slapped him across the mouth. She turned and stalked away toward the standalone home she shared with her husband on the estate grounds.

It's been one fantastic night across the board.

Rylan sighed and rubbed the underside of his chin, hoping to scrape away some of the dried ghast blood.

Maybe he could still turn the evening around.

Striding up the path to the main estate building, Rylan passed groups of mid-teen shadyrs moving about the lit grounds, running drills and sparring.

He remembered his early days at Darkfrey Estate, around that age, trying to stay awake through the long nighttime hours required, in awe of the braces heading out on hunts.

He'd been in awe of a lot of things back then. The castle-like mansion, ornate with crenelations and gargoyles, was impressive even now. But being a Darkfrey had lost some of its luster.

It was hard to feel all the warm, fuzzy team loyalty when there was a traitor in their midst.

And Master Mordan Darkfrey didn't believe Rylan.

The missing bodies of downed ghasts hadn't seemed important at first. Just rumors filtering in from cleaning crews. It was when more disturbing rumors started spreading that Rylan took notice.

When a shadyr grave had been desecrated.

The official explanation was that it was a bliv from in town, some dare taken too far from townies who thought the Darkfreys were all vampires.

And the rest of the Darkfrey shadyrs were fine with that answer and moved on.

But Rylan had known the shadyr whose grave had been robbed. A friend he had trained with growing up. And he wanted to make sure no further graves were dug up.

So he spent some time staking out the Darkfrey graveyard. Only to see a shadyr clear out another grave.

Rylan couldn't see who it was, but followed them back to the main building, only to lose them down one of the narrow hallways in the old section.

It was only later that Rylan remembered his mother once telling him how Darkfrey Estate was riddled with secret tunnels.

He hopped up the steps of the main entrance and squinted until his eyes adjusted to the fully lit interior.

There were a few other shadyrs moving around inside, but the main building was mostly used for classes and administration, and at that time of night shadyrs were either training, hunting, or sleeping.

Rylan wound along the corridors and intersections of the mazelike palace toward the place his target had disappeared. He hoped his second hunt of the night would go smoother than his first. He wasn't entirely sure how he was going to find a secret passage, but at least he knew roughly where to look.

He wished his mother had told him more. He wished she'd told him more about a lot of things. He glowered as he turned the corner to the hallway from the night before.

The dimly lit walls were unassuming. Carved wooden panels painted in maroons and gold on one side were contrasted with ancient bare stone on the other. Gilt-framed portraits of stern-faced shadyr ancestors hung in a line, their eyes seeming to follow Rylan's movements, scolding him for disturbing the silence.

"Now, where would a secret door be?" Rylan ran his hand over the paneling, tapping it a couple of times.

Some sections seemed more hollow than others, but he couldn't work out how to make them open and didn't want to explain the damage if he brute-forced his way in.

There had to be a mechanism, he just had to find it.

Man, Everly would love this.

The thought came unbidden, as did the memories of playing games of imagination and adventure in his backyard as a kid, pretending there was a secret door to another world under the steps of his front porch. The wide-eyed, enraptured expression on Everly's face as she led the way.

A stained-glass window featuring the Darkfrey crest of three skulls cast fractured rainbows on the antique carpet runner beneath Rylan's feet.

He stared at them, willing away thoughts of Everly. What was that, three times today? Four? Back in the diner, he swore for a moment he could almost feel her presence.

He had to get it under control.

That was when he saw it, right next to his boot, a strange join in the skirting board. He gave it an experimental nudge with his toes.

There was a subtle shift beneath his touch, a faint click resonating through the corridor.

A panel popped open, swinging on smooth hinges.

Rylan blew out a breath and smiled, then grew solemn. He peered into the revealed passageway, wondering what he might face down there. His heartrate picked up the way it always did at the start of a hunt.

Somewhere down in the inky darkness of that tight space, a traitor had taken stolen shadyr bones. Who and where and why were what Rylan wanted to know. He just had to find some proof, then something could be done about it, and Rylan could go back to being the best damn ghost hunter the Darkfrey shadyrs had.

Cold, stale air drifted out of the tunnel, smelling of damp earth and death, like a warning to leave dangerous secrets buried.

Rylan shook off the shiver tracing down his spine and stepped into the darkness.

4

Anxiety swirled like a building hurricane in Everly's insides, growing more ominous the closer they drew to Shroudhaven.

The campervan rattled and clanked as it took Everly back to the hometown she'd never wanted to see again. Harper was treating the journey like a fun road trip, but to Everly, they may as well have been driving headlong into the mouth of Hell.

It's just a place. A stupid, small town, filled with memories of trauma. What's the worst that could happen?

She turned to Harper in the driver's seat. It was tempting to beg her friend to turn the vehicle around, but instead, she said, "I owe you big-time for coming all the way out here with me."

"Like I was going to miss this!" Harper gripped the steering wheel with both hands and swerved to avoid the worst of the potholes.

The seat springs squeaked in protest and a cupboard door flapped loosely as they bumped along the craterous road.

"I could fix that cabinet for you when we get there, to repay you," Everly offered.

"It's fine. I'm not keeping anything in there anyway. And I'm sure you'll have plenty of other things to keep you busy once we arrive."

The picture-perfect baby-blue vintage Volkswagen had been purchased purely for a recent photo shoot. The sleeping area had been stripped out for prop storage, with only an ornamental throw over it to give it the appearance of a bed.

Behind the front seats, most of the space was filled with stacked suitcases, all part of a matching rose-gold set—Harper's. Just one well-stuffed khaki duffel plus a messenger bag and tool bag belonged to Everly.

She didn't need much. They weren't staying long.

The door panel continued to thump rampantly. Everly frowned back at it as though it were a war drum, beating a warning of danger ahead.

"Maybe we could stop right now. Just pull over, I'll get that door sorted, then we can turn around and—"

"We aren't backing out now. It's right around the corner!" Harper quirked her

perfectly glossed lips. "And you don't have to fix everything, you know."

Everly wished she could. For now, though, she wanted to fix the bad feeling that Harper was taking a week out of her busy schedule to drive her across the state to deal with her family dramas.

"If I could just—"

"It's fine. Seriously. I'm just excited that I finally get to visit the infamous Shroudhaven!" Harper panned her hand across in front of her as though reading a billboard headline. "Ghosts! Vampires! Mystery!"

"Trauma, abandonment, and heartbreak!" Everly cheered, her voice thick with sarcasm. "Wooo."

"So you have some bad memories of the place. But it's still your home, right?" Harper asked, tapping shiny chrome fingernails against the steering wheel.

Everly had been to Harper's home once, to have dinner with her parents and siblings, all at one table, a home-cooked roast with all the trimmings in a warmly lit space filled with of laughter and hugs.

She could understand why her friend was having such a hard time reconciling that *home* didn't always equal *good*.

Everly pictured her recently inherited family house. Quaint, narrow, two stories, with a shopfront downstairs, and a swinging sign reading *Boderleth Antiques*. Once painted in a charming lavender and cream color scheme, Everly mostly remembered it looking gray.

It had been four years since she'd left. It had been longer since it had felt anything like a home.

"I just want to get the place cleared out and fixed up so I can sell it off. Without me around to help look after things, who knows what state my mother left it in when she died."

Harper pursed her lips, silent for a moment. "It sucks that even in death she's making things hard for you. I'm sorry if that sounds harsh, but I want so much better for you."

"You can be as harsh to her as you want. We weren't close."

By a long shot, thought Everly.

She'd never been able to win her mother's love. Getting kicked out at fifteen had been just one of her many failures as a daughter. She was raised to believe if you worked hard enough and lifted yourself up by your own bootstraps, you'd succeed at anything.

And she tried. She got a fake ID and started doing odd repair jobs until she managed to lie her way into a role as a building super despite being underage at the time.

But no matter how hard she tried, she always messed up somehow, was always abandoned.

Harper reached over and patted Everly's knee. "Her loss. I can't understand for a second how anyone couldn't see how incredible you are. And I'm still positive you'll get something good out of this!"

Everly stifled a wry laugh. "If I can sell the house for enough to be able to put in my part toward us moving, that's all I need."

She had looked briefly into Shroudhaven property prices. It wasn't exactly a booming market. And the kind of apartments Harper had been window shopping for them weren't cheap.

"Do you think it's all still there, how you described it? Because I have to say, I'm super stoked to see this antiques store." Harper flashed a bright grin.

Memories of vintage dolls peering down from shelves, stacks of books like magical tomes, and a precious treasure dropped from tiny hands sent a chill through Everly's veins. She pulled her jacket tighter around her.

"I can't guarantee there's anything good in there. It's been sixteen years since anyone has stepped foot in those rooms. It could have all rotted away to dust for all I know. But you can help yourself to whatever remains," Everly said.

Harper's grin, if anything, only grew brighter. "My fans have been loving a bit of grungy vibe lately. And I really don't want to think about what they like so much about seeing me get all dirty. But it makes bank. So even if it is all dust, I'm sure I'll find plenty for some photo shoots."

"I just want this to be worth your time, too."

"It will be! We'll get the place fixed up in no time. Once it's all cleaned out and you've worked your magic on it, you might even decide you don't want to leave."

"Five days from tomorrow, Harper. That's what we agreed, and that's all the leave I could get from work. Five days in and absolutely out again."

They had already passed the small, historic village of Gorhanmere with its sandstone cottages and view over a black-water mountain lake and had come out of the mountains into the darker wooded area that surrounded Shroudhaven.

Along both sides of the road, massive, ebony-trunked trees shot up into the sky. They were so densely packed, it quickly became dark as pitch behind the first few rows, turning the forest into something mysterious and unknowable.

Everly's family home was north of the river—not far now—and the burble of anxiety rose in her the closer they got.

"Shroudhaven isn't a place many people stay by choice. And despite how exciting I may have made it sound, entirely unintentionally, it's honestly just a boring and vaguely creepy small town."

"Come on. There must be some happy memories worth keeping from your old place?"

"I doubt it." Everly's therapist had made it clear that dwelling on the worst of

the memories from her childhood wasn't good for her anxiety, which was currently climbing steeply.

She took a deep breath. *Be present. Be mindful.* Everly looked out the window, away from her friend.

Despite being midday, the sky was dark. Clouds hung low with unspent rain, and a strong wind tossed leaves around along the roadside.

Pretty normal Shroudhaven weather.

The whole world seemed dull and gloomy, making the forest look as sinister as the local legends suggested.

"I mean, this is the place townsfolk honestly believe is run by vampires who hang out in the big spooky estate on the hill. That's the kind of people around here."

"Vampires?" Harper sounded far too excited by the idea.

"No. Not vampires. Nutters who *believe* in vampires. Shroudhaven is where businesses go to die and some mundane tragedy or another manages to befall half the population. How many happy memories do you think I have?"

Harper tilted her head, pity overwhelmed by a sparkle in her bright-green eyes. "Don't judge me, but how cool would it be if there really were vampires?"

"You're thinking sexy, broody vampire boyfriends, aren't you?" Everly chuckled.

"Well, duh. Of course, I want some handsome bloodsucker action!"

Everly's laughter faded quickly. "I used to think the whole vampire thing was a dumb urban legend. Then the boy I loved moved into that estate and he ... changed. I'm not saying there really are vampires, but they turned him, somehow."

Harper made puppy dog eyes. "You mean Rylan?"

Everly gave a beleaguered sigh in return. "Yeah."

"Are you still dreaming about him every night?"

Everly hung her head, her voice small as she said, "Yes. Always. Ugh, it's the worst. I'm so pathetic. I should be over him by now!"

Harper squealed. "No, it's so romantic. I can picture it already, and I love this for you! We are going to do everything we have to do to get you two reunited. This is fate! Soul mates! I can feel it!"

She swung one hand into the air dramatically, keeping the other tight on the steering wheel. "The girl who only ever loved one boy, brought back into his life after years apart to discover that she was the only one he ever wanted too."

"Stop narrating my life. You're getting it wrong."

Harper clutched at her chest. "Their hearts, as one, together in their dreams for all the years they were apart!"

Everly giggled and slapped Harper on the shoulder. "Okay, enough! Look, it would be nice to see him again—"

"I bet."

"—but so much happened. I don't even know what he's like anymore. I used to think we were meant to be together, but I screwed up ..."

Harper whined, "But you still loooooooooove him!"

"I'm trying to say—"

Harper made grossly loud kissing sounds.

"That's it. I'm ignoring you now." Everly crossed her arms and stared out the side window.

There was movement in the distance, a shadow dancing between twisted trunks of trees. She frowned, squinting into the dark woods.

Harper sang, "Everly and Rylan, kissing in the sea. It's gonna happen 'cause it's des-ti-ny!"

"That's not even how it goes."

"I thought you were ignoring me."

The thing Everly had seen move became clearer and looked almost like an old woman, crone-like, flickering in and out between the trees in a hectic dash through the undergrowth.

"What on earth ..."

"What is it?" Harper craned her neck, staring over Everly's shoulder.

But nothing was there. Everly blinked, scolding herself for letting her imagination run wild. It must have been her heightened anxiety playing tricks on her mind.

The Wyrdwoods weren't a place many people went, especially old women.

"Thought I saw something. Never mind."

Everly turned back to face the front and gasped. A sleek, sandy-colored creature stepped out onto the road, right in front of the campervan's path.

Cat! was Everly's first thought. *Big cat!*

Quickly followed by, *Oh no, we're going to hit it.*

"Watch out!" Everly screamed.

Harper was still looking the other way. She flicked her head around. Shrieking, she slammed on the brakes.

Everly reached over, grabbing the steering wheel and trying to turn them away from the animal. The van swerved, wheels squealing as they skidded out.

Something thumped.

The girls were bucked in their seats. Limbs flailed and crashed against the dashboard as the campervan went off the road. Harper's head cracked against the steering wheel. Panic swarmed around Everly like a cloud of humming insects, darkening her vision.

She cried out, and a bright light flashed.

L ight engulfed Everly's senses.

No! Take control. Breathe. Count. You do not have time for a panic attack right now. You're in control.

The sensation battled to take over. Everly couldn't see, but she could sense Harper beside her. It was almost like the light tried to reach for her.

The light seemed to whip out toward Harper. Every instinct in Everly made her pull back, fight the strange feeling. It redirected, shooting out behind her and then retracting as Everly regained control and the world became clear again.

That was not a normal symptom Everly was used to from her anxiety, but as long as the panic attack had been pushed down, she didn't care. Mid-car accident, she had other things to worry about.

The campervan clattered to a rough stop.

"Ow." Harper groaned. "Are you okay?"

Everly checked herself, feeling around for any parts of her body that were in pain. A couple of minor aches.

"Yeah, I think so."

Harper's voice was a whining cry. "Am *I* okay?"

Everly turned to her friend, who had a hand pressed against her temple where blood ran freely.

"Omigod!" Everly moved quick, grabbing her leather messenger bag from between her legs in the seat well.

"I'm so sorry," she said as she dug through the contents of the bag.

"Did I hit it? Tell me I didn't hit it," Harper moaned.

Everly didn't turn back to look as she opened her mini first aid kit and unwrapped some gauze.

"We have to make sure you're all right first. You're bleeding like crazy."

She gently pried Harper's bloody hand away. Dabbing at the area to clear some blood, Everly winced.

This is all my fault.

Harper whimpered. "Is it terrible? Am I scarred for life?"

Everly pressed the absorbent dressing onto the split in Harper's temple and tried to smile reassuringly. "It's not bad. Only small. Looks like it might bruise a bit, but you probably won't need stitches. Here, hold this."

Harper took over pressing the gauze in place. "I have instant ice packs in my makeup kit."

The luggage had shifted and tumbled into a mess when they'd come to their abrupt stop. Everly spotted the glitzy crate behind their seats and started digging through it. The cut was small, but head wounds could be worse than they looked.

5

If something happened to Harper because of me ...

"Are you dizzy at all? Faint? Nauseous?"

"No. Just, ouch. And embarrassed. And worried about my sanity. Was that a *lion*?"

"A big cat of some kind, I think. Maybe a cougar?" Everly pictured it clearly, as though a freeze-frame of it was stuck as her mind processed the accident.

It had been small—not small enough to be a domestic cat, but not a fully grown cougar either. But there was no way she was telling Harper it was a *baby*.

"I thought they were only in the US. I know people always talk about panthers and things in the mountains, but they're just conspiracy freaks, right?"

"Aaand welcome to Shroudhaven," Everly muttered, rummaging through the pans of bronzer and eye shadow.

"Try not to break everything in there, please?" Harper pleaded.

"Sorry! Okay, got one." Everly held up the plastic pouch, skimmed the instructions printed on it, then gave it a sharp squeeze. After a quick shake, it became icy cold under her fingers.

"Thanks, babe. Concealer can do wonders, but I'd rather not be all swollen." Harper kept holding the dressing with one hand and took the ice pack with the other before pressing it over the top of the covered wound.

She leaned back in the driver's seat and sighed mournfully. "I can't believe I crashed."

Everly shook her head, wiping her hands clean with a wet wipe she'd also taken from the makeup kit. A few smudges of blood marked the cuffs of her jacket, blending into the dull red and existing stains.

"It's okay. The van seems fine. We're barely in the ditch. And it was my fault. I distracted you, and I saw the cat but didn't warn you fast enough, and you wouldn't even be here if—"

"Stop it. I was the one driving and not watching the road."

Everly just shook her head. She knew whose fault it was. Her fault that they were there at all. Her fault that Harper was hurt. Her fault an animal might be too.

"Stay here. I should go ... and see if ..." She trailed off, mouth gone dry.

She didn't really want to know if the animal was dead. Or worse, mortally injured but *not* dead. Everly shuddered.

Please don't make me be the one who has to put a kitty out of its misery.

She had failed the creature, and having its death on her hands was too horrific to imagine. But if she didn't check, she would be failing it again.

It could be lying there, needing help. It could survive as long as she got to it in time. Yet she didn't move from her seat. Her heart rate increased as panic tried to take over.

No, dragon, I know what you're trying to do. Not now, Everly told her anxiety firmly.

"If I hurt that poor thing, I will want to die," Harper said, and the blood smeared across her face made it all the more dramatic. "But we should go. We should check. I'll come with you."

Everly and Harper nodded in unison, braced themselves, then got out of the van. Everly took the lead as they followed the black lines of tire marks back along the road.

Harper held the dressing to her forehead and whimpered and squealed quietly the whole way, her eyes half-closed as though to shield herself from what they might see.

Everly peered ahead but couldn't see any telltale lumps on the tarmac that might be an animal. They reached the point where the skid marks began.

Nothing. No animal, no fur, no blood. Everly frowned. Where could it have gone? Was it back even farther?

Harper's expression brightened. "Do you think I missed it?"

"Maybe ..." Everly remembered the thumping sound the van had made as clearly as she did the dark-eyed face of the big cat.

She stepped into the overgrown weeds by the roadside, crunching them under her heavy work boots. She scanned around for any movement or pale-caramel fur.

The cougar could have been knocked off the road or stumbled there after it was hit.

Long tassels of grass swished in the crisp wind, but there were no other signs of life.

"It's not here." Everly tried to feel positive about that.

If the big cat had been badly wounded, surely it couldn't have gotten much farther away on its own. She tried not to imagine it dying alone of its injuries somewhere in the dark woods around them.

"So, it's okay?" Harper beamed, still pressing the first aid supplies to her temple. She stepped beside Everly and wrapped her free arm around her back in a cuddle.

"Yeah, we must have missed it. Can't see a sign of it." Everly matched her smile.

It would be good not to mark her return home with another death. She'd already seen enough death in Shroudhaven.

They wandered back to the van, and Everly gave it a quick exterior check, took the keys from Harper, and tried to get it started as they both held their breath. The engine ticked over and rumbled normally.

"I'll drive the rest of the way. You rest and keep that ice pack on there."

"Thanks, babe. Let's hope that's all the excitement we have on this road trip, hey?"

Everly sure hoped so.

As she rolled the campervan carefully back onto the road, a rustle of motion in the woods caught her eye again, gone before she could identify it.

As they drove closer and closer to the place she'd once called home, memories of death wouldn't leave her mind.

The nurse at the small main street clinic cleaned up Harper's wound and applied a butterfly bandage.

"It's a very clean split. Look at that, closing up nicely. Head wounds often look worse than they are." The matronly woman with bright-red lipstick handed Harper a fresh ice pack and then let her choose a lollipop out of a basket as though she were a toddler in for vaccinations.

Everly breathed a silent sigh of relief that Harper didn't need stitches. Her friend could gloat all she wanted about having the best makeup money could buy, but it was better to not be scarred to start with.

Harper asked the nurse for a photo with her, and since she wasn't busy she agreed, although she was confused when Harper fixed her makeup and pulled her portable set lighting from her handbag.

Everly stood off to the side, holding the high-powered LEDs as Harper and the nurse posed—Harper pouting adorably and the nurse pretending to reapply the bandage.

The nurse was a good sport, with both of them bursting into hysterics in between shots. The older lady even dug out a monstrously sized needle and pretended to terrorize Harper with it, perhaps a little too gleefully.

Everly was invited into the shoot too, but as usual, she declined. She didn't care about her weight, but she knew others could still be unnecessarily cruel, especially online.

The photo shoot ended when the nurse had to go and see to someone who had just come in after an animal attack.

Back on their way again, Everly stopped at the office of the administrator of her mother's estate.

She left the camper running so the heater would keep Harper warm. "Wait here and rest. This shouldn't take long."

Her friend poked at her phone, brow furrowed. "Thanks, babe. Ugh. I can't get my photos to upload. Reception keeps dropping out."

Everly had forgotten that charming part of Shroudhaven life—the dodgy cell phone service. "We'll get you connected again once we're in the house."

Everly was met by the administrator in his office. George Flitchworth. She was pleased to read the nameplate on his desk so she didn't have to keep bluffing that she had heard his name the first time.

He breathed heavily as he showed her where to sign—there, there again, on the reverse, and then he handed over the keys and offered his condolences for perhaps the hundredth time.

As she headed back out onto the footpath, Everly stared at the multitude of keys in her hand, wondering what they would unlock and fighting the tears in her eyes, when she walked face-first into a firm body.

6

"Oh, sorry!" Everly stumbled away from the person she'd collided with. Her eyelids fluttered as she tried to clear her vision.

"Everly?" The male voice, all gravel and growls, was filled with surprise.

Her eyes grew extra wide as his form became clearer.

I'm dreaming was her first thought.

But as a lucid dreamer, she had ways of knowing if she was dreaming or not. She was awake. And yet the man in front of her looked exactly like he did in her dreams.

"Rylan?" Everly squeaked.

They both stared at each other in silence for a drawn-out minute. In the dim light of the gloomy afternoon, Everly could see that Rylan had changed in the years since she'd left town.

His jaw was more angular, shoulders broader, and the foppish boy-band hair he'd once had was replaced with a soldierly buzz cut. Just like how he appeared in her dreams.

How weird.

She couldn't have known he'd changed his look. He didn't even have any online profiles she could stalk. She'd checked. Embarrassingly often.

The tight black T-shirt he wore stretched across a muscled chest. Over it was a gray-green military-style jacket with the Darkfrey crest embroidered on the pocket and a large hood falling over his shoulders.

He was so different, so much older, sterner, but the sight of him still made her heart patter like it had when she was younger. Like when she saw him in her dreams every night.

Everly scrambled for something to say. This was her lucky chance, could be her only chance, to reconnect with him. To get to know what he was like now. To find out if he'd forgiven her, or ever could.

Rylan spoke first. "I heard ... about your mom. I'm sorry."

His eyes were large pupiled and starry-swirled as though a nebula were caught inside, and his eyebrows furrowed over them. Everly remembered the exact shade of hazel–green they were even though none of that color was visible now in the gloom.

Everly shrugged. Rylan knew exactly what her mother was like, so she just said, "Yeah. That's why I'm here."

"I figured you weren't coming back when you didn't go to the funeral."

"No. I couldn't get there." Everly hadn't been able to bring herself to attend.

Mr. Flitchworth had organized a very basic burial, and Everly didn't want to see who else might—or might not—have been there. She wondered then if Rylan had gone, but before she could ask, he spoke again.

"Are you staying long?" Rylan's voice was a low, guarded rumble.

"Just this week. I have to sort out the old house." Everly jingled the keys on display.

"Right. Good." Rylan's shoulders dropped, and Everly was desperate to know whether it was in relief or sadness.

And good that she was here for a few days, or good that she'd be leaving soon? Even getting a few syllables out of Rylan was more than she'd had since they split ways, but the inability to decipher them was maddening.

She needed to hear more, say more. Seeing him there, in person, made her whole body hum with a strength of emotion that threatened to overwhelm her.

Everly's heart did some hectic maneuvers. Before she could back down, she took a deep breath and forced the words out. "It's really nice to see you. Maybe we could—"

"I have to go." Rylan lifted his chin, staring down the street toward nothing Everly could determine.

"Sure. Same. No problem." Everly's cheeks flamed.

He started striding away, then paused, glancing back over his shoulder. "It was ... good ... seeing you, too."

Everly blew out a long breath as she watched him go. "Oookay. Okay, okay, okay. Good, *Good*."

He said it was good. *Good*.

Everly made her way back to the campervan as her heartbeat pounded in her ears and her chest grew tight. She fought the urge to vomit.

"That was quick," Harper said as Everly collapsed into the driver's seat.

Her breathing was short. Her hands trembled, adrenaline uselessly claiming her whole body.

"Panic attack," she managed to say.

Harper, who had been leaning back with her eyes closed, slid up the bench seat to be closer. Taking her still cool ice pack, she pressed it to Everly's neck.

"Deep breaths. You're okay."

Everly counted while she inhaled, held her breath, then exhaled, going through the usual motions. She wanted to laugh and cry.

"I just saw Rylan, out on the street."

"No way!" Harper exclaimed.

She craned her neck around, trying to get a glimpse of the man, but Rylan was long gone. "Is he still gorgeous?"

Yes. Everly didn't answer aloud. She shook her head and did another breathing exercise. "A car crash and I manage, but *he* sets me off."

Her heart beat so fast her chest ached.

You're not dying. It's only panic. Just breathe.

"You know anxiety isn't logical. Remember, it's just your dragon, trying to protect you. But your dragon's a great big dumb-dumb and gets confused about what is actually a real threat."

Everly nodded.

Visualizing her screwed-up adrenal response as a protective-yet-stupid dragon had helped in the past, at least with the shame that often came along with the panic attacks. The shame of how she couldn't even control her own mind and body. Especially when it came to Rylan. Her eyes filled with tears.

If she couldn't even control her own body, how did she think she was going to make things right with Rylan again? Even if he wasn't planning on avoiding her until she left.

I'm such an idiot to have even thought there was a chance.

It didn't matter. Her dreams of fate and soul mates were childish. She was back in Shroudhaven for one job. Clean up the house and leave.

She had five days, then she'd never have to think about this town or the parts of her heart she'd left behind here ever again.

The campervan rattled to a stop and Everly turned off the engine, sitting for a moment to stare at the haunted house she'd once run from.

On the outskirts of town, her old home shared the space with other similar vintage buildings. The tree-lined road was lit by dull, ornamental streetlights, drooping like snowdrop flowers. It was late afternoon and the sun set early, taking away what little light had filtered through the thick storm clouds.

The whole area seemed deserted, with most superstitious locals staying inside as soon as the sun went down.

"There it is," Everly said.

"Wow." Harper breathed the word softly, sounding both impressed and sarcastic at once.

The narrow two-story building loomed in the darkness. Moonlight glinted off

the attic windows like ominous eyes.

The carved wooden ornamentation around the porch and windows should have been a nice feature, but was cracked and broken, looking more like giant cobwebs and claws gripping the house.

The picket fence posts were loose and hung askew like jagged teeth.

A brisk wind made the faded Boderleth Antiques sign at the front gate swing back and forth, creaking and banging. The front garden was an overgrown tapestry of sprawling miniature rosebushes and unpruned hydrangeas strangled by long runners of brown grass. Thistles and dandelions filled all the spaces between.

"Are we going in? Or ..." Harper let the word hang.

"Got any Molotov cocktails on you?"

"Fresh out."

"I guess we have to go in then," Everly said.

They made their way along the weedy front path, using their phones as flashlights, then Everly led them away from the front door, down a narrow side track.

"Ugh!" Harper gasped. "I just took a cobweb to the face!"

Everly quickly inspected her for stray spiders. "You're okay. All clear. That's what you get for being unreasonably tall."

"Why can't we use the front door? You have all the keys, right?"

Everly turned and continued toward the back. "The front door goes right into the antiques store. We go around to get into the living area."

It had been that way as long as Everly remembered—one half of the house sectioned off, closed up, unspoken of. She'd learned to pretend that part of the house didn't even exist.

The backyard was worse than the front. The rusty skeletal remains of a swing set had been smothered by ivy and grass. The porch groaned and gave softly under Everly's weight as she stepped onto it and faced the door.

Home. Or at least, the house she grew up in. A lump of sorrow filled her throat and she swallowed it away, unlocked the door, and flicked the light switch.

Candle-shaped lights lit up the small entry hall and the dull-brown floral wallpaper felt so familiar to Everly it sent her mind spiraling back into childhood. She denied the nostalgia, pushing it down before it could bring the bad memories with it.

"Kitchen and laundry are just through there on the right. That door leads to the basement"—Everly shuddered—"and everything else is upstairs."

Everly glanced toward the final option visible from the entryway—the back door to the antiques store. There was a frosted window in the top half of the door, but over the years it had grown so dusty and grimy, not a thing could be seen through it.

The whole section of the building had been closed since her dad had died when

Everly was three years old. It had been everything her father had ever cared about. And then no one had cared, or been allowed to care for it, ever since.

"I have no idea what state everything will be in, sorry." Everly cringed as she eyed the badly stacked piles of crushed-down beer boxes and moldy take-out containers in the hall.

Each step she took waded through rattling beer cans. The aroma was a mix of dry-dirt stale and warmly pungent rot.

A faint scratching sound came from the antiques store. Everly and Harper's eyes met, wide and alert.

"Probably just rats?" Everly offered.

She knew, in theory, rats were clever and generally harmless creatures, but the theory didn't stop them creeping her out. She shivered.

Harper put her arm over Everly's shoulders and squeezed. "Hey, it's going to be all right. We'll do whatever you need to do with this place, okay? Even if that means letting it all burn."

"Thought you were out of Molotovs." Everly's lips quirked up. "But thanks. Let's try to clean it up and sell it first before we resort to arson. I just hope I can fix it enough in the time I have."

"Babe, you can fix anything."

Not anything. If she could fix anything, she wouldn't have had to leave in the first place.

Everly forced a smile. "Come on. Let's sort out somewhere to get you resting, then I'll bring our stuff in, okay?"

Everly placed a foot onto the stairs, and they creaked. She tested her weight on it a couple of times before progressing farther. Harper followed close behind. When they reached the top, Everly clicked another switch, and a row of more faux candles lit a thin corridor.

"Living room was that way. Mom's bedroom—the main bedroom—was down the other end there. My old room was just across here near the bathroom." Everly paused at the door, where bits of old tape and ripped corners were all that remained of the poster from her favorite cartoon she'd once stuck there.

She turned the knob and pushed the wooden door. It stopped halfway, blocked by something behind it.

Everly put her shoulder into it, but it still wouldn't open fully. She ducked her head through the gap to see what was in the way. Harper, much taller, leaned over her and looked as well.

Piles of musty clothing, old magazines, newspapers, and shoes filled the space. If there was still a bed in there, if anything of Everly's old room was in there, it wasn't

even visible under the hoard of trash.

"You didn't like cleaning your room?" Harper whispered.

"This is Mom's stuff," Everly whispered back.

"Why are we whispering?"

"You started it!" Everly sighed, then spoke normally. "I have a skip bin booked for tomorrow, but we're not going to be able to pitch camp in there tonight."

Her voice echoed strangely in the old house, making her want to whisper again.

"I'm sorry about your room." Harper bumped her shoulder against Everly as they walked slowly toward the other bedroom.

"It wasn't my place. Mom could do what she wanted with it."

"Yeah, but it was *your* room. My old room at my parents' hasn't changed since I moved out. It's like this little memory shrine, you know? It feels like that's how it should be, like it's a part of you."

"I guess Mom didn't want any part of me hanging around."

Harper pouted. "Don't forget that your mom being an awful parent was on *her*, not on you."

Everly shrugged and broke eye contact. She pushed ahead and swung open the door to what had been her mother's room. It moved freely but whined all the way.

The stink of stale cigarette smoke smacked Everly in the face, coming from overflowing ashtrays scattered around the room.

She hopscotched across the trash-strewn floor and swung open the two sets of large windows. They squealed on old hinges. Below, the overgrown back yard looked like a shambling swamp monster, slumbering in the dark.

"At least there's a visible bed in here," Harper said, gazing around the space with her nose scrunched up.

The bed was a generous king-size with hand-carved wooden headboard that had additional tally notches literally marked down one side. Beside it stood a shoulder-high pyramid of empty vodka bottles. Everly's mother had enjoyed being brazen about her vices.

Everly's mouth twisted downward. "Shame we can't sleep in the camper."

"This will be fine. I have clean sheets and a heavy-duty mattress protector in the medium-sized suitcase."

"You think of everything."

"Number one tip for traveling to photo shoots—always bring your own linen. It makes all the difference to have a couple of additional clean layers between you and whatever the mattress has seen in the past."

Everly grabbed the car keys. "Things that we won't even think about, or arson will start looking like the best option again."

"It's not so bad. The air is clearing already. And the bed is big enough that we can share, if you want?" Harper offered.

Everly shrugged. "That's okay. You take it. I'll grab the couch for tonight. You need a good rest."

"There's really heaps of room. I promise I don't snore."

"Liar." Everly smirked. "It's no problem. I'll start bringing things in."

She backed out of the room. That space made her uncomfortable.

She was never allowed in there as a kid. Never allowed to interrupt her mom and her male visitors. She'd learned the hard way the consequences of breaking that rule. No way would she sleep easily in her mom's bed.

Harper sat tentatively on the edge of the old mattress, pointedly ignoring the stains. "Okay, you bring the bags in, and I'll try to order us some pizza. If I can get my phone working for long enough."

Everly chuckled wryly. "Good luck with that. Did I not do an adequate job of describing Shroudhaven to you?"

"I may have thought you were exaggerating."

"Since I wasn't, I brought some chocolate oat bars just in case." Everly dug two out of her bag and tossed them to Harper.

"You are a lifesaver, Ev! First priority tomorrow? Getting us online. First priority right now? Painkillers and a nap."

Everly made a couple of trips to the campervan, bringing in her tool bag and the two suitcases that she thought could have been the 'medium one' Harper had referred to.

After putting her work gloves on, she pulled the old sheets off the bed, then used them like a net to scoop as many of the dirty clothes, ashtrays, and beer cans out of the bedroom as she could. Once the sheet-bag was full, she hauled it out and dumped it outside on the back porch.

Harper was halfway through struggling to get the fitted sheet on when Everly came back in, hurrying to help.

With the bed made, Everly pulled a roll of heavy-duty garbage bags from her kit and ripped one off, clearing up the rest of the bottles and rubbish around the room.

"At least we can move around in here now."

Harper lay down with a groaning sigh. "Yeah, my head was really done with being upright. I'm just going to rest my eyes while these painkillers kick in, okay?"

"No problem." Everly ripped another trash bag off the roll.

Harper opened one long-lashed eye. "Don't go cleaning this entire place up without me!"

"I'll just do a little. Enough to get an idea of what we've gotten ourselves into."

Harper closed her eye again. "That's all?"

"Of course." Everly headed out again and carried the rest of their luggage in.

Once Harper had everything she needed, Everly hovered for a moment in the upstairs hallway. She was way too wired to settle in anywhere herself, and although it was dark out, it was still early.

She took her tools and supplies downstairs where she wouldn't disturb Harper. The kitchen seemed like the best place to start, since it gave off the most biohazard vibes.

At first, she went slowly, worried she'd throw away some treasure amongst all the trash. But as she excavated through grimy, broken dishes and crinkling snack wrappers, nothing of either nostalgic or fiscal value turned up.

Soon, Everly was piling rubbish into the bags by the armful. Within an hour, she'd filled ten bags and cleared the floor and all flat surfaces of the kitchen, attached dining area, and downstairs hallway.

There wasn't enough space near the back porch to pile all the refuse, so Everly began carrying the bags around to the front yard in anticipation of the skip arriving the next day.

The nearest streetlight flickered, making Everly's naturally bad night vision even worse. She fumbled her way down the side path to the front garden each time more on memory than sight.

Dumping the last bag on the teetering pile, Everly dusted her gloved hands off and stared up at the house that was now hers.

A loud squeak from the swinging Boderleth Antiques sign made her jump out of her skin. She marched up to it accusingly, giving the metal it hung on a jiggle to see how it was holding up. A bit of oil and it should be fine.

She stilled, wondering why she was thinking about fixing it. This place wouldn't be Boderleth Antiques for much longer. Either she or the new owner would have to take the sign down.

The thought of getting rid of it sent a mournful chill down Everly's body.

It has to be done. And then I can leave this town of ghosts behind for good.

Everly reached for the dangling panel to see what tools she'd need to disassemble it, when a low, rumbling growl emanated from behind her. She spun around, seeking the source of it, squinting into the darkness.

Down the road a dark shape prowled toward her, eyes shining like pale-blue stars in the darkness.

7

R ylan broke into a sprint, hammering down the street toward Everly's house.
What is that? Some kind of big cat?

Not a ghast. He couldn't sense one around at all. But whatever it was, it was going right for Everly. And without a ghast nearby, Rylan had nothing but his human body to defend her with.

He had the full length of the street to clear, and his legs felt too slow.

It was lucky he was there at all. He sometimes wandered past Everly's old home, even though she hadn't lived there in years. Even though they hadn't spoken for longer. It was his way of remembering her, of feeling close to her no matter how far apart they'd become.

He might not have been there at all tonight if he hadn't bumped into her on the street earlier. Once he knew she was back in town, he had to make sure she stayed safe until she left again.

He'd planned on just watching from down the road, making sure nothing dangerous was in the vicinity. Then he saw her wander out the front under the dim moonlight. He'd had such a strong longing for her presence that when he saw her, it felt as though he'd conjured her out of his imagination.

And then he saw the creature stalking her.

As he drew close, the feline form turned to him, eyes flashing an unnatural blue, then it skittered off into the darkness. Leaving Rylan skidding to a stop right in front of Everly with nothing to fight.

"Umm ... Hi?" She blinked up at him.

"Are you okay?"

"Fine?" It came out like a question, as though it was so obviously the answer she was confused to be saying it.

"Did you see ...?" She paused and frowned. "I'm not sure ..."

Rylan stared back at her, taking in the curve of her round face and her blue eyes that turned vaguely toward their dark surroundings. She probably didn't see a thing. She always did have trouble seeing in the dark compared to him, even compared to

39

regular humans. All the more reason she shouldn't be out.

"I didn't see anything. I was just ... out for a jog."

"You used to hate running." She half smiled in a way that seemed both happy and sad all at once.

"Things change."

"Yeah, they do." The sadness on her lips took over entirely.

Rylan had to tear his eyes away from them. He swore softly into the blustering night wind. She was more beautiful than he'd remembered.

But he'd distanced himself from her for a reason.

And that reason remained, now more than ever. Rylan's jaw twitched. He'd been on edge already, and Everly's reappearance was at the worst time.

It wasn't just the normal Shroudhaven threats that were a danger right now. Not after what he'd found down that secret passage. Not after the consequence of that.

Somebody was up to something, something dark and terrible.

His heart still raced from the worry at the danger Everly had just been in, and anger bloomed around it.

She shouldn't be here. She should be somewhere safer than Shroudhaven. His need for her to be safe was a painful, soul-deep longing.

"What are you doing out here?" he snapped at her.

She took a step back and pulled her arms up, crossing them defensively. "I was just putting the garbage out."

Rylan took in the mountain of overstuffed black trash bags. "It could have waited. Have you completely forgotten what this place is like? You've forgotten all the rules."

"I know it's not collection day. I have a skip bin coming. And a large amount of confusion surrounding why I'm being interrogated about it."

Rylan turned around, swiping both hands down his face and groaning before returning and trying to calm his voice. "It's not safe to go out in the dark. It can be dangerous."

Everly shifted her hands to her hips. "You did see something! Was it a cougar by any chance?"

She peered over his shoulder, as though she were going to follow the strange-looking big cat and offer it a saucer of milk. *Knowing her, she probably would.*

"You're not listening. You shouldn't be out here at night."

"You're the one 'out for a jog.' *Totally believable*," Everly muttered, eyeing his tactical pants and heavy jacket. She waved at the line of the fence beside her. "I literally haven't left my front yard, so maybe quit being so weird and aggressive about it?"

Rylan gaped at her, then clamped his mouth shut. She was right. He was acting very weird and aggressive.

Whether that creature was a close call or not, everything about Everly being back in Shroudhaven, there in front of him, had the blood in his veins burning.

He inhaled slowly, then locked his eyes with hers. "I'm sorry. It would just make me feel a whole lot better if you stayed in after dark. For me? For old time's sake?"

Everly seemed to chew over her response, a fiery, questioning shine in her eyes. "You're going to need a whole lot more reason than old time's sake if you want to be the boss of my after-dark activities."

Rylan's eyes widened, and he stared for a long moment. Then he cracked, a small chuckle of bewilderment escaping.

Ghast damn it, he'd missed her, almost every day since pushing her away, but seeing her there, hearing her voice ... it was going to be infinitely harder saying goodbye to her again.

"Ry?" A woman's voice came from the darkness down the road. It sounded like Annabeth.

Rylan's eyes were well adapted to the low light—a gift that came along with what he was. He spotted Vonny, Jasper, and Annabeth headed his way. A quick check of his watch and he grunted in frustration. He was meant to have met them an hour ago.

Everly had a strange, intense look on her face as the three of them approached, and her chest was heaving breaths. "It can't be ..."

The shadyrs were equally inspecting the newcomer Rylan had been found with. He didn't want either of his worlds colliding.

His expression closed up and he growled at Everly, "You shouldn't have come back to Shroudhaven. You should have stayed away for good."

Everly's cheeks turned berry red, as though they'd been slapped.

Vonny reached them first, looking Everly up and down. "Who's this?"

"Nobody."

"Nobody?" Everly gasped the word.

Annabeth spoke over her hushed voice. "Someone new to town? Do you know each other?"

Rylan put his hand on the small of Annabeth's back, guiding her to turn around. Everly watched with narrowed eyes.

"Just a bliv getting herself in trouble for being out in the dark." Rylan gave Everly one final, stone-hard look, then turned his back on her, leading his team away from the Boderleth's house.

Down the street, Rylan chanced a look back, but Everly had disappeared inside. He wasn't surprised.

I was so rude to her. Rylan rubbed a hand over his shorn hair. Better that way, though. Having his brace show up only complicated things.

"What are you doing in this part of town? It's not our normal beat," Rylan asked.

"We could ask you the same question," Jasper replied with a shrug.

He looked completely harmless in a beige knit cardigan, his black hair neatly combed back. Rylan knew better.

Vonny and Annabeth both had jackets like Rylan's, their hoods up, shadowing their faces. A normal look while on patrol. They would all have Darkfrey body armor on under their street clothes too, just as he did.

"We were looking for you, you dingus," Annabeth said with a bemused smile.

"Thought we'd come and check around your old haunts, see if you'd run off home with your tail between your legs like your little brother, to live with the freaks." Vonny's voice didn't have the same teasing friendliness the other two had.

Her narrow face was even more pinched, as though she'd tasted something sour.

Rylan turned his head in the direction of Howell House. It was only a couple of blocks away. He had considered going there, thinking he should tell them what he saw at the estate, that he could go to them for help.

But he hadn't been home for seven years. Not since his dad was killed, and he'd decided he couldn't live like a normal human anymore when that meant he couldn't protect the people he loved. He wasn't sure he'd be welcome at Howell House these days. But he was equally unsure who he could still trust.

He eyed the three standing in front of him. "So, you found me. What do you want?"

Annabeth pushed back her hood and tucked her bright-russet hair over one ear. She scrunched up her button nose. "Maybe to understand why you keep running off on your own? We're supposed to be a team. You're part of our brace, and our brace leader."

Annabeth used the term *brace* like it was something magical, still holding on to her youthful enchantment at the honor of being in one. She was the youngest of them by a couple of years. But once you were accepted into a brace, age didn't matter. You worked together, had each other's backs.

At least in theory. Rylan wasn't sure if he could even trust them anymore.

"You've been acting strange lately," Vonny scolded. "We were a good team. And you were, I suppose, a good leader. Until you suddenly decided to be a loner who goes poking his nose into everyone's private business."

"Is this new behavior a result of the the woman who's moved into the Boderleth residence?" Jasper asked, looking back down the street to the golden light shining through the upstairs window.

"An old friend of yours?" Vonny's eyes narrowed. "Is this what the new attitude has been about? You had some history with the Boderleths, didn't you?"

"Yeah, and history is all it is. I just need some time alone at the moment," Rylan said.

He cursed inwardly. He needed a better excuse but wasn't sure what he could tell

them.

As kids, playing games and getting into trouble together, Everly had always been the clever one, coming up with stories and excuses. He'd followed her lead. He wondered if she was still like that, how she'd changed since she got away from this town and her mother.

It doesn't matter. Stop thinking about her.

Jasper tilted his head. "Time alone? That's not how this is supposed to work. Four is the optimal number for a brace."

"Look, hopefully this is just ... temporary. I'll be back again soon." Rylan really did hope so. He was letting his team down by not being with them. "Just take the night off, okay? My orders."

"And what should we tell Master Darkfrey about whatever it is you're doing alone that you can't tell us?" Vonny shook her head, making her blond bob swing.

"Can you guys just cover for me for a bit? You know I'd do the same for you." Rylan pointed his words at Jasper.

Jasper frowned for a long moment. Then he turned to Vonny and Annabeth. "I think we should let him."

Annabeth put her hand on Rylan's arm. "Are you sure you want to do this? I know you're one of the best, but it's not safe to hunt alone. Not for anyone."

Rylan put his hand on hers, gently removing it from his body. "I'll be okay. I'm just ... looking into something."

"Not a beshadowing?" She pouted.

"Nothing like that. It's fine. I'll see you tomorrow."

She let her hand drop from his. "Okay."

"So you're all decided?" Vonny scowled, turning her back and heading off. "Have it your way, brace leader. But this is a bad idea."

Annabeth followed after the older woman.

Jasper shot Rylan a sideways glance. "You would really cover for me? If there were something that required it, of course."

"If there were, yeah, I would."

Jasper held out a hand, and Rylan clasped it briefly in return before Jasper nodded once and left to join the others. Rylan pulled his hood up to block the cold wind on his neck as his brace walked away. He looked once more toward Everly's home, then once more in the direction of Howell House, and then strode away from them both.

It was how it had to be. He had to do this alone. Even if he felt that he could still trust his team. Regardless of the risk to himself, it was the best way to keep the people around him safe—even if it meant he could never be with them.

Rylan couldn't let the darkness claim the life of anyone else he loved.

8

"I know you're scared. But we have to do this." Harper held both of Everly's hands in hers, her expression grim.

Morning daylight barely reached to the far end of the hall, and the candle-shaped light fitting closest to Everly was missing its globe, leaving her and Harper in a thick gloom.

"Do we have to?" Everly looked at the back door to the antiques section and scrunched her face. "I haven't been in there since the day my dad died."

"So you're going to leave it locked up like a time capsule so it can haunt you forever?"

"Yes."

"No," Harper countered. "We're ripping the Band-Aid off. You need to deal with this. Today. It's just stuff. It can't hurt you."

Everly sighed. Harper was right, but she still wanted to avoid it for as long as she could. Unfortunately, the waste management company had called that morning, apologizing that they couldn't make it today—something about an employee not showing up—promising to bring the bin tomorrow instead.

Everly couldn't keep piling too much garbage in the front yard, so they had to switch up plans.

At least the antiques store wouldn't be filled with her mother's trash. Still, she stalled. "You just want to see what's in there so you can start planning photo shoots."

"It's one hundred percent the reason I came here with you. Obviously. Chop, chop. Let's see what treasures I have to work with already!" Harper snapped her fingers.

Everly knew she was joking, or at least half joking. Harper had been pushing for Everly to return home since the news of her mother's death. Once Harper found out about the antiques, she'd decided they were going together.

Harper could work from anywhere as long as she could post photos online for her followers and keep in touch with her sponsors. And after the scandal that had brought her and Everly together, she needed a getaway as well.

Everly still wasn't sure coming back had been a good idea. But she owed Harper this much, to make the trip worthwhile for at least one of them.

She pulled the jangling collection of keys from her back pocket and checked through them until she found the old skeleton key she was looking for. "Let's see what sixteen years of abandonment does to a place."

We already know what it does to a person, Everly's brain wryly informed her.

"Seriously, no one went in there? For anything?"

"Nope. Mom locked it up and that was that. It was Dad's passion. Apparently one he was more passionate about than her, and I don't think she ever forgave him for it or for leaving her alone with me."

Everly inserted the key into the lock. It was sticky, needing an extra push and jiggle to go all the way in.

"She would tell me all the time that she was going to have a big yard sale or auction everything off or throw it all straight into the trash where it belonged. But she was never great at follow-through or getting rid of things. We're talking about a woman who couldn't even throw away dirty take-out containers. So it stayed locked up."

"Until now," Harper said ominously.

Everly turned the key and the lock clicked. "Until now."

Everly's memories of the antiques store area of the home were nebulous and dreamlike, too young when experienced to have a firm hold on them. As the door swung inward, those memories came rushing back.

The entry opened behind a dressing screen which was strung with feathery cobwebs drenched in dust. Everly suddenly knew the painting on the other side of that screen was of storks flying over a river and red sun, her mind serving up the memory that had been so long buried.

She tried the switch, and the pendant lights slowly bloomed to life, giving off a dull, egg-yolk glow. The unfamiliar illumination made things skitter away into the shadows.

Everly backed up into Harper. "Rats!"

"Aw, cute," Harper cooed. "Remember they're more scared of you than you are of them."

"Doubt it."

Harper nudged Everly forward, and they stepped out from behind the screen into the first room. Everything looked gray, coated in dust so thick it had stolen color from the world. The room was laid out like a maze, old dressers and desks lined up shoulder to shoulder with only a narrow path between them. Every surface was cluttered. Lamps, vases, photo frames, trumpets, brownie-box cameras, porcelain poultry, accordions, model ships, and butter churns were piled impossibly on every piece of furniture.

Framed oil paintings of country farmyards and whale hunting expeditions hung on the walls between rusty horseshoes, copper saucepans, ornate crucifixes, and more clocks than one might find through a looking glass. Ropey, tangled cobwebs were

strung across the room like bunting.

There were four rooms that made up the store in total, all joining together in one big loop. The front entry room with the counter, and the largest room which they stood in now, both held a mix of all sorts of antiques, big and small.

Another room was dedicated just to dolls and old toys, and the fourth room housed old books, with glass display cabinets tucked between each bookcase, presenting the most prized antiques.

That was the room where her father had died.

Harper gasped and gushed as she beelined from one treasure to the next, her hands turning gray as she brushed them over everything.

Everly bit her tongue and winced at the faded Do Not Touch signs. Her father's rules didn't apply anymore. This was all hers now. But following those rules was a lesson she could never forget.

They made their way around and looked into the room to the left. Everly tried the switch but the light didn't come on. Hundreds of porcelain faces grinned back at them from the dark.

"Nnnope," Harper said.

"It's just stuff. It can't hurt you." Everly echoed Harper's earlier advice.

Harper stuck her tongue out, but followed Everly in. "Just telling you in advance that I don't think being murdered by possessed dolls is a good look for us."

A sharp nostalgia clawed at Everly's insides, excavating memories. They were more feeling than substance. The longing to be close to her father, who had spent all his time with the antiques—selling them, sourcing more, fixing them up, keeping the store clean and well presented.

As a child, it had felt like her father had rooms and rooms of toys he played with all the time without her. Toys she'd wanted to play with too but wasn't allowed. Everly had been haunted by the feeling that playing with them could bring her and her dad closer.

Only a little morning light came in through the dust-covered window, along with what spilled in through the open doorframe from the previous room, but Everly could see enough sweet doll faces and wooden horses to bring back every childhood longing. Longing for toys and longing for a distant father.

She didn't touch anything. She kept her hands to herself. In one corner the dolls were all toppled over, their lace petticoats puffing out around them, interspersed with shredded paper. The pile shifted and bulged.

Everly felt the blood rush from her face. "Okay, I second your nope now."

"Let's get into our nope-copter and nope out of here. Next room?" Harper offered.

Everly eyed the entrance. The open door framed a rectangle of black. What windows there were in the next room were blocked by bookshelves and cabinets lining every wall,

with two more aisles of shelving through the middle of the space.

She reached out, feeling around for the light switch on the wall. When she clicked the toggle, the room illuminated.

"Lights, yes!" Harper exhaled. "Although, I'm kind of digging the horror vibe. I could do a whole spooky series. Oh! I could dress up like a porcelain doll and lie in a pile of creepy toys and let the rats crawl around on me. New viral hit for sure. I knew this would be inspiring!"

Everly's stomach churned at a memory of her own that was far too similar. "Don't ask me for help with that shoot, 'kay?"

"Are we going in or what?" Harper asked, as Everly remained still, blocking the doorway, an even worse memory holding her back.

She nodded slowly, not sure she wanted to enter that space. A tapestry of books patterned the bookshelves, everything from leather-bound tomes to dog-eared bodice-rippers and dated cookbooks. Many had tumbled free from the mismatched shelves, lying tattered in confetti piles of dust and droppings in each corner.

The glass cabinets were clouded with a film of grime, but inside, the precious objects glittered tantalizingly. However, it was something on the floor in the center of the room that caught Everly's eye.

She felt drawn to it, as she had been when she was three.

In the middle aisle, between looming dark-timber shelves, shards of broken crystal were strewn on the hardwood floorboards.

Everly knelt down in front of them as nausea overwhelmed her.

"No one cleaned it up," she said, her voice harsh and croaky.

Harper squatted beside her, staring at what was nothing but chips and splinters of glass glinting dully in the gloom. "What is it? Or what *was* it?"

It had been so alluring, so sparkly. Abstract spiraling fractals of intricately shaped crystal had danced around an inner form, barely visible through small gaps, like a whole world hidden within. A trick of the light and clever artistry had made it appear to glow.

"Some ornament, one of Dad's favorites. I loved how it looked too, although I wasn't allowed in here when I was a kid. But I used to sneak in and stare at it all the time. I just couldn't resist."

Harper blew a raspberry. "Like any kid has that much self-control."

"I should have. I should have tried harder." Her words echoed her mom's voice in her head. "But I just wanted to play with Dad's favorite toy. One day I came in and the cabinet was open. I just had to hold it. Then I broke it."

"Oops. Did you get in trouble?"

Everly shook her head. "Dad got so angry at me when he saw it broken that he had

a heart attack and died ... right here."

Harper smacked Everly hard on the arm. "What? Why didn't you tell me before? Like, I knew this was an emotional place for you, but I didn't realize we were dealing with this level of trauma!"

"Yeah, well, that might explain why my hair has been gray ever since." Everly gingerly touched one of the larger pieces of crystal.

Sickness jolted through her. She gulped it away and rolled backward to sit leaning against a shelf.

Harper reached out for her. "You okay? If you need to vomit, don't hold back on my account."

Everly took in long, shaky breaths to combat the wooziness, inhaling the smell of old paper and books. "I can handle it."

Fragmented recollections of her father's death were knotted together with the explanations and guilt-laden retellings of it from her mother—a blur of fact and constructed memories.

But what remained clear in her mind was the joy of holding something sparkly, the terror of it breaking, the fury on her dad's face. And ...

It was all so distant, and trying to bring it into the foreground only made her heart beat so fast she thought it was going to fail.

"You know it's not your fault, right?" Harper asked her in all seriousness. "I need to know you understand that, because it feels as though you're dealing with some guilt here."

Everly shook her head, her words cutting between short breaths. "How wasn't it my fault? I did the wrong thing and my dad died."

"You were three years old!" Harper yelled.

Everly winced.

"Sorry, but for the love of cookies, girl. You were *three*. You can't be held accountable. Shit just happens."

Everly shook her head. "It happens because people don't do the right thing."

"You can do everything right and bad stuff will still happen. And when you're three, *three*, it's not your job to protect yourself or others from that."

Tears formed in Everly's eyes, stinging them with their presence. "I still did everything wrong. I don't even really remember him, you know? I was so young. When I think *Dad*, I think *antiques*, mostly. But him dying just became such a big part of me that ... can I tell you something else horrible?"

Harper tilted her head. "We're sisters. We can share anything."

Everly raised her knees up and hugged them. "When Rylan's dad died, it was awful. Everyone was so sad, but ... I thought it would mean Rylan and I had something big in

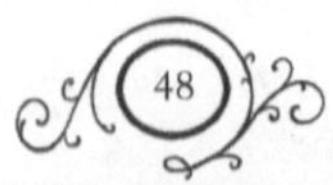

common, something we could bond over. We were about thirteen and had been best friends forever, but I was starting to want to be *more*."

Everly could remember how big those emotions were, as she'd started looking at her best friend in a different way. She remembered it vividly because she still felt that way when she saw him, alive or in her dreams.

"I had all these dumb ideas of how helping him get through his grief would help him realize he loved me too. Those feelings ... they ruined everything. I'm sure Rylan could tell what I was thinking, and he realized then how terrible I am. The girl who killed her own father and wanted to use his father's death for her benefit. I think that's why he stopped talking to me."

Harper turned around and leaned against the bookshelf beside Everly. "Kids can have messed-up and confusing feelings, especially at that age. That was also not your fault."

"I wasn't able to help him during his grief. I failed him and lost him because of that. I know you have some romantic idea that he and I will get together, but that's why it won't happen. I don't think he'll ever forgive me."

Seeing Rylan yesterday had left Everly reeling. He'd talked to her, at least. That was more than he'd done in years. But it was mostly to keep warning her away.

And those people he'd met on the street. The cardigan guy, the redhead, the blonde. Everly shivered. They were so similar to the characters in her dreams. How could that be? Did she know them from when she was a kid and it was just a coincidence her mind chose them to dream of too?

Everly rubbed her temples, her head aching and finding no viable answers.

Harper watched her with sad eyes. "I am so upset I didn't get a look at this guy yesterday. I want to see what's so special about him that keeps you dreaming about him. Maybe even give him a talking to."

"Don't you ever, *ever* dare," Everly hissed.

Harper hopped onto her feet, reached for Everly's hands, then pulled her up as well. "Come on. Let's lock this place up again for now and go eat cake for lunch."

"Best plan you've ever come up with." Everly smiled.

"You did good today, but now I'm seeing that you carry more baggage than I literally do, so how about I take over antiques-store duty until we're done here?"

"Yeah. If you're okay with that. I think it would be best. Thank you."

Everly looked back at the floor, scattered with sharp crystal. She wasn't sure she could ever accept that it hadn't been her fault, but it had felt good to face it, to say it out loud.

But another memory flickered, harder than the others to catch, leaving her chilled to her core.

A flash of bright light as her father fell, and a sensation of hunger being sated.

9

"I just need one more night." Rylan worked to keep the desperation from his voice.

"Again, Howell?" Vonny leaned against the side of the van and folded her arms, looking ready to murder him.

Jaw twitching, he nodded.

Last night had been a bust. After separating from his brace, Rylan tried to focus and keep searching for the shadyr who was robbing graves, but he kept finding himself drawn back to Everly's place. He wanted to make sure that creature—cougar or otherwise—wasn't still prowling around. That it couldn't get inside.

He had to know that she was safe. He'd watched her bedroom window, but it remained dark, the only light and movement showing in the living room, until that light went out too.

But even when he was sure she was asleep, he remained, unable to drag himself away.

Tonight, he had to make up for that lapse. It was his last chance to find something. He couldn't keep letting his brace down like this. He couldn't keep giving them nights off, and they shouldn't be out hunting just with the three of them, as good as Vonny and Jasper were.

He worried about Annabeth. She was competent but was far more passionate about the academic side of shadyr culture. She'd been pushed into brace duty by Master Darkfrey when they needed more bodies on the field after losing Callan and Cherry.

"One more night? For what? If you'd just explain what you're doing, maybe I could help out. You can trust me." The crunch of gravel turned Vonny's gaze sideways toward Jasper and Annabeth coming to join them.

Her eyes narrowed slightly, as though she didn't intend her message of trust to encompass the other two from their brace. "Or you could just let it go and get back to doing what you're supposed to do before someone gets hurt."

"It's important. That's all I can say. I can't just let it go." Rylan held her gaze.

Vonny looked away first. "Fine. But this is your last chance."

Jasper and Annabeth arrived beside them, suited up in their Darkfrey body armor.

Vonny turned away from them all and said, "All right, let's go."

Rylan stepped back from the van. "I'll see you tomorrow. Good hunting."

Annabeth paused with her hand on the door. "You're not—"

"No, he's not coming with us," Vonny answered for him.

Rylan turned his back on them so he couldn't see the disappointment in Annabeth's big eyes or the questioning interrogation in Jasper's.

The van doors swung and clunked and Annabeth whispered, not quietly enough, "What's going on with him?"

Vonny grunted. "He's probably just using the time for some secret hookup."

"Do you think that's what it is?" Annabeth rasped, scandalized, and the van rumbled away.

Rylan stalked toward the front entrance of the main building, feeling as though he was failing everyone. He needed to be split in three—hunting with his brace, finding out what was happening with the missing bones, and keeping Everly safe.

But he couldn't function as a good shadyr or properly protect Everly if someone had it in for him.

He still wasn't sure why they didn't outright kill him in that secret corridor after what he saw. The bump on the back of his head still ached. It could easily have been a killing blow, but instead they left him alive, unconscious, only to wake up with all the evidence he'd just found cleared out and no idea who'd blindsided him.

And he wasn't sure why they hadn't tried to kill him since, which made him all the more anxious to get Mordan's ear on this again, make him listen.

The tiny cage elevator rattled up to the floor with Mordan Darkfrey's office.

The lighting was dimmer up here, the warm glow of a few ornate lamps mounted onto the walls casting pools of light down the corridor.

A hulking figure stood at attention in front of the huge double doors.

"Nilson, is Master Darkfrey in?" Rylan eyed the man, having to turn his head up to do so even from his height.

"He's busy." Nilson barely opened his square jaw to spit the words out. His geometrically precise blond crew cut squared off the top of his head as well.

"It's important."

Nilson leaned forward, looming over Rylan, thick thighs and biceps straining the limits of his clothing. "He's in a meeting with Kole, and that's more important. Did you even get an appointment?"

Rylan smirked. "What, are you his secretary now?"

Nilson's hand shot out and slammed into Rylan's shoulder, pushing him and making him stumble back a few steps. "You can't just go walking in on Master Darkfrey. You should know your place, Howell runt."

Rylan stabilized his stance on the plush rug and rolled his shoulders. All the fire in his veins that had been burning him alive for days left him itching for a fight.

But laying out Nilson right outside of Mordan's office was a sure ticket out of the Darkfrey's for good.

He'd have to go looking for a fight elsewhere. "Fine. Be a good secretary for me and let him know I want to talk to him."

Nilson growled like a feral dog as Rylan strode away.

What was that all about?

Nilson was the finest specimen of jerk at the best of times, but since when was it his place to be playing guard at Master Darkfrey's door?

Was it on Mordan's orders, or was Nilson specifically trying to keep Rylan away?

Rylan shivered at the thought that Nilson was involved in the dark goings-on.

The man had the bulky build that matched the figure Rylan had seen robbing a grave. And he was strong enough to blindside Rylan like he had been.

But what would Mordan Darkfrey's own son be doing messing around with stolen bones?

No, it didn't make sense. Especially considering Nilson had even less mental capacity for conspiracy than Rylan did.

Rylan took the stairs down, heading back toward the secret tunnel, hoping to find something again there, something that was missed, but his confidence was waning.

Whoever his enemy was, they were clearly certain he couldn't catch them. Otherwise, he wouldn't still be alive.

Maybe they were right. He really wasn't the sneaky investigator type. He was the follow orders, take the hits, take the target down type. His investigation had only gotten as far as it had on luck and perseverance and he wasn't even sure where to look next.

It was all he could do to free some headspace from thinking about Everly and wanting to go to her, to be there, right outside her window, making sure nothing could touch her.

He'd had to satisfy himself by calling in a favor with Lucas's brace. His friend agreed to run an extra patrol or two down Everly's street. And maybe Rylan could check in on Everly himself later in the night.

Rylan gave the skirting board a sharp kick, popping open the wood panel entrance to the secret tunnel. He pulled the door closed behind him, left in almost complete darkness.

As good as his eyesight was in the dark, he pulled out his phone and turned it on for enough extra light to get a better look at every nook and cranny of the clandestine space. There had to be something left behind, something the grave robber had missed when clearing out their lair.

The air was damp and heavy with the smell of the ancient stone lining the path, carved in swirling patterns. The passage led him through the deepest corners of the estate, a maze that must date back thousands of years, back to the earliest shadyrs.

Annabeth would know. She'd probably know what all these carvings mean.

Shadows clung to every corner, a history of long-lost secrets held by every wall that had been built upon and built upon over time to create the labyrinth that Darkfrey Estate was today.

Heading back to the chamber he'd discovered on his last trip, he scoured every step, searching for a single fragment of bone, a footprint, or a stray hair. Were those the sorts of things detectives looked for?

He hoped for something more than that because he had no idea what he'd do with a single hair. Shroudhaven didn't exactly have a well-funded forensics department.

The chamber he'd found last time remained as empty as it was when he had woken up after being blindsided. He stalked around the carved stone boundary, checking every corner.

Nothing.

He was ready to rage-quit when a pale patch on the stone ground caught his eye. Moving closer, the brighter section turned out to be a scrap of yellowed paper, no bigger than a coin, pressed flat onto the ground until it seemed to be part of the stone itself.

One corner was marked by a boot print, as though it had been unknowingly walked in.

He gently pried it up with his fingernails. The boot print was only partial and seemed to be a match to the standard-issue boots all the Darkfreys wore.

On the flip side, only a few legible words remained. *Cast.* A cutoff list of names and characters. And the logo for Rook's Theater.

"Okay, that's something," Rylan muttered, examining the paper in the palm of his hand.

It was like a breadcrumb just waiting to be followed. Rylan's pulse quickened. The lead he needed had finally emerged from the shadows.

Rylan wasted no time making his way through the backstreets of Shroudhaven. He moved fast on foot, not wanting to take a vehicle that could be tracked, but wary of the many dangers of simply being out alone.

Rook's Theater sat on the main street, a mix of faded old-world glamour and rotting neglect. A street artist had once tried to revive the magic of the place, recreating vintage movie posters across the façade with spray paint, but those artworks were long lost under a mess of other vandalism.

The hairs on the back of Rylan's neck stood up. There was definitely something there.

Normally, he could tell what he would be facing, based on the way those sensations pulled his body toward change, but this was different, strange, too many confusing signals. Similar to how the bones he'd found in the secret chamber had made him feel.

This is it. They must have moved their operation here.

The street was windy, a chill slicing through from the nearby river, and Rylan pulled his hood up as he strolled around the side alley to the back entrance.

A heavy industrial metal door blocked the way, a padlock and chain wrapped around the handle. Rylan found a metal bar in the trash nearby, wedged it into the ring of the padlock, and the lock cracked.

Inside the theater was a riot of musty props and costumes and the refuse of decades left by daring teenagers breaking in to hold parties. Rylan stalked past it all, following his nose and the shadyr senses that had his skin trembling.

He was so consumed with the need to find his target, to get the evidence he needed to bring them down and end this, that he didn't realize until too late that his senses were also picking up a nearby ghast.

Rylan stood in the empty theater, staring down the aisle at the stage where a massive monster stared right back at him.

A harsh clarity broke across his thoughts.

His enemy didn't kill him at the estate because they were setting him up to be killed by something else.

10

E verly's dragon sat in the corner, a shining entity of destructive emotion.

The old couch on which her sleeping bag was rolled out was picture-perfect for real life, the old floral upholstery stained and yellowed. Her sleeping bag crinkled realistically as she shifted, blinking sore eyes at horrors playing out on the screen of the boxy, faux-wood-covered TV.

Nightmares within a nightmare.

"This is a dream."

On the TV, static snow obscured a black-and-white vision of Rylan, vampire fanged and monstrous, chasing after something shadowy, huge, and inscrutable.

Everly groaned, rolling her head around and stretching imaginary muscles.

"Vampires again? Great. Why not?"

At least this time she had a more comfortable viewing arrangement. Her dreams after a hard day were always dark and violent, so she wasn't surprised by the graphic visions on the screen.

She focused, holding on to the semi-lucid state she was used to having in her sleep. A state she could use to nudge the dreams toward being more favorable.

Her half-aware self pushed mentally against the reality of the dream, trying to adjust it.

An ocean of garbage surrounded the couch, and rolled out in a wave then back around her.

Sometimes a more physical approach worked better, so she got up and jiggled the bunny-ear antenna on the vintage set, then crouched in front of the screen and clicked the round channel dial.

The image flickered but wouldn't change away from its driving theme. Rylan and monster. Chasing.

One moment it was Rylan chasing a swirling creature; next it was Rylan tailing a monstrously tall man in a trench coat. But it was always him chasing, chasing. A never-ending chase.

Nightmares were much harder to control than more pleasant dreams.

Been a while since I had any of those.

On the TV, vampire-Rylan caught up to the shadow being. They clashed, a blur of violent limbs. Red blood splattered brightly against the black-and-white world. It sprayed out of the TV and hit Everly's cheek.

She cringed, then stoically wiped it away. Monsters and violence haunting her sleep was normal. She didn't like it, but she was used to it.

The fight ended and the chase resumed. She couldn't quite make out the form of whatever it was Rylan was after. It kept changing, shifting, made of feelings and vapors and dream-stuff too slippery for Everly's semi-lucid brain to lock down.

A cougar appeared, stepping out from behind the old TV, made of the same grainy black and white as the show and partially transparent.

A sudden sense of hunger jolted through Everly, but it wasn't her own. It was the dragon. Its scintillating shape slithered closer, prowling through the floating trash bags toward the cat.

Stop it, she scolded.

The glowing manifestation backed away. Everly wished she could just make the thing leave for good, but the best she managed was keeping it confined to a corner and ignoring it.

It was nice to see the cougar though. She hoped that was what she'd seen last night out on the street as well, that it was okay.

Everly reached out a hand. "Hey, kitty. I'm glad you weren't hurt."

It moved closer and sniffed at her.

Sparks glittered at the ends of her fingertips.

The cougar was gone. The couch was gone. The room was gone.

Everly and the TV remained, floating on a lightless sea. She balanced on a tiny island of refuse that sank quickly, and she had to hop from one trash-raft to another, over and over, to avoid going under. Things moved around her, a swarming oil slick of inky creatures, as the TV still played its horrible show.

Rylan and the creature, chasing, chasing. Out of the screen, into the darkness around her, small but getting ever closer and more real. Chasing, chasing. Everly's stomach churned.

This dream wasn't playing nice. She'd had enough.

Wake up.

Everly's tongue felt dry and swollen in her mouth, and she swallowed as she opened tired eyes. "Ugh."

Her sleeping bag rustled as she flopped her cocooned legs off the side of the couch. Her heart rate was up and the squelchy, sick feeling from the dream still filled her throat.

She hated that kind of dream—the stubborn, unchangeable nightmare her mind

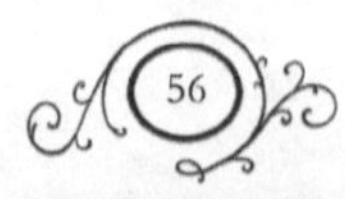

favored when processing a stressful day.

If she went straight back to sleep, it would only start up right where it left off. She had to break the connection before trying to get any more rest.

Everly slipped out of the sleeping bag, got up, and shuffled along the aged carpet that reeked of years of absorbed cigarette smoke. The air was chilly on her bare arms and feet as the warmth of the sleeping bag quickly faded, leaving just some leggings and a singlet to protect her against the cold.

She headed slowly down the stairs, trying to avoid any creaking sounds that might disturb Harper's sleep. At the bottom of the steps, she patted the bird sticking out of the broken cuckoo clock and wondered what the time was.

The light in the kitchen flickered and buzzed in a way Everly liked as much as she liked electrical fires, so she turned it off. There was just enough light coming in from the hall for her to find her way the sink.

A small, dark shape darted out from one of the cupboards. Everly swallowed a squeal as the rat jumped off the counter like a sleek dart and sped past Everly's bare toes, too close for comfort. She hopped up and down on the spot a few times to shake off the nerves.

Getting back to sleep is going to be so easy now.

She turned the tap on to wash a glass and a long howling sound startled her. Thinking it was the old pipes, she twisted the faucet off quickly.

But the sound didn't stop.

Crashing, ripping, crackling noises followed. Everly lifted the dusty lace curtain and peered out the window above the sink. She looked over the front yard to the street. The drinking glass fell from her hand.

Vampire-Rylan fought a shadowy beast.

The glass cracked on the floor, smashing beside her bare feet.

"That's okay. It doesn't matter. I'm still dreaming. This is a dream."

She bent down to swipe the glass away, erase the mess from her dream world, but a sharp shard sliced into the palm of her hand.

The pain was vivid, real. *Real.*

Wake up. Wake up. Wake up.

Nothing changed. Her eyes didn't open from sleep.

Instead, they stared, confused, at the blood on her hand and then out the window again. Where a man and a monster of living darkness fought on the street.

This can't be real.

Everly's mind scrambled as her eyes remained locked on the impossible violence occurring outside her window. She tried every self-test she knew to be sure she wasn't dreaming, but found she was more awake and more terrified than she'd ever been.

Have I lost my mind?

It was dark outside and everything moved so fast Everly struggled to follow what was happening. She couldn't make out many features on the man. But it felt like Rylan. It felt like how she'd just seen him in her dream.

Chasing, chasing.

The creature ... Everly stood paralyzed, mouth hanging open as she tried to process it. From a distance it cut the rough silhouette of a man in a trench coat, but too big. Too misshapen.

Draping shadows and writhing tentacles leaked out, lashing at Rylan. It lurched slowly, crookedly, as though injured.

Their fight moved them closer to a streetlight. The man who might have been Rylan wore the same clothes Rylan had when she'd seen him the night before. But he also seemed different, changed somehow. His jacket was torn and one of his arms dangled as though he had lost the ability to use it.

Everly's throat closed up. *He's hurt.*

He kept attacking the creature anyway, as relentless as he was in her dream. His actions blurred, moving faster than a human should be able to.

The creature slashed tentacles through the air and he dodged effortlessly, leaping high and landing behind it, panther-like.

He launched himself at it, trying to drag it away from Everly's home. The size of the thing dwarfed Rylan, threatened to consume him in its twisting shadows, but somehow he matched its strength, the speed of its dizzying attacks.

He shook out his arms—both seemed to be working again—and caught the largest of the whipping tentacles and wrenched. It tore off, and the thing howled—the same sound Everly had heard before.

Rylan stumbled back as though the effort had taken the last of his energy.

Dark smoke and mist poured from the creature's wound. It seemed to expand in size.

Tumbling and hissing, it flailed its whole body at Rylan, wrapping him entirely. Rylan was caught up in it, wrenching against the tangle of tentacles that enveloped him.

They tumbled together, and Rylan got back on top, but long ropes of the creatures flesh were bound around each of his arms, tight to the shoulder. Rylan cried out as the creature lifted him into the air.

A cracking sound pierced the night as the creature tore his chest open down the middle.

Rylan fell.

11

Everly didn't think, *couldn't* think about what she'd seen. She just knew she had to help Rylan. She ran.

She leaped over the broken glass and skidded out of the kitchen, through the back door, around the side of the house, and onto the street.

The street where Rylan had fallen.

Was it really him? It couldn't be. This couldn't be real.

But there lay a body, bloody and broken.

Hesitation froze Everly in place for a moment, staring from the body of the man to the mangled pile of shadows across the road where whatever it was had also slumped to the ground.

Her vision swam, sickness filling her throat. She couldn't deal with whatever *that* was right now.

She dashed across to the human form, breath turning to sharp spikes in her throat as she saw his face. All too familiar.

It was him.

Everly knelt at Rylan's side, holding one of his hands in hers as tremors raked through her.

"Ev …? No, no …" Rylan stared up at her with his galaxy eyes. Blood spattered from his mouth as he gasped out the words. "No. *Go.*"

Everly could only stare back, unable to speak, unable to breathe.

He was Rylan, just Rylan, no vampire or monstrous features of any kind. Just Rylan, torn open and bloody, the last of his life gurgling in his throat.

Everly, who had felt so capable and quick to act with Harper's small cut, now felt utterly at a loss.

I can't. I can't fix this. He's going to die because I can't fix this.

She couldn't put pressure on the wound because there was too much of it. The coppery scent of blood hit her nose. His shirt and some kind of underlayer of thicker metallic fabric was shredded, blood gushing around it.

She didn't know how he was still alive.

This can't be happening.

Everly hoped that her mind had broken with reality, that this was some kind of hallucination. She'd rather be insane than this be real, when this reality was enough to drive her insane.

I didn't see what I thought I saw. My night vision is terrible. Rylan is just Rylan and the other thing was probably some animal. But what animal could have done this?

The answer was it didn't even matter if the result was the same. If Rylan was going to die.

Rylan managed to raise an arm and touch her face. It was wet, the blood on his fingers painting her cheek.

He held her gaze intensely and pleaded, *"Go."*

Everly nodded, her voice still trapped in her throat. She should go, get her phone, call for help, call out to anyone for help.

Then Rylan's arm dropped, and his gaze held still, and his rattling breath stopped. His skin grew cold, pale, and hard beneath her hands.

She grasped at his face, lifting his head into her lap. "Rylan?"

There was no response. A rasping cry broke from Everly's mouth.

No, no, no.

Believing that she and Rylan would one day find each other again, that they were meant to be together, had once been her greatest dream.

Now that dream lay dead on the ground in front of her, and she'd give it all up, every chance at romance or love in her life forever, if it meant Rylan could live. Her face contorted as painful tears burst free.

A shadow grew over Everly as she cradled Rylan's head, screams wheezing silently from her mouth.

A cracking, slithering sound lifted Everly's eyes away from Rylan. The ghastly mound was no longer where she'd last seen it.

Whatever it was, it wasn't dead.

Whatever it was, it was right behind her.

She turned her head and found herself face-to-face with an uncountable number of gray tentacles—tentacles made of tentacles, bulbous and misshapen, sliding over each other, covered in teeth and eyes and dripping shadows.

Panic roared through her body. Adrenaline scorched her heart, lungs, and brain. She scrambled to stand. Bare feet skidding in blood, she ran.

A tentacle lashed out at her, smashing into her back with a force that lifted her from the ground.

She flew across the footpath and into her front yard.

She crashed into something spiky and brittle, some kind of sculpture left there among the weeds. It broke under her as she tumbled into it. The sound was lost under her heartbeat pounding in her ears.

Beneath her were what looked like black bones.

Tentacles slithered into view. A sickly gas oozed from them.

Everly choked on it and it made her dizzy, sleepy, clashing with her body that raged in adrenaline-fueled overdrive.

Every part of her was a knife's edge of nerves and frantic energy and she couldn't contain it.

She lost all control over her panic. Her mind snapped.

It felt as though her whole body exploded.

Wispy tendrils of bright light and sparkles filled her vision, searing her flesh. She lifted off the ground, hovering as the blinding bright threads lashed out at the tentacle creature. Caught in the web of light, the creature writhed, consumed within the blaze.

Everly's overworked heart was set to burst, and she almost embraced it, because how could she go on? If Rylan was gone …

But years of pulling herself back from the brink kicked in, automatically fighting back, trying to return to still and calm and control.

The light went out.

Everly fell into the overgrown garden. She gagged on the lingering vapors that swirled amongst the weeds. They fogged over her already failing consciousness.

She didn't know what was happening, what was real. Had she been hit by lightning? Was she dying?

She lay tangled in the rosebush, unable to move, to even cry out, as her consciousness faded. Through a small gap in the bushes, she could see Rylan's body, motionless on the pavement.

She tried to reach for him, stretch herself out to hold him, protect him, give anything she could to bring him back to life.

Some other form moved in the distance. A person, hobbling slowly up the street. Everly's eyelids drooped, fighting against her will to stay awake.

Save us. Save Rylan. Please.

Everly couldn't get the words out. Darkness edged in all around her.

The figure moved strangely. Silhouetted, hunchbacked, human-shaped but wrong. Dragging something. Coming closer.

"Everly!" Rylan rushed over to her as she sat up from the rosebush.

"Rylan? How?" Everly stumbled forward, clinging unashamedly to him.

His chest was firm and unbroken, his shirt whole and dry, his lips free of blood. Tears of relief hung in her eyes.

He grabbed her too, holding her briefly before he checked her over, brushing his hands along her face and arms. "Are you okay?"

Light crackled and glittered between her and Rylan where they touched. The roses didn't scratch her as she stood within them. She could see clearly, despite it still being night.

Her dragon swam through the air nearby, swallowing, smacking its jaws.

No ... Oh, no.

Everly's hands dropped and she stepped back, her heart aching.

He frowned. "What? What is it? Are you hurt?"

She stared up at him, his unmarred skin, untorn clothes. Her voice came out wan and lifeless. "I'm dreaming."

His lips twisted into a wry smile. "What? What do you mean you're dreaming?"

"I mean, dreaming." Everly waved a hand and daylight sparkled on the white miniature roses that surrounded them, fields and fields of them stretching on forever.

In the center of each tiny rose as a toothy mouth, dripping in blood.

Rylan jolted back, circling around to take in their surroundings. "What in the Everdark just happened?"

The nonsense words, as usual. Everly's shoulders slumped, and she didn't bother to answer. What was the point in explaining anything to a dream? But she didn't go anywhere, didn't try to rouse herself, too worried about what she might wake up to.

Maybe it was all a dream. But what if it wasn't?

"I don't know what's going on, but I'm not asleep—at least I don't feel like I am." Rylan stared at his surroundings, then his own hands, then Everly through narrowed eyes, as though suspicious of everything. "Are we caught in a beshadowing of some kind?"

"A what? No, never mind. Look, you can feel however you want to feel because this is my dream and you're a figment, saying whatever my sleepy brain decides it wants you to say. The real Rylan is ..." Everly choked on the words.

Was he dead? Had it all been real?

Her memory of it was so confused, with too many not-everyday-reality moments taking place to make sense of anything. Maybe she'd never woken up, never gone downstairs. Maybe she was still dreaming on the couch, more vividly than she ever had.

Or maybe she and Rylan were both dead.

Rylan had grown pale, forehead furrowed in thought. "The real Rylan is *what*?"

Everly clamped her mouth shut.

Tendrils of light swayed over the tops of the rosebushes as her dragon swam sharklike through them. It seemed bigger than usual. Everly wasn't surprised, given her recent anxiety-fueling experiences.

The dragon slithered closer, hungry. Everly stood between it and Rylan.

Go away!

The glowing, fractal-shaped creature caught Rylan's attention. He tensed. "What is that?"

"That's just my anxiety."

"Your *what*?" Rylan raised his eyebrows.

He rubbed a hand over his mouth and muttered something about maybe dreaming after all.

Her dragon pushed against her will in a way it didn't usually, and Everly pushed back until it cowered and shimmered away.

Everly remembered the similar tendrils of light that had surrounded her in the front yard. Only it couldn't have happened. Not if she was awake. Maybe she hadn't been.

"What do you remember?" she asked.

Rylan grunted, rubbing his temple. "I remember ... what was I doing? I was chasing a ..."

Chasing, chasing.

Everly swallowed away the sick sensation of the echoing words. "Chasing a what?"

Rylan looked at her from under low brows. "Nothing."

Everly tried to nudge him with her mind, to make him answer or change to a different subject. Nothing happened. It was strange that he was even there, talking to her, looking at her the way he was.

"You're not like how you normally are in my dreams."

Rylan pressed his lips together and made a quiet humming sound. "I'm ... normally in your dreams?"

"Maybe. Sometimes. It doesn't matter." Everly swallowed, growing flustered under the intense stare of his warm green eyes.

"What am I normally like in your dreams?" Rylan smirked, keeping her fixed in his gaze.

"Just, you know, *dreamy*."

Rylan's eyebrows shot up.

Her cheeks flamed.

She rambled on. "I mean, the way dreams are, not *dreamy* dreamy. More nightmarish dreamy if anything. For example, the dream I just had where you were a vampire chasing a big, weird, shadow tentacle thing."

Rylan's eyes grew wide, then were quickly schooled back into place. "That's one crazy dream."

"So you're not a vampire?"

"Of course not. There's no such thing as vampires."

Everly took in a long, frustrated breath. "Then what did I see? Tell me, in the frame of things that do exist, what did I see?"

Rylan turned away, staring out over the sea of roses as though there might be an exit in sight. "You said you were dreaming."

The dam broke and tears poured over Everly's cheeks. "What if I wasn't? What if you're really dead?"

"Dead?" The word dropped roughly from Rylan's mouth and he turned back.

Everly wiped her eyes on the backs of her forearms. "I saw you die. And if you're not some kind of immortal vampire, if that can't be real along with every other crazy thing I saw, then it means you're really dead."

Rylan stared at his hands for a long moment, saying nothing.

"I used to like dreaming about you every night."

Rylan looked up at her, a sadness on his face that was heartbreaking. "Every night?"

"But if you're gone, if you only exist in my dreams ..." Everly sobbed.

Rylan reached out for her, but she backed away. She didn't want to be comforted by her dream. She didn't deserve it.

"I'm not a vampire," Rylan said, his voice soft. "What happened, what you saw, it's not what you think. You have no idea what goes on in Shroudhaven."

"Then tell me. Tell me so I can do something for you."

Rylan shook his head, locking her in his gaze again in a way Everly thought could burn right through her heart. "When you wake up, no matter what happened to me, you have to leave and never come back."

12

Everly rocked back and forth. Shaken roughly by unseen hands, she roused from the clutches of deep sleep.

"Oh my gosh. Please, wake up!" It was Harper's voice.

Everly's eyelids snapped open, and her hands shot out so fast it made Harper squeak. "Are you *trying* to give me a heart attack?"

Everly's eyes darted around, trying to take in reality. The night-shrouded front yard was lit by Harper's phone lying beside them. A light rain fell, cold and tingly on Everly's bare skin. Her clothes were soaked through.

Harper had a blanket draped over her head, which gave them both some cover as she leaned over Everly, her mouth and eyes both wide.

"I'm so glad you woke up. I was freaking out. I got up to go to the bathroom, and you were *gone*. I found you here, completely out of it. I tried to call an ambulance but the reception is still dodgy. What are you doing outside?"

"I'm not sure." Everly rubbed her temple, but she was aching all over.

"Well, you look like you've been sleepwalking and picked a fight with a rosebush."

Is this real? The rain felt real. Harper's hands on her shoulders felt real. The sharp twigs and brambles sticking into her back felt real. Everly blinked once, twice, then sat bolt upright out of the weedy patch she'd fallen into.

"Whoa, slow down."

"Where's Rylan? Is he okay?" Everly scrambled to stand up.

Harper grabbed her arms, pulling her free of the overgrowth and onto the somewhat clearer path. "Rylan? There's no one else here."

"He was. He was right over there." Everly careened along the path and out onto the street where she had last seen Rylan, last seen his body.

The surface of the road was black and glistening in the rain. She couldn't see any sign of him, of blood, of the terrible fight she'd witnessed. Of his body, alive or …

"It sounds kind of like you've been sleepwalking and dreaming about him. Look, I knew you had it bad for this guy, but wow." Harper smiled and elbowed Everly gently.

Everly shook her head. "No, I know when I'm dreaming. I was dreaming, but then I was awake ..."

And then dreaming again. Or was I never awake?

She looked down at herself—pajamas spotted in washed-out blood, arms scratched by thorns, wet leaves and grass plastered all over her.

She remembered the creature throwing her into the garden—but maybe she'd tripped into it in her sleep? She remembered light coming out of her, destroying the shadowy thing—or had it just been her dragon in the dream?

"I don't know what's going on," she whispered. "It felt so real."

"Tell me what happened," Harper coaxed.

"Rylan was ... a vampire. And he was ... fighting a tentacle creature, but it killed him." Everly choked out a wry chuckle. "Wow, yeah. Okay. Now that I'm saying it out loud, it couldn't be real, could it? Ugh. I'm sorry for being such a head case."

"No wonder you decided to go toe to toe with the rosebush. Sounds like one exciting dream. Shame the rosebush looks like it won."

"It was less exciting and more mortal-terror-inducing."

Harper wrapped Everly in the blanket, her arm around her shoulders, guiding her away from the road.

"Come on. Let's get back inside. It's five in the morning, and I doubt I'm getting back to sleep after all this. We'll get you cleaned up, get some of the world's strongest coffee brewing, and pretend like we're actually morning people who want to be awake."

Everly nodded. She glanced back one more time at the road, needing to confirm again that it hadn't been real. Wind gusted, blowing the rain sideways. It sparkled under the streetlight, like the way the glowing tendrils had.

Anxiety churned within her, and she counted out some long, deep breaths.

She'd only ever seen light like that once before. So long ago it felt like a dream, like the confused memories of an infant.

And it had to have been a dream. Because if it was real, Everly didn't want to face what it meant.

Everly couldn't shake the feeling she'd seen Rylan die. But with everything pointing toward it only being a vivid dream, she worked hard to shut off the parts of her mind that replayed the horrific scene.

She and Harper sat together on the back step, warming their noses over mugs of black instant coffee. After some half-hearted rummaging through the kitchen cupboards, it was the best they could do.

They hadn't even found any sugar and had only bought cake when they shopped the day before. Harper added a proper grocery run to the list of priorities for the day.

The sound of clanging metal and rattling chains came from around the front, and they went to watch as the truck dropped off the skip bin.

Everly's breath stuttered from her throat as the bin was placed right beside where she'd seen Rylan die the night before.

No. It was just a dream.

"Time to get to work." Harper yawned.

"I'll keep going with the cleanup. You really don't have to get into the dirty work too." Everly had already changed out of her thorn-scratched pajamas into her regular outfit.

Harper was still in her satin nightgown and fluffy slippers.

"Any luck yesterday getting the house's internet connection going?" Everly asked.

"No. Might need a new router." Harper took a sip of coffee and grimaced. "I *neeeed* that wired connection. I can barely get online on my phone long enough to reply to a single comment. Being offline so long is making me physically itchy."

Everly patted her friend on the shoulder then left to get to work.

She had cleared the bulk of the rubbish out of the main living areas except her old bedroom the day before. The state of disrepair beneath the mess had become apparent then. Mostly cosmetic fixes, with the bones of the building remaining strong.

Everly lugged her tool bag from room to room, focusing on some quick and easy tasks—puttying small holes in the drywall, replacing a washer in a leaky tap, and screwing down some loose flooring. It felt good to work on things she could fix.

Deep cleaning was going to take a bit longer, but she figured she'd leave that until after repairs that would only add to the cleanup.

She unscrewed the switches and light fittings in the kitchen and found their loose connection before fixing them so the lights didn't flicker and buzz. As she turned them on again, testing her work, she froze for a moment.

It was when she'd woken up in the night that she noticed the fault. Right before she'd seen ...

No. She must have noticed it earlier. She'd probably forgotten, gotten confused, merged it into her dream.

It was just. A. Dream.

Harper had hooked up her modem, then sat on her bed, laptop and phone both at hand, tapping, muttering, and growling at the spotty reception.

"This is ridiculous! I'm going round in circles. How can I do two-factor identification if the internet isn't working but I need to do that so I can make the internet work! I give up! I'm going to have a shower!"

"I haven't finished cleaning the bathroom yet," Everly called back down the hall apologetically.

Years worth of spent shampoo bottles and moldy towels had been shoveled out the day before, but the space was far from clean. They'd both skipped showers the day before, worried they'd only come out of the space dirtier than they went in.

Harper stomped a foot petulantly and started grabbing bottles out of the cleaning bucket, piling them into her arms. "Then I'll hose down the whole room while I'm in there. This is all going to work out!"

It was an hour before she emerged again in a puff of steam, looking glamorous as ever, with the jade-toned bathroom tiles and matching bath behind her glistening and gleaming. It was the cleanest Everly had ever seen it.

While she'd lived at home, she tried to keep her own spaces and shared spaces like the kitchen and bathroom clean. But it had been a constant battle against her mother.

A mix of substance abuse, hoarder tendencies, and generally not giving a damn had meant the house was always filthy. The kind of men she'd brought home in a never-ending stream didn't seem to care about the mess either.

"Okay. I've calmed down, and I have a plan. I can't get through to the telecom to get the connection switched on here. I'm going to head into town, find some better reception, and better coffee," Harper said, jingling her keys on her way out the door. "Want me to bring you back anything?"

"No, thanks. I'm okay," Everly said.

Her eyes were gritty and lack of sleep made her body beg for some proper caffeine. But she couldn't impose.

She gave Harper directions for the best places to go, then had a drink of water and the last oat bar from her bag before getting back to work.

There was still a little room left in the skip bin, so Everly decided she needed to get the trash out of her old bedroom one way or another.

She propped the door ajar with her pry bar and began filling bags with whatever she could extract through the gap. Once she'd cleared enough refuse to open the door properly, she stepped inside.

Like an archaeologist unearthing lost ruins, it surprised her to find her original single bed under the layers of filth. As she sifted down through the mounds of garbage, that seemed to be all that remained of the bedroom she'd once known.

Digging her fingers under a pile of rotting clothing, something sharp poked her thumb, almost piercing through the thick work gloves. Scraping the rubbish away revealed a broken picture frame. The glass sat shattered within silver art nouveau edging. Everly shook the shards off into the trash bag and stared at the faded, scratched photo beneath.

Her dad and her mom were smiling in front of the brand-new Boderleth Antiques sign, holding a puffy pink baby with a gurgling grin.

Everly touched the photo and the surface peeled away under her rough glove, as though she'd taken a bite out of her father's shoulder. She inhaled sharply, then sighed.

This might be my one happy memory I find here, and it's ruined.

She considered just throwing it into the trash as well. Was it really worth holding on to, this token of a family she didn't even remember?

All she knew was a life of only herself, her mom, and the men her mother brought home—none of whom ever stayed long enough to even come close to earning a *dad* title.

The closest she'd had to a family, the only time she learned what a family was meant to be, was with the Howells. When she'd become friends with Rylan as a kid, his mom, dad, and brother all welcomed her in and showed her what love meant.

Everly's heart still hurt with the feeling that Rylan was somehow *gone.*

She wandered downstairs, put the photo away in a kitchen drawer, got out her phone, and stared at it.

I should try to call him, just in case.

Skimming through her contacts, she found Rylan's number—the last number she had for him anyway. She'd called it from time to time, and it had never been disconnected.

It never got answered, either. She gave herself a countdown so she couldn't back out and dialed.

It rang. And rang. And rang. No voicemail. No answer.

Everly sighed and continued her cleanup. It was late afternoon by the time she'd gotten most of the main rooms into what passed as a livable level of cleanliness. She hadn't yet unlocked the attic or basement and wasn't in any hurry to.

One rat nest had already been uncovered in the corner of the laundry and Everly had to spend a while standing on a chair as the rats relocated themselves. Probably into the attic or basement.

Everly tied up and lugged her latest bag of rubbish out to the skip.

On her way along the garden path, she looked over at the crushed rosebush. There was nothing strange there—no black bones, no weird light.

It was just a dream.

She grunted with the effort of hauling the heavy bag over the edge of the large metal bin. It clanged and echoed as it landed among the others.

She paused there, staring at the black road under her feet.

It was right here. Right here when I held him as he bled, then went still.

It had felt so real.

Frowning, she took off one glove, knelt down, and ran her fingers over the asphalt.

Her skin came away a rusty, blood red.

13

Everly gasped, standing quickly and backing away from the dark patch on the ground.

She stood there shaking as Harper pulled up in her campervan.

Harper hopped out of the driver's seat, balancing two takeaway cups from Pimey's Diner in one hand and holding a brown paper bag in the other. "Hey, are you all right? You've gone a weird shade of green."

Everly turned her reddened hand around to show her friend.

Harper ducked her face down and stared over the top of her sunglasses. "Oh no! Did you cut yourself?"

"No. No, I think it's Rylan's blood. It's from the ground ... there." Everly grabbed the rag hanging from her back pocket and wiped her hand mostly clean.

"What if it was real? I'm not saying vampire-and-tentacle-beast real ... but what if I saw *something* bad and real, and my sleepy, panicked brain processed it as a nightmare? What if it was an animal attack and Rylan really was hurt, is hurt?"

Harper pushed one of the coffee cups into Everly's hands. "I guess it's not completely unlikely. We did see a flippin' cougar on our way into town. I mean, how is there even a cougar here?"

"Keeping menageries was the done thing for rich people around Shroudhaven in the good old days. A bunch of animals got out over the years and have been spotted in the Wyrdwoods ever since. There was also the old zoo that closed down a while back under weird circumstances."

"You're telling me *anything* could be running around out here? No wonder no one goes out into the woods." Harper looked over at the spot near the skip that Everly was staring at.

"I feel like I need to do something," Everly said. "Tell someone. Just in case."

"Okay."

"Okay?"

"Yeah, let's head in and report it at the police station. Maybe they can look into it for you, make sure everything's all right." Harper waved her toward the campervan.

"Just got to unload some groceries first."

"Thanks," Everly said. She looked down at the coffee cup warming her fingers.

The red-and-white Pimey's logo caused a rush of homesickness to flow through her. "For this too. I told you I didn't need anything."

"You always say you don't need anything." Harper jiggled the paper bag in front of Everly and tossed it to her before grabbing one of the canvas tote bags full of supplies. "So I got donuts too. 'Cause I'm the best friend ever."

Everly returned a faint smile. Harper's support made it seem possible that last night's events weren't just a dream. But that was the last thing Everly wanted.

"**O**h, another *animal attack*, is it?" The police officer leaned over the front counter, sipping slowly from a mug that said *Boss Bitch*. She tapped it with long red fingernails in time to the tune playing softly on the radio in the background.

Everly remembered all the words to the folksy "There's a Mermaid in My Lighthouse" song that played. She'd heard it more times than she could count while growing up.

The officer called over her shoulder, "Hey, Holt! There's been another animal attack."

The balding man at the desk behind her didn't even look up. He coughed a laugh and muttered, "Do we look like bloomin' animal control?"

Everly stuttered, "Umm. Do you know Boderleth Antiques? It was right out the front there. Last night."

"Sure, sure." The officer rustled some papers around behind the counter but didn't appear to be taking any notes. She eyed the minor scratches on Everly's hands. "And you're the victim? Was it a Persian or a pug?"

Holt laughed again and Everly pulled her red jacket cuffs over her hands. "Not me. It was Rylan Howell, and he seemed really badly hurt."

"Really? One of the Howell boys? We didn't hear anything about that, did we? Nothing from the hospital?" Officer Eccleston, as her name badge identified her, directed the comment at Holt, who shook his head.

Everly looked to Harper for support, and she nodded her encouragement.

"That's the thing—he's missing. We were hoping you'd look into it."

"Missing? Just what is your relationship to the Howell boy?"

"Nothing. I just ... witnessed ... something." An ugly heat rose around Everly's neck and ears.

Eccleston seemed to size up Everly through her dark-rimmed glasses and smacked her bright-red lips. "Well, we haven't heard anything from anyone who *does* have a relationship with him. Did you check around? See if he's home? Talk to friends or family? No? Maybe think about starting there instead of wasting our time."

"I ... tried to call him, but he didn't answer. I saw—"

"I don't know what game you're playing, sweetheart, but getting the police involved isn't the way to track down a guy who's ghosted you. Go hire a private investigator to stalk the Howell boy for you."

"Like anyone would take *that* job." Holt chuckled under his breath.

"Go on. Out. We have our hands full with real troubles." Eccleston took a long, slow sip of her coffee.

"But this—"

Eccleston raised a sharp eyebrow.

Everly and Harper backed out of the station, the bell dinging above the door on their way out.

"So, that was utterly mortifying." Everly's shoulders slumped.

"Hey, you tried, right?"

"I think I need more donuts," Everly groaned.

The police station was on a side road from the main street of Shroudhaven, north of the river. Everly wondered about going to the estate and asking there, but it was south of the river in Shroudhaven Heights, the fancier part of town, and it was already late.

The sun, which had been barely visible behind rain clouds, had just dropped completely below the horizon.

Rylan had practically begged me not to go out at night. Everly worried why more than ever.

Down on the main street, half the shops were closed and boarded up. Especially the larger franchises and chain stores that had tried and failed to get a footing in the area.

The oddball collection of remaining shops had vintage frontages with weathered awnings and hand-painted signage. Pimey's Diner, Pimey's Grocery Store, and The Boutique All—a strange, labyrinthine bargain basement shop that had just about one of everything—were visible from the police station.

On the corner stood Cardboard Box Barry. Everly winced as the name they'd called him as kids popped into her head so quickly. To her more grown-up self, it felt so unsympathetic.

The wispy-white-haired, slim-as-a-whip homeless man with a braided beard stood alongside his large, blanket-covered cardboard box. He was as much of a town legend as the mermaid song. It seemed like no matter what part of Shroudhaven you were in, you'd see him.

There weren't many people out on the streets now that night bore down on them—Mr. Flitchworth chatted to a waitress in the doorway of the diner, an old woman in a muddy coat carried a large paper bag out of the pharmacy, and a young man loped on long legs down the opposite footpath to Barry. A young man who looked startlingly familiar.

Everly gestured to Harper to follow her and jogged down the street toward him.

"Callan?" she called out.

He turned, and when he saw her, his face broke into a broad smile. "Everly? No way! It's so good to see you!"

Callan was a year younger but towered over her. He caught her in a hug before she could awkward her way out of it. His dark hair was much longer than she remembered, as though he'd let it grow the whole time she'd been gone. It fell feathery and wavy around his shoulders.

"Yeah, I'm back, for a bit." Her voice was muffled by his chest.

He stepped out of their embrace and grimaced. "I heard about your mom. That totally sucks. I know how things were, but still."

"Yeah."

Callan's intensity made Everly gulp. He was so much more grown up now, but still had his familiar boyish charm and ever-present smile.

Harper cleared her throat during the lengthening silence.

Everly waved a hand at her. "Umm, this is Harper."

Callan turned his attention to the Amazonian goddess who matched him in height and froze for a split second as he took her in. "Harper? Not ... Harper Bells? Holy shit. *Bellsy?* Shit, sorry, I mean ... *shit.*"

Harper laughed and extended a hand to shake. "Not the worst greeting I've ever had, promise you. You follow me?"

She acted slightly surprised, but despite the fashion and makeup content of her business, she knew precisely how large a percentage of her audience were men.

"No ... sort of. I mean, there's a guy I know, he's a huge fan, kind of introduced us all to you."

Harper nodded knowingly, then indicated Everly with her thumb. "How do you guys know each other?"

"This is Rylan's brother," Everly said.

"Reeeeeally?" Harper drawled.

She raised her eyebrows at Everly as though silently asking, 'Do the looks run in the family?'

Apart from the hair length, and the friendly smile, Callan so resembled his brother it made Everly shiver. But they were also so different, in so many ways.

Callan was having a hard time ending his handshake with Harper, which Harper clearly found highly amusing.

His other hand roamed about, straightening his pale-blue shirt and smoothing down his hair. "What about you two? How do you two know each other?"

"Long story," Harper and Everly said almost in unison. They both laughed wryly.

Harper extracted her hand and nudged Everly. "You should ask him."

"Yeah." Everly cleared her throat. "I don't suppose you've seen Rylan today? Or heard from him?"

Callan's eyes didn't leave Harper. "Nope. Don't really see him much anymore. Not since I moved home about six months back."

"Home? Not a Darkfrey Estate boy anymore?" Everly was shocked.

Rylan and Callan had been inseparable. She was even more shocked about how much the timing lined up to her dreams, when Callan stopped showing up in them.

"Nah," he said, looking like he had a lot more he wanted to say.

Everly still remembered the day Rylan and Callan packed up and moved into the estate. It had felt like they'd been accepted into an enchanted academy without her.

She didn't know much about what happened at Darkfrey Estate or why they accepted some kids and not others. She'd never made it past the front gates.

"Look, this is going to sound a bit crazy, but I think I saw something last night, something weird, with Rylan fighting ... something."

Callan finally returned his gaze to Everly. "Something?"

"I'm not sure. Maybe a big animal?"

"There may have been tentacles," Harper added.

Everly shot her a glare, letting her know the comment wasn't at all helpful.

Callan frowned for a moment, studying her face. He dragged two of his fingers down his chin as though thinking, waited, then frowned again.

"I think he might have been hurt." Everly pushed the words out, feeling ridiculous. "Do you think you could check on him for me? Give him a call?"

"Yeah, okay. I mean, I'm sure it's nothing. Don't worry. I'll look into it." Callan's smile seemed forced.

His hazel eyes, sparkling in the dim light, were so similar to Rylan's it made Everly's heart clench.

"Thanks. It's probably nothing. I just wanted to make sure."

Callan frowned, looking along the street, then returning his gaze to her. "I can give you his number if you want?"

"Has he changed it?"

"No."

"That's okay, then." Everly's eyes sought her feet.

All the times she'd tried to call. All the times she never got through. Each one felt like a gut punch.

Callan pulled his phone out of his pocket. "Is yours still the same?"

Everly nodded, socked in the stomach again.

He put his phone away again, tilting his head bashfully. "Sorry we … sorry I never kept in touch. Really."

Everly shrugged. "No worries."

Harper thumb-pointed at the bargain shop across the road. "Does everyone else realize that shop's name sounds like The Booty Call?"

Callan's attention turned to her again, his expression brightening. "I know they say never meet your heroes, but this hasn't been disappointing in the slightest."

"Shucks."

"I'm not going to be weird and ask for a selfie. Yet." Callan grinned and started backing away.

He waved to Everly. "Don't worry. I'm sure Rylan's fine. I'll let you know as soon as I hear anything. You two better get home—it's late."

Harper lifted both hands in the air. "It's barely five o'clock!"

"That's Shroudhaven for you," Everly muttered.

A light mist had descended over them, glowing around the infrequent streetlights. There was no one else out on the street anymore, making it feel like a ghost town. Even Barry and his box were gone.

"Can you see yet why I'm keen to get out of this town as soon as possible?"

"Callan was nice, though. And he didn't seem worried about Rylan. Maybe we'll find him safe and sound, and then you'll change your mind?"

Callan had once felt almost like a younger brother to Everly. She and Rylan had been thick as thieves and Callan would chase them around, trying to be included too. Until everything fell apart.

Rylan had been the one good thing about her life in Shroudhaven. And whether real or in her dreams, he only wanted her gone.

Everly exhaled a puff of air that merged with the mist around them. "I don't think there's a happy ending for me here."

14

E verly shuffled along a crumbling path, partway up the sheer side of a deep, muddy ravine. Dry clay crumbled under one foot and dropped away from underneath her.

Rylan's arm shot out. He caught her around the waist then pulled her close to him. "Careful," he growled.

"It's okay. It's just a dream," she gasped, her heart racing from the feeling of his arms around her more than the threat of the fall.

Chunks of rock and dirt splashed into clear water more than three stories below.

"Right," Rylan said, shaking his head and letting go of her. "Just a dream. But is it your dream or my dream?"

"Mine. I thought I'd made that clear," Everly said, continuing along the ledge, clinging to brittle exposed tree roots to avoid tumbling off the narrow ledge.

"And why exactly are we doing this?" Rylan asked as she led the way.

"We're going to the day spa in that grass hut up ahead," Everly answered. "This is the only way there."

"Day spa," Rylan confirmed flatly.

"Yup."

"Don't you think it's weird a day spa would have such a treacherous entrance?"

"I mean, if it were real, sure. But this isn't real. Obviously." Everly wasn't surprised by the strange journey and wouldn't be if they had to go back and forth a few times either, just because. Dreams liked repetition and challenge. Better to just go along with it.

But she was surprised by Rylan's clarity and curiosity.

"Still feels real to me, Boderleth." Rylan checked his footing as a loose rock tumbled free. "Way too real."

Real like the way Rylan called her by her last name like he used to when they were friends.

"This is probably just a side effect of seeing you in person again," Everly said, more to herself than him. "My head's just all messed up."

"You think your head is messed up? I have no idea what's going on. I feel like I've

been asleep," Rylan said, his husky voice echoing in the ravine around them. "But now that I'm awake again, everything is like a dream."

"Yes. My dream."

Rylan reached out and grabbed Everly's arm, and she could feel a slight tremble in the firm grip. "It would really help me out if you stopped treating me like I wasn't real. This has to be some kind of beshadowing. Or ... I've been thinking about what you said, about what might have happened to me."

"You remember the last dream I had?" Everly stopped walking, but the grass hut still grew steadily closer regardless.

"Yeah, with the roses and scary anxiety dragon and telling me I might be dead? How could I forget?"

That hasn't ever happened before. Rylan acknowledging the entire dreamscape existence and previous dreams in a very meta way was a new development that Everly struggled to process.

"I was probably wrong about that anyway. When I woke up from that dream, you weren't even there." *But blood was.* Although Everly thought the words, they came out clear for everyone to hear.

"Well, whatever happened, whatever this is, this isn't being alive."

Everly turned to look at him, desperate to comfort him somehow, yet unsure if she'd only be comforting a dream. He shifted his eyes away from hers as though ashamed.

She reached for him but held back at the last moment. "Come on. Let's get somewhere more comfortable."

They were close to the end of the ledge now, and she could see a fruit stand outside the grass hut, but when she looked a second time, the colorful melons had become round, fluffy creatures. Her dragon appeared behind them, chasing and tearing into them ravenously.

Everly stepped off the end of the path and sat down beside a wide pool of still, aqua water at the base of the ravine, far below the grass hut and carnage above.

Rylan peered up at the cliff behind them, then at the water. "I can't get used to this dream logic. I feel awake and real. How do I convince you I'm not a dream?"

"Even the fact you're trying to convince me is just making me feel like this is just an especially weird trauma dream. I mean, you're here, in my dream; therefore, you are part of the dream."

"What about things only you and I know about?" Rylan persisted, taking a seat next to her on the lush green grass.

"Like?"

"Like that time we went fishing together and you were so excited, but when you actually caught a fish you cried the entire time I was getting the hook out and throwing

it back? Or when you got your head stuck in the banister and I found you there hours later, you tried to pretend it was all part of a cops and robbers game?"

"So your plan is to bring up only the memories that humiliate me?"

Rylan shook his head, thinking some more. "What about when we first met? Do you remember that? What you said to me?"

On the surface of the still pool, a memory drifted up, playing out in front of them.

Everly, her ashy-white hair tied in twin plaits, scruffy with snagged sticks and leaves, lay curled up on the ground under ancient trees, hugging a ratty, purple plush lion. Rylan, teary and angry and confused, approached.

Everly remembered running away from one of her mom's boyfriends. She got lost, was hurt, weak. It was just luck, or fate, that Rylan found her, also having run away. He never told her why he'd run, only that he felt like a monster.

"You're not a monster." Everly's five-year-old voice was high yet decided.

"Is that how you remember it?" Rylan asked from beside her at the water's edge.

"Pretty much. I was so young, though, and kind of out of it. I must have been seriously dehydrated at that point."

"You don't remember me looking ... *different*?"

"Different how?"

Rylan shook his head. "I remember finding you, helping you get home. I was amazed how strong you were, how quick you got better. I know we were young, but I remember it the same way, mostly."

"Yeah, but these are all things we *both* know. So this could easily be my sleeping brain feeding me information from my own memories."

Everly watched as their younger selves faded away from the surface of the water. A miniature fishing boat cruised by, throwing a net across their past.

"It is weird, though. I hadn't known you cut your hair but have been dreaming about you looking like this for a while, even before seeing you again. But you were always still dreamy, distant. Not full-on tangible inquisition-Rylan like you are now."

He thought for a moment, brows furrowed. "What if there are other parts of me that have changed, that you couldn't have known about? What if I could show you something new?"

Before she could answer, he stripped off his jacket and lifted his T-shirt up over his head. Everly flushed hot. Her jaw dropped, but she didn't look away. Rylan had invited the looking, after all.

"What exactly are you planning on showing me?" Everly's voice cracked.

Under his T-shirt was another layer, an unusual formfitting woven fabric sectioned into plates across his chest and shoulders, joined together with a sinewy elastic. Then he took it off too.

"Oookay. Yes. This is new."

"You never dreamed of me naked?" Rylan teased as he threw the garment onto the grass nearby.

Everly shook her head vehemently. Whenever she dreamed of Rylan, he was always distant, out of reach, doing his own thing—an elusive being she longed for but couldn't have. Just like in real life.

"You can admit it if you have. It's a pretty normal kind of dream."

"I really haven't. Normal? Wait ... *have you*—?"

"This is actually what I meant by new." Rylan turned his bare chest toward Everly, revealing a tattoo she'd never seen before—a coat of arms with the Darkfrey Estate crest.

But his skin was also a patchwork of scars. Some faded white hairlines, and others still puffy and red, drawn across his muscles in parallel lines like claw marks.

"What happened to you?" Everly whispered. She reached a hand out but didn't touch him.

"Nothing." He looked away from her, snatching his shirt and shrugging back into it. "Dog attack."

Everly dropped her hand and raised her eyebrows. "Dog attack? Really? Have you been employed training vicious guard dogs or something? Run an illegal dogfighting ring? Is that what goes on up at the estate? 'Cause that was a whole lot more than one dog attack."

"Forget about that." Rylan's jaw clenched. "I meant for you to see the tattoo. It is new, isn't it? Something you didn't know?"

"I didn't know there was a grass-hut day spa at the top of a muddy trail either, and yet here we are. Brains create weird things in dreams." Everly sighed and put her toes into the water which had risen closer to them.

Her head spun. Was he real or wasn't he? Did the scars mean anything or not? Unless she could see his real body out in the real world, she couldn't confirm anything.

"But ... something does feel different. About my dreams, since I saw you. You feel different."

Rylan nodded solemnly. "And if I'm not a dream, then I'm guessing I must be dead."

"Don't say that."

He raised exasperated hands to indicate the rising water and strange slant of the ravine around them and dragon flying high in the purple sky above. "I can't think of any other explanation for how I'm trapped in all this, not one that doesn't mean I'm dead either way."

Trapped. He thought being there with her was a trap.

Is that what he was? A ghost, forced to haunt the dreams of the person he only ever wanted to get away from.

Everly's dragon approached, still hungry after its decimation of the animals above, and she shook off the dark thoughts.

"There's no proof. I saw Callan today, and he didn't seem worried. The police didn't seem worried. And whatever happened, you're missing—not there at all. You probably just left, and these dreams are me dealing with that. Or it has all been a dream."

Everly stood up again as the ground she sat on narrowed and the pool dropped away. She was back on the clay ledge, heading to the grass hut. Always moving toward a destination she knew she'd never reach.

Rylan took hold of her arm, stopping her futile march forward. "I'll find a way to prove to you I'm real."

Because she was pretty sure he was a dream, Everly had the courage to say, "I used to think we were fated to be together. Whatever is happening, it's just proof I've been wrong my whole life."

Rylan bent toward her, and for a moment it seemed like he would kiss her. She froze, her breath caught in her throat as he stared at her in a way that could have cracked her heart into pieces.

"You never know what you're fated for until you reach the end of your story. I think my story has ended."

15

He's dead. He's dead.
    There was blood.
Was it blood? Was it his blood?
It all felt so real.
It couldn't have been.
Where is he?
Was any of it real?
Please … Rylan, please be okay.

Everly was scrubbing the linoleum in the kitchen when Harper stood in the doorway and made puppy-dog eyes and kawaii poses at her until Everly couldn't ignore her any longer.

"Do you need something?" Everly asked brightly.

"You're the one who clearly needs something. You've been scrubbing that same spot for forty-five minutes. You're going to wear a hole through the floor."

"Oh." Everly stared at the one wet patch in front of her, scrunched up her face, and dropped the scrubbing brush into the bucket beside her. "I may be a bit distracted."

Harper raised one shoulder. "Seeing the love of your life get brutally attacked and then go missing might do that to you."

"There's no part of that sentence that's necessarily true." Everly stood up and gave the bucket a gentle kick with her boot. The sudsy water blooped in a little splash.

"The whole vibe I've been getting from you ever since makes me feel like it is. You deal with anxiety and panic attacks every day, but this, this is different. Something is going on."

Everly pulled her work gloves off, tossing them on the counter. "I just need to clear my head. My dreams have been wild lately, and weirdly accurate."

"All the more reason we need to find Rylan. I believe that you saw something the other night. Whether it was a vampire, a prank, or an escaped wild animal, I don't know, but you need to find out."

Everly turned to the kitchen window, imagining again what she'd seen through

it. "Animal attacks really are pretty common around here. That's actually how Rylan's dad died."

"That's a great big yikes." Harper folded her arms over the shell-pink pirate shirt she'd paired with pinstriped dress pants.

"That's Shroudhaven for you."

Harper shook her head. "If my horror movie addiction has taught me anything, it's that an *animal attack* is never just an animal attack. Also, if that *is* all it was, how much of a jerk is Rylan if he got up and left without saying anything to you? What kind of guy gets mauled and leaves before you wake up, right?"

Everly couldn't contain a chuckle. "Thank you. For everything."

"I'm just getting started. By the time we're done in this crazy-ass town, there's going to be a whole new, less traumatized you. Starting with some closure on this Rylan business." Harper turned and swept out into the hallway, as though expecting Everly to follow.

Everly remained planted, calling after her friend, "We should just leave it. We only have a couple of days left and so much more cleaning to do. And I haven't heard anything from Callan. He said he'd handle it."

Harper leaned back into the doorframe, grinning impishly. "And you're really going to leave it up to him? I think it's time we paid him a visit. We're going to find out what's really going on around here."

Howell House sat in the middle of some fields like a clumped wedding cake, faded ivory wrought iron wrapping the all-around veranda like frosting. The veranda Everly and Rylan used to race laps around as children—races Rylan had let her win.

Everly and Harper walked up the lane leading to the aged homestead, lined with birch trees and lilies, their white blossoms glowing in the light of sunset ribboning through the trunks.

It was only a couple of blocks away from the Boderleth residence. Everly hadn't been able to get through on the phone to Callan, and she felt weird about showing up unannounced.

Her nerves were trying hard to get the best of her, make her turn back, but Harper urged her up the gravel drive.

Fields of long grass and blackberry brambles bordered the lane on each side. So much of it was just how Everly remembered it from her childhood.

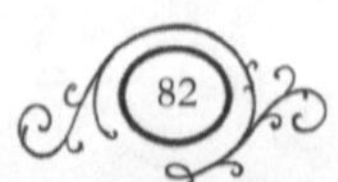

Long late summer days when she and Rylan would hide away together in their cave of thorned canes, gorging themselves on the fruit, faces and fingers covered in dust and sticky juice.

She looked into the brambles, hopeful to spot some of the dark, juicy berries, but it was the wrong season.

Instead, something glinted, two reflective eyes piercing through the foliage.

Harper reached out and grasped Everly's wrist sharply, making her gasp.

"Do you think they'd let me do a photo shoot here?" she asked.

Everly returned her gaze to the field, but if there had been eyes there, they were gone.

"Yeah, maybe. Rylan's mom, Lian, was always really nice," she replied as the house came closer into view.

It was much how Everly remembered it, but in a worse state of repair. Lian was a Pimey by birth—one of the older families of Shroudhaven that held claim over the naming rights of a hill, creek, and number of businesses.

It was only after she'd married that the homestead took on the name Howell House.

The front garden area was a mix of well-tended yet dated ornamental plants with white-washed garden edging. An unfamiliar, run-down RV was parked crookedly on one side between the house and the garage.

An equally unfamiliar small figure sat on the porch swing, all in black, cuddling their knees and shadowed by an oversized hood.

"If Lian even still lives here," Everly added, then called out, her voice timid and cracking, "Hello?"

The girl looked up slowly. She had a shaved head, pale skin, and the face of a doll—a doll that clearly hated the world. She unfolded hands that were stained as black as ink.

Her eyes stuck to Everly and Harper as they reached the front steps but she didn't reply.

The front door swung open, the screen door clattering and drawing Everly's attention away from the goth girl to a middle-aged man sporting a stained brown T-shirt and uneven blond beard.

"Hoooooly shiiit!" he sang like a crude game show host. He punctuated it by cracking the tab on a beer can and taking a swig.

"Uh, hi?" Everly began.

The man pushed past her to Harper. "It really is Bellsy! Callan said he saw you yesterday in town, but I didn't believe him. He also said you were as good-looking as your feed, and I didn't believe that either."

The goth girl grunted in disgust, but when Everly looked over, the girl was gone, as though she'd vanished into thin air.

"Always nice to meet a fan," Harper said, sounding almost like she meant it.

"Been following you forever! Callan wouldn't even know you if it weren't for me. When you got doxed, I considered coming to visit you—that's how big of a fan I am." He smiled beatifically as though providing the highest compliment.

The look on Harper's face was one of utter horror. "Please don't ever. Ever."

"Yeah, that is not okay. Look, is Callan around?" Everly asked.

"Probably." He shrugged like he couldn't offer anything more helpful. "I'm Denny, Denny Sketchman. You can call me Sketch; all my friends do."

He reached out for Harper's hand to shake, and when she didn't immediately extend hers, he reached farther and took it anyway.

"Ew," Harper squeaked.

"There are precisely zero people who call you Sketch." A tall woman with a tidy bun of salt-and-pepper hair appeared behind him.

She carried a tiny dog under one arm and a broom in the other, looking like she wanted to beat Denny with it. "How many times do I have to kick you out of here?"

"Come on, Mama Howell. You know you love me." He put on a charming smile, swiping his curly blond hair back.

"Is that my beer?"

"Busted." He winked at Harper and took another long swig.

"Out, now! Or you and your RV can go find somewhere else to park." Lian exclaimed, stamping the broom handle against the hardwood floor.

The dog, fluffy-haired and dim-eyed from age, started barking.

Holding up his beer can with his middle finger sticking out prominently, he trotted straight through a garden bed toward the motor home. All three women grunted in disgust at the same time.

"Sorry about that." Lian turned her attention to Everly. "I heard you were back in town. It's been a while. You look well."

Everly brushed a hand along her braided hair nervously. "You too. Is that Birdie?"

Lian left the broom leaning beside the doorframe and ruffled the white curls on the dog's head. "Yep, still with us. You here for a visit? I can put some tea on."

"That's okay. We were just hoping to see if Callan had found out anything."

"You just missed him. He went up to the Darkfreys to see his brother. Found out anything about what?"

"He didn't say?" Everly frowned at Harper.

Everly wasn't sure why Lian didn't know about Rylan's possible missing status, but felt that if Callan hadn't mentioned it, she probably shouldn't either.

"It was nothing really. Just about ... where we could get, umm, a weed trimmer, for cleaning up my old place."

"I have one in the back shed," Lian said, waving them both inside, her floor-length

gray knitted coat swinging behind her as she led the way. "The boy would know that if he ever helped out in the yard. Hey, Rushelle?"

A broad-shouldered woman with outrageous curves and white-gold hair piled on top of her head stepped into view at the end of the hall. She wore a marching band jacket over a sunflower-yellow leather corset.

"This is Everly and ..."

"Harper," Everly answered.

Rushelle beamed. "Are they—?"

"Old friends, from *out* of town," Lian said, and handed Birdie over to Harper. "Look after my guard dog for me. I'll go get that weed trimmer for you."

Birdie yapped once, then worked on licking every inch of the underside of Harper's chin.

"Great to meet you two! Let me pop the kettle on." Rushelle smiled cheerily and led Everly and Harper to the kitchen.

Everly breathed in deeply and the familiar scent of the home, one of laundry soap and baked vegetables, filled her chest with warm memories.

Everly was slightly heartbroken that the kitchen had been renovated, changed from the one she'd had some of her few happy memories in with the family that wasn't even hers.

Some parts of the original design were still present though—a unique mosaic backsplash and the historic farmhouse table, so thick and solid it probably couldn't be relocated if they tried. As familiar as the home was to her, it felt strange to find it crawling with strangers.

Rushelle bustled about cheerily, pulling cups from the cupboard.

What is going on here?

"Do you live here too?" Everly asked.

"No honey, I'm just a regular. Come by whenever I can to help out Ms. Howell. Just a sec—let me save my writing." She tapped briefly on a yellow laptop covered in rhinestone mermaid stickers that sat on the kitchen counter. "Tammy and Cherry are the only live-ins at the moment, and Callan's back now too. And Denny, albeit entirely unwelcome."

Harper shuddered and cuddled Birdie closer.

"You met him?" Rushelle barked a laugh. "That guy is *the worst*."

"Spoke to him for a whole of a few seconds and have to agree completely." Harper made a gagging sound. "What are you writing?"

"Fantasy romance satire mostly. The Far King series is my main one. *Taken for the Far King, A Virgin for the Far King, Hunted for the Far King*, and *A Bride for the Far King*." She ticked each title off on her fingers. "It's a good little side hustle."

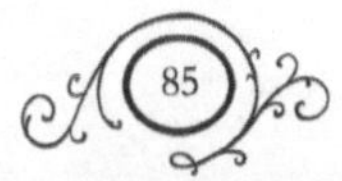

Harper laughed and patted Birdie. "I will absolutely be checking those out."

Rushelle winked. "Thanks, little duck."

"Is Lian renting rooms?" Everly asked.

She turned her head upward, as though magnetically drawn in the direction of Rylan's old room, hoping it hadn't been renovated or changed—or used as a hoarder's trash pile.

"No, she's an old softy, that marvelous woman. Brings in those who have nowhere else to go." Rushelle filled the vintage-style kettle and put it on the stainless-steel gas range. "What do you girls want? We have all the beverage basics covered. Hit me with your requests."

"We're fine, really. We'll just grab the weed trimmer and head off." Everly felt awkward enough already.

She didn't want to prolong the small talk. But she was curious about a few things. "Callan said he moved home six months ago. Does Rylan visit sometimes, too?"

"Not in years." Lian pushed the back door to the kitchen open from outside.

The sun had set and insects zoomed about in the porch light behind Lian as she kicked off her boots on the way in.

She thrust the weed trimmer out to Everly, who tried to take it, but Lian didn't loosen her grip. She put her other hand on Everly's shoulder. "But you know you could have always come by, if you needed anything, even after the boys left."

"Sorry I didn't visit you after … everything." Everly's face heated.

The funeral for Rylan's dad was the last time she'd really seen the Howell family together. Rylan was already not talking to her at that point, and Everly never thought she'd still be welcome in their home.

Had Everly abandoned Lian just as thoroughly as her sons had? Her childhood errors were so much clearer through grown-up hindsight.

"I'll try to stop in again soon, when we can stay for a proper chat, while I'm still in town." The offer felt hollow, knowing she only had two more days, but she had to offer something.

"That would be lovely." Lian let go of the garden tool and took Birdie back from Harper. "Now, you know you shouldn't be out so late. You need someone to walk you home?"

Harper looked at her watch and raised her eyebrows at Everly.

"I'm sure we'll be fine. It's not far." Everly gave Lian a stilted hug and thanked her for the loan.

On their way down the front steps, Lian called out from the front door, "Sorry about your mother."

Everly nodded, a pang of guilt passing over her. Lian had been more of a mother

to her than her own ever had.

Should I tell her about Rylan?

It didn't seem worth it until she had some proof. She rested the weed trimmer over one shoulder, getting a strong whiff of cut grass and gas, and waved goodbye.

As they reached the end of the lane and headed past the row of houses on the main block, Everly said, "You think Callan thought what I said about Rylan was so ridiculous it wasn't even worth mentioning ...?"

"Or did he think it was so serious he didn't want to worry anyone yet?" Harper finished the thought. "I mean, it could really go either way."

"He is looking into it if he's gone to the estate to try to see Rylan." Which made Everly think he must be taking it seriously, and that made her anxiety churn her insides into curds and whey. "I know it's late, but can I borrow the van to drive over to Shroudhaven Heights?"

"It's barely past six o'clock!" Harper laughed. "And no. I'll drive. I'm coming too, because if there's any chance of seeing a vampire tonight, I'm in."

Everly eyed the dimming sky and shivered. Rylan had begged her not to go out after dark. She wanted to laugh at Harper's joke, but the longer they remained in Shroudhaven, the more worried she became that they might really stumble across a vampire, or something far worse.

16

Everly squinted through the windscreen into the darkness, only able to make out four smudgy dark figures in the dim light. "Is that Callan? Who's he with?"

Harper spoke out of the corner of her mouth as though telling a joke. "A cute Asian guy with bright-red hair, a mean looking blond woman, and a guy in a cardigan? All walk into a bar—"

"Pull over."

"Huh? Why?"

"Pull over here!"

Harper brought the campervan to a lurching halt against the curb, down the street from the intimidating silhouette of the Darkfrey gates.

"Did they see us?" Everly asked, reaching over to turn the headlights off herself.

"They don't seem to be paying any attention our way. What's going on?"

Now that they were a little closer, Everly used Harper's description to clarify the vague shapes she was seeing. Callan and someone else on the footpath, and the blond woman and cardigan guy inside the gates.

The people from her dream again. They were Darkfreys?

"On our first night here, I saw Rylan again, after you fell asleep."

Harper swung around, resting an arm on the steering wheel and staring at Everly with high eyebrows. "Please, do tell."

"Not like that! Just out front while I was taking out garbage. I talked to him for maybe a minute before a couple of those people showed up, and he went all cold and rude, even more than usual."

"You think they have something to do with what's going on?"

Everly wasn't ready to tell Harper that she'd been dreaming of those people too, or how much it was starting to feel like her dreams were a lot more real than they should be.

She winced and shrugged. "Maybe? I don't know about the other guy with bright-red hair. Who did Rushelle say was living with them? Cherry?"

"It would fit. So what do we do? Wait for them to go before we talk to Callan?"

Everly chewed her lip, eyeing the couple of cars parked along the street near the gates. "I kind of want to hear what they are saying."

Harper's mouth dropped open and then broke into a wide grin. "Secret spy-like eavesdropping? Yes! Let's do this."

Climbing out of the van, Everly and Harper closed their doors softly, then ducked behind the parked car in front of them.

A whipping wind swirled through the leaves of tall trees lining the fenced-off Darkfrey grounds across from them, covering their footsteps as they scurried up to the next car, then the next, until Callan's voice reached them.

"Jasper, this could be serious. Just let us in."

Everly tilted her face to peer over the hood of the car she crouched behind.

Through the gate, the cardigan guy—Jasper—fidgeted with one of his buttons. "You can't come in. Sorry."

"You should be." Cherry shoved both hands aggressively into the pockets of his red-and-white racer jacket.

A brisk wind whipped his bright-scarlet hair into his face, and he scowled.

Callan leaned against the gate, but it didn't move, firmly barred.

A high-tech keypad and monitor to one side were in stark contrast to the ornate black twisted metal of the gate and the word Darkfrey lettered across the top in a curling script, entwined with sculpted bats.

Through the bars, past the dark wooded surrounds and up the long drive, Everly could barely see the massive mansion that sprawled on the cliffside in the distance. The glow from the windows was as small as fireflies from down at the gate, mere pinpricks of light lining the horizon.

She'd often imagined what it was like for Rylan and Callan, growing up behind that barred gate. She jealously pictured castles and feasts and secret passages and fancy boarding school uniforms.

Callan spoke again, the words cut off in a gust of wind before growing clear. "—see Rylan. Could you send him down since you're not letting us in and he's not answering his phone?"

The blond woman folded her arms. "He's not here."

"Then do you know where he is?"

"We haven't seen him for two days, since he chose to venture out alone," Jasper said.

Two days?

That lined up with when his body disappeared from Everly's street. Everly's heart jumped into her throat and she and Harper locked wide eyes.

The blond woman rasped, "Don't tell the Howell runts that. They aren't with us anymore. They don't need to know our business."

"It's his brother—he should know," Jasper said flatly.

There was a rattle of metal as Callan grasped the gate with both hands. "Vonny, you have to tell me what you know. Have you been looking for him?"

"Where would we look? Besides, Mordan's been on our asses about him being gone, blaming us for splitting up, losing his golden boy. He's grounded our brace. Like it's our fault your brother has been playing loner and running off doing his own weird shit," Vonny replied.

Everly's mind was stuck in a loop. *Two days. Two days. He really was missing.*

Callan shook the gate roughly, as though trying to push it open. "You're telling me he's been gone two days and you have no idea where?"

"If he was hurt, he'd have shown up back here. If it was worse, a cleaning crew would have found him."

Harper whispered, "*What the ...*"

"Who's there?" Callan yelled.

Harper's eyes widened. In an even quieter whisper, she swore. "Sorry! How did he hear that?"

Footsteps approached.

Everly raised herself to standing, giving a sheepish smile. "Umm, hi?"

"Her again? What's she doing here?" Vonny's nose wrinkled as though she were seeing something unpleasant.

Callan glanced between her and the gates. "Everly? What are you—?"

"Found it!" Harper popped up from behind the car too and pretended to put something away into a small case she pulled from her pocket. "Missing contact lens. What's going on?"

Everly half smiled at her. She wasn't sure it was even slightly convincing, but any excuse seemed better than nothing.

Everly moved closer to Callan. "We were hoping to catch you here."

Harper followed, arching her neck to take in the scene. "Wow, look at that gate! Gorgeous. Gothic. One hundred percent uninviting. I totally get the vampire stories now."

"Ugh, blivs," Vonny snarled.

"Gesundheit?" said Harper.

"Is Rylan here?" Everly asked, pretending she hadn't heard any of the conversation before being exposed.

"I was just checking in on him, like you asked." Callan smiled, but there was a dark gleam in his eye and a twitch in his jaw.

She looked at him expectantly, prompting him to continue.

Vonny glared at all of them. Jasper and Cherry stared at each other, wordlessly

communicating through a series of eye motions and tilted chins.

"And?" Harper sang into the silence.

"He's up in his room but doesn't want to see any of you," Vonny spoke over Callan.

"That's not what you said a minute ago," Cherry teased.

Jasper gave him a warning look.

Vonny eyed them all through the gate. "A minute ago I was ready to beat your runt asses. Do you really want to go back to a minute ago?"

A lean pole of a man cleared his throat from behind Vonny, and she turned around.

"In for it now," she whispered and ducked to the side away from him.

The figure stepped up to the gate, the satin lapels of his black and maroon suit shimmering in the lamplight. His arrival had been so silent it startled everyone. He lifted a goateed chin and stared down his nose at those outside the gate.

He addressed Callan but shot glances toward the two inside the gate as well. "I know why you're here. But unless you're joining us again, Callan, you are no longer privy to estate business. Your former peers should know this as well."

"Of course, Master Darkfrey." Vonny nodded and shot a spiteful look at Jasper. "That's exactly what *I* was saying."

Master Darkfrey ... as in head of the whole Darkfrey Estate? Everly tried to get a better look at the older man, and his eyes sparkled as they passed over her and Harper as though they were nothing.

Callan's jaw worked and his tone was flat. "No, I won't be joining you again."

"Then we're done here." Master Darkfrey turned and strode away so quickly, he seemed to vanish into the darkness.

Vonny threw those outside the gate one last sneer and chased after him.

Jasper turned as well and took a step away before hesitating. He tilted his head back, glancing at Cherry, then Callan. "Sorry."

"Don't be sorry, be helpful," Cherry snapped.

Jasper's eyes flicked from side to side a couple of times, then he moved toward the gate. Cherry and Callan stepped close, and he whispered to them, out of earshot of Everly. All she could catch was something about cleanup crews again.

Then Jasper nodded once, ignoring Everly and Harper, and strode away up the hill.

Callan and Cherry stared at each other, locked in some silent understanding.

"Well, that was *something*," Harper said, a nervous giggle in her voice. "If that old guy isn't a vampire, then I'm a bunny on a unicycle."

Cherry extended a hand. "Hi, bunny on a unicycle. I'm Cherry. Nice to meet you. Love your work."

Harper laughed and shook his hand.

"His introduction beat yours," she told Callan.

Callan only half smiled.

Everly could tell he was worried, really worried, as much or more than her.

She folded her arms and asked, "So is Rylan in his room like *Vonny* said, or is he missing like *Jasper* said earlier?"

"Shit, you heard that?"

She nodded shakily. "Glad we did too, since it's clear you weren't planning on telling us."

Callan put his hand on her shoulder and directed her away from the pool of light around the Darkfrey gate. His eyes flickered with thought and when they stopped in the shadows, he ran his hands through his hair and opened his mouth, then closed it again three times without managing to say a thing.

"If something's going on, you can tell me," Everly said. "I know you're worried too."

Callan leaned against the Darkfrey fence and groaned softly in defeat. "Yeah. I am. Rylan is missing, but the estate lot are being their usual closed-off selves about it all."

"It really seems to be their way." Everly pulled her jacket closer around her. She coaxed, "But you seem to have gotten out?"

Callan shrugged, looking back at his punk-hair-colored friend. "The estate was always where Rylan wanted to be. After a while, I disagreed too much with ... their policies. I figured Rylan didn't really need his little brother tagging along anymore, watching his back."

Callan swallowed visibly, and Everly felt the weight of his statement.

They both hoped he hadn't figured wrong.

"The estate, are they up to something shady?" Everly asked softly.

The corner of Callan's lip quirked up, but without any real humor. "What exactly did you see the other night?"

Everly felt the blood rush from her face as she tried to process things that didn't seem real, that were too terrifying to be real, but were starting to be confirmed. She was just getting Callan on her side; she didn't want to scare him off by sounding unbelievable.

"I'm not sure what I saw. It all sounds so wild."

"It's vampires. Vampires with tentacles," Harper said, joining them.

Callan raised an eyebrow at Everly and she sighed in return.

"There's no such thing as vampires," Cherry said, trailing after.

"You're obviously part of the cover-up, so you have zero credibility," Harper sassed.

Everly said, "Look, I can give you all the details, as weird as they are. If you think it would help find Rylan ... I don't mind sounding crazy."

"All right, let's hear it," Callan said.

Everly had just opened her mouth, starting with an explanation of the dream she'd had leading into the fight on the street, when Callan and Cherry shared a sharp,

wide-eyed look.

"Uh, Call?" Cherry cleared his throat. "I really need to go."

Callan turned back to Everly, smile wide and patently fake. "You know what, on second thought, what if we pick this up again another time?"

"Wow, do I really sound that ridiculous?" Everly frowned.

Callan waved nonchalantly, backing away down the street. "No, no, not at all. Just, you know, it's late ..."

"Well, do you guys need a lift?" Harper offered, pointing to the campervan with her thumb.

"All good. We parked around the corner," Callan said as he and Cherry picked up their pace, heading for the darker shadows on the other side of the street.

A strange, soupy, sickness filled Everly's chest. The same nebulous emotion she often had in her dreams when watching the dark, unknowable creatures that populated her nightmares, indistinct in form but clear in their presence.

The feeling she was looking at a monster.

It's just Callan. He's just the boy you've known most of your life.

Everly shook herself and called out, "What about Rylan?"

Callan's retreat faltered. "Do you know anything else you can tell me that might help find him?"

Everly thought for a moment. "Maybe. It's a bit of a long shot, but I might be able to find something out tonight."

"Don't do anything dangerous," Callan warned. "Just leave it, okay? For tonight. I'll come round tomorrow morning, and we can work it out then."

"Bye. Nice to meet you!" Cherry called from the shadows far ahead.

Everly and Harper stared in confusion as the two men vanished into the dark.

"What got into them?" Harper muttered.

Everly pressed her lips into a thin line. "I don't know. But there's definitely something they aren't telling us."

17

A harsh, nightmarish stretch of shore and sea solidified as Everly fell deeper into slumber.

When the dream scenery began to settle, she spoke her words, taking control. *I'm asleep. This is a dream. Oh no ... Not this one. Not again.*

Sand shifted under her toes, and she looked out at an endless, troubled ocean. The water twisted and turned, black and peacock green, flashes of white foam dancing across the high peaks of thunderous waves.

The scenery felt familiar, and Everly's brain labeled it as a beach up in Hartleydale, just north of Shroudhaven, despite it looking nothing like the real thing.

The coastline stretched too long, out to infinity, the horizon line lifting too high into the starry sky. Rolling sand dunes of sparkling silver, bare of trees or scrub, rocks or shells flowed into the dark, turbulent water.

Everly gave the waves an anxious look, knowing what was coming.

The dragon chased the shadow of a cougar up and down the argent hills, nipping at the big cat's heels. Toying with it.

Everly turned in a three-sixty, trying to find Rylan, hoping he'd be there again, and found him walking along the beach toward her.

Despite knowing it was a dream, a rush of relief filled Everly at the sight of him. If he went missing from her dreams as well, she didn't know what she'd do.

She held on to her plan, hoping that it wasn't ridiculous, that even having hope wasn't ridiculous.

"I saw Callan again tonight," she told him once he was within earshot. "You're definitely missing in the real world. Even he's worried."

Rylan just frowned, looking out at the water and the receding tide.

"There's something going on, isn't there? Something you know about, and Callan knows, and I don't know who else."

It felt like everyone she met was in on it. Callan's friend, Cherry, had the same dilated galaxy eyes that the Howell brothers had at night, and with his K-Pop idol features, he clearly wasn't related to them, so that didn't explain the resemblance.

Plus, both of them and the people from the estate had been giving off really vampy vibes. It was as though she'd almost been able to sense their teeth *growing*.

"If you'd just tell me, maybe I could—"

"No. There's nothing going on that you need to do anything about," Rylan snapped. Having glowered at the ocean long enough, he turned his frown on her. "Where are you now? If you saw Callan, you're still in Shroudhaven, aren't you? I told you to go."

Everly stood firm. "I know you want me gone, but I still have two days to finish up getting the house in order and a heap of work that needs to be done, so I'm not going anywhere until I run out of time."

The tide drew out farther and farther until the waves disappeared over the horizon and fish and crabs lay bare and flopping on exposed rocks, slick with writhing kelp.

Everly warily watched the bare sea floor. "And I need to work out what *this* is, this version of you here in my dreams and where you are in the real world. I don't know if leaving Shroudhaven will stop these dreams or whether you're ..."

Rylan growled, "It doesn't matter. About the dreams or me. You need to leave so you can be safe."

"From what? What's going on?"

Rylan didn't answer, his attention locked on the ocean.

The water returned, a wall of it in the distance, higher than a mountain peak and swiftly rolling toward them.

Rylan stared at it in horror. "Is that going to be a problem?"

"Come on," Everly said, jogging away from the beach.

Over the sand dune, a parking lot was filled with panicking tourists, screaming and running in all directions. Everly spotted Harper's campervan and led Rylan behind it. She pressed her back to the van, bracing for the wave to hit.

Rylan looked at the rushing water crashing toward them. "Are you crazy? The tsunami will smash this van to bits. This isn't going to work."

"Trust me, it will. I know it doesn't make much sense, but it's a dream, remember? Physics work differently here, if at all. Just keep close behind the van and hold your breath."

The tsunami broke over them. It hit the van and split, pouring past Everly and Rylan on either side in churning waves, only a small gap of air left around them. The protective rift within the tide closed, water pushing in closer and closer to Rylan and Everly. She held her breath as they were submerged.

For a few moments she was breathless, water lifting and smashing around her, trying to drag her with it. Then the wave dispersed, her head emerged again above the salty liquid, and she could breathe.

As the tide drained away as fast as it arrived, she found herself pressed against the

van with one of Rylan's arms around her soft torso, holding her safe.

Rylan drew a deep breath and let her go. Water dripped from his eyelashes and chin. He scrubbed it from his short hair.

"I can't believe that worked."

Everly's pulse quickened, her heart calling out to be held again. "Yeah. This is a recurring dream for me, so I know all the tricks. Just be ready—it will probably happen again."

Rylan wiped his face and watched the beach. "It all feels so real to me. I keep having to remind myself where I am. Are your dreams always so perilous?"

He hasn't seen the worst of it.

This was nothing. Her dreams could get much darker. She shrugged her lips.

"My therapist says that dreams are like our brain's way of testing us with challenges in a safe environment. Like hypothetical training for real-world problems."

"You have a therapist?"

"You don't?"

He shook his head, watching the receding water swirl around their ankles.

Everly looked him up and down. He still wore the same T-shirt, jeans, and jacket she'd seen him in the night everything went crazy, although now saturated.

In past dreams, he'd always been different. He'd be one of the actors in whatever play her sleep theater was putting on for the night, or sometimes just doing his own thing in the distance, ghostly, like the cougar. He didn't have this consistency, dream to dream—this level of awareness—that he did now.

Now, he seemed as real as he could be.

Maybe her long-shot plan could work.

"You said you wanted to prove you're real. Now's the time," she told him.

"How?"

"Tell me something you know that I *don't* know. But something I can confirm tomorrow when I'm awake." She could see as much turmoil in his expression as she had in the ocean.

"Like what?" he asked, guarded.

"Like about all the vampire weirdness going on, obviously!"

Rylan laughed through his nose. "There's no such thing—"

"As vampires. Yeah, yeah. So everyone keeps telling me. If it's not that, what is it? Give me *something*. Something that could help find out where you are."

A new wave approached, rumbling like a stampede of animals toward them, swallowing up everything in its path.

Rylan frowned at it, and his arms lifted to hold Everly. "I don't know what to tell you. I don't know where I am, and I can't tell you anything else."

"Can't or won't?"

His grip on her shoulders tightened. "I *can't* let you get caught up in something dangerous."

The water hit, rushing past on either side of them in deafening torrents as they looked into each other's eyes.

"And I can't watch you die and just go back to normal as though nothing happened!"

Rylan grunted through clenched teeth, then shouted over the swirling gush of water. "Okay. Fine. Tell Callan ... tell him to check the old Rook's Theater. It's where I was before ..."

Before you died? Everly's arms lifted as well, holding Rylan in return.

The wave closed in around them, rushing upward to submerge them entirely.

Rylan yelled, "Just tell Callan. Don't go yourself."

As they held their breaths and went under again, Everly already knew she wasn't going to follow Rylan's orders.

Everly couldn't hold on to the dream any longer and woke up gasping for breath. She could still feel Rylan's arms where they'd pressed against her, holding her safe within the raging tide, and felt an even deeper yearning for it to have been real.

But if he's real in there, does that mean he's dead out here?

She shivered into a sitting position, cuddling her sleeping bag tight around herself on the couch.

It would be better if none of it was real, if all of it was just her messed-up head. Better if dream-Rylan was imaginary, the violent death was just a hallucination, and Rylan wasn't missing, but just avoiding her completely. That had to be better than the alternative.

But she had to know. And now she had a lead—something that might offer proof. And she was going, regardless of what Rylan had told her.

She had to see what was happening for herself. She had to know. It was her second to last day of leave from work. There wasn't much time left to find out.

It was still early, so Everly sent Callan a text message to let him know she had a clue to look into, whenever he was ready. She half expected not to see him again until the sun set.

Am I really considering that Callan could be a vampire? What has my reality even become?

Still, she had only seen him after dark since she'd been back.

She shook her head. No, it was ridiculous.

After a strong coffee, Everly got to work doing some maintenance around her old home, making use of the early hours. It helped take her mind off her worries, and she had to get as much done as she could.

Her leave from her apartment-superintendent job was unpaid and she was watching her budget carefully. She'd just do what she could to improve the place in the five days she had, then hope for the best with a sale.

When planning the trip, Harper had offered, as she had numerous times since they'd first met, to bring Everly on as her paid assistant. Everly had done small construction jobs on some of Harper's photo shoots in the past but refused to be paid for it.

She was helping out her best friend. And she felt like perfect Harper's pet fixer-upper project at times already, without taking handouts from her as well.

Everly was in the kitchen, refitting a couple of cupboard doors that were loose, when Harper shuffled in on slippered feet.

She poked at the coffee maker that had been bought on one of her grocery trips and smiled sleepily. She'd been up late the night before catching up on work now that they had the internet connected.

"This place is coming along beautifully. Maybe I'll buy it off you and move in."

"I wouldn't let you do that to yourself." Everly tightened the last screw, then began clearing away her tools.

The side of Harper's mouth twisted cheekily. "No, really. I can picture it now. I'll marry Callan, settle down, and raise some cute little vampire babies."

Everly huffed a laugh. "I also noticed the way he was looking at you. A blind turnip would notice the way he was looking at you."

Harper picked up her mug and sipped the fresh coffee. "Pretty sure all turnips are blind, babe."

Everly kept reorganizing her tool bag even though everything was squared away. "Would you really? Go out with Callan?"

"He seems nice enough. But so did Bryce when I first met him. And we know how that turned out." The mention of her ex made all of Harper's cheekiness fade. She tossed back the rest of her coffee, shrugged, then set a bright smile on her face. "I'm just happy being man-free at the moment."

Everly smiled in support. What had gone down with Bryce had been not just ugly, but dangerous. As much as Harper loved to flirt, Everly couldn't miss the underlying vulnerability and fear hidden beneath it—scars left by Bryce's betrayal.

Everly said, "Hey, we've missed a couple of days of yoga. I think there's enough room out on the back porch. Might be a good start to the day?"

Harper left her mug in the sink. "Sounds like just what we need."

It was midmorning by the time Harper rolled out her custom-designed yoga mat and Everly laid out a towel over the worn gray timber of the back porch.

The long ribbons of grass and weeds that filled the backyard swayed back and forth along with the two women as they went through their usual routine together.

It reminded Everly of the waves in her dream, raising anxiety within her that she squashed beneath the peace and feeling of being present that the yoga brought with it.

Everly hadn't checked her phone since waking up, so she was surprised when Callan and Cherry wandered into the backyard in front of them.

"Wow, doesn't this place bring back memories." Callan stepped onto the porch, his voice holding the awe of nostalgia and an edge of sadness.

Everly and Harper both straightened up from their warrior three poses.

There goes the vampire theory. At least for them.

Everly studied Callan, who stood before her in the bright morning sunlight.

The feeling of something monstrous about him that she'd had the night before was gone. He was just Callan, the cute goofball who was like her younger brother. She must have imagined it. Unsurprising, with everything else setting her nerves on edge.

"Bellsy!" Cherry moved in and gave Harper a kiss on both cheeks, then he turned and extended a hand to Everly. "And Everly. We didn't really meet properly last night, but I've heard lots about you, too."

"Really?" Everly shook his hand with one of hers and tugged the hem of her tight tank top with the other, pulling it down over the bare roll of her stomach, feeling self-conscious.

"I might have forced Callan to give me the whole juicy story last night, under the threat of death. I love a good tale of crushes and—"

"So you said you had a lead?" Callan stepped in front of Cherry, looking somewhat pinker. "Ready to look into it?"

"Um, yes to the lead, no to being ready. Sorry, I missed your message. I figured it'd be later before you showed up."

"Why?"

It was Everly's turn to blush, glancing at the bright daylight around them.

"Oh ... oh right!" Callan turned his face toward the sun, shielded it with one arm. "Oh no. It burns. My fragile undead vampire flesh burns."

Everly punched him gently. "Fine, I get it! No vampires."

Callan smirked but didn't laugh. His eyes remained sad.

"Honestly so disappointing," Harper murmured. "I'm going to go and change, if all you non-vampires are okay without me for a minute."

Everly nodded, then watched Callan as he watched Harper go into the house.

Cherry watched Everly watching Callan watch Harper, and when she noticed, he gave her a subtle wink and eye roll directed at Callan.

Callan returned to the present and cleared his throat. "You said in your message you might have somewhere to start looking?"

Everly remembered Rylan's arms around her as the water swirled, his voice calling above the waves. "Right. Yeah. I want to check out the old Rook's Theater."

Callan's face screwed up in confusion. "Really? Why?"

"Just ... I can't explain it yet. And I'm not even sure if there will be anything there. But we have to at least check. Can you please just trust me, for now?"

Callan's eyes softened, and he nodded. "I think that's fair."

The back door swung open and Harper appeared, looking stunning in vintage overalls and a sheer lace blouse. Callan gulped like a cartoon character.

"Anyone want a hot brew before we head out to whatever plans you've planned?"

Cherry nodded, slipping past her to step inside. "I've always wanted to see what the inside of this place was like."

Everly urged Callan in next, then followed. "You guys sort out some coffee to go while I clean up. I'd like to get moving ASAP."

Harper herded them toward the kitchen as Everly bounded upstairs.

"Can I see the antiques store?" Cherry asked.

"No," Harper and Callan said in unison.

Leaving them to it, Everly changed into a clean set of her usual clothes. She didn't want to push any matchmaking but figured giving Harper and Callan some opportunities to get to know each other was okay.

Callan had been a good kid growing up. She hoped he was still a good guy now. Harper deserved at least one good person in her life.

Everly packed her phone, a couple of tools, and her mini first aid kit into the pockets of her navy work pants. She wasn't sure what she should be taking to prepare for where they were going.

Who knew what they would find, or if they'd even get in. Would they be literally breaking and entering? It would be trespassing at least.

Maybe we shouldn't. Maybe we should try to get permission from someone.

Excuses tried to take over. She already had threads of anxiety laying over her like a net, trying to hold her back. But there wasn't any time to get permission or let panic take over.

She only had two days, and if Rylan was hurt, who knows how much time he had. It scared her to follow this clue, but she had to know.

She had to know if Rylan was alive, at least in her dreams.

18

Everly stared at the aged façade of Rook's Theater. The place that could provide answers—answers she wasn't sure she wanted.

If they found something it could prove that the Rylan in her dreams was real. But what if that meant he was dead?

What if that's what I find here today? What if I find his body? What if he'd come back here, injured, and I was too slow to find him in time to help?

"This place is pure grunge coolness." Harper stared at the building in awe.

The theater was beautiful in its own decrepit way. Boarded-up doors and windows had decades worth of vandalism scrawled over the surface, a mess of scribbled tags making the faux columns and art deco frontage took on a look of black lacework, as though the whole building wore a mourning veil.

Everly swallowed down her rising heartrate.

The street they were on was a steep wind tunnel running all the way from the river, and an icy gust blasted by them, lifting scraps of paper and dry leaves around their feet, whistling and moaning like the ghosts of the past.

"Seen what you need to see, or are we going in?" Cherry asked.

"I think we need to go in," Everly replied, unsure she should even be suggesting it.

"We can probably find an entrance around the back," Callan said.

"What, you don't want to break into the place through the front door, right here on the main street? You're no fun," Harper teased.

"And you sound like you are." Cherry smirked back.

Everly looked over her shoulder. They were only a few blocks and around a corner from the Shroudhaven police station. "We don't really have to break in, do we? Or at least, anyone who wants to opt out should do so now. We don't need all of us becoming criminals in one hit. We should pace ourselves."

"If you think you're going to caper without me—you better think again. I want in on capers." Harper whistled innocently and headed off down the narrow side alley.

Everly, Callan, and Cherry followed. Around the back, the building had been covered in so many fragmented posters, stickers, and trash it was like the view through

101

a kaleidoscope had been projected over the walls.

The establishment had been closed for decades after a prank gone terribly wrong killed more than a dozen people.

The story was that someone had yelled 'fire' on a busy night, then locked the emergency exit door. They hadn't accounted for the steep stairs leading down to that door and how people tumbled and were crushed in the stampede.

That was the official story, but this was Shroudhaven, so there were a dozen other conspiracy theories about what had really happened.

That it had been vampires who had torn through the crowd. Or a giant satanic hound. Survivors' tales were mixed and wild with trauma and sensation.

Everly had always brushed them off, thinking that the simplest explanation was generally the correct one. But now, she wasn't so sure. Now she wondered how many dark mysteries that her hometown had shared as whispers were true all along.

Callan stepped up to the industrial-style solid metal door and nudged it with a foot. It swung open freely. "There we go. No breaking necessary, only entering."

A long, dark corridor faced them. Everly clicked on the flashlight on her phone.

"Sooo ... what are the odds we're walking into a crack den?" Harper asked.

"You can wait out here, both of you, while Cherry and I check it out. We should probably have someone as a lookout," Callan offered.

Everly grounded herself, locking down the creeping rise of anxiety. "No, I need to see what's in there."

Harper tapped a finger on her chin. "Stand around in a *boring* creepy old alley on my own, or go into an *interesting* creepy old building with you guys? Feels like a no-brainer to me too."

"I really don't know what could be in there," Everly said. Rylan had warned her not to go, and that warning should no doubt extend to her friend.

Harper pouted. "Aw. Don't worry. I'll protect you."

Callan's mouth twisted in a weird way, then he gave Cherry a worried look and took the lead into the theater.

Everly followed, trying to shine her light forward so they could all benefit from it. But Callan and Cherry moved confidently through the dark, and behind them Harper tripped on the randomly located furniture and debris.

Everly stepped back to walk with her, shining the flashlight where their feet fell and hoping not to see anything move in that beam of light.

Cherry jerked to a stop in front of them, grunting softly.

Callan put his hand up for a second and they all waited. He whispered into Cherry's ear, and Cherry hissed something back.

"Is that ... I don't know if ..."

"It's not … I think it's okay."

"What's going on? Are you feeling all right?" Everly asked.

Cherry smiled up from under a flop of bloodred hair. "No problem. Just a weird feeling. Probably something I ate."

Callan turned his gaze over all of them, his eyes starry and dark. "Maybe I should check this place out on my own?"

"Then if you go missing too, what am I going to tell your mom?" Everly tried to make it sound like a quip but failed.

Cherry nodded, slapping Callan on the back. "We stick together, tough guy."

Callan stared at him for a long moment, then shrugged. "Come on, then."

The back hallways led them through storage areas where the remains of stage sets and props had been piled in monstrous tangles.

The theater had put on a mix of movie screenings and live shows, mostly smaller local productions. A broken gargoyle watched them from the corner of a papier-mâché castle wall, leaning on a hand-painted swamp backdrop.

Dressmaker mannequins, half-stripped of their tattered costumes, cut creepy, headless silhouettes in the dusty gloom.

They pushed through to the main foyer area, where excess furniture had clearly been stacked, then toppled over, creating a sea of upturned chairs and cobwebs. A dank, nauseating stench floated around with the specks of disturbed dust.

"This place is wild," Harper said, flicking through a pile of old posters on the counter. They crumbled in her hands. "Anything in particular that we're looking for?"

"I don't really know." Everly shone her phone at the faded red velvet curtains leading off to the theater room.

The light fell on a statue of a cheerful round-capped usher with bulging, twitching eyes.

Did it just move?

She held the light on it, and despite the sculpture being terrifying in its own way, it didn't move at all. Fear was playing games with her imagination.

"Maybe there's nothing here."

"There's something," Callan muttered. He frowned deeply. "I mean, maybe. You two should keep looking in here. Cherry and I will go and check out the main stage."

Everly jogged over to meet him at the curtained entrance. "What have I said about splitting up? Not going to happen."

Callan's jaw clenched like he wanted to argue, but he didn't. Harper and Cherry caught up to them and they walked closely together through the short corridor toward the main theater room.

Statues of trumpeting angels lined the walls. The floorboards beneath them whined

a sighing song in musical concert.

The angels moved. Everyone else froze.

The statues swayed slowly at first, a gentle dance to the sighing song—such small motions, Everly wasn't sure what she was seeing, but from the looks on their faces, she was sure the others were seeing it too. Then the angels all spun in a jerky and hideously twisted pirouette and were still again.

"What the actual ghost just happened?" Harper squealed.

"We all saw that, right?" Everly said.

Callan had turned very pale. He approached one of the statues. "It's just ... just dated animatronics."

"Yep, definitely *animatronics.*" Cherry raised his eyebrows at Callan. "I always hated animatronics."

"Why would they still be powered?" Everly asked.

Callan rubbed the back of his head. "I really don't know but *anyway,* nothing to worry about! There doesn't seem to be anything here, so we should probably be heading off now."

He walked toward them, as though trying to herd everyone back the way they'd come.

"Are you in a hurry to get out of here so you can go get your eyes checked?" Harper stood her ground, folding her arms. "Because those statues did not move like animatronics."

Everly nodded in mute agreement. She reached out and touched one of the angels, and it felt hard as stone.

Are Callan and Cherry lying?

Something was happening here. Something Everly couldn't explain. But whatever was going on with the statues, they didn't give her any clues about Rylan or why he'd wanted someone to come here.

And if Callan had answers, she wasn't going to let him hide it from her. "We're not leaving yet. I want to see what's in the main stage room."

Harper nodded, and they both pushed past Callan and Cherry.

Muttering and swearing at each other behind them, the two men caught up as they left the rows of statues. Everly kept an eye on the angels just in case, but there was no more movement.

"Do you guys smell that?" she asked. The rotting stench from before grew stronger. Everly's stomach turned in on itself, swallowing her heart in the process.

What if the thing we find here is a dead body? What if that body is Rylan's?

"Yeah, weird smell," Cherry agreed.

"Like a cat vomited out an old diaper," Harped said.

"That's exactly how I'd describe it too!" Cherry replied.

Callan just continued frowning. "I really think we should go now."

"Why?" Everly demanded. "Do you have something to tell us?"

Callan winced and his voice came out high-pitched. "No?"

Everly turned on Cherry.

He held up his hands. "I'm just here in a support capacity."

"Then we keep going." Everly continued on, following her nose.

She had smelled dead things before. It wasn't the normal smell of death. She held on to that thought as they stepped into the main theater.

Holes in the ceiling allowed a few beams of light through, offering enough illumination to see the area in front of them. The folding chairs cascaded toward a shattered stage.

Through the center of the seating, a wide swath had been smashed, as though a boulder had rolled over them, crashing into the stage at the bottom. Splintered planks jutted out at all angles like crooked teeth.

"What happened here?" Harper whispered.

"This isn't from the stampede, is it?" Everly asked.

"No, I don't think so," Callan said, eyebrows low.

Cherry pushed out one of the folding seats and dropped into it. "Cal? That weird feeling is back. I think I'm just going to wait here, okay?"

Callan nodded. "We won't go far."

They stepped gingerly into the mess of the room. Part of the upper-balcony seating had also been broken away, and they moved quickly from under the structurally unsound section.

Harper picked her way over to the stage area, and Everly continued along the side of the room. She headed toward a small alcove off the side of one of the aisles. She wasn't sure why, but she felt drawn there, like a chilling thread of darkness reeled her in.

The alcove was surrounded by broken statuary of Shakespearean characters—not moving, Everly checked—and unlit neon-light tubing above it that read Snacks.

It no longer held snacks.

Bones, black as midnight and *rippling*, were strung together in a symbol that made Everly feel faint as she looked upon them. She stumbled away, gripping the aisle railing for support.

"What is that?"

Callan appeared beside her, looking in on what she'd discovered. He froze, staring.

"Are those bones real?" she asked.

Callan nodded.

"Are those bones ... human?"

Callan hesitated. His lip twitched ... in anger? "This is ... it's ..."

Everly wasn't sure why he'd be angry, but he seemed furious.

"Do you know what this is?" Everly tried to look at it again and her vision swam. "I've seen black bones like that before. Why are they black? Why are they *moving*?"

Callan either didn't have any answers for her, or he refused to give them.

All he said was, "We have to go."

Was this it? Was this what Rylan had meant for them to find? It was certainly *something*.

Something Everly couldn't have possibly known to find here herself. Which meant the Rylan in her dreams had known something she didn't.

It's real. He's real.

Before Everly could process that fully, Harper called out from near the stage, "Uh ... guys?"

She stood there with her hand over her mouth, staring down into the orchestra pit.

On their way to join her, Callan kept shaking his head. "It was probably just ... some idiot's idea of an art installation or something."

Everly narrowed her eyes at him. "Not even slightly convincing. What do we have to see to get you to admit weird shit is going on?"

"How about this?" Harper choked out the words, as though her voice was fighting with bile for the chance to get out of her mouth.

When Everly looked into the orchestra pit, she was glad she gasped, as the sharp intake of air helped stop anything else from rising out of her throat.

She had no idea what she was looking at, only that it was dead, that it wasn't human, that it wasn't any animal she knew of, that it was huge, and that it had been dead for a while.

The ripped and shredded carcass swam in a pool of smoky haze, as though it smoldered slowly in a lightless, decomposing fire. Everly couldn't identify body parts. There was no clear head or arm or leg.

Just *flesh*. A rotten avalanche of oozing, wrong-colored flesh.

"How do you explain that?" Harper demanded.

"Good question," Callan huffed.

He didn't seem surprised, but rather confused. His body shuddered and he muttered a string of swear words.

Harper pointed, as though any of them had missed the sight. "*That's* a dead monster if I ever saw one. Which I haven't and never expected to. But I will eat my own foot if that's not a dead monster."

Everly grabbed Callan's arm. "You know what that is, don't you?"

He groaned and wiped his hand over his mouth. "You guys shouldn't be seeing

this. You shouldn't know."

Everly tightened her grip gently. "But we have seen it."

"And we'd like to be told, please, what exactly we're seeing and knowing before our brains break, okay?" Harper added.

Callan's shoulders slumped. "That's ... yeah, that's a monster. Monsters are real. Happy now?"

"No," Everly and Harper replied in unison.

Everly didn't really want monsters to be real, but she wanted answers. "What about vampires?"

"Still not real."

"But it's more than just this *thing*, isn't it?" Everly watched Callan carefully. "Could Rylan have done this?"

"Killed it? Maybe. It looks like it's been dead a few days, so the timing lines up. But it doesn't make sense. You said he disappeared from your place."

Everly considered how much of her dreams about Rylan she could share now without sounding crazy. Rylan had told her this was where he was before he fought the thing at her place. Before he had possibly died at her place.

"You're expecting to find sense here?" Harper giggled madly and ran her hands into her hair. She froze, her face screwed up. "Are there any more monsters? Are there any more monsters *here*?"

Callan stared back up the rows of seating where Cherry was looking remarkably pale and waving to get his attention, then back at the grotesque corpse. He shook his head once before he paused, gasping in a sharp breath.

"We have to leave."

Harper chuckled as though he was having a go at her, but his expression had turned grim. He grabbed each of them and started dragging them up the middle aisle.

"What is it? What's the hurry?" Everly shone her light around but couldn't see any movement. "There's nothing else here."

"There is—there's something coming. Just ... believe me. You have to get out of here." Callan groaned and let go of them. His skin changed, wavered.

Cherry was on his feet too, coming back their way. "Is it what I think it is?"

"Yes!" Callan snarled. "I didn't notice at first because of the ... dead one ... it's too close now ..."

Cherry put a hand over his mouth. "Oh no. We can't—"

"I know!"

In the dim light, Everly thought she saw wisps of black smoke surrounding Callan. "Are you okay?"

Harper and Everly stopped, and he thrust both arms at them, pushing them away.

"I'm fine. Keep going!"

"No splitting up," Everly said. "Just tell us what's happening."

Callan groaned again, jaw set in determination, sweat beading on his forehead. His skin crackled and distorted, obscured beneath a mix of sparking glow and living shadow, like lightning within black storm clouds.

His voice changed, growing deeper, growling. "Don't worry about me. You have to *run*."

Callan was engulfed in darkness.

Snapping, stretching, sickening sounds emerged. Shadows and sparks swirled and grew larger, then faded away.

Where Callan had been standing, now a hairy beast loomed over them. Thick, powerful arms ended in razor-sharp claws. It stood upright on hind legs, barely covered in the remains of Callan's torn clothing.

The face was more wolf than human.

It opened its snout like mouth, baring vicious fangs, and growled, "Run!"

19

A roar came from behind Everly and Harper, spinning them around together. Another lupine form stretched and growled, dropping a red-and-white jacket from clawed hands.

"Callan?" Everly squeaked. "Cherry?"

Harper grabbed Everly's hand, her acrylic nails digging in. "Are they *werewolves*? I thought you said it was vampires!"

"I don't know!"

"Are they going to eat us?"

"I don't know!"

Callan looked like he wanted to eat them. Saliva glistened over his sharp teeth.

They should do what he'd told them to do. *Run*.

But Everly was more confused than ever. Was Callan really a monster? Nothing she'd seen in the last ten minutes felt real. It was all too much for her to take in at once and her body refused to act while her mind was in turmoil.

Werewolf-Callan lifted his head to the ceiling and howled, flexing massive, fur-covered muscles at the same time. Cherry howled in reply.

Everly ran. She pulled Harper with her, their hands still locked together, barging past the creature that had been Cherry.

Her heart raced and stuttered, feral, trying to punch its way free of her chest. Her body flushed and chilled, her thoughts swam. Every symptom of a panic attack flooded over her at once, threatening to incapacitate her.

This is too much.

Everly clutched at her chest and wooziness made her stumble, bringing both her and Harper smacking down onto the floor. Coughing out dust, Everly twisted around and looked back.

Callan and Cherry were right on their heels.

And something *else* was right behind them.

Something so big it was twice the height of werewolf-Callan. It had a vague wolfishness about it too, but in a way that was more from a feeling than from any visual cues, except the wicked grin of its mouth.

It was black all over. A black so dark and deep and slimy, it was hard to make out the forms and shapes, like looking into a living oil slick.

There were at least six legs but they were wrong and slithery, the joints bending in disturbing ways, boneless and deadly silent. There were no feet, each limb tapering to impossibly thin points that it balanced on.

It prowled toward them, its movements confusing and sickening, with no face or eyes to ground it as anything familiar.

But it did have a mouth. It opened slowly, slobbering, a strange green glow emanating from within as it kept opening wider and wider—so large it seemed half of the creature's body had split apart.

Everly stared, jaw slack, head aching from the sheer incomprehension of what was in front of her.

Callan let out another roar, but it sounded more frustrated, almost scared. He turned away from the fallen girls to face the nightmare.

Everly was sure she heard werewolf-Cherry mutter a colorful string of curses as he joined Callan at his side.

"Come on." Harper climbed back to her feet, pulling at Everly.

Everly forced herself up, despite the hitched, panting breaths that didn't draw in enough oxygen and the tremors in her legs.

Callan leaped onto the creature's back, tearing into it with his claws. As soon as he made contact with the slimy black being, there was a sizzle and the scent of burning hair. Callan wrenched one of his tree-trunk arms back and a slick coating of darkness covered his hand, burning patches in his fur like acid.

A spatter of ooze landed on Everly's hand, stinging and fizzing.

She gasped and wiped it away. "Watch out!"

Harper squealed, swatting at her bare arms. She dodged another spray of the slime and huddled behind the closest seat.

The creature swung around, smashing through the room with each step, spattering acid like rain and Everly ducked to the other side.

Cherry charged the creature, wolflike feet pounding down the aisle. He jumped and was struck midair by one of the dark mass's long legs. It flicked him, sending him flying over Everly's head.

He hit the crumbling upper balcony, smacking through the broken barrier and into the chairs above. Broken timbers and plaster shards exploded through the air.

Everly was on her feet again, staring up where wolf-Cherry landed, rubble still spilling down around her. She shielded her face from the pattering dust.

Was he ... could he survive that?

She wasn't sure what Cherry was, what Callan was, but she didn't want either of them to be hurt.

Harper screamed as a solid beam landed across the row of seating she'd taken cover in.

Her scream turned to a groan as she twisted on the spot. "My leg! My leg is stuck."

Callan tore into the back of the monster, and it didn't even seem to notice. Its boneless limbs flew upward, swatting and cracking against Callan, landing with bone-crunching thuds.

It's not enough. He's not enough. The monster is going to win.

It felt like watching Rylan die all over again—a memory that now felt horrifyingly real. She had entangled everyone in her curse, doomed to witness those she loved die. Again and again.

Everly stood frozen in place. Should she go and try to help Cherry? But she couldn't leave Callan to die alone. But if she didn't help Harper get out, Harper could die too. She was going to fail them all. She couldn't think through the pounding in her head.

The creature trapped Callan in one of its appendages and reeled him in, closer and closer to its glowing maw.

"Help!" Harper cried, tugging at her trapped leg.

"I can't. I don't know what to do. I can't fix this." Everly gasped out the words.

I'm going to get everyone killed.

Panic closed around her like a vise. She tried to move closer to Harper but crumpled under the pressure.

"You can fix anything. Don't let your dumb dragon take over. Actually, no, wait, *do* let your dragon take over," Harper yelled. "The dumb thing is right this time—this is *real* danger and a bit of adrenaline-boosted strength to get me out of here would be great right now!"

The creature had Callan at its mouth, a swarm of tongues lashing at him. He yelped, wolflike, thrashing to try to free himself.

Every instinct inside Everly screamed at her to not let her dragon take over.

It was wrong, went against every thread of her being, to let panic take control. But she could feel it raging inside her, wanting to burst free.

Maybe if she let it, if she gave in, stopped trying to hold it back, maybe her adrenaline would work how it was supposed to.

With a gulp, she let her barriers down.

Energy surged through her. Every part of her throbbed and seared with the riotous heartbeat tearing through her veins. She felt she would pass out entirely from the overwhelming intensity of the extreme panic attack.

Instead, she *lit up*.

At first, Everly thought the light filling her vision was her consciousness fading, a symptom of fainting, that she'd lost control entirely, but she quickly became more aware, the energy making everything clear.

A white glow filled the theater as sparkling tendrils emerged like lightning from her flesh, lifting her from the ground and carrying her toward the monster. An immense hunger washed over her, seeping deep into her bones.

She wanted ... needed ...

She surged forward down the aisle.

She couldn't control it—where she went, what she did. The light had taken over. The same scintillating, brilliant ribbons of luminance that had appeared the night Rylan was attacked.

It was real. All of it.

The blazing wisps lashed out toward the void-black monster, and it let out a heart-chilling, gurgling scream.

It flung werewolf-Callan free from its grasp. It moved so fast, it skidded on the spot in its attempt to flee.

Then it was nothing but a black flash. It smashed its way out through an exit too small for it, not even that slowing it down.

Callan rolled to a stop beneath Everly.

The hungry tendrils tried to reach for him, and Everly recoiled. She forced every scrap of control she had over herself into action.

An aching need to consume left her rattled to her core, and she battled against it, pushing it down, inch by inch.

The light faded and Everly drifted down onto her feet. Her legs wobbled and she fell backward onto her butt. Her vision swam, then cleared, and her breathing returned to almost normal. Her heart still pounded a rapid rhythm.

And she still felt *hungry.*

There was a clatter of debris as the werewolf who was Cherry slid down from above and thumped to the ground behind her.

He growled through his snout, "What the fuck was that?"

From where he still lay on the ground, Callan looked up at Everly with wide, bewildered animal eyes. "What the fuck are you?"

"What am I? What the fuck are *you*?"

Harper smacked her hands on the ground and cried, "What in all the fucks is going on?"

20

What am I? Everly remained still where she was sitting, but her mind raced. That happened. That wasn't normal. That wasn't human.

What am I?

Callan raised himself up in front of her, looming high above in his hairy, wolflike form. Everly shivered, still unsure if she should be afraid of whatever he and Cherry were. Or of what *she* was.

Callan prowled over to Harper, his paw-steps soft and silent for his size. He reached for her with a huge claw and Harper cowered back. He carefully lifted away the beam that had her trapped.

"Uh, thanks?" Harper gingerly got to her feet, then scooted over beside Everly. "You okay?"

"I have no idea."

Cherry stepped past them and bumped a clawed fist against Callan's shoulder. "Close one."

"Right?"

Everly gaped at the two of them. They both seemed to be themselves, on the inside, perfectly in control of their actions and emotions and speech, just changed on the outside. Callan turned to her, taking in her expression.

"It's okay. The weroth's gone." His voice was rough and not all the sounds were clear as he spoke through his snout-shaped mouth.

He wasn't what Everly expected a werewolf to be. If that's what they were.

And what was a weroth? Did he mean the other creature?

"Okay?" Harper squealed. "What is okay about any of this?"

"I don't understand anything right now," Everly said in a low voice. "Are you a werewolf?"

Callan crouched on his animal haunches in front of them. "No."

Harper eyed him up and down, gesturing at all of him. "But, I mean …"

"I know what it looks like," Callan growled wolfishly. "Just wait here a minute." He tapped Cherry's shoulder. "Come on."

With elegant, animal strength, Callan pounced across the rows of seating and into the upper level, Cherry right behind him, then they disappeared through an exit.

Harper and Everly turned to each other and spoke as one. "Let's get out of here."

After scrambling to their feet, they walked briskly out the way they'd come, Everly supporting Harper who had a slight limp, Harper supporting Everly who was shaking violently.

Everly caught Harper shooting her concerned sideways glances, but she didn't say anything. They were making their way across the foyer when movement froze them in their tracks.

Callan landed silently right in front of them, a snarl baring his teeth. Another thump sounded from right behind them.

"Wait," Callan growled.

Then he was surrounded by the spark-filled black haze, his body silhouetted within as it distorted and shrunk. As the shadowy mist faded away, he was himself again.

His clothes had been ripped badly, singed and dissolved, and he stuck a finger through a big tear in his jeans, pouting. "Aw, man, these were my favorites."

Still looking like a werewolf, Cherry stood next to him and dangled his racer jacket from one claw. "At least I saved this baby."

Harper and Everly just stared at them both, saucer-eyed.

"Normally, I'd strip off any good clothes I was wearing before dealing with a weroth. I just didn't have time."

"This isn't really the main explanation we'd like right now, but okay," Harper said.

Callan rubbed the back of his head and cringed at Cherry. "Yeah ... right ... I guess we have to explain."

Harper huffed. "You think?"

"Couldn't possibly be more busted than we are." Cherry shrugged a furry shoulder.

Harper looked him up and down. "Why are you still a werewolf? Could you stop being a werewolf, please?"

"Not a werewolf, and also, not all of us are as perfect as the Howell boys. Give me a few minutes, okay?" He rolled his wolflike eyes, a sight Everly never thought in her life she would see.

Callan started walking and tipped his head at them as a gesture to follow. Harper raised her eyebrows questioningly at Everly, and Everly shrugged.

He seemed like the regular Callan she knew—he seemed safe—but based on this whole new world of monsters and people not being what they seemed to be, Everly couldn't be sure. Still, Callan looked like he was heading to the exit which meant they'd be going the same way regardless, so she followed.

He led the way, speaking over his shoulder. "That thing back there, it was a weroth."

"One of a group of monsters called eidolghasts," Cherry added.

Callan shot back, "I'm trying to keep it simple. Don't overwhelm them."

"Expanding my vocabulary is the least of my overwhelm problems right now," Everly mumbled.

"Okay, eidolghasts are the monsters, and we"—Callan gestured between himself and Cherry—"are shadyrs. A kind of shapeshifter, I suppose. But we don't change into just one thing. We have a bunch of forms."

"Right." Harper nodded along, her face twisting with the effort to understand. "Monsters are real. Monsters are eidolghasts. A weroth is a kind of eidolghast. These are all words that don't come close to describing the full-blown brain-breaker happening right now."

Cherry put a hand on his barrel-sized monster chest sincerely. "I know. It's a lot to take in."

"Nah, nah, it's cool. Just the whole world not being what I thought it was."

Everly eyed the still hairy man. "So you, a *shadyr*, can become like a werewolf and other things too?"

"Yeah. What we become depends on what eidolghast is nearby. Weroths give us a form like what you'd call a werewolf." Cherry put both hands behind his head, tilted his hips, and did a shockingly model-perfect pose.

Callan gave a dramatic sigh. "Vasmires—big tentacle-y things, like the fleshy chunks back in the theatre—give us a vampire-like form. Those two are the most common eidolghasts, but there are others too."

Harper pouted. "So there really were no vampires?"

"Didn't lie about that." Callan turned back and grinned.

Everly folded her arms, frustrated. "But also, there kind of *are* because you basically become one sometimes."

"A technicality," Callan replied.

Harper asked, "So you're like, what, a monster hunter who turns into monsters?"

Callan frowned at the term *monster*. "We turn into something that gives us the weapons we need to fight a particular eidolghast type."

Cherry gestured to their ruined clothing. "You saw all the acid flying around back there. That's why we get thick fur when weroths are around, to protect us. Vasmires exude a kind of knockout gas, so our heart and breathing rates slow drastically, and our skin turns hard and cold to protect us from their mouths."

Everly's jaw dropped, remembering the strange gas from the night Rylan had disappeared, how she had fallen unconscious so quickly.

That was a vasmire, then.

Callan took over the explanation again. "So we don't turn *into* werewolves or

vampires really. It's more like what most people consider a werewolf or vampire to be is some mash-up of sightings and legends about shadyrs."

"No one's ever realized we're all the same thing," Cherry said. His snout crinkled up, and he grumbled, "Yes, finally."

Smoky magic swirled up around him, cloaking his body in a spray of embers and darkness.

The other three waited with an awkward, polite patience as he changed. When the mist cleared, he was Cherry again, shirt hanging in ribbons from the stretched-out collar and pants ragged from the thighs down.

Callan offered a fist and Cherry bumped it. "Good work, that was quick."

Harper rubbed her head. "Wow. This is not how I thought my day would go."

"You didn't have seeing your new friends change into wolfy-beasts scheduled into your calendar?" Cherry smirked.

"This is going to take some processing." Everly bit her lip, also trying to absorb all the new information.

She couldn't dispute that it was real after everything she'd seen. As outlandish as it sounded, it made a whole lot of things come together in her head. Including Rylan's vampire appearance the night he went missing.

Everly remembered the moment Rylan had gone still in her hands, how his skin had turned hard and cold so quickly. Too quickly for normal rigor mortis.

"Rylan is like you too, isn't he? A ... shadyr?"

"Yeah, him, Mom, lots of people in Shroudhaven."

Just how vampire-like did a shadyr's form make them? All the legends about immortality gave Everly some hope. Could Rylan have survived those horrible wounds?

"Oh, Darkfrey Estate must be full of shadyrs, right?" Harper asked.

Callan nodded and gestured for them to get moving again, herded them toward the exit. "Shadyr central. Kind of a shadyr school, boarding home—"

"And despotic military hellhole of bigots rolled into one," Cherry finished cheerily as he pulled his red-and-white jacket back on and fixed his hair.

"Is this shadyr thing like something you catch from a monstery love bite?" Harper flicked her hair, revealing her neck with a wink.

Callan gave it a longing look, then coughed. "Genetic inheritance, sorry. Okay, now it's my turn to ask the questions. What are you?"

"I'm a hella gorgeous influencer who is feeling a bit out of her depth right now," Harper replied.

"I think he meant me." Everly smiled wryly. "But I don't know. I thought I was human. I didn't even know there were alternative options."

Harper glanced sidelong at Everly. "She's not a shadyr-thingy too?"

Callan grabbed a fifties-style smoking jacket off a mannequin, shook the dust off it, and put it on over his shredded shirt. "Nope. What she did, I've never seen that before. How long have you been able to do that?"

"It's never happened before ..." Everly hesitated, traumatic memories churning, trying to breach the surface. "Before this week. I think it happened when Rylan was fighting the thing outside my house—"

"Probably a vasmire," Callan clarified.

"Okay, that. Well, I think that's how I survived, scared the *vasmire* off or maybe ... maybe killed it?"

"Even the best shadyr would struggle to take down an eidolghast on their own. No offense," Callan said. "You saw how that weroth back there hammered the two of us."

Everly lifted her hands in a shrug. "I don't know. And I don't know where Rylan went after that, except for ... well, kind of, *inside* me."

"I wish I was drinking so I could do a spit-take right now," Harper said.

Cherry snorted. "I will also refrain from what are totally inappropriate replies and just ask what that even means."

They reached the exit, and Everly stopped, squinting out at the glary light of the overcast day that felt so foreign to the world they'd just experienced.

A low blanket of clouds shone silver with blocked sunlight.

The sounds of cars and birdsong drifted in the cool air, undisturbed by the monstrous showdown in the theater.

The world seemed so normal out there, but Everly could already tell nothing would be normal again. "I mean, I've been dreaming about Rylan ever since that night, but very real dreams."

She turned back and looked at the theater. "It was Rylan who told me to come here. I had no reason to think anything would be here, but *he* knew. I think he, or some part of him, is really talking to me in my dreams."

"But he wasn't here, was he?" Harper asked, also looking back the way they'd come. "Should we have finished searching?"

Callan stepped out into the alley before turning on the spot and squinting back at the building. "He's not here. We checked the whole place while still in werewolf form—it has a nice speed-and-senses boost. I took apart that weird construction of black bones on the way out too, just in case."

"That was something, though, some proof that what Rylan told me in my dream means something?" Everly hated the pleading sound in her voice.

"I really don't know. I'm out of my depth here too now. We're going to need help." He paused, swore, and kicked an old can. "I'm going to have to tell Mom. Come on. Let's head back to Howell House."

Harper said, "Will you be in any trouble for letting the crazy out of the bag on your secret supernatural club?"

"I think we can be pretty sure you guys saw enough that you weren't going to blow this off as a trick of the light."

"Or *animatronics*?" Harper poked. "That place was haunted as all get out."

Callan raised his hands innocently. "Also, there's Everly probably fitting into the whole supernatural thing too, somehow."

"Yeah, somehow." Everly was still aware of the deep hunger within her that had stirred when the light emerged.

The shape of the light felt so familiar. As though her dragon was so much more real than she'd ever imagined. So much more monstrous than she'd ever thought.

Callan's eyebrows furrowed as he stared at her, and Everly noticed fear in his eyes. "Well, whatever you are, the weroth was scared of *you*."

21

Everly and Harper sat staring blankly, shock catching up as Callan drove them up the tree-lined drive to Howell House. Cherry sat in the front seat beside him, muttering about how much trouble they were in.

Harper had pulled the crocheted throw blanket off the prop storage bed area and wrapped it over her and Everly's shaking shoulders. Every time Everly looked over at Harper, she was staring at her and she'd give a small, supportive smile that made Everly feel worse.

Each one a reminder that she had done something unnatural, unexplainable. And she didn't know what that meant.

They had barely pulled up and unsteadily gotten out when Lian came through the front door to meet them.

She took one look over the four of them and her lips grew thin. "What's happened?"

Callan cringed. "There was a bit of an incident."

"I can see that. These two look like they've seen things that knocked the color right out of them."

"Monster tea spilled *everywhere*," Cherry said.

Everly and Lian locked eyes, and the silent apology and guilt Everly saw there made hot tears well up. She turned away, her own guilt over kept secrets stinging even more.

She should have known about Rylan already. I should have told her before.

Callan walked over beside Lian. She looked him up and down, frowning at the singed and torn clothing. She placed a hand on his cheek. "Weroth?"

"Yup. And there's more. There's ... a lot. Can you call everyone?"

"Rush, Tammy! Team meeting, kitchen, now!" Lian called out.

The door to the RV around the side clattered open.

"What's up?" Denny asked, beer can fixed in his grip.

"Did I call you?" Lian grumbled.

"I'm sure I heard my name. Team meeting, huh?" He winked at Harper as he swaggered in, cheap cologne overwhelming the area. "Don't worry, girls. Daddy is here to explain things to you."

"I'm not sure whether to be more traumatized by what we saw earlier or by that," Harper deadpanned.

Everly tried to smile, but the muscles in her face were too busy trying not to cry. Emotions overwhelmed her, swirling too fast to identify any one individually. She only wanted to weep and sleep.

And eat.

Denny headed inside first, and the rest of them followed. As Callan walked past Lian, she grabbed his shoulder. "What were you thinking getting Everly into this trouble?"

Everly's voice came out shaky. "The whole thing was my fault—"

"Nonsense," Lian interrupted. "How can it be your fault when you didn't even know what you could have been getting into?"

She shook her head at Callan. "I'm not happy about this."

Callan winced and pushed his hand through his long hair. "Then you're really going to be pissed about the rest of it."

In the kitchen, Rushelle already had the kettle going as everyone filed in and took a seat around the farmhouse table. When she found out that Everly and Harper were now privy to their shadyr secret, she gave them both enthusiastic bear hugs.

"Welcome to the dark side, girlies!"

Tammy was apparently the goth teen with the black hands. She sat away from the table, off to one side, silent and hidden by her hood, and had refused to shake anyone's hand on introduction. Obviously not a hugger like Rushelle.

Cherry slipped into the seat next to Harper before Denny could. When Everly sat on the other side, Denny grunted and raced around to get the seat directly across from Bellsy.

The skitter of tiny paws dancing around under the table drew Everly's attention, and she helped the elderly dog onto her lap.

"Hey, Birdie," she whispered and cuddled her close.

Callan laid out everything that had happened, from Everly seeing Rylan's encounter with a vasmire, to their visit to the estate, to the search of the theater and what they found there.

He hadn't yet gotten to how the fight with the weroth played out. Everly shook with nerves.

What were these people going to think when they found out she wasn't a normal human? Although they weren't exactly human either—all shadyrs, like Callan. Like Rylan.

Rushelle bustled about, clip-clopping on bright-yellow stilettos, bringing out hot drinks, biscuits, a cheese plate, and reheated pie, placing them in front of Everly and Harper.

"Comfort food time," she whispered with a wink.

Everly was ravenous, but no matter how much she picked at the food in front of her, the hunger didn't fade. Birdie whined, and she shared some small tidbits with the old pup.

Lian paced and fumed. "My son has been missing for days and you didn't tell me?"

Everly looked down at the table.

Callan's voice was low. "We only knew for sure last night, and even then, it was sketchy. The Darkfreys didn't give us much."

Almost everyone in the room scowled when he said Darkfrey. "We only ended up at the theater out of luck really. Everly can explain that part."

Everly gulped as every eye in the room turned to her. Birdie lifted her head and gave her a lick as though in encouragement.

"I ... Rylan told me to go there, in a dream."

"Ooh, fascinating!" Rushelle gushed.

Lian raised her eyebrows at Everly.

"Bet that's not all he did in the dream." Denny lifted a hand to high-five and everyone ignored him.

Callan continued with the story. "So she dreamed it, and there was definitely something there, some weird ritual bone thing, and a dead vasmire. Then the weroth attacked."

"Strange to get two different eidolghasts in the same place so soon," Lian said.

"There was one of those bone things at my place too, that first night back. But it was gone the next day." Everly was sure of it now.

Sure what she'd seen that night had been real.

"I think the ritual thing, I think it was made to attract eidolghasts," Callan said.

"Well, that's deeply troubling," Rushelle replied.

"How do you know?" Denny mocked, leaning back and swigging his beer. "Suddenly some shadyr black magic scholar? That shit isn't real anymore. Shadyr magic hasn't worked since they did the nasty with humans way back when."

He made a lewd gesture with his fingers.

"I think Rylan was investigating something too, and I think it has to do with those creepy bones," Everly said.

"And now my son is missing." Lian shook her head and pulled out her chair at the head of the table before dumping herself into it.

"There's also this son here who feels like he's not being cared about right now, despite having almost been eaten by a weroth." Callan gestured to his shredded clothing.

Lian sighed. "You're still here, barely a scratch on you, so I'm relieved enough to be angry about it."

"Love you too, Mom." Callan grinned.

Tammy spoke up from across the room, her voice dull, as though she didn't even care about the question she asked. "How did you even manage to survive? Just you two against a weroth?"

Cherry scoffed. "Is it really that unbelievable that Callan and I could take one down?"

Rushelle leaned over and patted him on his bright-red hair. "Aw, honey."

Callan tilted his head toward Everly. "So that's the next big thing. It wasn't just us."

Harper brought her hands up and waved them around beside Everly as though displaying a prize on a game show.

"Everly's a shadyr?" Rushelle gasped dramatically and flashed a huge smile.

"She can't be," Lian said without a hint of doubt.

"She's not," Callan agreed. "She's something else. Something I've never seen or heard of before. Something that the weroth ran screaming away from like a terrified bunny."

Silence fell around the room as everyone looked at Everly, expecting her to give some explanation or demonstration. She smiled awkwardly and shrugged.

Callan explained to them what he saw Everly do. The floating, the light—he made it all sound glamorous and not at all as freaky and horrible as it had been.

The mix of concerned and awed expressions pointed her way made her stomach churn. There she was, in a room full of shapeshifters with terrifying powers, who battled nightmarish monsters, and they were treating her as the oddity.

"She doesn't have a clue what she is." Callan spoke for her. "This has only been happening to her since this week."

"You haven't been back long enough to have been beshadowed." Lian took a slow sip from her mug and watched Everly through narrowed eyes.

Everly looked around for more of an explanation but it didn't come. "I haven't been back long enough yet to know what that means. What is being beshadowed?"

"Ah, blivs. So cute," Tammy muttered, sarcasm clear in her voice.

"That blonde at the estate called us the same thing!" Harper said. "And now I'm guessing it's not a nice thing."

Rushelle placed another plate in front of them, filled with hot oven-baked fries. She perched on one hip on the table beside them. "When an eidolghast settles into one territory for too long, the area and anyone in it becomes changed, possessed, and *weird*. Sort of like a haunting, all kinds of wacky things happen!"

She laughed like she was remembering a hilarious in-joke. "That's a beshadowing. Let it go on for too long and it can become permanent, including breaching a brand-spanking-new hole through to the Everdark."

"Oh hey, Everdark, another new term I had no idea about." Harper's eyes widened and she let out a single, "*Ha*. Blivs! Like oblivious, right?"

"Not just a pretty face," Denny said, reaching over and taking a whole handful of chips. "Bet you can cook too."

Harper cringed. "Why are you even here?"

"To be the sexiest man in the room. You're welcome."

"Just ignore him," Cherry said. "He thrives on any attention, especially negative."

Denny stuffed chips into his mouth. "He's right. Even your disgust fuels my ego."

"Ugh," Harper grunted.

"Mm, yeah, that's the stuff."

Lian pointed a finger at Denny, a chilling warning in her expression bringing the whole room to silence. With a long sigh, she turned slowly back to Everly and Harper.

"I think it goes without saying, but I'm going to say it anyway. The things you've learned today about shadyrs and our world must remain secret."

"Especially you." Cherry tapped Harper on the shoulder. "No sharing with your adoring cyber army."

"Her what?" Lian asked.

"I'll explain later," Cherry said.

"Yeah, of course. Lips and selfies sealed," Harper agreed, and Everly nodded along.

"Well, whatever is happening with Everly, she seems okay for now, other than being a bit shaken up," Lian said. "We need to focus first on finding Rylan. If he has some kind of dream connection with her, maybe he can also help us work out the rest, give us some more clues to find him."

If he's still alive.

Everly couldn't say that though. After the initial surprise, no one in the room seemed too worried about what she was, and she was letting that relief bring what little calm it could to her.

Maybe with beshadowings and eidolghasts and whatever else she still didn't know about their world, they were used to dealing with things a lot weirder than a woman with her own built-in light show.

There was more she should tell them—about her dragon, about how it had taken control, about how hard she had worked to rein it back in. About how scared she was that they wouldn't find Rylan alive. But Everly felt woozy under the weight of it all.

Lian stood up, prompting Birdie to yap and jump off Everly's lap to go and join her. "I'm going to give Mordan a call." She marched over to an old-fashioned phone on the kitchen counter.

"I still have so many questions. Do you guys have like, an introductory pamphlet or something?" Harper looked around as she tapped her fingernails on the table.

"You want the quick version of shadyr one-oh-one?" Cherry offered.

"Just, you know, the basics of why the entire world and reality isn't what I thought, yeah."

Rushelle and Cherry took turns running the no-longer-oblivious through a brief history of shadyrs while Lian talked on the phone.

"Lian, Lian Howell. You know who I am. Put me through to Mordan."

There was a whole other dimension, a place called the Everdark, where a race of shapeshifting beings once lived.

The dimension had been taken over by eidolghasts and the shapeshifters had to flee. They managed to break through a portal to the human world, right into what became Shroudhaven.

"No, I want to talk to him right now."

That was thousands of years ago. They took on human form to blend in and interbred ever since. Their descendants were shadyrs—mostly human, but still with some shapeshifting powers.

"Where is *Master Darkfrey*, then?"

The portal that brought the shapeshifters to the human world couldn't be closed, and eidolghasts followed them. Shadyrs considered it their duty to fight them back, to stop the eidolghasts from taking over this world as well.

"That's not soon enough."

Back in the dark ages, the eidolghasts had spread far beyond Shroudhaven and shadyrs fought them across the world, creating many of the sightings and tales of werewolves, vampires, and other monsters humans believed in to this day.

"I don't want an appointment. I want to know where my son is!"

And in those tales, the vampires and werewolves being hunted by humans were actually shadyrs.

Many times throughout history, shadyrs had been considered the monsters, rather than the ones fighting the true monsters, so they kept themselves and their powers secret.

"He is still my son. I don't care what you made your lackeys in the courts say."

Most of the shroudpools—the portals to the Everdark—were underground in Shroudhaven, with a few in protected areas aboveground too. There were also several shroudpools across the rest of the world, guarded by other shadyr groups.

"If you don't—"

There were shadyrs who chose to live elsewhere as normal humans, and many out in the world who didn't know what they were, and never would unless they came across an eidolghast.

But often they felt drawn back to Shroudhaven, as though feeling a sense of belonging for somewhere they hadn't found yet.

Most of them ended up at Darkfrey Estate, home to shadyrs and their lore from

the very beginning.

"No. I understand."

Everly stared at Rushelle, Cherry, and the others around the room. The secret history they'd shared changed her entire understanding of the world.

Is every monster story I've ever heard true, but got it completely wrong?

"Fine, *fine*. Tomorrow." Lian hung up the old corded handset violently. "Those ... *people*."

"Right?" Cherry woofed in agreement.

Lian looked over the room, settling her worried glance over Everly and Harper. She smoothed back her gray hair where fine strands had escaped from her bun.

"You two have had a big day and need some rest. You should stay here where you'll be safe."

Will we be safe here?

Knowing monsters were real, having just seen one, made nowhere feel safe. But Everly was exhausted.

The sun was only just setting outside, warm orange rays shooting in low through the back screen door. She was too tired to even try to argue about where they would stay that night. She trusted Lian, so she just nodded.

That seemed to signal the end of the meeting and everyone started moving around, clearing up the table. Tammy remained still, like a gargoyle in the corner.

Harper got up and stretched. She looked back at Everly with laughter in her eyes. "And we thought our little car accident was going to be the biggest excitement on this trip."

Lian bent over and picked up Birdie, cradling the furball in one arm. "Everly can have Rylan's room. Callan, Harper can have yours. You take the couch."

"She could bunk in my RV with me," Denny volunteered.

"Never in a million years." Harper scooted over closer to Callan and away from Denny.

"Leave her alone," Everly said firmly.

He sidled up next to her. "You're just jealous. Don't worry. I like chubby girls too."

"Get out!" Lian ordered.

"Aw, come on. I'm being nice." He waved dismissively at them and marched away. "Forget it. None of you deserve me. Best damn shadyr in this house of runts and what respect do I get?"

Everyone was silent as he stormed out and slammed the front door behind him, still ranting and cursing.

Callan grimaced. "Sorry about him. He's the worst."

"You could call the police to get him to stop squatting on your property," Rushelle

told Lian.

Lian sighed. "I know, I know."

"Then why don't you?" Everly cringed at the snap in her tone.

Lian brought Birdie closer to her face, looking into the little dog's eyes as though she were talking to her. "He has nowhere else to go. A place to stay is something everyone deserves, no matter how big of an asshat they are."

"Even the biggest asshat ever, doing nothing to dress up the even more mammoth ass underneath," Cherry said as he moved away from the table, narrowing his eyes at where Denny had exited.

"Plus, shadyrs are safest going up against eidolghasts in groups of four or more. We kind of need him." Callan sighed as though hating the admission.

Everly glanced around the room. Assuming Lian wasn't out hunting monsters, they still had Callan, Cherry, Tammy, and Rushelle. As her eyes settled on the sunny woman, Rushelle waved both hands in front of her.

"Oh no, I'm not a field girlie unless it's absolutely life or death."

Harper took a big step, winced, and wobbled. Callan reached out and grabbed her before she went down. "Your leg still hurt?"

She laughed, putting an arm over his shoulder. "Just a human here, remember? No fancy healing powers or whatever you guys get."

From the side of the room there was a soft grunt, and Everly turned just in time to see Tammy disappear into thin air.

22

Everly gaped wide eyed at the empty space where the goth girl had just been. "What ...? *What*?"

"Aw, poor duck," Rushelle crooned. She snatched up a jangly set of keys from a bowl on the kitchen counter. "I'll go and fetch her."

"From *where*?" Everly choked.

"Did Tammy just *disappear*?" Harper asked.

"Don't worry. It's normal. For her." Callan helped Harper back to a seat and went to the freezer, pulling out an ice pack.

"Normal. Right," Everly murmured.

She and Harper shared shrugs and 'what the fuck' looks with each other.

Rushelle passed Everly on the way out and patted her on the shoulder boisterously, a friendly grin brightening her face. "See, there are plenty of weirdos in Shroudhaven, not just you."

"Okay then. I think I'm done for the night." Everly pushed her chair back, standing up slowly and carefully in case she fell back down again.

Anxiety ran high through her system and she did her best to appear to be functioning normally. As normally as someone who had just learned that day that monsters were real, at least.

She knew where Rylan's room was and started heading out of the kitchen. Lian put a hand on her back and gave it a sympathetic rub. "How are you holding up?"

Tears filled her eyes again. "You know. A bit overwhelmed. Tired."

Hungry.

Lian nodded. "Understandably. Get some rest, but also ... if you see my son tonight, tell him I miss him and he better be okay. Let him know we're all trying to find him now."

Everly offered a smiling nod, but fear clogged her throat. She'd tell Rylan. She'd keep searching.

As long as it wasn't too late.

Everly made her way along a pathway of heartbreaking memories. Up the steps to the second floor of Howell house, she ran her hand along the time-smoothed banister, remembering the days when she and Rylan used to drag a mattress from his bedroom and ride it like a toboggan down those stairs.

The last time they'd ever done that she was thirteen. It had been years since they had played the game, and they'd revisited the childish activity on a nostalgic whim.

When Rylan sat behind her on the mattress and put his hands on her waist after pushing off, all new sensations had rushed through Everly. She'd known she was feeling differently about him, that she wanted to be more than just friends.

That had been about a month before his father died.

Rylan's bedroom was down the end of the hall, and she peeked inside each of the other bedrooms as she walked by.

The first was fairly bare, still very guest-room like, but there were some punk-style red-and-white clothes hanging in the open cupboard that Everly guessed were Cherry's.

Callan's room was next, looking as though it had recently been stripped of boyhood decorations but not yet adorned in any new way. The bed was made with military precision.

Lian's door was closed, and the next room had black block-out curtains, black bedspreads, and black clothes flung across every surface. Tammy's for sure. It had once been a guest room Everly used when she had slept over some nights as a kid.

Everly exhaled as she reached Rylan's closed door. She turned the handle and swung it open. She stood in the doorway, as though crossing that threshold would be stepping onto sacred ground.

It was almost exactly how she remembered it.

Everly ran her fingers over the glow-in-the-dark stars stuck all over the walls and the boxy old retro gaming console. She had been so jealous when he got that, in his own room no less.

He hadn't even taken it when he left for the estate. It looked like he'd taken nothing of his childhood with him.

Still on the wall was the poster showing an anime man in a space fighter uniform shifting into a purple lion. It matched the one Everly once had on her bedroom door. Their favorite cartoon she and Rylan used to watch together. It was a sci-fi adventure where the people used to turn into magical animals.

Did Rylan like it because he felt like them? How long has he known what he is?

Everly wondered if she would be second-guessing every part of their history now, both hers and Rylan's, and the world in general.

The bed had been stripped and covered in a mattress protector, and a thin covering of dust lay over the flat surfaces, only as much as a few months might have collected though.

In the middle of the room was an open cardboard storage box, half-filled with toys and books, next to a small stack of additional flattened-down boxes, also filmed with dust, as though someone had begun packing away and never finished.

There was some shuffling behind Everly, and Callan appeared with some clean sheets and blankets. "Bit of a flashback, hey?"

"It hasn't changed at all."

But everything else has.

"Mine was the same when I got back. Mom let me change it up however I wanted since then, but I think, you know, without us here, this was her only way of keeping us near."

Everly's mouth twisted, thinking of what had become of her own bedroom. Had anyone ever cared about her the way Lian cared for her sons?

"You left for the Darkfreys to learn about being shadyrs?" Everly asked, trying to make sense of a past that had changed all context.

"Pretty much."

"Your mom didn't teach you?"

"She's not all about the monster-hunting thing. More into living a balanced life. The Darkfreys ... dealing with eidolghasts is their entire mission. Rylan thought we needed that." Callan put the bedding on the desk and started shaking out the fitted sheet.

"That's okay. I can do it," Everly said, taking over from him.

"Thanks. I really need to go and spend a few minutes making sure there's nothing mortifyingly embarrassing in my room before Bellsy steps into it."

"I think I saw a dirty sock on the floor," Everly teased.

Callan's smile dropped. "Really?"

"Right next to the neck high stack of pornographic material."

His grin returned. "It's good having you back, Everly. I bet Rylan would think so too, will think so, once we've found him."

Everly's small smirk faded as Callan jogged away back to his room.

She closed the door behind him and brought the sheet close to her face. Lian must still be using the same fabric softener she always had. It smelled of springtime flowers, childhood games, and early awakenings of love.

It smelled of home. But it was never really the home she'd thought it was. It was a place full of shadyrs, people who knew the world wasn't what she thought it was, people who kept that secret from her.

Not that she was what she thought she was either.

Everly stared at her hands, wondering if she could make the light emerge from her again. But the only way she could think to do that would mean dropping her barriers of control. She had no idea yet what that would mean, what the consequences could be of letting her dragon take over.

Especially when it felt so hungry.

Everly finished making the bed and then sat there, staring at the poster on the opposite wall as her mind rolled all the new information she'd acquired over and over.

A vehicle rumbled outside and Everly pushed the curtain aside to watch Rushelle and Tammy get out of a yellow vintage sports car.

Tammy, arms folded tight and head low, marched into the house away from Rushelle. Seeing Tammy vanish into nothing being treated as a normal occurrence was one of the weirder things that had happened that day.

And in a day like the one she'd just had, that was saying something.

Tomorrow would be her fifth day in Shroudhaven, and her last full day before she had to get back or risk losing her job.

Can I just leave Shroudhaven, knowing everything I know now?

Through her sleepy thoughts, Everly could hear echoes of Rylan telling her to go. This dangerous world of shadyrs and eidolghasts and the Everdark was what he'd known all along.

What he wanted to keep her away from. Maybe she should just leave, turn tail, and go back to her normal life.

But how could she do that until she knew what had happened to Rylan?

Rylan awoke to darkness. It was still strange to him, waking up into dreams that belonged to someone else. He steadied himself, wondering what weird world he'd be faced with this time. He'd seen dragons made of light, grass-hut day spas, and tsunamis so far.

It felt like being caught in a beshadowing, twisting his mind. He didn't care though. As long as Everly was still dreaming, it meant she was still alive.

Though it would be nice to know I was still alive.

As the setting grew clearer around him, it seemed strangely, distantly familiar. Like a place he'd only been once or twice when he was very young.

Dim lighting shone through a single high window, revealing the floorboard ceiling, the stairs leading up to a closed door. Shelves were stacked with torn, overflowing cardboard boxes, old sporting gear, and tools. This was a basement.

Everly's basement?

Seeking her, he heard her before he saw her. Sobbing shrieks and gasps came from a dark corner. A small figure huddled into it, swatting and cowering away from swarms of rats.

Rylan strode over, then scooped the young version of Everly up and away from the rodents, kicking them with impunity.

They're just dream rats.

They puffed into clouds of dust where they landed. Everly, appearing around eight years old, wailed and clung to him. Her pale hair was stuck by tears to puffy red cheeks.

"Hey, hey, it's okay. You're okay. I'm here." He placed her onto her feet and kneeled so he was eye level with her.

She wiped her face furiously. Rylan wasn't sure if this was really *her* or just part of the dream. Either way, every fiber of him wanted to protect her.

"I hate rats. I hate them!" Young Everly balled her hands into fists, then grew before his eyes into the woman she was now.

I'm asleep. This is a dream.

Whispered words echoed around them. She took a deep breath and relaxed her hands, shaking them out. She didn't look him in the eye. "Sorry about that. Sometimes it takes me a while to know where I am."

Rylan was amazed Everly had as much conscious control over the dreams as she did. He'd heard of lucid dreaming before, but it was a whole other thing to experience it firsthand in someone else's mind.

Everly's face was still wet and red with fury. Rylan stood back up. He wanted to reach out and wipe her tears, but instead, he put his hands in his pockets.

"This actually happened, didn't it? You told me about it afterward. Is this what it was really like?"

Everly looked toward the corner she'd been saved from. "He thought it was funny. A funny way to punish a kid for interrupting his and Mom's private time. He rubbed peanut butter all over my clothes and then locked me down here. For hours."

One of her mom's many male visitors. Calling them boyfriends or even lovers was probably elevating their position. Rylan remembered this one in particular, although he wasn't the only cruel jerk Rylan had secretly chased away.

By that age, he'd already known he was a shadyr. His mom had been upfront about it all—it would have been impossible not to explain after the first time he changed—yet she had refused to train him to fight, to use his shadyr forms to go up against eidolghasts.

But there were some monsters he learned he could use his powers on.

The scene shifted into something straight from his memory. His eight-year-old self in vampire form—skin paled, eyes darkened, teeth long and pointed—chased the man through dark rooms in Everly's home.

Everly watched it with a frown. "Is this real? Is this from you?"

Rylan shook his head. He hadn't meant to take control of the dream, hadn't known he could.

"It's you, isn't it?" Everly demanded.

"Yeah, that was me. I was ... wearing a costume." His voice came out bashful.

He'd never wanted Everly to see the side of him he'd always felt was monstrous.

Everly eyed him for a long moment. "That man, he left Mom, not long after I told you about the rats. Yelling about how he wouldn't stay in a haunted house. You did that?"

For me? The final words echoed in the air despite Everly's lips remaining still.

Rylan shrugged. "I guess I always felt protective of you. I mean, anyone would have chased a scumbag like that away though."

"Except my own mom," Everly whispered.

"Maybe she was the scumbag I should have scared away. I don't know. I was young. I didn't know so much back then."

Everly looked into his eyes. "Even after you moved to the estate, the worst of the men never lasted long."

Rylan drew his lips tightly together.

"I thought you'd abandoned me, but you were always around, weren't you?" Everly's full lips were parted and glossy.

Rylan stared at them for too long before replying. "Sometimes. You didn't need my help that often though. You were always so independent, how you grew up looking after yourself."

"I had to. I didn't have any choice." Everly's voice was laced with bitterness.

"Still, you thrived despite all that. You were strong enough to get away, to live your life."

"If I thrived or turned out good in any way, it was what I learned from you and your mom and your family. It was you ... all who showed me what family was meant to be, what love was meant to be."

Unable to control the impulse, Rylan reached out and took the very tips of Everly's fingers into his own. His voice came out rough. "I missed you, when I left for the estate. But I only ever wanted you to be safe."

Everly's nose twitched and she sniffed, then took her fingers back. "I didn't feel safe. I felt alone. I felt like I had ruined everything."

How did she ruin anything?

Rylan was about to ask when light shimmered above them, and the strange fractalized, slithering thing that Everly called her anxiety drifted through the ceiling and rushed at him. Everly stepped between them, and power surged all around them in a battle of wills so strong, it made the hair stand up on Rylan's arms.

"Stop it. Go away!" Everly commanded, and the thing shimmered and rolled in the air before swimming through a wall. "Sorry about that. It's ... hungry."

"Your anxiety is hungry?"

"I'm not sure that's all it is anymore. A lot has happened today. I need to fill you in." Everly gestured for him to follow.

She walked up the basement steps, and when she opened the door at the top, bright light spilled in and they emerged on the main stage of Rook's Theater.

Only it wasn't run-down or destroyed. Everything was pristine, with stage lights shining over them. The cougar which showed up a lot stalked between the backstage curtains.

Rylan glared at Everly. "You went? I told you not to go."

"I'm sorry. But I had to know."

"And what *do* you know now?"

Everly ticked the items off on her fingers. "Shadyrs. Eidolghasts. The Everdark. Shroudpools. Weroths. Vasmires. All of that. But we still haven't been able to find you."

Rylan ran his hands over his head, huffing and stalking away from Everly. She knew. She knew all of it—a world he'd worked for years to keep her away from, safe from.

He wished he could have stopped her from finding out. But he was useless while trapped in this dream world.

Why hadn't he woken up? Why couldn't he?

Everly called out from across the stage, "Lian said to tell you she misses you. I'm there now, at your old place."

Rylan stopped his pacing and his shoulders sagged. He had a complicated relationship with his mom, but he didn't want to hurt her. Not any more than when he'd already ripped her heart out by leaving her and taking Callan with him.

"What if I'm really dead?" he asked softly. "I don't want to do that to her."

"Then we need to find you. You need to start telling me everything, anything that could help. And I need to tell you everything too." Everly walked over to him, a spotlight following her all the way, making her white hair glow bright against the black backdrop.

She told him again about the night he disappeared, how light had come out of her then and saved her from the vasmire.

And how it had happened again in the theater, chasing away the weroth. When she finished, she waited, a look of anxious expectation curling her eyebrows.

"That's ... new."

"Maybe. My dragon has been with me as long as I can remember. Maybe if you hadn't done such a good job of protecting me, it would have come out sooner."

She turned to look at it, swimming through the rows of seats. She narrowed her eyes as though giving it a warning to keep its distance. "I have no idea why your consciousness is here, and we still don't know where your body is. What really happened that night?"

Rylan stared out into the space, remembering his last night outside of Everly's dreams. "I was on my own. Usually, Darkfrey shadyrs travel in a brace when hunting—a group of four is considered the minimum safe number for dealing with an eidolghast. But I was investigating something and wasn't sure who I could trust."

"The weird bone statues?" Everly asked.

She knows about those?

"Yeah. I'd noticed some strange things with the Darkfreys. A shadyr grave being robbed, talk of other missing bodies and ghast remains. I managed to follow someone and came across a room full of bones and weird artifacts hidden at the estate."

"Do you know who it was?"

Rylan winced and shook his head. "I got caught snooping around, and someone blindsided me, knocked me out, and cleared up the evidence. I didn't know at first why they didn't finish me off then, but maybe it would have been too obvious. They wanted it to look like I was taken out in an eidolghast attack."

"This place?" Rylan swept his hand around the theater, and it changed to the decayed and trashed state it was currently in. "It was a trap, and I fell for it."

"But you killed the monster. You made it to my house."

"Do you know how hard it is to kill an eidolghast on your own? It was a miracle. I'm lucky it was a vasmire. The form we get has a small amount of regenerative healing. It was enough to keep me going, but I was wrecked after killing the one in the theater. And I couldn't go back to the estate, knowing someone had it in for me. I'd only hoped at that point I could drag myself to Howell House and beg them to take me back and help me."

Rylan put his hand to his chest, remembering the pain of being broken apart. "I was halfway there when I sensed another vasmire, heading to your place. I had to stop it. I had to. But I was too worn down at that point."

Everly inhaled shakily. "The bone statues—Callan thinks they attract the eidolghasts. There was one in my garden that night."

"They must have known—that I have a connection to you. They must have set it as another trap." Ice filled Rylan's veins. It was his fault. Just him knowing Everly had put her in danger. He should have stayed away, never even gone near her old home.

Everly's voice was barely a whisper. "Whoever it is that set the bone statues up, if they were also the grave robbers, could they have stolen your body?"

"Maybe? It doesn't help us much though, because I don't know who it is."

Everly had grown very still, a terrified look in her eyes.

Rylan opened his mouth to ask why, when his brain started catching up.

Everly had always been smarter than he was. She'd already connected dots that were still forming in his head.

That the people who made the statues, had made them from shadyr bones.

And what they might have done with his body.

23

Somebody bad could have taken Rylan's body, taken his body for horrible things. Everly awoke with a start, the realization she'd made in her dream shocking her into consciousness. She hugged the pillow around her head, willing herself to return to sleep, to be with Rylan again.

She couldn't sleep. She wanted to tear the whole town down searching for Rylan. But she didn't even know where to start.

They would be meeting with the Darkfrey's leader today. That had to get them somewhere. They would help find Rylan, wouldn't they?

Everly pushed out of bed and rubbed her face. She tiptoed by the other bedrooms, down the stairs, and past Callan sprawled and snoring on the couch, his long legs sticking out over the end.

In the kitchen she found Lian pacing, a steaming mug held under her nose. She looked like she hadn't slept at all.

"Tea?" she offered, moving toward the range and clicking on the burner under the kettle.

"Thanks." Everly finger-combed her hair and braided the white strands. She felt dried up and crumpled from a bad sleep in yesterday's clothes. Tea might help with that, but it couldn't help the ache in her heart or the burning worry for Rylan.

"Did you ... dream about my son?"

Everly blushed. "Yeah. And I'm worried."

Lian nodded and handed her a warm mug of tea. They each took a seat at the table. Everly explained everything Rylan had told her that night, from what he'd been investigating to his battle at the theater and again at her place.

"My boy," Lian whispered. "He always was a strong one. Strong and stubborn. Not many shadyrs could take on an eidolghast on their own."

"Almost two of them." Everly's nose twitched, and she sniffed the threatening tears away. "He'd almost beaten the one at my place too, before it ... It looked so bad, what it did to him."

Lian reached over, plucked a tissue from a cabinet behind her, and handed it to

Everly. "Shadyrs are tough. Especially in vampire form. It gives us stonelike skin and regenerative healing. And Rylan's one of the toughest."

She pulled out a tissue for herself too and blew into it fiercely. "I just wish he'd come to me sooner."

"What do you think it means? Being able to talk to Rylan in my dreams?"

Lian sipped her drink and shook her head. "All kinds of oddities can come from beshadowings. Dream connections aren't unheard of. The circumstances of this one are strange though, especially the apparent lack of an actual beshadowing. Sometimes, just a certain kind of exposure to an eidolghast or shroudpool can lead to a person ... changing."

"Like Tammy disappearing? What happened to her?" Everly asked.

Lian blinked sad eyes and spoke softly. "Stuck her hands right into a shroudpool a few years back. Ever since then she's had the bad habit of popping right out of existence. Luckily, she reappears in the same place every time so we know where to find her."

"Oh," Everly said, unsure what else she could possibly say.

Lian rubbed a thumb over her chin. "Your light powers, though, they're different."

Almost on cue, Everly's hunger manifested in a loud rumble from her stomach.

Lian chuckled. "Want me to put on some breakfast?"

Everly shook her head and finished the last of her tea. "I have more work I need to do at home. I should head back and do what I can until everyone else is up. I'm a bit behind, what with everything that's happened."

"I'm sorry, love. You don't need to be a part of all this. You shouldn't have been pulled into it. Best you finish up with your old house and get back to your life outside this town."

Everly nodded weakly. This was meant to be her last day in Shroudhaven. She and Harper weren't supposed to be part of the shadyr world.

It would be the right idea for them to just leave, try to go back to normal—pretend that this never happened. Would that even be possible?

Lian cleared up the mugs and started making herself another tea. "You don't have to come along today. We can handle things from here."

"No. I saw things about Rylan that no one else did. I need to be there."

Lian paused by the sink. "Won't be till midday that we can get into the estate. I don't want you alone all that time."

"Need a chaperone?" Rushelle popped her head into the kitchen, her platinum hair pinned back in retro curls. "I can keep an eye on the little duck."

"You don't have to, I'm sure it will be fine."

"It's really no trouble. I'm a morning person," Rushelle sang, as though it was possible she'd be anything else.

Lian nodded once. "Midday. We'll pick you up then."

Everly rose to her feet and gave Lian a quick hug. "Let Harper know where I am when she wakes up?"

"Of course." Lian stepped back, wrapping her woolen coat tight around her as she walked Everly to the door.

Rushelle gathered up her laptop and a few jangling items into a yellow purse and followed.

Everly was down the front steps and halfway through the yard when Lian called out, "You could have told me, when you came by the other day. You could have told me you needed help."

Everly stood out front, looking up at the old Boderleth building, wondering what else she could do in the short time she had left. The whole place needed repainting, but that wasn't going to happen.

Working that morning was more of a distraction than anything, an attempt to keep busy and keep nerves at bay.

Rushelle kept her distance, finding a spot where she could sit and tap away on her laptop, keeping the level of awkwardness at a bare minimum.

Everly finished up a few jobs and had a shower by midday, then Harper arrived in her van, bringing Lian and Callan with her. Everly wiped damp, nervous palms on her jeans and hopped in with them.

"Sorry I didn't come back sooner to help. Man, I was wiped!" Harper leaned around from the driver's seat as Everly took a spot on the bench beside Callan. "I guess redefining the structure of your whole world and seeing monsters for the first time deserves a big sleep in."

Everly nodded blearily.

Rushelle grabbed a seat as well, and Harper rumbled the camper on its way.

The drive across the river and up the hill to Darkfrey Estate didn't take long. It was agreed Harper would wait in the van.

There wasn't any point in letting the Darkfreys know more than one bliv had been let in on shadyr business. She parked out front and waved cheerily as Everly, Lian, and Callan got out.

Rushelle stayed with Harper. "Just in case. Never a good idea to be alone in Shroudhaven."

Harper called through her open window as they left. "Good luck!"

When they reached the ominous gate, Lian pressed a few buttons on the keypad, muttered her name, and the gates clunked and squealed as they rattled open.

Everly had to admit to a small amount of excitement as they walked up the steep drive and the first glimpses of the estate came into view. She'd always daydreamed about what was hidden up there.

What the place that Rylan and Callan had run away to was really like. Whether it was a luxurious palace or a haunted house.

It turned out to be a bit of both.

As they reached the peak of the hill, the dark woods around them fell away and the grounds opened up into formal gardens and sporting areas.

Clusters of grand buildings with crenellated towers, spires, and balconies of gray and white stone were joined with covered walkways and spread along the cliffside, looking down over all of Shroudhaven.

"I can't believe you lived here," Everly said in a hush to Callan.

"It's not as exciting as it looks."

"Really? Because it looks like a castle full of magic and adventure."

"The only thing true about both the appearance of this place and the reality of it is how old-fashioned it is."

A group of tweens jogged by, all in matching gray and maroon sportswear. They were led by an older man and ran in step with military precision. A few other groups of four, of mixed adult ages, also ran exercises around the grounds, from Tai Chi to fencing.

As they drew closer, a number of gardeners and cleaners became clear too. Everly couldn't help but notice a distinct divide between those training and those working. A divide of skin color.

Upper management and those in braces were distinctly paler than those in service roles. Only the cardigan-wearing shadyr Everly had dreamed of as part of Rylan's team stood out with his slightly darker skin.

"Is everyone here a shadyr?"

"Yep. Everyone except you." One of them waved at Callan and he nodded back. "Not everyone does hunting duties though. There are a lot of other jobs in the shadyr world and estate."

"And how are the jobs allocated?"

Lian snorted. "It's *supposed* to be on merit."

Everly didn't miss the emphasis on *supposed*. She knew Callan had left because of disagreements over how things worked here, and she wondered just how deeply their 'old-fashionedness' ran.

"Callan?" a voice called out, and a young woman with rich red hair jogged over to them.

She wore tight maroon leggings and the same plated undershirt that Rylan had showing under her loose singlet.

"Hey, Annabeth," he replied.

"What's going on? Is there news about Rylan?" She looked at him eagerly.

Lian answered, "Sort of. Going to see Mordan now."

Annabeth's eyes pleaded with them. "I wanted to be out looking, really. Master Darkfrey grounded our whole brace up until this morning. Rylan has to be okay though, hasn't he?"

No one answered, and they left Annabeth standing and staring at them in their wake.

They walked the rest of the way to Mordan Darkfrey's office in silence. Callan and Lian clearly knew exactly where they were going as they entered the largest of the buildings and marched along lengthy hallways lined with suits of armor from every era.

They rose a few floors in a Victorian-style caged elevator that barely fit the three of them inside and faced imposing double doors made from carved black wood.

The Darkfrey name and coat of arms—with crescent moon, twin fang-like blades, and three skulls—was detailed in high relief and well-polished.

Lian spoke through an intercom on the side and the doors swung open.

"Come in," Mordan's deep voice called. It sounded tired, although not unfriendly. "Finally come to return the artifact you stole when you left, Lian?"

"I certainly don't know what you're talking about or that anyone here would be able to do anything with it anyway," Lian muttered.

Everly shot Lian a sideways look, shocked. Who knew she had such a rebellious streak?

Mordan, in his glossy black and maroon suit, bent over the huge desk, signing paperwork. His office walls were covered in aged hunting trophies of a mundane variety—moose, lions, rhinoceros—and Everly wondered if there were any trophies of less mundane types hidden elsewhere.

The gold and maroon office looked like it could have belonged to a king from an earlier century.

Another person, or shadyr, stood at Mordan's shoulder. A slab of soldierly man with a face like a cinderblock, he wore body armor with no shirt over the top and a distasteful grimace.

Mordan Darkfrey glanced up at Everly as they entered. "I didn't realize you were bringing an *outsider* with you."

"This is Everly Boderleth. She's become aware," Callan answered with a level of formality Everly hadn't heard in his voice before.

His normally loose shirt had been tucked in, and he even stood at attention.

"Nilson." He nodded once to the shadyr behind Mordan, then leaned and whispered to Everly, "Mordan's son."

Nilson didn't offer a greeting in return. There wasn't a lot of family resemblance except for height and obvious annoyance at those they were meeting with.

Lian dragged out one of the seats across the desk from Mordan and dropped into it, gesturing at Everly to take the other. "Everly is an old family friend and can be trusted. She came to know most of what she does now on her own. And it involves Rylan."

Mordan clicked the cap onto his very fine pen. "Yes, Rylan. You have some information?"

Lian gestured to Everly to share what they knew. She gulped and stuttered her way through the night of Rylan's disappearance, her confusion, and the statue in her yard, right through to finding the other statue and facing the creature in the theater.

Callan helped fill in parts with what he knew and his theory about the statues summoning the eidolghasts. Everly left out any mention of her light or her dreams, as instructed by Lian, who had felt it best the Darkfreys didn't know about that yet.

When they'd finished, Mordan stared for a moment and then snorted a laugh through his nose. "You think there is some conspiracy? All based on the ravings of a hysterical bliv?"

Everly's hackles rose. "I know what I saw. I mean ..." *Do I?* "Others saw it as well."

"Where's your proof? Where are these bone structures?"

"The one at my place was gone the next day. Someone must have taken it away. But the one at the theater is still there," Everly said.

Callan shook his head, his lips tight. "I went back there this morning. It's all been cleaned up."

"It wasn't logged by our cleaning crews," Mordan noted, tapping one of the sheets in front of him. "Are you even sure that's what you saw? You know how areas on the cusp of beshadowing can trick your mind. It was probably just a pile of trash some kids were playing with."

Callan looked over at Everly, his jaw twitching. Her mouth moved weakly but she didn't know what to say.

Mordan continued. "Even if it was some ritual formation, shadyr magics don't work anymore. Only pure-blood shadyrs could use magic before they came to this world and interbred. This is all nonsense."

"What's nonsense, is that my son is missing and you're doing nothing about it," Lian snapped.

"Of course we're doing something. I have teams out searching even now. It's being treated very seriously. Rylan is one of our best and is like a son to me."

Lian shot forward in her chair, a scowl on her face.

A nasty sneer rose on Nilson's lips as well.

Mordan didn't flinch, just lectured on. "But he chose to leave his brace and go off on his own, which is a dangerous move. Shadyrs don't last as long when they don't have people they trust to look out for them."

Callan hung his head.

"I think you need to prepare yourself for the possibility that he won't be found alive. Not due to some conspiracy or foul play, but due to the dangers of *his* job and the stupid risk *he* took. The simplest explanation is often the right one."

"Then where's his body?" Lian demanded, her eyes glossy and furious.

"Given the activity being logged around your area, it's not impossible his remains could have been taken by wild animals. There do seem to be a high number of sightings, possibly even a beshadowing behind the growth in numbers and aggression."

Nilson gave a sharp nod and stepped forward. "Which my team are looking into. Let us Darkfreys handle shadyr business. We don't need a mob of misfits and blivs getting in our way."

Mordan waved a dismissive hand at him, and he took a step back again, scowling at Callan and Everly.

Lian pointed a finger across the desk at him. "You can't stop us looking for my son."

Mordan's expression grew dark. He straightened up in his chair with a threatening slowness.

"You know it's only your Pimey bloodline that affords you the privilege of staying on my good side, Lian. That means I let you play-act as shadyrs with your little team of runts instead of putting an end to it. So I wouldn't be pushing my luck."

He leaned back in his chair again, eyeing Lian.

The longer she gave him no reply, the larger his smile grew. "Now, you know the way out? Or should I have Nilson escort you?"

Lian stood up, dragging the chair harshly across the floor. "I know exactly how to get out of this place."

That was it?

Everly glanced around from Callan to Lian to Mordan. The looks on all their faces said they were done.

Everly felt humiliated, left with nothing. She wanted to scream her lungs out at Mordan Darkfrey as though somehow that could bring Rylan back, but she swallowed the urge and stood as well before following the Howells from the office.

"Oh, and Lian?" Mordan called when they reached the door. "Do be careful bringing blivs into shadyr business. It didn't work out so well last time with that husband of yours."

"Is that a threat?"

"It's reality."

Everly fought tears all the way out of the estate.

This couldn't be it.

Maybe she should have stayed home, just kept working there. Maybe if she, the hysterical bliv, hadn't gone into the meeting, Mordan Darkfrey might have taken it more seriously.

He'd said they already were. That they'd been looking. And if a whole estate of army-like supernatural monster hunters hadn't been able to find Rylan, what hope did she have?

24

The mood in the van was as gloomy as the weather as they drove down the hill away from Darkfrey Estate with nothing.

"We should go and see Crow. Maybe she has some insight," Rushelle suggested.

"You know she's hit and miss." Lian sighed. "And I hate sage."

Callan rolled his shoulders, a darkness clouding his expression. "Yeah, but if all else fails, at least we can have a drink. I for one could do with something strong."

Lian shot him the look of a mother not yet come to terms with her son having grown up.

"Crow, as in Crow's Nest?" Everly asked.

She knew the bar. It had been a local establishment as long as she remembered. But she'd left Shroudhaven before she was old enough to drink legally.

Not that it was the bar most kids wanted to go to. It was the dark, seedy bar everyone joked about as being the place only weirdos went. Everly was already starting to guess what those weirdos really were before Callan confirmed it.

"It's a bit of a shadyr hangout. Crowea, she's kind of the town witch. Not that anyone except for her believes in all the wiccan stuff she gets her kicks from, but she does have some powers."

"Worth a shot?" Rushelle encouraged.

"It's only two o'clock?" Harper said like a question.

Rushelle batted a hand at the air. "Shadyrs keep weird schedules. Crow's Nest is open all hours."

"What do you think?" Harper half turned to Everly, keeping her eyes on the road.

"I don't know. I guess. Sure." The way the others were talking made Everly feel like this was a last resort. A heavy pressure built behind her eyes, making them burn.

Callan gave Harper directions. They pulled up in front of a plain, flat-faced building with a dungeon-style door as an entrance. The bar's name glittered in small gold lettering across the front of the aged wood.

From across the road, Cardboard Box Barry watched them all exit the baby-blue van. A trash can clattered down a nearby alleyway, making Everly jump. A small creature

scurried out of the toppled over bin. Just a raccoon.

Lian grabbed her bag and from it pulled a strange sword scabbard on a belt and buckled it on under her long coat. "I'm going to go and look around on my own. See if I can find anything. You kids have fun."

Rushelle stepped beside her. "Right, I'll go with you."

"You know you don't have to."

Rushelle beamed sunnily. "I know."

"We'll let you know if we find out anything." Callan leaned on the door, pushing it open with his back as he waved.

Everly turned to say goodbye as well, but the raccoon caught her eye again.

It watched her, eyes glinting moonlight blue in the shadows. The headlights of a passing car shone over it for a brief second. Its fur was ragged, patches of the wrong colors in the wrong places. It hissed at the light and ran.

"Come on." Harper jiggled with excitement, dragging Everly by the hand into the bar.

The inside of the Crow's Nest looked nothing like the outside but lived up to the name far more. Trinkets and lamps, colorful scarfs and throws, fantasy paintings and figurines filled every space, making it seem more like a new age store than a bar.

The furniture was eclectic, not a single armchair or table matching another. About half the seats were occupied, and a low murmur of conversation mixed in with the tune of the mermaid in the lighthouse song playing in the background.

Every eye was on them as they stepped inside, and Everly got the impression they weren't entirely welcome.

Callan led them to the large timber bar that looked like something out of a western. A tall woman with massive, wild blonde curls shot through with gray streaks turned to greet them. Her bright, flowing hippy dress swayed and she wore tie-dyed silk gloves that covered her to her elbows.

Her peachy skin was a cobweb of wrinkles, and one of her eyes was covered by what seemed to be a large, broken fang protruding from it, surrounded by scarring.

Taking in the sight of them, she crooned, "Hello, babies. Look at these new faces."

Callan leaned on the bar. "Hey, Crow. This is Everly and Harper."

She reached toward his arm, but didn't touch. "I've been hearing talk of a missing face too, hearing it was your brother. I'm sorry that's all I've heard though, if you've come looking for more than a drink."

Everly couldn't hide the disappointment on her face, but Callan still seemed hopeful.

Crow leaned away from them. "Oh, you've come for a bit of Crow magic, haven't you?"

Callan nodded, and to Everly, he said, "Crowea has a sort of psychometry skill.

She can sense information from things she touches. I thought maybe she could touch you, find out—"

"Oh no. I'm not touching that. I can feel her from here. I don't know what is happening there but it's not something I want to get close to." She bent down behind the bar and returned with what looked like a fat, pale-gray, loosely wrapped cigar.

Using a lighter from her skirt pocket, she lit the end, and once it started smoldering, she waved the smoke around each of them. Then she pushed it into Callan's hands.

"Sage for cleansing. Best you keep that." She gestured at him to keep smoking Everly.

Everly coughed.

Callan pleaded, "Couldn't you—"

"No means no. You want to use my visions but don't trust my other senses? You get sage, and you can all have a drink on the house because you are clearly in dire need of it."

It was as though frigid water had been injected into Everly's veins. It was unclear how real whatever Crowea had sensed was, but the fact she refused to come near her didn't feel good. She felt broken, at a dead end, unable to fix anything.

Crowea didn't stop to ask them what they wanted to drink, just started mixing a large share jug with spices, herbs, flowers, blessings from the goddess, and generous splashes of alcohol.

She lit her lighter again and waved it over the top, invoking the elements, before pushing it over the bar to them, along with a stack of four highball glasses, then shooed them away.

Harper carried the jug and glasses and led them toward a free circle of armchairs in a corner.

As they crossed the floor, Cherry stepped out in front of them. "Oh! Hey, what are you all doing here?"

"Things didn't go great with Mordan, so this seemed like the next logical place to go," Callan replied.

"I can relate to that."

"You here alone?" Everly asked.

"Yeah, well, I guess it's solo-day-drinking kind of weather."

"Join us." Harper grinned. "We have a share jug of who-the-heck-knows-what."

"Ah, one of Crowea's signature cocktails," Cherry said.

"She even gave us four glasses. Ooh, that's spooky!"

Everly sunk into a vintage armchair and Harper poured the drinks. Cherry tapped away on his phone, keeping the screen close to his chest.

"Is she really a witch? Is that a thing too?" Harper asked.

Callan chuckled and snuffed the sage stick out on a used plate at the table across from them. "Jury is still out on the wiccan stuff, but the psychometry has proven real

in the past. You probably noticed her eye?"

"No!? Was there something in her eye?" Cherry cried, looking aghast.

Harper snorted her first mouthful of drink back into her glass.

Callan smiled around a sip of his drink. "It's an eidolghast tooth. From a dislimner, I've heard people say. Super rare. I've never seen one myself. She's had the psychometry power ever since it got stuck in there."

"Cool, cool, cool. So cool. Cool and normal." Harper nodded, then attempted again to take a drink. "This, however, is not bad at all."

Cherry tossed back a few mouthfuls of his drink, wiped his mouth, and checked his hair on his phone camera. "BRB, friends."

Everly tended to avoid alcohol, having seen the path her mom took to her early grave, but tried a small sip out of curiosity. It had a rich, honey flavor with a sharp, spicy bite that warmed her throat, but didn't warm her heart.

They were no closer to finding Rylan. It didn't feel like the time for social drinks.

"What are we going to do?" she asked quietly. "Rylan could be anywhere, and we're meant to be leaving first thing tomorrow."

Harper pouted. "You're going to find Rylan. Because you're amazing and can fix anything."

"I can't." Everly shook her head.

I'm not enough.

It felt over. Time to go back to their regular lives and forget all this ever happened.

"You don't understand."

I think he's dead. Either wild animals or bone-stealing grave robbers got to his body and ...

"I didn't do enough and it could be too late."

"This woman," Harper began, pointing at Everly and talking to Callan. "You know how we met?"

"I'd love to know," Callan said, leaning in.

"So, my malicious man-child ex doxed me."

"I remember when that happened. So wrong."

Harper took a swig of her drink and continued. "Everly was the superintendent in my building, and I was *flipping out*, trying to get her to install new locks for me and everything. When I explained why, without a moment's hesitation, she offered her own apartment to me if I needed somewhere to hide out. My first response was 'how weird' and 'should I be scared of *her*,' right?"

Callan sipped his drink, eyebrows raised at the turn in conversation.

Everly half smiled. "I'm sorry. It was weird."

"It was damned beautiful is what it was. Because when some creep started messaging photos of our building to me in the middle of the night and I ran to Ev's doorstep, she just let me in. Just straight up let a stranger who needed help inside and even gave me her bed. And still this woman thinks she's not good enough."

Everly remembered that night, how shaken up Harper had been. She hated to think what might have happened if she had sent Harper away.

Even without the close call, she hated to imagine a world where they hadn't become friends that night.

Harper looked at Everly, a fiery adoration in her eyes. "People see us and expect Everly tags along with me, but I'm the one clinging to this absolute goddess here."

Everly bit her wobbling lip. Harper leaned in and put an arm over her round shoulders and bumped her forehead to hers.

"She always was amazing," Callan agreed.

Everly sniffed self-consciously. "Please stop, it sounds like you're both eulogizing me."

Callan leaned forward in his chair and put a hand on her knee. "Really, you've been incredible through all this, and done everything you could have. We wouldn't even know about Rylan's disappearance if it weren't for you."

"And now we know just enough to know he's gone and we have no idea where and we can't help him." Everly gulped back a sob and stood up quickly to hide the broaching tears. "I'm going to the bathroom."

Harper popped to her feet. "I'm coming too."

Everly marched away, but Harper caught up. She spotted one sign and tried to follow it, but the back area of the bar was a maze of small rooms and curtained-off private areas.

Harper hurried to keep beside her. "You okay?"

"No, not really," Everly croaked.

"I'm sorry. I was just trying to cheer you up."

"It's not your fault."

Everly hit a dead end and tugged aside a curtain, hoping it led the way to the bathroom, and instead revealed a small storage area with Cherry and the cardigan-wearing shadyr from the estate neck-deep in each other.

Harper squealed.

"Whoa!" Cherry jumped away and put his hand on his mouth.

"Sorry!" Everly said, backing up and letting the curtain drop closed again.

From behind the curtain came the hiss of whispered arguing. "I told you we shouldn't."

"Ghast damn it."

The curtain opened again and Cherry grabbed Everly's arm. "Wait, listen, umm … You can't tell anyone about this. *Anyone.*"

"It's okay. No big deal."

"No, really, big deal," Cherry said.

Jasper stepped beside him, smoothing back his hair. His forehead remaining creased.

Cherry said, "No one can know. Not even Callan knows. Or at least he pretends not to for our sakes."

"Oh." Everly's eyes widened. "He said the estate was old-fashioned. Is it really that bad around here?"

Cherry rolled his head in a large, sarcastic nod. "Me being *me*, is what got me kicked out of Darkfrey Estate. Jasper is only still there because no one knows that he is who I was being *me* with. And for some ghast-forsaken reason, he wants to stay there. So no one can know."

Jasper gave Cherry a gentle, suffering look as though they'd had plenty of long conversations about exactly what his reasons were for staying at the Darkfreys.

"I'm riled up, okay? I know it's hard to leave. I know," Cherry said.

Jasper's eyes softened, and under his breath in a tone Everly expected was just for Cherry, he said, "And often it's also arduously difficult to stay."

Cherry reached for his hand, and Jasper's fingers squeezed around his for a second before he pulled away and straightened his cardigan.

Harper mimed padlocking her lips. "We will treat it as an even higher-level secret than our supernatural underworld knowledge."

Cherry gave her a quick hug. "Bellsy, you are the best."

"We won't tell a soul," Everly agreed.

Jasper cleared his throat. "Nice to meet you both again. I'm going to leave now before anyone else discovers our forbidden romance."

He gave Cherry a pointed look, and Cherry stole a peck on his cheek before he strode away.

"You weren't really here for solo day-drinking after all." Harper grinned. "How long have you two been together?"

"Almost a year," Cherry gushed proudly. "I know he comes across a bit stuffy, but he's ... he's amazing. I was so high on love for him after a few months together that I came right out to the whole world. Didn't take long for the Darkfreys to find a reason to boot me out after that."

"Was that around when Callan left?" Everly asked.

"Uh-huh. He fought so hard to make them let me stay, but when they wouldn't change their mind, he left too. I think we're better off away from there now."

Harper's tone was soft. "Jasper didn't leave with you, though?"

Cherry shrugged. "He has this whole internalized-shame deal going. Totally get it. Stuff he has to work through. Plus, he's super proud for ranking into one of the Darkfreys' best braces, considering he's not the most lily-white. That's hard for him to let go of."

"I did notice that about the Darkfreys," Everly mentioned, and Harper frowned.

"Still, Jasper doesn't want to lose that. And I'm okay with supporting him and sneaking around for now."

"Sorry we busted you," Everly offered.

Cherry waved the apology away. "Honestly, it's kind of nice to finally have someone who knows! But I could do with going back and finishing off that jug now. Phew!"

Harper asked Everly, "You still need the bathroom?"

"Never did really. I could do with heading back home soon though."

"Yeah, of course. Home it is. Whatever you need."

The need to sit in a corner and cry had subsided for now, and Everly thought she could probably make it home before it took over again.

It's not home, she reminded herself. She was leaving tomorrow to return to her real home. The one she'd made for herself outside of this place of shadows and grief.

Even if it tore her heart apart to leave with so many questions left unanswered.

They remained at Crow's Nest long enough to finish the share jug between them, then piled into Harper's van for the short drive home.

Except Harper insisted they take the scenic route back.

"Just one final tour around town to say goodbye, yeah?"

Everly nodded, but she knew Harper was just trying to hold on to hope for her sake, that they might still find something. Everly leaned her face against the glass of the passenger-side window and stared, watching the quaint town pass by as Harper cruised around.

The red-and-white awnings of Pimey's Diner had faded, but the warm glow of the interior stirred a homesickness inside Everly.

Cardboard Box Barry stood his vigil on a blustery street corner. The way the mountains rose up behind the rooftops, framing the town with their dark slopes, and the soft roar of the river and falls in the distance all felt almost like home.

She would miss it, a little. But she'd said goodbye to it once and could do it again.

Callan sat in the middle seat up front and Cherry leaned over from the bench behind them, offering Harper directions for streets to drive down and things to see, statues of town founders he provided the sordid backstories for, shadyr ruins mislabeled for the public eye, places he'd had his most epic battles against eidolghasts.

It was a side of the town that had been invisible to Everly, that made it feel less like home.

It was obvious that Harper was circling around every block between the theater, the Boderleth house, and the fringes of the woods that reached the edges of town.

The sky was a thick soup of low clouds, blocking any sign of the approaching sunset. Harper had been driving for over an hour, when they headed along a side street a couple of blocks from Everly's old home which looped around between the woods and the main road.

"I think we should probably go back now," Everly murmured.

Harper smiled, but her eyebrows twisted. "I just thought, you know, you might want to see a bit more of town. It's no problem."

Everly sighed. "We're not going to ..."

Up ahead on the side of the road, Everly noticed a familiar figure—silhouetted, human-shaped, hunchbacked, dragging something.

The night of Rylan's disappearance, when her mind swirled into unconsciousness, hadn't she seen the same thing? In the aftermath of all that chaos, she'd forgotten. There had been so much else to try to work out.

But now that she saw them again, she was sure.

The same person had been there that night.

Maybe they had seen something. Maybe they knew something.

"Stop the car!"

Harper slammed on the brakes. "What is it?"

Everly jumped out her door and ran toward the hunched figure. As she drew closer, she could see it was an old woman wearing a ragged, muddy coat. She bent over, picking something off the road and putting it into a large canvas sack.

"Hey," Everly called out. "Excuse me?"

The woman startled and dropped the sack.

"Sorry, could I ask you a few questions?"

The woman shied away and was reaching for the sack when Harper, Callan, and Cherry got out of the van too, rushing across the road to join Everly. The old woman spooked and bolted, dashing off into the forest faster than her age suggested she'd be able.

"I just want to talk," Everly called after her. The woman flitted between the dark trees.

Everly frowned. *Like I saw just before the car accident.*

"Who was that?" Harper asked.

"I don't know. But I saw her the night Rylan disappeared, and before our car accident."

"What's in the bag?" Cherry sniffed and kicked the corner of it.

Callan lifted the opening and glanced in. He inhaled sharply and his jaw dropped, tongue out and gagging. "That is messed up."

Everly braved a look. The smell hit her first—the overwhelming stench of death and rot. In the gloom and shadow of the sack, she could make out pieces of fur, messes of bloody gore, and bent and broken creatures.

Everly fought the urge to vomit. There was a stain on the side of the road from where the woman had just added another piece of roadkill to her sack.

Harper moved closer.

Everly blocked her view. "Better not. Can't be unseen."

"It's full of dead things. Animals, and I think maybe some bits of eidolghast," Callan told her and Cherry.

Harper frowned. "Little old lady has been collecting animal bodies?"

Cherry shuddered. "What for? Wait, do I even want to know?"

Everly's mind raced. If that woman had been there the night Rylan had fallen, if she had seen his body lying shattered on the road ...

"Do you think there's a chance she might have collected a *larger* body?"

25

Everly sprinted toward the tree line, crashing through the long grass and undergrowth on the verge of the forest where the old woman disappeared.

"Hello? Are you out there? Come back, please!"

There was no reply. Everly pushed further into the woods.

I have to find her. She could have seen what happened to Rylan. She could know. She could be our last chance.

In the low light, under the thick canopy of green-black leaves and twisting branches, it grew dark quickly.

Panicked, Everly blinked, trying to force her eyes to see better. "Which way did she go?"

Callan caught up first, his eyes massively dilated and sparkling in the dark. "You really think the old woman knows something?"

"She was *there*," Everly pleaded.

Callan squinted through the trees. "This way."

Harper and Cherry arrived just as Callan took off, leading the way.

Everly hesitated, frowning at Harper.

"Don't even think about warning me off. We're sticking together," Harper said, putting her hand out.

Everly nodded and took it. She held tight as they chased after Callan.

Within the woods it was dark as night, and the temperature dropped sharply. Harper took her phone in her free hand and switched the flashlight on, but it only cast light over the next few steps in front of them.

At the speed they ran, it barely gave them enough warning of when to jump a fallen log or duck a low branch. They each stumbled a few times, but when one did, the other caught her with their joined hands.

Callan raced ahead, clearly more concerned with not losing their target than not losing those behind him. Cherry made up the in-between, helping the women keep course, his shadyr eyes sparkling in the dark.

The tree trunks were densely packed and mazelike. Everything was moist, slimy,

and mossy, and muddy leaves squelched beneath their feet. Crooked branches and thorny vines seemed to reach out, tangling and tearing at them as they ran.

Everly lost track of their shadyr guides. "Which way did they go?"

Harper shone the light around. "That way."

Everly was sure she would have lost Harper out there too if they hadn't remained holding hands.

This isn't a forest I want any of us to get lost in.

Locals avoided going into the woods, and many of those who entered never came back. It was considered an unsafe place even without the truth of what could be creeping in the dark.

They sped forward again, and almost ran headfirst into Callan and Cherry, who had stopped beside a massive oak, its branches drooping, umbrella-like around them.

"Where is she?" Everly asked between gasping breaths.

"I'm sorry. I lost her." Callan pulled his long hair back, twisting it in his hands before tying it away from his face.

"I hope you haven't lost us, too," Cherry said, staring up at the obscured sky.

"No, I think we're pretty close to the main road still."

Everly frowned, thinking about where they had started and the direction they'd run. "That would mean we're pretty close to where we had the car accident."

Where another body may have disappeared from. Everly had been so sure she'd heard the car hit the cougar that day, and then there was nothing.

Her mind whirled. "We have to find her."

She turned on the spot, staring out into the twisted forest. Sounds of things moving in the distance, owls hooting and twigs snapping, came from all around. Two bright, reflective eyes peered straight at her.

Cherry gasped and hissed, "Is that a *cougar*?"

Harper looked at Everly, wide-eyed.

Everly could barely make out its silhouette against the shadows. But it was a shape she knew well from her dreams. Her skin tingled with goose bumps and a deep feeling of connection.

The creature turned and bounded away.

"Follow it," Everly whispered, rushing after the big cat.

It kept an easy pace, weaving between trees and skirting puddles, always just ahead of them as they sprinted behind it.

Deeper into the woods again, the cougar hesitated and looked back at Everly before springing up a tree trunk with its powerful claws and disappearing.

"No, come back!" Everly cried out, as though it would listen.

What had she thought would come from following it? It was nothing more than

a wild animal. She was getting all mixed up, her need for some final hope in finding Rylan making her chase wild geese—or wild cougars.

Harper caught her breath. "Did we lose it?"

Callan frowned at Cherry. "Maybe not. You feel that?"

"Yup."

"Feel what?" Everly asked.

"Eidolghast," Callan said.

"When they're near, we get this tingly kind of 'I'm about to self-combust and change form entirely' feeling," Cherry added.

"A vasmire, maybe?" Callan frowned, turning his head and rolling his shoulders. "But dull, like the dead one at the theater. Come on."

Callan took the lead again, moving slower this time, letting his shadyr senses guide him. Each of them had a try calling Howell House on their phones as they went, just in case they needed backup, but there was no coverage.

Callan seemed sure they weren't walking toward a full, living monster and tried to comfort them. But the idea that they were walking toward pieces of monster didn't make Everly feel any better.

Up ahead, the trees parted, revealing a log cabin perched on the swirling buttress roots of an ancient fig.

Smaller rooms and lean-tos of recycled doors and planks had been hodgepodged onto the sides, and an uncountable number of bowls were strewn around the ground surrounding the hut.

Most were empty, but a few held rotting remains, crawling with maggots.

The smell of rank meat filled the air. In the tree line surrounding the clearing, things of all shapes and sizes moved in the dark.

The old woman stood awkwardly near the front door, as though they'd caught her just arriving home. She stared at them with terror in her eyes.

Everly stepped forward quickly. "We want to talk. Just talk. It's okay."

The woman hunched over, as though it would make her invisible.

"Go away!" she pleaded, her voice gravelly and high.

"Please." Everly edged closer, reaching out a hand. "We don't mean any harm. We're looking for a friend of ours who is missing."

The woman turned hesitantly their way. Wiry copper-gray hair jutted out all around her face from under the hood of her ragged coat. Scars cut through the leathery skin on her face, cross-hatching her deep wrinkles. As her gaze passed over Callan, her expression drooped sympathetically, and then hardened again.

"You won't hurt me or my animals?"

Everly eyed the bowls and the shifting shapes in the trees, wondering what kind

of animals the woman was talking about.

"Of course not." Harper joined them near the front door, smiling cheerily. "We love animals."

The woman's face brightened. "Not all people do. They can be so cruel. I'm Nell. Missing friend, huh?"

Everly nodded and introduced herself and the others.

"Come on, then." Nell gestured to them with a blood-stained hand to follow her inside, but thankfully didn't extend it to shake.

The four of them warily went through the cabin door after her. On the way, Callan whispered, "There's definitely a vasmire here, but not a strong source. Can you keep yourself from changing?"

Cherry nodded.

Inside, Nell took off her coat and hung it near a stone fireplace. It was the only light source in the room, down to just a scattering of red coals. Everly had to step carefully between the bowls on the floor, and the odd small creature dashed past her feet.

Please don't be rats. Doorways hung with tattered fabric led off into a couple of other rooms.

"You have a lot of pets?" Everly asked.

"I'm a wildlife carer. I'm just trying to help the poor creatures people have hurt so much." Nell's clothes were a bundle of layered odds and ends, knitted woolens and tattered skirts over thick pants and gumboots.

There was a hand-knitted pouch slung around her chest, resting against her belly, where something squirmed and mewled.

There were two shredded armchairs. Nell took one, and Harper insisted Everly take the facing one.

Cherry and Callan stood behind the armchairs. They kept glancing at each other as though communicating silently, their muscles visibly tense.

"I've been running my little animal sanctuary out here for a while now. We take in all the animals we can."

"Is that what the roadkill is for? To feed them?" Callan asked.

The old woman squinted at him but didn't reply.

"We?" asked Everly.

"Me and Hubby." She smiled, eyes crinkling, and waved toward one of the doorways.

A dark figure meandered by within the other room, obscured by the threadbare curtain.

A low groaning sound came from him that resembled a "Hi."

Something the size of a small dog skittered across the ground, right past Everly, making her squeak and pull her feet in closer.

Its fur was ragged and its shape strange, making it hard to tell what it was in the low light. Callan put a hand on her shoulder, his eyes wide. What was he seeing that she wasn't?

"Honey? Can you bring in some firewood?" Nell called.

"Yeaaahh," Hubby moaned and continued to wander around the side room.

The corners of the room crawled with small shapes.

Everly shivered and swallowed her fear. "Where do you find the animals that you help? On roads?"

"Mostly. I help the ones that need my help the most. That no one else cares to help. That no one else *can* help," Nell said, pride in her tone.

Callan bent close to Everly's ear and whispered, "These animals ..."

"I think it's wonderful. I've sometimes thought about being a wildlife carer myself," Harper gushed, although Everly caught a wariness in her tone.

Nell smiled sweetly at her.

Callan hissed, "These animals are all *dead*."

26

"What do you mean dead? They're moving," Everly whispered at Callan. Her eyes darted around, unable to see whatever it was Callan could see in the low light. How could all these animals be dead? The place smelled of death, but that had to be from the roadkill the woman collected.

"I mean this is zombieville and we are surrounded by franken-animals."

Was Callan making some kind of sick joke?

Zombie animals? Is that even possible? She wasn't sure in this disturbing new world of monsters she'd fallen into.

Then something pounced onto Everly's lap.

A small black cat. But not just a cat—careful stitching held its patchy coat together, mixed with fur that clearly hadn't originally belonged to it, and sections that looked like the sickly gray flesh of a vasmire.

Lips that had rotted away exposed broken teeth. It stared up at Everly with milky-white eyes.

She gasped, freezing in place.

"See what I've been able to do?" Nell leaned forward, enthusiasm sparkling in her eyes. "I discovered things in Shroudhaven, amazing things, that I could never have done in all my years as a veterinary surgeon elsewhere. The countless lives I've saved with my new techniques."

Everly remained frozen, eyes on the zombie-like cat on her lap.

Its head whipped around, and Everly jolted, thrusting a hand between herself and the animal. The cat had begun to clean itself, but was startled by Everly's reaction, hissing. It lunged, jagged maw aimed at Everly's raised hand.

She shot to her feet, dropping the cat. It dashed off into a sooty corner.

"Sorry about Mittens. You know how cats can be when they are frightened." Nell chuckled.

Standing now, Everly could see out the window, could see all the shapes creeping around them. Like a sickly puppet show, silhouettes of big cats, bears, wolves, and more shambled around the cottage.

This was madness. This woman was stitching together roadkill with monster parts and keeping a menagerie of undead animals.

Everly looked at the small creatures skittering in the shadows underfoot. Were they dangerous?

The increased reports of animal attacks around Shroudhaven made her think yes. She almost laughed. It really had been animal attacks all along.

Undead animals.

But maybe not all of them were dangerous. Everly and Mittens had just scared each other equally, but the cat didn't actively try to eat her brains.

It was now sprawled in front of the fireplace, purring a disjointed rumble. A shaggy raccoon trotted over and curled up next to Mittens as though they were old friends. None of the other small animals scurrying around were trying to feed on their flesh.

Nell seemed proud of how she helped these beasts. How she could bring them back from the brink of death—or even beyond.

As horrifying as the concept was, Nell did seem to be doing a good thing for the animals. If the number of food bowls was an indication, she'd given a lot of creatures a second chance at life.

Okay, just try to ignore the zombie animals for now, Everly told herself, in a sentence she never thought she'd think.

She had to get herself under control and ask the question she came here for. Because she could only hope this old woman had saved more than just animals.

Callan and Cherry were on edge, as though ready to attack, and Harper was still smiling at Nell, but cuddled herself, the fear in her eyes clear.

Nell shifted in her seat, eyeing them suspiciously.

"Sorry, the cat startled me too." Everly settled back into her armchair again and nodded to her friends. "It's okay."

From over Nell's shoulder, Cherry gave Everly a sarcastic look that said, 'Really?'

Just to make sure she and her friends weren't about to become Mitten's dinner, Everly asked, "Your animals, they're ... friendly?"

"Friendly? Oh no. They are ... how do I say it?"

Everly gripped the armrests and waited.

"Not *domesticated*, mostly. Lots of wild animals in rehab out there, so don't go riling them up or trying to pat them or something."

Everly blinked a few times, glancing at the Frankensteined cat and raccoon sharing the last bit of warmth of the dying fire, then back at Nell. "Of course. We'll leave them alone, they'll leave us alone, right?"

Nell gave her an appreciative smile. "Exactly. Now, we don't often have guests, but would you like a cup of tea? Hubby can brew some."

"Teeeeeaaa," he groaned.

Everly eyed the curtain blocking the view of him. She fought off a shiver and shook her head.

"No, that's okay. The reason we're here ... a few nights back, out in front of the old Boderleth Antiques store, a friend of ours got badly hurt and has been missing ever since. I was knocked down in the garden. I don't think you saw me, but I saw you."

Nell's eyes narrowed. "So that's why you were chasing after me. I try not to be seen, when I'm out working."

Everly leaned forward in her seat, holding Nell's gaze. "Do you know what happened to our friend? Or maybe, did you help him too?"

Nell broke eye contact and looked down, her puckered mouth twisting. "I wondered if someone would come looking for him."

Everly's heart leaped into a gallop. "Is he here?"

Harper put her hands over her mouth. Callan crouched beside Everly, waiting for an answer.

Nell nodded slowly. "I saw the poor boy, all broken up like that. I don't normally work on humans, but I had to do something. Hubby helped carry him and what remained of the other creature back here."

"Heeerrre," came a grumble from the next room.

"I didn't see you, love. Otherwise, I would have tried to help you, too." Nell leaned forward and patted Everly on the knee with fingers stained in dried blood.

Everly found herself very grateful then to have been hidden by the rosebush.

"Where is he? Is he ..." Everly choked on the word *alive*.

Callan had turned very pale.

Nell pursed her lips, eyeing them as though weighing her answer.

Harper kneeled beside Nell. She asked gently, "Did you manage to save him?"

Nell shrugged, her lips turned down. "No."

The word hit Everly like a bullet, but then Nell continued. "Not really. His body just ... healed itself. I didn't even need to do any surgery. But he just won't wake up for some reason."

The breath that had caught in Everly's throat was chased free by a sob of relief. Rylan was alive.

Nell's shoulders slumped, and the creature in her pouch gurgled and hissed. "Sorry. I'm not good with people like I am with animals."

Hubby pawed at the fabric door hanging. "Goooood."

"Thank you for helping my brother," Callan said, his voice tight and hard. "But we need to take him home now. Where is he?"

"He's safely hidden away. I was worried someone would come and think the wrong thing. Can't be too careful when you have a human body lying around." Nell rose creakily to her feet and stretched out. "I'll take you—"

Something clattered and clanged outside, the sound of metal pet bowls being thrown around.

A man's voice followed. "What is this stinking mess?"

"I think we found our beshadowing," replied a woman.

Nell turned on Everly, eyes wide and fierce. "Who else did you bring here?"

Callan looked out the window. "It's the Darkfreys. Two braces. This isn't good."

"Why are they here?" Harper asked.

Her question was answered by a growl, then a loud thump and a whimper.

"What are they doing?" Nell howled and charged to the front door, Everly and the others close behind.

Outside stood what appeared to be a group of vampires. One, built like a soldier action figure with a blond crew cut, had a ragged fox pinned under his boot.

Everly recognized him from earlier that day. Nilson Darkfrey.

The young redhead who knew Rylan still appeared human for a moment before being engulfed in black smoke and sparks. When she emerged, she had the same long fangs, white skin, and sharp claws as the others.

"Monsters," Nell gasped.

"What are the Howell runts doing here?" Nilson bellowed.

Another shrugged and rolled up his sleeves. "Who cares? Clear off, kiddos. This is Darkfrey business. We have a beshadowing to eliminate."

Callan stepped in front of Nell. "I don't think there *is* a beshadowing."

Annabeth barked a laugh. "You're kidding, right? Have you seen this place?"

In her changed form, her features were sharper, less human. Everly could only identify her because she'd seen her change.

One of the others might have been Jasper, based on the cardigan, but she didn't recognize the rest. They all wore military-style jackets similar to the one Rylan wore, with their hoods up, shadowing their faces so only their sharp-fanged mouths showed, glinting in the low light.

"Vonny, get your brace onto finding the ghast. We'll take care of the collateral." Nilson twisted his foot, grinding down the fox pinned under his boot. There was a sickening sound of bones cracking.

Nell shrieked. "No, no, what are you doing?"

Harper looked like she was about to vomit. She marched forward, fury shaking her fists. "Stop it!"

"The beshadowed animals are dangerous and can't be allowed to remain," the one likely to be Jasper said bluntly.

Cherry moved closer to them. "It's not like that. Just wait, there has to be another way."

Jasper stepped back and looked down his nose. "It's our duty to keep the darkness from taking over."

Spooked by the shouting, a ferret sped out of the cabin between their legs, making a run for the tree line. It moved so fast it was just a small furry blur. But the shadyrs were just as quick.

In a flash, Nilson snatched out an arm and grabbed it. He held it up by its neck. "Look at this abomination."

Nell cried, "No, don't hurt it! The animals haven't done anything wrong. They deserve to live."

Around the clearing, glowing blue eyes surrounded them, from tiny squirrel-sized to ones at bear height. The beasts clung to the shadows, weaving through the trees, keeping their distance.

"Leave it alone," Harper cried. "The animals are ... okay, maybe they're a little undead, but they're just animals. You don't have to kill them."

"Shut it, bliv. You don't know what you're talking about."

Everly thought she did. The animals weren't attacking any of them, and if Nell could be believed, they weren't any more dangerous than regular wild animals. There had been more animal attacks, but if anything, it was the concentration of so many animals in one place that was getting dangerous, not the undead state of them.

Callan stepped forward. "Nilson, listen, man, there's more going on here—"

"Enough. Undead critters, eidolghast, and crazy, beshadowed old ladies all have to go." Nilson clenched his grip and broke the ferret's neck.

Nell flung herself at him—a flurry of shrieks and wild hair and clawing fingernails. He swiped his arm through the air, throwing her back to the steps of the cabin.

A deep growl cut through the air. A huge half-wolf, half-Labrador bounded into the clearing, landing in front of Nell. With its back to her, it roared ferociously at the Darkfreys.

And then from the shadows of the trees, chaos erupted.

Creatures of all shapes and sizes poured forward, a surging current of fur, feathers, and claws, launching themselves at the Darkfreys. Those people had hurt the woman who fed them, cared for them, who had healed them.

The animals didn't seem happy about that. Nell's warning about riling them up rung through Everly's mind.

Shouts went up from the shadyrs as creatures from massive stags to swarms of lizards charged at them, tearing through the clearing.

The beasts created a living wall between the shadyrs and Nell. Everly had remained

near Nell, but Callan, Cherry, and Harper were on the other side. Bodies scattered in every direction, human and shadyr versus animal. Hisses and howls and the crunch of impacts filled the air.

"Harper!" Everly screamed.

Everly tried to run for her friends, but hands grabbed at her, clutching fistfuls of her shirt and hair.

Nell was on her feet again, her face wild with anguish. "You led them here! They're killing everything!"

"I'm sorry. They aren't with us. Please, we just came for our friend."

Nell's fingernails dug into Everly's skin as she forced her backward into the cabin. "You'll never find him! Never!"

27

E verly grabbed at Nell's hands, trying to release herself from the terrifyingly strong grip.

They wrestled, back and forward, Everly trying to use her weight to her advantage, to push past the crone-like woman.

But Nell was much stronger than she appeared. She roared, lunging forward, and tackled Everly into the cabin, landing on top of her. Food bowls smashed and clanged around them. Others, caught under Everly's back, jabbed into her.

Ragged, bloody nails flashed in front of Everly's eyes.

"I'm sorry. We didn't want the animals to be hurt," Everly cried. She brought her arms up to cover her face as Nell pounded at her with gnarled fists.

"You're all monsters!" Nell screamed, her fingernails scraping across Everly's neck.

Everly rolled to the side, throwing the woman off her. She crawled backward to get to her feet. Nell landed on all fours and scrambled at Everly like a wild creature.

Everly dodged behind an armchair. "Please, stop. I don't want to fight you."

One of the Darkfreys burst through the front door, wrestling the Labrador-wolf. Its slobbering maw snapped close to his face. He put his foot into the animal's belly and kicked it back out of the cabin. There was a thud and yelp from where it fell.

Nell howled and rushed, banshee-like, at the man, flying across the room. She latched onto his back, hands clawing at his eyes and face from behind.

The shadyr swore and swatted at her, trying to shake her off.

Freed from Nells' wrath, Everly took her chance to dodge away from the grappling pair. Harper and the others were out there, somewhere amid the cacophony of animal and human cries, and she had to get to them and help.

She ducked to the side, under the man's swinging arms, and reached the front door. On the porch, she froze, trying to make sense of the scene.

It was a roaring tornado of animals. Tattered eagles, owls, and crows dive-bombed into the fray. Dogs, cats, foxes, and badgers dashed about, and in the center, three shadyrs fought to bring down the biggest bear Everly had ever seen.

One Darkfrey shadyr writhed on the ground, overwhelmed by a layer of smaller

animals, smothering them. Everly's eyes widened as a streak of orange flashed through the clearing.

Was that a tiger?

The battle had kicked up the bowls of rotting food and forest litter and the air had a rank, earthy odor like blood and dust.

Across the clearing, bright red caught Everly's eye. Cherry was there, changed into his vampire-like form, but recognizable by his vivid hair and matching red-and-white jacket. Back to back with him was Harper.

She'd picked up a couple of large steel food bowls and was using them as shields, holding her own against the rabid creatures.

A few animals nipped and chased them, but their defensive behavior wasn't drawing nearly as much attention as the Darkfrey's aggression.

Everly couldn't identify Callan in the messy battle. The undead animals were striking out at everyone who wasn't Nell. Anything human-shaped was their enemy.

Before Everly could make it out the door, the tangle of shadyr and Nell smashed toward her. The man tripped on a steel bowl, and Everly had to jump out of the way as the two of them came tumbling down.

They crashed through some shelving and upturned the armchair Everly had sat in earlier. From underneath it, a pulsating swarm of fur squirmed. Everly's stomach squelched and backflipped. Dozens of tiny bright-blue eyes stared at her from the swarm. Startled from their sanctuary, they rushed toward Everly.

Rats. RATS.

Everly's brain shorted out, overtaken by panic. Her skin crawled and her breath caught. She tumbled backward on pure primal instinct. Her back came up against the cabin wall, scraping against the rough wood.

The rats swarmed over the furniture, hopping across the room like speeding arrows, a flood of fur, coming her way.

Everly screamed and rushed to escape them, herded away from the exit, toward the other doorway. The tattered cloth curtain tore away as she pushed through it and she stumbled into the dark space beyond, barely able to see.

She ran into a bench, spilling plates and pans off it. They clattered and broke on the floor around her.

I have to get out of here, have to get back to the others.

She couldn't go back the way she'd come. She physically couldn't force her body to move back toward the teeming rodents.

A little light came through a window to Everly's side. She grasped at the latch, pushing and wrenching, but it wouldn't open.

There has to be another way out.

She squinted into the darkness. And inhaled a scream.

The rats, undead or otherwise, ran in, pouring through the door, and dashed under her feet. Then they *climbed up her.*

Everly felt their sharp claws as they scurried over her clothing, using her as a bridge from the floor to the sanctuary of the cupboards behind her.

Her whole body froze, completely petrified except for the uncontrollable shaking. Her dragon roiled within her like food poisoning, making her nauseous, wanting escape. She fought it back with everything she had. Her breathing had become staccato, faltering.

Go. Get out of here, she pleaded with herself.

She regained enough control to take one shaky step.

Movement flashed outside the window, then with the clash of thunder it caved in, the entire wall coming with it. The giant bear's back filled the space, twisting and swinging at the shadyrs trying to end it. Glass and splinters showered across the room.

Overhead cupboards tore from the walls and collapsed, smashing over Everly, bringing her down with them.

Her head hit something hard.

Everly twisted to the side, thrashing her arms out to push away the avalanche of timber and crockery that covered her. But there was nothing there.

There was nothing anywhere. Only inky darkness, only the barest sense of firm ground beneath where she lay.

Oh no. No. Wake up. Wake up!

"Hey, it's okay. You're dreaming." Rylan appeared in front of her.

He crouched down, hands on her shoulders to comfort her as she slowed her breathing enough to speak.

"No, I don't think I am." Everly held one of his arms for support and he helped her to her feet.

He frowned at her response. His warm green eyes met hers, stared right through her.

"I mean, it is … different than usual," he said, looking around into the empty void. "Normally there'd be more imminent terror manifesting around us."

Still clutching Rylan's arm, Everly tried again to wake up, but nothing happened.

Her voice trembled as she said, "I'm not dreaming. I think I got knocked out."

"You *what?*" Rylan growled.

Everly winced away from his anger. "We were so close. I thought we'd found you, but then everything went wrong."

"What hurt you out there? Are you still in danger?" Rylan demanded.

Everly just shook her head. She didn't know how to answer. Couldn't bear that Rylan was only worried about her and not whether they were going to be able to save him.

Nell's curse haunted Everly: *You'll never find him! Never!*

Rylan squeezed her hand. "Was it an eidolghast?"

"No."

She remembered the rats, the bear, the fighting, and destruction. She had no idea how badly she was hurt. Getting knocked out was not great though.

She wanted to wake up, go back out there, help her friends, find Rylan, but even when conscious, she hadn't been able to fix things.

"I couldn't do anything. I couldn't help anyone. I couldn't find you. I failed everyone." Everly covered her face with her hands, tears shaking loose from her eyes.

Everly felt Rylan's fingers over the top of hers, over her cheek. "You haven't. It's not your fault."

"You don't know what's happening!"

"But I know you." His voice came from close beside her ear. "And I know the world is cruel and dark, and terrible things happen, and that *isn't your fault*. You do the one thing that matters."

Rylan coaxed her fingers away from her face, and she looked up into his golden ocean eyes.

"You *try*."

Their hands remained locked together, fingers entwined.

"You always try so hard to help, to fix everything. And not everything is able to be fixed, but it's the trying that matters. It's the caring. In this dark, screwed-up world, compassion like yours is the one thing that can make the world brighter."

Everly's whole body convulsed, shaken by sobs. "It's not enough."

Rylan leaned in close, resting his forehead on hers. "You can't blame yourself for the darkness. You can't blame the sun for not chasing away every shadow. Believe in yourself, Evie. You *are* the light. And before you, the dark *will fall*."

Everly's sense of gravity lurched, tugging at her from within.

Am I waking up? Or am I dying?

She wanted to stay there with Rylan, with his hand in hers, with his face so close the temptation to kiss him was unbearable.

The pull was too strong, and she was dragged away, screaming, to face her fate.

28

“**O**w.” Everly groaned.

Her eyes cracked open. Splintered wood fell off her as she sat up. Gingerly, she touched the back of her head. Not bleeding, but tender. Alive. Awake.

Rylan ...

She'd woken up again so quickly. But this wasn't a situation where she could linger in dreams. Animals and shadyrs still roared in battle nearby.

Everly still felt Rylan's touch on her hands and face, longed to have him with her. And his real body was somewhere nearby.

She had to find him.

I am going to find him.

The fight with the bear had moved outside again, but another large shape stalked toward her, pale eyes glowing like small moons in the gloom.

Cat. Big cat.

The cougar. She had seen it enough in her dreams to know it right away.

It bared its sharp teeth, a growl low in its throat.

Things moved in the broken timber and kitchenware around her. Rats—panicked and fleeing around the room, around her. Everly held her breath, cringing away.

The cougar approached and Everly was sure it was the one from their car accident. Not yet full grown, it was big enough to be terrifying, but some spots from infancy hadn't yet faded to its plain adult coat, and its feet were too big for its body.

Rough sutures tracked across one of its shoulders and its eyes were milky blue.

It was Nell Everly had seen in the woods that day before the accident. Nell and Hubby must have taken the cougar. Healed it.

Poor thing. We did hit it after all.

“I'm so sorry,” Everly whispered as it reached her. She flinched back, waiting for it to enact its revenge.

Jaws snapped, and there was a shrill squeak. The cougar snapped up a rat that had been crawling along Everly's arm, then flung it away. It swiped its paw at another on her leg.

Everly exhaled in vibrato and stared at the young cougar, unsure yet if it was helping her deliberately or if it just hated rats as much as she did.

"Here's another one! I'll get it," a burly voice grunted the words. The big, cruel shadyr, Nilson, stepped in from outside, over the rubble, stalking toward the cougar.

"What? No!" Everly gasped, jumping to her feet and placing herself between him and the cat. "Stay away from it."

Nilson grinned, white lips spreading and baring razor-sharp teeth. "Or what? Have to go through you, will I? That's not much of a challenge, bliv."

The man towered over her and was built like a machine. Everly doubted she'd be able to match him. But she had to do something.

You try, Rylan's voice still echoed in her memory.

She had to try. She couldn't fight every darkness and shadow in the world, but even if she could save just one life—unlife?—it was worth doing.

"I won't let you hurt it."

He lowered his head and swayed it side to side as though thinking. When he looked up again, his grin dripped pure malice. "I think I see what's going on here. You're clearly beshadowed as well. Just a bit more collateral damage in the cleanup."

The man lashed out, faster than Everly could even react against. He grabbed her around the neck, his hands cold and hard as stone. Everly gagged.

A loud *clung* boomed through her ears, and the shadyr's grip released. His eyes rolled back into his head and he went down like a landslide into the jumble of shattered kitchen.

Behind him, a stout, elderly man stood, milky-eyed and slack-jawed. A large cast-iron frying pan still swung in his grip.

His shirt was too big for him, bulging out around suspenders, the sleeves rolled up to the elbows, revealing scarred hands and sallow skin. Another large scar puckered the side of his mouth, leading to his ear.

"Goooooood," he moaned.

"Umm, thanks?" Everly rubbed her neck.

Behind her, the cougar had vanished, hopefully finding safety. Hubby tilted his head in Everly's direction, but it was impossible to tell where he was looking or what he was seeing with his white-washed eyes.

He grunted loudly and Everly flinched. Then he raised an arm crookedly and beckoned her to follow him, shuffling into the main room. "Coooome."

Everly stepped in after him, finding the room completely trashed. There was no sign of Nell. Sounds of scuffling came from outside, and Everly heard her friends calling her name. She headed for the front door.

Hubby smacked his hand against the doorframe leading into a different room, flicking his head for her to follow him. "Boooy."

Rylan? It might be my only chance to find him.

Everly turned from the exit to the undead man before following him into the shadowy bedroom.

An overturned LED lamp cast a pale light over the area. A double bed was lovingly covered in embroidered pillows and crocheted throws. A framed photo of Nell and her husband in their youth, standing outside the gates of a zoo, sat on the bedside table.

The bed was off angle, pushed to the side and revealing a trap door that had been violently flung open, the wood cracked to pieces around the latch.

"Dooown." Hubby hobbled into the hole beneath the room.

Reaching out a shaking hand, Everly grabbed the lamp, took a few deep breaths, and followed him down.

The wooden steps creaked. They were slick with black ooze, sticking under her boots. The rough-hewn dirt walls of the stairwell gave off a peaty smell, which didn't quite cover the pungently sweet scent of rot coming from ahead.

Everly pulled her sleeve over her hand and covered her nose. She hurried after Hubby, along the short tunnel that brought them lower beneath the earth, and into a wide cavern. Hubby wobbled to the side, giving Everly a clear view into the space.

The dim light of the small LED lamp wasn't strong enough to breach all the darkness before her. But she could see in the center of the cave a makeshift operating theater.

Dozens of unlit lamps of all shapes and sizes hung from the ceiling, cables running in a spaghetti tangle to a generator on the side. An operating table stood beneath those lamps.

On it lay a human body.

Beside it was a Darkfrey shadyr, bent over the body.

At first, Everly thought they were attempting to revive the person, but then she saw their clawed hands, wrapped around the body's neck.

"No!" Everly boomed. "What are you doing?"

The shadyr turned. She couldn't make out who it was in the dark, with their distorted form and hood covering their head.

Everly flung the LED lamp down and charged the shadyr. She knew they were in vampire form. They were probably stronger, faster, and any blow she landed on them would magically heal.

She didn't care. She was just *angry*.

So much death, so much violence.

What is wrong with these people?

She bellowed wordlessly, coming in swinging. The shadyr dodged back, hissing. Everly's fist glanced over their Darkfrey jacket.

From beneath their hood, the shadyr growled, wilder than any of the animals up

above, then pushed Everly back with both palms, cracking against her shoulders and sending her tumbling across the rocky ground.

She rolled, hands scraping as she brought herself to a stop.

The shadyr turned their back on Everly as though she didn't even matter. Their head turned, seeking, and they picked up a large stone from near their feet. They raised it high above the lifeless body on the slab.

"Stop it! Why are you doing this?" Lightning seemed to flash behind Everly's eyes, the storm of her fury breaking.

She'd been trying to control herself, trying to reason with them. Now she just wanted to make it all stop.

And screw the consequences.

Something inside Everly cracked open. And she didn't fight it.

Roaring and rushing, gleeful in its hunger, light surged freely from her.

Brightness filled the cavern, stinging her eyes.

She soared above the ground toward the shadyr, a seething star of power and wrath. Tendrils drifted out of her skin, then struck forward.

The shadyr dodged and swatted at the starry strands, moving in a fast blur. They leaped away, taking cover behind shelves and stalagmites. The tendrils chased, whipping after them, relentless, ravenous.

The hunger in Everly rose. The shadyr seemed like nothing more than prey, than food. She wanted to eat them all up. She yearned for it.

No. This isn't right.

Everly tried to reel the light back into herself. The tendrils held still for the barest moment before extending again, swirling like the stingers of a jellyfish, out of her control.

In the brief pause of reprieve, the shadyr dashed to the side, making a run for it. Everly's body turned against her will, tracking her prey. She floated across the room, dragged along in the swell of voracious light.

The shadyr reached the exit, disappearing up the dark stairs.

Just let them go. That's enough, Everly pleaded with whatever was inside her, whatever this power was. Her dragon, taking over.

But it was hungry. Too hungry. It demanded sacrifice.

The wisps spread through the cavern, seeking, and found another victim.

"No," Everly gasped.

Hubby moved too slowly, hobbling away into a dead-end corner. A low, heavy wheeze came from his throat. The sparkling streams shot out at him like lightning, wrapping him entirely.

Everly could feel the life being sucked from him, drawn along those long strings of light, feeding her dragon.

No! Everly fought against it, struggling to make it stop. Her heart raged, searing light and pain coursing through her as she tried to force herself under control.

The hunger was too strong. Until it wasn't.

The tendrils detached, slithering slowly away. The glow faded.

Her dragon was satiated.

The old man's body slumped onto the ground. Everly stumbled over to him, her knees cracking as she fell in front of him. Glassy eyes stared emptily. Whatever essence, whatever life he'd had was gone entirely.

"No. *No.* What have I done?"

I've killed him.

Bile rose in Everly's throat. She tried to bargain, to justify. He was already dead, wasn't he? Undead? But he'd helped her. He'd been kind. He'd been loved. And now he was no more, and she'd done that.

The dragon inside her had done that.

The LED lamp still rocked slightly where it was discarded earlier, its glow obscured behind loose stones. The low angle made the shadows on Hubby's wrinkles and scars stark and strange, his face frozen in a mask of fear.

Rylan had been wrong. She wasn't the light. She was darkness.

She turned slowly, tearing her gaze away from the fallen soul. Only one hope kept her going, kept her moving. The body lying on the operating table. Her feet dragged, numb and heavy, as she edged toward it. In the low light, Everly tried to gather what she could see.

The body seemed whole. A tall man with short buzz-cut hair. His upper body was bare, a dark shape of a tattoo on his shoulder.

"Rylan?" Everly stumbled forward, tears blurring her vision.

It's him. It's him.

Please be alive.

29

Everly collapsed over Rylan's body, clung to his chest, and wept.

"Everly?" Harper's voice reached through the sounds of sobbing. "Are you down there?"

Everly lifted her head slightly.

She called out, her voice cracking, "I'm here."

Footsteps galloped down the wooden stairs and across the stone floor toward her. She turned to find two shadyrs, still in vampire form, and Harper following behind, holding a bright lamp. With more light, Everly could identify the two shadyrs as Callan and Cherry, mostly based on their hair and clothing.

"Oh, thank everything you're okay!" Harper wrapped Everly in a strong hug, the lamp banging into Everly's back.

"It's Rylan—you found him," Callan gasped.

"Oh, wow," Harper said in a hush.

She let go of Everly and held the lamp over Rylan. He lay still, completely unaffected by the noise around him. His skin was pale and firm, although not as white as the shadyrs in their full vampire form. Everly wondered if beneath his closed lips she would find fangs.

"Is he alive?" Cherry asked softly.

Everly nodded. She had heard a slow, soft heartbeat as she'd pressed her face to his chest and felt the barest rise and fall of breath. He seemed to be sleeping peacefully.

Harper turned back to Everly. "I was so worried when we lost track of you. That was craziness!"

"I was worried about you too."

Cherry snorted. "No need to worry about Bellsy—she was fierce."

"For a human," she added bashfully. "We came to find you as soon as it was clear enough. The Darkfreys, they killed just about everything."

The horror and fury in Harper's eyes made Everly's own sting.

Harper must have seen her expression darken, because she added, "We tried our best not to hurt any of the animals. Managed to chase some away. I'm sure some survived."

"They should have listened to us. None of that had to happen." Callan's pale face grew stern, and he squeezed his hands into fists.

Black mist surrounded him, and he returned to his normal self.

Cherry pouted over vampire teeth. "Show-off. Way too much vasmire ... bits ... nearby for me to change back now."

The extra light in the room showed the full extent of Nell's laboratory. Around the varying levels of the rocky floor, wooden shelves had been constructed to fit the spaces. They held body parts of all shapes and sizes, white labels hanging off them, black ooze dripping between them.

There were a lot of tentacles.

"You'll get there soon," Callan encouraged. "It just takes practice."

"Takes more than practice, runts."

Four Darkfrey shadyrs stepped out from the stairway passage. Nilson, Annabeth, Jasper, and another Everly didn't know.

Could one of them be the shadyr who tried to hurt Rylan? Everly clenched her teeth so hard they ached.

Nilson continued his sneering words. "Which is why you should leave it to us. Where's the vasmire?"

Cherry pointed at the shelves. "There. There. A bit over there. And also there."

"What in the Everdark is going on down here?" Annabeth asked.

"No vasmire?" the fourth shadyr asked. "Just bits? No wonder I felt weaker than usual."

Callan watched them warily. "Like I told you before, there wasn't a beshadowing here. Not really."

"So we could have avoided all of this mess if you'd listened for once instead of following orders blindly." Cherry glared at Jasper. Their gaze met for the barest of moments before Jasper turned away.

Nilson walked over to a shelf and kicked a tub of gore. "Alive or not, the eidolghast parts were affecting this area, the animals, and the crazy old witch."

"Where is Nell?" Everly demanded.

His pale teeth twisted into a dark grin. "The old hag? With her dead pets."

Everly's heart closed in on itself, and she spoke through clenched teeth. "You didn't have to do that! You're murderers!"

"She was ghast-twisted. She attacked us and had to be put down." In a puff of black mist and sparks, he shifted back into his regular form.

The other three followed, suddenly a lot less threatening, but no less monstrous.

Everly's voice grew loud. "You attacked her animals first. If you'd listened, you'd know she was only trying to help."

"You're just a bunch of bleeding hearts. That's why you shouldn't be messing around in our business. You're not strong enough to do what needs to be done."

Everly wanted to rage and fight and consume them whole. They were monsters and murderers.

But so was she. And if she gave in to that again, she didn't know what the consequences would be.

"Oh, is that Rylan?" Annabeth squeaked, running toward them.

"Yeah, it is." Callan stepped into Annabeth's path, blocking her before she could reach him. "That's why we were here in the first place."

"Is he alive?" Annabeth froze, her mouth open.

"Nell saved him," Everly spat, her words a weapon of guilt. "Nell saved him like she saved all those animals. And you murdered them all."

Annabeth seemed to shrink a little, taking a step back.

Nilson strolled over to Everly and poked a hard finger into her collarbone. "They weren't animals anymore. They were atrocities, and we did our job."

"Get your disgusting hand off me," Everly growled.

Harper, Callan, and Cherry pressed in by her side, staring him down.

Neither Annabeth nor Jasper moved up beside Nilson to match them, only the unknown shadyr, part of his brace, joined him.

Nilson cricked his neck and stepped back, his chin lifted, jutting out. "You shouldn't even be here. You're lucky we came along to put an end to this nightmare. Don't forget that."

"That's enough. It's over and done," Annabeth said. "We need to take Rylan home now."

The vision of one of the shadyrs trying to end Rylan's life flashed through Everly's mind again, nearly overcoming her control.

The cavern became almost imperceivably brighter, and Everly clamped it down. No longer hungry, the light was easier to contain, quickly fading again.

She exhaled her words through clenched teeth. "No. He's not going with you."

"Of course he is. He's one of us. He's part of my brace." Annabeth shook her head in confusion, her red hair, held back in a ponytail, swinging.

The remaining three Darkfrey shadyrs entered the cavern. When they saw everyone else, they shook off their vampire form as well, revealing Vonny and two strangers, the remains of Nilson's brace.

"What's going on in here?" Vonny snapped.

"They found Rylan, but they don't want us to take him."

"Found him? Alive?" She peered skeptically over their shoulders at his body on the table. "What's wrong with him?"

Everly glanced back as well. No matter the yelling and commotion, Rylan hadn't stirred at all.

Callan watched Everly, frowning. "We don't know."

Jasper tilted his head, looking at the body. "Then we should transfer him back to the estate for medical aid."

"Not a chance. Not after what I've seen." Everly shook her head.

Vonny narrowed her eyes. "What are you talking about? What did you see?"

Everly wished she knew, wished she could point out the shadyr who stood in front of her now as the one who'd attempted to take Rylan's life. But she couldn't.

"I saw enough to know there's no way I'm going to trust any of you with keeping him alive."

Vonny laughed her off. "He's a Darkfrey and he comes with us."

"He's a Howell and stays with us," Callan said, stepping in front of her.

"These guys are out of their ghast-damned minds," Nilson said.

Vonny huffed. "Fine, you know what? Keep him, then. He's been more trouble than he's worth lately anyway—running off on his own and ending up in whatever mess this is, leaving us to take the blame."

"Vonny, no. He's one of us. He's our brace leader," Annabeth argued.

"*He* made the decision to not be part of our brace anymore. And he can be replaced." Vonny marched away, out of the cavern, and Annabeth scuttled after her, still arguing and pleading.

"Looks like you guys have won yourself a vegetable." Nilson snickered. He turned to leave too, talking on his way. "Good luck with that. Whatever you do with him, better do it before the cleanup crew arrives. 'Cause he looks like he should go in the trash with the rest of the corpses."

The rest of the Darkfreys followed him.

Jasper frowned at the Howell team, opened his mouth, closed it, then left as well.

"I can't believe they did that. All that killing, like it was nothing." Harper's eyes were narrow and glossy. "And poor Nell ..."

Cherry sighed. "It's what they are trained to do—destroy a beshadowing, at any cost."

Harper said, "It's like they enjoyed it!"

Callan and Cherry nodded, sharing a sad look with each other. Everly wondered if they had seen far worse.

Harper cuddled her arms around herself. "At least we got Rylan back."

Everly's chest tightened. "At what cost?"

Callan said, "None of what happened here is our fault. They would have come out to deal with this whether we found the place or not. It was just bad luck we were

here at the same time."

Or good luck. They'd saved a few animals and Rylan. A few moments later, and Rylan would have been nothing but more body parts.

Everly's traumatized mind was still trying to turn back time, replaying every choice she'd made, every hesitation, pointing fingers at where she'd gone wrong.

If only she'd done this, if only she'd said that, if only she'd done better, been stronger, maybe there wouldn't have been so much tragedy. But she *couldn't* turn back time. She couldn't fix what she'd done.

She couldn't give back the life she'd taken.

Harper grunted. "How can they get away with this?"

"The Darkfreys own Shroudhaven. The cops, the courts. They do as they please and clean up the mess afterward." Callan looked around the room at the mutilated monster pieces. "Speaking of which, they're right. They'll have a cleanup crew out here soon. We should get moving."

"Whoa." Cherry spotted the crumpled body of the old man in the corner and pointed at him. "Who is that?"

Everly's mouth opened but was clogged by guilt.

"Is that Nell's husband?" Callan guessed. "What happened to him?"

Everly shook her head. Her voice broke over the words. "He's dead."

"Those horrible Darkfreys," Harper snarled.

Tears washed hot over Everly's eyes. She couldn't tell them, couldn't speak what she'd done. What would Harper think of her?

Harper turned away from the body to the two men. "You guys made the right decision getting out of that place."

Callan nodded slowly, his gaze on his brother. "I just wish Rylan had gotten out sooner too. Then maybe this wouldn't have happened."

They all turned toward Rylan, lying still on the table.

"He hasn't moved a muscle. Is he in a coma or something?" Cherry asked.

"He's so pale," Harper said.

"It's like he's only partly in vampire form, half and half," Cherry said, still in full vampire form himself.

Everly found her voice again. "He looked human, like this, the last time I saw him. In part of the fight he seemed more vampire-like, then he seemed human, then at the end he turned cold again."

"He must have changed back so you didn't see what he was. If his injuries were that bad, maybe he couldn't change again fully. But even like this, with all the vasmire parts around, he must have had just enough regeneration to heal himself," Callan whispered.

"What do we do now?" Harper asked.

Callan shrugged. "Try to wake him up, get him out of here?"

Despite it being what Everly desperately wanted the most, her hope of Rylan waking up had fallen low.

Still, she bent over him, speaking close to his ear, "Rylan? Can you hear us?"

Everyone seemed to hold their breath, but nothing happened.

"Hey, come on, man. Wake up," Callan said, patting his cheeks.

Nothing.

Cherry checked Rylan's pulse and rubbed his sternum with his knuckles.

Harper tried yelling and clapping her hands loudly in front of his face.

Nothing made any difference. Rylan remained as still as death.

30

E verly hauled a plastic tub of monster gore into her old bedroom, while Harper smoothed out the new sheets on the single bed.

Who would've thought this is where we'd end up today?

They'd found Rylan, but it didn't feel like a win.

Callan and Cherry carried his body into the room and laid him carefully on the mattress.

Since finding him, they'd made sure to never let his body be separated from the dead monster bits.

After making their way out of the woods, they had emptied out some tubs of props and photography gear from Harper's van and returned to Nell's laboratory to fill them with random chunks of vasmire anatomy off the shelves.

They assumed that as long as there were vasmire pieces nearby, Rylan's body would continue to renew itself enough to stay alive. That was about all they had to go on for now.

In the days he'd been missing, Rylan hadn't seemed to have lost any muscle mass or become dehydrated. It was like he was in a kind of stasis.

Given that he wasn't strictly human, and the remaining weirdness surrounding the situation, they all decided that a hospital wasn't the best idea.

Everly got checked over by Callan and Cherry, who both had medical training from their time with the Darkfreys, and they thought that despite briefly being unconscious, she didn't need a hospital either unless she started showing any other symptoms of concussion.

Everly and Harper had also cleaned up their minor scratches with some hand sanitizer from the van. It stung violently, but they were desperate to remove anything left by the filthy claws and nails that had made the marks. Callan and Cherry's vampire-tinted skin showed no wounds, completely healed already.

The vasmire parts helped Rylan, but they also presented a challenge, because not all the Howell House shadyrs had trained enough to have full control over their bodies in the presence of eidolghasts. Even dead ones.

Cherry, and Tammy too, Callan had thought, would be resigned to vampire form all the time if the vasmire parts were kept near them.

So they'd ended up at the Boderleth house.

Callan had allowed his vampire form to return to help carry his heavy brother up the stairs but went back to human again once the job was done.

"I can't believe we're doing this." Harper's voice had an edge of hysteria to it.

Cherry grinned over his still pointy teeth at Harper. "You didn't think to yourself this morning, gosh, it would really end the day well if we brought home an unconscious man and a few boxes of monster tentacles?"

"Maybe I did, but that's my own private business," Harper replied.

Everly leaned over and tucked the blanket up to Rylan's shoulders. She wasn't sure whether he could feel the cold, or anything at all, but it made him look more comfortable.

We found you. Please wake up. Wake up so everything can be okay.

"He's going to be all right," Harper offered, rubbing Everly's shoulder.

"Yeah, for now," Callan said, shaking his head as he stared at his brother. "I have no idea how long the vasmire parts will keep working. Those look pretty fresh, but I imagine they won't last long."

Faces turned grim, then Callan shook his head, smiling wryly at Harper and Everly. "We'll work something out. How about you two? Handling?"

Harper waved both hands in front of her, gesturing to the tufts of fur and splatters of blood across her clothes. "This, you mean? How am I handling *this*? I'm going to hold off on an answer until after I take the longest shower ever in an attempt to wash off all of *this*."

Cherry shrugged. "I'd tell you guys that tonight was crazy-out-of-the-ordinary, but I'd be lying."

Harper just stared at him for a long moment, then shuddered. "Okay, I'm going to hit that shower now."

She fluttered a hand and left. The sound of the bathroom door closing and shower turning on came faintly through the wall beside them.

"I want to get out of here too. I'd really like to have my own skin back." Cherry flexed his pale fingers. "You guys all right?"

Everly and Callan nodded, and Cherry headed for the door. "Good teamwork tonight. Including honorary members."

Everly tried to smile a goodbye, but her face fell. It didn't feel like the night had gone well. They'd found Rylan, but in every other way it had been a disaster.

I killed someone.

In brief moments of distraction, she managed to forget, but that weight crept into the forefront of her mind as often as it could, bringing cold chills and a stuttering heart.

"I'm sorry. I know that was all really hard, with the animals and Nell. I don't agree with what the Darkfreys did either," Callan said, his frown matching hers. "Beshadowings are tricky. Even partial ones. Nell had been working with eidolghast parts for who knows how long. It would have changed her. She wasn't really human anymore."

"And what are we?" Everly countered, tears in her eyes.

"We're not beshadowed," Callan said firmly. "Although Nell was doing the right thing now, beshadowings never end well. I'm not saying the Darkfreys handled it the right way, but if nothing changed, things would have only gotten darker."

It didn't end well.

Everly screwed her eyes shut. Then, worried, she opened them, staring at the semitransparent plastic tubs and the mess of flesh within. "Is that going to be a problem here? Is that going to affect Harper and me?"

Callan put his hands into his pockets and winced. "Maybe? We won't leave it long enough to find out. This is temporary, okay? We're going to get this worked out as soon as we can."

A soft knocking came from the bedroom door. Everly turned to find Lian there. "Cherry let me in on his way out. Thank you for calling me."

"Of course," Everly said. She moved out of the way, letting Rylan's mother come into the small space.

Lian stepped in and slowly walked to the bedside. Gingerly reaching out, she placed one hand on Rylan's chest and another over her mouth.

A moment passed as she stood frozen there, and Everly wondered if she was feeling for the dull beat of Rylan's heart, needing to feel that proof of life herself.

Then she turned around and hugged Callan. "You found him."

Callan returned the embrace. "It was Everly who worked it out."

They briefly explained Nell's animal sanctuary to Lian, her eyebrows rising at every new detail.

"Everly saw a Darkfrey shadyr trying to kill Rylan when she found him," Callan told his mom in a low voice. "She wasn't sure who. They ran as soon as Everly called them out."

That was the story Everly had told the others, anyway. She still couldn't put into words what she'd done to Nell's husband. She couldn't tell anyone what had happened. She could barely understand it herself.

Her mind swirled with confusing feelings of how much she'd been in control, or not in control, and she wasn't sure which option was scarier.

Lian sighed. "Whatever Rylan was looking into, it made him a serious enemy. I'll sort out shifts with our lot, make sure there's always someone keeping an eye on this place."

"I was thinking the same thing," Callan said.

"You really think they might try to come after him again?" Everly asked.

Lian shrugged and avoided eye contact. "Better to be safe, either way. We'll work out the rest later. For now, we have Rylan back. That's what matters."

The three of them looked at his body, and Everly knew they were all thinking the same thing. That he was only half back. And what really mattered was making him whole again.

"We'd better go, let you get cleaned up and rest after all of that," Lian said. "But we won't be far away if you need anything."

Callan followed Lian to the bedroom door, then turned back.

"Sure you're okay with this?" he asked, tilting his head to Rylan's still body.

"It's the least I can do. I'll look after him," she said. *Just like he always looked after me.*

Everly followed them downstairs and said goodbye.

"You done with this?" Lian asked, wrapping her hand around the weed trimmer that rested on the back porch.

"Yeah, thank you." Everly had never gotten to clearing the backyard, but it didn't seem important anymore. Her time limit in Shroudhaven had run out. But she wasn't going anywhere.

"You can borrow it again any time you like. Anything you need. You're family."

Everly swallowed. After the week she'd had, thoughts of her own mother's death had vanished entirely, especially in the face of the pragmatic, salt-and-pepper-haired woman who stood before her now. The woman who raised her more than Janey Boderleth ever had.

Everly felt her heart warming and breaking simultaneously. "Thank you, for letting me be part of your family. I'm sorry I was part of everything falling apart."

"Nonsense. What you are, is part of bringing it all back together again." Lian was already walking away, garden tool resting over her shoulder. She turned back briefly, her eyes full of emotion. "Thank you for bringing my son home."

Everly stood at the back door as Callan and Lian disappeared around the corner of the house, then she remained there a while afterward, hugging herself against the cold and staring out into the dark night. The murky shadows seemed so different now that she knew what could be creeping within them.

And something was creeping in her backyard. Everly startled as a blurry shape moved beside the garden shed, down near the broken fencing. She held her breath, hoping it was just her bad eyesight or her imagination and not some new horror.

The shape moved again, and Everly was sure she recognized it.

Moving slowly, on quiet feet, she stepped inside to the kitchen. She grabbed an old breakfast bowl off a shelf and put in some raw beef mince that had been intended as part

of their dinner that night. A dinner that had never happened due to other adventures.

Taking it outside, Everly placed the bowl in the long grass at the center of the yard, then quickly backed away again to the porch. She wasn't exactly sure what an undead cougar would eat, but she figured meat was good for both cats and zombies.

The grass shivered in a trail as the cougar prowled through it toward the bowl. As the grass cleared, it hesitated, milky blue eyes flashing toward Everly. Then it chomped the mince up in one gulp and pounced away.

Everly watched the darkness and found a small smile growing on her face. She had done that. She had saved the young cat's life. It was a small consolation, after all the carnage that night. But it was something—something she hoped was good.

"Hey." Harper stepped outside, patting the ends of her hair with a towel and yawning. "Everyone's gone?"

"Yep. Just us, Rylan, and the monster chunks now."

"So fun."

"I'm sorry about all this. I mean, when we came here, I knew Shroudhaven wasn't great, but I honestly had no idea this is where things would be five days later."

Harper put an arm over Everly's shoulders and they headed back inside. "Well, we did get you reunited with Rylan at least. You know. In a way."

"So fun," Everly muttered, echoing Harper's tone.

They both giggled, more in a shaky expression of relief than with any humor. Back in the kitchen, Harper got the kettle boiling and dropped a couple of teabags into mugs.

"Sooo ... I guess we're not heading home tomorrow?" Harper said.

Everly picked up a mug and slowly dunked the teabag up and down. The scent of chamomile filled the air. "I don't think I can. The dreams are too real. I'm sure there's some connection there, something that could help Rylan wake up. I can't leave him like this without trying. But you don't have to stay."

"Oh no, I'm sticking around. You can't have all the fun without me." Harper pouted. "Plus, I haven't even had a chance to do anything with the antiques yet."

Everly laughed through her nose.

Harper took a sip of her tea, regarding Everly. "What about your job?"

"It's okay. I'll work something out." Everly wasn't sure what a solution would look like.

Her savings were already almost gone due to cleanup expenses. And with Rylan's situation, she couldn't exactly rent out a spare room here.

"I can always try to sell off any of the intact antiques to get by until we move home again. Or there must be some repair work available around Shroudhaven."

"I bet." Harper yawned again. "My offer's still open too. I could really do with a partner in my work. Someone I trust."

Can you really trust me? Everly wondered. She didn't feel as though she even trusted herself anymore. "Thank you. I should be okay though. This is temporary. Just until Rylan wakes up."

Harper smiled and shrugged noncommittally.

They finished their tea and headed up the stairs. After peeking in to check on Rylan—still unmoving, still stable—Harper brought Everly into a tight hug. "We'll work things out. One day at a time, until he wakes up."

Everly stood at the doorway to her old bedroom for some time after Harper had gone to bed, staring at Rylan.

In the low light of the dimmed desk lamp she'd placed beside him, the lines of his still face seemed so familiar. It wasn't the face of the boy she remembered, but it was the face of the man she knew from her dreams.

She wondered how much she really knew him though. He'd lived and grown and trained with the Darkfreys for years.

Was he like them now? Did he share their attitudes? Their violence? Had he become a mindless soldier, or worse, one who relished in the spill of blood? Or did he still have the same kind heart from childhood somewhere beneath his Darkfrey tattoo?

Maybe she would find out when he woke up.

If he ever wakes up.

31

"Evie? What's happened? Are you okay?" Rylan's tone was frantic and deep with concern.

Everly heard him calling to her through the darkness before she could see anything.

The world shifted and turned. Petal-shaped fragments of scenery fell into place like puzzle pieces around Everly. Wherever she turned, reality blossomed to meet her observation.

A crinkling ground of autumn leaves beneath her. A night sky swirled with cotton-candy galaxies above. She sat on the edge of a sheer cliff, a dark forest at her back and an endless universe before her.

Rylan's shape emerged, crouched on one knee beside her. "Are you—?"

"I'm asleep. This is a dream." Everly spoke the words as she always did in her dreams, helping to ground herself, to take control.

Rylan dragged a hand over his mouth, eyes still stormy. "Asleep where? Are you safe? What was happening before?"

"It's okay. I'm fine." Everly looked up at him from under her eyelashes, her eyelids still puffy and tired despite being asleep. "And you're okay too. We found you."

Rylan moved slowly into a sitting position, his knees bent in front of him and his elbows on them. His voice was barely a whisper. "You found me? Am I ..."

"You're alive. Healthy even, except that you won't wake up. In a semi-vampire sort of state, it seems, which is keeping your body going."

"What in the Everdark has been going on? When you were here before ... what happened? Where were you? You were so upset and *unconscious!*"

Everly gave him the quick version of what had happened with Nell. Her lips wavered and eyes stung. She didn't mention Nell's husband, what she had done to him. She looked around, half expecting him to haunt her dreams as well, but he was nowhere to be seen.

"You did it. You saved me. I told you, you're the light."

He gave her a soft smile, but his words only brought a dark chill creeping through Everly's bones.

She knew now that the light within her was nothing to revere. It felt as monstrous as anything she'd seen since returning to Shroudhaven. What would Rylan do if he knew what she'd done? Would his Darkfrey training require him to treat her as a monster too?

In the nebulous sky above, her dragon spun its body in glowing wheels, and the cougar stalked in the shadows behind them. At her side, nestled into the leaves and stringy golden grass, was a playset of plastic zoo animals.

Rylan grunted. "I can't stand this. Whenever you're awake, it's like I've fallen asleep. I don't know anything that's happening. I can't do *anything*. You're going off into all this danger and I'm completely useless."

"I'm sorry. I don't know why you're trapped here. We'll do everything we can to wake you up."

Rylan shook his head fiercely, then turned and held her gaze. "That's not what I mean. You're not even supposed to be here. You're not supposed to know any of this. You're supposed to be somewhere safe, away from nightmares like the one you were just in because you were trying to help me."

Everly drew in a shaky breath and looked away. Beside her, the plastic animals came to life. Miniature lions and bears pounced over leaves, hunting. Tiny shadyr action figures emerged and rushed in terrified circles. In her dream, they were no match for the animals and were gobbled up, one by one.

Tears spilled from Everly's eyes as tremors shook her whole body. "It all went wrong. What I did … you don't understand. I have to—"

"Shh, it's okay. It's over now." Rylan shifted closer to her and put his arms around her shoulders. The arms she'd longed to have around her for her whole life. She felt their strength, their warmth, but it did little to comfort her. Sobs rattled the embrace.

He was only trying to comfort her, be the protective big brother like he'd always been, until he'd just want her gone so he wouldn't have to keep protecting her. She knew he still wanted her gone.

Everly swallowed away her feelings. "I'm going to make things right."

Rylan shook his head against her shoulder. "You've done enough. You found me, despite everything. You found me and you saved me," he whispered.

"Then why are you still here, in my dreams?"

Rylan's hold on her tightened ever so slightly. "Even if I'm not whole, you're keeping all of me safe—my body and my soul."

"Like you always kept me safe," Everly whispered. She sniffed and wiped her eyes. "It's my turn now."

Something nudged Everly's other side, and she turned to see the cougar nuzzling against her knee. It was only half there, shimmering and translucent, a gray mirror of its true self.

It settled down like a sphinx, belly squashing the plastic action figures and toys at war. They could be seen squirming through the cougar's ghostly body.

Everly moved slowly, tentatively at first. She reached out her hand and touched the back of a finger to the cat's forehead. Its pale-blue eyes closed, so she ran her whole hand over the soft fur between its ears. It rumbled a single, soft purr, then was silent.

The dragon swooped low, illuminating them with its glow. It had been satiated, for now.

She could control it again. She could keep it away from Rylan and the cougar, whatever part of them she had here with her, inside her. She would keep them safe.

Everly turned back to Rylan and found her face so close to his that she felt his breath across her cheeks. He watched her intently. Everly's tears had slowed, and her sobbing had ceased.

The smile she gave him tasted of salt. "I'm staying. In Shroudhaven. Until we can wake you up."

He frowned at that but didn't argue. He did let her go though, moving out of the embrace. Everly shivered, missing his warmth.

"I just wish I could do more." He glanced at her from the side of his eyes, then turned away. "But I can't. I can't have the people … around me be hurt when I can stop it."

"Sometimes we don't have that choice." Everly's heart fluttered, looking at him.

A rise of anxiety spiked through Everly, and her dragon seemed to relish watching her squirm.

Everly took a moment to ground herself.

Five things she could see: Rylan's green eyes, his eyes, looking into hers, his eyes, not turning away, his eyes, not shaming or blaming, his eyes.

Four things she could touch: the dreamlike fuzz of the cougar's neck, the silky strands of dream grass beneath her, the insubstantial press of dream clothes over her body, Rylan, if she only just reached out.

Three things she could hear: Rylan's breath, close to her ear, and her heartbeat, racing, driven thunderous by that breath. How loud it made her swallow.

Two things she could smell: Home, home. Howell house and Boderleth Antiques.

One thing she could taste: the saltwater of her tears.

The boy she'd loved as long as she could remember was gone. The man he was now was someone she was only just starting to get to know. But she could feel, deep within her, that he was still good.

It had been his words that had gotten her through the nightmare.

She repeated them out loud. "Sometimes the world is dark and cruel, and all we can do is try."

Everly raised her hand, as tentatively as she had with the wild creature beside her. She placed a single finger on Rylan's chin, then turned his face back toward her.

"Whatever happens next, we are in it together."

She had to get his consciousness back into his body. She had to wake him up. No matter what dangers and horrors this town threw at her next.

2

BESHADOWED

BLOOD BOUND

1

When Everly used to daydream about having Rylan Howell in her bed, this was never how she'd imagined it.

She used to fantasize about his warm green gaze on her, heavy with love. His body would fit against hers like they were meant to be together, like she'd always believed they were. It was an ever-present yearning. A dream she couldn't shake.

They *definitely* wouldn't have been in the childhood home of her nightmares. In the town shrouded in mist and loss, haunted by the specter of her father's death and memories of a mother who liked whiskey and one-night stands more than her own daughter.

And Rylan would also have been conscious.

"Yep. That's probably the biggest difference." Everly halted just inside the door and stared at Rylan's still figure lying on the single bed in her childhood bedroom.

No change. She hadn't expected there to be, but she'd hoped. Every moment of the last week, she'd hoped to walk in and find Rylan awake, alert, back to himself. She'd been certain that now he was safe, he'd come out of his supernatural stasis. But as time wore on, it became obvious that something else was wrong.

Now, instead of hoping his eyes would spontaneously open, Everly wondered about the long-term effects of this state on his mind and body.

This can't last forever. He can't last forever, like this.

Everly ventured farther into the room, her steps hesitant. She lifted his wrist. The skin was cool and firm to her touch, almost corpse-like. But his pulse was still there.

It tapped a slow and lazy beat, as though holding onto life was an afterthought for his body. As if some automatic, paranormal process of regeneration brought on by his shadyr powers kept him alive, rather than a mind fighting to live.

If it weren't for his semi-shifted form, giving him the semblance of a vampire, it might almost seem like he was sleeping. His head was tilted ever so slightly toward the door, and his expression was blank and unbothered. Pale, unblemished skin showed no visible injuries, no bruises to indicate that not long ago he'd been flayed open by a vasmire and left to die.

"Are you even in there at all?" Everly squeezed his cold hand.

The one place Rylan seemed most alive was in her dreams. He still appeared to Everly nightly, a conscious prisoner in her dreamscapes. How he ended up there, how to get him out again, and whether that would bring his body back to life, were all questions no one had been able to answer. Everly was sure most of her friends didn't even believe that he was there.

Harper appeared in the doorway with a clattering of beaded bracelets. She peered around the scratched wooden trim with all the panache of a celebrity posing for a headshot.

"Hey, you ready? Callan's pacing out front. He wants to get there ASAP so we don't miss our chance."

Of course, Everly's best friend had chosen to wear a glittery pink plaid flannel over high-waisted, stonewashed denim shorts to go hunting for vasmires. As far as Everly knew, Harper Bells had never appeared before a living soul without a full face of makeup and attire fit for a fashion model.

"Yeah, good to go. Just wanted to check Rylan before we left." Under Harper's gaze, Everly quickly removed her hand from Rylan's.

She zipped up her faded red bomber jacket. Maybe not the height of fashion, but as comfortable to wear as her own skin.

Also doesn't show up bloodstains too much, Everly thought, her anxious mind serving her up visions of the risks they were about to face.

Harper's nose wrinkled, and she cut her gaze across the shelves at the back of the room where the rotting vasmire parts lay in transparent plastic crates. One bloated, gray tentacle had slipped over the edge, leaking fluids onto the hardwood floor.

"I kind of hoped they would stop smelling after a while," Harper said.

"I think when they stop smelling, they'd be so rotted away they wouldn't be helpful to Rylan anymore."

"Great, great, so no chance of our place not smelling like dumpster vomit anytime soon then?"

Everly tensed.

Harper lifted a hand to her mouth. "It's not that I *don't* think he's going to wake up soon. And I'm totally supportive of him and his monster-gore life-support being here however long is needed. I'm cool. I'll just get a peg or something."

She pinched the bridge of her nose and offered Everly a smile.

Everly slid past her through the doorway, grabbing her by the elbow. "Come on, let's go. You don't want to spend too long in there. You know what Callan said."

Harper sighed, blowing an errant chunk of her long, dark hair from her eyes. "Yeah, yeah. 'Even deteriorating eidolghast bits could cause a beshadowing effect on humans.'

Blah, blah, supernatural woo-woo, blah. I don't see you avoiding the room though."

Everly turned away and took the lead as they headed down the narrow staircase. "I'm ... different."

"Sure thing, Sparkles, but we don't know what you are or that you can't get beshadowed."

"But keeping you safe is my responsibility."

"Babe, I know that's coming from a place of love, but I'm my own grown-ass woman and can keep myself safe, thanks very much."

Everly grimaced. She knew Harper Bells was the highest of all high achievers, able to excel at anything she set her mind to. But this wasn't contouring or kickboxing or becoming a successful online influencer.

Harper seemed to be approaching the deadly supernatural side of Shroudhaven with the same enthusiasm she did any new pet project, and Everly didn't like that at all.

"And how are you supposed to do your next photo shoot if you've lost your mind because a monster's rotting corpse has turned you into a mindless zombie?"

Harper gasped in a way that made Everly turn back to face her. Lips trembling, Harper reached out and took Everly's hands and held them up to her heart.

"Promise me, if it comes to that, *promise me* ... you'll take lots of photos and upload them to my socials for me? Because a mindless zombie photo shoot sounds *amazing*. What a way to go."

Everly chuckled and shook her hands out of her friend's grasp. "You're such a goof."

Harper blew her a kiss. Everly couldn't stay mad at her, and couldn't control her. But she would do everything she could to keep Harper safe.

Stepping off the staircase into the downstairs hallway, Everly took a moment to admire how hard they'd worked to clean the place up.

A week and a half ago, they'd hardly been able to navigate the house, it had been so full of her mother's garbage. And *rats*. The plan had been to clean all evidence of her mother's hoarding tendencies and destroy any remnants of the substance abuse that killed her, then sell the place off to the first interested buyer.

Now ... Everly sighed and turned to leave out the back door. Now their stay was indefinite. Something Harper seemed far happier about than Everly was.

Everly worked at braiding her pale gray hair out of her face as they headed past the jungle of a backyard, and up the side path that led to the front of the house.

The last vestiges of the evening sun still colored the horizon rosy, but the shadows in Shroudhaven had always seemed darker than most, so the glow barely touched the street. Fog had already crept in off the water, shifting and morphing through the cool evening like ghosts.

Everly shuddered, glancing at the cluster of semi-dead rosebushes where she'd

been knocked unconscious the night Rylan was hurt. She vividly remembered the "sculpture" she'd crashed into, and the sensation that all of the black pieces that had broken beneath her had been bones.

Except the pieces had all been gone the next day.

More questions than answers, Everly thought, tugging her jacket tighter against the cold night.

Callan Howell waited on the sidewalk beside Harper's vintage Volkswagen campervan, his nebulous gaze staring into the darkness down the block. Everly could see nothing but blurry shadows, but she knew he had a shadyr's near-perfect night vision, so if anything came at them from the dark, he'd be able to see it. If he didn't sense it first.

He shook his long dark hair back, and it settled around his face in messy layers as he turned his gaze on her. He was like a ganglier version of Rylan, but smiled in a way his brother never did. Especially when he looked at Harper.

Everly hadn't seen Rylan happy since they were kids. Since his father died, and he'd taken the entire weight of it upon himself. Something Everly thought she could relate to, but it had only driven them apart.

"Got you a present," Callan said to Harper, hefting a shiny new axe off the ground beside him and presenting it to her.

Harper took it reverentially, inspecting the chrome-bright sharp edge.

"It's beautiful," she gushed. "And it matches my nails!"

"What? Nothing for me?" Everly said it teasingly but she wished she had some kind of weapon too.

The shadyrs' shifted forms came with inbuilt, natural weapons that she and Harper didn't have. Everly had her dragon, but she couldn't control it. And when it was out of control, it did terrible things. Like taking Nell's husband's life.

She still hadn't shared that secret with the others. How could she tell them what a monster she really was?

Before Callan could reply, a lazy drawl declared, "Don't worry, sexy. I'll protect those sweet curves of yours."

Denny's head poked out from around the back of the campervan door, and he made a clear show of looking her and Harper up and down. Everly rolled her eyes and kept her gaze firmly trained on Callan, who took the opportunity to mouth an apology.

A step behind Denny came Cherry, who slapped the leering man on the back of the head. "Can you stop being the walking embodiment of sexual harassment for even five minutes?"

Denny rubbed his blond curls where he was hit. "You're just sour 'cause you're no good with the ladies."

"I'm *gay*, you complete waste of sentience."

"Whatever."

"Does he have to come along?" Harper grunted, resting her new axe up on her shoulder.

A smaller figure lurking in the shadows behind Cherry huffed in monotone. "How funny. I was going to ask the same thing about you two blivs."

Tammy leaned her petite, goth-styled self on the back of the campervan. In the faint glow of the streetlamps, her skin had the eerie pallor of a shadyr in vampire form. At sixteen, she was the youngest of the group, and still hadn't mastered keeping control over her form. Even the presence of the rotting parts in the room upstairs had changed her.

Harper jangled the keys to the campervan and headed to the driver's seat. "I've got the only vehicle that can fit all of us, and our potential booty of monster parts. You're welcome."

Tammy unfolded her arms, revealing her ink black hands. She droned, "Not like it matters if you get killed anyway, or if you get us all killed. Makes no difference to me. All got to die one day."

With a lazy eye roll, she flicked her hood up over her buzz-cut head and climbed into the van.

"She's so cheery and sweet," Everly whispered to Callan.

He shrugged, casting a frown in Tammy's direction.

Everly had started making her way to the front passenger seat when Cherry jumped into her path.

He grabbed the door handle. "I call shotgun. Sorry. I get carsick in back."

Everly held up both palms.

"No worries," she said, then went around to the side door, ignoring Denny's leering gaze as she hopped up the shallow steps and into the camper.

Tammy was already perched up on the back bed area, beneath which Harper kept most of her portable photoshoot belongings and wardrobe overflow. The girl looked uncomfortable being the only one stuck in shifted form. Her skin resembled smooth, pale marble, and her fangs had elongated enough to dent her lower lip. She sat so statue-still, she looked dead.

With her lip curling involuntarily in disgust, Everly took a seat on the bench beside Denny. Callan entered the van last, tugging the door shut behind him.

He slapped his hand against the wall and called, "Hit it, Harper."

He slouched back against the side of the van, clinging to the railing next to the staircase as the van lurched forward. In front, Cherry gave Harper directions between their gossiping in hushed whispers.

Everly frowned as they drove away from Boderleth Antiques, and Rylan.

"Don't worry." Callan nodded as though he understood her expression. "Mom

and Rush are on their way to keep an eye on him while we're gone."

It wasn't only monsters from the Everdark that were a threat in Shroudhaven. Someone had tried to kill Rylan, and might still want him dead.

Callan's gaze swept the world outside. Everly had a feeling those shadyr eyes missed nothing. It was still new to her—the idea that the two boys she'd grown up with lived in a completely different world than she'd ever known.

The knowledge that Callan, Rylan, and their mom Lian were all shapeshifting monster hunters who could take on different classical creature forms, like vampire or werewolf, to fight extra-dimensional demons called eidolghasts, was still taking some getting used to. There was a woosh of black smokey shadows and sparks as Tammy shifted back into her human form.

"There you go, managed to change back already." Callan smiled encouragingly at the silent girl.

The streetlights flashed by as Harper picked up speed, illuminating Tammy's scowling face in harsh relief.

There was a hint of pink on her cheeks, and she ducked her head farther into her hooded jacket. "Don't treat me like a baby."

Tammy had kept her distance from everyone and had barely spoken during the time they'd been in the same spaces. Everly really wasn't sure what to think of her, except that she clearly had a problem with the world at large and acted like every minute she was alive was a hardship.

Everly knew she had some history of losing someone, and the weird magical side-effect of random teleportation that the same event had left her with. The details were sketchy, but the deep hurt the girl held was palpable.

Beneath Tammy's black lace and leather shirt, the high-tech body armor Everly had seen on other shadyrs showed through. Everly glanced at Callan and Denny and could just make out the form of their armor underneath their shirts and jackets, too.

The Darkfrey shadyrs all wore the same stuff, and Everly realized that the Howell team must have taken theirs with them when they either left or were cast out from the Darkfrey estate. She wondered whether they had any spare sets.

Harper should really be wearing something more protective. But this mission was a rush job, and they hadn't had long to prepare.

Denny lurched off the bench and started poking around some storage crates at the back of the van. "There's got to be some booze stashed in here. Where are we headed again?"

"Rooks Hotel," Callan said. "Our inside at Darkfrey Estate says they've had a report of weirdness happening at the hotel, likely vasmire related. Only just came in, so hopefully we'll get there before the Darkfrey team does."

Cherry hissed a sigh, and his face appeared in the space between the two front seats, bright red hair haloed by the glow of the headlights passing on the other side of the road. "If *the Darkfreys* would just help us out properly, we wouldn't need to go hunting. It's not like their cleanup crews haven't picked up a dead vasmire this week. You know they would have."

Callan grunted his assent, then returned to staring out the window.

"Honestly, I'm getting a little bit sick of *the Darkfrey's* attitude," Cherry grumbled to Harper.

"Aw, no don't say that," Harper cooed.

Her voice lowered again, whispering between them. Their private conversation was quickly interrupted.

"Denny Sketchman!" Harper snapped. "Put that dress back where you found it!"

He lifted the glittery material to his nose and took a deep breath. "But it smells like you."

Callan stepped away from the wall with preternatural quickness and snatched the dress from Denny's hands.

He tossed it through the aisle into Cherry's lap. "Sit down, Denny."

The burly blond muttered curses under his breath, but he obeyed.

Rooks Hotel.

Everly remembered the place from her childhood as a dashing red brick Colonial that sat outside of the downtown area, a little more off the beaten path than most places in Shroudhaven. She could still picture the giant white letters that spelled out the name across the top of the building.

Two chimneys, she thought, as she recalled her younger self thinking the place had horns. It had always had a stellar reputation for customer service and cleanliness, and an old-world charm that wasn't out of place in a town like Shroudhaven.

But when Harper pulled up outside the hotel, and the team disembarked from the van, Everly stared up at a building she didn't even recognize.

Gone were the bright red bricks—they'd turned dull gray, as if the entire building had been covered in ash. The white letters were still in place, but the *S* in *Rooks* had turned sideways, and the *T* in *Hotel* had fallen away entirely.

"What on earth happened here?" Everly asked under her breath as she stopped on the sidewalk beside Callan.

His expression turned hard as he gazed up at the roof. Everly followed his line of sight to see a foggy mist rising from both chimneys. Not smoke. Something else, something heavier. Something otherworldly.

Callan's starry gaze was haunted as he murmured, "A beshadowing. The worst I've ever seen."

2

A low, inhuman moan echoed out of Rooks Hotel, making the hairs on Everly's neck stand on end.

"A beshadowing? What exactly does that mean? What are we going to find in there?" she asked.

Callan waved them all forwards again. "Could be anything. Things get weird. We've seen stuff that would make the best horror movie director weep."

Everly distanced herself from Callan as he led them up the wide front sidewalk to the hotel. If he needed to transform in a hurry, she didn't want to be caught at his heels. The memory of the first time she'd seen him in shadyr form as a monstrous, werewolf-like beast still sent a pang of fear through her.

Faux torches shone from regular intervals along the facade of Rooks Hotel, and the flickering lightbulbs inside that mimicked flames hardly shed any light on the cracked sidewalk.

The glow of a single streetlamp set several yards down the road was nearly swallowed by the fog. Beyond it, Everly could barely make out the half-empty parking lot.

Enough cars squatted low in the shadows to indicate that the building was occupied, but when she traced her gaze up the outside of the hotel, she noted that all the curtains and blinds were closed, and none of the rooms appeared to be lit from within.

Creepy.

Her heart thumped a skittish pulse. The whole situation felt wrong in a way that made her skin crawl. More than the discolored bricks, broken letters, and mist rising from the chimneys. More than knowing they were purposefully walking into a fight with a supernatural monster. The wrongness went deeper.

To the dragon, stirring in her chest.

Shivering despite her jacket, Everly shoved that thought away. She couldn't deal with the dragon right now, or even think about the light that somehow lived inside her and wanted to consume everything it came into contact with.

Just focus on fixing one disaster at a time, she thought, her work boots heavy on the stone steps that led to the front doors.

First and foremost, they needed a dead vasmire to put beside Rylan's bed to keep his regeneration powers working until he woke up. Then, she could figure out what in this ever-loving hellscape of magical madness was going on inside her own body.

Sometime in the last decade, Rooks Hotel had replaced their old wooden entry doors with a glass and chrome revolving unit. It glinted in the night, and a bit of interior light shone through onto the front landing.

As they drew nearer, they found the glass was completely misted over so that everything inside appeared to be nothing but blurry colors.

"I see movement," Callan muttered.

"Yeah, same," Cherry agreed, his shadyr eyes also sparkling like a miniature galaxy.

"Do you think there are people alive in there?" Everly tried to peer through the doors but couldn't see what they'd seen.

The two men exchanged a glance, and Everly didn't like the unspoken words that passed between them.

Callan shrugged. "If there are, you and Harper can work on getting them out while we go hunting."

"Don't try and sideline us." Harper pointed her axe at Everly. "You don't sideline your nuclear option."

Is that what I am? Ultimate destruction, waiting to explode? Everly practiced her calm breathing. *Just focus on one disaster at a time.*

"So is there a vasmire here or what?" she asked.

When Callan looked back to answer, his transformation had begun. Shadows swirled and eddied around his body, dotted by fiery sparks of light. Beneath the magic, his skin turned ash-white, his teeth elongated, his body morphing into a hard, powerful form that hardly looked like his anymore.

"Yep, that would be a vasmire," Everly said. Exactly what they needed.

Denny, Tammy, and Cherry changed as well.

Callan looked them over, striding along like an army sergeant checking his new recruits. Except as vampires.

"Good work. Hold your forms, this place looks rough. Visibility will be poor, and a building like this will have plenty of places for the vasmire to hide out. We can't let it slip past us or we might not get another chance. Taking it down, and fast, is our priority."

Tammy and Cherry nodded, and Denny gave a mocking salute.

"And us?" Everly asked.

Maybe being sidelined isn't a bad idea.

"Stay close. Watch out for the knock-out gas the vasmire can exude—you don't have protection from it, so get out fast if you have to. You two are strictly support, not frontal attack." He directed his final instruction at Harper. "So no Leeroy Jenkinsing."

"Fiiiiine," Harper agreed.

Tammy grunted in disgust.

Callan eyed her sharply. "Come on."

The motor on the revolving doors was broken, so Callan pressed his palms against the glass and shifted the doors manually.

Everly and Harper leapt in behind him, and the rest of the team filed into the next section as it spun around. Everly shuffled carefully over the carpet so as not to tread on Callan's feet, and then they spilled out into the lobby of Rooks Hotel.

The ceiling soared high overhead, lost in a thick, heavy mist that hung over everything.

"What were you saying about avoiding the gas?" Everly tried to breathe shallowly as the fog swirled around her ankles and up to her waist.

Callan sniffed the air. "This is something different. Probably more to do with the beshadowing than coming directly from the vasmire. You feeling faint at all?"

Everly steadied herself, taking a moment to be mindful of how she felt. She was no fainter than usual with her anxiety.

"No, seems okay."

Harper shook her head too.

Callan swung his arm in a sharp gesture, and the three other shadyrs followed him slowly as he continued in.

Harper whispered to Everly. "That means we follow."

"When did you learn military field signals?"

"Last night." Harper grinned.

"Of course you did."

They moved into the vast and misty foyer as a unit. Over to the right, an unattended reception desk was marked by hanging signs for *Check Ins* and *Customer Service*.

To the left, through the churning haze, Everly could trace the hint of an alcove with a bar and shelves of liquor. The space in between reception and the bar held scattered comfy chairs and coffee tables. Everly squinted, unsure if any were occupied. Then behind the hulking, black bar counter, she saw movement.

Callan lifted a fist and everyone froze.

Out of the dark swirls, a man stood at a strange angle, leaning heavily to one side. He moved a metal cocktail shaker slowly up and down as he stared off into space. There was no sound of ice or liquid sloshing within. His bared teeth glinted in the gloom.

"Is he ... okay?" Everly already knew the answer but thought that 'okay' sounded better than asking if he was human, or if he was lost beyond any chance of saving.

"Maybe we should che—Holy shit!" Cherry gasped.

A short, curvy blond woman in a navy-blue skirt suit appeared right in front of them.

Tammy inhaled sharply and seemed to flicker. With a deep gulp, she stilled again. "I'm *fine*," she preempted.

The woman swayed in a small circle, the mist following her like a whirlpool. Her eyes were riveted somewhere over Everly's shoulder. A rectangular gold nametag on her jacket read, *Brooke, Assistant Manager.*

Cherry waved his hand in front of her glazed eyes. "Hey, hi there? Are you hearing me?"

"Welcome to—" Her voice crackled.

Her head twitched. She smiled wider than humanly possible.

"Welcome. Welcome to to to to. Welcome ttttttttttttttttt." Her mouth gaped open.

A hushed, unhuman static emerged, like a stifled scream. Then the blond woman sidestepped him and continued a slow journey across the room, seemingly without a destination in mind. She hadn't even reacted to Cherry's very obviously *not human* appearance.

"Wow, that was creepy as all get out," Denny said, cracking open a beer can.

"Did you steal that from the bar? For ghast's sake, dude," Callan hissed.

"What? They aren't going to miss it. Look at them. Too far gone."

He flicked his chin toward the foyer. The haze had cleared just enough to show the silhouettes of half a dozen people, shifting about. Their movements were jerky and repetitive, caught in a nightmarish loop. Soft mutterings came through on croaky voices.

"Non-smoking. Non-smoking. Non-smoking."

"My room issssss ... room isss ..."

"Hell ... hell ... hell ... hello, do you have ... have ..."

Some moved closer. They trudged as if they couldn't lift their feet, eyes glazed over and bodies stiff. Almost zombie-like, but with the most chilling, wide grins plastered on their faces.

"Can we save them?" Everly asked.

"We can save them, and Rylan, by taking out the vasmire." Callan shook his head and pointed across the side, toward a sweeping staircase. "We have to act fast. This is the latest stage of beshadowing I've ever seen."

"How long do you think it's been like this?" Cherry said, as he and Denny moved up to join their team leader.

Callan shrugged. "Don't know. The place is family run—live-in staff. I doubt they've been answering the phones and taking new reservations. Everyone here is non-responsive. Any drop-ins pulling up out front may have assumed the place was closed. It's still weird it got like this without anyone noticing though. It normally takes ages for things to get this bad."

Tammy droned, "All these people, and no one even noticed they were gone.

Sounds about right."

Everly shivered. "Can the beshadowing still be reversed?"

"It can, up until when a permanent shroudpool forms," Callan said darkly.

"Let's stop that happening, shall we?" Cherry said.

Callan led them up the wide staircase to the second floor. Everly got the sense he was following something only the shadyrs could feel—whatever magic warned them that an eidolghast was nearby.

Harper whispered, "Are beshadowings always zombie fun-times like this?"

"Oh no, they come in all kinds of nightmare fuel flavors. Anything you could imagine, and all the things you wouldn't want to imagine." Cherry grinned at them in a way that mimicked the zombified hotel guests.

"Quiet," Callan snapped. "It's close."

Harper nodded seriously, lifted the axe off her shoulder, and held it in front of her with both hands.

Everly wished she had a weapon to hold onto, too. Rather than one she had to hold back.

The farther they walked, the more the proximity of the creature strengthened the Howell team's transformations. Their skin hardened and smoothed to resist the vasmire's toothy tentacles. Their breathing slowed to almost nothing to protect them from the noxious gas that oozed from the monster.

Callan had explained that the fangs they grew were venomous and could be used to fight back. But most modern shadyrs found biting their repulsive enemies a bit distasteful. Their vampire form luckily also came with strength that could rend the monsters tentacle-from-tentacle.

Callan stalked down the hallway, his head turning this way and that as he seemed to note the monster's movements. They stepped around an overturned cleaning cart.

The mist was thicker up there, and it undulated around them as the group moved, casting disorienting swirls and shadows. A painting of a lighthouse hung on the wall beside them, dripping black ooze.

A guest emerged from the mist ahead—a man with gray-streaked hair and unfocused eyes. He was in a bathrobe, a business suit underneath, dripping wet as if he'd just showered fully dressed. He dragged a white bedsheet along in one hand.

Something else swirled in the darkness behind him.

"You see it?" Cherry hissed.

Callan nodded.

"Hey, check this out," Denny said loudly from a few feet back.

Rolling his arm like a baseball pitcher, he flung his empty beer can at the catatonic guest. It plinked right off his forehead.

"Score!" Denny cheered.

Callan, Cherry, and Tammy all hissed at him, fangs bared.

The vapor shifted violently, like an ocean parting around a swimming creature.

Everly caught a glimpse of something long and writhing stretching down the hallway, and then before she could scream, it wrapped around the businessman's torso and yanked him away into the pitch-black mist, disappearing again in a split-second.

"You idiot," Cherry growled, pushing Denny against the wall.

Tammy sped off, racing after the escaping vasmire.

Callan yelled, chasing after her, "Not on your own! Damn it!"

From a distance, a soft crunch echoed through the hall, followed by wet, gurgling, slurping noises.

Harper grabbed Everly's arm with a gasp, and Everly's head reeled, nausea rising in her belly. She could feel Harper's long talons biting into her bicep through the heavy fabric of her jacket, but she'd lost the ability to comprehend anything else beyond those sounds of a human body being consumed.

Another wave of nausea hit her. Their target was getting away. They were split up. People were being *eaten.*

Cherry and Denny need to go after the others. They have to get the vasmire. Why isn't Denny saying something dumb?

It wasn't like him not to fling an insult right back again. She looked for them in the mist, and found them frozen in place, Cherry's fists still bunched into Denny's shirt. Both smiling.

Everly choked on panic.

"Harper? We have to get out of here! We have to get—!"

3

"We have to get one of those cocktails!" Harper squealed happily.

"Huh?' Everly jerked, startled by the bright light. She blinked away a foggy haze in her eyes to find that she stood at the Rooks Hotel front desk. Harper leaned beside her, wearing an oversized floppy sunhat and eying the bar.

A pretty blond clerk smiled over the counter. *Brooke.* The name floated to the surface in Everly's mind.

"Was that a single or double bed, Miss Boderleth?"

Leaning in like it would help her understand, Everly said, "I'm sorry, what?"

"Do you need a room with a single or double bed?" the clerk repeated pleasantly, as if she had all the time in the world.

Everly's gaze darted as she tried to ground herself. A nameplate confirmed that the clerk was Brooke. Assistant Manager.

How did I know her name?

Memories of swirling darkness, unresponsive victims, the crunching of bones came back to Everly.

She grabbed Harper's arm. "Something's wrong. This place is beshadowed."

Harper chuckled. "Are you okay? Is this PTSD?"

"No, we were just there ... here ... but it wasn't like this."

Harper lifted the brim of her hat and squinted down at her. "Babe, that was weeks ago. Really, are you okay?"

Weeks ago? Everly's brow wrinkled.

She turned away to look around the hotel lobby, astonished to find the sun was high and bright, shining in through wide windows.

No more mist hovering over the hotel. The floors and surfaces were all sparkling and new, and a crowd of guests meandered around, laughing and chatting. No zombified snacks-in-waiting to be seen.

The rest of the Howell gang were nearby, too. Tammy and Denny sat across from each other in cushy armchairs, while Cherry and Callan were playing catch with some car keys.

Everly nodded. "Right. Yeah, I'm fine, sorry, just got confused for a minute. Go grab your cocktail while I sort this out, okay?"

Harper gave her a final assessing frown, then pranced over to the bar.

"I'm dreaming. This isn't real," Everly whispered to herself, using the words that had always been able to keep her lucid in her nightmares. "Wake up."

Nothing happened. *Okay, maybe not? But how did I lose weeks?*

A moment ago, she'd been standing in the upstairs hallway hearing a man get eaten by a vasmire. Had the monster come for her next?

Am I dead?

Brooke cleared her throat. "Do you need to check with your party?"

Everly flushed red, realizing the woman no doubt heard her talking to herself.

"Um, yeah. I do." She gave the woman an awkward smile, then crossed the pristine carpeted floor to her group.

Callan came over, intercepting her halfway. "Don't tell me they're out of rooms. I know it's, like, the only hotel in Shroudhaven, but I was really looking forward to a spontaneous vacation."

"A vacation?"

"We deserve one after everything, don't we?"

"I guess. But, don't you think something seems off? What can you remember from the last few weeks?"

Callan frowned, then shrugged and laughed. "Not much, but that's why we need a break."

"You don't find that weird? I can't remember either. Like we were just investigating the beshadowing moments ago. Remember the guy in the bathrobe? The munching sounds?"

Callan smiled. "That was ages ago. We're safe now. Everything is fine."

Everly nodded vaguely, but his reassurance only creeped her out more. Either she'd somehow fugue-stated her way through the last few weeks, or something else was going on. She looked around for other signs this was a dream. Anything strange or out of the ordinary, even a small detail.

But the proof she got was much bigger.

"Everly?"

She whirled, her heart hammering at the sound of Rylan's voice echoing through the cavernous lobby.

He jogged toward her from the front door. He was still clad in the clothes he'd worn the night of his attack: a tight black t-shirt beneath a gray-green military-style hooded jacket embroidered with the Darkfrey crest. His gaze raked the lobby, taking everything in.

Could he have woken up? Could this be real? Or ...

"Dreaming about my brother now?" Rylan smirked.

"So this *is* a dream?"

"You didn't know? I suppose it is the most completely mundane setting I've ever seen your brain conjure up." Rylan's gaze still swept the space, as though the armchairs would come to life and try to eat them at any moment.

Callan had grown very still beside Everly.

He looked at his brother with an intense expression. "You ... You're here. When did you wake up? I can't remember."

Everly stared at him. "That's a weird reaction for a dream figment."

"What did you call me?"

"Look, just, give us a second, okay?" Everly rubbed her forehead, completely confused about what was or wasn't real.

She grabbed Rylan by the arm and dragged him away from Callan.

They stopped off to the side of the revolving door, near the luggage trolleys. One of them held Harper's set of rose-gold suitcases.

If this is a dream, the details are amazing.

Rylan stared at Everly's hand around his bicep. "You're worrying me. What's going on?"

Everly took her hand back and bit her lip. "You really haven't woken up? This isn't real?"

He gestured to his appearance, which had seemed locked in since his near-death experience. "I don't remember waking up. I remember your last weird dream about the train filled with blood—not one of my favorites by the way—and now we're here."

"Yeah, okay, it was a longshot, but I needed to check. Last thing I remember we were here, at Rooks Hotel, but it was beshadowed. Late stage, Callan said. We were hunting a vasmire because the pieces we've been using to keep you safe are deteriorating and losing their effectiveness."

"They brought *you* to a *beshadowing*?" Rylan barked, tossing a glare at his brother.

Callan remained where they'd left him, still staring back their way with a pinched expression.

"The point is, when we got here everyone was walking around all zombie-like, mist everywhere. Then suddenly I'm here in this dream with you."

Rylan tossed one more glare at Callan, then turned his attention fully to Everly. "You mean, you could still be there, asleep or knocked out? You've got to wake up and get away. Can you wake yourself up? Like I've seen you do before?"

Everly shrugged. "It was the first thing I tried. I can try again, but I think ... Rylan, I think it's an outside force keeping me here. It feels different."

The hard, determined look of a shadyr on a mission faded, and he reached out to take hold of both her arms. "Try."

She drew strength from the dreamy warmth of his hands.

Closing her eyes, she spoke. "Wake up. You're dreaming. Wake up!"

Nothing changed.

A muscle ticked in Rylan's jaw. He turned and studied the Howell team.

"What about them? Can they help? I mean, are those actually my brother and his friends, or are they figments of your imagination?"

"Callan did react weirdly to seeing you." She turned towards the other people in the foyer who were enjoying the warm light and happy atmosphere. "What if this is a dream, but it's not *my* dream."

"Umm, explain?"

"It's not just me here, it's the whole Howell team, Harper, all the hotel staff and guests. Everyone who was in the hotel before."

"And me?" Rylan asked.

"You've piggybacked along with me, but whatever this is, it's not my dream. I think this *is* the beshadowing. Maybe all of us at the hotel are caught in this dreamworld, and our bodies are still out there, bumping around like zombies waiting to be eaten."

Rylan brushed a hand over his face and the look of abject disbelief there. "Could you have gotten into a worse situation?"

"Who knows. I've had to figure most of this out on my own because you and your brother kept so much from me to begin with," Everly snapped. "Maybe I'd have had a better handle on all this beshadowing stuff if you'd just been up front with me years ago when you packed off to Darkfrey Estate."

To his credit, Rylan looked suitably chastised, but his voice came out stern. "I know. I'm sorry. But the secret was bigger than just you and me. I wanted—"

"Later. We don't have time. We have to find a way out of this mess before the vasmire eats one—or all—of us."

"Then let's go see if the others are themselves enough to help."

They went back to Callan first, who stood with his arms crossed, foot tapping. "You two have some explaining to do. How is Rylan here?"

"You don't remember the last couple of weeks because they didn't happen. We're still in the beshadowing, trapped in this dreamworld. Rylan has somehow hitchhiked along with me, what with him living in my dreams. I don't understand it better than that."

Callan nodded slowly. "If this is a dream though, why would I think he's even real?"

Rylan crossed his arms to match his brother. "Want me to prove I'm real? On a scale of one to wetting yourself in front of Alexis Darkfrey, how embarrassing of an anecdote from your childhood do you want?"

The two brothers stared at one another for a long moment, Rylan with watchful expectation. Several emotions crossed Callan's face—embarrassment, confusion, dawning horror.

"Ghast damn it. We're zombies, aren't we? Like all the others?"

Everly nodded. "That's my best guess."

Callan pointed at Rylan, but looked at Everly. "And he ... You *were* telling the truth. That's actually Rylan. He's *in* your dreams. Like, real in your dreams."

Everly put her hands on her hips. "What, you thought I was psychic when I dragged you to the theater to find the eidolghast he'd killed?"

Callan stared at his brother. "I guess, maybe I thought you'd just gotten lucky. I didn't know what to think."

He gave his head a sharp shake, his eyes glossy.

Stepping forward, he flung his arms around Rylan. "It's so good to see you."

"You too."

Stepping back, Callan couldn't seem to take his eyes off Rylan. "Wow, this is ... How'd you get trapped in Everly's dreams?"

Rylan shrugged. "We don't know."

"Can we discuss theories later?" Everly said. "More escaping now."

Callan nodded. "Let's clue in the others."

They rejoined their group by the armchairs. Movement caught Everly's eye, and she saw her spirit-cougar dash skittishly up the stairs, spooked by the different atmosphere. It had ended up here, too, and clearly didn't like it.

Everly hadn't seen her dragon yet and hoped it wouldn't show up. She had no idea how it would behave in this dream realm, with so many people around. Another reason to get out of there fast.

"Hey, Harper?"

Harper didn't look up from where she lounged in her chair with her legs crossed over the armrest.

She tapped away on her phone with one hand and sipped a peach-pink cocktail from a martini glass with the other. "Hey babe, yours is on the table there. Reception here is amazing."

Denny sat across from her, reading a magazine, and Tammy had wandered away over to the bar, probably when Harper sat down. She seemed to especially have an issue with Bellsy.

Cherry saw Callan and Everly approach first, saw Rylan with them, and his jaw dropped.

Callan lifted his chin. "Yeah man, Mordan Darkfrey's my sugar daddy."

Everly raised an eyebrow. "What?"

Cherry's face changed immediately, as if a veil had been stripped away from his mind. "Whoa. We're beshadowed?"

Rylan looked at Callan, bemused. "Mordan Darkfrey is your sugar daddy?"

Callan shrugged. "We needed a warning phrase for when things really went off the wall, something we'd never normally say. I like to plan for every possibility."

Denny put his magazine down and slapped his thigh. "No way! I didn't think we'd ever need that one."

Callan scowled at him. "We only needed it because you screwed everything up for us with that dumb beer can stunt."

"Oh, come on. It was a perfect bullseye!"

"You know what your problem is?"

"Yeah, my dick's too big."

"Wait, wait, wait, what? Who is who's sugar daddy?" Harper put her phone down and glanced up. Then she caught sight of Rylan. "WHAT?"

Rylan seemed to be key at jarring people to their senses. Whatever constructed reality surrounded them, lulling them into feeling safe, it hadn't accounted for his presence.

Everly reached down for Harper and pulled her to her feet. "Trapped in a dream, wacky dream magics, yadda yadda. Can you wake yourself up?"

Harper's pretty face screwed up. "The vasmire ... the guy in the bathrobe and the ... It *ate* him, didn't it?"

"Yeah, and it's going to eat us if we don't get the hell out of here. Can you wake up?" Everly repeated.

Harper jumped on the spot and pinched the backs of her hands and screamed, drawing the attention of the other guests. "That would seem to be a no."

Rylan patted his brother on the shoulder. "Good idea setting up a phrase like that. I'm impressed."

Callan turned to him with a glowing grin, and they clapped one hand each into a tight grasp, pulling in for another brief embrace.

"This might be the hottest bromance I've ever witnessed," Harper whispered not at all quietly to Everly.

"Who is she?" Rylan asked.

"Harper? I've mentioned her. I'll introduce you two properly once you wake up for real." Everly rushed out. "We need a plan *now*, and we need a plan *fast*. I already tried to wake myself up, but I can't. Whatever the vasmire has done to us, we're in deep."

Cherry's expression twisted. "We're all just sleepwalking the halls, waiting to be picked off and eaten by the monster. The vasmire's own personal buffet. Yeah, not loving this."

Everly chewed her thumbnail, thinking. "If we can get even one of us awake, they

could have a chance to save the rest of us."

Rylan's voice came out deadly serious as he said, "I'd bet that as long as your bodies remain in the beshadowing, no one's waking up."

"Tammy," Callan said suddenly.

Rylan frowned. "What about her?"

"She has this ... I don't know, I guess it's an ability, but not something she seems to control. She can teleport to the Dark Corner shroudpool."

Rylan glanced over to where she stood with her back to them at the bar. In her all-black outfit, she looked out of place in the bright and cheery foyer.

"Tammy Kyrstelle? The kid that got kicked out of Darkfrey Estate after she had some part in the Mesman boy's death? She can *teleport*?"

"Only to that one place," Callan went on. "But yeah, like, poof, gone."

"So, what?" Rylan said. "We get Tammy to teleport out of this dream, and she goes right to another dangerous, beshadowed place? That doesn't seem helpful."

"At least she'd be dealing with it while conscious, unlike here. Plus it happens to her every other day, so she's familiar with the area and its effects," Callan clarified. "Once she's out of here, she can bring back up."

"If we can get her to teleport on purpose. I thought it was involuntary," Everly said.

"She just needs a good scare," Denny said, chuckling. "Once I farted loudly and she popped out of existence."

"Your farts would make anyone want to pop out of existence," Cherry scoffed.

"Your general presence would make anyone want to pop out of existence," Harper added, and Cherry high-fived her.

Callan shot them a look. "Great, so we have a plan. Now we just need to convince Tammy this is a dream and make her zap herself away from here."

"I'm hoping for a two-birds-one-stone situation," Everly said. "Just learning it's a dream might set her off."

Callan nodded, and led the group over to the bar.

The sullen girl leaned heavily on the counter, making a pyramid of empty shot-glasses with her ink-black hands.

Everly cast a concerned look as the bartender poured out another row of five tequilas. "Um, hey. Tammy? Can we talk?"

She side-eyed them, peering at Everly, Callan, and Rylan in turn through narrowed, smokey eyelids. "If you're about to tell me we're in a dream, don't waste your breath."

"You know?"

"I'm just taking the opportunity to get dream-trashed since this dream-bar doesn't card me." She reached over and downed another shot.

Callan pushed the rest out of her reach. "How did you—?"

"Mordan Darkfrey is your sugar daddy. Your voice carries. It's grating."

The signs of a mammoth effort of patience played out over Callan's face. "Did you hear the plan then?"

"Yeah, and it's not going to work. I've never been able to teleport on purpose. And yes, I've tried." She stretched past Callan, reaching for another drink.

When he wouldn't budge, she leaned over the counter and took a whole bottle.

"Just give up. We can happily dream-drink ourselves into oblivion while our bodies become vasmire-food. There are worse ways to go." She moved to take a swig of the cheap whiskey.

Callan snatched the bottle from her hands and threw it against the wall. The glass shattered in a loud explosion. Everyone in the foyer turned to stare as one. Then as though nothing happened, they returned to their happy selves.

"We're not giving up," Callan growled. "I'm not giving up on you."

Tammy stared up at Callan with a look of pure, teary petulance only a teenager could muster.

Callan scooped both of her hands into his and held them between their chests. "Work with me here, please."

Everly thought she saw a pink tinge rise in the girl's neck and cheeks, but it disappeared almost immediately, as if Tammy had willed it away. "Fine. I guess. Whatever."

"Close your eyes. I want you to picture Dark Corner shroudpool."

The skin at the corner of Tammy's eyes tightened. "Great. My favorite place."

"I know it's hard for you," Callan said gently. "But you're our only hope right now, okay? You're the only person with the ability to leave."

Tammy took a deep breath, and her perpetual pout and angry glare was smoothed away, replaced by a hint of determination.

"Imagine the place where you typically show up when you teleport," Callan went on. "Picture it in your mind."

Tammy breathed deeply in and out, and her eyelids flickered as if she were seeing exactly what Callan told her to see. "Okay."

"Imagine you're there, standing in that spot. Really visualize it, down to every last detail."

Her shoulders rose and fell slowly with her breathing. She leaned forward, her head dipping as if she were falling asleep. Callan leaned in, too, and placed his forehead on hers.

Tammy gasped, and her eyes fluttered open to zero in on Callan's face so close to hers.

Then she was gone.

"She did it?" Everly gasped.

Callan dropped his hands and leaned on the bar with a long, low sigh. "Well, it either worked or—"

Or Tammy disappeared from the dream for another reason, one no one wanted to say out loud. That she was the first to have been taken by the vasmire.

Callan shook his head. "There's no way to know."

Everly turned to Rylan to find him staring back at her. He frowned and looked away. "I don't like this." His voice was gravelly.

That they were relying on a surly, nihilistic sixteen-year-old to teleport herself across town to a beshadowed danger zone, make her way alone out of there, get help, and get back to them in time before anyone else got eaten?

Yeah, I don't like it much either.

All faces were grim surrounding Everly. "All we can do now is wait and see."

4

I didn't think I'd ever be happy to see this place.

Tammy blinked, clearing the hazy dream world away and taking in the eerie corner of the Wyrdwoods that had ruined her life.

She'd appeared flat on her back, a few yards from the semi-dormant shroudpool that drew her to it like a bath-toy down a pulled plug.

Her heart hammered from the phantom sensation of Callan's forehead pressed against hers. She brushed the tips of her fingers over the place where their skin had touched and shivered. It hadn't taken any visualization or deep thought to send her teleporting out of the hotel and into Dark Corner.

Only the touch of Callan's skin and his face infinitely close to hers.

Ugh. I don't like him. I can't.

Tammy grunted, placed her hands on the cracked, barren ground, and shoved to her feet unsteadily as she tried to come to terms with reality. Getting drawn to the shroudpool always left her dizzy and disoriented, and getting there from the dream left her head spinning.

"And of course, I'm completely sober. Brilliant."

Nothing grew close to this shroudpool. The circle of dead earth reaching twenty feet all around was ringed by dark trees that seemed to move in ways trees weren't meant to.

Tammy rubbed her temples as her gaze was drawn to the shroudpool itself. The rough circular patch of darkness was big enough to drive a car through. A heavy mist seeped from the void-like black mess.

When it was still a fully active portal to the Everdark, it had writhed with a strange depth that could send you mad from looking into it. She remembered thinking it looked like a tunnel filled with shag-pile carpet made from oily black worms. One that would frequently spew out monsters from another dimension.

That doorway was now closed, but not gone, and a haze of evil still oozed out.

Because of what she'd done.

Getting her unsteady feet moving, Tammy stumbled past the one massive tree that stood in the middle of the clearing. Its bark was warped and twisted, its roots encircling

the shroudpool. It didn't grow anymore, but sometimes, it screamed.

The interdimensional portal may have been mostly dormant, but this area was still dangerous, so she knew better than to let down her guard. Dark Corner was permanently beshadowed to the point where nothing and no one came in or out—except Tammy.

All because she'd stuck her hands into that shroudpool.

"It's not going to work. We shouldn't be here alone."

Blaise flashes a perfect smile. "Come on, be more positive. Imagine if we can do this, we'll be the heroes of Darkfrey Estate!"

His blond hair flops over one eye. It shouldn't be possible to be that pretty. Tammy smiles, heart in her throat.

Tammy shuddered. The last moment she saw her friend, with his eyes wild and mouth wide and screaming was a memory that tormented her far too vividly.

She'd latched on to his hands. Sunk into the shroudpool up to her elbows. His fingers slipped through hers. She was nearly pulled in after him.

I should have been.

Pain rushed to the surface, and tears swam in her vision. She swiped both blackened hands across her eyes, jaw clenched.

She didn't have time to stand there wishing she'd done something different. Wishing she'd saved her best friend. The past was the past. She'd screwed up, and this special little punishment of always teleporting to the place of her heartache was her curse to suffer.

But this time, maybe her curse could save some lives.

Fishing about her pockets, Tammy pulled out her phone and tapped to turn it on. The screen remained dark. A crack split across the glass, and when she gave the device a shake, it rattled.

"Ghast damn it. When did that happen?"

Wetness smudged over the phone screen, faintly red against the black. Examining her inky hands, Tammy noted a rip in her jacket, a sting on her forearm, a bite mark the same size as the toothy mouths that covered a vasmire's tentacles.

She shivered.

Was it really that close? I almost got eaten … Oh well. Better luck next time.

Without a phone, she only had one other option. She rubbed the velvet-short hair on her head and shook the tingles out of her limbs. Then struck out at a sprint for the rusted, locked gate.

There were a couple of permanent shroudpools around Shroudhaven, and each had been fenced off with warning signs stating *Mine Subsidence Area* or *Dangerous Gases* and *Landmine Field, Keep Out.* Anything to strike enough terror into the blivs to keep them out of trouble.

Plus, the Darkfrey gang did their best to patrol the surroundings and get rid of

any teenagers who looked a little too daredevilish.

Tammy slithered through the narrow, nearly invisible slash in the chain link fencing while she went over her options. Dark Corner was on the outskirts of Shroudhaven, much too far from Rooks Hotel for her to make it on foot. But close enough to Howell House, and just around the corner from it, the Boderleth home.

Callan had told her to go for help. Lian and Rushelle were there, keeping an eye on Rylan's body. She straightened on the other side of the fence and for a moment, she thought about going straight to the hotel to try to wake up the team on her own. But she knew better than to pretend, even to herself, that she could do anything to help her friends alone.

She hadn't been able to save Blaise.

She was useless. Cursed.

The team needed someone capable.

With the sun gone over the horizon and not a shred of light to shine through the thick, gnarled branches overhead, the woods were pitch black around her. Anything could be lurking out there.

Normally when she disappeared, someone would come and pick her up, but no one conscious knew she was there now.

Running is the worst.

Two deep breaths, then Tammy took off at a sprint down the uneven dirt road toward civilization.

She kept her gaze glued to the horizon, cursing her humanity. She had access to powers that could make her strong and fast, but without an eidolghast nearby, she couldn't transform and *use* said powers.

It was a crappy clause in the shadyr contract. Though in her estimation, the whole package of being a shadyr wasn't worth the hype. They were literal monsters half the time.

She cast out her senses, hoping to catch the scent of an eidolghast close enough for her to transform. In Shroudhaven, monsters were so common you couldn't sneeze without hitting one, and she usually couldn't go anywhere without coming up against their familiar energy.

She didn't have great control over her shadyr side, so even a hint of an eidolghast could trigger her transformation. Just like the dead one keeping Rylan alive had.

Of course, when she *needed* a monster, there wasn't one to be found.

Her lungs burned and sweat clung uncomfortably around her body armor. Soon, the small side lane met with a larger road. In one direction lay the main highway that connected Shroudhaven to Gorhanmere. Relief flooded her at the sight of brake lights in the distance, and a cluster of streetlights that marked the intersection up ahead.

Maybe hitchhiking was a possibility.

A feeling bloomed within Tammy like a ball of fire in her chest.

Nope, hitchhiking wouldn't be a possibility, unless there was a furry convention happening tonight.

There was a weroth nearby—a terrifying creature of void-like blackness with six legs. They were vaguely wolf-like but too boneless and slithery to ever be confused for something earthborn. They had too many joints, most of which bent the wrong way, and Tammy had always thought they looked like slimy, eyeless spiders.

She steered clear of where it lurked in the woods beside the road, but took full advantage of its presence for her transformation.

The burning shadows engulfed her body as she shifted. Her chest and arms widened, tearing her clothes and putting pressure on the custom built, flexible shadyr armor beneath. It was getting too small for her.

She'd grown since she left Darkfrey Estate with it a few years ago, and the Howells didn't have the same resources. It pinched badly but didn't tear. Her legs lengthened and fur sprouted all over her skin.

Tammy ran her tongue over the sharpened teeth in her now snout-like face and flexed her refreshed muscles. On strong, clawed feet, she tore through the dimly lit streets with startling speed.

Up ahead, she spotted the round, swinging sign for Boderleth Antiques.

The closer she got, the more she could sense the pieces of vasmire upstairs, and dark shadows swirled around her werewolf form. She tried to fight it, had to fight it. Her body ached and shifted, trying to be more than one creature at once.

"Liaaaaaan!" Tammy buckled over at the front gate.

The gray-haired woman appeared within seconds. She wore a floor-length knitted cardigan over pajamas, her sword strapped by a belt to her side.

"Tammy? Is that you? What's happened?"

"Trouble," Tammy mumbled.

It was hard to form words around her snout. Though she could feel the weroth's influence finally fading. The vasmire's presence was taking over.

"At Rooks Hotel?"

Tammy nodded.

"They need help?"

She nodded again.

That was all Lian needed to know.

"Rushelle!" she hollered toward the house. "Go get a car, fast!"

Rushelle's face appeared in one of the front windows, her pale golden hair piled atop her head. "Yes, Mam!"

Dark whisps of change surrounded the woman as she vanished from sight. The back door slammed, and her footsteps echoed away as she leaped across backyards toward Howell House.

Tammy slumped down on the pavement, wheezing, and turned her furry face to the sky. She focused on her breathing, several breaths in and out, counting to five each time. Callan had taught her mindful breathing as a method for controlling her transformation. A way for her to be in charge of when she changed. It never seemed to work for her though.

Lian adjusted her sword hilt and squatted beside her. "Tell me everything. What are we going into?"

Tammy struggled through a quick and dirty explanation of what they'd found and what had happened, words slurred by her mouth full of razor-sharp teeth.

Every second that passed as she waited for Rushelle to return felt like two seconds too long.

I'm already too late. I failed them all. They're probably dead already.

Just the journey from Dark Corner could have been enough time for someone to be hurt. Or eaten. It was another fifteen-minute drive to get from there to Rooks.

Tammy's face scrunched up and she shifted from werewolf to vampire, her body shuddering, exhausted, soaked in sweat.

Lian mumbled and started scrolling through her phone. "Damn it. This is too big for us. Bloody Darkfreys are always telling us they've got things covered and don't want our help. If that's the case, they shouldn't have let a beshadowing get that bad!"

The phone rang on speaker. Lian held it up in front of her face, the light casting deep shadows over her wrinkled skin.

"Darkfrey Estate," a female voice crackled over the line.

The last word vanished in a snap of static. Shroudhaven's motto might as well have been *Dangerous Creatures, Foggy Nights, and Constantly Bad Reception!*

"Vonny? It's Lian."

The static eased enough to hear Vonny's audible sigh. "What do you want, Howell?"

"Our team is in trouble out at Rooks Hotel. A late stage beshadowing. Need all hands on deck."

"We aren't—" *crackle, crackle.* A line of white noise, and then sudden clarity: "—our problem, Howell."

"My son is in trouble!" Lian insisted.

"Your sons always—" *hiss, crack.* "—in trouble, don't they?"

"Von—"

"Stop interfering," Vonny snapped. "Stay out of it, and we will—"

The static cut off. Vonny had hung up.

Tammy bit her lower lip, thinking of Callan trapped in that nightmare while a

vasmire stalked around his sleep-walking form.

She spoke up into the sudden, charged silence. "We can't stay out of it."

"We aren't," Lian said briskly.

A roar sounded around the corner, and a vintage yellow sportscar, roof down, squealed to a stop in front of them.

Rushelle leaned out from the driver's side, grinning over vampire fangs. "Good to go."

Lian didn't hesitate to swing herself over into the passenger seat, long cardigan flying out like a cape.

Rushelle adjusted her sunshine yellow corset-top as she checked Tammy over with a glance. "You okay, duckling? You look like you went spelunking."

"If by spelunking, you mean I ran all the way here, then yeah."

"From Rooks?"

"From Dark Corner."

Rushelle cringed. "Man, oh man. I hate that you have to go through that."

Tammy's bones still ached from the run, and her heart still ached from the feeling they would be too late. She groaned off the ground and stepped toward the car.

Lian put her hand up, stopping her. "We need someone here. We can't leave Rylan unattended. Don't worry, we've got this."

Heat stung Tammy's face. *Of course. I'm not going. They don't need me.*

She fought the tears back with a roll of her eyes. "Whatever."

5

Everly awoke to chaos.

Somebody tackled her down onto hard concrete. An explosive clattering burst behind them.

She opened her eyes, staring up at the front entrance to Rooks Hotel. The glass of the revolving door flew through the air, landing like hail all around her. She covered her face with her arms.

The body that was on her moved away, leaving bursts of bright yellow in Everly's clearing vision.

"They're waking up!" The voice was familiar. *Rushelle?*

Everly sat up in a cascade of glass shards. She craned her neck to glance up.

The buxom woman in her sunshine yellow halter top grinned down at her, showing off her pointed fangs. "It's okay, duck. It's us, you're out."

Her face was pale, strange, and monstrous, but there was no mistaking Rushelle.

Everly looked around for Rylan as reality settled before her darting eyes.

I'm out of the dream.

A hint of movement to Everly's left drew her attention. Denny and Callan stirred beside her, both still in vampire form. No Cherry. No Harper.

Where are the others?

Denny's eyes opened, staring straight into Everly's. The corner of his mouth turned up. "Look at us, waking up next to each other."

Ignoring him, Everly got her feet under her and stood up with Rushelle's help. "Where's Harper?"

"I don't know, honey. Found you three first, bobbing about like the world's happiest zombies. Herded you out quick smart. I was just about to go back in for the others, but I think Lian's found the vasmire."

Something crashed, and a deep, inhuman howling followed. Everly turned to the gaping, shattered entryway to the foyer. Within, the mist swirled and forms moved inside it.

Callan stumbled to his feet. "We have to go help."

219

Rushelle grabbed his shoulders to steady him. "Whoa there, sugar. I'm going. Take yourself a moment to recover."

Callan bared his fangs and shook his head, long hair whipping. He knocked her hands away.

"I'm ready. I'm not losing anyone on this mission." He took off at a run.

Rushelle raised both arms and groaned. "I just dragged your zombie asses out! Run back into that beshadowing before you've recovered and who knows how long you'll last a second time."

"Don't worry about me. I'm good here. Not planning on going anywhere," Denny said, pillowing his hands under his head.

Everly winced an apology to Rushelle. "I have to find Harper."

She dashed back into Rooks Hotel, leaving the woman behind swearing about *these crazy kids*.

Everly was met with a face full of dark mist. It parted, and the vasmire loomed right over her.

Bulbous gray flesh swirled and whipped past her eyes. Toothy circular mouths covered the tentacles, grinding and snapping. Multiple sets of coal-black eyes opened and blinked at her. Three wormy tentacles shot out toward her with an odd crackling sound.

A figure burst into Everly's field of vision with an animalistic snarl, bringing down a jagged black sword on the slithering appendages. The sword clanged against the floor, and the monster screamed as those limbs were separated from its body.

After striking, the newcomer froze in place, statue-like, head tilted as though in concentration. When transformed, the shadyrs sometimes became so different from their usual selves that Everly could never tell their identities unless she knew what they were wearing.

But she knew this was Lian. Her sword. Her salt and pepper hair. Her long, knitted cardigan. Her ... pajamas?

The vasmire withdrew, whipping around the room frighteningly fast. A second shadyr, Callan, lunged at it, digging his hands deep into the creature's flesh.

"Great googly-eyed gods, I've never seen one so big!" Rushelle joined the fray, skidding to a stop to take in the mess, then yelled, "Lian! To your left!"

Like clockwork brought back to life, Lian slashed, her sword flashing in a strong and precise movement. More dismembered tentacles fell. She returned to a holding stance, as zen as a samurai.

Everly couldn't fit the Lian she knew—caring mother, homemaker—with this violently beautiful creature. She tore her astonished gaze from Lian, searching for Harper or Cherry in the misty shadows.

As big as the foyer was, the vasmire almost filled it. Not in solid mass, but in its

length, a web of writhing tentacles. Rushelle took a running leap, flying across the space and landing close to Callan.

"Welcome to ... to to to."

Everly jumped out of her skin as Brooke appeared in front of her again. She gave the sleepy-eyed clerk a gentle push toward the open front entrance, hoping momentum would carry her all the way out. Then she ran for the staircase.

Everly dodged the vasmire's whipping limbs, dashing through the foyer, her eyes darting for signs of her best friend. Would she still be upstairs? She could have wandered anywhere while trapped in the dream.

A wet *thunk* was followed by an explosion of pain in Everly's shoulder. One of the vasmire's wildly flailing tentacles struck against her back and sent her toppling forwards.

Sharp pain lanced up her knees and wrists as she hit the floor. She paused long enough to force back the surge of her dragon's light trying to escape in her moment of weakness. As soon as it was reined in, she rose back to her feet, wobbling and gritting her teeth.

She couldn't wait for the pain to ease or the fuzzy black edges around her vision to fade—she needed to find Harper.

Everly raced up the long, shallow steps to the second floor as the thunder of battle in the lobby grew. She glanced back to see how the Howell team were doing. Pale skin and teeth flashed in the mist and gloom. A chorus of muffled shouts as the team communicated were punctuated by the howling creature.

Lian, Rushelle, Callan ... only three shadyrs against the eidolghast. They always said at least four was best to take the monsters down, even ones not as big as this. They were holding their own for now, but for how long?

They need help. But I have to find Harper first.

A sick feeling squirmed in her stomach. She'd brought Harper to Shroudhaven. She'd exposed her best friend to this world. If the vasmire got to her ...

"There's Cherry!" Callan yelled from somewhere below.

"I'll get him out," Rushelle replied.

Everly spun back around, hoping to spot Harper there too.

Lian's sword flashed like a beacon in the low light. Callan danced around the creature's strikes, moving boldly and loudly, clearly attempting to distract the vasmire from Lian so she could land a killing blow.

Then more movement shimmered through the mist near the bar.

Shuffling like a lost marionette, Harper's grinning face emerged from the murky shadows.

She was entirely too close to the vasmire's flailing tentacles. Even with the shadyrs keeping it distracted in battle. And she obviously wasn't in a good frame of mind to get the hell out of the way herself.

Rushelle rejoined the battle, but the time she took to get Cherry clear had put them on the back foot. Lian took a hit to her chest. It flung her clear across the foyer. She landed among potted palms, ceramics and foliage clattering around her.

Everly couldn't distract them again, she had to get to Harper herself.

Harper didn't have a shadyr's tough skin and sharp teeth to fight back. She was a fragile human, and with one chomp, she would be vasmire food just like the guy in the bathrobe.

Everly looked over the railing, but it was way too risky to jump. She broke into a run, arms and legs pumping, skipping down the stairs so fast she nearly fell.

But not fast enough.

Everly skidded to a halt with just a few stairs left, staring in horror.

Something else moved behind Harper. Larger than another possessed human. Larger than anything that had any right to be there. Its form swirled in the shadows, a tangle of snaking flesh.

"There's another one! THERE'S TWO OF THEM!" Everly yelled with every bit of oxygen in her lungs.

The fight seemed to still for just a second, as swear words spilled from every shadyr in the room.

"We've almost got this one, just keep back!" Lian hollered.

That wasn't an option. Not with Harper standing defenseless right beneath the thing.

It expanded behind her friend, growing ever bigger in a mass of lashing flesh. The way the one Rylan had fought had, right before it landed its killing blow.

Please, no. Please, no.

"Over here, you bastard!" Everly leaped over the railing.

A tentacle shot out and wrapped around Harper's waist.

"No!" Everly screamed, chills racing across her skin.

She set off in a sprint across the floor, desperate to reach Harper before the beast swallowed her whole. How did the vasmire eat? Were the tiny mouths on its tentacles biting Harper even now?

I've got to get her out of there.

The shadyr team attacked their target even more violently, trying to finish it off. The monster was already a mess of bloody stubs, oozing black instead of red, but still it lashed at them, persistent and deadly. All their attention was on it.

Harper dangled five feet off the floor, limp and still grinning disturbingly within the vasmire's grip. In one of her hands she clutched her axe, the sharp edge bumping and scratching bloody marks on her leg.

Everly reached the floor beneath her best friend just as the vasmire pulled Harper out of reach.

"No!" Everly screamed, leaping after her friend's boots. Her fingers fell just short. *Not Harper. This can't be happening.*

Several tentacles moved away from the vasmire's central mass, revealing a mouth that was wide enough to eat a small car, icicle-point teeth glinting.

"Callan, help!" Everly screamed, panic surging. "I can't reach her!"

She glanced around for his tall shadyr form but couldn't find him. Nearby, a blond head that could only be Rushelle's was obscured, wrapped within a squeezing tentacle, and just beyond her, Lian continued to slash what seemed to be a never-ending number of limbs.

The vasmire was too strong. Too big.

They can't beat it. They can't beat two of them.

Anxious breaths clogged her throat and her heartbeat raged, deafening her. Her dragon roared within, ramming itself against the cage she held it in.

No. Everly used every skill in her mental toolkit to keep her panic attack at bay. She wouldn't let it incapacitate her. Not now.

She grabbed bottles from the bar, flinging one after another at the beast. It paid them no attention. They shattered against it, raining down alcohol and glass.

If I could light it on fire somehow, if I had Harper's axe, if I had something, anything … Anything except the dragon.

Whatever those powers were, they weren't powers for good, and she couldn't control them.

A deep breath, a firm stance. Everly blinked.

Can't I?

She held her unruly adrenaline back by sheer force of will. She regulated her anxiety through years of hard work. It was always there, but most of the time, she kept it in check.

Maybe she could control the ravenous being of light inside her. Maybe she had been for most of her life.

If she let the energy flow through her, she could use it to save Harper, but then it might as easily turn around and eat her friend, too. The adrenaline spiking in her system made Everly woozy. She felt faint and worked harder to shake it off.

No, not just adrenaline. This is like before. I'm being pulled into the dream. I have to act, now.

The vasmire pulled Harper ever closer, its dangerously sharp mouth widening.

Everly would not be lost to the beshadowing again. Everly would *not* let Harper die.

She did the only thing she could.

Okay, dragon, let's do this.

6

Brilliant light blossomed from Everly's chest and streamed down her arms, illuminating the darkest shadows of the hotel lobby, burning away the mist. Sparkling tendrils emerged from within her, slithering quickly to the ground to take control.

It wasn't really a *dragon*.

Not in the actual sense of the word. But that was how Everly had always personified her anxiety. When the thing appeared in her dreams—a magnificent, coruscating, snaking body of fractal light—she'd labelled it the same way. Just a mental embodiment of her panic trying to break free.

The tendrils of light lifted her up into the air, putting her head at the same height as the vasmire's alien face. They propelled her forward with a smooth, even gait that almost felt like floating.

Everly had lived with the dragon her entire life, using a therapist to get control of the "feelings." Breathing exercises, mindfulness meditations, growing her field of tolerance, learning to accept her emotions ... It took all that and more to quiet the dragon.

Then one day, it had come *out* of her.

The day she saved herself, Harper, and Callan from the weroth at the theater. Then she learned it wasn't a metaphorical manifestation of her anxiety at all. It was a *thing*, some monstrous, fierce entity that no one could identify.

One that wanted to consume anything it could reach.

A ravenous desire washed over her hard and fast. It was a gnawing, aching need that seemed to come from her very essence, as if it had been locked up inside her and left to fester until it exploded. As the tendrils maneuvered her toward the vasmire, she was nothing but light and hunger.

Whoa there. I'm the one in control.

She asserted her willpower onto the force, directing it to take down the vasmire. The light had other plans. Several arms wavered out toward Harper, and foreign excitement filled Everly at how good the mortal girl would taste.

Back off!

Everly snapped at the dragon, shoving her consciousness between Harper and the light. It took an immense amount of control to steer the dragon away.

Eat the monster!

The light turned its focus away from Harper. Tendrils that had been reaching for her whipped out to wrap around the vasmire. But with it still holding Harper, entangled in its tentacles, Everly didn't trust letting her light have its way. She forced it to hold, to wait.

It roared with yearning. She pushed back, pain splitting through her head from the effort.

Everly noticed with detachment that the Howell team had backed away. Cherry, and even Denny, were with the others now, and their vasmire lay broken and twitching, its last few tentacles still whipping wildly.

There. You get two meals. But don't touch anything else.

With a rush of delight, light streamed to the second eidolghast as well.

Everly closed her eyes, trying to block out the part where the light ate the vasmire's life force. No matter how much power the light consumed, filling her, making her stronger, it still felt *wrong*. Abhorrent and abnormal. The beaten vasmire was gone within seconds.

The one holding Harper lurched and twisted, trying to break free. The void-black eyes and no obvious facial features in its central area made it hard for her to read its expression, but she could sense waves of fear rolling off the beast.

Like the weroth at the theater that had stumbled over itself in its haste to get away from her.

In its effort to escape, it dropped Harper.

She hit the floor on her feet and then fell forward onto her knees. There was a startled cry, and Harper looked up at Everly with awe, yellow sparkles shining in her green eyes. She was at least alert enough to scramble out of the way.

Everly held the light back until Harper had leapt behind the watching shadyrs, then she set it free. More tendrils emerged from her and wrapped around the vasmire. The creature thrashed and screeched but was no match for her dragon. The light began to consume it.

"No, no! Release me," a new voice said. A voice of screaming bats and gurgling lava. "Curse you! Vile monster! Beast of teeth and stars!"

Caught in her stasis behind the light, Everly blinked at the vasmire.

Had it just called *her* the monster? Most importantly, the thing could talk, though she didn't see its giant mouth moving at all. The voice had almost seemed to come from inside her own head.

Vasmire tentacles pressed against the light, sizzling as if the flesh were touching

flame. The light took pleasure in the vasmire's fear, and purred sickeningly as it dragged the monster's essence into it.

Everly imagined the dragon inside her, licking its salivating lips. It had eaten, but it was not sated. It would never be sated.

Finally, the vasmire was nothing but a blob of quivering flesh on the carpeted floor. Dead.

You're done. Time to go.

Resistance, growling defiance, and then the light faded. Everly drifted down to her feet, as if the sparkling tendrils were setting her down with utmost care. She leaned forward and rested her hands on her knees, gulping in air as if she'd just finished running a race.

Lian stepped in front of Everly, her gaze shrewd. "That was some light show."

Everly flushed. Lian knew about the dragon, but this was the first time she'd seen it in action. Could the others tell, just by watching, that the dragon was consuming its victims' lifeforce?

She hadn't really explained the sensation to the others. The tendrils seemed strong enough to physically defeat its foes, to crush the life from them rather than absorb it. Maybe that was all that was happening.

But Everly couldn't shake the sense that something, somehow, was being *eaten*. And it wasn't the physical bodies, which still lay before them.

Everly straightened and rolled the kinks out of her shoulders. Being possessed by the light left her feeling weak and achy for a couple of hours afterward. She hoped that was what she felt now, not her mind being sucked into the dreamworld again.

She asked, "Is it clear? Is the beshadowing gone?"

Cherry kicked one of the dead vasmire bodies. It oozed a little dark gas, but otherwise the mist that had filled the space had vanished. "Dead, and dead."

"Good work, team," Callan said.

His skin was covered in vasmire-black and human-red blood, but if he was injured anywhere, his vampire form must have already closed the wounds.

Cherry scoffed. "Team? We didn't even finish off this one ourselves. Both kills land on Everly's scorecard."

"I was counting Everly as part of the team," Callan replied.

"And the MVP I'd say." Harper still had the axe gripped in white knuckled fingers. "I can't believe how useless I was. I didn't even get to use my new toy."

Everly shook her head. "You were trapped in a dreamworld, it wasn't your fault."

Harper tsked. "Excuses. Next time I'll do better."

Everly barely had time to brace herself before Harper threw her arms around her neck and squeezed painfully. "Thank you. You saved my life."

"Might have saved us all," Cherry added. "I was starting to fall back into that dream world again. Can't believe we all made it, especially with also dealing with this fool."

He threw a fistful of vasmire at Denny.

"Watch it!" Denny swatted the gore off his shirt and grumbled about not being appreciated.

"We did good, for what this was. That beasty was an especially big fellow." Rushelle chuckled, picking something out of her hair. "And then another one shows up! Like, whaaat?"

Callan squatted down beside the second vasmire to examine it. "No wonder this beshadowing wasn't caught sooner. It probably turned dark much faster than normal."

Lian wiped spattered hands on her pajama shirt. "We were lucky to have Everly with us."

A harsh, sudden clapping interrupted them.

A Darkfrey team stood just inside the busted revolving doors, concealed in the low light. They'd obviously been there a while. Several of them leaned against the wall like spectators, and the one man out front—bigger and more muscular than the rest—was slow clapping with extreme irony.

"Wow, just, wow. I mean, we always joke about how useless and messed up the Howell runts are, but seeing it in person is something else," he said, his voice thick and growly.

Callan muttered under his breath and shifted ever so slightly to put himself in front of Everly and Harper.

Everly peeked around him to see if she recognized any of them, but in their shadyr forms, silhouetted by the streetlights behind them, they were total strangers. She counted eight of them. That meant two braces, as she'd heard their four-person teams called.

"How nice of your pet human to take care of everything for you. Although, she's not exactly human, is she?"

They saw? Everly almost wanted to ask if they knew what she was, but from the man's tone, she guessed it was a no.

Lian swung her long cardigan so it obscured the sheathed sword at her side, then stepped ahead of her team. "You were there long enough to watch, but you didn't bother stepping in to help?"

The Darkfrey shadyr shrugged. "And miss the show? Figured we'd wait and see. Could always mop up if you ghast-lickers bit it."

His flippant tone brought a flush of hot fury to Everly's face. It reminded her of that day in the Wyrdwoods when they'd been ambushed at Nell's animal sanctuary.

The Darkfreys had come in, treating it like a black op. All those animals, the poor, eccentric old crone... And when Everly found Rylan's unconscious form lying beneath the house in Nell's laboratory, she'd also found a Darkfrey shadyr there, attempting to kill him.

If she hadn't shown up when she did, she had no doubt that they would have lost Rylan that day.

One of them wanted Rylan dead. And it could be one of them in front of her now.

The bulky cut of the man who mocked them—the sound of his voice was familiar.

Everly stalked straight toward them, anger glittering in her eyes.

She approached so quickly, so surely, that the huge man backed away from her.

It was him, the one with the blond crew cut and body of an action figure soldier, who had led the ambush at Nells. She'd seen him before too. Nilson Darkfrey.

Even in his shadyr form, she could tell it was him. Closer now, she also spotted Vonny, Annabeth, and Jasper to one side of him. The four faces on the other side were unfamiliar.

It could be any one of them.

Everly didn't know what to say to them. Fury had burned away all her words.

Vonny snapped, "Howell, come and leash this freak of yours!"

"Don't call her a freak, you murderers!" Harper yelled back.

"We just do our job and do it well."

"You sure replaced Rylan fast," Callan said, striding up beside Everly. "Nilson is part of your brace now?"

The soldier-man snickered. "I'm leader of this brace now, and it's one of the best since the Howell taint is all gone."

Vonny's face twisted into even more of a scowl at the word *leader*.

Cherry hollered from behind them, "Yeah, best at letting a beshadowing get this far along and not even noticing. You guys are sooo great at your jobs."

Nilson snarled. "Shut your mouth. We know what we're doing. Shroudhaven is the Darkfreys responsibility. You're the ones showing up with your little team of useless misfits trying to get yourselves killed."

Both teams erupted, voices on each side rising over one another.

The din echoed through the high ceiling and stone lobby. Fangs were bared. Any moment now someone could strike the other team.

They didn't have time for this. They needed to get back to Rylan, not get into a fist fight with the larger and better resourced team of supernatural beings.

"Enough!" Everly cried, and a burst of light flashed through the room.

Silence fell as all eyes turned to her.

Vonny stepped forward to stand next to Nilson. She tossed back her blond bob and narrowed her gaze on Everly.

"Jasper told us that your pet human had some kind of freaky power. We didn't believe it at first. If you aren't shadyr, you're human. If you aren't human, you're a monster. So, girl, what are you?"

Before Everly could even consider answering, Cherry pushed his way past her. His hands balled into fists at his sides, and his face was menacing, still transformed into his vampire-like visage.

"Oh, *Jasper* mentioned it, did he? Good little soldier boy. I should have known where your loyalties lie."

Everly glanced at the man in question, and he swallowed visibly. She and Harper were the only people who officially knew that Cherry and Jasper had been secretly seeing each other.

The Darkfrey shadyr was a good-looking guy of average height and build, with silky black hair he usually wore combed back, and dusky skin. Even when on the hunt for monsters, he wore bland, neutral-colored cardigans and pressed khakis.

But the hint of emotion that touched Jasper's face fled, and he said coolly, "I might have mentioned something you brought up while we were talking the other day."

"Talking." Cherry spat the word. "Yes, of course. *Talking.* As friends do. But you know, I think we're done *talking.*"

Everly had never heard him sound so angry.

"Lose my number."

Jasper's eyes flashed, but the reaction was chilled by an icy expression. "Fine. It's no loss at all."

If Everly hadn't known the truth, she wouldn't have seen the sharp look of pain that crossed Cherry's face before he schooled his expression back into emptiness.

The two of them had heated exchanges about their different approaches to being a shadyr in the past, but this felt different. Had the two of them just broken up?

In the distance, the few hotel guests that remained shuffled around, calling out with confused pleas.

Lian turned to her son. "Callan, I think we've said all that there is to say. Let's gather up what we came for, and the Darkfrey team can deal with the rest of this mess. It's *their* job, after all, isn't it?"

With grunts and muttered curses, the Howell shadyrs each scooped up as much vasmire as they could carry.

Nilson spat at Denny's feet as he passed by. "Told you that you suited being in cleanup crew."

Everly was surprised when Denny didn't bite back. He hoisted a large tentacle over his shoulder and walked out, head hung low.

A cold smile crossed Vonny's face. "So Rylan is still unconscious, is he? I heard you were keeping him alive with monster bits. What a shame. He was a good fighter.

Must be the Howell in him that made him weak."

Lian's spine went ramrod straight. She whirled on her heel and stalked toward Vonny, her face like fire.

She jammed a finger against Vonny's bulky jacket. "The Howell in Rylan is what makes him strong. It was the Darkfreys that broke him."

Then she turned back and strolled away before Vonny could reply.

Vonny's face was thunderous as she pointed at Callan.

"Get your shit and get out," she said in a low, deadly voice. "And when you give up trying to keep your brother alive, go ahead and bring him home to us. Then maybe you'll learn to start leaving things to the experts."

7

Curse you. Vile monster.

Everly barely paid attention to the low hum of conversation between the rest of the campervan's occupants. The night had grown darker and more imposing as Harper steered them back to Boderleth Antiques.

Beast of teeth and stars. A shudder rippled up Everly's spine.

It's like the monster knew me. Knew the dragon.

She needed to talk it out with the others, see if any of them knew what it meant. Rylan's mom was older, had been around the shadyr block a time or ten, so maybe she'd have an answer, or at least know *something*. Right now, though, Callan was busy chewing Denny out for his role in the mess at the hotel.

Everly clutched the cold metal railing and watched Shroudhaven pass out the window, wishing she was anywhere else.

Lian and Rushelle had taken their own car from the hotel to return to Howell House, stating the "gore duty" could be handled by the young people.

Callan made some futile attempts at eliciting remorse from Denny, but overall the mood in the van was much lighter than it had been on the way to the hotel.

Despite everything, their mission had been successful. They were all still alive. Callan and Denny continued ribbing each other, but it almost seemed playful now. Harper laughed from the driver's seat as if she hadn't almost died. Cherry was the only one that remained quiet.

Denny went on a mournful tangent about the desk clerk and how he'd only gone back into the fight to impress her. Apparently, the woman had run off screaming before he could show off properly. Everyone in the van threw things at him until he shut up.

Swinging to park in front of the Boderleth home, Harper cut the engine and remarked, "We made it. Now, please get that foul-smelling monster out of my vehicle, stat."

"You mean the vasmire bits, or this guy?" Callan pointed at Denny.

"Yeah, yeah. Laugh it up, chucklehead. You just lost my help hauling your gore." He clapped his hands once in Callan's face, hopped out the side door, and wandered off down the street.

"*How* can we smell it? The crates are sealed!" Harper grunted.

Callan grinned wryly. "I think we're the ones that smell."

They evacuated the van, taking a moment to breathe fresh air.

A small figure hovered midway up the front path, a petite shadow, hugging themselves.

"I ... um ..." Tammy took a small step forward, then backed off again into the shadows. "Took you all long enough. None of you died then?"

"Don't sound so disappointed," Cherry snapped.

"Hey," Callan barked at him. "Cool it. We did all survive and we can thank Tammy for that."

"Do I get a medal or what?" A subtle, bitter tone laced Tammy's words, one Callan seemed to miss.

"Don't get too cocky. I still want to talk to you about breaking rank and running headlong at that vasmire. Later."

Tammy rolled her eyes. "You're not the brace-leader of me."

Kicking at gravel on the sidewalk, Cherry said, "Wow, with that attitude no wonder we're a mess. I swear we spend more time babysitting her and Denny than getting the job done."

"Cherry, that's enough. It's this kind of in-fighting that made us such an embarrassment in front of the Darkfreys." Callan squared up in front of him, then put a hand gently on his shoulder. "I don't know why you're in such a mood."

Everly and Harper's eyes found each other's, and their lips thinned.

Cherry's voice was low and exhausted. "We'll always be an embarrassment. We're just the runts after all, the unwanted losers and misfits."

"We can be a good team. We did good tonight. For one hell of a ghast-blighted situation, we survived, we ended the beshadowing, and we got what we went for. I know, Ev here stepped in and finished things off for us, but I'd bet my teeth that even without her, we could have gotten there the long way."

"Hope you like soup." Cherry picked up one of the crates and headed toward the house.

Callan sighed and scratched both hands across his scalp, ruffling his long hair.

"Come on, let's finish up so we can wash this stink off us. Everyone take a crate straight to Rylan's room," he ordered. "Swap the new crate out for an old one, and I'll have the fire ready in the backyard to burn the rotting bits."

Tammy took her crate, lifting it easily in her vampire form, then Harper took hers.

Everly offered Callan a sympathetic smile as she picked up the last crate from the campervan.

He huffed a sardonic laugh. "Back at the Darkfreys, braces are carefully selected for skill level and temperament, so each member complements the others. A brace becomes a perfect, efficient unit. I'm trying hard with these guys but maybe we're just an incompatible group of shadyrs. I don't know what else to do."

Everly offered gently, "Maybe remember sometimes that they are humans too?"

Callan's dark eyebrows lowered and he chewed his bottom lip. Then he nodded and wandered off to the backyard.

They'd started their mission at sunset and it was only mid evening by the time the new severed tentacles were in place beside Rylan and the old had been tossed onto Callan's roaring bonfire.

Everly was dead on her feet. All she wanted to do was kick out the Howell team and then stand beneath the shower until the water turned cold and her fingers pruned. Even the mystery of the words the vasmire had spoken wasn't enough to overcome her exhaustion. It could wait until the morning.

Then Callan suggested a drink at Crow's bar to celebrate and debrief, on him. Harper so enthusiastically agreed that Everly wasn't even given a chance to bow out. She also figured this was maybe Callan taking her suggestion, so she should be supportive and join in too.

"I guess you'll need someone to babysit the almost-corpse again," Tammy grumbled.

Everly bristled. *Rylan's not a corpse.*

She turned to glare at the goth-girl, but when she did, there was such vulnerability on her doll-like face, barely concealed beneath the lazy contempt, that her anger dropped away.

"Yeah," Callan nodded.

Tammy's lips twitched like she'd been slapped, revealing her fangs.

Then Callan continued. "I'll call Mom, see if she can keep an eye on him. Team drinks means you're coming with us too."

For a split-second, the scornful mask slipped right off Tammy's face and only the vulnerability remained.

Then her lips closed into a pout. "Sure. Whatever."

With gore duty done, the shadyrs headed back to Howell House, and everyone split off to get cleaned up. Not long later, Rushelle showed up at Everly's front door with her glittery laptop.

"Hey sugar," she said, grinning. "I'm on Rylan watch tonight. Lian's heading to the bar with the others. Said she wanted to have a chat with you. I'll be right here. It's a good chance to get some words in."

"Oh, okay." Everly hovered near the door as Rushelle walked in like she was at home.

Seeing the blonde bombshell fight earlier, it seemed to Everly that Rushelle was a

natural, a force of nature. It was odd that she wasn't part of the team too. She always appeared by Lian's side, willing to help her with anything, but otherwise seemed more interested in her writing than in any kind of shadyr activity.

I guess we can't choose what powers we're born with, but we can choose what we do with our lives.

And now Lian would be at the bar too. Everly could ask about what the vasmire had said. The thought of doing so left her with shivers.

She was considering how she could back out of the festivities, when a freshly showered Harper bounced down the stairs and dragged her out of the house.

After dark, Shroudhaven turned quiet and cold. They didn't pass a single oncoming car on the journey through town, and the dark peaks of the mountains that cradled the buildings looked remote and lonely. Everly might have attributed the overall feeling of desolation to her own emotions, but this was just typical Shroudhaven.

"Take a left here," Everly said as they neared the downtown block where the bar was located.

"Yeah, got it," Harper replied, already turning.

Everly shot her a sidelong glance. "You're becoming awfully comfortable with the roads here."

Harper scoffed, tossing a perfectly curled lock of dark hair from her face. "It's not like it's New York City. Shroudhaven's too small to get lost in."

Looking back out the window, Everly murmured, "Yeah, but there are other ways of getting lost."

Harper found an empty spot along the curb half a block down and pulled into it, muttering under her breath as she attempted to wedge the camper between two small hatchbacks.

"Ugh, I can't get anything right lately!" She was normally a great driver, but the spot she'd chosen was precarious. Everly hopped out and helped guide Harper in from the curb.

As Harper straightened the van a final time, Everly glanced down the street.

It was mostly businesses down this block, including a solicitor specializing in wills, a dodgy looking small-claims lawyer, and a print shop advertising discounts for lost pet posters.

At nine in the evening, they were all long closed for the day, and this late, very few pedestrians could be found on the streets thanks to the unofficial curfew of sundown. Since returning to Shroudhaven, Everly had spent more time out after dark than she ever had growing up there.

Across the street from their parking spot, Everly saw movement in the shadows and jumped, her mind immediately going to eidolghasts.

Harper joined her on the pavement. "What? What is it?"

Everly squinted into the darkness and then breathed a sigh of relief. "It's Cardboard Box Barry. I mean, Barry."

The rail-thin, white-haired man stood outside his large cardboard box, swaying as if to a silent song. His long, braided beard brushed back and forth over his heavy-metal shirt.

Harper stared at him, the streetlight setting her profile into sharp relief. "You know what's weird? I haven't seen a single other homeless person in Shroudhaven. Is it terrible that my first thought is that they don't last very long, what with the you-know-*monster*-whats?"

Harper was right, Everly hadn't seen anyone else either. "Barry's been around as long as I can remember though."

She shivered, watching for a moment longer, wondering. Barry twisted his hips and swung his arms to an unheard song. Then, behind him, another form appeared, crawling from behind the blanket covering his box.

Barry stopped dancing and opened his eyes, holding out a hand to help the man to his feet. The newcomer had pale hair, and wore khaki chinos and a polo shirt. He didn't appear to be another homeless man, given the glint of a gold watch on his wrist.

"Does Barry often have visitors to his, um, box?" Harper asked softly.

Everly watched the stranger glance furtively around, offer Barry a brief embrace, and then take off at a quick walk down the street.

As he vanished around the corner, she said, "I really don't know."

"I'm not even going to start to guess what that was about then," Harper said.

A gust of blustery wind raced past Everly. She pulled her bomber jacket closed against the cold as she fell into step beside Harper, surreptitiously glancing at Barry again. He'd vanished, presumably into his box.

The Crow's Nest had occupied the same space in a plain, flat-fronted building for as long as Everly remembered. Its tall, arched wooden door was decorated with iron studs and elegant, black iron hinges. If it weren't for the glittery golden letters spelling the name, the place would look less like a hole-in-the-wall bar and more like a dungeon.

Harper latched onto Everly's arm. "I hope Crowea makes us that concoction she made last time. That might have been the best cocktail I've *ever* had. I think it was the added witchy magic."

Everly opened the heavy door and motioned Harper to precede her, then followed her best friend into a burst of warm, sage-scented air.

The Crow's Nest might have been boxy and boring on the outside, but the inside was a different story. An array of antique lamps graced end tables between mismatched armchairs, couches, and age-stained dining tables.

Colorful scarfs were draped over the lampshades, spilling a soft, warm glow through the room. Fantasy paintings and brightly colored Celtic tapestries hung from the walls and angled ceilings. Curtains and low bookshelves loaded down with books, trinkets, and witchy memorabilia separated the wash of furniture into some semblance of order.

"There's a Mermaid in My Lighthouse" played low on the sound system.

There's a mermaid in my lighthouse, and her heart belongs to me.

There's a mermaid in my lighthouse, and she's staring out to sea.

Like Cardboard Box Barry, just another backdrop to life in Shroudhaven.

Callan, Cherry, and Tammy already occupied a curtained-off space near the corner of the room, and Lian stood at the long timber bar, chatting with Crowea.

Other than the Howell team, only one other group sat drinking on the other side of the room. Everly didn't recognize their faces as anyone she'd seen since getting involved with the shadyrs, but she definitely recognized the Darkfrey crest on their matching shirts.

Great, Everly thought, wincing. *Hopefully they leave us alone.*

"Hey, girls," Lian said, leaning her hip on the edge of the bar to turn and greet them. "There's already a pitcher of Crow's signature blend at the table. I'll meet you over there."

"Welcome back, babies." Crowea grinned and leaned on her glove-covered arms on the bar.

She was a tall woman with a wild blonde/gray curls and a penchant for long, flowing dresses. Though that wasn't the most striking thing about the old Wiccan.

Harper gave the bar matron a friendly wave and then grabbed Everly's arm and tugged her toward the team.

Under her breath, she whispered, "Okay, she's even more creepy the second time around."

"It's the tooth," Everly whispered back.

"No, really?" Harper sassed.

At some point, Crowea had come up against an eidolghast and lived to tell the tale … but she'd walked away from the encounter with a sharp fang stuck in her left eye.

Scarring fanned out from the tooth, intermingling with the wrinkles on her wise face, giving her an almost villainesque appearance. But she wasn't a villain. In fact, she'd saged Everly so thoroughly the first time they met, that Everly had walked away thinking she herself was, in fact, the villain.

Luckily, Crowea had already fallen back into conversation with Lian, and Everly wasn't subjected to another full body smudging.

"About time you ladies showed up," Cherry said as they approached. "We were just discussing whether or not to leave you any alcohol."

Tammy squinted at him. "What? We were not."

"Okay, fine, I was internally debating whether or not to leave *any* of you any alcohol," Cherry said, pouring himself another glass.

Harper dropped her giant handbag onto the floor next to one of the two empty armchairs and flopped onto the overstuffed cushion. "Sorry we're late."

Cherry gave Harper an indulgent smile, but it didn't really meet his eyes. "I bet Bellsy getting ready is a long and meticulous process."

Despite his flame red-hair, he seemed colorless and subdued tonight, in basic sweatpants and a black sweater. Nothing like his normal, crisp red-and-white racer jacket look. Everly didn't think it was an accidental pick. He was mourning the end of his relationship with Jasper.

Harper returned his smile. Hers didn't reach her eyes, either.

"I also had some open wounds to bandage up, but sure, lets blame the makeup."

Everly shot Harper a worried glance, then slipped into the other armchair, sinking into the soft depression in the cushions until she felt like her knees were above her head.

"What'd we miss?"

"Just basic debrief stuff." Callan picked up an empty glass, offering it to Harper as he reached for the pitcher.

"By which he means, a very *cheery* pep talk about our team tactics, and our *attitudes*," Tammy droned.

After filling Harper's glass, Callan offered Everly one too, with a side of a long-suffering expression.

Everly shook her head and held up a hand, indicating she didn't want any of Crow's potent mixture. She'd had a taste out of curiosity last time, but she had a volatile relationship with alcohol after seeing how it had destroyed her mother's body, mind, and moral code.

Everly's head was such a swirl of dark thoughts tonight that drinking seemed like the last thing she should do.

Tammy picked up an empty glass and held it out. "I'll have hers."

"No, you won't." Callan pointed at a second pitcher across the table. "You've got your mocktail over there."

Everly raised her eyebrows at Callan. As Rylan's younger brother, he must only just be barely legal drinking age himself. Harper was probably the oldest of them all at twenty-one.

"Joy," Tammy muttered. "I was better off back in the dream-trap. Could have died happy and dream-drunk, but nooooo, someone had to go and spoil it."

"Thanks for that, by the way," Cherry offered. "Sorry I was being bitchy before. We wouldn't have gotten out of there without you."

Harper lifted her glass. "To the hero of the night!"

Tammy shot daggers at Harper, as though expecting a sarcasm that wasn't there. Then everyone else joined in the toast.

Tammy clutched her refilled mocktail glass to her chest, a red tinge rising up her neck and into her cheeks. She had the hood of her black jacket up over her head, and sank back into it like a turtle.

"It wasn't anything. I didn't even get to come back and finish the fight."

"We had Everly—wondrous one-woman-light-show—there for that." Cherry lifted his glass again.

"Which I couldn't have done if not for Tammy getting out and sending help," Everly deflected, just as uncomfortable with being singled out as Tammy.

Callan extended one long leg and nudged Tammy's black boot with his toes. "Quit beating yourself up. You saved the day."

Tammy flickered slightly, then groaned out a fake-barfing sound in response.

Cherry leaned over the arm of his chair toward Harper. "Truth though, I am so upset that I didn't get to see you go all lumberjack with that axe."

Harper huffed. "I know, right? Do you think it's really a good look for me, though? I've been wondering about training with weapons more, and my heart keeps getting drawn to dual-wielding sickles. Ooh, or maybe a whip sword!"

While Tammy and Callan argued about the legitimacy of Tammy's actions, Harper and Cherry continued to get louder and louder about best weapon options, both for killing eidolghasts, and for perfecting Bellsy's look.

Everly listened, observing the here and now as she worked on her calm. The tightness at the corner of Cherry's eyes spoke to the hurt he was hiding. Everly had noticed that since she sat down, he hadn't once pulled his phone out of his pocket, when before he was *always* texting Jasper.

As for Tammy, there was something different about her when she talked to Callan. Her sullen glare had softened, and instead of staring at the wall or ground as she often did, she made eye contact with Callan as he piled on the praise.

And, Everly could hardly believe it, there was even a tiny *smile*.

Lian rejoined the group, carrying a mug of something steaming hot. She settled onto the couch next to Callan and crossed her legs before taking a dainty sip. She'd changed out of her pajamas, but still wore a long, chunky-knit cardigan and sheathed sword.

The memory of the older woman slicing so deftly with that weapon still surprised Everly.

This was a lady who changed into her pajamas by sunset. She had probably been curled up half asleep with her yappy little dog Birdie when they called her round to watch Rylan so they could leave urgently on their mission.

And yet she was so formidable, when required. Much like Rushelle, she had her priorities decided. She'd never wanted her sons to give their whole lives to shadyr duty as the Darkfreys did. She wanted for them a life as normal as possible. For some reason, that had fallen apart when their father died, and she had only just gotten them back. One of them broken.

Everly offered a small smile to Lian and took control of her nerves. "You wanted to talk?"

Lian took a sip from her mug and nodded. "Callan told me he saw Rylan, that they all did."

"Oh, yeah. In the dream." Everly let out a sigh of relief.

She wasn't being accused of being a monster.

"He's really there," she muttered as though to herself. "How are we going to get him out? We don't even know how he's there, or what you are."

"Actually, about that ..." Everly inhaled deeply and rushed out her next words. "Something happened during the fight that I wanted to talk to you about."

Lian inclined her head. "I'm listening."

"Did you know that vasmires could speak?"

The two conversations taking place around them petered off as Everly's friends clued into hers.

Lian nodded. "Yes, it's been thought they have ways to communicate. But it's some kind of eidolghast language. Only other monsters seem to understand it. We haven't exactly had a chance to study it and learn over the centuries."

Everly swallowed hard. *Only monsters understand it.* As if she didn't worry enough she was one of them.

"*I* understood it. One of them spoke to me."

Lian lowered her mug to her knee, her face impassive. "What did it say to you?"

"It called me the 'beast of teeth and stars.'"

"That's ... something," said Callan.

"Yeah, but what?" Everly asked.

Lian stared, her gaze sharp as though it could dissect Everly. "It called you that, like a name? Was that all it said?"

"Pretty much," Everly murmured with a shrug.

"Is that what Everly is, or has in her, or whatever? The beast of teeth and stars? What even is that?" Harper rambled.

"It was so long ago, but I think ..." Lian lifted the mug to her lips, her eyes going unfocused. "I don't know that phrase, not exactly, but there is an artifact at the Darkfrey Estate with a similar name. The Bane of Teeth and Stars."

"That can't be a coincidence," Cherry said, leaning into the conversation.

"But what is it? What am I?" Everly's voice was breathy, anxiety building within, compressing her lungs.

Lian placed a hand on Everly's knee. "I'm sorry, I don't know. That's the only thing I know of that's similar to what the creature called you. It's an ancient shadyr artifact, stored beneath the estate in the protected archives."

"Where you plundered your sword?" Callan pried.

"Slander." Lian covered a sly grin by sipping her drink again. "I may or may not have *obtained* my sword there."

Callan's grin widened for the briefest moment as he and his mother faced off, then he went on. "Can we assume this artifact has something to do with Everly? With the weird light powers?"

Lian's eyes narrowed, and she chewed at her lower lip. "It's not exactly a common phrase. There is merit in the idea that whatever causes Everly's powers might have something to do with the Bane."

"So, how about we 'obtain' this thing, too," Harper suggested. "See what we can learn about it, or from it?"

Lian gave her an amused smile. "It's worth considering. But it and anything related to it are Darkfrey property and well protected."

She polished off her drink. "Let me think on it, maybe ask around a bit. I still have some connections. But that's enough for tonight. It's late and time for me to leave you youngsters to it."

Wiping her palms on her jeans, she stood up. "Be careful on your way home."

Callan shot up awkwardly, as though he were about to either salute or kiss his mother goodbye but couldn't decide which. The rest of the group bid her goodnight, then she wove through the maze of shelves, chairs, and tables, disappearing out the front door.

"This is awesome. We have a name, and a lead," Harper said with great enthusiasm.

"A name no one knows except that one lead," Everly countered.

"Pretty cool name, though," Tammy mumbled. The slight turn at the corner of her lip seemed almost sincere for once.

That smile dropped quickly when Callan reached over to refill Harper's drink, and she touched him on the wrist as a silent thank you. Tammy clenched her ink-black hands into fists and folded them under her armpits.

"Hey, thanks," Everly said, leaning toward the scowling girl.

"It's just a dumb name."

"I meant for saving my life, all our lives. I know you're not a huge fan of your power. I know it seems weird and hard and wrong. But you got it under control and kicked ass."

Tammy's lips twitched, but she rolled her eyes. "Projecting, much?"

Everly chuckled and lifted a hand for a high-five. "Go us, team freaks."

Tammy narrowed her eyes, assessing Everly.

"Don't leave me hanging, it's seriously awkward."

Tammy huffed, smiled, and released a dark hand to slap Everly's palm.

A flash of light burst between their touch.

A crack of thunder and howl of nightmares. Sparks shot out from where their skin made contact. Everly hissed at the sudden pain and yanked her hand back from Tammy's as the entire bar was plunged into darkness.

8

The bar fell silent. Every eye in the place turned to the source of the explosion. Like slow-motion rain, mist descended over the tables and chairs in the darkness, obscuring everything and everyone except for those closest to Everly. Tammy's face scrunched up, mirroring the socked-in-the-gut sensation Everly was hit with.

From the general direction of the bar, Crowea's thick, raspy voice spoke, "Oh my stars."

"What just happened?" Harper shone her phone around their group like a flashlight.

An icy breeze filtered past Everly, shifting her pale hair. It tickled her skin as if someone had brushed their fingers against her. Crow's collection of wind chimes jangled in a mournful tone, each one somehow keeping time with the others in a hideous symphony.

Everly's palm tingled with a million pins and needles in the aftermath of the high five. Her hand still hovered in the air. She jerked her arm back and tucked her palm against her stomach, horrified.

Was that the dragon's light?

Had it manifested somehow? Without her knowledge or permission? Just the idea filled her with bone-deep horror. It was every nightmare she'd been harboring since the moment she realized a monster lived inside her. She shivered, and she didn't know if it was from the growing chill in the room or her own fears.

Tammy groaned and slouched in her chair, tucking both of her blackened hands back into her armpits. "I'm so sorry. My hands are *cursed.*"

Surprised, Everly turned her gaze on Tammy. The shadyr thought *she* was the issue? Everly opened her palms and looked down at her hands, a churning pit opening in her stomach.

"I don't think it was you, Tammy. Or, not *just* you."

"It is me. It's always me. I'm always going to be cursed. I ruin everything I touch."

Callan appeared out of the mist, kneeling in front of Tammy's chair. "Not true. Remember, you're the hero tonight. The world needs you. *We* need you."

Tammy's head shook in small, shuddering movements from side to side.

"All right, party's over," Crowea called.

Feet shuffled nearby on the patchwork of rugs covering the floor, then a high-powered beam of light cut through the misty darkness, aimed at the front door.

"Everyone out. Make your way carefully to the exit."

A chorus of groans filled the bar, but the clink of glasses and the scrape of chairs proved the occupants were obeying their bar matron. Everly stood, her elbow brushing Harper's.

"You okay?" Harper asked in a low voice, taking hold of Everly's jacket sleeve.

Everly shrugged, her mouth too dry to speak.

As one, their group moved in the general direction of the front door. They were intercepted halfway there by Crowea. She formed from the shadowy fog like a demon, the eidolghast fang in her eye socket and the scars around it harsh and unforgiving. She had a fat roll of sage burning in one hand, and a military grade flashlight in the other.

"You children all right?" she asked, her one eye sweeping over Everly.

Tammy's face held no emotion and her voice was flat. "I'm sorry, Crow. This is my fault. My stupid cursed hands. Can I stay and help you clean up?"

"No, baby, I got it." Crowea tucked the flashlight under her arm and put a hand on Tammy's shoulder.

The elbow-length gloves she normally wore were gone.

Tammy's eyes popped wide and she tried to back away. "Don't, I'm cursed, you—"

"Hush baby, it's okay. Your pain, however deep and piercing, is not a curse."

Everly exhaled roughly. What was Crowea doing? Was she somehow reading Tammy right now, with her psychometry? Her power to know things about objects and beings she placed her hands on?

The power she flat out refused to use on me.

A tear spilled down Tammy's cheek and she fled the building.

Crowea's singular gaze swept across the rest of them and landed on Everly. "Keep an eye on that one."

As she waved them toward the front door, it was unclear whether she was instructing Everly to keep an eye on Tammy, or the others to keep an eye on her.

"Don't worry about all this, babies. A bit of smudging, some banishment charms, a new protection ward, we'll be good as new."

As they filed from the bar and into the cold night, Crowea's shrewd gaze remained on Everly. The dungeon-like door slammed shut behind them as they gathered on the sidewalk outside.

Tammy was leaning on the wall in the shadows of Crow's Nest, and Callan sighed when he saw her. "At least she didn't try and run home on her own."

"Sounds like she's done a lot of running tonight already," Cherry added, softly.

Across the street, the uniformed Darkfrey group glared back at them as they left. Everly tried to ignore them, but their looks of judgement were red-hot brands on her skin.

Callan stepped closer to Harper. "You guys want to come back to our house? We could pop some beers and watch bad movies."

Exhaustion washed over Everly, but she didn't miss the twitch of Tammy's lips and wrinkle of her button nose. The goth girl folded her blackened hands and turned away.

"We're going to go home," Everly said, then to Harper, she added, "if that's okay."

Harper linked her arm through Everly's and nodded. "Yep. Maybe another time. This has all been some swell life-threatening fun, but we should really go and relieve Rush from Rylan watch."

The group shared goodbyes, and the two girls headed for the campervan, faces down against the sharp wind rolling in off the mountains. They were silent until they'd gotten in, where Harper locked the doors and asked, "So ... What happened?"

Everly stared at her still tingling fingers. "I'm not sure. Tammy and I high-fived, and it caused some kind of ... reaction."

Harper turned the key in the ignition, her face thoughtful. "Have you ever come into contact with Tammy before?"

Everly thought back over the past few weeks. "No, I don't think so. She's not much of a toucher."

"Like the opposite of Rush," Harper gasped with enthusiasm. "Maybe when Tammy got cursed, her personality split in two and became like a light and dark version of herself!"

Everly snorted a chuckle through her nose. "That sounds weird, even for Shroudhaven, and also Rush is like thirty years older than Tammy. We can probably chalk Tammy's lack of touchy-feely-ness down to her being a troubled teen."

Harper pulled away from the curb and smirked, clearly proud she'd provoked Everly into a laugh. "Or that she knows weird stuff happens when she touches things. Maybe it was just Tammy. She seemed pretty sure about that."

"Maybe," Everly murmured.

Whatever it was, she was just glad no one got hurt.

Everly rested her forehead against the window and watched the streets pass the rest of the way to her old family home, feeling sorry for herself.

It wasn't a normal emotion for her. She'd learned early on that life was hard, and it was her job to put on her big girl panties and keep moving. But everything had changed so fast these past couple of weeks. Even Everly herself. She just wanted to go back to the way things were. When things were normal.

But if she'd been expecting any kind of normalcy back at Boderleth Antiques,

she was sadly mistaken.

Rushelle sat on the front steps, illuminated by her laptop screen. Once the van was parked, the woman closed her computer and met them on the front garden path.

"Had to come and write outside," she said, grinning happily. "Oh boy are things going wonky bonkers in there!"

Everly and Harper cast side-eyes at each other.

Rushelle fanned a hand limply at them. "Oh, nothing serious, just a bit distracting. Although it did give me some ideas for a new book! *A Ghost Lover for the Far King.*"

"Great, another one for my to-be-read pile!" Harper laughed.

"Have a good night, ladies," Rushelle cooed, and wrapped her long arms around them both at once, squeezing them in, then wandered off down the street.

"Well, this is our first night with spanking fresh eidolghast bits in the house. Shall we go and see what Rush was talking about?" Harper said.

"I'm not sleeping out in the rose-bushes again," Everly replied.

Around on the creaky wooden porch, she shoved open the back door. A thin fog rolled down the stairs from the second floor. On their level, it had settled into a hip-high cloud down the hallway, stretching in an ocean of pillowy white from the back door through the rest of the house.

Everly hit the switch to turn on the candle-shaped lights that lined the narrow hallway, but their dull bulbs barely penetrated the gloom. Coupled with the brown floral wallpaper, they almost seemed to make everything even darker than if she hadn't turned them on at all.

Harper blanched and waded into the fog so that it moved like liquid around her legs. "This permanent smoke machine thing is not my favorite part of having dead monster chunks around."

Everly locked the back door. "You have a favorite part of having dead things around?"

"Well, it's not the smell either. But keeping Rylan alive is good and watching the little googly eyes you give him every time you walk by his room is a solid bonus. Five stars."

"I'm glad my remnants of a childhood crush on what is now a non-responsive stranger is entertaining to you," Everly replied.

She reached past Harper and flicked the old-fashioned switch on the wall to illuminate the kitchen.

"He seemed rather responsive to you in the beshadowed dream-world—*what in the fresh hell?*"

All the kitchen cabinets were open and swinging, as if in an invisible breeze.

"Okay, that is pretty wonky bonkers," Everly murmured as she crept into the kitchen.

"Are we being haunted now? How exciting would that be?"

"Not exciting," Everly said. "Not at all. But I think this is just the minor beshadowing effect. Like that's what beshadowings are—haunted weirdness caused by eidolghasts."

She grabbed for the first cabinet door and gently closed it, then waited several seconds to see if it would stay that way.

When it did, she started closing the rest. "I don't know, Harper, maybe you should go stay at Howell House. These fresh eidolghast pieces are doing way more than the old ones."

"Not gonna happen. And quit acting like you aren't just as human as me." Harper opened the fridge and pulled out a yogurt. "You want one?"

Everly nodded, closed the last cabinet, and accepted a tub and spoon from her friend. "That big vasmire is probably extra potent too. It was strong enough in life to beshadow an entire hotel full of people super quick, along with its friend. Even its dead bits are going to be a problem. I don't want to see you get hurt."

"I'm not going to be. Not by this try-hard poltergeist, anyway. A little bit of beshadowing doesn't scare me." Harper peeled the top off her yogurt and spooned herself a large mouthful.

Everly sighed. *That's what scares me.*

Harper had adapted to the weirdness in Shroudhaven *way* too easily and had been approaching it all with her usual high-achiever attitude. But the longer they stayed, the stronger Everly's sense of foreboding became. For the first time, she could understand Rylan's need to distance himself from the people around him, to protect the humans in his life. To protect *her*.

"The only thing that worries me is if the cops show up here for any reason," Harper quipped as she headed for the door. "Imagine trying to explain why we have a body in the upstairs bedroom surrounded by chucks of giant monster-calamari? Or cabinets with minds of their own?"

She motioned behind Everly with a grin.

Everly glanced back and groaned. The cabinets were all open again, swaying in that invisible breeze.

She turned away from the dancing doors, too tired to deal with it again. "I hope he wakes up soon. This life has become a little too weird for me."

In the hallway, Harper paused by the antiques shop door. "Did you have any luck with the carousel music box?"

Taken aback, Everly frowned. "Oh, um, yeah. Early this morning, while you were still asleep. It just had a gear knocked loose. Didn't take much to open it up and put things right."

Since they'd been in Shroudhaven, the two of them had cleaned every living area of her old home—though Everly had steered them away from tackling the basement or the attic just yet. Her childhood phobias ran deep.

Once the house was mostly done, they'd turned their attention to the antiques store.

The place had been boarded up for nearly sixteen years with everything exactly as her father had left it the day he died.

They were tag teaming the project, with Everly repairing and cleaning the better looking antiques while Harper used her skills at sales and marketing to sell them online. As far as Everly was concerned, it was a temporary arrangement, but one that they could be equal partners in.

"Perfect. I think it might be a real collector's item," Harper said excitedly. "I did some research with the pics I took last night. I have a ticket in with this big antiques website to help with verifying it. The thing's over a hundred years old, and the last one in the public eye sold for over twenty thou."

Everly blinked. "What? No way."

"Your dad left you a treasure trove, Ev." She took a few steps toward the door that separated the living area from the store. "I'm going to go do a few mock-ups for the carousel, see if I can't get a stunning portrait to woo potential buyers. You coming?"

"Not tonight." Everly loved working alongside Harper, but she didn't have any energy left. "I'm going to call it a night."

"Suit yourself. Pancakes in the morning, my treat."

"Like you'll get out of bed before me," Everly teased, then watched as her best friend disappeared into the antiques store. She still found it weird to be coming and going through that door. Her entire life had been spent pretending that door, and what lay beyond it, didn't exist.

After her father's death inside the shop, Everly's mother had locked it up and left it to rot. Day after day, Everly had passed that door as if it weren't even there—dark mahogany wood, a frosted glass window covered in dust and grime, and an old skeleton keyhole that kept it closed forever.

Not forever, Everly thought, standing for a moment to listen to Harper puttering around on the other side.

All the tragedies this house had seen, all the neglect Everly had experienced, all the secrets hidden—one day, they'd be nothing but history. Everly would sell the house to someone who could breathe new life into the place and bring a family to fill it with light and laughter.

Everly finished off her yogurt and it sat heavily in her stomach. She felt a pang of regret for the childhood she wished she could have had, then headed upstairs, fighting against the flow of fog, and the chilling fear that there were only more tragedies still to come.

9

Everly didn't really need a second shower that night, but *wanted* one in order to chase away the icy butterflies that had made a home in her chest.

Tonight, she'd controlled her dragon. They'd beaten a beshadowing and provided Rylan with what he needed to stay alive. Monster parts for days.

But how many more times would they have to repeat this? How many more times *could* they?

They'd barely survived, even with calling in backup, even with using the ravenous power within Everly. What if Rylan didn't wake up this week, this month, this year? How long would it take before everyone had enough of hunting Vasmire for his life support?

I won't ever give up on him. I'll keep him alive, no matter what.

Everly towel-dried her hair and checked the bedroom. Harper still hadn't come upstairs from the shop, though with the way she nitpicked every last thing about her photography setups, Everly assumed she'd be there half the night. Inching the lighting to the left. Trying different colored gels. Finding the perfect angle to show off the carousel's bright colors.

Harper hadn't earned her status as an influencer without the eye, talent, and hours worked late into the night to back it up.

Dressed in clean leggings and an oversize, threadbare t-shirt, Everly snuck downstairs with a gurgling hunger in her belly. Her own hunger, this time, and not the all-consuming hunger of the light. They had missed dinner, and one yogurt wasn't enough of a replacement.

She tiptoed past the antiques shop so she wouldn't disturb the artist at work, then pushed through the door into the kitchen, not bothering with the light switch.

The cabinets all hung open, though they were no longer swaying with their synchronized, haunted dance. Everly took a moment to close them all, again, and glared at them in a silent dare to pop open one more time. She'd take the damn things off their hinges if she had to.

Everly pilfered a granola bar from the box on the kitchen counter and stood over the sink, munching on the chewy chocolate and oats mixture. She hoped it would be enough to quell her stomach so she could sleep, although the churning inside her wasn't only from hunger.

She had almost lost Harper tonight. An eidolghast spoke to her, calling *her* a monster. And whatever that thing was between her and Tammy.

How has life gotten so crazy?

The lacy white curtains hung open over the window, revealing the quiet street outside and the dull glow of streetlights. All the neighbors were tucked inside their dark houses, seemingly sound asleep by the lack of glowing windows.

Trees shifted and bent beneath the breeze, and even through the old, wavy glass, Everly could hear the clack of their branches beating against one another.

Movement broke the stillness.

Everly stopped chewing and leaned forward, her gaze raking the street. The night Rylan had been attacked, she'd watched him get struck down through this very window.

At first, she'd thought he'd been fighting a tall man in a gray cloak, but things had been … off. She knew now, of course, what a vasmire was, and how they lurked around Shroudhaven.

But instead of a vasmire slinking through the shadows on her street, she saw a familiar long, sleek tail and a flash of predatory eyes pass through the streetlight, then vanish down the sidewalk next to her house.

The cougar.

He was one part of all this craziness Everly actually liked.

Everly smiled and hurried to the fridge, pulling a slim packet of ground beef from the bottom drawer. She'd picked up several slabs of meat a few days before just for such an occasion. She ripped the plastic off and carried it to the back door on silent feet.

The smoke of the gore-burning bonfire, still smoldering in the bare far end corner of the yard wafted to Everly as she stepped outside.

The cougar lurked near the old, overgrown swing set, peering out through the weeds and ivy. His tail flicked and he marked Everly's every movement as she stepped down off the porch and walked up to him cautiously.

He'd clearly been young when he'd died, because he was still much smaller than a normal cougar. His coat still showed some of the spots juveniles have which are lost as they matured. He was still big enough to be a threat, but considering he had been brought back to some kind of undead life by Nell, Everly wasn't sure he'd ever grow another inch.

Everly crouched and set the plate of meat in front of him. "Heya, Zozo."

He leaned down and sniffed at the meat, then moved up to snuffle at her fingers. He'd been getting tamer by the day. The first few times she'd brought him food, he'd run off when she got too close, and she'd left his plate in the weeds for him.

But still he kept coming back, always nearby, as though drawn to Everly. And still his hazy visage haunted her dreams. Connected, somehow.

Zozo snuffled her fingers, then dug into his meal, snapping at the bloody meat with sharp teeth.

"You'll never believe the day I've had," Everly told him, settling down on her knees.

Though he didn't look up at her, he huffed as if to let her know he was listening.

"You wouldn't judge me, would you, if it turned out that I was a monster?"

A low, satisfied growl rumbled from Zozo as he ate.

A lump formed in Everly's throat. If she could tell her zombie cougar friend all her worries and fears, could she tell the others?

But before she could open her mouth to speak again, the back door creaked open and the porch light flashed on.

Harper's voice called, "Ev? Is that you out there?"

With the barest rustle of grass and leaves, Zozo was gone.

Everly frowned after him, sad to see him go, then got to her feet and waved. "Yeah, it's me. I'm here."

Harper stood on the porch, haloed by the dim glow of the candle lamps in the hallway behind her. She'd pulled her long dark hair into a messy bun that looked effortlessly classy. One suspicious eyebrow lifted toward her hairline.

"Whatcha doing?" she sing-songed, in a tone that also held an unsaid *"Should I be worried?"*

Everly walked back up the cracked concrete path, dodging weeds higher than her ankles. One of these days, she'd need to tackle this jungle. For now, though, it gave Zozo plenty of places to hide.

But how would she explain to Harper that she was feeding an undead cougar?

She could already imagine Harper wanting in on a pet kitty, no matter how Frankensteined. But just because Everly felt some strange connection to the beast, didn't mean it was safe.

She hopped up the three shallow stairs leading to the porch. "There's a stray cat I've seen around. I've been leaving it food."

Lying to her best friend left a gritty feeling in her mouth. But Everly didn't like the way Harper had adjusted to the dangers of life here, or the way she dove headfirst into the paranormal as if it were her goal to experience it all, as if it were just another thing to master. The more Everly could keep her separated from that world, the better.

The last thing she wanted was for Harper to get attached to Zozo.

Like I have? I shouldn't have named him.

Neither of them should be forming attachments there. Because as soon as they were able, as soon as Rylan was awake and well, they would leave Shroudhaven and all

this danger behind forever.

Unless I'm one of the dangerous things.

Harper's eyebrows lifted a little higher. "I'm not sure if leaving meat out for random wildlife is a smart thing to do in this area, babe. But I love the sentiment."

"How'd your shoot go?" Everly grabbed her elbow and tugged her back into the misty house.

"I got some beautiful shots of the carousel. I'll list it and start marketing tomorrow. This one is going to be such a winner."

"Great." Everly clicked the deadbolt into place behind them. "I'm going to check on Rylan one more time before I go crash."

"Mm hm." Harper's full lips flattened into a smirk. "I bet he can't wait to see you again too."

"What do you mean?"

"I mean he's clearly into you."

Everly huffed. "He's in a coma. I don't think you can tell anything he's into right now."

Harper stuck her tongue out. "Stop being obtuse. I mean when we were in the beshadowed dream, duh. He looked at you like you were the only person in the room."

"He's probably just gotten used to ignoring other people since being in my dreams, because normally any other people aren't real," Everly pointed out.

She led the way up the stairs, fog parting around her ankles, weirdly warm in places in a way that felt even creepier than the cold spots.

Harper slid her hand up the banister with a dancer's flourish. "The way he looked at you was real. Like every muscle in his body—which is a whole gorgeous bunch by the way—seemed to tense up when you were near."

"In irritation, maybe?" Everly rebutted.

"Did you not hear me telling you to stop being obtuse? Should I say it louder?" Harper cupped hands around her mouth as though about to yell.

Everly lifted a hand in front of her. "Rylan just wants me out of this town and out of his life, and he's made that perfectly clear. He's changed so much from the boy I used to lo—know."

Everly coughed, a futile attempt at covering up her slip.

Harper tilted her head innocently and fluttered her long-lashed eyelids. "Well, if I were you, I'd be taking this remarkable opportunity you've been presented to get to know him again. Like, I'm surprised you haven't gone to sleep already. Honestly, now I've seen what you see in your dreams, I'm surprised you're awake as often as you are."

Everly blushed. She had to admit, she spent many of her waking hours counting down to when she could fall into her dreams with Rylan again. But she didn't have to admit it out loud.

Having Rylan all to herself in her dreams was a bad, guilty sort of pleasure Everly refused to indulge in.

"It would be much better to see him up and around again in the real world," Everly said.

Whether he likes me or not.

"Obviously that is the ideal outcome, but don't dental-check your gift horse, you know?" At the top of the stairs, Harper air-kissed Everly's cheek. "Sweet dreams!"

Everly stuck her tongue out in reply.

Harper wriggled her fingers in a wave and took over the bathroom for her nighttime facial cleansing ritual.

Everly stopped by her old bedroom to peek in at Rylan.

He lay as still as stone in the fall of golden light from the hallway, his skin pale, and his breaths apparently nonexistent. The fog was even denser in his room, billowing from the crates of dead vasmire bits and turning every corner dark. Shadows crept in nightmarish patterns along the walls, shuddering and slithering like snakes.

Everly steeled herself and ignored the weirdness as she ventured into the room. At Rylan's side, she placed the tips of her fingers beneath his nose. His soft breath fanned over her skin, sending goosebumps up along her arms, and her heart into a gallop.

She pulled her hand away again before the urge to stroke his cheek became too strong.

He was still breathing. That was all she needed to know.

That was all she could hope for right now, but didn't know how long it would last.

10

The boxy old TV showed Rylan hurrying down a sidewalk, his hands shoved in his pockets and his eyes trained on Everly through the screen. As he moved closer, the streetlamps behind him went out, chasing him with a sticky, malevolent darkness.

"I'm asleep. This is a dream," Everly said out loud.

The dreamlike haze resting over her senses vanished. Without significant effort, the setting of the dream would do whatever her subconscious felt like doing, but at least she would have control of herself.

Everly found herself in the living room, on the couch where she'd fallen asleep. She sat up and shoved the sleeping bag away, putting her feet down on wet floors.

Water poured through the open doorway behind the couch, and lily pads floated past her on the currents. Hundreds of frogs swam and hopped around, jiggly and shiny, filling the wet space.

Zozo splashed after the largest of the vivid green plants, batting at it with one of his oversized paws. He was still ghostly in the dream world. Everly wished the cougar could speak, so she had some idea of whether it was really its conscious self, like Rylan was, or just an ever-present dream figment, like Rylan used to be in her dreams before his near-death experience.

She guessed it wasn't the cougar's complete life essence trapped in here like Rylan, since it was still able to move around normally out in the real world.

Looking up at the ceiling, she could see her dragon turning lazy circles in the sky above, even though the roof wasn't transparent. She simply *knew* it was up there, so entwined with herself she could sense its motion, its feelings. It almost seemed to be sulking at the control she'd exerted over it.

That's right. Just keep your distance.

On the television screen, the darkness chasing Rylan had solidified into black water, filling the world behind him as he increased his pace to a sprint. He grew larger, his face taking up the entire television as the inky liquid filled in around him. He reached out, his hands coming through the glass.

Everly lunged forward and grabbed a hand in both of hers, pulling back with all her strength. Frogs squirmed around her knees and despite knowing it was a dream, Everly hoped she wasn't crushing any.

Rylan's head and shoulders pulled free of the saturated TV world, and he gasped a deep breath. His hands were slick and Everly's grip slipped. She fell back onto the lounge.

With a slurp and splash, Rylan hauled the rest of his body out of the television. He rolled face first, doing a graceful somersault across the lily-pad floor that thumped him right up against Everly's legs. A few frogs that had been in his path shook themselves off and hopped away.

Dripping wet, Rylan glanced up at her and remarked, "Your mind is a terrifying place, Boderleth."

"Tell me yours is much better," Everly shot back with a grin.

"Touché." He wore the same hooded jacket and jeans he'd worn the night the vasmire nearly killed him.

He hopped to his feet in one smooth movement, his body all hard angles and grace, and then turned to dump himself onto the couch beside her. Dark liquid clung to his eyelashes and made his clothing cling in messy wrinkles to his skin. Droplets sparkled as he rubbed his head and face, then he leaned back with a tired groan.

Everly readjusted to make room for him, and as he hit the cushions, she was struck with the acute sense that she felt naked.

Oh my ghost, don't be naked, don't be naked.

She glanced down at herself and sighed in relief to see she wore a close approximation of what she'd gone to sleep in. Only the threadbare t-shirt felt entirely too thin.

Better than nothing, she thought, glad she'd yet again been spared the humiliation of *that* kind of dream while Rylan was around to watch.

Rylan's eyes were on that shirt as she turned back to him.

He threw his arm over the back of the couch and cleared his throat. "Glad to see you made it out of the beshadowing situation in one piece. Everybody okay?"

"Yeah, everybody's good." She gave him a basic run down of all the waking moments since she'd last seen him, as she'd become accustomed to doing since he was separated from the real world. The TV had emptied of its black liquid, and played through a strange, birds-eye view of time-ramped scenes from Rooks Hotel.

Once the basics were out of the way, Everly looped back around to the hard part. "When I used my light powers on the vasmire ... it spoke to me. And ... I understood it."

Rylan remained silent, his brows lowering over olive green eyes.

Everly sighed out the words. "It called me the beast of teeth and stars."

"Did it call you that, or the *dragon*?" Rylan glanced around as though checking for it, but it had remained at a distance.

"I don't know. Are we separate? Am I the dragon or is it something else inside me? Either way, I don't know how I got like this. My parents aren't around anymore to ask them whether they were something other than human."

"They weren't shadyrs," Rylan said.

Doesn't mean they weren't something else.

Everly shrugged. "Even with this name, we've only got one lead. Your mother thinks we might find answers with some kind of relic that's being kept at Darkfrey Estate that has a similar name. Unless you learned anything while with the Darkfreys that might give us some insight?"

"No. I haven't heard that name before. But I was never very good at shadyr history, that was more Annabeth's thing. Put most of my effort into learning how to kill eidolghasts, honestly."

Everly shivered as the water around her feet slowly soaked up the fabric of her pants. But the chill that left her shaking was more due to the fact the boy she used to know had spent his life training to be a killer.

When he'd left home at thirteen years old for Darkfrey Estate—when they'd stopped being friends—she would never have guessed that was the reason why.

Rylan rubbed a thumb over his chin as he watched her. "I think it's clear you aren't a shadyr, but you're definitely not entirely human."

"What other options are there? Eidolghast?" Everly asked quietly.

Like the things you kill.

He reached out and placed his hand on her knee, squeezing gently. "You're not an eidolghast."

"But I am a monster." Everly let the words fall between them with all the weight of her worries.

All the things she hadn't been able to tell anyone. The way she seemed to consume things that left her feeling sick right down to her marrow.

Before he could argue with her and make her feel worse, she went on, "At least I could help get the vasmire for you."

Rylan turned away from her, his jaw and arm tensing. "I hate that you had to do all that just to keep me alive."

"Nobody who went today had any qualms about what we needed to do," Everly pointed out. "Your mom loves you. Your brother adores you. The rest of the Howell team cares about you. I ... care about you."

His eyes flashed up at hers. "I care about you too. Which is why I hate you putting yourself in danger to keep me safe. I need to find a way back into my body."

Everly rubbed at the goosebumps that sprang up all over her arms. "Any ideas?"

"None." He leaned forward and placed both hands over his face as he slouched down.

The motion made the cushions sink so that Everly angled in toward him, and their sides pressed together.

He didn't make any move to pull away.

Everly's breath shuddered. Even in the dream, she could feel his warmth, smell the familiar soap scent of his skin, hear the breaths in his body. He was long and lean, his muscles hard against her full curves. She was certain he could feel the way her heart pounded being so near to him.

As if in response to how she felt, the lily pads still floating by on the watery floor began to look suspiciously heart-shaped. With a bit of will, Everly managed to change their surroundings until water became sand and a purple sun beamed down from overhead, casting everything in a hellish glare.

Though they were still on the damn couch. Touching.

"What have you tried so far?" Rylan asked, his gaze sweeping the glaring horizon.

Giant, lumbering shadows walked just out of sight, nothing more than dark shapes despite the sun. They reminded Everly of Nell's undead animals darting through the trees of the Wyrdwoods.

Everly blew out a breath. "Well, we stuck needles between your toes."

Rylan looked over at her, horrified. "Ow."

"That was Callan's effort," Everly added, and thought, *his lips are so close.*

Everly shifted away from him in the guise of pulling her legs into a crisscross beneath her. She needed space from him. Room to breathe. Room to wash all the desire from her mind before it drove her crazy.

I don't even know who he really is anymore. These feelings are just a hangover from my childhood. Calm yourself the heck down, woman.

"We've also tried smelling salts, adrenaline injections, and throwing water on you—scalding and iced," Everly said, ticking each of the options off on her fingers.

An amused grin quirked up the sides of his lips. "What I'm hearing is that my supposed friends and family have been torturing my unconscious body."

Everly grimaced. "It does sound a little like that, doesn't it?"

They shared a laugh, and as Everly watched his face, her heart skipped a beat. She hadn't heard that laugh in what felt like a lifetime.

A true laugh that trickled up from deep within him and illuminated his face. It transformed him from the buzz cut, military Darkfrey shadyr into someone more familiar. A shadow of the boy he'd been years ago, when he was her best friend, first crush, loyal protector.

She wanted him whole again back in the real world.

But a deep, secret, selfish part of her wanted to keep him here in her dreams, where he belonged only to her, where his time could only be passed in her company.

A yearning hunger that wanted to hold onto him forever.

We won't let him go.

Everly's eyes widened.

We? This wrong, selfish desire to hold onto Rylan ... was it coming from her, or the dragon?

She glanced up at the sky. She'd sensed the dragon there above them, but had studiously ignored it. Instead of a ceiling, there was a canopy of leaves overhead now, and the dragon stared down at them both through the shivering foliage.

Somehow, she, or her dragon, was holding Rylan's spirit within her. In a way, she'd felt like she and Rylan were connected on some metaphysical level ever since that day in the woods when they met as children, both of them lost until they found each other. Connected the same way she and Zozo were now.

But something changed when Rylan almost died. That connection became a full-blown soul-kidnapping.

Is that related to the feeling of consuming things I get when using my powers?

But the other beings whose lifeforces she'd consumed—Nell's husband, the vasmires—they hadn't ended up in her dreams. They were just gone. Or maybe never eaten at all.

I should tell him.

The self-rebuttal came fast. *And have him think I'm a soul-sucking monster?*

"Okay. What other options are there for getting me conscious again?" Rylan said, interrupting her reverie. "Let's talk pop culture and literature. Rip Van Winkle. What woke him up?"

"Um, nothing. I think he just woke up on his own."

"Might still be a possibility," Rylan said, "but not one I'm willing to wait for."

"Odin from Norse mythology had a sleeping thing happening, but again I think he woke up himself."

Rylan huffed. "Who didn't wake themselves up? Sleeping Beauty?"

She woke with a kiss.

Everly flushed from the roots of her white hair to her toes. "Yeah, I guess, but these are just fairytales."

Rylan looked her right in the eyes. "Just hang on a moment. I mean, have you, uh, touched me, much, since you found me?"

Everly straightened in her seat and stammered. "What? No! I mean, no, your brother and Cherry carried you. Your mom, she makes sure you're clean—"

Rylan winced. "I guess that's the least mortifying option of many?"

Everly continued rambling. "I haven't ... I just, I check your pulse, signs of life, but that's all."

Rylan ran a hand over his short hair. "Okay, but it could almost make sense, right? If my consciousness is here, in you, and my body is out there ... what if more direct contact between your body and my body is needed, to put me back?"

Everly's skin turned molten. She suddenly found herself super glad she'd moved away from him, because if she hadn't, right now he'd be feeling her go up in flames. She burned in a way that could turn the sand around her ankles into glass.

"You want ... me to kiss you ... like you're Sleeping Beauty?" she clarified.

He shrugged, looking embarrassed himself. "I guess. I don't know. But it's worth a try, right? We're in new territory here."

A kiss just to save his life, Everly thought, crestfallen.

She wanted to kiss him for real, and for him to kiss her back like he meant it. Not stand over him like some savior princess and hope her lips on his cold, hard mouth would bring him back from the dead.

The sand around them shifted, rolling like waves coming to shore at the foot of the couch. They started growing, pulsating in time to her heartbeat, and Everly hoped this wouldn't evolve into a twisted version of her tsunami dream. She closed her eyes, trying to control the world in her mind, and calm the emotions shivering through her.

"I'll try it," she promised, carefully keeping her emotions from her tone. "But there's got to be another option. Isn't there some local legend about a place you can make wishes?"

Rylan's face darkened. "Absolutely not."

The wishing stone was a story Shroudhaven kids told each other, but as with Santa, generally grew out of quickly. It was a large stone, jutting out from the small island in the middle of Myrkur Lake, rumored to grant wishes—if you could get to it.

But since she'd learned that nothing in Shroudhaven was *actually* just rumor, and most of the weird stuff had a basis in shadyr fact, she was assuming the wishing stone might be real too. Rylan's response seemed to verify that.

"But maybe it could help us," Everly argued. "Maybe one wish could bring you back."

"It's not what you think it is." Rylan grabbed both of her shoulders and turned her to face him, his gaze serious. "The whole lake is beshadowed. A shroudpool formed out there, and in a effort to block it off, shadyrs had the area dammed and flooded. But that water and island are still ghast-twisted and deadly. Promise me you won't go out there."

"But what about the stone? Could it be something, something real?"

Rylan grunted. "Put it this way. Have you ever heard anyone say they went out there and had their wish granted?"

"No, but—"

"And how many tragic, accidental deaths by drowning have you heard about

from that lake?"

"Some. A lot. Okay, I get it, bad place."

"Bad place," Rylan echoed. "Like most of Shroudhaven."

His hands slipped away from her shoulders as though exhausted, and he stared out over the rolling dune-waves. "A place I wish you'd just leave."

Everly's nose wrinkled with the effort to hold back tears. She'd considered it. Giving up, leaving Shroudhaven to return to where she and Harper weren't at threat of death-by-monster every day. If she gave up, Rylan could remain like this, hers and only hers in her dreams.

No. She couldn't do that to him. She refused to stop until he was back in his body.

But scarily, part of Everly wanted to keep him trapped. Part of her wanted to never, ever, let him go.

11

J asper and his brace stayed at Rooks Hotel only until the cleaning crew arrived, but Jasper struggled to stay focused.

Don't let anyone see. No one can see that you're hurt.

As part of a hunting brace, they were at the top of the Darkfrey pecking order. That was where Jasper liked being, where he'd worked hard to be—a place of power no one else in his family tree had ever achieved.

Braces didn't have to do the dirty work. The cleaners would deal with removing any trace of monster remains, help any lingering civvies out of the building, and make some excuses about a gas leak or explosion.

The hotel staff and guests would still have some strange stories to tell about their experience, but who in Shroudhaven didn't?

Their sleek black van trundled up the steep drive of Darkfrey estate. In the back seat, Jasper clenched his hands together to keep them from shaking.

It's over. Really over.

None of his team gave him a second glance. They couldn't see through his calm exterior to his malfunctioning heart inside. It jittered and thumped and cracked against his rib cage, frantic to beat itself into oblivion in its pain. Jasper grimaced.

Get it together. It's better this way.

Vonny pulled the van up to the gates and rolled down her window to key in the security code. A burst of chilled night air rushed in, and Jasper inhaled it deeply as though he hadn't breathed since his final words to Cherry. The gates opened, and Vonny closed her window as the van rolled into motion up the long drive.

Dark forest thinned the higher they rose, and then the trees opened around them on a wide, angled plain covered in the estate's training areas. The hulking shadow of Darkfrey Estate sat atop the hill, windows blazing with light like something out of a gothic horror movie.

A hint of movement atop the crenellated ramparts proved that the night's guard had already set to work. Ghasts didn't typically try to barrel onto Darkfrey's gated property, but it wasn't unheard of, either.

A group of shadyrs in maroon sweats played basketball beneath glaring white lights on one of the courts, but they were the only visible occupants at this time of night.

The other illuminated training areas were empty, fog wisping over concrete and turf to give the grounds a desolate look. Most of the estate had already retired to their rooms. After his brace debriefed with Mordan, Jasper had every intention of shutting up in his own room.

And not crying. *There will be no crying.*

His throat tightened. He couldn't lose it in front of the others. He dug one thumbnail into the other.

Red welled up in the crease of his nail, shiny in the passing lights. The pain helped him chase away thoughts of his boyfriend. *Ex*-boyfriend. Jasper was a Darkfrey, and that meant he was strong, in control.

Only the mission mattered. Only the fight. Nothing else.

Vonny pulled the van up the circular drive before the front door and threw the vehicle into park with more force than necessary.

She'd been in a mood ever since her run-in with the Howells, and most of the brace had given her a wide berth so they didn't get caught up in her ire. She may have been barely over five feet, but Jasper knew intimately that she could kick his ass.

He had learned early. The hard way, with the scars to prove it.

The tiny overhead light bloomed to life, chasing away some of the darkness pressing in from outside. Vonny opened her mouth, her face clearly ready to bark orders, but Nilson stepped in front of her.

"Straight to Master Darkfrey's office," he commanded. "He's expecting us."

The big, blond brute had replaced Rylan in their brace, and he'd come in with a bang, vying with Vonny for control—something Vonny thought she'd finally claimed. Even for someone as imposing as him, Jasper didn't think Vonny would have ceded command. But being Mordan Darkfrey's son counted for something.

Jasper avoided Nilson's shrewd gaze and stayed close to Annabeth's heels, the two of them following Vonny into the building. Something about the older man set Jasper's nerves on edge—like he could see through Jasper, straight to his secrets.

Secrets that could get him kicked out of Darkfrey. Being gay wasn't overtly against the rules, but being different in any way often ended in expulsion. Mordan Darkfrey liked traditional people and traditional methods, and his values seemed to trickle down to most of the shadyrs in residence. Jasper wasn't willing to play the odds.

He kept his gaze firmly on Annabeth's auburn hair as they navigated the maze of halls toward Mordan's office. The oppressive walls of Darkfrey's lengthy corridors pressed in on him more than usual.

It wasn't the suits of armor that disturbed him, or the oil portraits of white-faced old shadyr families, or the dull, flickering glow of the lights, all of which could be somewhat spooky on a night like tonight.

It was the way Jasper didn't quite belong.

Jasper's brace piled into the Victorian cage elevator. The rickety shaft was barely big enough for the four of them, which made it claustrophobic with Nilson's oversized bulk.

Vonny yanked the metal folding door closed and smacked the button. Nilson glared down at them from above, breathing like a bull. Rumor was he hadn't been pleased with his last brace, and the way he looked at them, Jasper wondered if anyone would hold up to his standards.

They exited the elevator in the long, shadowed hallway outside Mordan's office. The lights never seemed to be on at any point except right in front of the elevator, giving the entire floor a kind of "hands off" vibe.

The double doors to the office soared high overhead, made of black wood and both decorated in intricately carved knots. Formed in the center, where the two doors met, was the Darkfrey coat of arms, made of a crescent moon, twin, fang-like blades, and skulls.

Vonny tapped the button on the intercom. A moment later, the lock on the door clicked, and the doors opened outward to admit them.

Mordan sat behind his huge mahogany desk with his back ramrod straight while he perused an open file. He wore his typical garb of a well-tailored smoking jacket in deep shades of purple and gold, and his silver hair was tied back in a low ponytail.

The walls framed him, covered in built-in shelves loaded down with books, statues, trophies, and other artifacts, while the massive wall behind Jasper held an array of animal heads forever frozen in death. Any time Jasper stood before Mordan in this room, he could swear he felt their eyes on him.

Between the lush maroon carpet and the thick drapes over the windows behind the desk shining like gold, Mordan looked like a king lording over his kingdom.

Jasper often felt like that was the truth, too.

Mordan didn't look up right away, continuing to read whatever paper was on his desk that merited his full attention.

Their brace stood like soldiers, hands clasped at their back, feet spread shoulder width apart, waiting patiently for him to acknowledge them. In the time he took, the other brace who attended Rooks trickled in and posted up behind them, ready for the debriefing.

After a few long, silent moments, while the richly appointed grandfather clock behind him ticked away the seconds, Mordan flipped the manila folder closed.

He raised a gaze as nebulous and silvery as his hair, and remarked, "Proceed."

"Rooks Hotel has been secured, sir," Nilson exclaimed.

"Good work," Mordan said, giving a single nod. "Any trouble with the Howells?"

Nilson took a second to snarl, and Vonny stepped in before he could reply. "Yes, sir. There was a notable event involving the Boderleth woman."

Her voice always went lower, more raspy, around Mordan, as if she felt like she needed to exude a more masculine vibe to be taken seriously.

She probably does, Jasper thought.

Mordan's old-fashioned values made him favor the men under his employ.

Mordan leaned back in his chair, his weight resting on one arm. "Oh?"

"The rumors appear to be true," Vonny said shortly. "She's not human."

Jasper kept his expression neutral as Vonny described in detail what they'd seen. Guilt made his skin crawl, and he fought the urge to dig at his nails again.

He knew that what they'd seen had to be reported. It was too big and too *weird*, even by Shroudhaven standards, not to report it. But it still felt somehow like a betrayal. If only they'd gotten there too late to see, it wouldn't be any of their business.

It could remain a secret, like some things should. But he'd hurried them to the site, secretly worried about Cherry's safety. And they all saw what Everly could do, the light, the sheer power. And Jasper lost Cherry anyway.

When Vonny finished her explanation, Mordan leaned back in his chair as though bored of the proceedings. "Interesting. Well, if that's all, Vonny, I'd like—"

Jasper startled, his gaze moving between Vonny and Mordan. That was it? She wasn't going to bring up Rylan and why the Howell team ended up in that situation?

"Um, sir?" Jasper's heart beat faster as he stepped forward.

Mordan's silvery gaze turned on him, surprise visible in his eyes. It wasn't done for one of the subordinate brace members to be so bold, and Jasper knew he was risking undue attention by stepping out. Nilson and Vonny shot him narrowed stares.

But Rylan had been part of his brace. A good fighter, good shadyr, and good friend. The Howell team were risking their lives to keep him alive with a resource the Darkfrey cleaners were incinerating daily.

Jasper cleared his throat. "Sir, if I may speak?"

Mordan raised an eyebrow, but made a flippant hand gesture indicating for him to continue.

"The Howell team have submitted multiple requests for vasmire remains to assist keeping Rylan Howell stable in his strange coma. I can't see the logic in denying them. Approving those requests would at least keep them out of our way in situations like this, and I also feel as though helping to keep Rylan alive is a worthy cause."

And that maybe the only reason not to, is that someone doesn't want him to remain alive. That was something else Cherry had once whispered to him, something so crazy and scandalous Jasper didn't even consider passing it along.

"It isn't your job to 'feel,'" Mordan said sharply. "Your job is to fight back the forces

of darkness and do as you're told."

Jasper inhaled sharply. "Yes, sir!"

"I don't appreciate my logic being questioned. Remember your place, shadyr." He paused and looked around the room. "Vonny, please remain so you and I may talk privately. The rest of you are dismissed."

She nodded, then turned to glare at Jasper, her lips curling in a snarl that promised retribution.

Jasper looked down at his boots, shame racing through him. He fell into line with his brace and headed for the elevator, berating himself for speaking up. He shouldn't have said anything. He knew better than to step out of line.

But Cherry had that effect on him. As the elevator trundled down to the first floor in silence, he thought of the way being with Cherry had made him feel.

Cherry made him want to be different. Better. Braver. That had been the most intoxicating part of building their relationship, when he'd discovered there were qualities hidden deep inside himself, if he only had the courage to bring them out.

But he didn't. He couldn't. As upset as he was to lose the person who made him want to be more, Jasper knew his place was with the Darkfreys. He was on the right side, the side of power, the side fighting for the very existence of their world. He was going to be fine.

As long as Cherry didn't out him in revenge.

The thought sent a tremor down his spine. He said good night to his brace, avoiding Nilson's gaze, and then took the staircase that led to his tower dormitory.

Darkfrey Estate was his home.

If he wasn't a Darkfrey, he was nobody.

12

Rylan and his family are shapeshifting monster hunters. Someone from Darkfrey estate tried to get him killed. Someone who is doing creepy things with black bones. Rylan needs to get back in his body. Plus, I need to find out what's going on with the light inside me. What is the beast of teeth and stars?

And did Rylan really ask me to kiss him?

After waking up from her conversation with Rylan, Everly's mind raced with everything she knew, everything she'd learned since coming back to Shroudhaven. She couldn't shut down the endless swirl of information.

Everly finally gave up on rest as the sky outside the window was beginning to tinge with morning pinks and reds.

She rubbed sleep from her bleary eyes and shuffled downstairs to brew a coffee, adding an extra shot for a little more *oomph*.

She sipped from the warm mug, standing over the kitchen sink as she watched the neighborhood awaken.

Across the street, a bent-over old woman emerged from her house to water the flowers in her front garden. A few houses down, the dentist who worked out of his three-story Victorian hung his *Open* sign, his sapphire blue scrubs a startling splash of color on the gray, misty morning.

Farther down on the corner where the street ended, school kids trickled to the stop sign in twos and threes—never alone—to wait for the bus.

Normal, everyday life in Shroudhaven, Everly thought. *And it's a total lie.*

These people had no idea that monsters roamed their town after dark. They had no idea that a mad witch in the woods had been bringing dead animals back to life, or that there were portals throughout the area connecting Shroudhaven to another dimension full of horrifying beings.

There were stories, rumors, but overall they were blissfully unaware. Oblivious. Especially in the light of day when intuition whispered it was safe because the things that went bump in the night were sleeping.

Everly herself would have been in the dark still if her mother hadn't died. She wished she were back in her city apartment, ignorant of all of the shadows in Shroudhaven. Back when her only worry was keeping her anxiety at bay and making sure Harper was safe from her ex.

Back when people like him were the only real monsters.

"You're up early."

Harper's voice broke through the silence of the kitchen so abruptly that Everly jumped. Coffee sloshed over her fingers into the sink, and she hissed, quickly putting her mug down and reaching for a towel.

Harper raised her eyebrows as she reached for the cabinet door to extract a mug. She still wore her cream-colored silk matching night set under her open robe, but her feet were bare, toenails colored in a glittery pink.

"Sorry. Jumpy this morning, huh?"

"Thinking about monsters," Everly replied, drying away the spilled coffee on her fingers.

Harper carried her mug to the coffee pot. "Literal or metaphorical?"

"Yes."

"I suppose both is an option. We're spoiled for choice, aren't we?" Harper filled her mug, adding a heaped spoonful of her flavored creamer. "Do we have plans today? Monster related or otherwise?"

Does kissing Rylan count?

Everly cleared her increasingly dry throat. "Not that I know of."

"Good. I'm going to get an early start in the shop. I didn't like the way the Waterford crystal pics came out. Too many rainbows."

Everly laughed. "Since when do you put a limit on rainbows?"

Harper made a face and picked up her mug. "When you can't even see the vase for the sparkles. Meet you there?"

"Yeah. I'll join you in a few."

Everly listened to her best friend's light footsteps pad down the hall, then the creaky back door to the antiques shop opened and clicked shut. In the ensuing silence, the school bus arrived at the end of the block, lights flashing while kids piled on.

She envied them for still being kids. Her most treasured memories were still from the time before Rylan's father died, when it was him and her, best friends against the world.

A time when they could spend their days trying to teach Birdie tricks, or building a fort down by the creek, or sitting in a mulberry tree, staining their mouths and hands blood-red and pretending to be vampires.

Did he know then? Did he always know what he was?

Rylan's questioning of her memory of when they first met now had a deeper meaning.

At five years old, she had run away from home to escape her mom and her male companion, and gotten lost in the Wyrdwoods. A place many people didn't come back alive from. Rylan had run away too, although she was never truly clear on the reason why until learning about shadyrs filled in the blanks.

He was worried he was a monster.

She remembered telling him that he wasn't. She'd felt so sure about that, because it was the grown ups in her life who were the monsters.

In her dream when they'd talked about it, he'd asked if she remembered him looking *different*. Everly tried to bring a clear vision of him at the time forward.

But it was so long ago, and she had been weak and delirious by that point. But maybe he had been in a shifted form then. Only five himself, he'd carried her all the way out, back to his mom for help. That wasn't normal.

He'd known at least that long, what he was.

He'd done everything he could to protect her since that day, too.

She knew what Rylan expected of her. He'd been clear that he wanted her to kiss him in the hope it would wake him up. The idea thrilled her and frightened her all at once, and she knew she needed to get on with it.

But she dawdled over the sink, taking her time with her coffee, procrastinating by washing the few dishes left from the night before. When her cup was empty, and there was nothing else to distract her, Everly took a deep breath, let it out slowly, and then headed back upstairs.

The door to her old room hung open, but the sunshine beaming in from the rest of the house couldn't penetrate the darkness that lay beyond. The beshadowed weirdness had eased already, but the worst of it remained in there, oozing across the bedroom walls.

Everly's skin crawled from the cold rolling out, and as she stepped up to the threshold, she waded into a knee-high wall of mist.

On the bookshelves along the wall, the vasmire pieces seemed to hum with unrestrained tension. The tentacles pulsed like they were alive and breathing, though Everly knew it was just a symptom of the minor beshadowing caused by their presence.

She stared at Rylan in the dim room, her heart pinging against her rib cage. Was she really going to do this? Kiss him while he was in a coma?

Sucking in a steadying breath, she took a step into the room and tried to turn the overhead light on, but the switch flicked uselessly. She considered getting a flashlight. So she didn't have to be alone in a dark room with strange things happening all around her, and it would be handy to check for signs of life and—

Stop it. Stop putting it off.

Everly walked up to the edge of the bed quietly. He lay atop the covers, eerily still, his pale skin nearly glowing in the dark.

Should she just … lean over him? Sit beside him?

She waffled between her options, unsure whether she was doing the right thing. The idea was silly—she couldn't fix him with a kiss. She needed to find a way to get Rylan's spirit out of her head and back into his body, but there was no way a kiss was enough.

Whatever metaphysical thing had happened to put him inside her dreams, she needed a reversal of that.

Plus … what if this was the only kiss they ever shared? And he wasn't even awake to kiss her back.

Just do it, she chastised herself.

A person couldn't win the lottery if they didn't buy a ticket. She'd never know if this crazy plan would work unless she just went for it. Rylan must have thought it had at least a small chance, or why else would he have suggested it?

She took a few more deep breaths to calm her racing heart, and gave her hands and arms a good shake to brush off the jitters. Then she sat down on the edge of the bed, put her hands on either side of his head, leaned over, and kissed him.

Though his shadyr skin was hard like stone, his lips were soft, and cool. They parted ever so slightly under the pressure of her mouth, and for just a moment, she imagined he was kissing her back.

She'd imagined her lips on his countless times, imagined how fireworks would explode around her, how she'd melt into him, turn to liquid heat, fall to utter pieces beneath his touch.

None of that happened.

He didn't move. He didn't wake up. He remained as cold and immoveable as a statue.

Everly ended the kiss and pulled away, though she didn't sit up. She stared at his closed eyelids for any hint of movement, but they remained still, as her own eyes filled with tears.

"Dammit." She shoved away from the bed, turning her back on him as the hot tears spilled.

Harper stood in the doorway.

Everly froze in mid-stride, halfway between the bed and the door.

Embarrassment flooded her neck and cheeks with heat. "It's not what you think."

Harper leaned her hip against the frame. "You were trying Sleeping Beauty's kiss."

"Oh. Then it is what you think. It was Rylan's idea. He asked me to try."

"Didn't mean to interrupt, just came for my slippers."

"Didn't work, anyway." Everly wiped her wet cheeks, only spreading the salt-water as more and more tears fell. "I just want to fix him. I *need* to fix him."

"I know," Harper said gently. "And you're going to."

"What if I can't?" Everly's voice cracked on the last word, and pain blossomed

in her chest, shooting numbing chills down her arms. "What if this is it? What if he's just broken for good? What if he's trapped in my mind forever and we can't continue keeping his body alive?"

With every word, her tone got higher pitched, the words came faster, her heart beat painfully loud in her ears. Tremors rattled her hands.

"What if he *dies*, Harper? For real this time? It'll be all my fault because I couldn't find a way to let him go. What if I never—"

She cut off. Her throat closed and all the breath in her body had vanished. The tension in her chest extended upward, shooting pain through her neck and scalp.

The dragon shifted restlessly, and she could see its light just out of sight inside her. Feel it scraping at her walls, waiting for this weakness to set it free.

"N-no, *no*," Everly stammered, backing away from Harper.

She backpedaled furiously, all the way into the corner of the room, where her back slammed against the bookshelves that held the vasmire tentacles.

The force of the hit kicked her legs out from beneath her and she slid to the floor, reaching desperately to catch herself on the shelves. Instead, she grabbed a crate of putrid monster flesh and dumped it on the floor beside her. Foul-smelling fluids spattered her leggings, and she cringed away from the pile with a short, sharp cry.

The light was everywhere. Inside her, all around her, brightening this dark, beshadowed corner of the room. Her heart pounded, and the grip around it tightened even more. Despite the cold, misty air, sweat broke out on her forehead, even as her skin felt frozen solid. She heard a frightened voice and some part of her recognized that it was *her own*, but it didn't sound right.

"No, no, I won't let you. Stay inside. No, no, no."

There was nothing, nobody, there that she could let the dragon consume.

Her vision tunneled until all she could see was Rylan's corpse-like form on the bed.

Harper's fingers dug into her shoulders, drawing Everly's attention. "Ev, hey, Everly, look at me. Breathe. You're okay. You can control this."

"I ... I can't!" Everly gasped the words out, her breaths like knives in her throat.

"Yes, you can," Harper said firmly. "You will. You do it every day. Look at me. Breathe with me."

Everly forced herself to look into Harper's bright green eyes. The two women stared at one another for a long moment as Everly anchored herself in Harper's gaze, and then Harper took a deep breath and let it out.

"Nice and slow. Press your feet down, ground yourself," she said, then pulled in another deep breath. "Come on, you know what to do. You've got this."

I've got this.

It was hard, in the moment, to feel as though she wasn't dying, to feel as though

anything could help, that everything wasn't pointless. Everly struggled to maintain her hold on reality, as the dragon wailed to be released.

But she'd survived this before. She'd lived through every panic attack that had ever struck her down. She would survive this too. She knew how. She set her trembling legs as firmly as she could onto the ground. She pulled back her shoulders, expanding her chest.

She focused on Harper's breaths, on mimicking her, one breath at a time until her heartbeat slowed, and the sparkling lights and dark edges of her vision widened.

"There," Harper said, like she'd put the finishing touches on her grandest photographic masterpiece. "Are you all back together again?"

Everly nodded. Her hands still shook, but she no longer felt on the verge of her heart giving out. The exhaustion that hit on the other side of a panic attack felt like slurry filling her veins. She wanted to crawl into her sleeping bag and snooze for the next week.

"Thanks. I'm sorry for freaking out."

"Psssh. What you should be apologizing for is making me crouch down in these nasty vasmire parts. Look at my slippers, Everly. Just look at them." She wiggled her toes with an audible squelching sound.

"I'll buy you new ones."

"Babe, I have five pairs and I didn't like these ones anyway." Harper grimaced and held out a hand. "Come on. Let's get away from the dead monster for a while. I'm sure it's not the best for a happy state of mind."

Harper pulled Everly to her feet then tossed an arm around her shoulders. "You're going to be okay. And so is Rylan. You'll figure out how to free him. I know it."

Everly nodded, giving Rylan's sleeping body one last glance before Harper steered her out the door.

Will I?

It was going to be hard to free him when an essence deep in her being screamed that it would never let him go.

13

After pulling herself together—plus a shower and a little more coffee—Everly joined her friend in the antiques shop. Maybe if she focused on working with her hands, she could get a break from the overwhelming worries beating at her mind, and the echoes of the eidolghast's voice screaming *monster, beast.*

And the building evidence that the vasmire was right about what she is.

She and Harper had set up a temporary workshop-slash-photo studio in the front room, since it had the most natural light and available surface area.

Harper had made use of an antique table in the corner for her photography and tech needs, while Everly had turned the old L-shaped checkout counter into her repair station. The monstrous wooden bench was covered in paint splattered drop cloths she'd found in the storage room, and the entire contents of her toolbox were scattered across the surface.

It had taken more than a few rounds of dusting, sweeping, and vacuuming to remove the gray tint of neglect from the antique store. Of the items that could be salvaged, most still needed individual cleaning as well, but the cobwebs no longer dangled like ribbons across the rooms and the air was more breathable. The rats, also, had been banished.

Every time Everly sat on the old barstool behind the counter, she flashed back to her dusty memories of her father.

Being in that forbidden space had been painful in those first few days of cataloguing the store. As though her father's specter hung in the air, accusing her of his death, of dismantling the store that had been everything he'd cared about.

His presence was everywhere: in the selection of antiques he'd curated, in the 'Do Not Touch' signs, in the corners and shadows and slants of light. Her father's heart and soul existed there, even though his body didn't.

She'd been only three years old when he suffered a heart attack right in front of her, just next door in the books and collectables room.

Everly still blamed herself. She'd broken one of his favorite pieces, and his fury had sent him into cardiac arrest. Her mother had done a great job of piling on the guilt, too, so it had been a pain she'd lived with all her life.

Though her memories of that day were fuzzy, like she was looking through a translucent veil, she remembered light. A flash of brilliant light.

A flash she'd discounted as faulty memory for most of her life. But in the new awareness of all she'd learned and experienced in Shroudhaven, all her old memories were being scrutinized.

There had been a light.

Like the dragon had been there then, too.

Maybe it had always been part of her. The thought made her shudder and she put those dark musings out of her head.

For several hours, Everly threw herself into repairing the old German cuckoo clock Harper had tasked her to fix. She was no clock expert, but she had the internet—spotty as the connection could be—and an eager ability to teach herself how to fix anything.

It had served her well when she'd been kicked out by her mom at fifteen and bluffed her way into adulthood early, scoring maintenance jobs with a couple of forged documents and online tutorials.

Focusing on something she *could* easily fix helped ease the knot of tension in her chest.

Around noon, a shadow appeared on the other side of the lace-curtained front windows. The silhouette passed the window like a wraith, then appeared on the other side of the frosted glass window at the front door.

Everly froze, miniature screwdriver hanging in the air over the open door on the clock.

Three sharp knocks echoed through the high-ceilinged room.

Harper straightened and lowered her camera, brow furrowed as she glanced at Everly. "Are we expecting company?"

"No. And any company we *know* would use the back door." Everly slipped off the stool and went to answer the knock.

"Um ... Hello?" Everly squinted into the daylight at the red-headed shadyr on the front porch.

Annabeth was in her usual uniform of black pants and a Darkfrey jacket, the hood up over her auburn hair. She was taller than Everly by a couple of inches and had a cute button nose and a galaxy of ginger freckles on her cheeks.

She offered a wobbly smile. "Everly, right?"

"Yeah, we've met before."

"Oh, I know, but not really, well, only ..."

"Only when it was our-team-versus-your-team fun times?" Everly offered the stuttering girl.

Annabeth gaped but recovered quickly, her lips firming into a straight line. She

extracted a small maroon envelope from her pocket and held it out. "From Master Darkfrey."

Harper peered over Everly's shoulder. "You sure it's not poisoned?"

Annabeth's brow furrowed. "Um. No?"

Harper flashed her teeth in a mockery of a smile. "No, it's not poisoned, or no, you aren't sure?"

"Harper," Everly admonished.

"What? It's an important distinction," Harper said, laying on the mock innocence.

The envelope felt heavier than its size allowed, and the front bore Everly's full name in spidery gold script. She turned the envelope over to find it sealed with wax in the shape of the Darkfrey crest. The tiny skulls with their hollow eyes stared up at her, threatening.

Slipping a finger beneath the lip, she opened it and withdrew a note made of thick, textured cardstock. It was as dark maroon as the envelope and held the same spidery gold handwriting.

"Dear Miss Boderleth, please accept my regards and welcome to Shroudhaven," Everly murmured. She read onward, each word furrowing her brow further. "He wants me to come for tea."

"Why?" Harper asked, drawing out the word suspiciously.

"Since my first visit to Darkfrey Estate wasn't 'under the best circumstances' he wants to 'welcome me properly,'" Everly quoted.

She exchanged glances with Harper and wondered if her best friend had the same thought she had: Mordan Darkfrey wasn't interested in a social call.

"Right. Nothing to do with you glowing up Rooks Hotel then?" Harper murmured.

It seemed she and Everly were on the same wavelength.

Everly nodded, then took hold of the door. "Well, thanks for bringing this by. I'll give it some thought and call the number he left if I decide to go."

But the shadyr stepped forward, putting the toe of her boot against the wood before Everly could close it. "Wait. I ... can I see Rylan? Please?"

"He's still not awake."

"I know," Annabeth said, subdued. "I just ... wanna see him, you know? He is—was—my brace partner."

A sudden flash of jealousy and protective fury coursed through Everly's veins, and the feeling was so foreign, she felt like she'd stepped outside her own body.

"If you cared about him, you'd help us keep him alive," she snapped.

Annabeth's eyes widened and her mouth pursed. "I know. I would if it were up to me. If you just gave him back to us, I'm sure—"

"That's not happening."

Annabeth's face twisted as though something had broken inside her, and she put a hand over her eyes for a few seconds.

When she withdrew it, her expression was calm and neutral. "I just want to see him, just for a moment."

Everly turned to Harper, unsure. Despite the firm line of the shadyr girl's mouth, there had been a hint of pleading in her tone. Harper shrugged.

Annabeth had never been outright antagonistic to her and her friends like other members of her team. She seemed innocent enough, for a Darkfrey. Why should Everly be so rude as to deny her simple request?

Except ... Annabeth could be the shadyr who tried to kill Rylan the night of the raid at Nell's animal sanctuary. She couldn't let her guard down around *any* of the Darkfrey residents. But she could let the girl see Rylan. Accompanied. It could be a chance to try to trap the shadyr into revealing herself, if she was the one.

If she did want to kill Rylan, would I have a chance to stop her? She could use the monster bits to shift into vampire form and then I'd be no match for her.

But I do have my dragon.

And if Annabeth tried something on Rylan, Everly knew she wouldn't hesitate to let out her light.

Everly shrugged as casually as she could, and stepped aside to let her in.

Harper stayed behind to keep working, saying she'd had enough of the vasmire tentacles for one day, so Everly led Annabeth through the house alone. They didn't speak, though Everly could sense Annabeth's curiosity about the house, and the quiet, contemplative way she studied her surroundings.

At the door to her old bedroom, Everly motioned to the darkness beyond, then let Annabeth go inside first while she waited at the threshold. She held her breath, watching for any sign of change, or attack.

Annabeth's steps faltered halfway into the dark room. Ambient sunlight from the living room down the hall illuminated the back of her military jacket, casting her shadow over Rylan's face.

"He looks dead," Annabeth said quietly.

Everly wanted to question whether that was what Annabeth wanted, but the dull tone hadn't hidden the fear in her words.

She sighed and said softly, "He's not. The pale skin is because he's partly in vampire form, regenerating."

Annabeth nodded slowly, turning to the crates, nose wrinkled. Some had popped their lids, the gore inside expanding as it decayed.

Everly watched the woman carefully, but there was no sign she was going to shift. She seemed younger than her, more like Tammy's age, but clearly had complete control over her abilities. Everly guessed she wouldn't be part of an active brace if she hadn't.

Annabeth looked around the room at the strange black shapes pulsing along the walls and the mist pouring from the crates. "This is dangerous for you and your friend."

"We're managing just fine." The words were snappier than she'd intended, but the Darkfrey shadyr had no right to lecture her about the vasmire pieces keeping Rylan alive, and wasn't about to scare her into letting them take Rylan away.

Annabeth walked up to the edge of the bed, and Everly jolted a step forward after her, breath hitching. The shadyr reached out and pressed her fingertips to Rylan's neck. Checking for a pulse, but also something more, something lingering. Everly shifted uncomfortably at the sight, jealousy surging. She wanted to scream at her to stop touching him.

What is going on with me? He doesn't belong to me, in any way.

Rylan's presence in her head must be doing this, making her possessive, thinking of him as hers and hers alone. But it wasn't true. It never would be.

"The two of us, we ended up at Darkfrey estate in the same circumstances," Annabeth said without looking back at Everly.

Her voice was soft, as though it were more for Rylan than anyone else. "An eidolghast attacked my home, too. Killed my mom. Years after it happened to Rylan, but I think the pain was still fresh for him. It connected us."

A deep chill ran up Everly's spine.

Rylan's dad was killed by an eidolghast?

That wasn't the story she'd been told. But now she found it hard to be surprised that it wasn't just an animal attack. She'd wanted to be there for Rylan when he was grieving, but he'd shut her off, pushed her out of his life entirely. But he didn't shut out Annabeth.

"I'd only been in his brace since Callan left, but we were so good together." Annabeth's fingers slid up to his cheek and then down his jawbone, hovering just below his lips.

Oh.

Everly drew a sharp breath. "You're in love with him."

Annabeth turned toward her, vulnerable, watery eyes hardening fast. "What does that matter to you?"

Why didn't I see it, why didn't I think?

Of course there would have been someone in Rylan's life who loved him.

Why wouldn't it be this stunning, capable, hard-edged young woman? Why wouldn't he love her back?

I have to know. But I don't want to.

Everly's lips opened and closed a few times before the words got out. "Is ... is he

in love with you?"

Annabeth laughed bitterly. "No. I worked out pretty quick that his heart's buried under a brick wall. It belongs to someone else."

Everly's heart skipped a beat. "Who?"

Annabeth's wry grin spread as she took Everly in, as though seeing her for the first time. "Huh. I'd almost guess you had a thing for him, too."

"We were friends." The denial came too fast, too off pitch.

Annabeth strolled up in front of Everly, eyes soft with sympathetic solidarity. "Right. Sure. Good luck with that. But I'm telling you, his heart is already taken."

Everly folded her arms, as though that could hold in the churn of acid burning her insides.

Annabeth straightened up, almost at attention. All the softness had gone from her face again.

"Thank you for letting me see him. Look after him. He's a good man."

As the shadyr passed by her into the hallway, Everly glanced at Rylan's sleeping form. Was Annabeth right? Did he love someone else?

Of course he could. In all the years they'd been apart, of course he would have had relationships, could have been in one right now. She knew there was at least one reason why Darkfrey shadyrs kept their romances secret.

After all the other massive secrets he'd kept from her, one more wouldn't be a surprise.

Everly didn't hesitate to get in touch with Lian to let her know about her invitation. It was decided she should come over for dinner that evening to discuss options.

Callan showed up at dusk, tag-teaming them for Rylan watch duty. Everly and Harper left in the campervan to drive to Howell House.

Up until recently, she would have just walked the couple of short blocks, but now that she knew what came out after dark, she wasn't interested in tempting fate. The campervan drove like a tank, and if they came up against a wandering vasmire or weroth, Everly intended to use it as a weapon.

She was much too aware of Mordan Darkfrey's fancy invitation in the inside pocket of her red bomber jacket. She didn't like that he knew her name or that he knew what his shadyrs had seen at the hotel. She needed Lian's advice.

Howell House sat alone in a large field at the end of a birch-lined drive. When

Mr. Howell had been alive, the place had looked like a palace—white gingerbread trim always freshly painted, ivory siding as bright as the sun, the flower and herb gardens like something out of a fairy tale.

While Lian had maintained her gardens with the same colorful eye for detail as all those years ago, the rest of the house had faded and cracked. As if her husband had taken the vibrancy with him when he died.

They hadn't even knocked on the door when they heard Rushelle's voice. "Come in!"

Everly shoved open the creaky screen door to find the house filled with the smell of cooking. Lian's bolognese. She knew it immediately and the scent was so familiar it sent an ache of nostalgia into her chest.

She and Harper headed to the kitchen, where Rushelle set the huge, farmhouse table, and Tammy sat slumped in her seat, hood up, ear buds in, a patch of darkness in the warm space. Across the room, Cherry and Denny argued.

"Bellsy is, like, my new best friend," Cherry said, waving his hands around. "And no offense, but I'm pretty sure she hates your guts, so … I'm sitting next to her, and that's that."

"Nope. No, siree," Denny said, rocking back on his heels with a little smirk on his bearded face. "I got dibs."

"You can't dibs a person!"

"But I did, so suck it up. Hope she wears something low-cut. Girl's got nice—"

"Girl's here!" Harper interrupted loudly.

"Tits," Denny drawled, unperturbed.

Tammy made a far too realistic gagging sound.

Harper tossed her perfectly curled hair back. "I've got a nice AVO lawyer too, happy to show that off."

Denny opened his mouth, but Rushelle straightened, looking like a vengeful Norse goddess as she slammed her fists on her hips and glared. "Do I need to serve your dinner to go, mister?"

"Was just a compliment," Denny grumbled under his breath.

Under the continued pressure of Rushelle's stare, he gestured zipping up his mouth and dropped into a chair, slouched and sulking.

Cherry put his arms out and welcomed an embrace from Harper. Over her shoulder, he stuck his tongue out at Denny, before taking a seat as far from him as possible. The hushed conversation between him and Harper started up immediately.

Across the kitchen, Lian hefted a huge cooking pot to the sink, momentarily disappearing into a cloud of steam as she drained off the pasta.

Everly sidled up to the counter across from her and pulled the envelope from her pocket, tossing it next to a cutting board. "Here it is."

"Fancy." Lian set the pot down and opened the envelope, raking her gaze over the short message. "What a polite way to invite you to an interrogation."

"My thoughts exactly."

Lian tossed the envelope and card back on the counter. Grabbing a ladle, she spooned a thick, red sauce into the pasta.

"Even if we did know what caused your powers, that's information we don't want the Darkfreys to have. And we certainly don't want them working it out first."

"Do you think they'd hurt me?"

Lian stared into the pasta as she stirred the sauce through. The silence grew heavy before she looked back up and tossed Everly a small, encouraging smile.

"We wouldn't let them. But still, you're different. Mordan and his army don't treat 'different' well."

Everly glanced over at Cherry. He and Harper had stopped their conversation. Despite a casual smirk, there was a darkness of pain in Cherry's gaze.

"Then I should decline the invitation?"

Lian's smile widened. "Oh no. We're going to accept."

"We?"

"Yes, you and me. You're not entering that place on your own. We'll approach the meeting with caution, keep up appearances for Mordan," Lian said. "Because this could be our one and only opportunity to get inside Darkfrey Estate."

She put the ladle down in the sink and chuckled almost mischievously. "Mordan thinks he's going to get info from us, but this is our chance to get something from them."

"The Bane of Teeth and Stars?" Everly said.

For some reason, the phrase turned her stomach sour, but a hint of excitement followed. This could be her chance to find out what she was, what the dragon was.

From over at the table, Harper squealed. "We're going to do a heist?"

Lian grinned as she took the cordless phone off the wall and held it out to Everly. "Let's go to tea."

Tea, with Mordan Darkfrey. Everly may as well be walking into the lair of a monster.

14

In the light of day, Everly expected the gates to Darkfrey Estate to be less foreboding.

Of course, the "light of day" in Shroudhaven was often dim, gray, and misty, so instead of bright sunshine glinting off the black wrought iron gates, the atmosphere was more that of a gothic movie.

Low-hanging, gunpowder gray clouds threatened rain and cast the forest in a haze that made it look darker than it should be. Everly shivered in her seat at the presence of those gates, and what lay beyond.

Lian rolled down her window and pushed a button on the intercom.

A beat of silence passed, and then a crisp, authoritative voice said, "Yes?"

Lian leaned out her window. "Lian Howell and Everly Boderleth to see Mordan."

"Do you have—"

"Yes," Lian cut in. "He's expecting us."

After a drawn-out pause, the voice at the other end said, "Pull around to the front door and an escort will be waiting for you."

The gates began to creak open, and Lian hit the toggle to roll her window up.

"An escort," she scoffed, carefully pulling through the gates before they'd finished opening. "Sounds like someone is feeling a bit threatened."

By me?

Everly didn't like that idea. "Is that going to be a problem?"

"No, we'll work it out. This isn't my first rodeo."

"Your sword?" Everly fished.

Lian flashed a mischievous grin.

They fell into silence as Lian navigated the twisting driveway through thick, dark woods.

Everly lay her head back against the headrest and thought about how strange it was to see this side of Lian. When she'd been a kid, Lian had just been Rylan's mom, and Everly had been so focused on her relationship with Rylan that she'd almost missed how much of a mother Lian had been to her, too.

How there was always a place at their dinner table when Everly's own mother had neglected to keep any food in the house. How Lian accidently bought a pair of shoes in the wrong size for Rylan that managed to perfectly fit Everly when the soles had come off hers. How Lian had her over for sleepovers on nights when Everly's mom had male guests in the house.

But the truth was Lian had an entire life she'd lived before Everly ever showed up on her doorstep. This Lian was older physically, but with all the secrets out in the open, she seemed ... freer. Younger at heart, maybe, though she still carried an undercurrent of sadness from the tragedies she'd experienced.

The trees thinned, and the castle-like building of Darkfrey Estate appeared at the apex of the hill like a craggy mountain, dark and imposing, casting a long shadow over the rolling lawn.

A chill raced up Everly's back as Lian's SUV rolled into the circular drive before the main building.

An unfamiliar shadyr with a bald head approached and opened Everly's door.

"Welcome to Darkfrey Estate," he said in a monotone. "I'll be escorting you to Master Darkfrey's office."

"For ghast's sake, Bob, you know I know the way," Lian groaned from the driver's seat.

"Just following orders, Lian."

Everly noticed that Bob didn't look right at her. His gaze locked over her shoulder on the upholstery, and she wondered if he knew about the light. Word traveled fast around Darkfrey Estate. She unbuckled her seatbelt and exchanged nods with Lian, then exited the vehicle.

Lian grabbed the large canvas tote from the back seat and put it over her shoulder, patting the side. As they fell into step behind Bob, Lian leaned in and muttered, "Don't eat or drink anything he gives you."

Everly raised her eyebrows but nodded. Her skin chilled even more, and she tugged her jacket tighter around herself as they walked into the building.

She'd followed this same path before with Lian when they were trying to find out what had happened to Rylan, so she was familiar with the suits of armor, the oppressive entombment of the dark stone walls and floors, and the cage elevator that led to Mordan's office.

She'd been excited to see the inside of Darkfrey Estate that day. Now, she was nervous. Nervous that Mordan was dangerous. Nervous that he intended to uncover her secrets and use them against her.

What if he already knows what I am? What if it is something terrible? What if this is a trap?

When they walked into his office, Mordan immediately rose from behind his desk and straightened the lapels of his smoking jacket. The fabric was maroon and embroidered with golden threads that looked like stars. His tight-lipped smile seemed a little too wide.

"Miss Boderleth. Welcome," he said grandly, sweeping out from behind his desk to offer his hands. "I'm delighted you could meet with me."

Everly hesitated, but she didn't want to be rude, so she lay her hand in his. He clasped her fingers with smooth, cold hands and kissed her knuckles. Everly shuddered but kept her mouth firmly shut. It was agreed Lian would do the talking, and Everly didn't think things would start off well with her declaring how grossed out she was.

When Mordan straightened, he didn't immediately release her.

He studied her with shrewd gray eyes. "Such a lovely girl, aren't you?"

His unnecessary assessment of her physical appearance made her squirm, and Everly glanced at Lian, begging for help.

Lian leaned forward and batted Mordan's hands off Everly's, putting out her own in replacement. "Hello, Mordan. Don't you think I'm lovely, as well?"

Mordan glared at her hand for a few seconds too long. The two stared at one another with such open enmity, Everly could feel the tension rippling across her skin and filling the office like the charge in the air before a thunderstorm.

"Lian," Mordan said stiffly. "When I invited Miss Boderleth, I didn't know I was inviting you, as well."

"What kind of person would I be if I sent a friend into danger on their own? But you wouldn't know anything about that, would you? You refuse to do the very things you send your charges to do."

"I did my time on patrol, as you well know," Mordan said, an edge to his voice. "And this is hardly a dangerous situation. Please, have a seat. I'll send for our tea service."

"Cut the shit, Mordan," Lian said, dumping her tote bag beside her and slouching lazily in her chair. "We both know you didn't ask Everly here to serve her Earl Grey and scones."

Everly took a seat beside her, trying not to smirk.

Mordan didn't reply right away as he settled behind his desk. His thin, craggy face was an emotionless mask, but a glint of irritation flickered in his gaze. Lian seemed to know all his buttons and how to push them, though whether doing so was a smart idea, Everly couldn't say.

"Indeed," Mordan relented. "Since you'd like to dispatch with the pleasantries, yes. My team returned from Rooks Hotel with the most intriguing tale. As such, I'd like to know more about Miss Boderleth's powers."

"Sadly, your team is woefully misinformed," Lian said, opening her palms to

the ceiling in a loose shrug. "All they saw was the result of a conveniently timed gas explosion that caused an intense electrical surge, killing the vasmires."

Everly had to work hard to keep her expression from changing. They hadn't discussed what would be said beyond Lian's directive to let her do the talking, so this cover story was news to Everly. Whether it was believable was beside the point. Lian clearly wasn't handing over a scrap of truthful information.

Mordan's eyes narrowed. "A gas explosion electrocuted the vasmires. To death."

Lian shrugged. "Great timing, too, as we were admittedly struggling, what with there being two of the huge beasts. Meanwhile, your people just stood by and watched. Is that a new course here at Darkfrey? 'How to watch other shadyrs die'?"

"I'm sure had the 'gas explosion' not happened, you and your *team* would have had the situation well in hand," Mordan said dryly.

"Perhaps!" Lian said brightly. "But it all worked out for the best. Everly narrowly escaped getting hurt in the explosion. The only power she has is good luck."

Mordan huffed and directed his question to Everly. "That's really what happened?"

She shrugged, innocently. "How else would you explain it?"

"How indeed."

Mordan didn't believe her. Everly could see it in the tight lines of his face. But it was also clear he didn't have answers either.

She imagined he was weighing his options of whether to argue with Lian and demand she tell him the truth. Everly didn't know anything about their past together, but there was certainly no love lost, and neither of them had a problem goading one another into a fury.

But Mordan's gaze slid to Everly, and he straightened, seemingly coming to a decision.

"What news of Rylan?" he inquired.

The smile fell off Lian's face. "Don't pretend you care about him."

Mordan's eyebrows furrowed and his hand fell limply onto the table with a thump. "Of course, I care. And if you'd only let him be brought here, he'd have every resource available to us to treat his condition."

"Or make sure he never wakes up," Everly countered.

"I don't know what lies the Howells have poisoned your mind with, but we aren't a den of monsters trying to kill our own. We only do what must be done to keep our world safe. Rylan knew that more than anyone. He understood the nature of sacrifice."

Everly shivered at the word. "You aren't making a great case for his safety."

Mordan sighed, running a hand down his chin. "I truly do care for him and his health. Rylan is one of my favorites. A great soldier, one of the best. He's like a son to me."

"A son?" Lian leaned forward and smacked both hands down onto Mordan's huge timber desk, rattling the lamps. "A son you stole from *me*."

"Rylan and Callan wanted to be here. I could never have made them stay otherwise," Mordan snapped. "We've been around and around with this, Lian."

"They were *children*. Their actions were a direct result of your manipulation, your, your ..." She waved her hands, her eyes as wild as her gestures. "Your *brainwashing*!"

"This isn't a cult, Lian," Mordan said stiffly, leaning back in his chair away from her.

"Isn't it?" she shrieked, tugging at her gray hair.

She stood abruptly, snatched her tote bag up, and glanced at Everly. "Come on. I can't even stand to look at this man!"

Mordan reached to an antique-styled phone on his desk. "Let me get you an esco—"

"I don't need a ghast-damned escort, Mordan! Or are you trying to hide something? Well? Are you?" She turned her scathing glare on him, swinging her bag like a weapon.

He put his hands up, away from the phone. "Lian—"

But she didn't let him speak, howling into the room, "If I find out that Rylan's situation had *anything* to do with you, I'll kill you!"

Lian grabbed Everly's arm, dragging her from the office.

Mordan stood motionless behind his desk, glaring down his nose at them. "You and the runts you surround yourself with? As if you ever could."

15

The moment the rickety elevator was in motion, Lian unzipped her tote bag and whipped out the two Darkfrey jackets from within, loaned to them from Callan and Cherry.

"That was close." Lian stripped off her long cardigan, swapping for the disguise. "Sorry you had to witness that. I knew we wouldn't get out of there without an escort if I didn't distract him. He freezes up when confronted with a hysterical woman."

Everly took the second jacket and grinned in appreciation of Lian's ruse, but even if it all was just for show, her mind was still on the idea of Mordan "stealing" Rylan and Callan.

Everly remembered as a teenager being surprised when she learned that custody of both Lian's boys had been granted through the courts to Mordan, but she figured she just didn't understand the legal system.

Rylan and Callan had seemed like they wanted to leave. Like they were just going to a full-time boarding school, where they were too good for those they left behind.

And Rylan wanted to leave everything in his life behind to come to this estate. Especially me.

The elevator rattled around them as Everly took off her faded-red jacket and replaced it with Callan's Darkfrey one. It was a little tight, and there was no way she'd be able to zip it up, but it would serve its purpose.

Everly said in a low voice, "Can I ask, what really happened to bring Rylan and Callan here?"

Lian let out a short, bitter chuckle as she slipped into Cherry's jacket easily, the fabric swimming around her tall, thin figure. "You didn't hear that I was an unfit mother?"

Everly nodded slowly. She'd heard that rumor when her own mother, in one of her rare lucid moments, had questioned Everly about whether or not Lian Howell had ever hurt her. Even then, Everly had been aware of the irony of her questioning. Janey Boderleth was the only unfit mother in her life.

"I did. Didn't believe it then, definitely don't believe it now."

Lian's eyes glittered, and she cupped Everly's cheek for a moment before she sighed and got to work stuffing their jackets into the tote bag.

"My boys ... I tried to raise them in such a way that didn't *hide* what they were, but that would allow them to have a normal life, too. I didn't want them to be mindless soldiers like the shadyrs here at the estate. Just bodies used up in the service of Mordan's war on the Everdark. Kids come here, and they just ... they stop being kids."

The elevator groaned to a stop. They both flipped up their hoods, and Lian opened the gate, ushering Everly out and to the left—the opposite direction from the door they'd entered upon arrival.

In silence, Lian led Everly down several halls, moving with a sense of purpose and an uncanny knowledge of the mansion's layout. Lian clearly wasn't a stranger to Darkfrey Estate.

They passed a few other shadyrs—groups of children and teenagers—but with their Darkfrey jackets on, the pair didn't get any double takes.

Lian darted into an uncomfortably narrow side hallway and slowed down, her gaze raking the wood-paneled walls.

There were only three dull globes set in the stone walls to light the way down the windowless hallway. The few visible doors lining the short hall were closed tight, and the thick floral carpet beneath their feet looked like it got a lot less traffic than other areas.

Everly stuck close to Lian, half of her attention on the larger corridor behind them. If a Darkfrey student showed up and saw them loitering weirdly, they were sitting ducks down there.

Lian halted suddenly and grinned, then reached over her head to press against a carved nodule in the wood.

A hidden door sprang open.

Everly quelled a startled gasp.

Secret door, secret door!

Its very existence delighted her, calling to mind every adventure movie she'd ever seen, and every ghostly, gothic novel she'd ever read. The fact that a *real* secret passage existed made her grin from ear to ear.

Harper was already annoyed she couldn't do the heist with us. She's going to flip that she missed out on this.

Lian ushered Everly through the dark opening, then slid the door shut behind them, cutting off what little illumination there had been. A moment later, Everly had the flashlight on her phone turned on, casting pale, colorless light over their surroundings.

The secret passage was even narrower than the hall, though the ceilings were still just as high, disappearing into darkness overhead. The belly of the building was all exposed beams and dense shadows, reminding Everly of ribs and blood. Her boots scuffed the stone, but the cocoon-like area muffled the sound, almost like the hushed atmosphere of a snowfall.

"I was out one night," Lian said softly.

She motioned with her head for Everly to follow her, and they moved off into the gloom, their phone lights barely chasing away the darkness.

"An eidolghast showed up, attacked my family. The boys shifted. They defended themselves as best they could. But they were so young and untrained. That was my fault. Not theirs. None of it was their fault." Lian shrugged helplessly. "My husband, he wasn't a shadyr. He knew about us, of course, but he was human."

Annabeth's words about how she and Rylan had ended up as Darkfreys the same way came back to Everly.

"That was the night your husband died," she whispered.

Lian nodded. "He called me, as soon as he saw the boys had changed, he knew something was nearby. I got back as fast as I could. My boys, they fought so hard ... but ..."

She trailed off and it was a while before she spoke again, leading in with a long, exhausted sigh. "Mordan got to them, put it into Rylan's head that if he and Callan had been better trained, perhaps they could have saved their father. Once they started thinking that way ... I don't think they've ever forgiven me for keeping them from being fighters."

"So they left to come here."

"To be monster hunters through and through," Lian said. "I wished ... I wanted them to know that even the best fighters in the world can't shield themselves entirely from tragedy."

Everly hugged herself, remembering how broken Rylan had been after his father died.

"That it wasn't their fault, or mine either, really. That terrible things just happen sometimes and can't be prevented, and that's awful, but they didn't have to give their lives in the pursuit of trying to stop it happening again." Lian's voice broke, and they moved along in silence.

When she spoke again, her voice was soft and apologetic. "I think, maybe, that's why Rylan pushed you away too. To protect you from all of this. I hated seeing him do that to you. It wasn't your fault."

Everly's cheeks flushed and her eyes stung.

It wasn't my fault?

She'd spent so long believing that she'd wronged Rylan after his dad's death, that it was the reason he'd left her behind. If it weren't, that could change everything.

Everly wasn't the only person Rylan shut out though.

"I'm sorry, that Mordan made them think they had to leave you," Everly offered, feeling as though it wasn't even close to enough. "That they did, leave you."

"I tried to win them back." It almost sounded like an apology. "When I tried to

use my parental rights to force them home, Mordan used his power with the town justice system to take me to court for custody. I'm not the first mother he's done it to, and I certainly wasn't the last."

"How can he get away with that?" Everly's own mother probably deserved to lose custody of her early on, but nobody batted an eye when she was found to be drunk or high with a five-year-old around.

How could such a bad mom have no repercussions for her actions, while Lian lost her kids to a stranger?

"Mordan Darkfrey operates under his own set of rules. All the Darkfreys consider themselves above human law, and they've built up a support system in town to make sure they stay that way."

Lian paused as the passage hit an intersection, then looked both ways before choosing to turn right.

"We're talking generations and generations of wealth and influence controlling this region and everyone in it. Nobody stands a chance against them. Even with my Pimey heritage, my family's power is nothing compared to the Darkfreys. It's just enough to keep them from running me and mine out of town entirely."

Everly thought of Tammy, Cherry, Rushelle, even Denny, all outcast for one reason or another. If Lian hadn't taken them in and given them her protection, what would their lives be like now?

Callan left the Darkfreys of his own choosing, and Everly got the impression he'd be welcomed back, but after recent events, him returning seemed highly unlikely.

Everly asked, "Has it been good, having Callan home again?"

"Hmm. He's a grown man now. I missed out on so much. But yes. Yes, it's wonderful."

Lian stopped and turned to the wall, running her fingers over a crack in the plaster. The barest hint of light seeped through a slim rectangle, and when Lian found the catch and depressed the button, the crack became a door.

Everly watched the web of wrinkles around Lian's shrewd eyes, sparkling with the effects of her shadyr night vision, and maybe something more. Everly nodded to herself, making a small, silent oath. She'd do anything to bring Rylan back to his mother as well, so she could have both her sons with her again.

The room beyond the secret passageway was dim and empty of occupants. Glass cases lined the walls, each illuminated by warm amber lights sparkling down from overhead. On the shelves inside, trophies and plaques gleamed like flame beneath the lamps.

Several freestanding podiums throughout the middle of the room held plaster busts of people—presumably shadyrs who had once walked these halls and done something noteworthy. The wood floors were laid out in a geometric pattern polished to an unnatural sheen.

"There are secret routes all over this estate, but they aren't all connected in an easy path," Lian explained. "We're going to have to cut through some areas. Keep quiet and inconspicuous, okay?"

Everly nodded under her heavy hood.

Lian strolled out into the room, moving with the speed of purpose. Everly kept to Lian's side as she glanced around for surveillance cameras from the corner of her eye, trying not to reveal too much of her face.

She couldn't spot anything. Maybe Mordan's traditional values extended into also being a luddite. She had noted that his desk only ever had papers on it, no computer. Or maybe he was just so sure of his control over his shadyr army that he didn't think interior surveillance necessary.

"That's my great, great grandad," Lian whispered as they passed one of the busts, who looked as precisely old-white-guy as the rest of them.

Everly raised her eyebrows, feeling out of her depth in all this shadyr history. "Oh. Cool."

On the opposite wall, Lian found another notch and toggled it, then they slid back into another hidden passage. It seemed older than the last. Strange lichens and soot marked the ancient stone walls.

Lian seemed to know every secret of the sprawling manor.

"How long were you here before you left?"

Lian spoke softly, although the solid rock walls blocked all sound. "Until I was twenty-two. Long enough to learn the ropes, be assigned to a brace, get into a bunch of trouble. It was Mordan's father who was in charge back then, but things were much the same. Some stuff happened ... and I decided this wasn't the life I wanted. I left, met Quinn Howell, and tried to live as much of a normal life as Shroudhaven allows."

The winding passageway seemed to lead them down into the earth and back up again. "Why didn't you leave town?"

"There's something about this place. When you're a shadyr, it's like it calls to you. Maybe it's the shroudpools, connecting this dimension with the one the original shadyrs came from, or the sense of duty so many of us are indoctrinated with. I don't know. But leaving just felt too hard."

They exited and re-entered the passages three more times, and each gave Everly a glimpse into life at Darkfrey Estate. Beyond the trophy room, they passed through a quiet study where only one student worked, headphones looped over bright auburn hair and her nose in a thick textbook.

Is that Annabeth?

Everly's nerves went on high alert, and she and Lian hid behind tall bookshelves until they reached their tunnel re-entry point. The red-headed shadyr didn't look up once, and they passed out of the room without her notice.

They skirted down a long, more modern, hallway where Everly caught glimpses of small lecture rooms.

Projected onto their screens up front were things like "Anatomy of a Nyevmer", "The Coruscare and Pre-Transition Mythology", and "Serving your brace."

Farther down was a rec room with a dark flat-screen television and multiple cushioned armchairs and couches—mostly empty, since it was the middle of the school day for the estate shadyrs. The most occupied area they passed was a training room where a dozen grunting students were sparring and throwing each other onto thin mats.

A few times Lian had to turn them away from their chosen path to avoid passing a group of Darkfrey shadyrs head on, but she seemed to always know another route to take in the labyrinthine building. Everly was utterly lost when Lian stopped at yet another hidden door and reached for the release.

She paused to glance at Everly. "This is it. The archives are accessed through the armory."

Everly nodded with a rush of excitement. But a strange sensation that they were being followed left a curling tension in her gut. She glanced back and around but saw no one nearby.

The door opened on silent hinges, revealing a pitch-black room beyond. Lian lifted her flashlight to light the way, and Everly fell into step behind her. She couldn't see much beyond the dim glow of the phone until they entered an aisle flanked by two tall metal shelving units loaded down with weapons, extending into the distance.

Broadswords, pikes, vicious daggers, modern compound bows and antique longbows, a range of deadly tools Everly imagined a ninja would use—every possible type of historical weapon that existed was represented on the armory shelves. Guns and more modern weaponry were sparse.

"This is some collection," Everly puffed under her breath.

If the Darkfreys had to go to war, or if the apocalypse came to Shroudhaven, they'd certainly be in a good position to defend themselves.

"Shadyr's shifted forms come with their own inbuilt weapons, and most are happy to rely on them alone. But sometimes it's good to have more options."

"Like a sword?" Everly asked.

"That's my preference," Lian agreed lightly.

Everly eyed a rack of handguns. "I haven't seen any shadyrs carrying. Do bullets not work on eidolghasts?"

"Oh, they work well enough. It's more of a secrecy issue. Can't be going around

firing off automatic rifles and RPGs around town every night and expect people not to notice."

Lian and Everly walked all the way across the room, their footsteps eerily loud. At the end of the main aisle of weapons, a set of wooden double doors was inset in the stone wall, secured by a high-tech fingerprint lock.

"Won't they know we were here?" Everly asked, eyeing the keypad.

"They would," Lian agreed, "if I tried to get through those doors. But we aren't using that entrance."

She led Everly a few feet away, reached her arm through to the back of a weapon rack, and tugged gently. The whole shelf pivoted forward in a wide arc to reveal a plain metal door, half an average adult's height.

"Does *every* room have a secret passage?" Everly whispered, amused.

Lian shrugged. "Probably. My older brother showed me the most. I think Dad showed him. And I had fun trying to find even more myself. This place has been here in one form or another since shadyrs first came through from the Everdark. It's a building built around another building on top of ten other buildings."

Crouching low, they entered the claustrophobic space behind the walls. Lian left the door open behind them, and Everly wondered if she did so in case they needed a quick getaway from the archives room. That sent a shiver of terror streaking up her spine.

Pipes and cables filled the space, perhaps some sort of maintenance access. They weaved between them slowly, hunched over.

They seemed to reach a dead end and Lian pushed on the pock-marked brick wall. It rolled slowly, crunching dust and debris beneath hidden wheels, and revealed a room filled with a strange, blue glow. A puff of cool air met them as they stepped inside.

While the rest of the estate was old-fashioned, channeling a medieval castle's aesthetic, this room was something out of a sci-fi movie. Glass-encased metal podiums scattered the room like trees, each illuminated by its own little spotlight. There were dozens of them, each occupied by some kind of artifact. The podiums connected to the ceiling on a series of tubes and cords, and a low-level hum echoed through the room.

"Each case is vacuum sealed and climate-controlled," Lian explained. "Most of these artifacts are several thousand years old, at least, brought over from the Everdark."

Everly followed her through the sea of narrow cases, too busy peeking inside the glass to pay attention to their path.

Some cases held statues so old and worn by time and weather damage that she couldn't make out what they'd once represented. Others held strangely shaped weapons, formed from the same black material as Lian's sword.

There were also books made from thick sheets of carved bone, a black-glass orb that glowed inside like molten lava, and all types of jewelry, from archaic metal pieces clearly wrought by hand to thin, crystalline objects more likely to have been woven by some otherworldly spider.

A few cases held skeletons, and Everly knew at first glance that they weren't human.

Lian stopped abruptly and Everly slammed into her back. The older woman had enough inner balance in her wide stance that the hit barely nudged her. She was staring into an empty case, a concerned wiggle between her brows.

"What's wrong?" Everly asked.

"There are artifacts missing," Lian said. "This is the third empty case we've passed."

"Do you think they were stolen?"

Lian blew out a low breath. "I don't know. These were all filled last time I was here, but that was a long time ago."

With her brows still pressed together, Everly continued searching. Lian was right—there were *a lot* of empty podiums.

Lian halted again and let out a low moan of distress. "Dammit!"

The case she stared into wasn't empty. A sheet of crumpled parchment lay across the white satin cushion, stained with a rust-colored substance. But Everly could see the rough outline on the parchment where something heavier had sat, its diamond shape marked by blood.

Something that was now gone.

"This is it," Lian murmured. "It should be here."

The Bane of Teeth and Stars was gone.

16

*G*one. Everly stared at the bloody parchment. A light-headed queasiness swelled through her, then drew together into a hard lump in her throat.

They hadn't known *for sure* that the Bane of Teeth and Stars held the answers they needed regarding Everly's powers. Maybe the name of the artifact had been a total coincidence. Maybe the vasmire's dying words didn't mean anything at all. But this artifact was the only possible lead they had.

In its absence, Everly watched all her hopes for figuring out how to deal with the dragon fade away.

She couldn't live like this, in this constant state of worrying that she'd slip up and kill someone else.

Nell's husband may have been some kind of resurrected zombie, but he'd been a moving, breathing person when Everly's light ended him. He'd saved her, led her to Rylan, showing a heart that was still good, a mind that still comprehended the world around him.

And the thing inside Everly destroyed him with glee. The guilt of his death still hummed like a swarm of hornets inside her.

The thought of anyone else getting hurt by her ... Lian, Callan ... Harper ...

She swallowed past the lump in her throat. "Are you sure this is where it's supposed to be?"

Lian nodded and pointed to a small bronze plate on the side of the podium, engraved with the name. She then pressed her palm against the corner of the glass. The case popped open and released a blast of cool, dry air, smelling faintly of old meat and loose change.

"This is the place. And whoever took it left this behind. It belongs with the Bane." Lian reached inside and grabbed the parchment.

Small flakes of dark red crumbled and fell from the ancient material.

Everly turned on the spot, seeking any available answer. "Could it just be, I don't know, out for maintenance? Getting repaired or cleaned? Or being used or something right now, by someone at the estate?"

"The things in here, they don't get used. They're considered too precious, but mostly, no one actually knows what to do with them." Lian shook her head as she pulled a clean square of canvas from her tote bag and wrapped the bloody parchment in it. Up close, it looked like soft leather made of a dull, pale skin.

"Nobody studies them?" Everly thought about Annabeth with her head in a book.

"They've been looked at in the past, sure. But they aren't in any kind of regular use. Plus most of these are just basic relics, kept for their historical, not magical, value. Others may have special magic as yet undiscovered, but it takes a bit of trial and error to work that out, and Mordan doesn't like sharing his toys."

Lian glanced warily around at the sea of illuminated podiums. "It is weird, though, how so many artifacts are missing from their cases. Maybe you're right. Maybe someone has taken them out for some reason and we just have bad timing."

Everly nodded, but there was little hope to be found.

Lian tucked the wrapped parchment into the waistband of her jeans at the back. "What are you doing?"

"If we find the Bane, we'll need this," Lian explained, releasing her jacket so that it fell over the parchment, hiding it from view. "It's somewhat disturbing that it's not with the Bane now."

Everly closed the glass case, the lock clicking as it closed. "We're still going to try to find it? How?"

Lian shrugged. "I don't know. Having the wrapper is a start though. Maybe whoever has the Bane will come to us to get it. Otherwise, things will get pretty messy."

Everly's forehead wrinkled. "Messy—?"

A hint of movement in her peripheral vision caught her attention. She whirled around, her heart leaping into her throat. She was not prepared to have to fight their way out of there if they were caught.

In the shadows, a figure moved. One in a beige cardigan, with neat black hair. *Jasper?*

The moment Everly spotted him, he turned on his heel and disappeared through the room, vanishing like a wraith beyond the glow of the cases.

"Busted," Lian muttered in a low voice. "We better make a speedy exit before he tells Mordan where he found us. We stand a better chance facing the master's wrath *off* his property."

Lian took the lead, rushing them out of the room with Everly close behind. They took a different path out of the estate than they'd taken in, using secret doors and hidden passages only until they were away from the archives room.

Then Lian led Everly at a swift pace in the most direct route toward the exit. There was no point hiding anymore. They hurried down large hallways and through open courtyards. Neither woman spoke as their shared sense of urgency kept them moving and alert. Everly's anxiety peaked with every person they passed, with every voice that drifted their way, waiting to be called out, captured. She didn't want to think about what their punishment might be.

But if Jasper was loyal enough to the Darkfreys to give up his relationship with Cherry, he definitely wasn't going to hold back tattling on them for breaking into the cursed archives.

They could be ambushed at any second. Expedience won out over remaining hidden.

They were ten steps from the exit of the main building when a sharp, commanding voice called out, "Howell!"

Lian waved toward the voice without looking. "*So* sorry, can't stop, just leaving."

Two bodies moved in from their side and came to a halt in front of them like a wall, blocking their path.

Everly's heart was already beating at a rapid pace, and it shuddered into overdrive as she sized up the Darkfrey shadyrs in front of them.

She recognized Vonny from multiple run-ins with the hard-faced shadyr who led Rylan's old brace, but the muscular man beside her was a stranger. He had long blond hair slicked back over the crown of his head—milkier than Vonny's golden bob, but nowhere near as colorless as Everly's own white hair.

Age-lines marked his furious, red-veined eyes. His long-sleeved button-up shirt stretched so tight over his muscles the fabric was tortured, sitting strangely against his body, lumpy in places that didn't seem right.

"So close," Lian murmured to Everly, before plastering on a fake smile. "Vonny, lovely to see you again so soon."

"Can it, Howell," Vonny snapped.

She crossed her arms and her gaze shifted between Lian and Everly, the pinched expression making it no secret that she wasn't happy to see them. "What in the Everdark are you still doing here? You left Master Darkfrey's office almost an hour ago."

Lian's eyes snapped across to Everly, then blinked to cover the silent message.

They don't know.

Had Jasper not told anyone yet, or had the news just not reached the two in front of them? Either way, they were on borrowed time. The doorway lay right in front of them, standing open, their car still parked just out the front.

"Oh, I was just feeling nostalgic, felt like taking a little tour. But we really must be going now," Lian said pleasantly. "Don't want to overstay our welcome."

"Why are you both wearing Darkfrey jackets? Those don't belong to you. Especially not to a bliv." Vonny's eyes narrowed on Everly.

Lian drew her attention back. "Oh, this? It's my son's. I thought I'd borrow it, to

fit in. Isn't that what you Darkfrey are all about?"

Vonny scoffed. "You never understood what it means to be a Darkfrey."

"You're right. I never did get the Darkfrey lifestyle. Which is why I left, and why we're leaving again now." Lian took hold of Everly's jacket sleeve and tugged, edging around from the couple.

"Don't walk away from me!" the man roared.

His shout was loud enough to shake the delicate chandelier over Everly's head. She glanced up at the shivering crystal pieces, then turned her wide eyes to Lian.

Lian left her fingers on Everly's sleeve and they both turned back.

"Kole. Sorry I didn't acknowledge you there. Everly, this is Kole Mesman, Vonny's husband."

Everly knew this would normally be the point some hand-shaking would be done, but no one moved.

Lian continued, "It's been ages. How long has it been since you left the estate and saw the light of day?"

Kole only snorted in response, like a bull about to charge.

Lian eyed the man up and down, her smile becoming crisp. "You're looking ... *bigger*."

Veins pulsed around his bulging eyes as he glared down at them. His gaze was disturbingly both fixed and distant at the same time. Filled with simmering violence and something inhuman.

"You ... *you* ..." he growled.

"Kole," Vonny said under her breath.

Though her empty expression indicated boredom, there was an undercurrent of warning in her words, laced with fear.

The massive man stepped closer to Lian, his giant, ham hock-sized fists clenched at his sides. "You don't get to leave here without answering for what you've done."

Everly shot Lian a worried look. Maybe they did know after all.

"And what, precisely, have I done?" Lian asked coldly.

"You took in that ... *cursed girl*. After what she did to us."

Everly's thoughts whirled, confused for a moment that he might mean her. But whatever her dragon was, whatever curse was going on inside her, she'd never done anything to the Mesmans.

"Tammy?" Lian's shoulders lowered with a long breath. "She's suffering enough for what happened. I'm not going to leave the poor kid out on the street. You know what happened to Blaise wasn't her fault."

With an animalistic growl, Kole launched for Lian, his fingers curled into claws.

Vonny stepped between them in a flash. She placed a hand on each side of his face, drawing him down to look at her. Still growling and breathing hard, spittle flew from the corners of his mouth, but he stilled.

Vonny's fingers stroked his jaw lovingly. "Kole. It's not the time. We don't want to get on Mordan's bad side. Not now. These are his guests today."

Lian's hand which had remained clinging to Everly's arm released, and she took a single, tentative step toward the shadyr couple.

"I know what it's like. How hard it is." For the first time since the Mesmans had arrived, Lian's tone sounded sincere. "I lost my children, too."

"Oh, like that's the same." Vonny whipped around, her face twisting with hatred. "Your boys only left you for a better home."

"Excuse me?" Everly's temperature spiked, and her hands balled into tight fists, fingernails digging into her palms.

How dare they say that.

Lian, however, remained calm. "I know it's not the same. But it still hurts. It still gives me perspective. If my sons had died—"

"He's. Not. Dead!" Vonny hissed, her voice going low and hard.

"You will never be able to move on until you accept that." Lian raised both hands up in front of her, stepping back again. "You have to let go, one day."

"Never." Kole snarled, pupils jittering against wide, white eyes. "I should kill you right here, so you can't protect that cursed girl a day longer!"

Vonny pressed a hand against his chest. There was no way she'd have the physical strength to hold the huge man back, but the gesture slowed him down.

Vonny glared at Lian and her lips twitched. "Just get out. Both of you. Go!"

Lian grabbed Everly's hand, and they fled the hallway for the cold, misty day outside.

They remained silent as they buckled into the SUV and sped down the shadowy drive.

Everly watched the trees thicken out the window, and breathed easier as they passed the threshold of the gates that took them off Darkfrey property.

But not even leaving behind the walls of Darkfrey Estate could make Everly forget the unstable fury and murderous glint in Kole Mesman's eyes.

17

S tanding in the shadows of a large tree, Jasper watched as Cherry and the new bliv girl sat in the open side door of a baby-blue campervan.

They chatted in hushed whispers, sipping from steaming Pimey's Diner paper cups. *Are they talking about me, about us?*

Except there was no *us* anymore, Jasper reminded himself. Still, Everly and Harper knew what he and Cherry once were to each other. They may have been the only people who did.

Callan and Tammy were there too, leaning against the back of the van. Jasper was pretty sure they didn't know, yet. And he was going to make sure no one else knew.

After seeing Everly and the Howell woman snooping around where they shouldn't have been, he'd followed them until they went right into the most forbidden and sacred part of the manor. Then he'd hurried down to the gates of Darkfrey Estate. He'd planned on confronting them on their way out, but then he saw the small squad hanging around out front.

What are they supposed to be here for, back up? What were the four of them going to achieve against all the shadyrs of the estate?

So he hid, and waited, and watched.

He tried not to notice how Cherry's fire-engine red hair dye hadn't been refreshed recently. Or how his lips met the coffee cup and blew out steam after sipping. Or how Harper wrapped an arm around his small waist, and squeezed, and Jasper immediately knew exactly how that waist felt.

It was a relief when Lian's SUV finally pulled through the gates. He wouldn't have to watch anymore. He wouldn't have to worry.

Lian parked behind the camper and opened her door to get out, though she left the engine running. Everly followed suit, shoving her hands into her pockets against the chilly morning.

Jasper slipped through the gates before they closed and approached the chatting group. He took in what he could of their conversation along the way.

"I can't believe I missed out on secret passages! You owe me, big time."

Callan laughed at the bliv. "They're lucky they weren't caught and locked away in the dungeons."

Harper's jaw dropped. "There are dungeons?"

"Especially lucky since we were seen," Everly added, looking at Cherry. "I think it was Jasper."

Cherry's lips pursed tightly. "Guess the whole estate will know soon, then."

"And we didn't get what we were after. It wasn't even there." Lian sighed. "There were quite a few missing—"

Callan barked, "We've got company."

They all quieted and turned to Jasper. He stopped a good distance from them, looking over their group. They were such a mess. Borrowed, ill-fitting uniforms, slack stances, none of the precision and strength a team of shadyrs should have. But the way they stood together against him sent a chill across the back of his neck.

A rotation of strong emotions crossed Cherry's face before he settled on pinched irritation.

He crossed his arms and vibrated with tension. "What do you want?"

"Come to drag us in yourself since the Mesmans didn't do it for you?" Lian accused, hands on her hips.

Jasper blinked. "I don't know what you're talking about."

Everly frowned at him. "You didn't tell them to stop us on our way out?"

"I didn't tell anyone anything."

Everly eyed him warily. "You saw us in a place we shouldn't have been and didn't tell anybody? Why?"

Jasper took a shaky breath. His gaze slid past Cherry for the briefest moment before he looked Everly in the eye. "Because now I know a secret of yours. Much like you know one of mine. I want to make sure neither gets out."

Lian shot Everly a questioning look, as did Callan and Tammy. Even mentioning that there was a secret was risky. But no bigger than the risk of Cherry or the other two using that secret against him.

He needed some assurance, a deal made so he wouldn't have to spend every moment worrying he'd lose his place at the estate, and today had given him just what he needed.

"I won't tell anyone where you were, what you were doing, or what you took," he said. Then he directed his words at Everly, Harper, and Cherry. "And you all keep quiet in return."

"You're blackmailing us?" Cherry spat. "Of course you'd think that way."

He crossed the wide distance between them and huffed quietly. "Jokes on you because you should know I would never, ever do that to you. You could break my heart ten times over, and I'd still never do that to you."

Jasper's cheeks flushed with heat, and he broke eye contact, too uncomfortable under Cherry's dark-eyed gaze.

"Come on. This fool is wasting our time," Cherry grunted, spinning around and marching back to his team.

"Wait." The word came out unbidden.

Cherry stopped, but didn't turn around. "What don't you get? We promise your secret is safe. I know that's all you care about."

Harper and Everly closed ranks around Cherry, staring Jasper down.

"I ... I know you didn't get what you were after today. You were looking for an artifact that's missing, right? I know what happened to them. All of the missing ones." The saliva in Jasper's mouth dried up.

What am I doing? Sharing information is a betrayal of the Darkfreys.

But he owed Cherry and his friends something more. He could never stop owing them.

Everly raised a pale eyebrow. "And what will this information cost us?"

"Nothing."

Cherry half-turned, but his lips remained pressed tight in a crooked line, and his narrowed eyes darted, scrutinizing, burning Jasper down to his core.

Whatever. It's not like I'm trying to win him back. It isn't worth the risk.

"What do you know?" There was an eager edge to Everly's voice.

Jasper fixed her in his gaze, trying to block away the view of Cherry beside her. "All of the missing artifacts disappeared ten years ago. Around the same time the Gorhanmere group split off from Darkfrey Estate."

"Gorhanmere," Lian mused. "I heard about them incorporating their own shadyr group. Thought it was weird Mordan would let them out from under his control. Weirder still if he let them run off with the artifacts."

"Some odd rumors have been coming out of Gorhanmere since then," Callan said, frowning as though filling in the blanks. "That they've become extra powerful."

Jasper nodded. "From what I've heard, Mordan didn't think the artifacts were worth starting a war over."

"No, maybe not," Lian agreed offhandedly.

"Thank you," Everly said. "That's helpful."

Jasper's eyes were on Cherry again, who still hadn't turned around.

His heart shrunk painfully. "Just keep your promise."

Callan and Lian still looked confused, and Tammy seemed like she couldn't care less about anything going on around her.

With a few waves and goodbyes, they headed over to the SUV, and the two new girls and Cherry headed to the campervan. He hadn't said goodbye, hadn't even glanced

back, and a rush of yearning filled Jasper just to see his beautiful eyes one more time.

"Hey," Jasper called out, halting their climb into the van.

Cherry's gaze met his then, and Jasper's breath hitched.

He swallowed nothing, dry mouth sticking as he found his words. "If you go after them ... be careful. The Gorhanmere shadyrs aren't just powerful, they're dangerous, even a little unstable. Whatever it is you're after, try not to get yourselves killed."

Everly and Harper spent most of the day at Howell House, eating, planning, and lounging around with the team.

It was comforting to do something so innocuously normal for a few hours, despite the fact that they were talking about infiltrating a supposedly "dangerous and unstable" group of shadyrs in between snacks and video games.

By late afternoon, they had a basic plan. Rushelle and Denny would remain behind to look after Rylan, and the rest of the team would leave bright and early the next day to travel to Gorhanmere.

They would pose as shadyrs dissatisfied with the Darkfreys—not a stretch—who were looking for a new group to join, and see what they could find out from there. Once that was decided, Lian sent everyone off to rest up.

If Jasper's warning about the Gorhanmere shadyrs was legit, they'd all need it.

The sun had already dipped below the mountains when Everly and Harper got back home. The backyard was deep in shadow beneath a purple sky, but Everly caught a flash of glowing eyes in the thick brush around the swing set.

Zozo.

She locked eyes with the little cougar, willing him to stay there while she went in and grabbed him some food.

As Everly unlocked the door, Harper leaned a shoulder against the aged timber and sighed. "Hopefully this trip will be good for Cherry. Poor guy is in a rough place. Can you imagine having to keep such a big part of yourself secret like that?"

Everly shivered. "Yeah, that must be hard."

"I might run a bath and soak for a while. My pores need to steam. Do you want to grab a shower first?"

Everly shoved the door open. "No, you go ahead. Just going to grab a drink and then I'm keen to get to sleep."

"Bet you are." Harper flashed a cheeky smile and then veered off up the staircase.

"If I could go back in time and never tell you Rylan was in my dreams, that would

be a secret I'd be okay keeping!" Everly yelled after her with a laugh.

Harper ducked back down to peer at her through the railings. "But you wouldn't keep secrets from me, would you?"

Her cheeky smile remained, but there was a slight edge to her tone.

"Of course not," Everly replied, chuckling as though the idea was ridiculous. "Goodnight."

Harper blew a kiss and disappeared up the stairs.

Everly's smile faded as she continued down the hall toward the kitchen.

The fog filling the house was lighter than it had been, and the kitchen cabinets were all blessedly closed. Everly hoped it meant that the beshadowing effects were dying down as the vasmire pieces decomposed, though the faster they broke down, the sooner the team would have to find more to keep Rylan going.

How long can we keep this up?

This town felt like it was dragging her down into darkness. Since being here, there had been too many secrets and dangers and questions she wasn't sure she was going to like the answers to.

She extracted a fresh tray of ground beef from the fridge. Even just trying to focus on one thing at a time left her feeling overwhelmed. They couldn't keep following an endless cycle of killing vasmires, stocking Rylan's room, and just hoping he'd wake up.

At some point, Callan's warning about the beshadowing effects on the two of them would come to pass, and if Everly herself was beshadowed, she couldn't very well keep Harper safe.

Everly tucked her chin into the collar of her bomber jacket, warding against the cold as she skipped down the back stairs. Shroudhaven's nightly mist had filtered into the backyard, turning the shadows heavier and more menacing outside the small globe of light from the porch.

She kept her gaze trained on Zozo, studiously ignoring the idea that there could be other things roaming in the dark.

"Hey, Zozo," Everly cooed, stopping a couple of feet away on the cracked and mossy path.

She sat cross-legged on the concrete and slid the styrofoam tray out for him. "Dinner?"

The cougar dipped his nose to the beef, sniffed at the meat, then started chowing down.

"Why do you keep coming here?" Everly asked him. "I know Nell is gone, but you were wild before, weren't you? I can't keep feeding you forever."

Everly wasn't sure if Zozo was lingering nearby because of the food or something else. But she liked being able to feed the big cat. Even with all the madness of the situation, helping Zozo made her feel more like herself, like she was doing something good, and less like everything in her life had come untethered.

She reached out carefully and ran two fingers down the cougar's silky forehead, across a carefully stitched scar. A low rumble emanated from the young cat, and her adrenaline zinged through her veins before realizing it wasn't a growl.

Zozo was purring.

Warmth tingled through her, and she added the rest of her fingers, smoothing her palm over his head.

The click of a door opening echoed through the backyard.

Zozo lifted his head, his ears flattening as he zeroed in on the house. His purring ceased, and Everly yanked her hand away before he got spooked enough to bite her.

She craned around to glance back at the house, her heart racing.

Harper stood in the glow of the porchlight wearing her fluffy pink night robe.

Everly scooted to the right in a vain attempt to hide Zozo from sight. "I thought you were taking a bath."

"Thought you were going to bed." Harper folded her arms, squinting into the darkness at Everly. "That's one awfully big stray cat. Is that one of Nell's rescues?"

Everly frowned at her casual tone. As though finding a zombie animal in their backyard was no different than spotting a sparrow on the fence. "I, um, didn't really see him until tonight. This is the first time he's come up close."

"Come on. You two are far too familiar for that. Why have you been keeping this cutie from me?" Harper put her hand on the railing and started down the short staircase in her bare feet.

Zozo growled at her approach.

Everly snapped, "No, don't come down here! It's not safe."

Harper paused mid-step. "I'm confused. Safe for you, but not for me?"

"It's complicated—"

"Then why don't you explain it to me?" Harper asked, her voice growing louder. "Because it seems pretty basic to me. You're keeping secrets and then having double standards. It's okay for you, but never for me."

Amidst the raised voices, Zozo's growl rumbled. The cougar sprang forward and landed on the path between the two women. His shoulders and head were down, teeth bared, and haunches tensed as though ready to pounce.

"Zozo, no!" Everly yelled.

The cougar looked back at her, a question in its ghostly blue eyes.

Is he trying to protect me? From Harper?

Harper remained frozen in place, her hands out in a calming gesture and eyes darting back to measure the distance between her and the back door.

"Leave her alone, she's not an enemy." Everly moved to her feet in a slow, smooth motion, making calming sounds.

The cougar's pose softened, tail twitched, and it circled back around behind Everly where it kept her friend locked in its vision.

Harper's face was scrunched up. "What is going on with you? Secretly training zombie cougars to attack your friends?"

The accusation made heat sting through Everly's eyes. "It's not like that."

"Then you'd better tell me what it is like."

Everly rubbed her eyebrow, chasing away the growing tension. "I'm not sure. I think there's some kind of connection between me and this cougar."

"Clearly. And maybe if you'd let me do some of the night-time feeds, I could have had my own attack cat, too."

"It's not just that."

"Then *tell* me. Stop keeping secrets!"

Zozo growled again, and Harper lowered her voice, almost pleading. "You can tell me. Whatever is going on, I'm here for you if you're just honest with me."

Everly shook her head. Harper was right, but that didn't make it easy. She swallowed, her body wanting to chase away the words as they rose from her.

"Remember when we ran over something on our way into Shroudhaven?"

Harper hugged herself and nodded.

"But we didn't find a body or evidence we'd actually hit something? That's because Nell got to him first. This is the cougar we hit. And I've been dreaming about it too, ever since."

Harper's face softened. "Like Rylan?"

"Sort of. But not as strong of a connection. But that's why I think Zozo is safe for me and not for you."

Harper nodded.

Her lips were tight and voice hard when she asked, "Do you know how you're making these connections?"

Everly opened her mouth, ready to deny knowing anything, but Harper's gaze pierced deep, as though waiting and watching for any sign of something withheld.

"I think it's the dragon," she mumbled.

"Your powers?" Harper urged.

Everly lifted her hands, staring at them instead of making eye contact. "I think it has somehow absorbed some, or all, of the cougar and Rylan's spirits. When the light comes out of me, it doesn't just attack. It's not just hitting things. I think ... I feel like it's also absorbing them. Like it's *eating* them. Eating their lifeforce."

Harper just stared, and Everly's voice shook as more words tumbled out of the

broken dam. "And I can't control it. Not always. It does what it wants, and what it wants is to eat things. It wanted to eat you, at Rooks Hotel. And at Nells ..."

Everly's voice shuddered to a halt with a sob.

Harper stepped forward, moving closer despite Zozo's soft rumbling. "What happened?"

"It wasn't a Darkfrey who killed Nell's husband. It was *me*. Can't you see now why I'm worried about you? This whole place is dangerous. *I'm* dangerous!"

"No, you're not."

She sounded so certain it made Everly gasp, her sobs drying up.

Harper continued her steady pace up the path to her. "Whatever is doing those things, it's obvious now that it's not you. *You* would never have done that. You wouldn't choose to murder someone! That light power you have is something, but it's not *you*. And if you'd told me all this bloody sooner maybe you wouldn't have been going around thinking it was all this time!"

"I don't want to hurt you," Everly whispered.

"I know you don't. That's why I trust you." Harper stopped right in front of her and eyed her for a long moment, then her shoulders slumped. "But you have to stop keeping secrets from me, Ev. I never thought you would ..."

"I'm sorry," Everly murmured.

Zozo nudged her arm with his nose, and she put her fingertips on his head, reassuring him that everything was okay, that she didn't need his protection. He pressed back against her hand for a moment, and then backed away, vanishing into the long grass.

Harper stared at where the big cat had disappeared, then shook her head and leaned into Everly, giving her a tight hug.

She mumbled into Everly's ear, "We're a team. We're together in all this weirdness. Stop trying to shoulder the burden alone."

Everly nodded back into Harper's silky hair. But it didn't matter whether Harper wanted to share the weirdness or not. As soon as Rylan woke up, they were leaving the weirdness behind. Because every day they remained in Shroudhaven could be their last.

18

Rylan opened his eyes in a gleaming shopping mall. Stark, bright, and as unnerving as any dream he'd shared with Everly so far.

Shroudhaven, as small and undeveloped as it was, only boasted a dinky little strip mall. The only actual mall was two hours away, outside of the larger Shroudhaven region.

But this wasn't any mall he'd ever seen in real life.

Rainbow lens-flares sparkled, obscuring the details of cotton candy-colored shops. On the other side of the frosted glass in the ceiling, vivid sparks ebbed and flowed like fireworks, blurry and abstract.

Maybe this was based on a mall in the city where Everly had lived after leaving, or maybe it was purely her imagination, but at least some parts seemed familiar.

A bright, upbeat J-Pop song played loudly throughout the space. The singer's sweet voice was mournful and yearning, contrasting with the energetic metal guitar riffs and electronica beats.

I know that from somewhere.

Rylan frowned, unable to remember why. The lyrics were all in Japanese.

He stood on an escalator, taking far longer than was realistic to get to the next level. As he climbed, the stairs flowed downward beneath him, twisting into a dizzying illusion that threw him off balance.

Not that Everly's dreams ever made him feel any other way. Her presence had the same effect on him, making everything upside down and confused.

He was supposed to protect her. It was what he'd always wanted, why he'd made the decision to push her out of his dangerous life, keep her as far away from the world of monsters as possible. But with all this time together in her dreams, all he could think about was holding her near.

If I can't do anything anyway, if I might be stuck here forever, would that be so wrong?

It sounded like Lian, Callan, and the others at Howell House were doing their best to keep Everly safe, which offered him some comfort. But as long as his body was still out there, and he was in here, he knew Everly would keep putting herself in danger to fix it.

Maybe it was worth trying to get her to give up.

Rylan turned a circle on the moving staircase, searching for her. If he was "awake," it meant she was here, too.

The mall was unoccupied, all the stores were gated, and interiors were obscured by a blurry swirl of glow and darkness.

When viewed from the corner of his eye, he saw familiar shapes moving behind the locked shutters—like monsters walking in the depths of the Wyrdwoods, just out of sight. He shivered and hoped the rickety metal would keep the monsters in.

As he got closer to the second-floor landing, he caught sight of Everly's striking pale silver hair sparkling in the overhead lights. She stood with her back to the escalator and her hands clenched into fists at her sides. Her body vibrated with tension.

When he crested the top of the escalator, he hopped off onto smooth white marble floors and walked over to join Everly. He was used to coming up against weird things in her dreams, but he wasn't fully prepared for what he found this time.

Dolls. Dozens of creepy, broken dolls.

They were arranged on tables at differing heights, like they would have been displayed for viewing in a toy store. Except rather than being locked away behind a store's gate, they were in the middle of the landing, all of them facing the escalators and the second-floor balcony, the latter of which didn't have a safety railing.

The dolls were ... *wrong*.

Many were missing limbs, or had battered, bloody clothes. Several of the porcelain dolls had gaping, jagged edges where their faces should have been.

Rylan side-eyed the creepy display and swallowed hard. The dolls stared back at him.

"Taking inspiration from classic horror tonight?"

Everly made a small sound of agreement.

"They're moving," she muttered without turning to look at him. "The one in the purple dress with the shattered arm blinked at me."

"You're dreaming," Rylan reminded her.

She rolled her eyes. "Yes, *I know*. That doesn't make them any less terrifying."

Near the front of the row, a black-haired, porcelain doll with a too-wide, crooked crack where her mouth should have been, turned his way.

Rylan's heart hammered. Dream or not, Everly was right—they were terrifying. He stared at the now-unmoving doll, calculating his options. If it moved again, he was going to break it limb from limb. Was he imagining a soft giggling coming from that direction? If so, it was swamped beneath the song playing throughout the chamber.

"Does the music have to be up so loud?" he asked.

Everly winced, keeping her eyes on the dolls. "Sorry, it was stuck in my head when I went to sleep, like, really locked in there. It's going to be a hard thing to change."

Rylan listened again, the chorus somehow taking him back to his childhood.

"What song is it? It seems familiar."

She cleared her throat—*embarrassed?*

"Closing credits of *Akima and the Animatrons*, season three." She smiled bashfully in a way that brought an automatic smile to Rylan's lips, too.

The sense of nostalgia the song filled him with suddenly became a clear memory. Him, Everly, and his brother, bundled in blankets on the living room floor in front of the TV, binging their way through the neon-bright animation.

When they had run out of episodes, they'd play acted their own stories as the characters. "Oh yeah, we used to watch it all the time when we were kids, right?"

"Before you left home."

Home. That was a place the Darkfrey estate never felt like. There were no lazy morning cartoon marathons there. He'd left so much behind.

Still turned away from him, Everly's voice sounded small. "I know why you left. I know about your dad. Is that why you pushed me away?"

Rylan huffed. "Mom's been talking, huh?"

Everly nodded, her eyes shifting briefly to his then back again to the dolls. But not fast enough that Rylan didn't notice the pain there.

He scrubbed the back of his head with his hand. "I just ... wanted you to be safe."

Everly's shoulders dropped as though letting out a breath she'd held too long. "The *Akima* poster is still up on the wall in your old bedroom. It's all the same in there, from before you left."

"I haven't been back there in so long. I've almost forgotten what it's like."

Everly turned to him properly then, locking his eyes with hers. "We'll get you home soon."

Rylan returned his gaze to the demon dolls and tried for an easy tone in an attempt at levity. "So, what's the news from the real world?"

"Not anything good." Everly jolted as another doll near the highest of the display tables stood up with abrupt, jerky movements. "The Gorhanmere shadyrs took off with a bunch of artifacts from the Darkfrey archives, including the one we wanted."

Rylan blew out a breath. "Well, that sucks. What's the plan now?"

"We're going to Gorhanmere to follow up. The Bane is our only real lead. If we can figure out what I am, maybe we can figure out how to free you from ..." She waved a hand vaguely in the air. "This."

The standing doll hopped off her display square onto the marble floor and began to hobble toward them. She was missing half a leg, which gave her a swaying, uneven gait. Her eyes were black and hollow, and her frilly pink dress had been slashed to ribbons. She left a smeared trail of red blood behind her on the pale floor.

Rylan glanced back at the escalator. The first floor had moved farther away so that it was more like ten stories down instead of one, and the escalators stretched and narrowed until they were as thin as ropes.

Everly's breaths came fast and her eyes were so wide the whites were visible all the way around. "No way down."

Everly usually seemed calm and collected in her dreams—at least the ones that were recurring. She'd mastered what to do to stay sane during even the worst of them. But now ... Rylan realized that she was legitimately frightened and without a plan.

"You haven't had this dream before," Rylan guessed.

Everly shook her head, biting her lips.

More dolls clambered off their pedestals and began to jitter stiffly across the smooth marble.

"I don't know what to do," Everly whispered.

"They're just dolls." *Bloody, terrifying dolls.* "How bad could it be?"

Everly raised her eyebrows over fearful eyes, expressing how bad she thought it could be.

"Okay then." Rylan stretched out his arms and cracked his knuckles.

He stepped in front of Everly, ready to fight the miniature army.

"Hang on, I want to try something." Everly searched about until her eyes landed on their target.

The ghostly cougar that was also trapped in her dreams, skirting around near the closed shopfronts.

"Zozo?"

It paused, turning to her voice.

"Get them!"

With a growl, the cougar changed its path, slinking toward the dolls in a low-bellied trot. Once it was near enough, it put on a burst of speed, sprinting in and pouncing into the thick of them.

"Huh, how about that." Everly didn't seem entirely happy about the outcome.

Rylan's lip quirked up. "You named it Zozo?"

"Not really, it's just short for Zombie Cougar." Everly shrugged as she watched it dismembering the dolls.

Despite the carnage in the main huddle of demon dolls, a large number still dragged themselves closer.

Everly pointed beyond them to a long corridor. "Come on, it looks like there's an exit over there."

The first doll reached them. Rylan kicked it viciously in the head. The doll sailed away like a football and careened over the edge of the balcony.

It hit the ground, smashing far louder than something its size should.

"We're going to have to go through them."

Everly nodded, smiling grimly.

Together, they waded into the ambling dolls.

"So, no luck with the kiss?" Rylan asked, in an effort to pretend they weren't fending off possessed toys.

"No luck," Everly agreed, her voice shaky. "I tried, though."

It had been a silly idea to start with.

I don't know why I even suggested it.

The fact that it didn't work left Rylan with a dull hollow in his chest. Or was it the way he was now imagining Everly leaning over his motionless body, kissing cold lips, and suddenly, bizarrely jealousy of himself? She'd kissed him. And maybe he'd never know what that was like. And why did that hurt so bad?

Rylan sent two more creepy dolls sailing off the landing. "What else can we try? I'm out of ideas."

"We'll work it out. The Bane could still be something, or I'll convince Crowea to touch me and give us answers, or we'll try every other fairy tale cure out there if we have to." Everly's eyes glistened fiercely.

They dodged the worst of the dolls, Rylan booting away the ones that reached him. He was happy to have something to take out his frustration on, and he searched for more. They seemed to be avoiding him, trying to circle around him, only one target in their sights.

Everly lifted her heavy work boot to kick the one closing in on her. But it moved in a flash, leaping over her foot and latching onto her thigh. Two more joined it, rushing up at startling speeds.

Rylan grunted. They didn't care about him at all. They were putting all their energy into reaching Everly.

The doll on her thigh plunged its jagged mouth deep into her flesh. She cried out, sending Rylan's pulse into overdrive.

Rylan grabbed the monstrous toy and tore it off her, throwing it back toward the cougar. The other two dolls clambered like spiders around Everly's body, biting chunks as they went. She stumbled.

Wrenching the dolls off her, Rylan scooped her up into his arms and charged through the remaining toys and down the corridor.

She wrapped her arms around his neck, helping support herself as he ran. Her warm blood seeped through his clothing. His heart hammered.

It's just a dream.

Ramming the exit door with his shoulder, they burst out into a parking lot that extended into eternity.

Above them, a bright magenta aurora shimmered, and the dragon swam amongst it, shimmering and sparking as the two came into contact. Everything was a warm, purple tone and smelled of the candy aisle at The Boutique All.

Everly shivered against his chest, her arms tight around his neck.

The door slammed behind them, and no further sound of scraping porcelain or J-Pop music followed them through.

"Are you okay?" Rylan's whisper cracked in the silence.

Everly nodded, shifting her weight as a signal to be let down. He placed her back onto her feet, but wasn't ready to let her go. As his fingertips drew away from her, they felt somehow hollow.

"I'm sorry about that," she said, head hung and cheeks pink.

Although she didn't appear to be in pain, she still bled freely.

Rylan groaned, running a hand over his mouth. "I know it's not real, but it *feels* real. The danger feels real. Your *blood* feels real. And the worst part is knowing you're out in the real world doing even more dangerous stuff trying to keep me alive. I hate that so much, you can't understand."

Rylan's heart continued its raging beat but did nothing to shake off a sense of finality that was settling upon him. Maybe it wouldn't be so bad, if he no longer had a body to go back to. He could imagine a lifetime with Everly in her dreams. "Maybe you should just let my body go. Cut the life support."

Everly's plump lips widened into a circle. "You can't give up. Just because the kiss didn't work, doesn't mean nothing will."

"It was a dumb idea anyway," Rylan huffed, failing to turn his gaze away from her lips, once again imagining them pressed to his. "I mean, how was a sleeping beauty kiss supposed to work if I wasn't even there to experience it?"

Everly frowned, questioningly.

"I mean, when you're awake, it's like I don't even exist, so if it took any effort on my part to get out of here, how could I know what was happening enough to get back into my body?"

"It's not like I can kiss you while I'm asleep."

Rylan's heartbeat pounded in his ears, so deafening he couldn't hear his own words. "What if you did?"

"Sorry, what?"

Rylan focused on keeping his expression unchanged, as though he was asking for something perfectly rational. "What if we tried the sleeping beauty kiss here? Now?"

Everly turned scarlet, her cheeks burning against the white of her hair. "I guess. Yeah, I mean, we could do that. If you think it could help."

Rylan licked his lips, his head shaking. It was a stupid suggestion. The logic for

how it would work was a stretch, at best. But what else was there?

"If there's even a small chance it will work, we should, shouldn't we?"

"Oh. Yeah. Of course. We should." Everly took a deep breath and let it out slowly.

"We should," Rylan echoed, and stepped slightly closer.

"Just in case." Her voice was a breathy whisper.

Rylan bent toward her. He swallowed against the thud of his heartbeat in his throat and pulled her into him.

The moment Rylan's lips pressed against hers, he knew it was a lie.

If the sleeping beauty kiss was going to wake him up, it would have done so in reality. This wasn't going to wake him. That wasn't why he'd asked for it, why he wanted it.

He just ... wanted it.

Her mouth was soft, lush. She tilted her head back and her lips parted ever so slightly, maybe even unconsciously. But Rylan took it as an invitation, deepening the kiss, opening her lips with his, his tongue teasing hers.

Even though they were in a dream, he felt everything—the curves of her body pressed into him, the warmth of her, the satin touch of her skin beneath his fingers as he cupped her face and then slid his fingers into her hair.

He was fairly certain sleeping beauty hadn't been kissed quite like this.

She turned him mindless. He wanted to soak in every part of her, run his fingers over every full curve. This was the moment, the dream he'd denied himself his whole life. He was lost in every sensation, every touch, wishing for more.

He'd missed their first kiss, in the real world where his body was numb and unconscious.

Here, though ... He could touch her here. He could kiss her here.

Here, maybe he could admit that he wanted her.

And she'd agreed. She wanted this too. Desire rose inside him and he squeezed her tight.

Her arms entwined his neck, pulling him toward her. Did she want him too? Or was she doing this only to try to help him wake up? The thought that she might was like a stab to his chest.

The pain shot his mind back to reality with the force of whiplash. The words he'd spoken to himself for years shouted through his mind.

You can't want her. You can't love her. You can't be with her. Not if you want to keep her safe. Keeping her safe is all that matters.

He pulled away abruptly.

Everly stared up at him, chest heaving and cheeks pink. He wanted to reach for her again, but he forced his hands to his sides.

"It ... didn't work." His voice came out low, husky.

Everly blinked three times and swiped a finger to the corner of her eye in a swift motion.

She smiled on shaky lips. "Don't worry. We'll figure it out."

Rylan turned his face to the unnatural sky above them, trying to calm his body.

And if they didn't ... He'd have to convince Everly to let him go.

If keeping her safe was the last thing he ever did, it would be worth it.

19

*H*e kissed me. We kissed each other.

Everly pushed away the memories of last night's dream as they interrupted her for the millionth time that morning. It was just a test, an attempt to wake Rylan up. It didn't mean anything. But the sensation of his lips on hers had felt so real, still haunted her, made her feel drunk and woozy and wanting to return to sleep forever. The way he had kissed her …

Doesn't mean anything if I can't wake him up.

Everly sat near Callan, both of them anchored to the hand railing as the campervan bounced along the rough road. She'd driven past the highway turnoff that led to Gorhanmere a dozen times or more in her life while heading in and out of Shroudhaven, but she'd never taken it. Never actually stepped foot in the nearby town.

For good reason, clearly. No one in their right mind would have wanted to travel this way.

The road twisted up the side of a mountain, cutting through a thick tunnel of dark evergreens. The fall off on one side was vertigo-inducing. There were times Everly held her breath and prayed the van wouldn't tip backward off the steep road. Through the gap in the front seats, she could see Harper's knuckles turning white on the wheel.

Everything outside was dusky and silent. Glimpses of a churning gray sky could be seen through the forest canopy. Everly hadn't spotted a single bird or hint of other wildlife since Harper had turned off the main highway.

Something about their surroundings felt … wrong. Like they'd left safety behind and driven into madness. The farther they continued up the winding road, the worse Everly's sense of foreboding.

In the passenger seat, Lian hummed, breaking the charged silence. "There it is."

Harper slowed and curved to the right onto a dusty one-lane road.

The small town appeared up ahead. Gorhanmere sat on the banks of a wide lake, with water so dark it was like a bottomless hole in the earth. From afar, the village was picturesque—a grouping of half-timbered colonial cottages with low gables and aged sandstone walls, surrounded by thick forest and backed by the mountain's craggy peak.

But as the van skirted the edge of the lake and drew closer, it wasn't quite so vacation perfect. The cottages had weathered to dull grays and off-whites. Weeds rambled, leafless and thorny over fencing and walls.

Many of the exposed timbers were crumbling away, bits of wood sticking out like broken bones. Several windows had cracked panes or lacked glass entirely, like gaping, soulless eyes.

"The village continues into the trees," Lian observed, pointing at a few visible rooflines between the thick pines.

Everly squinted through the windshield, noting the hanging signs on the nearest buildings. A bakery, town council, and a farm supplies shop, where they seemed to have selected all the deadliest looking farm tools—scythes, pitch forks, huge, toothy saws—to line the display up front. But the place seemed deserted.

"Where is everybody?"

"There's a car behind us," Harper said, leaning to get a better view of the side mirror. "A dark minivan."

In the back, Tammy and Cherry turned to look.

Lian checked in the passenger side mirror. "They weren't following us on the way up?"

Harper shook her head. "They popped out of the trees after we turned off the main road."

Lian sighed. "Everybody on their guard. We don't know what to expect. Harper, the motel's down that way. Take a right here."

The campervan trundled over a sparsely graveled road toward a long, low building shielded beneath overgrown trees. Harper pulled into the parking lot and chose a spot near the door marked *Reception*. Like every other building they'd passed, the place looked deserted.

The other van pulled in a few spots down.

Cherry whistled. "Isn't that a coincidence. It's a Darkfrey van."

"Just what we need," Callan said as he reached for the door handle.

When he opened the door, a brisk, mountain wind blustered through the vehicle. They were quite a bit above sea level, and the temperature had dropped dramatically.

"You think they're here for us or something else?" Everly shivered and zipped up her jacket before she followed Callan out.

She hopped off the staircase onto dry dirt, and dust billowed beneath her boots. The Darkfrey team unloaded out of their van at the same time, the two groups sizing each other up.

"Hey, man!" Callan held out a hand toward one of the new arrivals. "Long time, no see."

"Look what the ghast dragged in," the guy replied with an open, honest smile.

The two men clasped hands and did one of those manly back-clapping, single-armed hugs, then stepped away to appraise one another. The Darkfrey shadyr was tall and thin like Callan, but older, with a hard glint to his eyes and buzzed strawberry-blond hair.

Callan motioned to the man. "This is Lucas. I trained under his brace."

"You and your brother. I still say Darkfrey's worse off without the two of you," Lucas said, his grin widening.

He nodded to the rest of them, eyes passing over Tammy and Cherry without acknowledging them, then lingered on Lian. "What brings you lot to Gorhanmere?"

"Thought we'd have a weekend getaway," Callan replied, smoothly.

"Ha, sure. No one comes out here unless they're looking for something. Normally trouble."

Callan smiled. "The only thing we're looking for is a place to relax. What about you? Is it normal for a Darkfrey brace to be so far from Shroudhaven?"

Lucas nodded, glancing back at his team. They were unloading equipment from the van into one of the motel rooms.

"Yeah, unfortunately. We're investigating a beshadowing."

Lian spoke up. "I thought Gorhanmere had its own group of shadyrs to look after it?"

Lucas inclined his head. "Well ... it *does*. Mordan keeps it hush-hush, but the leader of the group here has gone a little mad, and we can't rely on them to keep the town safe."

"You know where we might find this leader? Just to steer away from that area, of course," Callan said.

Lucas frowned slightly. "We keep clear of them and they keep clear of us. We only come up every so often to clean house. Got reports a couple days ago of strange sightings. I've put my money on it being an auerdax."

Cherry gasped. "No way!"

Lian tensed, her hand twitching at her side.

"A what?" Harper asked.

Lucas frowned at her and Everly for a moment before his grin returned. "Oh, these are your new bliv friends. Heard about them."

Everly stuffed her hands in her pockets and tried to make herself small.

"An auerdax is a rare kind of eidolghast," Callan told them, his mouth thin and downturned.

"Rare and tricky," Lucas agreed. "We were out all night hunting for this thing. Came back to grab some shut eye before nightfall, then we'll head back out."

"Need any help?" Callan asked.

"Nah, we've got it. Just keep your eyes peeled so you don't end up in trouble. We

can't be babysitting you lot." He still grinned widely, but the warning was clear beneath his playful quip.

"We'll be fine," Callan assured him.

"Good to see you, man," Lucas added, offering up a hand once again. "Don't be a stranger."

As the Darkfrey team disappeared into their rooms, Lian grabbed her purse from the passenger seat and shut the door. "I'll go check us in."

Everly watched her vanish through the creaky door that led to the small office, then turned to Callan. "That's two warnings about the unstable shadyrs in the area. The shadyrs we're meant to be infiltrating in order to steal from. Should we be worried?"

"*Pshh.*" Callan waved a hand. "The Darkfrey mob also call us crazy. How bad could they really be?"

"Famous last words." Tammy shifted closer to the group, her lips barely moving as she murmured, "Welcome party approaching."

Callan stiffened and followed her line of sight.

Everly did the same.

Five figures emerged from the shadows beneath the thicket of trees, ambling slowly into the parking lot with their gazes locked on the Howell team. There were two women and three men, all of them wearing stained, battered overalls and muddy boots.

All of them had clean-shaved heads, showing off the dented, scarred skin of their scalps. Dirt smudged their wide, bulging-eyed faces. Two of the men carried shotguns holstered on their backs, and one woman had a rusty machete resting on her shoulder.

Harper hissed. "Are we about to be axe murdered? Because this feels like the beginning of a gory B-horror, and I am *not* dressed for murder."

"Looks suitable to me," Tammy muttered under her breath.

"You had the option to stay behind with Rush and Rylan," Everly said.

"Together in the weirdness, Ev." Harper's expression grew serious. "Also Denny is back there too, so, ew, no."

All five of the townsfolk were covered in scars. Dozens of white lines showed anywhere their skin was visible. As the group got closer, the eldest of the men stepped ahead of his companions, eyeing the Howell team warily. His bald head peaked strangely, ovaloid, off center, and too large. He loomed over them, staring with icy-blue eyes.

"Shadyrs, or just creepers?" Cherry whispered.

"I'll check," said Callan.

He stepped forward and casually ran two fingers from the corners of his mouth, straight down his chin. He'd done the same thing to Everly and Harper when they'd first met him again after returning to town and had been questioning him about weird stuff.

He'd since explained that this was an insider symbol for shadyrs, a way to check

whether someone was in on the secret without having to come out and ask. The gesture represented the growth of two sharp fangs.

The man grunted at him and casually swung his shotgun around to the front.

"More Darkfreys?" His voice was deep, with a disturbing gurgle in it.

"No." Callan gave the man a knowing look and said meaningfully, "*Independent* shadyrs."

The man's fingers danced over the barrel of his gun as he took each of them in slowly, through bloodshot eyes. His arms, neck, and face were covered completely in thin, white lines, some of them crisscrossing at junctures where the skin had knotted and bulged while healing.

The younger woman and man of the group had fewer scars than the others, but the leader looked like his skin had melted off and only been half-pieced back together.

Finally, he said, "You have no business here."

"We were hoping maybe we could." Everly used her calmest, friendliest voice.

The man terrified her. It was unlikely any level of friendliness was going to get them far with him.

Still, she tried. "We'd heard maybe there was a place for shadyrs, up here. Shadyrs who didn't want to be Darkfreys anymore."

The man spat on the gravel, then sucked at his teeth while he glared at them one by one. "I *said* you have no business here. You're not *welcome* here. New blood is tainted. Old blood is pure. Our family is strong."

"Our family is strong," the four others intoned behind him.

Everly swallowed.

Harper pressed against Everly's side, uncharacteristically silent. Everly slipped an arm around her waist, horrified to find her best friend was trembling. She'd nearly been eaten by a vasmire and joked about it later, but when it came to people—shadyr or not—Harper had a real fear.

Callan caught Everly's eye, his brow raised. He cleared his throat. "Our family is strong too, maybe we could be—"

"You've been warned." The scarred man's fingers tightened on his gun.

20

The feral shadyr led his shaggy group back into the woods, and Harper watched them go with a shudder, still clinging to Everly's arm. She'd never been that close to a crazy man with a gun before. She'd been lucky not to be, the one other time. Still, the whole encounter had left a sick, sinking feeling in the pit of her stomach.

The terror it had stirred in her was *a lot* like when her ex betrayed her. She'd tried her hardest to push all those old fears and emotions down, and it was easy to pretend she was fine when she was surrounded by all this supernatural madness.

A straightforward, evil creature from another dimension was somehow simpler. But sometimes, even shadyrs and eidolghasts couldn't keep her past from haunting her thoughts.

Especially not while staring down the barrel of a shotgun.

Fear of what other humans could do, the pain they could inflict on each other, had overwhelmed her when Bryce doxed her.

Once her home address was made public, the graphic threats that flooded her inbox, the *things* she'd found left on her doorstep, and then the man with a gun the police had caught breaking into her apartment the night she'd fled to Everly's—it all taught her that real people were capable of terrible things, and it was hard to distinguish the monsters from the rest.

To have had that caused by a man she'd loved was like him saying, "I hope someone uses this information to hunt you down. I hope you die."

It had shaken her whole world.

Everly's shoulders drooped in a sigh beneath Harper's grip. "Something tells me we're not going to be making buddies with the Gorhanmere shadyrs any time soon."

"What tipped you off?" Tammy scoffed.

Cherry shuddered physically. "For me it was the intense, evil cult vibes."

Callan wandered back toward the van, hoisting out his black duffle bag. "We've got options still. It might just mean a stealthier incursion on evil cult HQ."

"Sure, or better yet, let's just frontal assault an unknown quantity of unhinged shadyrs on their home turf," Tammy said, feigning enthusiasm and punctuating it with an eyeroll.

Harper squeezed Everly's arm again before letting her go. "Don't worry, we'll work it out."

The creaky registration door opened, and then slammed shut behind Lian. She held three keys in her hand and a perplexed expression on her face.

"Weird people," she said, passing one key to Everly and another to Callan. "The registration office smelled like mothballs, and I'm nearly certain the clerk had spiderwebs in her hair."

"We just had a run in with the locals too. Weird would be a dire understatement for them." Harper shuddered, glancing back at the woods.

She couldn't wait to get behind the protective walls of a motel room. The weight of eyes, watching from the trees, still lay on her.

"Not friendly?" Lian asked.

"I'd prefer to face the auerdax than deal with them again," Tammy muttered.

"No, you wouldn't," Callan snapped. "We all have to take the risk of its presence seriously."

"Why's that, exactly?" Harper asked, directing the question to the group at large in an attempt to distract herself from thoughts of guns, ex-boyfriends, and betrayal.

"Auerdax are a really rare, badass eidolghast," Cherry replied.

"Don't sound too excited," Callan said wryly. "Auerdax are hard to locate and even harder to kill. They're only tangible in darkness. They turn completely incorporeal in the light."

He squinted at the overcast sky, filling the parking area with an even, dull glow. "It could be here, right now, and we wouldn't even know it, until night comes and it kills you in the dark."

Lian fixed Callan in a tight-lipped stare. "Let's all just hope it keeps far away."

"Speak for yourself," Cherry said. "I've never had a chance to shift into auerdax form before. I've heard it's awesome."

"Oh yay, a chance to be a new kind of monster," Tammy groaned.

Harper's mouth opened as she processed the details. "So weroths turn you into werewolves, and vasmires turn you into vampires ... what form do shadyrs take around an auerdax?"

"Hopefully it doesn't come close enough for you to find out," Callan said darkly.

He left the conversation, shoulders hunched, and let himself into his room.

"Just wait and see," Cherry grinned at Harper, then followed after Callan.

Lian and Tammy shared the second room, and Everly and Harper would be bunking together in the third. They unloaded their bags and went to settle in.

Lian managed to get them side-by-side rooms connected by interior doors, which helped Harper feel slightly more protected, given she didn't need to leave her room to mingle with the shadyrs.

Harper stayed behind to chat with Cherry while Callan and Everly drove back to the main strip of town to check for hot food options.

It was mid-afternoon, too late to be called lunch, too early to qualify as dinner, but most of them had skipped breakfast that morning before they set out for the mountains. After learning of the auerdax, they also wanted to have everyone behind closed doors before sunset.

When the van returned, Harper went to help unload.

"All we found were some pies and pastries at the truck stop," Everly said apologetically.

As they unpacked their make-shift feast in the middle room, Harper cringed at the warm canned sodas. "We're going to need ice."

"I'll go with you," Callan offered quickly.

He picked up the plastic bucket, holding it out for her.

Harper eyed him, concerned by his eagerness, but she accepted the bucket and headed for the door, glad she didn't have to go outside alone.

She shivered and wrapped her arms around her torso, wishing she'd brought something heavier than a distressed, off-the-shoulder sweatshirt to keep her warm. Not the first time she'd sacrificed warmth for fashion, and it definitely wouldn't be the last.

She caught Callan's eyes on her a few times, and made a quick, silent wish that he wasn't about to make things awkward. She enjoyed his company, and—minus Denny—enjoyed the company of everyone in the new group of friends they'd found with the Howell team.

Even Tammy, with her gothic nihilistic attitude, was growing on her. But she had lived enough years in her skin to know *the look* Callan was giving her, and romance was the last thing on her mind these days.

They turned into the enclosed alcove where the ice dispenser sat between a soda machine and snack machine, the latter of which had a huge *Out of Order* sign taped to the glass.

"Looks like a midnight junk food raid is out of the question." Harper shoved the ice bucket beneath the dispenser.

Callan peered into the dark machine and scoffed. "All that's in there are spicy fries and sesame snaps. I think I'm good."

He reached past her and depressed the button to dispense the ice.

Harper tensed at the nearness of him. *Just relax. He's not one of the monsters.*

Over the racket of the ice hitting the bucket, a tinny sound system mounted in the corner near the ceiling played "There's a Mermaid in My Lighthouse."

Harper chuckled, humming to the beat then singing along. "Hungry light shines over the waves, and my merrrr-maaaaaid, she yearns. When will I return? When will I return?"

She trailed off at the intensity on Callan's face. "What? Did I get it wrong?"

Callan shook his head and blinked, focusing on her. "No. It's just … You have a beautiful voice."

"Oh. Um, thanks." She checked on the progress inside the bucket then glanced back at him. "I took vocal lessons for years. Got to be that triple threat, you know."

"I think you've got all the threats covered." Callan's cheeks flushed. "Surprised you know the lyrics to that one though, it's kind of unique to Shroudhaven."

"It didn't take me long to pick up, they play the bloody song over and over everywhere."

Callan chuckled. "Yeah, I used to wonder if every speaker in the region was beshadowed, cursed to only play one song, because seriously, it's everywhere you go. But if you know it, that means you're a true local now."

Harper rolled her eyes. "Don't say that in front of Everly. She'd freak. She's *so* uncomfortable in Shroudhaven."

"What about you?"

Harper half-smiled and tugged the bucket out of the cubby hole before the ice overflowed. "There's a certain charm to this area, monsters and all. I mean, I'm not dumb. I know this place is dangerous. But there are monsters everywhere in this world, you know?"

Callan nodded, but she wasn't sure he really understood. "I'm glad you guys have stayed a bit longer. I wanted to, umm, ask you …"

Harper cringed internally, freezing in place.

"You wouldn't want to … I mean …" Callan avoided her gaze and rubbed the back of his neck, staring at the *Out of Order* sign like it held the mysteries of the universe. "Dinner. With me. You know, when all of this with Rylan is over, and we can go back to normal. Shroudhaven normal, anyway."

Harper took a long breath, lifting her lips and putting on the picture-perfect manners she'd practiced for years as though it were armor.

She played it naïve. "Are you asking me on a date?"

"Yes. I'm doing an awful job of it, aren't I?" He laughed.

"Nooooo. I mean, yes, but no. You're adorable. Really," she cooed as if he was some unknown fan on the street asking for her number.

Callan was already nodding slowly, head hung and chin bumping against his chest.

"I'm sorry," she blurted out. "If it were any other time in my life, you'd be getting a yes, I swear. It's just … I'm not ready for another relationship. Not with anyone."

He looked up at her from under his lashes.

Harper clutched the cold bucket to her chest, and let her act drop. Callan deserved more.

"I hope you can understand that it *truly* is not you, it's me. The whole experience with my last boyfriend, it's put me in a place where I've been rethinking *everything*."

Harper swallowed, wishing she had the answers to give him, but she honestly hadn't found them yet herself.

She tried to dig out the words to explain. "I'm questioning everything, about me, what I want, what love is. I don't even know if ... I don't know what I want any more."

Callan frowned. "I'm sorry, I should have realized. I knew what had happened to you but didn't think about how that could make you feel, which makes me a complete idiot. I get it, why you'd need time."

Harper's heart swelled a little, and she pouted a smile at him. "Thank you, for understanding. Friends still?"

"Of course."

Harper winced bashfully. "You sure?"

"Absolutely," he said, smiling broadly.

But she could hear the let down in his voice. She hated being the one to make him feel like that.

He turned to head back toward the rooms and she caught up to walk beside him.

"But, you know, if you are looking for romance in your life, I think maybe Tammy might be interested in a little something more," Harper pointed out with a sly smile.

"Tammy?" He raised an eyebrow and coughed a laugh. "She's more like a little sister. Like the kind of little sister who can't stand her older brother."

"Really? I got the impression there might be something there. But what would I know?" Harper bumped her shoulder against his. "The only thing I'm an authority on is what's *not* a happy-ever-after."

21

Tammy leaned face first against the cold bricks just out of sight, fighting hot tears in her eyes as the mountain wind cut through her black hooded jacket. *Like a little sister. Great.* She closed her eyes and ground her teeth.

She didn't care if Callan *liked* her. She just wanted to be taken seriously. Instead, she was treated like a child. Sure, she played into that, with the sullen teen groans and eye rolls, but it was the easiest way she'd found to get people off her case, to stop them babying her. Keep them all at a distance.

But she wasn't a child. She'd known loss. She'd known grief. She'd known death. In terms of suffering, she was just as far advanced down this pointless mortal coil as the rest of their miserable party.

And why does that infuriating influencer chick think I have a thing for Callan?

She'd been sure she hadn't shown anything—because there wasn't anything to show. It wasn't like Callan had ever given her reason to think he was interested. Even if he did, it wasn't something that could happen. Not for her.

She dug her fingertips into the corners of her eyes, annoyed that the tears wouldn't stop.

What is wrong with me?

Everything, a dark voice inside answered.

Callan and Harper's conversation continued as they left with the ice bucket, voices growing quieter as they headed back to the rooms.

The paper bag holding the veggie pie Tammy had taken for dinner crumpled in her tense hand. She'd picked it up and stepped outside, wanting to be alone after the long drive stuck in the van with everyone. Instead, she got to be the secret audience to Callan and Harper's little soap opera moment.

I should have stayed inside.

With her paper-bagged dinner cradled against her chest, she turned around, sliding her back down the wall until she landed on the concrete.

And saw that Everly was standing right behind her.

The unexpected company jolted her. She half expected to disappear to Dark Corner

but managed to keep it together. Since going on purpose from Rooks Hotel, it seemed a little easier for her to hold onto herself.

"What the ghast?" Tammy snapped. "How long have you been there?"

Everly's gaze moved over Tammy's face, where tears must have left smudgy tracks on her cheeks.

She shrugged one shoulder. "About as long as you have. Lian didn't want you to be alone."

Tammy swiped her sweatshirt sleeves over her face and looked out at the trees behind the motel so she wouldn't have to see the pity on Everly's face. "Completely defeating the purpose of why I came out here."

She kept her gaze on the dark, eerie forest as Everly came closer. If she thought the bliv would get the point and leave, she was wrong.

The white-haired woman lowered herself down to sit next to Tammy on the ground, leaning against the motel wall. She had a paper bag in her hand too, and fished a sausage roll out of it, snapping off a bite-sized piece with her fingers and popping it in her mouth.

"I don't need a babysitter," Tammy growled.

"I know." Everly dusted crumbs off her jacket.

Tammy would have never admitted it, but she liked Everly's trademark red bomber jacket. She wished she could wear red like that, but black was the only color that matched her anymore.

"But what about some company? Especially after eavesdropping what just echoed our way."

"I don't know what you're talking about," Tammy snapped, but her voice came out thick with tears.

"You don't have to be strong with me," Everly said quietly. "I've been hopelessly in love with Rylan for what feels like my whole life."

Her fingertips drifted to her lips then were chased away with a small shake of her head. "And he's done everything in his power to keep me away from him. I understand how it feels."

"I'm *not* in love with anyone."

Everly eyed her for a split second then shrugged. "Maybe not, but feeling unwanted still sucks."

Tammy sighed and opened her paper bag, pulling a bit of crust out to nibble on. "Yeah. Yeah, it does."

"You and me, team freak, and team rejected by Howell boys." Everly chuckled, lifting her paper-bagged food as though making a toast.

Tammy's first instinct was to spit another denial, but it didn't matter. Not really.

Whether or not she had any feelings for Callan, Everly was one hundred percent right about the rejection part. Tammy hmphed and lifted her bag to join the toast.

Before she got close enough to touch, the strange sensation sizzled in her fingers. She snatched her blackened hand away again.

"Team freak all right," she grumbled.

"Yeah. I felt that too," Everly agreed, swapping her food into her other hand and flexing her fingers. "It wasn't a one-off thing that happened at Crow's then."

"Guess not. Lucky you, got an excuse to keep your distance from me."

Everly shifted around, moving to sit cross legged in front of her. She reached out both hands, holding them palm up between then, a few inches away from Tammy's.

"Come on. Let's test this again. Slowly."

Tammy pressed back into the wall behind her, horrified. "Why?"

"Scientific curiosity." Everly wriggled her fingers like an invitation. "We should try and understand what is happening with this reaction, and why."

"Except that we know exactly why. I'm cursed." Tammy dropped her bag on the ground, staring at her Everdark-stained hands.

Everly caught her gaze, and her voice came out firm. "You are not defined by what happened to you. You're so much more than that."

"Speak for yourself," Tammy murmured. "Aren't you just as haunted by your past? Your curse?"

They stared at one another in silence for a long moment.

Tammy sighed and lifted her hands closer to Everly's. Their palms were only inches away from each other, and a low-level hum rose between them from the proximity.

Something supernatural was at work, something she was starting to think took *both* of them to happen, since it had never happened with anyone else. Not that many people had touched her blackened hands. But Lian had, Rushelle had, without flinching, without any reaction.

She hesitated. "You think it's safe?"

Everly's hands closed-up, pulling back toward her chest. "I ... don't know, actually. I'd probably bet that it's not. Maybe it's not a good idea after all. I just thought—"

"Whatever, let's do it."

Tammy closed the space between their hands until their fingers touched.

This time, there was no big flash or loud bang like an explosion, but brilliant sparkles did sizzle between their palms, chased by what looked like black flames.

Tammy yelped at the fiery pain in her fingertips, and the two released each other quickly. Energy hung in the air for several seconds, casting an arc of blue light around them that glittered off Everly's wide eyes.

A gray mist rolled in, and the late afternoon light grew darker. It took less than a

moment for the day to completely disappear in the fog and shadows. The billowing mist thrummed around them with unnatural sounds as it heaved and churned.

They both got to their feet, to avoid being submerged entirely. The cloudy substance was thick and tangible, scraping against them like sand within waves.

"So weird," Tammy muttered, her gaze roaming the thick blanket of mist. "It's almost like a beshadowing effect."

Everly nodded, her bottom lip between her teeth.

Her voice was a tiny whisper, "Like what an eidolghast causes."

"It has to be caused by my hands. I mean, I'm *literally* poisoned by shroudpool magic."

Everly flexed her fingers as if shaking away the memory of the stinging electricity. "I don't know. I think I'm part of it, too. Whatever that light is, inside me ... when I touch you, it roars."

Tammy raised her eyebrows. "Okay then. So I think we can scientifically conclude never to do that again."

A new voice cut through the gloom. "Everly? Tammy? Girls, where are you?"

"Lian," Tammy said under her breath.

Everly nodded, then called out, "We're over here!"

A few moments later, Lian appeared from the mist like a mirage. The fog parted around her, and she moved with an elegant grace that Tammy was used to seeing around Howell House, her long cardigan swirling at her ankles.

"You girls okay?" Her gaze swept around the thick fog, the cold, paranormal wind, and the static electricity on the air. "We were worried when you didn't come back."

What was with the babysitting?

Tammy narrowed her eyes. "We've only been out here like five minutes."

Lian blinked, then glanced down at the delicate gold watch on her wrist. "Sweetheart, you've been out here almost an hour."

Everly's jaw dropped open.

Tammy lifted her blackened hands, staring at her fingers in shock.

Lian crossed her arms, her expression grim. "I'm guessing then that you weren't just getting along so well you lost track of time?"

Everly shrugged. "We were testing the weird reaction that happens when our hands touch."

"You two caused this?" Lian turned slowly on the spot, taking it in. "Thought it seemed like something more than usual weather. It's almost like a minor beshadowing. Maybe that's what caused you two to lose time."

"Creepy," Tammy muttered, shoving her hands back into her pockets.

Everly did the same. "Agreed. No more touching."

Lian motioned for them to follow her. "Come on. It isn't safe out here. Especially with all of this mist dimming the lights and an auerdax around."

Tammy fell into step beside Everly as she asked, "We could beat it though. Right? I mean, especially with the Darkfrey team close by. That's what, ten of us against one of it?"

"Don't underestimate an auerdax." Lian frowned deeply as she led them back toward their motel rooms. "Though, we do have an advantage with my sword."

"Ah, the famous sword," Everly teased. "How did you get it again?"

Tammy smirked. It was an ongoing joke at Howell House that it had been stolen from the Darkfrey's archives, but Lian had always played it coy. She'd also always made sure not to let any Darkfreys see her with it, despite keeping it on her person almost constantly. It hung at her side even now.

Lian's pace slowed, and she spoke to them over her shoulder. "I stole it from the Darkfreys when I left them. More as an act of rebellion than any thought-through plan. I was young and dumb like that once."

Tammy's mouth opened, stunned. Everly caught her eye, looking equally shocked.

Lian continued. "Everyone thought it was useless anyway, a cursed weapon, which is probably why I got away with it."

"Why do they think it's cursed?" Tammy asked quietly.

"Because it blinds you as long as you are wielding it."

"What? No, I've seen you using it," Everly scoffed.

Lian looked a little farther over her shoulder, one side of her mouth pulled up. "You have. And yes, I was blind at the time."

"Why would you even use it then?" Tammy grunted. "That does sound useless."

Lian turned away from them again. "I thought so too, at first. Then came the night an auerdax attacked my home."

"You mean, the night ..." Everly's words cut out.

Lian continued. "After what it had done ... I was so desperate to kill the thing that I grabbed the sword off the display where I kept it like some stupid trophy. Hoping I could just get one good slice in. It fled into a lit room and I just lunged, blindly, furiously, and the sword impaled it, even though it wasn't really there. That's when I learned the sword's power."

Tammy blew out a slow whistle. "It can harm an auerdax even when it's incorporeal?"

Lian nodded, still facing away from them. "If only I'd known sooner ..."

Tammy shivered, and pulled her hands into her sleeves. She knew Lian's husband had been killed by an eidolghast, but she'd never known what kind. That must have been terrifying, for her, for her boys.

They reached their rooms again and Lian stopped at the door, hesitating a moment with her fingers on the door handle. "Since that night, I've trained with it every day, learned how to fight without the use of my sight."

"That's amazing," Everly said in a hushed whisper.

It's totally badass, Tammy thought, but didn't say it aloud.

It seemed somehow strange, to praise a skill that had emerged from such a tragedy. Like the way the others had called her a hero that night she'd helped them escape Rooks Hotel.

It almost felt like they were saying, "Hooray, isn't it great Blaise died in a shroudpool so that Tammy can do this!"

A sharp pang of grief hit her chest and her face twisted. She smoothed it out again when she noticed Lian watching her shrewdly.

With a small smile, the older woman said, "It goes to show, that sometimes things that people consider cursed can prove to be the most valuable."

Tammy turned away, staring back at the mist. *And sometimes, they're just cursed.*

22

Everly turned on every light in their motel room. Both bedside lamps, both reading globes over the beds, the hanging lamp over the corner table, and the strip of lighting above the bathroom mirror. All the Howell team would be sleeping with the lights on that night, to stay safe from the auerdax.

The thought of a monster that would strike only in utter darkness left a cold chill running down Everly's spine. Even worse was the idea that it could be there now, lurking around them unseen and untouchable, just biding its time. For all their sakes, and especially Lian and Callan's, she hoped the thing stayed far away from their brightly lit rooms.

With a plan in place to canvass the town for intel starting early tomorrow, they all retired for the night not long after dinner. Everly crawled beneath the covers and rolled toward Harper, who was staring at the ceiling from her own bed nearby.

Right next to her pillow, leaning on the wall, was the axe Callan had given her. She'd painted her name up the side in a flowing script with glittery pink paint.

"It's so bright in here!" Harper whined, rubbing her eyes. "I forgot to bring my eye mask. I'll never get to sleep!"

Everly squinted at the brightness too, feeling far from slumber herself. She hit the power button on the remote for the television and started scrolling through channels. Most only showed snow. The way Harper glared at her phone screen without tapping away told Everly that reception was out for everything.

She wanted to ask about what had happened with Callan. Everly had heard the end—Harper needing time, agreeing to remain friends, then her suggestion of something with Tammy getting shot down. Everly could guess what had led up to that point.

Should I confess that I overheard? Or just wait until she's ready to tell me about it?

Harper threw a spare blanket over her head and rolled over with a frustrated grunt. Everly settled on waiting. It left her uneasy, and saddened, that there was one more secret pushing in between the two of them.

She hadn't known Harper that long, but the way they had bonded quickly over their various traumas meant they'd shared everything at first. Everly didn't want that

to change, but life since they'd arrived in Shroudhaven had been so volatile. She didn't know where it would leave their friendship.

Taking inspiration from Harper, Everly grabbed a spare t-shirt from her bag and tied it into a makeshift blindfold. Light still poked through the gaps, but it was enough to help her settle.

And then she was at Howell House.

Upstairs, in the hallway connecting all the bedrooms. The colors were dimmer, grayer than real life, and thick beams protruded from the woodwork into the hallway at strange angles, making it hard to move along the space without ducking and weaving.

"I'm dreaming," she said out loud.

A reply echoed to her in return. The deep rattle of a train, combined with the howl of wind and growl of hungry wolves.

Oh no, not this dream.

She spun on the spot, eyes wide. Through a window over the staircase there was the flash of something black and twisted, shooting by like the reverse of lightning.

"RYLAAAN?" Everly screamed.

Where was he? She needed to keep him safe. What if it had already found him?

"Down here." His voice drifted up from the stairwell.

Everly ran to the landing. "Get up here, quick!"

A second later he emerged, jogging up to her with his forehead furrowed. "What's wrong?"

"This dream. This is bad. We have to hide." Everly kept her eyes on the windows for movement.

The garden outside was ashy and swayed like seaweed in a tide under a ghostly sun.

Rylan scoffed. "Bad? I'm not sure how it could be worse than some of the other dreams you've had."

"It's worse. There's something outside ... something dark, and twisted, and ... empty. It's hard to explain, but if it sees us, if it touches us, it will turn us into nothing."

"Nothing?" Rylan's eyebrows raised and he checked the window too. "And that's happened to you before?"

"Yeah, but it's just a dream, for me. It feels awful, like what I imagine dying to feel like but worse, but I then I wake up in the real world after it happens."

Rylan stared into her eyes. "What answer did we end up landing on with the whole, *if I die in your dream do I die for real* question?"

Everly swallowed and shrugged. "Really not something I want to risk testing."

The shadowy thing flickered past a window again, a swirl of null, of void. It roared its strange, clattering sound as it brushed by an old oak, and the tree was obliterated into ashy snowflakes that faded into nothingness.

"Right. Okay, so how do we stay unseen?" Rylan grunted.

"We have to hide." Everly rubbed her forehead, trying to clear her panic and think. "All the rooms have windows."

"Closet." Rylan pointed down the hall, to the narrow door at the end.

They bolted, crashing into each other as they dodged and clambered over the uneven levels and barricades the protruding beams created. Rylan's hands pressed against Everly's waist, helping lift her over one, and Everly pulled at Rylan's arm as he ducked under another.

The shadow creature's roar grew deafening as they rushed into the closet and slammed the door behind them.

Everly's eyes spun in the darkness, seeking chinks of light that identified holes they could be seen through. It was pitch black. She sighed, relieved.

Everly had gone in first, her back cushioned by hanging jackets, and her chest pressed against Rylan. His warm breath drifted down over her, and every part of her body remembered the kiss they had shared the last time she dreamed of him.

The space was tight, and she tingled everywhere his body rested on hers. One of his knees was between her legs, entangled and trapped amidst clutter on the floor, keeping them entwined. His strong hands moved on either side of her, tickling along her waist, her arms as they searched.

There was a soft click, and a small bulb above them illuminated. Rylan's hand still rested on the pull cord. His face was barely an inch from hers, hunched close in the cramped closet.

The railroad howl of the creature sounded again, rattling the walls and coat hangers.

"Are we safe in here?" His voice was soft and husky.

Everly tried to answer but her voice got stuck. She licked her lips and nodded. It felt like the closet got smaller every time she thought about it. Knowing how her dreams liked to test her limits, it probably was.

"I think so," Everly forced the answer out. "I'm sorry. That you're trapped in here."

"It's okay. It's not so bad." Rylan shifted his weight, leaning a shoulder into the hanging jackets to one side. He brushed the fingertips of his other hand over her face, pulling stray strands of hair off her cheeks.

"Scary creatures of darkness aren't that new to me, after all. There are a lot worse places to be than in a closet with you."

His touch traced lines of fire on her skin, like she'd stood too close to a candle's flame and it would melt her. She leaned in, unbidden, wanting more, wanting him closer.

I can't do this. I can't be this close to him.

It'll break me.

Rylan dropped his hand away again, frowning.

He cleared his throat. "So, what's new in the real world? Did you guys make it to Gorhanmere?"

"Yeah, we're there now," Everly replied, struggling to get the words out.

Stop looking at his lips.

Her gaze dropped, lingering instead over the strong lines of his neck and chest.

Everly blinked rapidly then turned her eyes to the jackets beside them. "We met some creepy local shadyrs already, and there's a Darkfrey brace up here too, hunting an auerdax."

"An *auerdax*?" Rylan's body tensed, pressing Everly harder back into the coats surrounding her. "What time is it? Is it night? You need to get out of there."

"We left all the lights in the room on," she assured him. "So even if it does show up, we're safe."

"You can't be safe enough from a creature like that. You don't know ..."

Everly's eyes flushed with tears at the pain in his voice. "I do. I know what happened."

Muscles twitched in Rylan's jaw. "Then you should understand how serious this is."

"I promise you I'm doing my best to stay safe. I feel like ... It's not only my life at risk, you know? You're a part of me, somehow, so I have to be extra careful. If I died, maybe you would, too."

She paused, struck by a sudden thought, then laughed bitterly. "Although, for all I know, me dying might be the thing that actually frees you."

"Don't even joke about that." Rylan grabbed her, both of his hands sliding up her arms, over her shoulders, then cupping her cheeks as he glared down at her.

There was so much worry, so much pain in his eyes it made her ache.

"You are *not* going to die," he said sharply. "I don't care if that's the answer. I'll live in these dreams with you forever if I have to, as long as that means you're *alive*."

Everly shivered, unable to speak, to move, unable to do anything but stare at his eyes, his lips.

Rylan's gaze swept across her face as if he were memorizing every aspect of her. His thumbs brushed close to her mouth.

"Being freed from here because you died wouldn't be a victory. It would be a nightmare. I'd rather walk every one of your nightmares *with* you than live my own without you."

They stared at one another for an interminable amount of time. Everly was distantly conscious of the dark being roaring outside, shaking the house in its hunt for them.

But her every sense was overwhelmed by Rylan's presence—the warmth of his hands on her skin, the intense glint in his warm-green eyes ... *the way he had kissed me.* The way she wanted more than anything for him to kiss her again.

"Evie ... I need to tell you something," Rylan murmured.

Everly's heart raced so fast, she choked on her words as she said, "O-oh? What is it?"

His gaze drifted to her lips. "Something I should have told you a long time ago. I haven't been honest with you for so long. I haven't really been honest with myself. But you deserve to know how I—"

The dream shattered.

Everly awoke with a jolt, sitting straight up in her motel bed with her heart beating out of her chest and her skin prickling with unease.

Everything was black. She ripped her makeshift blindfold off, taking in her surroundings and trying to work out what woke her. It took her several moments to surface from the dream world, to leave all her emotions surrounding Rylan behind and figure out why the room felt ... wrong.

It wasn't morning. It was still night, and everything was dark,

Everything was dark.

Panic struck through Everly's nerves like electric sparks. All the lights she had left on were out. Even the television had gone off, leaving the whole room shrouded in deep, unending shadow.

Everly blinked away the last vestiges of sleep, rubbing her eyes as she searched the darkness for danger, for a monster, waiting to attack.

Movement caught her attention.

A shimmering, translucent ghost was walking through the room—coming right for her.

23

The ghost lifted a hand and put a finger to his lips.

It looked like Callan.

Shock rooted Everly to the mattress as he stalked past the end of her bed toward Harper's side of the room.

Callan's a ... ghost? Her stomach flipped over inside her.

Had he died? Had the auerdax showed up and killed her friend while she slept?

Two more forms came through the walls, stepping right through the cheap wood paneling as if it didn't exist. Tammy and then Lian, who held the hilt of her sword as if ready to draw at a moment's notice. Even in their luminous, translucent form, it was clear they were all in pajamas, jackets thrown on over the top. Their faces were grim and alert.

They didn't look dead. They looked ready for battle.

It's their shadyr form, Everly realized in awe. The auerdax turned them into *ghosts*.

And that meant it was near.

A short, sharp gasp echoed through the silent room, and then a flash of light. Harper sat up in bed, shining her phone at the 'ghosts.' Her eyes were so wide her whites gleamed in the dim light.

Everly caught her friend's gaze and shook her head once, putting a finger to her lips just as Callan had done. Harper reached out with her free hand and wrapped it around the axe handle.

Lian broke away from the others and stepped between the two beds.

Her voice came out low and echoey, as if she were whispering down a long tunnel. "The auerdax is here. It must have tripped the motel's fuse box. I didn't think they were that smart ..."

She glanced at the door to the room, where Tammy and Callan were peeking through the wood.

Their heads were *outside* while their bodies were inside, as if the door was nothing but a waterfall.

Lian continued in an urgent, hushed tone. "The Darkfrey team is outside with

Cherry. They're going to distract the ghast. We need to get you out of here to safety."

Everly shoved the covers aside and rooted around blindly on the floor for her shoes. "What do we do?"

"Wait until it's clear." Lian's movements were slow and fluid, like she existed on a different plane of existence while under the influence of the auerdax. "Then run to the camper and get the Everdark out of here. Go into town. Find light."

"We have some light in here," Harper said, shaking the phone in her hand.

"It's not strong enough. Even when partially corporeal, the auerdax can kill."

Everly helped Harper find her designer sneakers in her mess of a suitcase, and they both tugged sweatshirts on over their pajamas, anticipating the cold outside.

Near the doorway, Callan's head popped back into the room. He motioned to them, his ghostly face grim.

They tiptoed silently to the door and stood behind the three shadyrs. Callan raised his hand again, signaling them to wait.

Seconds trickled into minutes. Everly shifted on her feet, her heart like a frightened bird in her chest. She could hear *nothing*. No sounds of battle. No creaks or groans of a large monster sliding past their motel door. Just empty silence.

Then Lian pulled back into the room and snapped, "Now. Run."

Everly didn't hesitate. She slipped the bolt and snatched at the flimsy doorknob, throwing the door open to the inky night.

Outside in the motel's parking lot, the Darkfrey brace had surrounded something, as far away from the building as they could get without disappearing into the trees.

Everly glimpsed Cherry a few doors down, evacuating a sleep disheveled family from their own room, and one of the Darkfrey girls was doing the same with a young couple even farther down the sidewalk.

"Go!" Lian snapped.

Everly startled, then clasped her fingers in Harper's and yanked her in the direction of the campervan. Lian, Tammy, and Callan sped the other way to join the Darkfrey team.

Everly's feet pounded on the asphalt. The shadyrs were shouting in strange, echoing voices. Harper screamed.

The auerdax appeared before them, blocking their path.

It loomed out of the shadows with an unearthly growl that shook the ground.

Everly skidded to a stop, stunned by the sight of it.

She hadn't known exactly what to expect, but anything she could have imagined wouldn't have come close to the truth.

In the meager light of Harper's phone, and no moon above, it was almost completely solid, with only a hint of blurry translucence.

Of the eidolghasts Everly had seen so far, it had the most humanoid form, but

could never be mistaken for a person. It towered over her, three times her height, with a massive, asymmetrical torso.

It had no head, no face, but dozens of empty eyes stared back at Everly. Skulls. Its chest area was full of them.

Bones, black as the night sky, filled the monster, as though all that made up this creature was the gruesome skeletal collection and the strange, sickly goo that held them together.

Like a malformed blob of melted flesh and shadows, with uneven, lumpy legs, and whip-like arms with deadly talons at the ends.

It seemed as if someone had created the beast from all the world's night terrors.

Fear come to life.

"You ..." the auerdax hissed and growled, but Everly understood its meaning.

Every skull in its torso turned to track her, jaws opening in time. "You I know ... familiar essence. Loathssssome light. Dessssstroy ... Again!"

The tendril of bones and slime protruding from one shoulder whipped out, rocketing toward Everly's head.

With a loud cry, Harper swung her axe. It shimmered in the night, slicing through the mishappen limb. A harsh screaming sound filled the air, as though every bone Harper had broken cried out in pain. Pieces fell to their feet, still jiggling.

Harper beamed. "Yes! Did you see that?"

The auerdax wobbled and morphed, bones crunching as it reshaped itself, growing a new arm.

Harper's smile dropped. "Oh shit."

"Get out of here!" Cherry yelled, catching up to them.

The rest of the shadyrs arrived too, a crowd of ghostly shapes flanking them, and the fight began in earnest.

The auerdax lashed out again, and Everly ducked the new bony arm. Harper hoisted her axe over her shoulder, and Everly grabbed onto her. She hauled Harper along with her, making a beeline for the van.

"We need more light!" an unfamiliar voice called out. "It's too strong when it's this solid!"

An answering reply got lost on a brisk wind that rolled off the mountains and buffeted past Everly's ears.

They need more light.

If they could get to the van, they could turn on the headlights and point them at the auerdax. She and Harper couldn't really do much to help fight the monster, but they could do that.

They reached the van, and Harper threw open the driver's side door and clambered

into the cab.

Everly leapt into the passenger seat. "Turn it on! We need to light up the parking lot!"

Harper dropped her axe into the seat well and stabbed the keys into the ignition.

The van rumbled to life. Harper jammed it into reverse, spinning around to light up the battle.

Something large slammed into them, rocking the camper almost off its wheels. There was a *bang* as one of the tires blew, and the side window cracked like broken ice.

The auerdax had landed on the driver's side. With the headlights so nearby, it was faint and ghostly, but still strong enough to shake the whole vehicle. Slippery, barely there, it oozed slowly right through the driver's door of the van. Harper shrieked and slid across the front bench toward Everly's side.

"Teeth and starsssss. Mussst ... dessstroy!"

It wants me.

If she ran, she could keep Harper safe. It was a risk, for her, and for Rylan, but the auerdax was a claw's reach from Harper.

Throwing open the door, Everly leapt out of the van.

"Everly!" Lian cried. "What are you doing?"

Everly ignored her and raced past the group of shadyrs surrounding the van and the eidolghast. She headed for the opposite end of the lot, praying that the monster would take her bait and get the hell away from Harper. Then she'd do whatever she needed to do to keep herself safe.

Shouts filled the air, and a scuffle broke out behind her. Everly whirled around to see the creature had turned away from the van to her direction, fighting through the shadyrs blocking its path.

Lian took a blow from one of the monster's semi-solid, bony arms. Her wiry body hit the ground. She sprawled out on the concrete with her sword thrown out of reach. Everly's breath caught, but Lian was already getting back to her feet.

Tammy kicked the sword back to her and Cherry helped to extract Harper from the van.

Lucas leapt, landing on the auerdax's bulbous top. It didn't seem substantial enough for him to stand on, but his own partially-intangible shadyr form was designed just for that, somehow on the same wavelength. Lucas tore into the beast with his bare, ghostly hands, flinging handfuls of bone and gooey flesh away into the surrounding darkness.

Another Darkfrey shadyr and Callan joined him, clinging to the monster and tearing it apart.

The auerdax gurgled and grated its bones, moving straight into the beam of the headlights.

Then it was gone, and the three shadyrs fell to the hard ground.

No, where is it?

A second later it reappeared on the other side of the light, rushing straight toward Everly. The shadyrs cried out, trying to surround it, hold it back, but as it moved out of the light it seemed to grow stronger.

And it only had eyes for Everly.

Light, we need more light, she thought, glancing around at her surroundings.

The best opportunity for the shadyrs to destroy the thing was to have it in a semi-solid state. Too bright, and the being disappeared entirely. Too dark, and it outmatched them for strength. A medium level of light was the Goldilocks zone, the one the shadyrs' ghost forms could fight it in.

At this end of the parking lot, there had been a streetlight, but Everly glanced up at the backdrop of swaying trees to find it was dark and useless now. A trail of white smoke still seeped from it and glass glittered on the ground below.

The auerdax charged, railroading every last shadyr in its path to reach her.

There was only one source of light left for Everly to use.

Her shock at the auerdax's presence and disturbing appearance had overridden all her other senses. But as her anxiety grew, her dragon began to awaken, too. She felt it stirring inside her, felt the light pressing against her skin and bones, stretching her until her body felt detached from her own mind.

Her dragon was made of brilliant, blinding light. It should be enough. Or maybe she could take out the monster entirely.

She set the dragon free.

Pale blue light burst from her like a waterfall of exploding sparks. Her feet left the ground and she soared into the air as the motel parking lot lit up, bright as day. The dragon roared inside her, and hunger swept through her like a sickening tide.

Everly fought to surface from the light's sudden takeover, determined to keep it at bay. She refused to be just a passenger, unable to control her own body, much less anything the dragon did. If she let the dragon have that level of control, it would do whatever it wanted.

Including consuming her friends. Everly's gaze swept the parking lot for the monster and found nothing. Shadyrs, wispy and ghost-like, moved around her, but the auerdax was ... gone.

Horror grew in the pit of her stomach. She was giving off *too much* light.

"Find the monster!" Everly pleaded with the dragon. "Eat the monster!"

The dragon purred at the idea of a meal, and hunger rumbled through Everly's body. But on the heels of the hunger, a new sensation—confusion. The dragon couldn't see or sense the auerdax either.

Dammit!

They were safe from the auerdax as long as she kept the area lit, but she didn't know how long she could keep the others safe from *her*. The dragon surged against her attempts to control it, bellowing its frustration.

It was hungry now, and it had been promised a meal. If it couldn't find the ghast, it wanted something else instead. Or someone.

"Back down!" Everly bit out through her teeth, shoving with all her might against the dragon. It was a battle of wills, and the dragon was strong enough to win if she dropped her guard for even a second.

Then, finally, the dragon relented, withdrawing into her. Instead of letting her down gently, it dropped her like a kid throwing an unwanted toy. She crashed back onto the parking lot, her knees buckling beneath her, landing across the asphalt in an inelegant sprawl.

"Ow," she groaned, shoving up to her elbows.

She'd taken the force of the fall on her knees and right hip, and all three throbbed in agony. Someone yelled, and she glanced up to see the auerdax—visible again in the dark—across on the far side of the lot. The Darkfrey girl who had evacuated the couple knelt on the ground below it, bleeding from a gash in the side of her neck.

Everly couldn't guess the ghast's intentions, whether it had fled there from her light, or had pounced on the chance to take out a shadyr isolated from the rest of the group, but the girl had clearly been caught unawares. The other Darkfrey were all too far away.

The auerdax whipped a violent tendril of bones, spear-like talons shooting at the girl's back.

Callan appeared, flying through the air in a spin. He grabbed the arm across his chest and brought it into the turn of his body, wrenching it free from the ghast's shoulder. It howled and turned from the girl to him, the skulls swiveling in unison.

Callan dropped the dismembered limb, scattering the bones across the ground. They smoked and melted under his feet. Everly could make out the shadows of the motel straight through his semi-translucent form, and his skin was luminous. Pale. With his battle face on, he looked so much like Rylan.

He put himself between the auerdax and the girl, and yelled across at Everly. "Take Harper and go! Find light and stay there!"

Tammy appeared at his side, lifting the injured girl and scurrying with her to take cover in the van's headlights. Everly launched to her feet, limping as she regained her footing. She fought past the bruised ache in her limbs.

Harper stood at the back of the van, watching wide-eyed as the shadyrs descended on the eidolghast once more. She clutched her axe in front of her, looking ready to run back into battle.

Everly didn't slow. She linked her arm through Harper's and yanked her away

from the camper, into the night. Behind them, the shadyrs swarmed the creature, like ants on a carcass.

Lian stood before the auerdax, her hand on her sheathed sword and a grimace on her face. She couldn't risk swinging at the monster with the other shadyrs attacking it. She yelled at the Darkfrey to get clear, but they ignored her.

Everly and Harper bolted down the drive from the hotel, around the corner onto the main road, leaving the skirmish behind. There was a streetlight on the corner not far ahead. A quaint, black iron lantern-styled light that beckoned them like a sanctuary.

Everly's bruised knees ached and her footsteps landed unevenly. Anxiety tangled like a knot in her throat, and the dragon's hunger was all-consuming.

She focused on just her next breath, her next step, surviving the next ten seconds of pain. But she didn't breathe easier until they left the darkness and reached the comforting glow of the streetlamp. The cries of battle reached them dimly through the trees.

They leaned against the ornate lamp post, catching their breath.

"Are ... you ... okay?" Harper huffed out between breaths.

"A few bruises, you?" Everly panted.

She put her back against the pole, using it for balance. Her knees and hip trembled. Shooting waves of pain left her nauseated.

"I'm only hurting for my poor van. My baby was mint condition." Harper smiled wryly, but her voice shook.

Everly eyed their small circle of light on the ground. The brightest part seemed to barely cover their bodies where they huddled in the center. It dropped off quickly around the edges.

"Hey, listen. The auerdax, it wants me. Or rather, the beast of teeth and stars. If it comes after us again—"

"What? No! Don't even suggest what I think you're getting at," Harper snapped.

"I just—"

"No! I don't want you to martyr yourself for me. You think I'd be happy living with myself after that? Hot take, but I feel like that wouldn't be fun. If it does come back, you can use your light powers to glow this place up and we'll *both* be fine."

"I told you, it's not safe for you."

"I trust you," Harper said.

Maybe you shouldn't.

Harper lifted a finger and tilted her head. "You think they're okay back there?"

Everly paused, listening. Things had gone silent.

"Is it over?" Harper whispered.

With a crash and crackle of bones, the silence broke apart around them.

The auerdax charged through the trees, toward their small sanctuary of light.

24

"Just stay in the light. It can't touch us in the light," Everly said, as much to herself as to Harper.

Harper hoisted her axe, ready to swing. "Yeah, and we can't touch it either."

The auerdax barreled toward them, shadyrs trailing in the distance. It moved *fast*, its body of bones and fleshy ooze somehow as fleeting as shadows.

Everly latched onto Harper's wrist, worried her friend was about to charge forward and play chicken with an eidolghast. "What time is it? We just have to make it to sunrise."

Harper rested her axe on her shoulder and pulled her phone from her pocket.

With a groan she said, "Three a.m. Look at that thing! It's already grown back everything the shadyrs have done to it."

The ground shook as the auerdax reached them, halting beyond the sphere of bright, clear light that came from the streetlamp. With a growl like scraping gravel, it lashed at them. Everly winced, but as its whip-like arm moved into the light, it vanished. Claws that could have shredded them to bits harmlessly passed right through.

Everly gasped. It couldn't touch them. The shadyrs were on their way, if they could just hold out—

In an explosive crash, shards of glass and rocks rained down over them.

Harper shrieked and darkness fell like a cloak.

No, how did it do that?

"Run for the next light!" Everly screamed, fear for her friend stronger than any fear she had for herself.

She launched into the shadows, following Harper's silhouette for the next sphere of light about twenty feet away. The ground shook. The auerdax was right behind them. Halfway along, Everly veered, away from the light and her friend. Harper's hand shot out, latching onto her arm, her sharp nails digging in, dragging her into the glow.

"Don't do that!" Harper growled. "We stay together."

"It's too fast, we can't keep outrunning it!" Everly panted, wincing at the pain in her legs.

A glance back confirmed they'd only made it because the first of the ghostly shadyrs had caught up. The auerdax shook them off as if they were nothing more than annoying fleas and barreled toward the two women.

"Desssstroyyyy ..."

It swiped a boney arm along the ground then flung a hailstorm of gravel at them. Everly shielded her face from the pelting stones, and the lamp above them shattered.

Not again. Her whole body ached as she pushed it to keep going.

By some miracle they reached the next streetlight, only to have it shattered before they could catch a single breath. The monster cackled inhumanly, relishing how it whittled away their protections.

They ran again, Harper's hand still tight around Everly's arm. Ahead, there was only one more streetlight at this intersection, then a huge gap of darkness before the light of the town.

Everly's anxiety peaked. When the auerdax took out that last light, they'd have nowhere else to go.

They couldn't make the next gap. Her fear mounted until she couldn't breathe, couldn't see. Her hands began to shake, and the trembling moved into her arms, her legs, her body.

Still she ran for the final light.

Harper's fingers detached roughly from where they held hers, followed by a thump, and a scream.

Everly stopped running, staring back with pure, abject terror.

"No!"

The auerdax had Harper's leg wrapped in one whip-like arm, reeling her in. Harper twisted and turned, trying to get a hit in with her axe, kicking with her free foot.

Everly released a feral growl. The only way to save Harper was to let the dragon loose. But as soon as she did, the auerdax would vanish, leaving Harper as the only edible soul within striking distance.

A ghostly figure broke ahead of the rushing shadyrs, sprinting at breakneck speed.

It was Lian. "Let your light out, Everly. Do it!"

She did.

The dragon roared happily as it was given free rein once again. Its hunger had grown exponentially, and it took every inch of Everly's will to keep the light from reaching for Harper.

Gorhanmere lit up as if a new day had dawned. The light washed over the auerdax, and it vanished from sight, turned completely incorporeal by the illumination. Harper stilled on the ground, set free from the dragging grasp of the auerdax. She quickly rolled over, scrambling away.

"Hold it steady!" Lian called as she bound toward the place where the auerdax had

vanished, then leapt high. Mid-air, she unsheathed her sword, and struck.

A screeching cry pierced the night.

Lian hung there above the ground, gripping the handle of the sword which seemed to float, stuck into nothing.

With a victorious grunt, she yanked her sword free, landing on her feet, only to slice the sword again in a wide arc in front of her. Again it made contact, the momentum of her strike lost as the blade passed through the invisible monster. It gurgled and hissed.

"I've almost got it!" Lian yelled. The other shadyrs reached the boundary of Everly's light, hanging back, unable to strike the incorporeal auerdax.

Everly was losing her tenuous hold on the dragon. The light hungered, cataloguing every living soul around her, trying to decide which it most wanted to eat.

Every time, it went back to Harper, who crawled toward her as though she were safety.

"Not going to happen!" Everly snapped.

She couldn't last any longer. With a battle cry, she jammed the light back down inside her, ignoring the dragon's irritated squeals, ignoring the debilitating hunger that clung to her, the ringing agony in her head. Each breath raked across her throat, painful and insufficient.

I'm. In. Control! She crumbled onto her hands and knees, gritting her teeth for one final shove.

The light finally relinquished, slithering back inside of her.

All illumination winked out, and the auerdax reappeared.

Broken and oozing from its wounds, it raced off into the trees.

Lian sheathed her sword, blinked, and watched it go, looking almost as though she were ready to make chase.

Harper offered Everly both hands and helped her to her feet.

"I knew you could do it. When are you going to stop doubting yourself?" Despite the encouraging words, Harper's expression was icy.

Everly sighed. Hunger sat like a brick in her stomach, so strong her whole body shook. She could feel the dragon's fury at how she'd shoved it back into its cage.

The Howell and Darkfrey teams circled up around the two girls. It was strange to see ghosts panting, doubled over while catching their breath. In a cascade of shadows and sparks, one after another swirled with shadyr transformation magic, returning to their human forms.

"You going to go after it?" Callan asked Lucas.

"Ghast no." He laughed, then switched quickly to a frown as he took in his team.

The girl with the gash in her neck had kept fighting, but looked woozy, skin pale against her jet-black hair. She'd lost a lot of blood, if the amount on her clothes were

any indication. Lian had a cut and bruise blooming across her temple, and Callan had sustained several scratches on his arms and chest, shredding his pajama shirt. He didn't have his armor on underneath.

The Darkfrey team were in a similar state, clothing ruined and lacking the protection of their armor. The auerdax's ambush caught them all unawares.

Only Tammy and Cherry seemed to have made it out mostly unscathed.

Lucas shook his head. "I told Master Darkfrey this was at least a two-brace job. We were lucky you guys were around."

The Darkfrey girl put a hand gingerly to her neck, wincing. "Very lucky. Thanks. Pretty sure you saved my life."

Callan shrugged bashfully. His battle face was gone and suddenly he was back to his gawky self again.

"Happy to. Anytime. I mean, not that I want another chance to."

She chuckled, watching him as she tucked her hair behind her ear. Everly shot a glance at Tammy, but she was looking the other way, scowling.

When Everly turned back, Lucas was staring straight at her. "Having someone around who's a walking daylight source came in handy too. What's the deal with that?"

Everly wrapped her arms around her middle, swallowing away her hunger. "Still trying to work that out."

"And our business, either way," Lian added, eyes narrowed.

"No problem. Not like we haven't seen weirder in this line of work." Lucas gestured to his team. "Come on. Let's get back and patch up."

With groans and sighs, both teams turned around to trudge back toward the motel.

Everly stumbled, and Harper looped her arm around her waist, taking some of her weight, but didn't look at her. Callan and Lian took position in front of her, with Tammy and Cherry at the rear.

The injured girl and two other Darkfreys took the lead, but Lucas hung back to walk with the Howells.

He elbowed Callan softly. "Hey, I really do appreciate your help tonight. Molly only just joined our brace, and it would have been terrible to lose her, especially so soon after Adrian."

Callan said, "I thought she seemed fresh. I'm sorry."

Lucas's shoulders dropped. "You know how it is."

Everly frowned. How often was it that Darkfreys didn't make it home from a mission?

Luca lowered his voice. "You're here looking for the stolen artifacts, aren't you?"

Callan exchanged glances with his mother. "Why would you think that?"

Lucas smirked. "Your poor deception skills, for starters. Look, going after them has crossed my mind a few times when we've been on missions up here, but orders are to keep our distance from the Gorhanmere lot. But I've got no such orders not to help you out. I was thinking, if I point you in the right direction, you could get what you want and maybe we can get something out of it too? Split the booty?"

"If that did sound like something we'd agree on, what direction would you point us?" Callan asked.

Lucas slapped him on the shoulder. "There's a ruined mansion out off the old mountain pass. Mostly falling apart, abandoned, but something's up. We've seen the Gorhanmere shadyrs going in and out. Haven't been able to get close enough ourselves to check it out, but I'd bet it's worth a look."

"Thanks, man."

"No, thank you. Again." The two shook hands before Lucas picked up speed to join his team.

Callan seemed to trust Lucas, but Everly wasn't so sure she could trust any of the Darkfreys. Still, they had somewhere to start looking tomorrow for the Bane of Teeth and Stars.

Everly clung to Harper on the journey back to the motel, thankful she'd been able to control the dragon long enough to keep her best friend safe. But would she always be able to? Every time she let the light take over, her hunger grew, and she knew there would come a point when the dragon demanded its meal and wouldn't take *no* for an answer.

She had to be careful. Not use the light anymore. At least, not until they could find answers and she could understand more about how to control it. On the bright side, Lian had definitely wounded the auerdax, so hopefully the beast would limp off into the woods and die.

Back at the motel, the lights burned radiantly, power restored. All except the streetlamp at the end of the lot, which had been destroyed rather than just tripped in the fuse box.

Everly knew the auerdax was smart, able to work out how to destroy the streetlights, but being smart enough to trip the fuses was something else.

She cast her eyes over the motel frontage and spotted a large metal box hanging on the wall near the office. It was partially in shadow, around the corner, but seemed too brightly lit still for the auerdax to have gotten to it.

Everly frowned, her body still rattling with nerves and hunger. The golden glow of the porch lights and the illumination behind the gauzy white curtains in their rooms sent relief rushing through her.

She never wanted to be in the dark again.

The Howell team walked into Lian and Tammy's room together, then stopped short.

Their belongings were strewn all over the floor, clothes torn, and furniture smashed.

Up behind their beds, there was writing on the wall, in thick, dripping letters that looked an awful lot like blood spelling out *LEAVE OR ELSE*.

"Someone's been in here," Callan grunted.

"Really? You don't think that wrote itself?" Cherry said.

"I mean, okay, obviously."

Tammy squeaked, holding out her blackened hands. Shadyr magic swirled around her, the black smoke uneven and thin, juddering strangely.

She was shifting, parts of her skin turning smooth and hard like in her vasmire form, while her legs grew ghostly and insubstantial. Fur sprouted on her face, and her claws grew and curved. Patches of skin were covered in scales. Behind Callan, a similar reaction was taking place for Cherry.

"Something's wrong," Tammy said, her voice coming out thick and muffled by long vasmire teeth.

Concern knit Lian's brow together, and she held out an arm, indicating for the rest of them to stay back. With one hand resting on the hilt of her sword, she stalked forward to investigate the blood.

She sniffed at the wall, her nostrils flaring. "It's eidolghast blood. But it's ..."

"A mixture," Callan finished, his gaze locked on Tammy. "It's a mixture from a bunch of different monsters."

Lian nodded. She slid a finger over the letters. The blood spread beneath the pad of her fingertip, and her form shifted seamlessly. First, ghostly auerdax, then stone cold, fanged vasmire, then dark fur sprouting and bones popping as she grew into the larger weroth form.

"Where did they get it all?"

She returned to human form. Plucking a tissue to wipe her hand clean, she continued to stare thoughtfully at the message.

Everly considered the words too. "Someone really wants us gone."

"Unless this is from the woman at reception reminding us about check out time, I'm guessing it's from our friends in the woods who are too friendly with their razors," Harper said.

It wasn't just the words that scared Everly, but the possibility that the Gorhanmere shadyrs had also tripped the fuses. They would have known about the auerdax, known how light affects it. They could have purposefully stripped them of their protection.

"I can't sleep like this," Tammy griped. "I have no control over the change. I look like a monster."

"You can have my bed," Harper said, still avoiding eye contact with Everly. "I can handle being in here."

Everly wanted to talk to Harper, apologize, explain what she was trying to do,

how she was trying to keep her friends safe in the only way she knew how. But Harper had her back turned, already moving to remake the ripped off sheets of her new bed.

Tammy stared at Everly as though waiting for her approval too.

Everly worried at her lip but nodded her agreement. Regardless of bedding arrangements, something told her that none of them would be getting back to sleep, knowing the horrors lurking around them.

25

Everly rubbed gritty eyes as she crouched between Lian and Callan, hidden inside the tree line. Before them loomed a hulking mansion—the place that may hold her answers, or a whole heap of scary shadyr cultists.

Harper, Tammy, and Cherry remained a few steps behind them as they watched for signs of movement.

Everly felt every inch of her sleepless night. She wished she'd said "yes" to the third cup of coffee Cherry had offered her from the pot that morning. But the motel coffee had tasted like sludge and choking down the first two servings had been a chore. Considering she wasn't particularly picky about her caffeine to start with, that was saying something.

The mansion before them had been abandoned a long time ago and left to go to seed. It was three stories tall, cross-timbered like the rest of the village, and missing at least half the glass in its windows. Two wings, tangled in ivy, angled off from the main building. The leaves blew in the wind, swirling and moving as though the vines grew before Everly's eyes. Four chimneys stuck up from the aged, moss-covered shingles, and the front door stood wide open—a gaping, screaming mouth.

"Maybe Lucas has sent us on a wild ghast chase," Callan said, glancing at his mother. "This place is clearly uninhabited."

Harper scoffed, her gaze flicking about the trees surrounding them. "Did you see those crazies yesterday? They didn't have the presence of people concerned with health and safety."

"They're exactly the kind of people I'd expect to hole up in a place like this," Cherry agreed.

Everly swallowed hard against nausea. She'd been trying to ignore the strange feeling welling up inside her from the moment they'd left the campervan back on the old dirt road. They'd walked half an hour to get there, and with every step, a sick sensation rose inside her.

"Something's there," she said, her voice cracking. "I don't know what. But I can sense it."

Callan caught her gaze, and Everly winced, touching her solar plexus where the nausea sat like a stone in her gut, right next to the hunger that remained from the night before.

Lian sucked at her teeth for a moment, then lay her fingertips on the hilt of her sheathed sword. "All right. We have to check it out. Keep an eye out for tripwires, surveillance, anything that screams we're walking into a trap."

"And hope no one is home," Harper added with a chuckle.

She'd regained some of her usual bravado, but a haunted vulnerability filled her eyes that hadn't been there before.

Everly hadn't seen that expression since Bryce had torn her world to shreds. Her hand rested on her axe head at her hip. She'd fashioned a sort of holster for it so it could hang on her belt. Everly had wanted to talk to her that morning, but she had refused any help when changing the blown tire on the van.

Everly still worried about her but had to admit she'd gotten a pretty good hit in against the auerdax the night before. It shouldn't have surprised Everly that Harper would excel at monster hunting just as she did every other aspect of her life. She just wished it wasn't a part of her life at all.

Callan took the lead beside his mother, with Harper and Everly behind them. Tammy and Cherry took up the rear. They entered the house through the open door, moving slowly and silently.

Everly noted the front door hanging off its hinges, never closed, and the severe water damage just inside the threshold that caused. She hissed a warning and steered their crew away from the worst of the rot with a hand on Callan's shoulder. Falling through decayed floorboards would be a great way to announce their presence if anyone were around.

The foyer opened on a grand staircase that had become a cascade of ferns and vines. At the top, a raven sat, pecking at something. It didn't startle or caw at their entrance, but stared at them with glassy blue eyes.

A huge hole in the domed ceiling overhead likely dumped buckets of rain on the steps every time a storm rolled through, which meant going upstairs wasn't a safe option. A glass and crystal chandelier had shattered on the wooden floors, and weeds grew around the glittering pieces.

Harper let out a long, low sigh. "This would have been beautiful in its day."

"Let me guess, you'd love to do a photoshoot here," Everly whispered back with a grin.

Harper returned a small smile, but didn't reply.

Callan peeked into a dusky doorway to the right, then called back in a hushed voice, "Clear. Living room. It's empty. Not even any furniture. Just a fireplace."

Tammy, who had crossed to the opposite archway, answered, "Clear. Dining room. With a table that could easily seat twenty freaking people. Like anyone has that many friends."

Callan turned a circle, his gaze sweeping over the broken railings and the obvious dips in the floorboards where water had pooled for decades. "Should we split up? Search the rest of this floor?"

"No." Everly shook her head and pressed her hand tighter to her belly.

The ground had a heartbeat. One that thrummed through the soles of her feet.

"It's below us. Whatever I'm feeling, it's below us."

Lian nodded, her gray bun swinging. "A place like this probably has a basement. Let's check the kitchen for stairs."

They moved in single file through the darkened dining room. Splintered chairs lay in cross-hatched piles in the corners. Tammy had been right; the massive mahogany table was a little worse for the wear, but in its heyday had been capable of seating more than twenty guests.

Everly could almost sense their specters hanging around, a dinner party of the dead. The memories of every person who had once lived within these walls.

Shadows flittered in the darkest parts of the room. A gilt-framed painting of a man on horseback seemed to move. The horse's nostrils flared. Blood dripped from the man's eyes. Everly blinked and it returned to normal.

"You guys see that?" Everly asked, hoping she wasn't going crazy.

"Yeah," Callan said. "There's some weird stuff going on here."

"A beshadowing?" Harper asked.

"That would be my guess. But I can't sense an eidolghast nearby." Lian turned her eyes to Everly.

Because I'm sensing something.

Down another short hall, filled with dust motes and cobwebs that seemed to reach out like tiny hands in the dark, they found the kitchen. It hadn't fared much better over the years.

All the appliances were still in place—a stove, fridge, dishwasher, fancy coffee machine, all relatively new. The place hadn't been abandoned too long, despite the accelerated takeover by nature. The tile floors were cracked and moldy beneath timber cabinet doors that hung crooked on their hinges.

Out of nowhere, the faucet gurgled and coughed out black ooze. Tammy jolted and flickered out of reality for a moment before stabilizing herself again.

"You're getting better at stopping yourself dissappearing," Callan noted with an affirming nod.

"Also getting better at not shoving my fist in the face of people who patronize

me," she muttered.

"Over here." Cherry stood in the corner of the room.

He'd opened one doorway through to an empty walk-in pantry, and then next to it a second door with stairs leading down into darkness.

Everly flashed the LED light on her phone down the stairs. "Looks sturdy enough. Looks ... *new*, actually. There's no way these cheap pine planks are original."

Lian leaned past her. "Seems like good evidence this place isn't as empty as we thought. Careful now."

They descended into the dark bowels of the house with Everly's phone light leading the way. At the bottom of the staircase, a small, dank cellar stretched around them, bare of anything but a few empty, wooden workbenches and an ancient water heater in the corner.

The floor seemed to have been carved from one solid piece of smooth, pale limestone, and moisture dripped down the paneled walls. In places where water ran in larger rivulets, it almost seemed as though stalactites were forming, but Everly knew that couldn't be possible. They took millennia to grow.

"Nothing," Callan remarked, his sparkly shadyr eyes taking in the room despite the darkness. "A bunch of black mold, though. We shouldn't stick around here long."

"No ..." Everly let the word trail off as she picked her way across dusty, debris-strewn floors.

She circled the staircase, following the nagging feeling that something was nearby. It was like the closer they got, the farther away she wanted to be. She fought the sensation. In the corner beneath the stairs, the wall panel sat crookedly, less than an inch out of line.

Moving closer, the distinct tickle of cold, moving air flowed through the crack, and her nausea spiked.

She wrapped her fingers around the warped edge of the wood and tugged. It scraped loudly over the stone floor, and she cringed at the way it screamed through the quiet house.

On the other side, a natural, rocky tunnel curved away into the darkness.

"Whoa," Callan said softly as the rest of the team gathered around them to peer inside.

Harper squealed. "Yes! I get to do a secret passage after all!"

The shadyrs all exchanged worried glances.

"I'm not sure we should be going down there," Callan said.

Harper pouted. "Of all the crazy adventures you guys go on, you don't want to go into a cave?"

Callan shook his head. "Caves are bad, bad news. Shroudhaven is full of interconnected, subterranean caverns."

"Which we affectionately call the underdark," Tammy added.

"And they are filled with eidolghasts and shroudpools. Shadyrs lost that battle centuries ago. We just let the underdark be enemy territory and avoid it at all costs."

Everly squinted down the long tunnel, wishing she had the night vision of a shadyr. She felt so close to finding something, even if it was something the light inside her seemed to despise. Maybe that was a good thing.

She couldn't turn back now. "There's no proof that this tunnel connects all the way back to Shroudhaven though, is there?"

Callan shrugged.

"And are you sensing any eidolghasts nearby yet?"

Lian wrinkled her forehead and closed her eyes for a moment. "There's something ... You're right that there's something nearby. But no, not eidolghast. Not exactly."

The others shook their heads too.

"Then I'm going in."

"If you're going in, we're going too," Harper snapped.

Callan glanced from her to Tammy. "Maybe you should—"

The glare Tammy returned was so intense his words seemed to dry up.

Harper unholstered her axe. "Let's move."

Callan took the lead, ducking his tall, lanky form through the small door and into the cave beyond. Everly followed, praying that this would be worth it.

Whatever she sensed ahead, it was powerful. It had to be the stolen artifacts. Even if the Bane of Teeth and Stars didn't do anything, maybe one of the other ancient shadyr items would. There had to be a solution there to what she was, how to save Rylan, how to keep the dragon under control.

She glanced back at Harper who was right behind her. She knew Harper could take care of herself. She'd never known anyone more capable than her friend. But Everly was still filled with fear that something terrible would happen to her and it would be her fault.

They moved by the light of Everly's phone, keeping it pointed low. Only she and Harper seemed to need it, the shadyrs moving confidently in the darkness. Fog drifted around their feet, and the walls clung close, pale limestone shiny with perspiration.

The tunnel twisted left, then right on a steep decline, as if they were moving toward the bowels of the earth. If the house had seemed eerily quiet, the cave was a riot of sound. Dripping water and the rushing of the wind barreling through stalagmites and stalactites made for a symphony of noise that even covered up the scuff of their footsteps.

Which was likely the reason they snuck up on a Gorhanmere shadyr without being noticed.

The man rested on a flat-topped stalagmite, staring forward into the darkness.

No—into the *light*. There was a deep, pulsing red light ahead, and the moment

Everly's gaze locked onto that light, nausea rolled through her and she gagged.

Harper stepped forward, making a series of hand signals that Everly still didn't understand. Callan raised his eyebrows, and nodded, looking impressed.

The man was huge, with thick, corded muscles beneath his dirty overalls. He carried an automatic rifle on a strap around his shoulder and a vicious knife buckled to his muddy boot. In the red glow, crescent shaped scars over his arms and shaved head gave him an odd, zebra-striped pattern.

Harper silently handed her axe to Callan. He rushed forward on silent feet and cracked the butt of the handle into the back of the guy's neck.

He grunted, pitching forward. Then with a low growl he straightened himself up and turned on them. His eyes were bloodshot and wild.

"Shit," Callan muttered, before taking a swiping blow across the chest.

He was knocked backwards so fast he cartwheeled over himself and crashed into a veil of limestone. The axe clattered out of his grasp.

Lian sprinted across the space with surprising speed. Before the Gorhanmere man could get his hands on his rifle, Lian unsheathed her sword and cut through the air gracefully, severing the nylon strap and sending the gun catapulting across the ground. Lian sheathed her sword and dodged a punch.

Callan leapt back to his feet, joined by Tammy and Cherry as he rushed back into the fray.

"They aren't changing," Harper said, her eyes narrowed. "Come on, this is an even human V human fight for once."

Everly reached a hand out for balance, buckling at the waist and dry retching. "Can't."

Harper hesitated, looking back at Everly with concern.

"Except, not actually sure this guy's human!" Cherry yelled across to them.

The four shadyrs grappled with the huge man as he swung his tree-trunk arms at them. Callan and Lian grabbed for his meaty fists, trying to keep them pinned.

Tammy scrambled up the man's back, like scaling a mountain, and wrapped her blackened arms around his neck, squeezing tight. The man's breath gargled and his face turned red, but still he raged at them.

"Use your light!" Harper insisted, motioning to their friends. "That guy is like a grizzly on steroids had a lovechild with a pro-wrestler. He's wiping the floor with them!"

"I can't," Everly said, shaking her head a little too long and hard.

Between the nausea from whatever strangeness lay ahead, and the dragon's hunger consuming her thoughts, unleashing the light in this state would be a bad idea.

On top of worrying about the dragon consuming any one of her friends in this cave, she worried about Rylan's essence being consumed, too. As though every time she refused the dragon a meal it grew hungrier, and it was starting to turn that hunger inwards, to the lifeforce trapped in Everly's dreams.

Too many unknowns and not enough answers stayed her hand. She knew the Howell team could defeat the Gorhanmere goon. He was just a man, wasn't he?

She hoped.

The battle was short but brutal. Tammy remained latched around the man's neck while the others did their best to keep his hands off her. Finally, he went down onto one knee, then the other, then face first onto the ground.

Lian checked the man's pulse and nodded. "He's out. I thought we were going to have to kill him for a moment there. Best we don't, though. There's clearly some kind of beshadowing here, so these guys aren't themselves."

Cherry brushed his fingers beneath his nose, and they came away as red as his hair. "How many of these guys do we think there are hiding out down here?"

Tammy shook her head, her normal scowl shaken off her pale face. "It took four of us and way too long to bring him down."

Twisted in unconscious slumber, the man's face wasn't familiar to Everly. "He's not one of the five who welcomed us last night."

"At least that many then, so we just need—" Cherry pretended to count on his fingers. "Twenty of us."

"And even if we're not trying to kill them, I don't think they are going to return the favor," Tammy groaned.

Harper bent to collect her axe. "That guy didn't go down quietly. If there were any more nearby, they'd be on us by now."

Callan nodded. "We've come this far. There's a light coming from just ahead. We check there, then get out."

Everly swallowed the sickness in her throat and followed on wobbly legs as Callan led the way.

"You okay?" Harper moved close beside her.

Concern seemed to have overridden any iciness or grudge she'd been holding from the night before.

"I feel like the dragon is trying to vomit itself out of me to escape this place. It's pushing so hard. I'm worried I can't control it."

"If this feels wrong, we should go. Something that is hurting you shouldn't be the answer. We can find another way."

"No. I'm fine. I can do this."

Harper just frowned in response.

The tunnel ended around the bend, opening to a large cave with soaring ceilings. Unlike the limestone tunnels that had led them to this point, the cavern was absolutely

covered in giant crystals.

Bone white and glass-clear pillars stuck out all around the walls and ceiling like jagged teeth, as if the cave were the mouth of the giant beast about to swallow them whole.

The cave billowed with fog and pulsed with that strange red light, ebbing and flowing like waves between the crystal shore. The cold breeze Everly had been sensing since they found the hidden door grew stronger. The prickling on her skin that raised goosebumps head to toe told her the beshadowing came from something in this cave.

Lian's eyes gleamed in the pulsing red light. "That's it. The Bane."

Everly's heart leapt. She followed Lian's gaze toward the center of the cavern, to the source of the glow.

A black triangle stuck out of the moving clouds.

Everly forced herself toward it, each step a battle.

The fog parted, revealing a pillar, jutting out from a dark, sludgy pool.

Liquid covered the crystal podium, and the black object was wedged into the top. The triangle turned out to be a diamond-shaped item as large as a head. Made of intricate filigree black metal, it oozed red liquid continuously through the gaps in its rune-like curlicue designs.

The edges of the diamond weapon looked razor-sharp.

It was the source of her sickness. Bile rose in the back of her throat, and she stumbled away from the Bane, retching.

Harper was at her side in a heartbeat, pulling her hair back even though nothing came up. Everly had skipped breakfast, and her coffee had long since moved through her system. She dry-heaved, dimly conscious of the Howell team gathering around the Bane.

Finally, when the heaving stopped, Everly leaned heavily against Harper, and they turned to survey the quietly chatting shadyrs.

Tammy and Cherry had both moved away from the bloody Bane in a state of semi-transformation, like what had occurred in Lian's motel room the night before.

"That damn thing is bleeding the same weird mixture of ghast blood," Cherry snarled.

The red light strobed on his face, highlighting his high cheekbones and casting the shadows of his shifting face into harsh relief.

Callan glanced down at the fog, obscuring the sludgy pool Everly had seen beneath. "Explains the beshadowing. There's so much blood."

Tammy explored the far corner of the room. "Woah. Apocalypse central over here. Road flares, canned goods, bottled water, ammunition, extra guns. It's like my crazy Uncle Teddy's doomsday bunker."

To the other side, a massive stalagmite had been sawed off, forming it into an altar-like surface stained with dry, dark splotches.

Lian moved around it, shaking her head. "More blood here too. But it's different. Just weroth and vasmire. What dark business are they up to?"

"Business you should have kept out of!"

The new voice startled Everly so bad she jumped, and Harper tightened her arm around her waist to make sure she stayed on her feet.

"We warned you. What happens now is your own fault." It was the wild-eyed forest man.

The older, more scarred leader of the little pack that had approached them when they arrived in Gorhanmere.

He was alone, but Everly had a feeling his minions were right behind him. The way Lian caressed her sword's handle, she must have figured the same.

She spoke firmly. "We're taking the Bane, and the other stolen artifacts. You are beshadowed. If we take this away, you'll be cured."

"Cured? We are strong!" The man cackled breathily, lifting his bulging arms out to his sides and raising his hands into the air. "You arrogant Darkfreys, thinking we need help."

Lian opened her mouth as though to argue their misclassification, but the man's voice boomed over her.

"Can you not see? We have all the strength we need to cut the darkness from this land. Eidolghasts fall at our feet." He flung a hand toward the altar. "We bring a new sacrifice even now."

Everly's heart pounded as a monstrous wail echoed down the tunnel.

Tammy gasped, her hands flying up before her. Shadyr magic swirled as her body shifted into a ghostly, translucent form.

She whispered, "The auerdax."

The scarred man smiled. "It comes."

26

For a moment, nobody moved.

Then the Gorhanmere leader cackled like a wicked witch—high-pitched and maniacal— as he was consumed in black mist, shifting into a ghostly form.

A roar shook the crystal pillars and sent debris sifting from the ceiling. The Howell team backed up closer to each other. Tammy, Cherry, Lian, and Callan all shifted.

The auerdax burst into the cavern, rushing through so fast it slammed into the wall. Crystal shards exploded from beneath its giant, misshapen body of bones.

On its heels charged five shadyrs. They had stripped back their overalls to the waist and were painted in blood. From the wide range of strange forms they took, Everly guessed it was the blood that had spilled from the Bane.

Their twisted bodies were part vampire, part ghost, part werewolf, and part other things Everly couldn't even identify. They taunted loud cries as they clawed and lashed at the eidolghast, driving it farther into the cavern.

No ... They herded that thing here?

The man had mentioned sacrifices, but Lian had only sensed weroth and vasmire blood on the stone altar. If auerdaxes were rare, maybe they'd never killed one before. Maybe they were in for a much bigger fight than even they were prepared for.

The skulls in the ghast's chest swiveled wildly. It ground to a halt, surrounded by shadyrs on both sides, Howells at the front, Gorhanmere behind. With a shout that was part raven's caw, part thunder, it whipped out a tentacle of bones, knocking down two of the five shadyrs that had chased after it into the cave.

The red light that pulsed from the Bane didn't appear to affect the auerdax's tangibility. It was rock solid and deadly in the dim glow.

The cult leader cackled again, as though delighted by everything before him. "New blood is tainted. Old blood is pure."

The knocked down shadyrs returned quickly to their feet.

Their words echoed in harmony through the cave. "Our family is strong."

Two of them launched themselves onto the auerdax. The other four made straight for the Howells.

"Come on," Harper cried, tugging at Everly's jacket.

Everly stumbled, still nauseated and wobbly on the uneven cave floor which was obscured by the swirls of fog.

Something smashed behind them. Dozens of pieces of crystal shard rained down, hurtling toward Harper and Everly. Everly threw her arms around her best friend, turning them both away as pieces ricocheted off her back.

Edges sliced across Everly's neck, causing hot blood to well up on her skin. She hissed and put a hand to the scratches, though they were more annoying than painful. The two of them ducked behind a thick row of stalagmites.

A roar filled the cave, then the auerdax's shifty, shadowy voice whispered, "Starteeth beast … You are here … Show yourself and die."

Harper straightened, brushing the glittering slivers off her clothes as she turned wide eyes on Everly. "You okay?"

Everly swallowed, glad she was the only person who spoke eidolghast. "Not great."

"That Bane thing is really doing a number on you. You need to keep safe. You're in no state to join in."

"We need light."

Harper pulled out her cell phone, but Everly shook her head. "That's not enough. Tammy said there were road flares in the stash in the corner. Come on."

The two girls ducked behind a giant pillar of crystal. Everly peered around the edge to survey the battle taking place and plan a safe route around the auerdax.

Tammy was in hand-to-hand combat with one of the cult women, mostly just doing her best to dodge her wild attacks. Three monstrous men had backed Callan and Cherry into a corner.

They fought hard to bring the cultists down, but still seemed to be pulling their punches.

The Gorhanmere shadyrs were still people, and all the eidolghast blood in the cave and on their bodies had likely made them crazy. If the Bane were taken away, they had a chance to heal and return to normal. Killing them wasn't the answer.

Unfortunately, they weren't giving the Howell team the same treatment.

One of them caught Cherry with a blow to the chin. It knocked him upwards and back, tossing him onto a cluster of painfully sharp looking crystals.

Lian, standing beneath the auerdax with her hand on her sword's hilt, grunted and ran back to help Callan. With a precise strike, she slashed her sword across the ankles of two of the Gorhanmere shadyrs, toppling them to the floor.

Everly winced. *Ouch. Survivable, but ouch.*

The cult leader and another woman clung to the auerdax, pulling at its limbs, dragging it toward the altar. The auerdax whipped at them, shaking them off and

throwing them away, only to have them pounce back on again.

With everyone's attention occupied, Everly motioned for Harper to follow her. She fell into a stooped sprint, darting from pillar to pillar, keeping her gaze locked on the eidolghast.

She wasn't certain where Tammy had found the Gorhanmere prepper stash, but she remembered her general location. Once there, she scanned the forest of small, jagged crystal pillars until she found what she was looking for: several wooden crates full of supplies. The two women began flipping off lids.

"Got them. Road flares," Harper explained, passing a red tube over to Everly.

Everly stared down at the flare. "Do you know how these work?"

Harper grabbed one for herself and popped the cap off, then twisted the striking pad open. She held it up beside the end of the flare. "Just like a match."

She struck them together, and the flare sizzled to life. Bright light bloomed from the flaming tip, sending red sparks spilling from the tube.

Everly half-smiled. "Of course you know."

Harper held her flare up with a grin. "Best thing is the auerdax can't break this like it did the globes last night."

"No, but these won't last long, will they?"

"So we have to hope the others slay the monster before our lights run out." Harper unholstered her axe again, peeking over the top of their cover. "And also deal with the army of crazy strong cultists. Easy peasy."

"Hey!" Lian circled and dodged around the feet of the auerdax, hand on her sheathed sword, trying to find an opening to strike. "Throw some of those flares over here! I can't get a hit in on this thing when it's at full strength."

Everly and Harper dug into the chest of supplies and found four more flares. One by one, they struck them to life and tossed them out into the melee. Each one made the auerdax a little more ghostly, putting him on the same plane as Lian and the rest of the shadyrs.

But it also drew the ghost's attention. Every skull in its bulbous chest turned toward the source of the glowing projectiles, toward Everly.

"Dessstroy."

Callan still tangled with one man and Tammy was busy with her opponent. Their scarred bodies were nothing but muscle, and they fought like they hadn't even lost their breath. Cherry still hadn't returned to the fight, and Everly worried, unable to see where he was.

The auerdax tried to move toward Everly, but it was held back by the two shadyrs clinging to its torso, and Lian taking neat slices at its legs.

Lian kept her feet planted, head cocked for every sound, as she turned and struck

with her ancient sword. One of her blind attacks caught the lead cultist in the arm, dropping him off the beast. He rolled out of sight into the shadowy, red fog.

The auerdax growled in a way that made the crystals shimmer and sing like wine glasses. It grasped at the shadyr woman on his back again, but instead of throwing her, it gripped her in its boney tendril and slammed her straight up into the cavern ceiling.

With a sickening crunch, a stalactite impaled straight through her chest. She hung there, pinned like a fly, twitching and dripping blood.

Everly gagged and retched, tears hanging in her eyes. The shadyr numbers were dropping fast, and still the Gorhanmere group were turning against them instead of the monster.

The auerdax prowled toward Everly, out of the range of Lian's blade. Lian sheathed her sword, blinking as her sight was restored. She took in the situation—and stared upwards in horror.

Then the flare that glowed at Everly's feet began to sputter and dim.

"That's not ideal," Harper groaned.

They both watched in horror as their flare died.

Everly glanced out at the fight. "We have less than a minute before the other four are going to go out, and we'll all be back in the dark with the auerdax."

"Ev," Harper said, her expression serious. "You're going to have to use the dragon."

"No," Everly snapped. "Bad idea. I'm not at a hundred percent, and it's already feral with hunger. I can't guarantee I could control it at all at this point."

Harper pointed at the auerdax. "I *can* guarantee that this is about to kill us if you don't."

In the center of the cavern, Tammy let out a pained yelp, and both girls whipped around to see her fall to the ground, out cold.

The Gorhanmere leader had joined the woman sparring with Tammy. He stood over the girl with an evil, victorious grin on his face.

The woman joined him in her gleeful expression and lifted a taloned claw, ready to deliver a killing blow against their downed friend.

The flares sputtered out.

There was no time left. No options left.

"Harper? Run," Everly commanded, and she let the dragon loose.

White light exploded from her body, and she shot off the floor into the air as the dragon took its form around her. Tendrils of blinding light unfurled and guided her forward, quicker than she expected, as if the dragon had just been waiting for her to free it.

One glowing thread shot toward Harper before Everly even sensed the dragon's intentions, but Harper was already on the move and darting behind a pillar. The tendril slammed into the column of translucent crystal and shattered it.

Everly opened her eyes wide and struggled to gain control of the beast inside her. *I'm in control!* she roared in her mind.

The dragon didn't respond. Hunger washed over her in debilitating waves. Everly had refused its desires for too long, her body was too weakened by exhaustion and sickness. The dragon's influence was all-consuming, and it wouldn't be denied any longer. It *would* take what it wanted.

Terror shot through Everly as a coil of light whipped out toward Harper again. Harper lunged away and sprinted across the cavern, right into the battle, axe grasped in both hands.

Everly clenched her hands into fists and tried to get a grip on the dragon's consciousness, but it moved without her. She dangled uselessly, merely a puppet in its luminous grasp.

Everly's light suffused the cavern, filtering through the crystals to form an even, low glow. The auerdax had faded into a see-through ghost of itself.

Lian blocked its path, lunging and striking left and right as it tried to dodge past her. Shattered bones and tar-like ichor spread across the floor as it backed away from Lian's deadly assault.

The Gorhanmere shadyrs stood in awe of the dragon's imposing presence. Cherry was back on his feet, a little wobbly but alive. He took the opportunity to strike, taking out Callan's opponent with a large chunk of crystal that thunked against the side of the man's shaved head. Callan turned to take on the remaining woman.

They were hurting, exhausted—the dragon sensed it like he was scenting a weakness. Its hunger had reached an uncontrollable point. Tendrils danced on the air in anticipation.

The leader of the Gorhanmere shadyrs had been distracted by Everly's light, but his attention whipped around to Harper, fleeing across the cavern to stay away from the dragon's grasp.

He rushed to intercept her.

No!

The dragon shot into motion, spurred on by the sudden rush of fear and adrenaline through Everly's body. They barreled across the cavern, Everly's only thought to reach Harper before the Gorhanmere shadyr did.

But when Harper saw the dragon's light coming toward her, she darted away again, right into the murderous man's arms.

He howled with that eerie, maniacal laughter and grasped each side of her head in his monstrous hands. Harper screamed silently as he lifted her off her feet, trying to crush her skull.

Tears streamed down her compressed face. She shifted her grip on her axe and swung. The man dropped her, dodging the sharp metal. She landed hard. He reached out, snatching the axe out of her hands and lifting it over his head, ready to bring it down.

Get him, Everly told the dragon. *You can have him!*

She let the hunger fill her every cell until she was blinded by bloodlust, and directed every part of it toward that man.

The dragon roared with glee at being let off its metaphysical leash.

The tendrils of light latched onto the man and fed.

27

The axe fell from the man's fingers.

His eyes bulged and his mouth gaped wide with horror. His body shook and shifted, his shadyr form changing through a range of shapes before reverting to a normal human. Thin tentacles of brilliant light wrapped tightly around the shadyr, like a jellyfish trapping its prey, until he vanished behind the illumination.

Harper scuttled away from the man and the dragon's coruscating attack.

The bile rising in Everly's throat no longer had anything to do with the Bane. She hated this part. Hated the strange sense of chewing and biting, even though nothing of the sort *physically* took place. She could sense the way the dragon consumed the shadyr's life force like a monster chomping on a victim.

Like the vasmire at Rooks Hotel eating that poor man in the bathrobe.

And she had sanctioned it. She had chosen this shadyr to die.

It had to be someone, she tried to justify to herself. *It was him or Harper.*

But it still left her insides twisted with guilt.

Within moments, it was over. The tendrils retracted, dropping the man. His body slumped to the floor and collapsed, still and pale with lifeless, staring eyes.

A loud, earth-shaking scream vibrated through the cavern. Everly jerked her gaze away from the dead shadyr. Lian was poised atop the auerdax, her sword hilt-deep in its center.

With a battle cry, she wrenched downwards, splitting the monster down the middle. It staggered and oozed ichor as it tried to reform, failing to reconnect its halves. Its pieces crumbled to the floor. Whatever life had animated it was gone, leaving nothing but unmoving bones and shadows.

Lian sheathed her sword, breathing hard. She looked over the dead eidolghast with hard, glittering eyes. Callan and Cherry chased off their final foe, high fived, and bent at the waist to catch their breath. Beside them, Tammy stirred.

They'd survived. They'd *won*.

But still the dragon wanted more. Before Everly had even realized it, the tendrils had reached for another of the Gorhanmere shadyrs who was crawling across the floor with his cut hamstrings. An easy target.

No, no more!

It was too late. Everly was overwhelmed with a sickening feeling of *fullness*.

She focused all her willpower onto taking control, as the dragon turned again to take another victim. It shot toward Harper, who remained on the ground, clutching her head.

With a feral growl, Everly snatched at the light, putting a mental shield between it and her friend. *Enough! Leave her alone.*

Irritation poured off the dragon, and it returned her growl. The light coming off it surged, brightening the cave blindingly. She couldn't control it.

Bile rose again, and Everly's eyes widened. *It hates the Bane.*

Everly grunted, summoning just enough strength to force herself closer to where the diamond-shaped artifact was pierced into its crystal plinth. Nausea surged through her and the light dimmed. She latched onto the stubborn beast, dragging its tendrils back toward her body. The dragon hissed and kicked.

You've eaten! Everly yanked harder. *You're done!*

The light burned hot around her, manifesting its fury. She clenched her teeth and closed her eyes, pushing it back where it belonged.

Or rather, where it resided against her will.

Her body absorbed the light with an audible pop, and the cavern went dark.

Prepared for the drop this time, she fell to the floor on her feet in a crouch. Every muscle and joint ached. The cave had dimmed once more, but the red pulsing flash of the Bane made her eyes burn. Across the space, Lian helped Tammy to her feet, and Callan and Cherry fussed over Harper.

"I'm fine. I'm fine!" Harper pushed their assistance away with a grunt, standing up by herself.

Everly got up with a groan, shuffling to join them. She kept her eyes turned away from the woman impaled on the cave ceiling, the two men dead and drained on the ground. Three lives, lost. Two by her hand.

Lian caught her looking away from the dead bodies. "The other three scampered off, if that's who you're looking for. It's over."

Only me and the auerdax, the two monsters, killed people today.

In the dark cavern, lit only by the red light, the eidolghast had reverted to its corporeal state. The giant pile of bones looked a lot less deadly when it was silent and unmoving. But no less creepy.

"Do we leave it here?" Callan said, as Everly limped over to join the circle of her companions.

Lian nodded. "I think so. This cavern is far enough away from people to cause no

harm in the time it takes to rot."

"Ev!" Harper shoved away from Cherry's supportive grip and threw her arms around Everly's shoulders. "I knew you could do it. I knew you could control it. You're a freaking glowing goddess."

Everly whispered into her friend's hair. "But I ... it killed them."

Harper pulled back and gave Everly a knowing look. She knew what Everly's light had done to those men. How it consumed their lifeforces.

Everly wished she could take it back, that she'd never explained how it felt like she *ate* things. But from the proud smile Harper gave her, she wasn't even entirely sure her friend believed her. To her, and the others, she was just their bright super weapon. A good thing.

But Everly felt as far from good as possible.

"You did what you had to," Harper said firmly. "You saved us."

"You still got hurt."

A bruise blossomed around Harper's left eye, and there was a split in her eyebrow above a trail of dried blood down the side of her face.

Harper grinned and probed the skin next to the cut with a grimace. "It'll make for a cool story. I was thinking—mauled by a goose in the park. My followers would love that. I can work with my graphic designer and launch some naughty goose merch."

There had been real fear in Harper last night when they'd been running from the auerdax. And again today when Everly's light had attempted to grab her. But there she was, laughing and making plans for her next publicity stunt while blood still dripped down her cheekbone.

"You shouldn't have even been here," Everly said hotly. "We should have made you stay back at the motel."

Harper's green eyes grew fierce. "I beg your pardon? 'Made me stay'? I'm not a toddler you can just boss around. I chose to come here."

"And look what that got you." Everly motioned to the cut on her face. "That's probably going to scar. How's that going to look in pictures?"

"Wow. Would you chill?" Harper rolled her eyes. "First of all, makeup companies make incredible concealers nowadays. I'll probably land a deal *because* I have a scar they want to prove their product can cover."

"But—"

"*Secondly,*" she pointed at the others, who awkwardly watched their argument, "both Tammy and Cherry got hurt, too. Should they have been left back at the motel?"

Cherry raised his hand. "I believe I win the prize for getting knocked out of the fight first. We were all getting our asses kicked."

Harper gave a sharp nod. "I had things under control. I'm not some fragile princess,

and I thought of all people you'd know that by now."

Everly's emotions swirled, every thought a raw nerve. "It's not that I don't think you're capable, but you're only human—"

"You think I don't wish I was all special and magical like everyone else here? I have to work with what I've got, and I *know* I can do it. But thank you sooo much for making me feel like not enough."

Lian stepped between them and spoke up before Everly could respond. "Sorry to interrupt, but we should get what we came for and get out of here before any of our cultist friends return."

Callan cleared his throat. "And I'd like to touch base with Lucas and let him know what happened before rumors start flying."

"Of course," Harper said, backing away to rejoin Cherry.

She brushed her fingers down the fresh trail of blood on her face and turned away from Everly.

"Right then. Would you like to help me release the Bane?" Lian asked.

"If it's okay with you, I'd like to stay far, far away from that thing for now. It makes me ill." Everly stared at her feet, fighting against hot tears.

Lian crooked a finger at Callan, pulling the rolled parchment from inside her jacket with her other hand. Once the parchment was spread across Callan's arms, she climbed up onto a natural nodule in the crystal pillar, wrapped her hands in the hem of her t-shirt, and then reached for the artifact.

It made a sharp metallic scrape as it pulled free from its resting place. Then she placed it on the blood-stained parchment across Callan's hands.

The moment it touched the parchment, the continual oozing of blood ceased, and as Callan wrapped the parchment closed, Everly's nausea ebbed to a more manageable level.

"And that's why we needed the parchment," Lian said. "It's the only thing that stops it bleeding."

The nearness of the Bane no longer affected Everly as it had, muted by its wrapping. Lian climbed down, wiped off her hands, and then made a disgusted face at the eidolghast blood on her shirt.

"Take a look around," she said to the group. "See if you can find any other artifacts. Ghast knows what will happen if they're left in the hands of these beshadowed shadyrs."

Though the group searched the supply trunks and every dark corner of the cave and ruined mansion, they found nothing else of note. Wherever the other shadyr artifacts were, they weren't in the cave, which meant the Gorhanmere shadyrs would have them for a while longer.

And as Lian had said, there was no way of knowing just what kind of damage they could do.

When Harper pulled the van into the lot at the motel, the door to Lucas's room popped open. He stood in the frame, watching the Howell team disembark. As though he'd been waiting for them.

Everly shivered as she hopped out of the campervan. The afternoon had turned cold and breezy, and a light misting rain fell from a charcoal sky.

There was something sinister about Gorhanmere that sent chills up her spine. She'd be glad to see it in the rearview mirror. All they had to do was pack and go, but the way Lucas eyed them left her worrying that wasn't going to go smoothly.

The Darkfrey shadyr approached, his hands shoved into the pockets of his cargo pants like he was just out for a stroll. His blue gaze cast over their general sense of dishevelment and injuries, then landed on the blood-stained parchment bundle clutched in Lian's hands.

"Seems like you found what you were looking for," Lucas remarked, catching Callan's eye. "But you know that's Darkfrey property, right?"

"Finders, keepers," Cherry jeered, and Lian shushed him with a glare.

Callan squared up against Lucas. "It *was* Darkfrey property, before Mordan allowed it to be stolen by someone else. Now it's ours, because we fought for it, risked our lives, and won it."

"We had a deal, that you'd hand over what you found."

Callan scoffed. "The deal was we'd take what we needed and share the rest. There was nothing else. Go look for yourself if you want."

"Really? Maybe we will go and check. But still ..." Lucas folded his arms and raised his voice. "We really can't let you leave here with that."

The rest of his brace filtered out of the motel room and took up stances behind him. Everly wasn't sure if they meant to look so menacing, or if that was their standard appearance, but it set her heart racing.

She had no misconceptions that she could take a Darkfrey shadyr in a fight.

Not without using the dragon, which was something she wanted to avoid again for a long, long time.

Callan leaned around Lucas and smiled. "Hey, Molly. How's your neck?"

Everly recognized the girl who'd almost died the night before. She looked fresh-faced today with only a small, raw scratch where the ghast had almost slit her throat.

Molly tucked her hair behind her ear. "Oh, um. Great. All healed up. Thanks again."

"Wonderful." Callan cut his gaze back to Lucas and his smile fell away. "It's so lucky you're alive, Molly."

"Touche," Lucas murmured, a sly grin turning up one corner of his lips. "I get the point. We owe you. Fine, keep your ill-gotten goods. But you know I'll have to report it to the estate."

Lian scoffed and brushed past him on her way to the rooms.

She tossed her final thoughts over her shoulder. "I can handle Mordan. You go ahead and tell him we did something he *couldn't*. I'll celebrate that victory. Also, the auerdax is dead. You're welcome."

Lucas raised an eyebrow at her retreating back, then looked at Callan. "Your mom's kind of a badass."

"I only recently figured that out myself," Callan replied wryly. "If you want the auerdax body for a safe cleanup, you'll find it in the cellar of that abandoned mansion. Little triangular door under the staircase leads to a cave."

"Will we find more than just a dead eidolghast body?"

Callan shrugged. "Maybe. Maybe not."

Lucas sighed. "I should make you do the cleanup."

"That's one of the advantages of not being team Darkfrey anymore. You can't make me do anything." Callan's grin widened. "It was good to see you, Lucas. Keep in touch."

"You know I won't." Lucas saluted him, then turned around and ushered his minions back toward their room.

Everly took a few steps forward to stand at Callan's side.

Under her breath, she asked, "Is Mordan going to be a problem? Once he knows we got the Bane?"

Callan's gaze turned troubled as Lucas's door closed behind him. "I don't know. But I'd venture to say we're going to find out."

28

Everly sat in the passenger seat, all too aware of the Bane's closeness. Even though it was at the back of the van with the others, the sick, dark energy it spilled that made her want to roll down the window and puke.

The Howell team passed the artifact between them, examining it, trying to form any understanding or meaning from the runes and shapes etched into its sides. The only thing they knew for sure was that it made Everly sick.

They'd chosen to stop and see Crowea on the way back to Howell House. They'd been able to shower and get into clean clothes back at the motel, and they were all in need of a solid meal. Dinner at Crow's was a unanimous vote, and Lian wanted to touch base with the old witch and see if she knew anything about the Bane.

The street outside Crow's Nest was quiet for a weekend night, which was probably explained by the heavy, driving rain that soaked through Shroudhaven. The storm had started not long after they left Gorhanmere, and their trip home had been fraught with slippery close calls on the mountain descent.

Harper pulled the campervan up across two parking meters, clearly unconcerned about tickets at that point. She'd barely spoken to Everly since their fight in the cave.

They'd have to talk eventually, but Everly had little hope of trying to fix their friendship when she couldn't even fix herself.

Everly slid from the passenger seat and shoved her hands into the pockets of her jacket, walking quickly away from the van before the others.

She didn't want to be anywhere near the Bane.

She squinted against the downpour and jogged toward the lit door to The Crow's Nest. The door opened on a wave of sage-scented heat mixed with the smell of fried foods. They were early enough for Crowea's nightly dinner special, and it smelled divine.

Crowea sat at the bar with a paperback in one hand and a coffee mug in the other. She glanced up when Everly stepped inside, shaking her silvery hair free of raindrops.

"Blown in on the storm, I see," Crowea drawled, setting down her mug.

Everly gave her a wan smile. "You could say that."

Crowea placed her book face down on the bar. Her lone eye traced the edges of

Everly's face with a concerned look.

"Oh no, what's wrong, baby? You need to chat about it?"

About how her only hope to discover the source of her powers was a dark, bleeding weapon that made her sick to her stomach?

Or how her relationship with her best friend was falling apart because of this horrible, dangerous town? Or how she'd taken lives that day, *chose* them and allowed them to be taken? Everly swallowed hard, tears sitting along her lower eyelid.

She was saved from having to respond when the door whipped open behind her, and the rest of her friends piled into the bar, carrying the scent of wind and rain with them.

Lian greeted Crowea with a hug. "Dinner special all around, please. Got some tired and hungry shadyrs here."

Crowea smiled, crinkling her eye. "Sure thing. Go on and sit. I'll get the kitchen started on your order and make sure they pile the plates up good."

Lian hovered a moment longer. "Think you could come sit with us for a bit?"

Crowea nodded, her good eye flicking toward Everly again. "I'll do what I can."

Joining the others, exhaustion washed over Everly as she sank into a comfy armchair and let her limbs melt into the cushions.

Even though they'd only been in Gorhanmere for a day, so much had happened that she felt like she'd run a marathon. For the first time in forever, she was actually looking forward to returning to Boderleth Antiques.

While everyone else chatted in a somewhat subdued manner, Everly closed her eyes and drifted in a place between sleep and wakefulness, wishing she could let herself dream.

Wishing she could dream of Rylan.

But her over-stimulated mind only served her visions of the Gorhanmere leader's face contorted in dread as he died. And other strange flashes of the Bane. Like distant memories, too hazy and ancient to view clearly. Just sensations of closeness, of cutting, of falling apart.

"Hey," Callan murmured, nudging her shoulder. "Food's here."

Everly blinked open her eyes. Not only was there now a pitcher and several full glasses on the table, but a meal waited for her, as well. There was a pile of crinkle cut fries on her plate, and a golden-brown stuffed pastry.

When she bit into it, the buttery crust flaked away, and the concoction of veggies and spices exploded inside her mouth.

Hints of curry, thyme, and dill, and some kind of yogurt sauce. But Everly's stomach churned, too close to the Bane, still feeling too *full*, to enjoy the food.

Crowea was settled in a chair beside Lian with her coffee mug, now steaming with fresh brew. Her expression was stern as Lian muttered to her between mouthfuls of chips.

"All right. Let me see it then," she said.

Lian reached down near her feet and her hand returned with the Bane, still wrapped in its thick, blood-stained parchment. Crowea made no action to take the bundle from her.

She sucked in a breath and put her mug aside. "I can already feel magic."

Lian nodded. "It was with the Darkfreys for a long time. It's called the Bane of Teeth and Stars."

"Isn't that lovely and ominous," Crowea murmured.

"It's almost the same name a vasmire called Everly," Lian added. "The beast of teeth and stars."

"Speaking with eidolghasts now?"

Everly shrunk into her armchair. "I can understand them, sometimes."

Lian's voice became strained. "The similar name is why we thought it would give us some clue about her. But we can't work anything out about it ourselves. We were hoping—"

"That this old witch would place hands on a thing obviously corrupt and dangerous in order to answer some questions for you?" Crowea's eye was wide and her lips pursed.

Everly should have known this would come to nothing. Crowea had also refused to use her psychometry on her.

Does that mean I'm something corrupt and dangerous, too?

She didn't want to believe it, still hoped there was some other answer, but everything kept pointing that way.

Lian's voice trembled. "This could be what wakes up my son. What saves him. Please."

Crowea lifted her face to the ceiling, and her gaze flickered lightly over Everly. "Very well. I'll see what I can see. But I do not like this."

Eating around the table ceased, and everyone watched as Crowea peeled off her elbow length gloves and reached for the parchment.

She paused, her fingers hovering over the weapon as she gave Lian a pointed look. "Safe to touch?"

"We've all handled it. Just avoid the sharp edges."

Crowea pinched the edge of the flimsy parchment and unwrapped the Bane as carefully as if she were unswaddling a baby. She inhaled sharply.

"My, my, my." Crowea tugged aside the second flap of the Bane's stained wrapping, her one good eye raking over the weapon beneath a narrowed brow. "Powerful. Deadly."

Everly gagged at the sight and presence of the Bane. She tossed the remnants of her veggie pocket onto her plate and curled back in her chair.

"What can you tell us about it?" Lian asked.

Crowea took two deep breaths, letting them out slowly and deliberately. She closed

her one eye, then she placed her fingertips on the black metal, well away from the sharp edges of the diamond's sides.

Her eyeball could be seen flickering and rolling beneath its eyelid, and from her other eye, dark liquid started oozing from around the edges of the eidolghast tooth. She sucked in a breath, snatching her fingers away from the Bane. Her one eye fluttered open, bloodshot and dilated, zeroing in on Everly.

"You." Crowea returned her gaze to the Bane, her fingertips bouncing lightly in the air above the artifact. "Oh, this thing knows you, baby. Intimately."

Everly opened her mouth to ask more, but it had dried up entirely.

"So they are connected?" Lian urged.

"It remembers ..." Crowea muttered, closing her eye once more. "That *thing* ... The thing inside the Boderleth girl is only a piece. It's not whole."

She tilted her head, wincing painfully, and her wild gray curls shivered. "So, so many destroyed ... It was this weapon that broke that *thing* into pieces."

Everly wrapped her arms around herself, trying to hold off a chill that had formed deep in her chest.

"But what is it, Crow? What is in Everly?" Lian urged.

Crowea's eye shot open. Her pupil narrowed and focused on Everly.

Don't say it. Don't say it. Please don't say that I'm a monster.

"Soul eater," Crowea whispered.

Every eye at the table turned on Everly then, staring with a mix of pity, awe, horror. Everly's head shook, wanting to deny it. But what could she deny?

Into the absolute silence that fell after Crowea's declaration, Callan asked, "Is that some kind of eidolghast?"

Lian shook her head. "Not one I've ever heard of. Though there is always the chance a new one has ventured through a shroudpool to wreak havoc on the world without us knowing about it. Can you tell us anything else, Crow?"

Crowea shook her head. Her skin had paled, and she stood up, shaky on her feet.

She slipped her gloves back on. "No, I can't. That's all I've got. That is all I'm willing to bear."

Lian placed her hand on Crowea's covered hand and squeezed with a kind smile. "Thank you."

Crowea left them to their meal, and Lian wrapped the Bane back up. While everyone else brainstormed what this could possibly have meant, Everly stared blankly at the bundled weapon, too upset to finish her food. The one theory that kept returning and coming back around was that Everly was possessed.

Possessed by a "piece" of an eidolghast that ate souls.

And just like that, her absolute worst nightmares were confirmed.

By the time they left the bar, the rain had slowed to an annoying trickle—enough to wet eyelashes, but not enough to justify an umbrella. Everly and Harper walked out of the pub last. Harper tapped away at her phone even though Everly doubted she had any service.

It was just an excuse to ignore Everly.

The rest of the team climbed into the camper, still talking about the artifact and Everly's supposed secret identity.

Everly grabbed Harper's arm and tugged her around. "Hey. Talk to me. I know you're mad."

"Oh, I'm not mad." Harper hit the button to turn off her screen. The ambient glow cut off, leaving them in the dark. "I'm upset. There's a distinct difference."

"Why don't you explain it to me then?"

"You really don't get it? You can't see how it would be upsetting that my best friend thinks I'm so useless that she has to act like a damned *martyr* to save me?" Her tone was harsher than anything she'd ever used with Everly before, and it stung no different than if she'd slapped her.

"And you know what? It does suck that I don't have all the glowy swishy powers the rest of you have, but that doesn't mean I'm worthless. But everything you've been doing is making me feel that way. You're shutting me out, lying to me, leaving me behind. I had to bust you with your freaking pet zombie before you'd even open up to me a little!"

"You think it was easy for me to tell you that stuff? That I like being this *thing*?"

"Of course not! But it's the difficult things we should be telling each other, otherwise how are we supposed to survive this? But any time the issue has to do with this place, all the supernatural woo woo, you ice me out and remind me that we're not staying, like you have every say in the matter." Harper waved her arms wildly as if to encompass the whole town.

"Because it's not safe here. There's no reason for you to still be here."

"No reason? How about being here for my best friend?" Harper jabbed a shiny-nailed finger toward Everly's chest.

"What happens when Rylan wakes up? Are you coming home with me, or are you going to ship me off alone, get rid of the useless human? I don't know what weird entity has latched on to you, but in case you need a reminder, you're human, too, Ev." Harper's voice had risen during her tirade, echoing through the rainy street.

"Beg pardon. I don't mean to intrude." Cardboard Box Barry appeared beside them.

He wore his usual uniform of holey jeans and heavy metal t-shirt, but he'd covered his arms with a stained, khaki jacket. His long white beard dangled in a smooth, freshly woven braid down his chest.

Everly stared at him, astonished. She couldn't remember a time he'd ever approached her or any group of people she'd ever been with. She'd never even heard his voice before, which didn't match his appearance at all. Smooth, cultured, and a deep bass tone.

Barry glanced at the camper, where the shadyrs were watching the exchange through the windows. Then he sized up Everly, before his gaze slipped away to settle on Harper.

"Are you all right, little lady?" he asked gently.

Harper huffed. "I'm just *fine* apart from being called little lady."

Barry shifted back and forth on his feet a couple of times, his gaze marking the shadyrs and Everly. "I just thought, maybe you need to get away from this lot?"

"No. No, these are my friends ..." Her expression softened. "I'm fine. Really. Thanks."

Barry shrugged. "Suit yourself."

Everly watched him disappear back into a nearby alley, stunned by the exchange.

Harper pointed after him and whispered, "Did he just try to save me from you?"

Everly shook her head. "No idea. That was so weird."

Harper grunted a frustrated squeal. "Why does everybody think I need saving?"

Everly snorted a laugh, and Harper joined her, shaking her head. For a moment, it was just the two of them again. No anger. No frustration.

Then Harper sighed and looked up into the drizzling rain. Her smile fell away, and she put her hands on her hips. "What do you have to say? I talked to you. Now talk back."

"I'm sorry," Everly said without hesitation. "I don't think you're useless. You're on the entire other end of the spectrum from useless. But you don't *have* to add monster hunter to your resume. You don't have to excel at every single thing in this world."

Harper laughed again, but there was no humor in it. "If you think that then maybe you don't know me at all."

"I just ..." *I want to keep you safe.*

Everly exhaled and looked over at the van, thinking of Lian, her husband, what had happened to the Howell brothers.

Even the best fighters in the world cannot shield themselves entirely from tragedy. "And I just realized I'm doing to you exactly what Rylan did to me. Shoving me out of his life to keep me safe. That's not fair."

"You're right. It's not. Because we're a team," Harper reminded her.

"We are. A damn good one."

Harper stepped forward and hugged her. "So don't do it again, okay? Promise?"

"Promise." Everly squeezed her back.

As they released one another, she was struck by an idea. "Hey, I'd like you to be the one who looks after the Bane. We need to keep it from ending up back with the Darkfreys, and I know you can do that."

"Seriously?"

"Seriously. Considering what it is, how its connected to me, there's no one I'd trust more to keep it safe." Everly glanced at the van, then lowered her voice. "But there is something I want to try before you put it away."

29

The back porch globe couldn't dispel the gloom behind Boderleth Antiques. The small, square yard pressed in on the ambient light like it was nothing more than a candle flame in the void of space. Shadows turned the overgrown weeds and the ancient swing set to monsters, and to Everly that felt too soon. Too raw. Monsters *were* real, and they were everywhere.

Even inside her.

"Is he here?" Harper asked quietly, her voice stealing through Everly's dark thoughts.

Everly nodded, motioning to the darkness beneath the broken swings. Zozo's reflective eyes blinked at her, then glanced warily at Harper.

"Are you sure about this?" Harper's knuckles had turned white on the parchment-wrapped Bane.

Misty rain clung to her long, dark eyelashes. True to form, though, her mascara wasn't running at all.

She clutched the artifact to her puffy pink jacket, her face pale. "This thing is dangerous. Look what it did to those crazy people in Gorhanmere."

"That was the eidolghast blood. Not the Bane." Although the blood did come *from* the Bane. Everly frowned. "I think."

"Always fun to play with ancient, cursed artifacts we don't understand," Harper said, laughing nervously.

Lian had handed the Bane over to them in a gesture of trust that left Everly teary. It had been scrubbed and disinfected, and they worked out that as long as one part of the Bane was in contact with the parchment, it didn't bleed. So that was one more thing they knew about it.

As Harper slowly unwrapped it again there in the backyard, Everly gagged.

Harper blanched, folding the parchment closed again. "How is this supposed to work?"

"I get sick when I'm close to the Bane, but I think it's the dragon ... the soul eater"— the name was bitter on her tongue—"that's reacting to it. I don't understand the thing inside me, but I can sense how it feels."

The dragon roiled within her.

"It wants to *consume*, and the Bane makes it want to vomit. I think I ... *it* somehow partially consumed Rylan and Zozo. And it doesn't want to let them go. I want to try and release Zozo first because he's only partially trapped inside me. It might be easier to get him out."

"So what? You think the Bane will help you vomit them out?"

"Maybe?" Everly tugged up her hood against the rain. "Or maybe it will help me get enough control over the dragon to set them free. I know it's a long shot, but I have to try. Rylan can't stay inside me forever."

Harper flashed a sly grin. "Oh, I bet he'd want to try."

Everly groaned and punched her lightly in the arm. "Inappropriate."

Harper adjusted her grip on the Bane. "Right then. Do we just hold the Bane near you while you toss your cookies and hope for the best?"

Everly winced. "I think it needs to be more than that. We know the Bane can hurt the soul eater, that it can, and has, even broken it apart. To get it to lose enough control, I think we need to hurt the dragon."

"Hurt the dragon. Like ... we use it to hurt *you*?" Harper shook her head. "Nope, we've reached bad idea territory now and I'm not keen to trespass."

"You can either help me, or I'll do it myself."

Harper's gaze grew fierce. "I don't like either of those options. You're being a wannabe martyr again."

Everly rubbed the rain off her face and sighed. "Please. This has gone on long enough. Zozo and Rylan both deserve freedom. I want to do this for them, and I want you by my side while I try."

For a long moment, the two women faced off on the backyard path. The rain continued to mist down, coating everything in a glossy sheen. The porch light gleamed off the sprinkling rain like there were thousands of tiny diamonds falling to the pavement. Beyond the creaky wooden fence at the back of the property, the trees shifted and swayed in a whispered lullaby.

Harper groaned. "Fine. What kind of friend would I be if I let you experiment with a dangerous weapon from the Everdark alone?"

Everly put her hands on Harper's arms, squeezing them through the puffy pink fabric. "Thank you."

Turning away, she rolled up her sleeves then knelt on the concrete. "Come here, Zozo. Come see me. Don't mind my friend, Harper. She won't hurt you."

Although, she was driving the van when it hit him. Luckily, he didn't know that.

Zozo came out from under the swing set timidly, his eerie blue eyes bouncing between the two of them. He nudged Everly's hand with his nose and let her pet the top of his head. A strong purr rumbled inside him, though it stopped when Harper kneeled next to them.

"It's okay," Everly soothed the skittish animal.

"What now?" Harper whispered.

Everly kept one hand on Zozo then offered her other arm to Harper. "Cut me."

Harper made a slashing, stabbing gesture in the air above the bare forearm. "Just like … do it?"

"Did you want to say a few words first?"

"Should I say grace or give your eulogy? 'Cause we have a wide range of potential risks here."

"Sorry. I'm nervous, too. But I have to know if this will work. Can we just get it over with?"

Harper sucked in a breath and unwrapped the Bane without releasing it entirely from the parchment. Her hand shook as she brought the sharp edge of the artifact over to Everly's arm.

Everly swallowed down the urge to vomit and braced herself for the slice. She had a high tolerance for pain, mostly, but there was something psychological about knowing what was about to happen that made it hurt much, much more than when it was an accident.

"I'm sorry," Harper whispered.

The Bane's sharp edge bit into Everly's forearm, and fire licked up her skin.

Light flared, though the dragon itself didn't manifest. Sickness overwhelmed her. Then Everly felt a huge expulsion of energy, like some part of her had been torn asunder and tossed aside. Lightning crackled between her hand and Zozo's fur where they touched.

Everly screamed, overwhelmed by the pain and illness raging from the cut in her arm, and the violence of having a piece of her ripped away. She collapsed sideways onto the concrete, her bleeding arm twisted beneath her chest. She flushed hot from head to toe and grew lightheaded. Disoriented.

Everything seemed to dim.

"Did it work?" The words were a mere crackle in Everly's throat. She curled on her side, and her eyes sought the dark space for the cougar.

Zozo snarled and backed away, his tail flicking irritably.

She reached for him. "Zozo?"

He growled and snapped at her fingers, and she pulled her hand back quickly. The cougar backed away several steps, then he turned tail and sprinted away.

"Ev?" Harper's voice shook.

"I think it worked," Everly whispered.

Then she launched to her knees, crawled to the grass, and emptied her stomach.

She lost track of time for a little while. Fever wracked her body, and nausea ebbed and swelled. The dragon howled and swam within her, charging the walls of her mind, a wild, wounded beast. It was furious.

Everly was too weak to move her arms and legs, so Harper had to support her and drag her into the house. There was a bit of confusion where Harper couldn't carry her up the stairs to a bedroom, and then Everly was on a fainting couch in her father's antique shop. Her eyes closed, then opened again to Harper's distant voice and the press of ibuprofen in her palm.

Everly managed to choke down the pills. At some point, Harper had removed her shoes and covered her with a blanket.

"We need to go free Rylan," she murmured, nearly dropping the glass of water Harper had given her.

She closed her eyes, more comfortable in the darkness beyond. Her head felt like it was splitting in two.

"No, you need to recover." Harper's voice rose, strained. "Rylan isn't going anywhere."

"The dragon is angry. About Zozo. Rylan isn't safe."

"Tomorrow, Ev. Please. For me. Just rest."

Everly made a small sound of disagreement, but sank deeper into the cushions, unable to hold her train of thought, let alone a conversation.

Harper's fingers entwined with hers, and they both fell silent. Everly drifted somewhere between sleep and waking for several long moments, until Harper must have assumed she was asleep.

Because the last thing Everly heard before she finally passed out was Harper saying, "Lian? I need your help."

Everly was back in the crystal cavern, surrounded but jutting outcrops of shimmering stone.

She couldn't remember how she'd gotten there. They'd driven home from Gorhanmere. Stopped for dinner at Crow's Nest. Left this cave far behind. Plus it looked ... different.

The clear and translucent crystal pillars were red now, all of them pulsing with an inner light. So many flashes at once made the whole cave look like a blood-tainted ocean reflecting moonlight. The Bane was gone.

But there were padlocks. *Everywhere.*

Ancient, heavy, rusted ones. Clinging to the crystal pillars. Hanging from stalactites. Cemented into the floor beneath her feet. Even locked onto small, broken chunks of crystal scattered across the ground.

Padlocks everywhere she looked. Some of them were broken, but most of them were locked up tight with no keys in sight. Something scintillated softly in the far corner, growling in a low rumble. The dragon, knotting itself into a tight glowing ball, sulking.

"I'm dreaming," Everly muttered.

Rylan's gruff voice echoed through the chamber. "Boderleth? You in here somewhere?"

She stepped out from behind a larger pillar that blocked her view.

Rylan stood near the entrance to the cavern, lips twisting into a half-smile when he saw her. "Is this place some kind of metaphor?"

"I wish," Everly said with a shudder. "This is where we found the Bane in Gorhanmere. It was just like this, but without all the padlocks. They're new."

"You found it?" Rylan rushed forward, halting just a step away from her. "Have you worked anything out yet from it?"

The Bane, the blood, her plan, and the slice down her arm all rushed back into her memory. Along with the name. *Soul eater.*

"Yeah, I've learned some not great things." Everly's voice wavered in a way that she hated, and tears sprung up in her eyes.

"Hey, it's okay." Rylan stepped closer, pulling her into his arms.

Everly sank into him, her face pressed against his shoulder, trying to hold down a shaking sob. She breathed deep, surrounded by the scent that was so singular to him. A scent that took her back years and years to a happier time. That took her back home.

Her *real* home—the one she'd made with him and the Howells, not the broken mess that her mother had created around the hole where her father once was.

"It's okay," Rylan repeated, stroking her hair. "If it doesn't work, if you can't put me back—"

"No. I think I can. Maybe." She released him. "Hang on just a second."

Rylan arched a dark brow in question, but she ignored him and wandered off through the pillars.

"Zozo?" Everly searched among the red columns, looking for the little cougar.

He was always nearby in her dreams, even if she only caught a glimpse of him. And he'd come to her when she called, when he'd pounced on the creepy dolls in the shopping mall for her.

But he didn't come this time.

His ghostly form didn't stalk the edges of the dream space.

She could feel his absence.

He was gone. Whatever part of him, his soul, that had been trapped in her dreams had been expelled.

"It worked," she said out loud, astonished. "It actually worked."

"What worked?" Rylan had followed her and spoke over her shoulder.

Turning back to him, it startled her how beautiful he was. The red light glittered off his short hair and his warm green eyes. His jaw tensed as his lips pressed together then parted in a way that brought back every single sensation from the kiss they'd shared.

Whether Rylan cared for her or not, whether he wanted her near or not, he was and always would be an anchor in Everly's life. One solid point in a world that too often felt like a tumultuous ocean. He was the embodiment of *home* Everly had never found anywhere else.

Now it's time to bring him home.

Locking her gaze with his, Everly's smile wavered. "Do you remember that game we used to play when we were young? The one where we'd get every kid in the playground who would join us, and all hold hands in a huge ring. Then we'd run around like crazy, all linked together, tugging and shoving at each other."

In a mirror to her words, faceless, silhouetted children appeared around them, skipping together in a wide, jostling ring-a-rosy.

Everly lifted her hands between her and Rylan, palms up and waiting in invitation.

Rylan frowned but took her hands in both of his without hesitation, sending a jolt of warmth through Everly's chest.

"Yeah, I remember. If you fell over, or let go, you were out. But what does this have to do with anything? *What worked*?"

Everly shook her head and continued, "As kids got out, the circle got smaller and smaller. There was that one time when it came down to just you and me. And we just, stood there, holding hands."

Rylan's frown morphed into a smile and he chuckled. "Oh man. How could I forget? It was so awkward. But I didn't want to drag you over just to win."

Everly was sure as well, even back then, that he could have if he wanted to.

She squeezed his hands in hers. "And I ... I just didn't want to let you go."

Rylan's smile faded and she could see him swallow.

"But now I have to. I have to let you go." Everly let Rylan's hands fall from hers. "And I know how. I know how to put you back in your body and get you out of this nightmare."

Rylan covered his mouth, his voice muffled beneath it. "How?"

"The Bane can help free you. If I cut myself with it while touching you, you'll be free."

"Wait, what? Cut yourself with the ..." Rylan's teeth bared. "No. Do you realize how bad that sounds? There has to be another way. Don't go doing anything dangerous for me. How many times do I have to beg you not to?"

He reached for her, and Everly backed away from him, shaking her head. "It's what I did for Zozo, and I'm ..." She remembered vomiting, collapsing, burning up from the inside. "I'm fine."

The unlit children ran faster, spinning hectically around them, a dizzying chaos of ghosts.

Rylan's gaze pierced straight through her. "Evie, no—"

"You can't stop me." She had to do this for him. She had to free him.

She had to let him go.

"I'm dreaming! Wake up!"

30

Everly sat up with a sharp inhalation. Her heart raced and a cold sweat covered her skin. Goosebumps ran up her arms and the back of her neck.

The antiques store was quiet, lit by a stained-glass shaded floor lamp that sat next to the fainting couch. She felt disoriented for a moment, then remembered Harper half-carrying her into the house and getting her settled in there.

Being in the antiques store after dark with only a single lamp to chase away the shadows and ghosts sent a chill down Everly's neck. She shivered and stretched, trying to rouse herself and push away the pain and wooziness that overwhelmed her.

She rubbed the sleep from her eyes, but she couldn't do anything about the flu-like symptoms that had begun after she'd released Zozo with the Bane.

Leaving her shoes where they lay, she quietly left the store, passing through the frosted-glass door, which Harper had left open. She heard voices from the doorway to the kitchen and the sound of the coffee machine running. A quick glance showed Harper and Lian over by the sink, hands waving animatedly and conversing in harsh whispers.

Only snippets reached Everly's ears.

"... he's my son."

"And she's our Everly. We can't ..."

"I know. *I know.* Ghast damn all of this."

The Bane didn't seem to be with them.

Where is it?

Everly blinked her sore eyes and narrowed them as she searched. The candle-shaped bulbs were dim, and the doors to the laundry and basement stairs were closed as usual.

But one of the drawers of a small buffet-and-hutch by the back door was slightly open, a pale shape jammed in the closure. It looked like the parchment the Bane was wrapped in. Harper must have shoved it in there between moving Everly inside and calling Lian.

Holding her breath, Everly crossed the open kitchen doorway in one swift step, hoping they wouldn't see her.

Their conversation continued without interruption, and Everly gingerly opened the drawer. As it edged open, her sickness increased. It was the Bane.

Reaching for it, a wave of guilt caught Everly's hand back. She'd promised. She promised Harper they were a team, that she wouldn't keep any more secrets or take risks on her own. And here she was, stealing the Bane in secret, after giving it to Harper as a gesture of trust.

What if they try to stop me?

The way they were arguing, Everly worried they might not give her another chance to do this. And she had to. For Rylan.

She couldn't leave him trapped inside her with something that ate souls for a moment longer.

She snatched up the Bane, wrap and all, and headed for Rylan's room.

Everly tiptoed up the stairs, carefully avoiding the warped boards that she knew would creak under her feet, then passed down the upstairs hall in the dark.

Inside her old bedroom, she eased the door shut behind her. She flipped the light switch. Nothing happened. The vasmire pieces were still doing their level best to beshadow the space.

Sighing, she turned and carefully worked her way across the room to the window. In the pitch black, she could sense the vasmire parts billowing with power, and cold fog parted around her bare ankles as she skirted the bed.

It smelled horrific, like a slaughterhouse in high summer. Coupled with the proximity to the Bane and her leftover illness from earlier it left her wobbly and weak. But she pushed on.

At the window, she ripped open the curtains. The glow of moonlight filled the room, illuminating the body on the single bed with silver light. He lay exactly as he had since they brought him home from Nell's laboratory. He looked gray and ghostly pale, like a colorless statue lying atop the mattress.

Everly's heart was in her throat as she sat on the edge of the bed and rested the Bane in her lap. She touched his face, his skin frigid beneath her warm fingertips, then she slipped a finger beneath his nose to reassure herself that he was still breathing.

The tickle of his breath on her skin reminded her of all the times they'd been close in her dreams. All the times she'd wished it had been real.

Could it be real, once he's awake again? Will he treat me the same?

Everly didn't give her questions time to search for answers. She had to wake Rylan up for *him*, not for any of her own desires.

She unwrapped the Bane and stared down at the weapon in the dim light. For such a dangerous creation, it was quite beautiful. She wrapped her left hand around Rylan's, their fingers intertwined, and rolled up her sleeve.

Hefting the head-sized object in her right hand, she positioned the blade over her

left forearm. She would have matching cuts on her arms—one for Zozo, one for Rylan.

And they'd both be free.

Then another thought emerged. Maybe, if she cut deep enough, could she cut the *thing* out of her? Expel the soul-eating dragon from her entirely? It would be worth it, to not be a monster anymore.

I could be human again. Just human. In control of myself.

Everly lingered on the thought, torn between hope and the fear of hoping. Her hand shook, unwilling to cause self-harm. She felt frozen in time, willing herself to act, but afraid of the consequences.

The door slammed open.

The light switch clicked loudly in the silence. The bulbs, which hadn't worked for Everly, snapped on, flooding the room with harsh yellow light.

"Ev!" Harper snapped, looming in the doorway like an avenging angel. "What the hell are you doing?"

It has to be now. Everly gritted her teeth, looked back at Rylan, and plunged the Bane deep into her arm.

Harper was across the room in a split second, frantically yanking the diamond-shaped blade out of the wide wound it caused. She cried out as the sharp edge tore into her fingers, and Everly watched, mind blurred by agony, as blood welled up on Harper's hand.

Then everything splintered to shards.

Everly wandered a world of dark, shattered glass.

She found nothing and no one but herself. It didn't even seem like a dream. Just empty, unending black, the vastness of the universe, broken by the glint of sharp edges as crystal broke and fell like rain around her. Over and over. Endless sparkling shards in an eerily soundless deluge.

She was alone. No Rylan. No Zozo.

Is the dragon gone, too?

Her heart clenched as a shimmering ribbon of pale light flashed by her field of vision.

No. NO!

Everly crumpled. She couldn't remember a life without Rylan in her dreams. Even before he'd become trapped there fully, he'd always been around.

She'd lost him. An empty pit opened in the center of her being.

But that thing, that soul eating *thing* was still there. She felt shattered and lost, and no matter how many times she demanded to wake up, she couldn't. So she walked. She cried. She screamed at the emptiness, at the terrible creature that swam like an aurora around her, and she begged for mercy.

Until finally, her eyes opened.

Early morning daylight filtered into the bedroom. She recognized the off-white plaster relief ceiling, the brown, floral wallpaper, the chest of drawers directly across from the bed, and the bookshelf beside it which they'd loaded down with vasmire pieces.

Except ... The crates were gone. And the room smelled like disinfectant, not rotting eidolghast.

Everly sat up with a start, throwing her arm out to touch the other side of the mattress, where Rylan had lay lifeless.

He was also gone.

Everly pushed back the covers and put her bare feet on the floor. But as she stood, a wave of dizziness washed over her, and nausea ripped through her guts. Her skin flushed hot, too hot, and her legs wobbled underneath her. She keeled over and hit the rug on her hands and knees, knocking everything off her bedside table in an attempt to catch herself.

A glass of water and bedside lamp crashed to the floor. Loudly.

Racing footsteps echoed in the hall, and a moment later, Lian barreled through the door, her gaze scanning the room.

When she saw Everly on the carpet, she *tsk*ed. "Got up too fast?"

Everly nodded, tears blooming as pain roared through her arm. "Rylan?"

Lian smiled. "He's awake."

Everly closed her eyes and let out a single, thankful sob. The pain in her arm, the sickness in her body, none of it mattered if Rylan was back.

Lian tucked her arms under Everly's shoulders and hauled her back to sit on the bed. "You need to rest. You were in really rough shape last night. There were moments we were worried you wouldn't pull through."

There were times Everly had also wondered, in that world of darkness and shattered glass, if she'd already died.

Lian's smile fell away. "That was a stupid, dangerous thing you did."

"But it worked," Everly pointed out weakly.

Lian's eyes turned glossy and she pulled Everly in for a hug. "It did. Thank you."

Everly's head swam, trying to grasp onto reality. She worried about Harper being angry with her, and how she'd been cut with the Bane too. She worried about the throbbing pain in her arm, and how long she'd been out. But only one thought kept emerging to the surface.

She needed confirmation, she needed to see with her own eyes. "Can I see him?"

"There were some ... complications." Lian fluffed the pillows up, avoiding Everly's gaze. "I'll ask him if he feels up to it."

"Complications? What complications?"

Lian shook her head. "I'll let him tell you."

After she disappeared through the door, Everly leaned back onto the pillows for a moment, working through a breathing exercise to fend off what felt like a killer panic attack. Voices sounded from downstairs, too many to be just Lian, Rylan, and Harper. It sounded like the whole team was down there.

He's awake.

Everly lifted the hem of the bedsheet, intending to dry the tears from her eyes. Pain lanced up her left arm and traveled through her body, making her momentarily blinded from the agony.

She grunted painfully under her breath as she lifted the sleeve of her sweatshirt.

Her arm had been bandaged where the wound was, but there were marks on her skin, extending out around the edges of the dressing.

She was cracking apart. Like the glass in her dream.

The damage was faint. Paper-thin, jagged red lines showed beneath her skin, spider-webbing outwards. She pressed a finger to the cracks and stifled a scream as it felt as though glass shattered beneath her skin. The cracks grew darker and spread farther.

That can't be good.

Heavy footsteps filtered through her despair, and she yanked her sleeve down. If they hadn't seen it when treating the wound, then no one needed to know.

It'll heal. It'll go away, Everly assured herself, watching the doorway in breathless anticipation.

Rylan stopped outside the threshold to the room, his warm green eyes latching onto hers.

Everly let out a breath she'd been holding since the night he was attacked. All that they'd been through since that moment felt insubstantial, unimportant. The goal had always been to bring him back, and here he was. Whole again. Whole and beautiful. And angry.

"Hey," he said, voice gruff and eyebrows low.

"Hey," Everly replied, cheeks flushing hot. "Come in."

His gaze flicked away from hers and latched onto the floor. "I can't."

"What do you mean?"

He scrubbed at his face, then ran a hand over his short hair, blowing out a breath. "I don't know how to explain … I … Just watch."

Rylan took a single step into the room, and immediately began to swirl with black, sparking shadyr magic.

His body juddered and twitched. He sprouted fur. His limbs lengthened and hardened, and vasmire fangs grew past his lips, then retracted again, reforming into a wolf-like snout. His clawed hands turned milky translucent until the wall appeared behind them.

It was the exact thing that had happened when Tammy and Cherry came in contact with the eidolghast blood mixture that had once covered the Bane.

"Oh, no." Everly's good hand fluttering to her mouth. The wound in her left arm ached and throbbed. "I don't understand ... We cleaned the Bane."

Rylan backed out of the room, stopping a few steps behind the threshold. His body contorted and with an almost painful groan, the shifting magic ended, and he returned to his human form. He still hadn't looked at her again.

"We're not sure what's causing it. For some reason my shadyr form is reacting to you. Or more likely the soul-eating being inside you. Maybe there are still some essences of the eidolghasts it's consumed in there."

"But it doesn't affect anyone else." Everly's voice cracked.

Lian had sat right next to her, held her. If the Bane had changed something, why was it only happening to Rylan?

Rylan shrugged. "I'm free now, but my spirit spent a long time in there, caught up with you and the dragon. Maybe that changed something. I don't know. I just can't be close to you right now, not without becoming a monster. But it doesn't matter ..."

He trailed off and cleared his throat. "Because you're leaving."

Everly's heart froze in her chest. "What?"

"You should never have risked your life the way you did," he snapped, finally meeting her eye. "I told you I didn't want that."

"But it worked!" Everly said desperately, feeling as if her entire world were turning upside down.

She tried to stand up to move closer to him, but didn't have the strength, didn't want him to feel as though she made him a monster.

"I don't give a damn! I woke up to see you lying lifeless on the floor, blood everywhere, Harper screaming. I thought ..." His tone was cold and remote. "You shouldn't have had to do that. You shouldn't be *here*."

Where was the Rylan from her dreams? The one who had so casually chatted with her? Who had touched her like old friends, who'd laughed with her, fought by her side, comforted her ...? The Rylan who had kissed her until the world fall away.

"I don't understand," Everly said in a small, devastated voice.

But she did. It had been too much to hope that any of the closeness they'd shared in their dreams would continue into the real world.

Rylan had become himself again.

He half-turned away from her, staring again at the floor. "You did what you said you were going to do. There's no reason for you to stay."

Everly swiped at the tears in her eyes before they could fall. "No reason? None at all?"

She wanted to beg him to stop acting like this. Rylan was every reason in the world

she wanted to *stay*.

All along, she'd said over and over that when he was safe, she would go back home. But a part of her had always known that it wasn't the truth. It was a pretty lie she'd told herself to make it easier to walk the halls of her haunted home.

Leaving him wasn't what she wanted.

She wanted *him*. It had always been Rylan. It would always *be* Rylan.

But clearly, he didn't feel the same way about her. He looked at her like she was a monster. And maybe she was. She was possessed by a monster, after all.

Of course Rylan didn't want her. Of course he'd only want her to be gone.

Rylan turned away. "Go home, Everly. Before you really get hurt."

She took a shuddering breath, praying she could hold it together until he left. "If that's what you want."

"It's what you need," he replied, and then he was gone.

The day outside the back door was blustery and gray, and a heavy fog had rolled in off the mountains. Everly couldn't even see the swing set in the backyard for the thick clouds.

Lian stood on the warped boards of the back deck, looking in the door at Everly, who leaned heavily against the doorframe, panting with the exhaustion of just getting downstairs.

The rest of the Howell team had come up to the bedroom to check on her before heading home. Rylan had already left without even a goodbye. But Everly insisted on getting up to see Lian off.

Lian cupped Everly's cheek in one hand and smiled sadly. "I wish you'd stay."

Everly fought against her rising emotions. She refused to cry in front of Lian. If word got back to Rylan that she was emotional about leaving, she'd have been humiliated.

So she lifted her chin and said, "There's nothing left for me here."

"That's where you're wrong." Lian patted her cheek. "You will always have a home here with me."

Everly blinked back tears and stepped away from Lian's hand. "I appreciate that. But I have a new home now, one that it's past time I got back to."

Lian stared at her for an interminable moment, looking as if she wanted to say something else.

Instead, she just smiled again, even more sad than the first, and said, "Well. Call me and let me know when you get home safe."

With tears finally cresting over her cheeks, Everly watched Lian disappear around the corner of the house.

Her own mother had never once requested such a thing.

Closing the back door, Everly gingerly hobbled up the hallway, doing her best to seem fine and not pass out at the same time. The only person she hadn't seen yet that morning was Harper. That was the other reason she'd worked up the strength to get out of bed.

Everly found Harper bent over the table in the antiques shop, her camera beeping as she took photos of a jewelry box with a delicate, dancing ballerina inside.

"Hey," Everly said.

The camera beeped again and Harper didn't look up. "I'm glad you're alive but I'm not talking to you."

She certainly seems okay, other than angry.

Everly sighed and slumped onto a small two-seater couch beside her. "I just wanted to know how your hand was."

"My what?" Harper glanced up.

She was in full makeup this morning, her thick dark hair down in the kind of messy curls only girls like Bellsy could pull off. She was wearing soft pink overalls with gold buckles that hugged her hips and a baby doll tee that said *Ask me how much I care* in gold letters.

"Your hand," Everly repeated. "You cut it on the Bane last night."

Everly was ninety-nine percent certain the strange reaction taking place beneath her skin had to do with the soul-eating beast inside her, but a small part of her had been worried about Harper ever since she woke up, despite reassurances from the others that she was fine.

Harper shook her head and returned to her photos. "I didn't cut my hand. You must have imagined it."

"No, I saw—"

Harper let the camera hang from the strap around her neck and lifted both hands. She wriggled unmarred fingers at Everly. "No cuts. I promise. I'm perfectly fine. You, on the other hand, look like you need about five months of sleep."

"Feels accurate," Everly said dully.

I must have imagined it. Everything is so blurry. Pain lanced through her arm again and her face crumpled.

Harper straightened and set the camera down next to the light box she had built on the table. She sat on the couch beside Everly, her expression soft and understanding.

"You okay?"

"Yeah. Everything is good. Everything is done." Everly looked away as tears spilled

out of her eyes.

She swiped at them and shrugged. "It's time to go home."

"What? We have so much to do here!" Harper swung her arm around, gesturing at the mountains of antiques.

"We'll hire someone, send a moving company to pack it all up," Everly murmured. "Your last sale was huge. I've got more than enough to pay for it. We can get a storage unit back home and work out of there. Or not. You can go back to your normal work and I'll go and beg for my job back. Whatever. But we don't have to stay here."

"What about Rylan?"

"What about him? He's awake. It's over." Everly couldn't see Harper's face through the blur in her eyes. "He made it pretty clear that he didn't want me here."

"Well screw him then." Harper rested a hand on Everly's. "Forget him and what he wants. Do *you* want to be *here*?"

Everly shrugged. "I didn't think so ... No. It's better this way. Maybe away from Shroudhaven, I'll get a better handle on the dragon, like I did before. We can get back to normal."

Harper pouted and leaned her head on Everly's shoulder. "I'm sorry, Ev. I really thought there was something between you two."

"There was never anything there. He's just some kid I used to know, grown up into a man I don't know. Any feelings were probably just the weird connection caused by the dragon. And that connection is gone now."

Harper brought her head back up and looked at Everly with piercing green eyes. "I think you should talk to him—"

"There's nothing else to say," Everly said. "We pack up and we go. That's that."

"Okay, Ev. If that's what you want."

The mirror of what Everly had said to Rylan almost sent her over the edge into full-on, heaving sobs. But she'd spent her entire life mastering her emotions, learning to function even when everything seemed too hard to carry on. She'd mastered the art of surviving trauma much earlier than most.

"When will we leave?" Harper asked.

Everly straightened and took a steadying breath. "Tomorrow. If that's all right?"

"Of course. I go where you go."

Everly smiled, though even she could tell it didn't meet her eyes. "Where's the Bane?"

Harper's expression hardened and she crossed her arms over her overalls. "Hidden where only I can get to it. Because clearly *you* can't be trusted."

"But it worked!" Everly waved her hands wildly in the air, feeling like a broken record. "Not to mention, it's not like I have another soul inside me still to remove. It's just me in there now."

Wandering through a dark and broken emptiness.

"Regardless," Harper said firmly. "The Bane is my responsibility. You stay away from it."

"Fine." Everly glanced around her father's store.

A hint of bittersweet sorrow filled her bones. She had grown to love this space. She wanted to stay. She'd enjoyed building a fledgling business side by side with Harper. She wanted to get to know more about this store and what it held, to be close to the spirit her father had left behind in his beloved antiques.

Leaving meant giving up the friendships she'd formed with Callan, Cherry, Rush, and Tammy. Even Denny. It meant turning her back on a home with Lian and dinners at The Crow's Nest. No more Cardboard Box Barry sightings. No more Zozo. No more "There's a Mermaid in My Lighthouse." No more coffee on the back porch as the sun rose over the misty mountains.

No possible future with Rylan.

But leaving was her only option. Staying would only hurt more.

3

BESHADOWED

SHADOWS AWOKEN

1

For all of Rylan Howell's years as a Darkfrey, only the mission mattered. Fighting the darkness, keeping the world and those he loved safe. No matter the cost.

Now Rylan's world had been turned upside-down, but it felt right.

Being home at Howell House felt right.

Reuniting with his mother felt right.

Heading out on a hunt with his brother by his side again felt right.

Seeing Everly again, outside of her dreams ... was temporary. Rylan had made sure of that.

His new team—a band of runts and outcasts by Darkfrey standards—chatted noisily in the back of Lian's SUV as Rylan pulled over on Main Street of downtown Shroudhaven.

Fog shifted and parted as they came to a halt. He could hardly see five paces ahead of the vehicle, even with the headlights shining bravely into the night.

The asphalt was wet from an earlier rainstorm and drops flecked the windshield. Rylan twisted the key to turn off the engine, and the headlights extinguished. He shushed the others and they responded instantly. Maybe they weren't as hopeless as he thought.

The eerie silence of the early hours greeted them. A flickering illumination pierced the mist from the direction of their target location, causing strobing effect.

In the passenger seat, Callan eyed the flashing light with nebulous shadyr eyes, his dark hair feathering around his face. It was already longer than Rylan considered suitable back when they were both still at Darkfrey Estate, and it had been allowed to grow even longer since.

Callan smirked. "The Boutique All seems like a weird place for a beshadowing. What ghast wants to hang out in a dollar store?"

From the very back seat, Denny leaned forward to the middle row where the girls sat. "Come on, we all want some booty call action now and then. I'm open to it any time, just so you know."

Light flashed off his blond beard as he grinned toothily and waggled his eyebrows.

Tammy's grimace shuddered through her whole body. She'd tucked herself into the corner of the seat so that her lean face was half in shadow and her shaved, dark hair looked like a bruise spreading over her skull.

Everly's friend, who Rylan didn't even think should be there, finished applying some lip gloss as though nothing had been said.

Cherry, sandwiched between the girls, whipped around and snarled, "Read the room, you deluded swine. No one thinks you're booty call material, no one thinks you're funny, no one will ever want you until you quit being such a selfish bigot."

Woah. That was not the Cherry that Rylan remembered.

There was pain and a level of viciousness in his voice completely unlike how he'd behaved while still a Darkfrey. He'd been more subdued back then, shy even, before he came out. Things changed after that.

Rylan figured he'd be bitter about it. He was right to be. But the way Harper patted Cherry's shoulder supportively, it seemed like something more was going on.

There's so much I don't know. How are we supposed to be a team?

Harper flung the side door open like a cannon blast in the silence. "Come on. Let's get this party started! I want to be done and dusted before Everly wakes up."

And how did this bliv end up on our hunt?

Harper had shown up at Howell House in the middle of the night, just as the team had stepped out to deal with the weroth report. She carried a bundle of shiny gardening tools under one arm and wore an even shinier smile, and an apron.

"Bellsy? What are you doing here?" Cherry had greeted her with matching enthusiasm.

Rylan glared at those smiles and the out-of-towner. Surely she'd experienced enough of Shroudhaven to know she shouldn't be wandering around at night on her own.

"Just returning these to Lian. I've cleaned and sharpened them all for her, too."

"It's almost two in the morning?" Callan said it like a question, one Rylan was wondering as well.

"Is it? Time got away from me. Everly went to bed early, I think she's still feeling a bit off, you know."

Rylan's teeth ground against each other.

Harper shrugged in a jangle of saws and secateurs. "So, I thought I'd get a few more things done."

Tammy's eye roll could be heard in her words. "Why are you wearing an apron?"

"Oops, I forgot to take it off. I was just baking some muffins."

The whirlwind of a woman left Rylan confused. "I thought you were packing to leave?"

"Yeah, I was packing, too. The muffins are for the drive tomorrow." Harper hummed with energy, vivid green eyes bright and alert. "Hang on, if it's 2 a.m., where are you all off to?"

"Shadyr business," Rylan said at the same time Callan said, "Weroth hunt, at The Boutique All."

Harper's grin turned supernova. "I'm in! I'm coming, I'm coming too!"

"Well, there's a sound bite for the spank bank."

A chorus went up.

"Gross!"

"Inappropriate."

"Denny!"

Harper ignored him, dashing over to put the gardening tools on the porch. "One last dose of Shroudhaven spookiness before it's all over. It's perfect!"

Rylan grunted, "That's not—"

"Cool," Callan said over him. "Did you bring your axe?"

"No," she pouted.

Turning back to the tools, she plucked out some hedging shears and tested them with a few quick clips. *Sshhhckt Sshhhckt.*

Her grin twisted up and her eyes narrowed wickedly. "These should do."

"I don't think—" Rylan tried again.

"Bellsy gets what she wants," Cherry snapped.

Harper bounced on the spot, then filed into position with the rest of them. "You know, I don't normally wear an apron when cooking but thought I could get one more photoshoot in. I was trying a more cottage-core look. Turned out super cute. Repainting the cupboard doors really helped. I'm going to miss shooting in that old house ..."

Right. Yeah. That's how she ended up with them.

Rylan didn't like the idea of a bliv he barely knew tagging along. Everly trusted her, and so it seemed did Callan and the others, but trust wasn't enough to save her from being turned inside out by an eidolghast.

Rylan gritted his teeth and opened the driver's side door, stepping out into the cool night. Misty rain wet his skin, and he ran a hand over his shaved head, glancing at the SUV as Harper stepped out like a star arriving for a Hollywood premier. Perfect makeup, perfect silky hair, perfect warm-brown skin, perfect Pilates princess figure.

Rylan couldn't see how this *influencer* fit into shadyr business. Even if his brother vouched that she was capable.

Capable or not, Harper was a human, and as far as he was concerned, she had no place joining the team on a hunt.

"You're going to stay close and keep your head down," Rylan told Harper as he stepped onto the sidewalk to join her and the others. "We can't be responsible for

keeping you safe while we take down the eidolghast."

"Save your over-protective 'keep you safe' bullshit for Everly. I'm here to hunt. I'm not weak." Harper shrugged and tossed her dark tresses over her shoulder. "And neither is she, FYI."

"Roast his ass," Denny guffawed.

Cherry high-fived Harper.

Rylan clenched his jaw. If this team showed him no respect, how was he supposed to lead ...?

I'm not, he reminded himself. *This isn't my team.*

All eyes were on Callan, who was diligently checking over the street and shop front while the rest of them squabbled. His little brother had grown a lot, and leadership suited him. But Rylan was left feeling lost. He had no idea who these people really were, or what his place among them was. They seemed to have accepted the bliv more than they accepted him.

"Just don't let your human need for 'one last adventure' get you killed, all right? Or we'll see how strong Everly is when I deposit your corpse back home."

Harper glared him down, tall enough to meet him eye to eye. "I do *not* know what she sees in you."

A pang lanced through Rylan's chest, and he battled to keep his expression even.

Cherry's bright-red hair flopped over his eyes in a blunt fringe, matching the red and white leather jacket he tossed back into the SUV.

He draped an arm around Harper's shoulders. "Leave Bellsy alone. She's already been through several missions. She knows the game. Just chill already. You aren't a Darkfrey anymore so quit with the arrogant asshole attitude."

Rylan frowned and turned away from them, shrugging out of his jacket and shirt and chucking them back into the car before closing it up. All the shadyrs now wore only their flexible body armor and tactical pants, prepared for what was to come.

Everything Rylan knew told him that Harper was a human and a liability.

But doubt stirred within him. How true was what he'd been brought up to believe by the Darkfreys?

That deep-seated certainty that humans were weak, and that shadyrs in a hunting brace, shadyrs like him, were the best, the strongest, the only hope for the safety of their world from ever-encroaching darkness. Top of the food chain. But recent events left him questioning everything.

Maybe those Darkfrey biases he was only now starting to acknowledge ran deeper in him than he knew. Maybe he *was* being an asshole.

He'd still keep an extra eye on the human, though. A dead best friend wasn't the going-away gift he wanted for Everly. The pang in his chest returned.

There was a moment when trapped with Everly in her sleeping mind that Rylan had thought maybe they could be together. That all his self-imposed rules of the living world could be ignored, and he could just *be* with her, in her dreams, forever.

Then his soul had been hurled back into his body and he'd woken to screams, and blood, and Everly, cold on the floor.

She'd come back to him from that death-like faint, but it was the real wake-up call. Everly couldn't be part of Shroudhaven, and shadyrs, and danger. He couldn't handle seeing her hurt like that. She couldn't be part of his life.

The mission remained. And there was no room for anything else.

Rylan checked his watch: twenty to three. Still several hours till dawn, but they didn't have time to dawdle. The eidolghast—a weroth, according to Cherry who had sensed it during a late walk and returned for backup—needed to be taken down before sunrise when the street would be filled with potential victims.

He cut himself off halfway through thinking they should just report it to the Darkfreys and let them handle it.

That's how Darkfreys think. I'm not a Darkfrey anymore, but I'm still a shadyr. I still have my mission.

The Boutique All had a wall of glass windows and doors on the first floor of the building that gave passersby an internal look at the chaotic madness of the emporium. Normally there would be holiday-themed scenes and mannequins wearing *I Dropped a Call in Shroudhaven* T-shirts, or a view of dozens of packed metal shelves leading off out of sight.

Tonight, though, an eerie, strobing light pierced outward, silhouetting everything inside so the shapes juddered like possessed shadow puppets.

Callan returned from his recon down a side alley. "All set? We have potential access down here. Let's move in."

The team followed quickly and reached a locked metal door beside two dumpsters overflowing with broken-down cardboard boxes.

Rylan was used to the privileges of being a Darkfrey, one of which was having access to almost anywhere in Shroudhaven if needed for a hunt. Having to force their way in seemed wrong, but he put his shoulder up beside his brother's and the door gave under their combined strength. Callan grinned at him, then ushered everyone inside.

Rylan's boots squeaked on the white linoleum, scuffed by years of foot traffic. He kicked them off, as did the other shadyrs, leaving them in a pile by the door. The pull of his change already churned within him, and of any shadyr form, the weroth transformation was the least kind to clothing.

The door brought them inside where a divider wall separated a basic kitchenette from the main store. They emerged from the alcove between shelving piled in wicker baskets of all shapes and sizes, and drooping, floor-to-ceiling synthetic flowers that seemed to be rotten.

The store was deathly quiet except for the low, musical bars of "There's a Mermaid in My Lighthouse" playing over crackly speakers.

There's a mermaid in my lighthouse, and her heart belongs to me.

There's a mermaid in my lighthouse, she keeps staring out to sea.

Up ahead, the aisles seemed to stretch onwards into infinity. The more Rylan stared, trying to see the end, the more they wobbled and twisted in his vision. Thick, flickering fog pooled around his bare feet.

All the signs of an eidolghast in residence.

The weroth's presence prickled over his skin like hot embers. It was close but not too close—somewhere farther in the depths of the labyrinthine store.

Rylan had no doubt it could sense them, too.

2

At the first intersection of aisles, they stopped. Something cold and smooth touched Rylan's foot, and he reached down to pull it from the heavy mist so he could identify it. A loose fluorescent tube. It buzzed incessantly, light strobing, despite having no power source.

Across from him, Callan gently kicked another one, and it swirled beneath the low fog. The lights lay scattered throughout the store.

"Watch out for broken ones," Callan told his team.

Cherry and Tammy had already become engulfed in the black, cinder-spotted smoke of their shadyr transformations. In gaps between the dark magic, their arms and legs jutted through, lengthening. Claws pierced from the tips of their fingers like curved blades.

Wiry fur sprouted from every inch of their bare skin, and by the time it covered them, it would be thick enough to protect them from the weroth's slimy acid. Or broken glass.

Tammy and Cherry were still young, less practiced at containing their shadyr forms. The rest of them—Callan, Denny, Rylan himself—wouldn't change until they chose to.

The potential for standing on a fluorescent tube with a bare human foot made Rylan consider changing now, too. But in the highly competitive Darkfrey braces, it was a point of pride to see who could hold off their change the longest.

Callan, though, nodded in solidarity to Tammy, and began his change, too.

Denny, whispering a mini wolf howl, followed.

The shadyr form when in the presence of a weroth had birthed the age-old legend of the werewolf. For good reason, too, since when the transformation was complete, they looked exactly like the beast of lore.

"I feel like I should have brought some doggy treats," Harper muttered.

"You changing already?" Rylan asked.

As his change stabilized, Callan's snout-like mouth twisted into a wolfish grin.

"We do things a bit differently." He elbowed Rylan, strong enough that it almost knocked him down. "Hey, just want you to know, it's good to have you back."

Rylan hesitated, suddenly feeling awkward as the only shadyr left in human form.

"Glad to be back."

"Feels great to be hunting together again, doesn't it? As long as you're feeling up to it."

Rylan rolled the kinks out of his shoulders and shrugged. "Yeah. I'm feeling better by the minute."

"You were in a death-like coma for weeks," Callan pointed out. "It's okay if you're a little rusty."

Rylan didn't miss the sly smile, even on the wolfish snout.

"Could kill more ghasts than you in my sleep, little brother." He returned the smirk.

"Wanna bet who takes this one down first?"

Harper stepped between them. "My money's on Callan. Soldier boy here is too busy pretending he doesn't want Everly around to have his head in the game. He hasn't even suited up yet!"

Rylan hid his grimace, trying to keep it light. "Who invited you into our smack talk?"

Callan barked a laugh. "She's got you there though."

"She doesn't, because I'm not pretending anything."

Harper pushed past them and took the lead, poking through the shelves as she went. "Methinks he doth protest too much!"

Rylan eyed Harper as she plucked items from the shelves around them, arming herself with a thick canvas raincoat, leather work gloves, and a plastic face shield.

She laughed flippantly at how ridiculous she looked, but she clearly knew enough about what they were up against to be planning ahead. She didn't have a shadyr's natural protection against weroth acid, so she was making her own. Maybe she did know what she was doing.

"She doesn't know what she's talking about," Rylan grunted to Callan as they broke into a fast stride to keep up as Harper continued around a corner, Denny, Cherry, and Tammy close behind.

"Sure. Suuure." Callan grinned, all fangs. "I for one liked having Everly around again and I'm totally comfortable admitting that. You know I had a crush on her as a kid too, right? Hot older friend of my brother's? Maybe I'll ask Everly to stay."

Rylan's fists clenched and he smiled over equally clenched teeth.

He's just having a go at you, ignore him, you did the right thing telling Everly to leave.

In a shadow nearby, Tammy grunted. "Are we going to kill a ghast or fight over a woman who could literally suck your soul out of your body? To be honest, I'm in either way. Both sound like a great chance to opt out of this mortal meat-suit."

Anger swirled out of Rylan's control, and he spun toward the goth girl.

Restraint slipped away, and his change exploded around him violently. Flames of pain scorched his fingertips as his claws extended, and the entire expanse of his skin itched and burned as the fur burst from his pores. He grunted in pain and frustration.

When he emerged from the change, Callan stood between him and a wide-eyed Tammy, a concerned, warning look on his face.

Hot air puffed from Rylan's wolf-like mouth, and he shook his head, denying his anger. He hadn't lost control of his change since he was fifteen.

I must be weak from the coma, that's all.

He held Callan's gaze and muttered, "Everly's safer far the hell away from Shroudhaven. End of story."

Callan's expression calmed, and he let out a slow breath. "I dunno. Look, jokes aside, seems to me life can take away what we love—"

Rylan shot the darkest of looks at his brother.

"—at any moment for all kinds of reasons. So, why should we be the ones that push them away?" Callan turned as he spoke, his gaze falling for a second onto the sullen wolf-girl behind him.

"Come on, let's hunt already!" Harper all but yelled from up front, snipping her garden shears. "Which way? This place is a maze."

Callan slapped a clawed paw onto Rylan's shoulder. "You want to take the lead on this? You know ... if you're up to it."

Rylan snorted a laugh, sighed, then nodded. Best to focus on the hunt. Closing his eyes for the briefest moment, he opened his newly enhanced senses and tried to home in on the sensation of the weroth lurking somewhere in the store.

"This way," he said, inclining his head as he took off to his left.

The team fell into line behind him, moving past school supplies and a wall of greeting cards. The occasional sound of a toe-claw tapping the floor or Harper's sneakers squeaking marked their passing.

The next section held cleaning supplies: bottles of bleach, brightly colored containers of detergent, and more brands of floor cleaning fluids than seemed necessary. The lids on some had popped, and black fluid oozed and bubbled out the tops. The temperature grew colder the farther they moved into the store.

The aisle took a right-angle turn, then another, turning left, then left, then left and left again in an ever-shortening spiral, before branching out impossibly into seven different paths that cut out at strange angles. The beshadowing was already messing with space and dimensions, turning the cluttered store into more of a labyrinth than it normally was.

Still the song played, warbling over the tinny speakers.

Hungry light shines over the waves and my mermaid she yearns,
When will I return, when will I return?

With a squeal of static, the music cut out, and a pre-recorded voice chirped,

"Don't forget to join our frequent buyer club for The Boutique All bonuses! Enjoy your time at The Boutique All, and remember, no matter the deed, The Boutique All has everything you need!"

Rylan always wondered if the name was intentional or a naive mistake.

They must know how it sounds.

He could hear muffled chuckles from Denny farther down the line.

The recording ended in a glitchy crackle, and the mermaid song began again.

Somewhere nearby, something hard clattered to the floor.

Rylan stilled, his entire body going on alert. He held up a fist.

The strobing light made it hard for his eyes to adjust to their natural night vision, but his sense of hearing had sharpened until he could hear even the mice roaming through the walls.

And the weroth's six needle-pointed feet tapping on the linoleum. It was on the move.

Signaling the others, Rylan put on a burst of speed and bounded along another aisle filled with pet supplies, shelves piled high with metal food and water dishes. The floor seemed to slope downward, and as they passed through, the bowls jumped off the shelves like popcorn in a skillet, clattering down into the distance.

The clang of each dish hitting the floor ached in Rylan's ears. "I've lost the trail. Can't hear which way it's gone."

"There's something," Callan said, pointing.

What seemed to be a pile of mannequin legs that had merged into a strange, flesh-colored plastic insect, ambled past them in jerky, disjointed steps. Harper squeaked at the sight and skidded to a stop.

"Woah." Her phone was out of her pocket in an instant and she snapped a couple of photos, the flash merging with the strobing light around them.

"What? I'm not going to post them! Just for my personal mood board, I swear."

Rylan growled. "This isn't a game."

"I *know*. But that doesn't mean life has to be spent as grumpy Mr. Serious Pants a hundo percent of the time, either. Tammy, can you eye-roll at him for me? You do it best." Harper poked at her screen, blue light reflecting off her face shield. "Aw, they turned out all weird and blurry."

"Sorry, babe." Cherry patted her gently on the back. "Beshadowings are almost impossible to capture."

Harper pouted.

"Hurry up," Rylan snapped, speeding up again. "We have to find this thing."

A large, black silhouette stepped into the aisle ahead of him.

"I think it found us," Denny said.

Rylan slid to a stop on his clawed feet.

The weroth balanced on six legs, each tapering to a point so thin it seemed physically impossible for the monster to be standing. Though it had no visible eyes, Rylan knew it had no trouble "seeing" him and his team in the foggy darkness.

It hissed in deep, undulating syllables. A disturbing green glow emanated from inside a toothy mouth, opening so wide it split its entire body in half.

Then it charged.

Its strange legs bent at unnatural angles as it slithered in a rush at Rylan. The force of impact threw him off his feet. Gravity vanished as he rolled through the air, and then he bounced off the unforgiving floor.

He rolled twice before coming to a bone-jarring halt against an endcap of dryer sheets. Two dozen boxes that smelled like eucalyptus rained down on him, and he batted them away irritably, surfacing from the overwhelming scent with an immediate headache.

I am off my game. This is embarrassing.

Cherry, Tammy, and Denny leaped over his body and bounded toward battle with the weroth. As a team, they well outnumbered the ghast, so Rylan wasn't too worried about Cherry and Tammy's novice abilities or Denny's tendency to preen and prance when he should be fighting.

Callan didn't seem worried either as he casually helped Rylan up.

As Rylan stumbled back to his feet and fell into a loping run to join the party, he caught sight of Harper.

She let out a powerful battle cry and wrenched the garden shears in her gloved hands. They snapped right in two, and the bolt that joined the halves pinged onto the floor. The feverish glint in her eye and confidence in her shoulders was ... not normal. Not for a human coming face-to-face with an eidolghast.

Surprised by the brutality in her expression, Rylan found himself slowing. Watching her.

Harper dashed into the fight, keeping speed with the werewolf-shaped shadyrs beside her. Her twin shear blades flashed in the strobing lights.

She was under the beast first. She swirled the shears elegantly, each slice accompanied by a tennis-player's grunt. One, two, three legs, cut out from beneath the beast.

What the ...

That wasn't paper she was chopping through. No matter how spindly they appeared, a weroth's legs were all bone and sinew, hard as steel.

Black acid spurted from the wounds, and the eidolghast staggered and stumbled, smashing into the shelves beside it. An avalanche of basketballs and tennis rackets rained down. Harper dodged back, landing as spry as a cat. Cherry, Tammy, and Denny reached the weroth next, each targeting a leg of their own.

Rylan and Callan followed, racing in time. As mirror images, they leaped into the air, flying for the monster's bulbous body.

Rylan slammed into the beast, digging his claws deep into the ghast's black-hole-colored fur as its filaments waggled around his hands. Callan landed beside him, shooting him a grin. Rylan found himself smiling back.

The creature wobbled wildly on half its remaining limbs, bucking and trying to throw them. Rylan reared back, slicing his razor-tipped claws across the black expanse beneath him. Slimy, deep-green blood appeared, and the weroth let out a short, sharp cry of fury.

Callan swiped next, dislodging a hunk of acidic flesh that splattered onto the low ceiling.

"You trying to steal my kill?" Rylan scoffed.

Callan got another swipe in first. "Gotta show my team I'm as cool as the legendary Rylan Howell."

Rylan's wolf-like mouth turned up on one side, and he dug faster into the oozing flesh of the monster.

A crash came from the other side, and Callan looked down. Another smash clattered as the weroth rammed one leg and the shadyr attached to it against the shelving. Tammy cried out.

"Careful!" Callan hissed at her.

"I'm fine!" she snapped back.

"How do we finish this thing off?" Harper called from below.

The sound of a blade slicing was followed by the spatter and sizzle of acid.

The weroth kicked out, shaking Cherry free from another leg. It stabbed that same limb forward, attempting to skewer him on the floor.

Cherry skittered out of range, then yelled, "There's a weak spot, deep in its back! That's what those two are digging for."

Rylan thrust both arms into the hole they had created, tearing backward in an attempt to wrench the gash wider. Callan shouldered into him, jostling for the best position to get his claws into the kill spot.

A figure appeared, flying toward them, silhouetted in the stirred-up fog and strobing lights. In a flurry of flying, silky hair, and sizzling raincoat, Harper landed with a ferocious cry. Both shear blades plunged deep into the hole the brothers had made.

The weroth stilled. A harsh, susurrus gurgle escaped its glowing maw. Then its remaining legs crumpled beneath it. It slammed down onto the floor.

Callan and Rylan jumped off to the sides. Harper tumbled in a backward somersault, skidding on all fours on the blood-slickened floor.

Her chest heaved as she grinned and panted, straightening herself up. "Did you

see that? I did it! I took it down!"

"I think it was really a team effort," Rylan muttered.

With the eidolghast defeated, he brought forth his shift, swirling in shadowy magic until he'd returned to his human form. Callan and Denny followed suit, but Cherry and Tammy remained changed.

"Don't diminish this for her!" Cherry snapped, giving Harper a furry high five. "You were amazing, but I never had any doubt."

The weroth corpse sizzled, melting in its own acid. The shear blades oozed upward out of the gore, worn and pockmarked from the caustic onslaught.

"Aw, I liked those. I think dual wielding is definitely a good look for me. Remind me to replace them for Lian."

Harper shed her outer protective layers and brushed herself down. Her cheeks were flushed and her eyes gleamed bright with a strange mixture of excitement and something that looked a little too like bloodlust. As she took her gloves off, a faint scar line shimmered on her wrist in the low light. She pulled her sleeves down again, covering it.

Tammy rolled her shoulder, wincing and tugging at her body armor that was too tight for her. Rylan frowned. She must still be wearing the same Darkfrey armor she had from when she was kicked out years ago.

He was so used to having access to new resources whenever he needed them, but he realized now that the armor he wore, that he'd left the Darkfreys with, might be the last he'd ever own, too. At least he wasn't still growing, like the goth teen.

Callan moved closer to her. "You okay?"

"Ugh, I'm not a baby. Go check on Denny or something for once."

"I'm fine, thanks for asking," Denny yelled from a pile of sports drinks nearby. "Except for this raging boner from watching Bellsy in attack mode."

"I swear he makes me want to barf out my ovaries," Harper grunted, and Tammy snorted a laugh that left the others shocked.

She quickly schooled her animalistic face back into a scowl. "What? I mean, she's right."

Harper squealed in glee at Tammy's approval and skittered over with a hand up for a high five from her, too.

Tammy folded her wolf claws, just as black as her normal hands, under her crossed arms. "No."

Smiling regardless, Harper let out a long, satisfied sigh. "What next? We left this place in a real mess. Should we clean it up for them? I can fit on some cleaning. Won't take long at all."

Cherry sniffed. "I think we should call in the Darkfreys and have them handle clean up. They have to be good for something, after all. Plus, I'm wiped."

Rylan's muscles also held an aching tiredness despite the enhancements of the werewolf form, but he wasn't about to admit weakness.

"Sounds like a good plan to me," Callan nodded, punctuating it with a yawn.

Tammy lifted her snout to the ceiling. "Do you hear that?"

Rylan shook his head. "Hear what?"

As if to answer him, police sirens wailed to life.

Rylan groaned. "Ghast dammit. I bet this place had a silent alarm. We gotta get out of here before the cops show up."

"What about the body?" Harper asked. "Won't they find it?"

Rylan turned back to the corpse, but it had mostly melted into a disgusting black puddle by that point. "I'm more worried about them seeing a couple of werewolves running around than what's left of that."

The group headed for the exit at a quick clip—easier now that the beshadowed fog was dispersing and aisles ran in straight lines again. The fluorescents had ceased their strobing, plunging the store into darkness.

The shadyr night vision kicked in properly for Rylan and the others, and he checked for Harper in the gloom, but she seemed to move with as much confidence of sight as the others. Something weird was going on there ...

But it didn't matter.

He'd already done his duty in chasing Everly, which meant Harper too, out of town. Tomorrow, they'd both be on their way, and whatever Shroudhaven weirdness had taken root in Harper would likely fade away. Even the entity inside Everly had only shown itself when she'd returned to Shroudhaven. Hopefully, it too would die off, outside of this darkness-tainted town.

Reaching the back door, Rylan snatched up his boots, and still the song played on an eternal, eerie loop.

There's a mermaid in my lighthouse, and her heart belongs to me.
There's a mermaid in my lighthouse, to her I own the key.

3

The ice-and-fire adrenaline crackling through Harper's system was heightened by the arrival of flashing blue and red lights that shone down the alleyway to meet them.

Rylan and Callan, who'd been ahead of her on their journey through the store, came to an abrupt halt several feet out from the exit. Still pulling their boots back on, they checked up and down the alley.

Harper stepped toward the main street and lights. "Want me to go hold them off? I can distract them."

Callan grabbed her arm and twirled her around before she could walk any farther. "No. I think there's another way out down here. Better if we can all get away unseen."

"Especially the young'uns with their shadyr hangover," Denny said.

Tammy's shimmering galaxy-eyed gaze landed on him, and her face—barely recognizable in werewolf form—contorted with effort. A hint of blackness swirled around her, then faded again without any change. She groaned fiercely. She and Cherry carried their boots with them, clutched in their front paws.

"You'll get there," Callan offered.

She eye rolled.

"But for now, let's get out of here."

The store exit wasn't far down from the main street, and the flashing lights were way too close to the left, so the group turned right and jogged along the grimy, narrow path between buildings. Sodden, slimy scraps of cardboard and newspaper slipped under their feet, and rodent-shaped shadows darted away from them up ahead.

Harper knew the team was fully visible as long as they were in the alley. The moment an officer appeared at the entrance, they'd be seen, and there was nothing they could do about it.

She didn't exactly relish the idea of being arrested for breaking and entering, but the excitement of running from the cops, and being so close to being caught, made the situation that much more exhilarating. Power rippled through her veins and made her feel capable of *anything*.

What I could have done with this power six months ago ...

Maybe her entire life wouldn't have been blown to bits. When Bryce had doxed her and all the internet had access to her home address, she could have done with a magic boost.

She wouldn't have felt so vulnerable in her own home. She wouldn't still have nightmares about how close the gap was between her fleeing what should have been her safe haven and the moment when that random man showed up with a gun.

She could have fought back, not felt so ... powerless.

But then you wouldn't have moved in with Everly, she reminded herself.

She disliked the idea of life without her bestie. But she refused to be powerless again. Refused to get anything wrong, do *anything* below the highest of standards. Refused anything other than total control.

Finally, a turn in the alley showed itself up ahead.

But not before a gruff, angry voice called out, "Hey! Stop! Stay where you are!"

The group ignored the directive and put on another burst of speed. Harper followed Callan around the corner, her blood pumping as fast as her sneakers on the ground. Excitement pulsed through her, and she smiled broadly even as heavy boot falls chased after them.

The dingy alley was crisp and bright in Harper's eyes, and she kept pace easily with the three soldier boys and two werewolves by her side. Their sheltered path ran out quickly, expelling them onto a brightly lit street.

At that time of night, the street was still and empty, and it would be a long run to the shelter of the next alley. There were barely even any parked cars to hide behind.

Harper still didn't know the town as well as the others. "Which way?"

"Where can we hide?" Cherry asked, wide-eyed as he scanned the relatively bright and barren view.

Callan's eyes searched the roof tops, settling on the lowest. "You think you two can get up there? The rest of us ... I don't—"

"Running from something?" A voice muttered.

From the shadows of a shop entrance beside them, a figure stepped out.

Tall, lanky, with a hint of a potbelly beneath his black skull-and-lightning T-shirt. The older man had a beard that hung down his chest and ended in a thin braid, and his eyes were surprisingly blue. Harper had met this Shroudhaven legend once before.

Barry.

Tucked under a streetlight a little way down the block was his ever-present cardboard box.

Everyone seemed too nonplussed to reply.

To their credit, Tammy and Cherry attempted to hide their werewolf forms

behind the others, in complete futility. But Barry didn't seem at all surprised at their monstrous appearance.

"Go on. Quick. Into the box."

"Um. What?" Harper managed.

Barry's cardboard box sat against a red brick wall with a tarp and a floral sheet dangling over the opening. He grabbed the corner of both and ripped them back, exposing the inky abyss inside. There was no way it would be big enough to hide them all, not even if they lay on top of one another like they were piling into a coffin.

No one moved until a glance back showed three police officers turn down the alley their way.

"Get in," Barry hissed, one pale hand flapping erratically.

With a shrug, Callan dove in first. Cherry and Tammy went next. Harper expected to see a furry elbow or foot jutting out, but somehow, they all fit. Denny and Rylan shared a look and followed as well.

"You have got to be kidding me," Harper muttered, getting down onto hands and knees.

Only seconds after Harper crawled in, Barry's lighthearted voice filtered through behind her. "Good morning, officers! If you're seeking the children who passed through, they've gone down that street and around the law office."

The odd old man really *had* protected them.

With hardly a grunt of gratitude, the officers stomped off into the distance.

Harper expected to come to a quick halt and need to climb into someone's lap—*not Denny's, please not Denny's*—but instead, the darkness kept going.

And going.

And going.

Until the cardboard above her head vanished, and a space tall enough to stand opened around them.

Harper straightened, and a flashlight popped on behind her as Barry joined them.

He stood up with a wise smile beneath his fluffy gray mustache. "Welcome to my box."

Callan arched his neck, looking all around. "This ... is some box."

Barry chuckled and joined Callan at the front of the group. "Damn straight, boy. My box is a special box."

Denny coughed, but even he was apparently too shocked to pick that low-hanging fruit.

"But you kids are a bit special too, aren't you?"

Tammy cowered, hiding her werewolf form behind Callan. "You're not scared of us? Of how we look?"

Barry gave a raucous laugh. "I know about *everything* going on in this town. I'm not scared of you scamps."

Rylan returned to them, having walked off a little ways. "How far does this thing go?"

"Woah, woah, slow down. Don't go wandering off without me. You could get lost forever down here."

"It's a straight tunnel," Rylan said flatly.

"That's what you think. Follow me. Let's lay low for a bit to make sure the cops are gone, then we'll pop you back out wherever you need to be."

"Wherever?" Callan raised his eyebrows. "So, this is how you always show up everywhere."

"Did you know?" Harper asked, wondering why he'd been willing to lead his team into the box for shelter.

Callan shrugged. "I'd heard some weird rumors that made me think it was worth a shot in the squeeze we were in. Figured it was regular Shroudhaven weirdness but didn't quite realize the scope of the weirdness. Does this system extend all over town?"

Barry nodded and combed his fingers through his beard. "Only a few places I can't get into, or don't want no truck with."

He pointed a finger at the straight tunnel ahead of them and made a gesture as though selecting a direction to take. Waving his flashlight like an airplane conductor, he walked away at a slow, leisurely pace.

With a few shrugs and wary glances, the team followed along. There was enough room to walk two abreast, and Harper ran her hand along the wall to her side.

It was cardboard, all of it, scrappy squares and torn-off sheets layered over each other with staples and tape. Disconcertingly, it gave under her fingers, just like being within a cardboard box, rather than some solid tunnel through the earth. She shivered, wondering what might be on the other side if it tore.

In the middle of the group, Cherry and Tammy's shadyr hangover must have expired because they swirled up in magical smoke and emerged again as themselves. There was a large acid burn on Cherry's pants, and he poked at it, muttering how he hated weroths.

The memory of the man in nice slacks crawling out of Barry's box and giving Barry a hug came to Harper, and the time he approached Harper during her argument with Everly. "Um, Mr. ... Barry?"

"Juuust Barry."

"You've helped other people too, right? You do this a lot, don't you?"

"Ah well, I got a good setup here for avoiding danger, which never seems far off in this town. Filthy with monsters, as I bet you know." He trailed off, his blue eyes going unfocused for a moment.

Then he shook off the reverie, his braided beard swishing as he took long-legged strides. "Figured I could put this place to good use."

"This place ... Just how did you get it?" Rylan asked, frowning at the cardboard around him as though it could attack them at any second.

Barry tilted his head and hummed. "It was so long ago. I collect things, you know."

Like that explains it.

Harper shook her head. "Why'd you help us? We were being chased by cops, not monsters."

"Not monsters?" Barry guffawed.

When everyone only stared back, he cleared his throat. "Well, I'm not much of a fan of law enforcement. Whose laws, anyway? Nothing more than a system of oppression ..."

Barry's muttered rantings continued as the single long tunnel went on. From time to time he would pause, seem to ponder which direction to take, then follow along the only available route again.

He moved too slow for Harper's liking. Adrenaline arced like electricity through her veins, heightened by the Bane's magic.

The first time she was cut by the ancient blade was an accident when she'd snatched it away from Everly. The rush of power was so intense she'd almost pulled a door off its hinges in her panic. But then the cut healed, faster than possible. And Harper tested the effect of the Bane on her skin again.

She'd lost count of how many times since then she'd refreshed the magic with another small slice ... She'd been on a high of productivity and strength and energy.

Now the eidolghast was dead and the cops were long gone, the lack of exciting things to do made her itch for more.

The rush of her pounding pulse when she'd sliced into the weroth's tough skin ...

The exultation that sung in her veins when she'd cut off three of its gross, spidery legs ...

Fighting monsters and crawling into magical cardboard boxes—how was she supposed to go back to normal after this? Back to a life she'd been so powerless in.

It will be different this time.

This time, she'd have the Bane. It had been agreed by the Howells that it should remain in Harper's care. Because it was somehow related to the Beast of Teeth and Stars, they decided it should stay close to Everly, but not *too* close.

Since Harper had already taken possession of it, the decision was easy. Lian also liked the idea of how Mordan Darkfrey would react when he found out they'd allowed an ancient shadyr artifact to be taken out of Shroudhaven by a bliv. She'd chuckled about it for hours.

Still, having the Bane didn't feel like as much fun without also having monsters to hunt. As much as Harper would love to dismember some of the human monsters in her life, that was generally frowned upon.

"I'm going to miss all of this so much," Harper said with a pout. "I feel like I just got a taste of the good stuff, then was told, 'No more monster hunting for you, little missy!' and sent back to my room."

Up ahead, Rylan grunted. "Don't go getting any ideas. You're leaving Shroudhaven. Everly, too. Neither of you belong here. It's not safe."

"Not safe for the eidolghast," Harper retorted. "Remember who took the kill tonight?"

"You got lucky. Most of that luck being that you had five shadyrs backing you up," Rylan said.

Harper stomped over a fold of cardboard. "You're lucky I respect Everly's decision to go because I would otherwise be staying just to spite you."

She glared at his back to show him she meant it, but he didn't turn around. He'd been grumpy since he woke up from his strange coma. Harper studied the subject of her best friend's uber-crush. He could no doubt be considered hot. Strong brow, chiseled jaw, darkly good looks, about three of every muscle.

She didn't really think Everly would be into that broody alpha personality though. Maybe he was different when they were kids, before the Darkfreys got their hooks into him.

But Harper couldn't see the appeal in him at all. The more she thought on it though—and Bryce's betrayal gave her plenty of time and reason to think on it—she couldn't seem to remember the appeal of any of the men she'd ever had in her life.

In front of her, Cherry caught her eye over his shoulder.

"We're going to miss you too, Bellsy. I don't know what I'm going to do, losing you as well—" he choked on the last words.

Harper reached forward to take his hand and squeeze it. "You're going to call me. And I'm going to call you. As much as Shroudhaven reception allows it."

Up ahead, the tunnel stopped at an apparent dead end. Barry pushed against the cardboard, and a door that had been unevenly cut into it popped open. Flakes of kraft paper shed from the rough edges.

Stepping through the narrow doorway, they emerged into a cavernous room. Flattened cardboard and pegged-up sheets broke the space into sections. To the left, ragged old mattresses with bedsides made of boxes created a rough dorm area. Lamps of all shapes and sizes sat beside beds and in corners, brightening the patchy brown space with warm light.

Harper couldn't tell how they were being powered. A large dining table with

eleven mismatched chairs could be seen down another path. Straight ahead, a range of threadbare armchairs sat in a circle, over which on a long rope hung an asymmetrical, arty, single-piece crystal chandelier, glowing softly.

Various oddities clearly straight off garbage collection piles filled every other space, from old bicycles to boxy television sets. Stacked tinned food and old soda bottles filled with water created trip hazards in between.

Harper turned on the spot, taking it all in. "You really have been collecting."

Callan raised his eyebrows. "This is some setup."

"My uncle Teddy would love this place," Denny agreed. "If it had more firearms."

Tammy gave him a distasteful look.

Barry shook his head, making his long beard swing. "Not really my groove. I'm a pacifist through and through. Anyway, welcome to the heart of my maze. Stay as long as you want."

"Thanks, but I think we can probably get back to the street now we're all, um, ourselves again," Callan said.

"No problem, I can let you out round the block from where we started." He waggled a finger at them, leading them through the center of the cardboard bunker.

As Harper moved between the armchairs, she paused to admire the light fitting hanging there, not far over her head. Light sparkled prettily from its intricate forms. She'd been reading up on crystalware for the antique sales and wondered whether it had a maker's mark on it. She reached out a hand to turn it and check.

Barry slapped her fingers away with a roughness that made her gasp. "Don't touch that!"

"Okay!" Harper stepped back beside Cherry and hissed, "So much for being a pacifist."

Barry walked them in a small circle, then back out the same doorway they had come in. The path they followed led as straight as before, and soon grew smaller until they had to move on hands and knees. Like a strange caterpillar conga line, the group crawled out. They emerged from the cardboard box through the floral bedsheet and tarp curtains in a completely different location than where they'd first entered.

Getting to his feet, Callan held out a hand to Barry. "Thanks, man. We appreciate your help."

Barry stared at Callan's arm as if he didn't understand social niceties, then placed the very tips of his fingers around Callan's thumb.

He gave one floppy shake, then released the shadyr. "You're most welcome. I typically don't help ... well, your type. Only the normal folk. But I've been watching you. Lian's kids," he added with a nod. "You're better than the other lot."

"The other lot?" Rylan asked.

Barry's blue eyes gleamed, and he looked beyond Rylan into the night. Without another word, he ducked back into the cardboard box. A second later, the sheets and cardboard folded in upon themselves like an origami magic trick and vanished without a trace.

"No matter how weird things get, Shroudhaven always finds some new way to surprise me," Harper muttered.

"Let's aim to get back to the car with no more surprises tonight," Callan said, taking the lead down the footpath.

Shroudhaven's usual dark mist pressed in on them, and the street stretched into the eerie fog, silent and empty this late at night.

Harper wondered how many monsters were roaming the fog out there, and her fingers twitched. But her energy levels were dropping. The walk back to the car left her exhausted.

A deep yearning grew inside her. She needed to get back to the Bane soon. She needed … more. The sensation concerned her, remembering the glassy-eyed gaze of the more-scars-than-skin Gorhanmere cultists.

She knew the risks, but she needed this. She needed the power, the control. Would she be strong enough to keep herself from crossing that line?

4

Jasper tugged the hood of his jacket up over his head against the cold of the night, then checked his phone again.

Six days.

Only six days since he'd lost Cherry, and each one had been more interminable than the last. Every second that passed was pain, and that pain was a failure of his ability to move on.

Why won't it stop hurting?

Even though they'd had to keep their relationship hidden, he'd had something good with Cherry, but part of him knew it could never last, not if he wanted to remain a Darkfrey.

I knew. I should be able to let it go.

But without Cherry in his life, everything that had felt right now felt wrong. Before, he could be a good Darkfrey and be secretly in love. Now, it seemed he could be neither.

Jasper tapped the icon for his text messages. Before he could get his emotions in check and stop himself, he chose Cherry's thread.

Cherry's last message drew his attention like a magnet.

Seven letters. That he couldn't stop looking at, no matter how they made his heart sting.

TTYL. ILY.

"Eyes up, Jasper," Vonny said in her clipped, bossy tone. "I'm not going to die because you feel the need to check your socials while on patrol."

Only the hood hiding his face gave Jasper the nerve to roll his eyes in reply. He dropped his phone back into his pocket without a sound. Arguing with Vonny Mesman was like doing a round in the ring against a tornado. It wasn't worth the damage.

Beside her, the newest member of their team, Nilson Darkfrey, did have the nerve to visibly roll his eyes. He never missed a chance to make it clear he was above everyone and everything around him. Entirely too big, too violent, too casually cruel, and Jasper had no doubt that if the brute found out he was gay, Nilson would kick his ass into the Everdark without blinking twice.

There were half a dozen shadyrs who could have replaced Rylan in their brace, yet somehow, they ended up with Mordan Darkfrey's son.

Life just kept piling on lately.

Jasper focused on the thud of his sneakers against the asphalt as the four of them moved briskly along the main street, marching two by two. To his side, Annabeth pressed both her fists to her lips, huffed breath into them, then rubbed her palms together. She seemed to suffer the cold more than others, just like Cherry did.

Fall in Shroudhaven wasn't picture-perfect. Winds howled and buffeted, and rain left everything soggy and gray. When discussing the approach of winter, Jasper had told Cherry he'd be there to keep him warm. But now ...

Jasper managed to stop an inch away from ramming into Nilson's brick wall of a back, where he'd come to an abrupt halt in front of him.

Get over all of that and focus, Jasper scolded himself, taking a step back into formation.

Only a huff came from Nilson as any indication as to why they'd stopped.

Several people approached through the fog. A few familiar faces, a few that were slightly less familiar.

And one that was Cherry.

Sweat broke out across Jasper's skin and his chest stung as if someone had planted a knife in his solar plexus.

Like the other Howell shadyrs, Cherry wore only his body armor and acid-burned pants. Battle-worn, exhausted, and entirely gorgeous.

Their eyes met and under his red hair, Cherry's gaze was as brittle and icy as the weather.

Jasper wanted to reach for him, to yank him into his arms and try to ease the suffering between them.

But he remained silent. Frozen.

The two groups faced off against each other in the misty darkness.

Vonny spoke first, her voice harsh in the quiet night. "You're awake?"

Huh? Jasper blinked, dragging his eyes from Cherry to see Rylan standing at the front of the Howell pack.

Annabeth leaned to the side for a better look.

"Rylan?" She took a step forward.

Vonny swiftly raised a fist. "Awake, and went out on a hunt with this lot? He's clearly chosen his side."

Annabeth stepped back into place, her expression turning hard and blank.

Rylan stared the Darkfreys down, animal rage in his eyes. He made no move to rejoin them, to argue his case, or to explain.

Jasper had seen the braver side of Rylan when they were on the same team. He was a soldier, through and through. His every action had a purpose, his every movement was calculated and strategized. He didn't do or say anything without a reason.

But there was also something new to Rylan. A kind of jagged edge or shattered piece to him that wasn't there before his coma. Something had changed. It weighed on him, visible even to Jasper. He was a Darkfrey no more.

Cherry, Callan, and now Rylan too? So many choosing to leave the Darkfreys. Not that Cherry had a choice, really. But the Howell brothers were on equal footing with Mordan's own offspring as some of the best shadyrs at the estate.

Could I leave too? Could I be beside Cherry, instead of stuck on the other side of party lines?

It felt too hard, too much. Cherry had always been the brave one. Jasper had drawn on that courage when Cherry was by his side, but even if he did leave the Darkfreys, he doubted Cherry would take him back.

Nilson crossed his arms over his barrel chest. "When are you runts going to stay out of shadyr business? I found the stinking mess you left at The Boutique All."

Denny coughed from the sidelines. "Sounds like what your girlfriend says about you."

Not a hint of humor or understanding crossed Nilson's face as he turned to Denny. "You? You should be there with the cleaners now, slop boy."

"You know I'm not a cleaner! You know I deserved a brace rank," Denny snapped back.

"You'd be better off as a Darkfrey cleaner than as a Howell runt. Dregs and outcasts from *our* training, pretending to be something you're not. You're all nothing."

Jasper tensed as Cherry caught his eye, then dropped his gaze to the ground.

"Oh, they are something, all right." Vonny's voice was low and hard.

Her eyes were fixed on the small goth girl skulking at the back of the group. "Two half-breeds, a moronic pervert, a useless misfit, some random human pet."

She cut a scathing glare across Callan, Rylan, Denny, Cherry, Harper, and back to Tammy. "And last but not least, that stain on existence."

All the color drained from Tammy's face—which wasn't much, considering how pale she already was.

Callan put a hand on her shoulder, but she flinched away.

"How dare you stand there after what you did to my son?" Vonny stalked forward, closing the distance.

"I—" Tammy's lips wobbled.

"*You* are a curse that stole my boy from me!"

Callan stepped into Vonny's path. "What happened to Blaise was an accident. We all wish things could have been different, but—"

"Do you?" Vonny shoved him, but he remained solid.

Rylan, Cherry, Harper, and, to Jasper's shock, even Denny, closed in, forming a wall between the young shadyr and Vonny's rage.

She stilled and glared through the protective line as though she and Tammy were the only ones there. "Do you wish it was different? Would you wish it with all your heart that you could bring my son back? Would you wish to take his place?"

"I do, I would," Tammy replied in a small, frightened sob.

"That's enough," Callan barked.

Tammy gasped at the air as if it were drowning her.

Then she vanished.

Jasper blinked at the space where she'd been standing. *What in the Everdark?*

Beside him, Annabeth sucked in a quick breath, and she reached out to grab Jasper's arm. It wasn't just him seeing things, then.

Cherry sighed and pulled his phone from his pocket, taking a few steps away from the crowd as he dialed.

Vonny's irritation faded, and she raised an eyebrow at Callan. "Did she just ... disappear?"

Callan scowled back darkly, and there was a sharp danger in his tone that Jasper had never heard before. "Wouldn't you be happy if she did? She's been through enough. You have to leave her alone."

Vonny's bitter laugh rang through the night. "*She* has been through enough? No, only I get to decide that."

Cherry's low voice drifted over as he murmured into his phone, "Hey, Rush. We need a Dark Corner pickup."

Vonny took a step back as though struck. Her eyes narrowed.

Jasper clenched his teeth. Dark Corner was the shroudpool that Vonny's son, Blaise, had fallen into. Was that where Tammy had ended up, and how? He stared at Cherry as he ended his call. This seemed like an everyday occurrence to him but was something they'd never discussed when together.

Why did he keep this a secret? This is the sort of thing the Darkfreys should know about, it could ...

Jasper's chain of thought cut off with the blunt recollection of how his relationship with Cherry ended. Because he'd passed along information about the Howells that Cherry had provided him to the Darkfreys. It hurt that Cherry hadn't told him everything. As though Cherry never truly trusted him all along.

I did the right thing. The Darkfreys needed that info. For the mission. For the good of all against the Everdark.

Cherry moved closer to Callan but didn't quiet his voice when he said, "Come on, let's go. They don't deserve any more of our time."

"We're not done here yet." Nilson stalked forward, putting himself into Rylan's personal space. "We know you're in possession of stolen Darkfrey property. Lucas told us. The artifact belongs to us."

Rylan opened his mouth, but before he could say anything—

"Like hell it does," Harper said.

Nilson turned to her as though to a yapping puppy.

He grinned, the smile stretching his meaty face. "Shut it, bliv. You've got nothing to do with this."

She stepped up to him.

Tall as she was, he still dwarfed her, but fire filled her eyes. "I have everything to do with it. The Bane is where it belongs, which isn't with some entitled sock stuffed with rocks like you."

"Harper," Rylan growled in warning.

Nilson thrust a hand toward her chest in a shoving motion. She snatched it from the air, faster than sight, and twisted it away from her.

With a grunt of disgust, Harper dropped his arm and raised her fists.

"I'm not afraid of you," she spat, and swung.

Jasper held his breath. He'd already spent the last hour and a half hoping tonight would go smoothly so he could go home and get some sleep, forget his feelings for a while. Now, there was about to be a brawl between the Howell and the Darkfrey teams.

Jasper couldn't honestly say which side he'd fall on. Not with Cherry's big dark eyes watching him.

With a smack, Vonny caught Harper's punch in her grasp.

She put up a hand to warn Nilson back, and wrestled Harper's arm downward, grimacing with the effort. "You're a strong one."

"You have no idea," Harper snarled.

Vonny grinned, her profile skull-like beneath her blond, bobbed hair. "The shadyrs at Gorhanmere were especially strong, too."

Harper inhaled sharply and snatched her hand away. Callan reached for her, and she let herself be pulled back into the protective circle of Howells.

"Wow, you runts never fail to surprise me with the trouble you get into." Vonny shrugged, then motioned with two fingers to her brace. "Come along. Someone has to keep the town safe while this lot falls apart from the inside."

Nilson snarled at her for edging into his role as leader, and at everyone else for merely existing. He took the lead away from the other shadyrs.

Letting loose a ragged breath, Jasper whirled on the ball of his foot to follow his brace leader. At least it was over.

But it wasn't, because he was powerless against the urge to look back.

To see Cherry staring at him, with all that pain, and judgment, and loathing.

Jasper cursed between gritted teeth and turned away again. He trudged after Vonny and Nilson as they muttered under their breaths about the Howell team. Their brace had once been a family, but that family had been broken then broken apart again.

Jasper did his best to now separate the working aspect of hunting eidolghasts from the emotional aspect of being a part of the team. They weren't a family anymore, but it didn't matter if they could still get the job done. As long as he held brace rank, he was someone, worth something.

He may have to live a lie to remain part of the Darkfreys, but at least there he made a difference in this dark world. Even if he could never truly belong.

5

Blearily, Everly rolled her sleeping bag up off the couch. Only the softest hint of morning light showed in the sky through the living room windows, but after waking in a panic, Everly only wanted to leave, and leave now.

A knee-buckling sting shot through her arm as she tried to push the silky fabric into its stuff sack. She exhaled through clenched teeth, trying not to whimper.

Peeling back the sleeve of her shirt, Everly eyed the damage the Bane had done to her, disheartened to see that it looked even worse than it did last night.

She'd cut her right forearm to free Zozo's soul, then cut her left to free Rylan's. She'd managed to release them both, but not without consequences.

Those two cuts had done a lot more damage than expected.

Thin red lines spider-webbed beneath her skin, cracks marring the pale expanse of her arm as if she were fractured glass, waiting to shatter.

It felt like she was breaking apart from the inside. Every movement sent more pain shooting along her nerve endings.

I just have to get out of here, out of this house, this town, and then I'll have time to heal.

Moving more carefully, she gave up on the sleeping bag and left it flopped loosely on top of her already-packed duffle bag. She tiptoed out to collect the last of her toiletries. Even the walk down the short hallway left her breathless and sheened in sweat. The door of the bathroom swung open to reveal Harper leaning in close to the mirror, wiping something dark green off her neck.

"Sorry, I didn't know you were up already."

"No probs, I'm all done in here if you want the bathroom," Harper said. "I wasn't expecting you to be up so early either, sleepyhead."

They shuffled past each other in the doorway, switching places. Everly leaned heavily on the basin, ran the tap, and splashed her face with water.

Harper hovered in the hallway. "Are you okay? You look pale."

"Yeah, just didn't sleep well." Except she had, deeply, so deep she couldn't wake herself from the terrifying and vivid nightmares that plagued her.

Everly stood up straighter and put on an *I'm fine* smile. "It's good you're up, I'd like

to get going soon. I have a few more things to pack, then I'm ready to leave whenever you are."

Everly scooped her toiletries into their case in one handful and zipped it closed.

Harper's face fell. "Oh. I was kind of hoping you might have changed your mind about leaving."

"Staying was never the plan," Everly said firmly.

"Yeah, I know, but I kind of like it here. We could totally make this our home."

"No!" The word dropped between them with explosive power.

A rush of heat and nausea washed over Everly, and she swallowed hard. This place wasn't home. It was good they were leaving. She carried a lifetime of bad memories of Shroudhaven—her mother's mental and emotional abuse, her father's death, plus Rylan pushing her out of his life, twice.

There was nothing more for Everly here.

As soon as they were ready, she intended to lock the door and never return. She'd already found a team of movers willing to come in and pack up the antiques shop, and she'd also found a good storage place back home where she could rent a garage for it all as they continued selling it off.

Her time in Shroudhaven was *officially* over.

She should have been ecstatic to get out. Away from there, the dragon would remain firmly locked away. She could live a normal life. Forget about eidolghasts and shadyrs and the man with the nebulous eyes who'd stolen her heart only to break it.

Instead of feeling happiness or relief, she felt hollow, slowly shattering apart.

Reining in her emotions, Everly murmured, "This isn't my home. It hasn't been for a really long time."

Harper's long lashes fluttered and her lips lifted in a smile. "Then we leave. I go where you go. You know that. The only thing I need to grab is the you-know-what and then we can hightail it out of here."

Everly's mouth popped open. "Really? You're all set?

"Mm-hm."

"Your makeup and camera gear?"

"Done."

"Final sales we need to post out?"

"Done."

"Fridge emptied?"

"Done."

"Did you even sleep last night?"

Harper tittered a high-pitched laugh and skipped off down the stairs.

Everly took a deep breath and let it out slowly, slumping over the sink again as she

waited for a wave of dizziness to pass. Then she grabbed the last of her belongings and hauled her duffle bag downstairs, sleeping bag dangling under her arm.

Harper was waiting with her laptop bag over her shoulder and one small rose-gold suitcase by her side.

"Is that it?"

Harper nodded. "The rest is all loaded, ready to make our escape."

Everly wasn't sure when Harper had done everything but was grateful it meant no waiting. Maybe she really had been up all night, although she certainly didn't look like it.

Following Harper down the entrance hall, she did one quick doubletake back through the kitchen doorway. "Um, when did you repaint the cupboards?"

Out on the back porch, Harper just shrugged.

Stepping outside, Everly dug in the pocket of her blue jeans, pulling out the bundle of keys the estate attorney had given her. She reached back into the hallway and flipped the switch, extinguishing the candle-shaped lights. She needed no greater ritual than that to farewell the haunted abode. Turning the key, she listened to the lock tumble on her life in Shroudhaven.

"Goodbye, spooky house," Harper sang.

Not one for goodbyes, Everly just walked away, as she had once before.

In the backyard, the swing set was still overgrown because she'd never had a chance to tackle the worst of that jungle. Maybe the next owners would.

A plate tucked into a small clearing in the weeds held only the barest dredges of watery blood from the raw meat left out the night before. She hadn't seen Zozo in real life or her dreams since she'd freed him, so had to hope it was him who'd consumed the meal. Maybe leaving the plate there would give the next owners the hint to put food out, too. She hoped Zozo would be okay.

Everly's duffle bag weighed a ton by the time she'd walked around the house. At least the front yard had cleaned up well since Everly first returned. Much less overgrown and wild than on the night when everything had gone to hell, right there, and her whole world changed.

She would never be able to rid herself of the vision of Rylan being torn apart. Of how she'd run to him, taken him in her arms, seen his blood glistening on his broken body. Of how something had also split open inside her, releasing the dragon. That *thing*. The soul-eater.

Her friends, the Howells, they'd all heard it. They had all heard Crowea call the thing inside Everly a soul-eater. Yet they went about as though it was no big deal. Maybe none of them truly believed it. None of them could *feel* the thing inside her like she felt it, its hunger, how close they were to becoming its next meal.

For all they knew, Rylan was the only soul that had gotten caught up in any *eating* business, and she'd gotten him back out okay. No harm, no foul, right?

They had no idea how hard it was to stay in control, or the cost of extracting souls back from the being's grasp.

And they wouldn't know. Soon, Everly would be too far away.

Everly glanced up the street, shuddering at the way the fog drifted like ghosts beneath the dim light of dawn.

"I'll drive," Harper said as she unlocked the campervan and tossed her bags in, "so you can rest."

"Thanks." Everly grunted in pain as she set her duffel bag on top of Harper's matching suitcases.

She climbed into the passenger side as Harper took her seat behind the wheel.

The campervan's engine rolled over and Harper gently pulled away from the curb. "It wasn't all bad though, right? I think I'd like to come back sometime. To visit."

Everly slouched further into the chair and shoved her hands into the pockets of her red bomber jacket. "You'll have to come without me."

A beat of silence fell over them.

At the end of the block, Harper took a right turn, and Everly sat up, confused. "You're going the wrong way. The highway's the other way."

Harper squeezed the steering wheel between both hands, her green eyes glinting in the backwash from the headlights. "We've got farewells to make."

Everly's skin prickled. "Harper, no."

"You seriously thought we were going to zoom out of town at the crack of dawn without saying goodbye?"

Everly rubbed the growing tension between her eyebrows. Escaping without a word was *exactly* what she wanted. She didn't have the energy to deal with goodbyes, or the strength to listen to Lian telling her she should stay. Her arm hurt like crazy, and she felt hot and cold at the same time.

She just wanted to *go*. "We said everything that needed to be said yesterday."

"Did you say *goodbye*? No? Then you didn't say everything."

Everly turned to the window, avoiding Harper's eyes. "I don't want to wake them up."

"I'm sure they're still awake."

"Huh?"

"We're going. Driver's rules! And look, we're already here."

What was a short walk between the Boderleth residence and Howell House was even shorter by car. The campervan trundled down the long drive lined by silvery birch trees, and Lian's ancestral home emerged at the top of a low hill, all the porch lights shining in welcome.

The glow illuminated the weathered siding and flaking ivory paint on the trim. The hundred-plus-year-old house hulked against the pink-blushed sky, still quite lovely in its decay.

In the shadows beyond the porch lights, something moved and rustled in the underbrush, and Everly's head whipped toward it. A curved, tan tail that looked suspiciously like Zozo's poked above the bushes but vanished almost instantly.

It seemed the Howell gang was awake, and a few of them sat on the porch. As the campervan drew closer, they rose to meet it. Callan, Cherry, and Lian came down the steps, but Rylan remained at a distance.

And there's the instant regret. Everly groaned pitifully.

Harper shut off the engine and leaned over, giving her a one-armed hug. "You can do this."

"I'm not sure about that." *Emotionally or physically,* Everly thought as another wave of nausea left her head spinning.

"Look, I'm not saying that this is my last-ditch effort for Rylan to pull his head out of his sculpted ass and beg you to stay, but I'm not *not* saying that."

"You just said it!"

Harper sighed, then squeezed Everly one more time before reaching past to open her door, practically pushing her out.

As Harper hopped out her side and they walked up the path together, the door to Denny's trailer slammed open and he appeared in his tiny porch light, shirtless and carrying a beer.

"Ugh," Harper said.

"We could have avoided him entirely," Everly pointed out.

"Stop dodging your issues. These people love you. I mean, maybe not this guy, not in a way we want, anyway," she amended with a glare at Denny's leering grin. "But the rest of them do."

Lian reached them first and wrapped her thin arms around Everly, tugging her in for a hug. Her long cardigan sweater was as gray as her hair, and the fabric smelled like a mix of citrus and eucalyptus.

It was the smell of home.

Well, Everly's surrogate home, anyway.

Everly raised her arms to return the hug, wincing at the pain it caused.

When Lian released her, the older woman stepped away and studied Everly with worried gray-brown eyes. "You're not off already, are you?"

"Yeah, making an early start." Everly studiously kept her eyes from turning up toward the porch. "We just stopped to say a quick goodbye."

"Oh, I thought we might have more time! We haven't even properly celebrated you

bringing Rylan back to us. Can you at least stay for breakfast?"

Before Everly could refuse, Callan said, "We've got waffles! We can do a farewell feast. Don't leave without waffles."

He reached for her, and Everly let him bring her into a brotherly hug. Her chest ached at the thought of never seeing him or his mother again. They'd been her family when her own hadn't been capable. Them, and Rylan.

Everly could see Rylan's feet up on the porch through the corner of her eye. He was just standing there, wouldn't even come close to her. Shame and queasiness heated her face.

"That's okay, I don't want to trouble you with all that. We should keep moving." Everly thumb pointed back to the car, then reminded herself through gritted teeth to restrain the hand gestures.

"I'm going to miss you two." Cherry leaned in and hugged them both, adding in a whisper, "My confidants."

"Oh, but Rush and Tammy aren't back from Dark Corner yet!" Lian declared. "You have to say goodbye to them, too. And you might as well grab a coffee for the road while you wait."

Everly could feel prickles of sweat breaking across her forehead, and stars floated in her eyes.

She needed to get back into the van, to sit down, to be leaving. "I don't think we have time ..."

Lian raised one thin eyebrow. "Are you on the clock or something? Another twenty minutes won't hurt anything."

Everly wobbled on her feet, shaking her head.

Lian's shrewd eyes locked onto her. "Are you feeling okay? You still look unwell."

Swallowing, Everly put energy into her smile. "Oh, no, I'm fine, it's just that the Bane is in the van."

"Well come inside away from the thing!" Lian waved them on and led the way back up into the house.

Everly's gaze followed her for too long, catching Rylan's eye for a moment. She hastily turned away, but not before seeing the seething distaste there. Maybe the others didn't look at her like the monster she was, but he knew.

Harper hooked arms with Callan and Cherry and like the traitor she was, she followed Lian up to the front door.

"No, Harper, we really should—"

"Maybe a beer for the road, too," Denny crowed.

Twenty minutes, I can do twenty minutes.

Everly took a step forward, crunching the gravel under her boot. Her feet were

heavy, and the heat that had been radiating in waves from her arm seemed exceptionally hot. Her eyesight wavered, blurred, and a tiny chill of panic snaked up her spine. Nausea swelled inside her. Her head pounded and swam.

I can't do twenty minutes.

"Harper—" her voice failed.

She stumbled.

Black edges pressed in on her vision.

Then her legs gave out and she collapsed.

Through dimmed vision and thunderous agony, she saw Rylan, his face like white marble, close to hers, his teeth long and sharp. She felt as he caught her in his unyielding arms.

Voices surrounded her as all went dark.

"Evie!"

"What happened?"

"What is that on her wrist?"

6

E verly's eyes fluttered open to a cool, dim room.

Shock rushed through her, chasing away the last of the cobwebs from her dreamless sleep. She swallowed through a cotton-dry mouth. The shapes of people moved nearby, but her vision remained blurry. She blinked to clear it.

Four navy walls cradled her, each of them dotted with dozens of stars—glow-in-the-dark stickers that she'd helped put up a lifetime ago. A vintage television still hunched on the small dresser next to the equally aged gaming console they'd once spent hours playing.

She could still recall the theme song of their favorite platformer so clearly.

The room, Rylan's room, was like a childhood dream, at once achingly familiar yet so distant. Much like the man her childhood sweetheart had grown into.

As her sight cleared, she realized that the poster of their favorite anime show that had been taped to the wall—that had been there when she'd last been in the room—was gone.

Rylan had only been back in his childhood bedroom for one night, and that was the change he'd chosen to make.

Did Rylan tear it down because it reminded him of me?

The thought brought hot tears to her eyes, blurring them again.

"Shh, it's okay." Lian appeared at the side of the bed, holding out two little white pills as she reached for a bottle of water on the nightstand. "Here. Take this."

Everly considered refusing them and saying she'd just had a panic attack, but the way she felt, she needed whatever pain relief she could get. Propping herself up on her better elbow, she accepted them.

Her other arm burned as she popped the pills in her mouth and took the water bottle. She gagged as she washed the pills down her dry throat, then tried to hand the water back to Lian.

"More," Lian ordered. "Drink at least half."

Everly made a petulant face but obeyed.

Lian waited patiently, then took the bottle back and set it on the table.

Everly spared a glance at the clock on the nightstand. Barely ten minutes had passed

432

since she showed up at Howell House then fainted, but she felt as though she'd been under for days. She tried to get into a more upright position.

Lian stepped closer to the edge of the mattress, crossed her arms, and her motherly concern morphed to a glare. "You're not going anywhere."

"I'm fine, really." Her entire body felt like it was running several degrees too hot.

All it took was a light push from Lian on her shoulder to send her flopping back against the pillows.

The glaring continued.

Meeting Lian's icy gaze, Everly asked, "What?"

"Why didn't you tell us about your arm?"

Everly's cheeks heated even more. "What about it?"

"Ev. We know." Harper's disapproving tone drifted from the doorway.

Everly found Harper standing in the glow of the hallway light, and beside her, Rylan.

All three of them looked at her as though she'd been caught kicking an orphan's kitten.

She was used to that disappointed distaste from Rylan, but the vampire form he was in made it more vicious. His lips were spread, revealing his fangs beneath, and his bone-white skin made him seem like an ancient, judgmental statue.

Generally, shadyrs didn't take that form unless there was a vasmire close, but not in this case.

In this case, Everly was the problem. Since releasing his soul, Rylan's shadyr senses now reacted to Everly like they would an eidolghast.

And nobody knew why.

But it gave him yet another reason to not want to be near her.

Lian, clearly tired of waiting for Everly to own up to the situation, sighed. "Were you going to tell any of us about this?"

She brushed her fingers lightly over Everly's wrist.

Everly intended to keep playing innocent and ask, *About what?* since the last she'd looked, the damage from the Bane was hidden beneath a bandage beneath her sleeve.

But a quick glance showed that the red cracks had spread downward, creeping over her wrist and into her palm. "Oh."

"Oh? That's all you have to say?" Rylan's voice was gravelly.

Everly shrugged, the movement awkward in her prone position. "It's nothing. Don't worry about it."

Harper stepped closer. "That wasn't there yesterday. I saw the bandage you put over the cuts from the Bane. Whatever is going on, it's coming from those cuts and it's spreading."

"I'm sure it will heal," Everly said, frowning at how it had grown.

"It's clearly getting worse," Rylan grumbled. "There's more than there was even ten minutes ago."

Lian gently picked up Everly's hand, studying the strange pattern. "It looks as if you're cracking apart from the inside. Like a broken mirror."

"We have to fix this." Rylan took a step closer, and his skin rippled, black smoke swirling around him as he shifted away from vampire and toward werewolf.

With a grunt, he stepped back again. "From what I understand of what Crowea said, the being inside Everly is only a piece of something that had been broken in the past by the Bane."

He pointed an accusing finger at Harper. "And you let her hack into herself with that same artifact? No wonder she's falling apart."

Harper gasped. "Let her? As soon as I saw what happened the first time, I tried to stop her the second. You're the reason she was dead set on slicing herself up again."

"What's done is done!" Lian snapped. "Let's focus on a way to fix it."

Harper harrumphed and folded her arms, a begrudging pout on her lips. "Look, I think Rylan's probably right. This isn't just about the Bane, it's about the thing that's inside Everly, how it is reacting to it. Cutting normal humans with the Bane doesn't do this."

"How do you know?" Lian asked.

Harper's mouth twisted and she huffed, "Okay, fine, so I might have scratched myself with it while trying to wrestle it away from our stabby martyr over there."

Everly's mouth dropped. "You said that didn't happen."

"I didn't want you to worry! You'd been through enough. Anyway, it was fine, completely a nonissue."

Everly knitted her brows. There hadn't even been a mark on Harper's skin ...

Harper continued briskly, "If it's the dragon that's breaking and taking Everly's body with it, we need to somehow strengthen and heal it. Find another piece of it maybe."

A chill ran down Everly's spine. "That sounds risky. I already have trouble controlling the thing. If it were even stronger ..."

Staring down at the floor, Rylan said, "If making it stronger will save you, then we need it."

A loaded silence filled the room, and Everly fidgeted with the blanket between her fingers. All three of the others stared at her expectantly. She sighed.

"Fine. But how would we even do that? We're at a dead end with whatever my dragon is." Other than *soul-eater*, a term Everly noticed everyone had been skirting around. "Or how and why it's in me."

Harper perked up. "If monsters are a thing ... is necromancy? Is there any way to speak to the dead, maybe bring back Mr. or Mrs. Boderleth? They might know something about why Everly is this way?"

Rylan let out a short, sharp laugh. "Even if they knew something, which I doubt, that isn't possible. Any secrets they may have had died with them."

Lian reached over and gave Everly's hand a gentle squeeze. "Our only other info is what the eidolghast referred to: the 'Beast of Teeth and Stars.' We're in possession of the *Bane* of Teeth and Stars, but as far as I'm aware, there are no other artifacts associated with that very specific phrase."

Harper gasped. "Oh! What about *other* artifacts? Surely there's something at Darkfrey Estate that can heal? I'm all in for round two of raiding that place."

Lian shook her head. She still hadn't released Everly's fingers, as if she knew how much her helping hand had eased the shame inside her.

"I'm unaware of any 'healing' artifacts," she said regretfully. "But I do think there is one other clue we've overlooked."

Everly tensed, expecting *soul-eater* to finally come into the conversation.

"The being inside you is made of *light*, while the eidolghasts are creatures of darkness. That seems relevant, don't you think?"

Everly *hadn't* thought of that before. She'd always assumed that the creature in her was a monster, an eidolghast of some kind.

She asked, "What does that mean? I thought the Everdark was just that, all darkness. Could a creature of light come from there? Or does that mean it's from somewhere else entirely?"

The floorboards creaked as Rylan shifted position, leaning against the doorframe. "Actually, the Everdark wasn't always dark."

"I mean, it's in the name," Harper muttered. "It's not like they called it the *Recentlydark.*"

Rylan shot her a glare.

She rolled her eyes. "But what do I know?"

"A lot for a bliv," Rylan said, sounding more frustrated than approving. "Honestly, most shadyrs would think the same. Only history nuts like Annabeth really talk about how the Everdark didn't start out as a realm of darkness and monsters. She would always go on about that, along with all the other pre-crossover history theories and religious studies most shadyrs aren't interested in."

"Too busy fighting monsters to care where the monsters came from and why," Lian said.

Rylan continued, "Anyway, the point is it was the ghasts that *made* it that realm dark."

"How?" Everly asked, not sure she wanted to hear the answer.

"That's what eidolghasts do—they come to a dimension and slowly take all the

light away until it's entirely beshadowed. That's why it's so important we fight them back. That's why our shadyr ancestors from that dimension fled to this one when all the light was gone. Annabeth lectured our brace on it all the time." Rylan's voice grew stronger as he talked, more excited and intense.

While he'd been lying in his strange coma, Annabeth had shown up at the Boderleth residence and asked to see him. During her visit, she'd revealed to Everly not only that she had a thing for Rylan, but that she believed his heart belonged to someone else.

The way Rylan looked as he spoke now, Everly wasn't convinced it didn't belong to Annabeth.

"So there may have been creatures of light like my dragon in the Everdark at some point? It might still have come from there?" Everly wanted to feel some relief, that she didn't have an eidolghast possessing her body.

But regardless of what label the being had, she knew deep in her gut that it wasn't *good*.

Lian nodded thoughtfully. "That would make the Beast of Teeth and Stars an enemy of the eidolghasts. Which tracks based on what we know. Still, the ghasts won that realm, with no other trace of creatures of light having survived. We can only make guesses. They predate our history."

"Which means," Everly said, her voice sharp with irritation, "that we haven't gotten any closer to knowing what this ... *soul-eater* inside me really is."

The name hung heavy in the room. Holding back a grunt of effort, Everly sat up, pushed the blankets away, and swung her legs over the edge of the bed.

"Look, I'm fine, really. We don't know that the wounds won't heal themselves in time. I'm sure they will. I just need to leave, and recover, away from all of ... this."

Rylan caught her eye on the last word. He opened his mouth to speak.

A light trilling sound shot through the room, and Lian jumped, then shoved her hand into the oversized pocket of her cardigan. She extracted her phone, glanced at the screen, then frowned.

"It's Rush," she informed them as she accepted the call. "Hello?"

Lian listened intently for a moment, her expression changing, and all the color faded from her so that she was nearly as gray as her cardigan.

"We'll be right there." She hung up, face grim. "We have to go. Tammy's missing."

7

Rylan clutched the handle above his head as his brother careened the packed SUV through the empty, early morning streets of Shroudhaven.

He was half-transformed into his vasmire form, thanks to Everly's presence at the very back of the vehicle, which heightened his senses and made his brother's wild driving hurt his head.

"Do you have to take corners like that?"

Callan didn't spare a glance at him, all attention on the road. "We might not be a brace in the Darkfrey's sense, but we are a team. They are *my* team and my responsibility. And unlike the Darkfreys, I care about losing one of them."

"Ouch. Point taken, right to the heart."

Lian, who sat directly behind Rylan, leaned forward. "Keep up the pace. She's not just team. She's family."

Rylan turned and caught her eye. Yesterday, when he'd risen from apparent death, she had been all motherly love and welcoming arms, but now, there was something harsh about how she stared him down.

She spoke in a low voice, close to his ear. "I know it's only been a day, but you need to start shaking your Darkfrey habits. We do things differently."

Yeah, I'm getting that impression, Rylan thought, but before he could say anything his mother continued, "And your misguided hostility to Everly has to end."

Rylan tensed, a million arguments and excuses firing through his brain. But he didn't owe those to anyone, even his estranged mother.

"I know what I'm doing."

"No, you don't."

Rylan spun in his seat, staring the woman down. "Don't treat me like a child."

"Then stop acting like one."

Beside him, Callan coughed a laugh, but quickly schooled his face and gave his brother a sympathetic look.

So this is what it will be like being back at home, is it?

"Ha, sick burn from your mom," Denny chortled from beside Lian.

She smacked him on the shoulder.

Callan leaned across and not subtly whispered, "Not sure if you noticed, but Mom is hardcore now."

"Well," she muttered, "losing your kids will do that to a person."

Callan's grin failed. "We're back now."

Rylan nodded. "Both of us."

In his youthful hot-headedness to become the best monster hunter there was, in his bitter anger in the belief that it was his mother who had kept him from that path, it had been easy to distance himself from the pain he caused her when he left and took Callan with him. She had changed because of that. They all had. He could only wonder what sort of family they would be now.

"And I'm so glad you are. But let's not lose anyone else," she said sternly.

Callan refocused on his driving, putting on a boost of speed, but Lian held Rylan's gaze.

Rylan's eyes turned to Everly, who was sitting in the back between Harper and Cherry. She still looked so pale, wearing that rigid smile that wasn't fooling anyone.

No, I can't lose her. That's why she can't stay in this dark and deadly town.

He already couldn't forgive himself that she was now falling apart from what she did to save *him*. He would fix that. Save her. And then say goodbye. This little excursion was just delaying the inevitable.

Dark Corner shroudpool was close to Howell House, in a section of thick forest that butted up to the Wyrdwoods—a place full of eidolghasts and other things that prowled beneath a sunless canopy. Rylan didn't think anyone went there, until he learned about Tammy's curse when the Howells used it to escape a beshadowed nightmare in Rook's Hotel.

Rylan hadn't known Tammy prior to waking up, but she seemed like a good kid. A little younger than his brother, on the darker end of teenage attitude and sullen, but considering what he knew of her past, he couldn't blame her.

He didn't know the details but remembered when Tammy had been exiled from the Darkfreys. She'd had some part in the death of the Mesmans' boy. Her Everdark-blackened hands had been seen as the visible mark of her guilt. He'd only learned later that this was the price she paid for trying to reach into a shroudpool to save her friend.

She'd only been around thirteen. Rylan had been secretly glad when he heard Lian took her in. The way the kid looked when she left, he wasn't sure she would've survived otherwise. It was clear some Darkfreys hoped for that outcome. That had been the first time Rylan ever questioned his place there. It took him another three years, and an attempt on his life, to finally break from that establishment himself.

Callan pulled to an abrupt stop behind Rushelle's yellow sports car and cut the engine. The buxom blonde leaned on the back bumper of her car, fire-engine-red lipstick glowing in the darkness. Her beehive hairdo and the sharp black wings on her eyes made her look like a vintage pinup.

She straightened as the team piled from the SUV, her usually cheerful face drawn and tight.

"I've tried to call her five times," Rushelle greeted them, her hands twisting with worry in front of her tight yellow tank top. "It rings, but she's not answering. Poor duck, I hope nothing's happened to her."

Lian glanced at the tree line. "Did you go in?"

Rushelle nodded, and the typewriter charm on her gold necklace clinked against the chain. "Nothing looks out of place. The signs are all still up on the fence, and the opening in the chain-link where Tammy comes through is still hidden. I did a quick turn around the shroudpool, and it hasn't changed either. She's just ... not there."

"She always teleports here," Callan said. "She's never gone anywhere else."

Lian ran her fingers back through her graying hair, her gaze darting over the forest.

"I'm not sensing any ghasts nearby. So something either happened to her within the beshadowed area, or she somehow teleported somewhere else. Okay." She puffed out a breath, rubbing her eyebrow. "Okay, we're going to split up—"

Before she could complete her thought, a chorus of tinny sounds chimed within the group. Rylan watched as Lian, Rushelle, Cherry, and Callan each checked their phones.

A group text. A group Rylan wasn't yet part of.

Rushelle perked up. "It's from Tammy."

Lian's voice shook as she read, "Don't worry about me—I'm off to see about making a wish."

Harper, who had been fussing over Everly, glanced up, confused. "That's it? What does that mean? Is Shroudhaven harboring a genie?"

Cherry shook his head, his voice haunted. "No. No genies."

Harper lifted her palms upward. "I feel like I have to ask these things, you guys are always holding out on me."

"No genies," Callan agreed through gritted teeth. "But we do have an island in the middle of a dangerous lake with a rock that supposedly grants wishes."

Lian stared past them all, unfocused and pale. "*If* you survive the swim."

Phones were pocketed again, and they were back on the road within seconds.

Rylan understood the rush—Myrkur Lake was a death trap. But he also detested that they were on this trip in the first place. This was an unwanted distraction. Everly was fading by the second.

Rylan forced back his anger before he put his fist through the passenger door. Tammy didn't know, had no reason to know she was stealing time from Everly. The

kid must have been in a bad state to be heading in a direction nobody came back from. She must know that. Every shadyr knew that about Myrkur Lake.

It was a legendary place among Shroudhaven teenagers. In a small town, there wasn't much to do except hang out and make their own fun. Some of the more daredevil teens liked to do that by challenging each other to take a harrowing swim across the black depths.

The legend stated that if you survived the dangerous swim to the island in the center, you'd find a strange stone there. Touching it was said to grant a wish.

The problem was that the island was a known shroudpool location, and the beshadowing that accompanied it had spread throughout the lake. The water was inky black and frigid, full of currents that seemed to have sentience, and twisted, possessed sea creatures looking for their next meal.

Thankfully, most kids chickened out after dipping their toes in the water.

Most.

Rylan had heard of at least three drownings during his lifetime, and not a single report of anyone who made it to the island and returned.

Morning had broken, but the sun was hidden behind heavy black clouds and thick fog. The SUV zoomed down the highway as Rushelle followed in her coupe, headlights shining into the rearview mirror.

Callan slammed his palm on the steering wheel. "Vonny put this into her head, the way she was digging in this morning, telling Tammy she should wish things were different."

"She did?" Lian asked. "I'm going to need a word with that woman. She knows damn well there're no wishes to be granted in this town."

Harper leaned forward from the back.

"But how do we know for sure the wish thing isn't real? 'Cause maybe that could help, you know ..." She flicked her gaze across to Everly beside her.

"I'm fine," Everly said with a crackly voice.

"I know because that's why I left the Darkfreys in the first place." From her spot in the middle, Lian turned from Harper to stare out the side door.

"I grew up training there like most shadyr kids, alongside my best friend. Sidney ... She was different, you know? People used to put a whole bunch of harmful labels on others back in the day. Still do, I guess, and I don't feel like it's fair for me to slap a label on her now without an approval from her I can never get. But for a place that kicked someone like Cherry out, Darkfrey Estate was *bad* for her."

Harper tutted and looped an arm over Cherry's shoulder. He grumbled something incoherent, still sullen since the run-in with Rylan's old brace.

Lian continued, "Still, being a shadyr was everything to Sid. She fought against

every true part of herself to fit in there."

Rylan swallowed. He'd never had the full story on why his mom split from the Darkfreys back before he was born.

From the distracted look in Callan's eyes, maybe he hadn't either. "What happened?"

"No matter how Sid tried to hide herself, the in-crowd took a disliking to her," Lian said sadly. "She was kicked out, on a technicality, like Cherry, but everyone knew why. She was exiled. She swam Myrkur Lake because she wanted to wish herself 'normal.' She just wanted to be accepted by her own, and she ended up getting dead, when there was nothing *wrong* with her!"

The last words burst from her.

Rylan's hand twitched to reach out to his mother, but Everly reached forward first, putting her hand on the older woman's shoulder. "I'm sorry you lost her."

"Loss … happens. But I didn't lose her. They killed her, them and their awful, unfair, hateful ways." Lian took a shuddering breath and smoothed back her hair with one hand. "That's why I left the estate and never looked back. She's why I take in anyone who defects from the Darkfreys. Anyone."

All eyes in the van turned briefly to Denny, who seemed completely oblivious to any shade thrown his way.

"Shame that they're no better now," Cherry grumbled from the back, this time just loud enough to hear.

Lian shook her head. "A damn shame. Thirty years have passed and *nothing's* changed. You either fit the Darkfrey mold, or you suffer the consequences. Some of you more than others."

Cherry sunk further into Harper's embrace. Rylan knew the consequences were many. He knew Cherry's parents. Both shadyrs, both fully indoctrinated Darkfreys.

As were Tammy's.

And now the two young shadyrs had been disowned for who they were, not just by their kind, but by their own family.

Rylan's shoulders grew tense with tangible contempt for the Darkfreys. Did the others still see him as one? He had been until so recently that part of him felt like he was. He'd had similar concerns and disagreements about Darkfrey ways, too, but had always been—he could hardly admit it—too scared to say any of it out loud.

His voice wavered as he said, "If anything, they've gotten worse."

Callan shot a glance at his brother, then returned his eyes to the road. "The whole world is changing, for the better. The Darkfreys can sense that they're a dying breed and they're digging their claws in deeper, screaming louder in denial. You're not like them. Just so we're clear though, I made the right decision to get out first."

"I hope I'm not going to regret this." Everly's voice drifted up to the front, low and a little strained. "What about you, Denny? Why did you leave the Darkfreys?"

There was a soft sympathy in her tone that twanged a string in Rylan's chest. That her heart was big enough to even care about that tone-deaf meat sack ... even when she was suffering herself.

Why does she have to be like that? Why can't she just think about herself for once?

Cherry cracked a grin for the first time in a while. "Because he's too big of a jerk even for them."

"That's not why!" Denny said gruffly, as though Cherry had offered the reason seriously. "Those asshats put me on a cleaner team. Me! Refused to give me a spot on a brace. I'm better than that. I chose to leave."

Callan scoffed. "You're such a liar. Everyone knows you were hitting on Alexis, and she tattled to Daddy that you were harassing her."

Harper gave a desperate-for-gossip gasp. "Who's Alexis?"

"Alexis Darkfrey," Callan clarified. "As in Mordan Darkfrey's only daughter."

"No way!"

"That's right, no way," Denny said hotly. "You've got the story wrong. What me and Alexis had was mutual."

"Could you be more deluded?" Cherry snapped. "She's an eleven—"

"So we're right in each other's league," Denny said, gesturing to his body.

"—And she's married. With children. To someone who isn't you."

Denny smirked and shrugged. "Forbidden fruit is *always* better."

"Oh look, here I am, regretting it," Everly muttered.

"Gross!" Harper squealed, and the rest of the van burst out in insults.

Rylan exchanged amused glances with his mother, who remained silent.

For a moment, things felt almost normal.

Unfortunately, there was nothing normal about their situation. Rylan was exhausted. He'd wanted to shower and hit the sack after the hunt but had been waylaid by Everly's collapse. Now they were driving all over town to try to help Tammy, who clearly didn't want their help to begin with.

Being stuck in the SUV with Everly, which kept him in a constant state of half-transformation, was wearing him down. Her injuries were clearly wearing on her, too.

Callan swung off the highway onto a rough service road. Rylan knew it well, having done patrol out there in the past. Much like the other known shroudpool areas, the Darkfreys had worked secretly within the community to have the lake marked unsafe for public access, with some story about hazardous chemicals.

Not that it stopped everyone.

Sneaking in and scaring each other on the water's edge was something of a teenage rite of passage. That's why the Darkfreys kept the lake on their regular beat.

Rylan half hoped there would be a Darkfrey brace out there now, to have already stopped Tammy from entering the water.

But when the end of the road and the tall chain-link fence came into view, there were no other vehicles.

Once the SUV stopped moving, Rylan hopped from the passenger side as the others piled out around him. Callan, Denny, Lian, Cherry …

The other two were taking their time.

Rylan hovered uncertainly by, fighting against the change as best he could, as Harper reached back into the vehicle. Everly leaned heavily on her as she climbed out of the back seat.

The headlights of Rushelle's car coming to a stop behind them washed over Everly.

She looked … rough. Shadows grew beneath her eyes, purple against too-pale skin. Back in his bedroom, she'd piled her silvery hair into a messy bun and demanded to join them. Even though he and his mother had attempted to convince her to remain behind and rest, they'd failed.

He wished she had *listened*. She was in no shape to be out, much less on this wild goose chase to stop Tammy from doing something terrible.

Everly met his gaze and she straightened, linking arms with Harper.

She rolled her eyes, likely at the hard look on his face, and hissed, "I'm fine."

Tammy needed to be stopped before she became the lake's next victim, there was no doubt about that. But her recklessness pissed him off since it could be dangerous for Everly. Not just for her *being here* and insisting to help, but for the fact that her injury needed to be the top priority right now.

She wasn't fine.

Rylan didn't want her there, but he also didn't want her to be alone, out of his sight. Not until she was better. He'd only just gotten his arms under her when she'd fainted that morning …

If it happened again, would he be there to catch her?

8

Tammy hadn't expected the water to be *so* cold.

Granted, Shroudhaven and its surrounding areas weren't known for sun-kissed weather, but Myrkur Lake wasn't just cold—it was bone-numbingly frigid.

As soon as the water reached her knees, she began to shiver, which made moving forward harder and slower than it should have been.

Not a lick of morning sunlight pierced the heavy sky to offer her warmth, and a soup of fog swirled over the surface of the lake. She'd left her boots back on the bank, and her bare toes sank into deep, squelchy silt as she trudged farther into the water. After several moments, she couldn't feel her toes at all.

But what was a little frostbite if there was *any* possibility she could bring Blaise back? She was coming away from this with him, or not at all.

Either way, the rest of the world would be better off.

Vonny's hardened face and verbal assault were seared into Tammy's mind. She could take the hatred. It was the pain beneath that cut her to the quick.

The guilt Tammy lived with on a daily basis had built into a painful throbbing in Vonny's presence. When her curse brought her again to Dark Corner, right to the scene of the crime, she knew Vonny was right. She did wish things were different.

Vonny and her husband, Kole, wanted nothing more than to have their son back.

Tammy would give anything for the same.

When the water level reached up to touch its icy burn to her ribcage, she pushed off and fell into a shivering, painful swim.

The wind cut over her face and shaved head like thousands of tiny knives.

She jolted as something like bony fingers brushed against her leg, and her heartbeat pounded madly as she imagined a dozen terrible monsters beneath the black water.

She put on a burst of speed to get away from whatever it was.

The island sat dark and silent ahead. Her limbs burned and ached. It still seemed so far away.

A strong current passed beneath her, tangling her legs.

Tammy let out a yelp and lost her buoyancy, bobbing beneath the choppy surface.

The dark water swallowed her like a hungry weroth, sucking her down. Tammy kicked and flailed her arms, swimming furiously for the surface. She was in total darkness—not even the barest hint of morning light from above penetrated the water.

She managed to splash back into the air, gasping frantically for oxygen.

Turned around, she saw the headlights of two cars arriving.

Before they'd even fully stopped moving, doors opened and slammed, and several familiar silhouettes lined up on the shore.

Two led the charge, both of them jogging for the edge of the lake faster than the rest of the crew. A blinding spotlight popped on and swept the water.

Tammy threw up a hand as the beam landed on her face.

"Tammy!" Callan yelled. "Get out of there!"

"Come back," Lian called. "Please!"

Tammy pursed her lips in irritation, then turned around and started swimming again.

She'd already come this far. She intended to finish the journey.

The light jerked madly for a minute, and over the splashing of her arms, she thought she heard arguing on the shore.

Then the sound of more splashing joined hers.

Tammy halted and turned to see Callan, illuminated by the flashlight now in his mother's hand. He swam with Olympic swiftness toward Tammy.

"What the Everdark are you doing?" Tammy shrieked. "Don't follow me."

Callan kept swimming, so Tammy turned away, trying to get away from him. But she couldn't outpace his longer limbs.

As soon as he surfaced within arm's reach, she lashed out at him, splashing water his way. "Get *out* of here, Callan! I don't need you to babysit me."

"That's not ... Just stop, you have to go back, it's not safe." He eased forward, treading water with an irritating finesse—like everything else he did. *Infuriating.* His long hair was plastered to his face, putting his sharp cheekbones on display, and Lian's spotlight danced over him, making his concerned features sharper.

"Ugh, I told you not to worry about me. Just go."

Water dripped from his eyelashes as he stared her down. "I'm not leaving without you."

Tammy's heart fluttered, but she firmly shoved it down and away. "I've got to do this."

"What, die? Because that's all that's going to happen."

"Who cares?" Tammy said hotly.

She lifted her hands from the water, brandishing her blackened fingers. In the flashlight's beam, they looked even more charred and horrific than usual.

"I'm already cursed. Who cares what happens to me?"

"*I* do."

Tammy blinked the water from her eyes and a shiver ran from the nape of her neck to her toes.

Her teeth rattled as she spoke. "No, you don't. You just want to be a good little team leader. Just let me do this. I *have* to do this."

She whirled around and swam for the island once more. Hard fingers snatched at her arm and dragged her back. Tammy thrashed against Callan's grip.

Their legs tangled beneath as they both treaded water, and Callan didn't release her arm. His irises, shadowed by his brows, appeared black, but they sparkled like tiny universes.

"You aren't at fault for what happened to Blaise."

"I'm not? Gee, how dumb of me to think it was me, there, in my body, being at fault." Tammy attempted to yank her arm from his grasp to no avail.

His gaze landed heavily on her. Devastating. Judging.

He tugged her closer until their chests brushed together. Tammy froze, legs and arms going weak as his warmth came through their body armor.

"What happened to Blaise was an *accident*," Callan said softly.

"I couldn't hold on!" The words burst from her, raw and ragged as tears stung the back of her throat. "*We* went to Dark Corner. *We* started a ritual thinking we could close the shroudpool. *We* wanted to be big damn heroes. But *I* lost Blaise. *Me.*"

"So, what? You're just going to give up? Swim head-on into a beshadowing?"

"It's worth it." If there was a chance, any at all, she would sell her soul, she would trade places, she would *not* be careful what she wished for.

Nearby, the water splashed.

Callan and Tammy both whipped toward the sound. Tammy held her breath as her gaze swept the black surface.

"That wasn't you?" Tammy clarified, turning her wide eyes on Callan.

He shook his head and released her arm. "No."

Another splash. This time from behind Tammy. She turned around, arms knifing through the water as she searched wildly across the lake. Lian's spotlight pierced through the fog all around them, but under the glittering surface, the lake was a total blackout.

More movement—behind Callan.

His back bumped against hers. "We need to get out of here."

Lian's voice drifted from the shore. "Cal? What is it?"

Before he could respond, the water separated next to Tammy's elbow and a slick form crested over the surface. The water churned. Tammy let out a startled cry and darted back—into the empty space where Callan had been.

"Callan?" Tammy cried, whipping her head side to side.

There was no sign of him. She dove. Headfirst, down into the inky, skull-chilling water.

A burst of released air bubbled up against her face. Fingertips brushed against hers. She grabbed on, tight.

A slimy, snake-like thing wriggled past her, sliding across her lower back. Tammy pulled at Callan's hand, but could only feel them being dragged farther down, faster than she thought possible. The water whipped past her like a strong wind.

Something wrapped around her thigh, smooth and slippery but with a vice-like grip. It jerked at her body, pulling against the bond between her and Callan. She clung tight, adding her second hand. He squeezed back in return.

Lungs burning, Tammy kicked out with her free leg, trying to detach the creature, but she couldn't find the body beyond the tentacle. She didn't even know what the creature was, but considering she hadn't transformed into one of her shadyr forms, she knew it wasn't an eidolghast. Too bad, since if it had been, at least she'd have some way of defending herself.

A second slithery tentacle tangled around her foot, and something sharp sunk into her calf. A gasp of precious air escaped her mouth.

Don't panic. Don't panic. Don't panic.

If I vanish out of here and leave Callan alone, if he dies here because of me ... I could never ...

Her renewed kicking and struggling made no difference. The creature had an iron grip, and she was quickly losing feeling in her leg. She was losing feeling everywhere.

Oh my ghast. I'm going to die.

She wasn't afraid of death—not really. Not for her.

But she didn't want *him* to die.

Callan's fingernails dug into her skin and her small, blackened palm slipped through his. *Not again.*

She fought against the crushing emptiness of her lungs, putting all her energy into holding on as her senses faded. *I can't do it. I can't hold on.*

Blinding light flashed all around her, turning her eyelids pink.

Tammy's stomach lurched, and her eyes popped open. Golden illumination filled the underwater world around her, fading off into a murky horizon. The glow highlighted the shiny, ghost-pale hide of two oversized, squid-like creatures wrapped around her and Callan. Gaping, beaked maws detached in shock from their victim's flesh. Their bulbous eyes were a strange, milky white.

The squid things released Tammy and darted away, disappearing into the darkness beyond the light with a high-pitched squeal that sounded like a cry of pain.

Her gaze darted down, following them, and she watched, horrified, as dozens of hideous silhouettes beneath Callan swam away from the light in a cacophony of alien moans and screeches. Through the water, she could feel their screams in her bones.

Callan kicked up to her level, grabbed onto her, and together they swam for the surface. It was so far away. She flailed, real panic setting in as her lungs burned for oxygen. Callan gripped her arms and yanked her upward, dragging her alongside him.

Tammy breached the surface and sucked greedily at the air, her chest feeling like it was on the verge of exploding. She took two more deep breaths before Callan urged her forward with a gentle shove.

"Swim for the shore," he said, coughing out water.

Tammy blinked at him—he was glowing golden from beneath. Her eyes dropped to the water, which only moments before had been blacker than midnight, and realized it wasn't some spotlight up above shining into the water.

The lake was lit up from *within*.

"Tammy, go!"

The second shove woke her up, and she whirled around, throwing her already-tired, aching body into the fastest swimming she'd ever done. She swam without looking ahead, arm over arm, sucking in air between bursts of energy.

Her feet hit the ground, and she surged forward, digging her toes into the muck for more speed. Water splashed wildly around her body as she pumped her arms and legs for the shore, only turning briefly to check that Callan was still behind her. Once her feet were on solid ground, she managed to raise her head and look at the Howell team waiting on the banks up ahead.

Even though they were all there, they were entirely eclipsed by Everly.

She stood on the shore, her body a kaleidoscope of shimmering, white light. Her silver hair floated on an invisible breeze, and her eyes beamed like two small flashlights through the last remnants of morning fog.

Her feet hovered several inches off the ground, her body supported by multiple tendrils of light. Those same tendrils arced out of her fingertips and into the lake—the source of the glowing.

Tammy sloshed through the last of the shallows, a prickle of awe opening inside her. Everly looked otherworldly and magnificent. It wasn't the first time Tammy had seen her wield the strange power, but it would never be something that didn't leave her awestruck. She was like a goddess.

The light vanished before Tammy and Callan had fully left the water. The tendrils sucked back into Everly in a flash, and she dropped. Her legs crumpled beneath her. Rylan leaped forward, grabbing her before she could fall face-first into the lake.

Shivering in a way that made her eyeballs ache, Tammy prepared for an onslaught

from the team about her behavior. But all attention remained on Everly.

Everly was attempting to get her feet under her and push Rylan—whose body was mid-shift between vampire and something scaly—away. But her legs didn't seem to want to hold her up. Rylan kept his arms around her, and Lian stepped forward to peel back Everly's collar, exposing something red on her shoulder beneath the jacket.

"The cracks are spreading."

Harper gasped.

"Cracks?" Tammy asked, taking several more steps along the muddy bank in her bare feet. She noticed her shoes were clutched in Rushelle's arms like a teddy bear.

Everly coughed. "I'm fi—"

"Don't you dare say it." Rylan swept Everly into his arms, one arm behind her shoulders and the other behind her knees.

As he straightened, he glared at Tammy, looking even more dangerous in his strange, combined form. "I'm taking her to the car."

Then he stomped off with Everly.

Tammy watched them go, her stomach roiling with upset and swallowed water. Everly had saved her life. Callan's too. What had she paid for that?

Neither of them would have been in danger if Tammy hadn't come here.

It's always my fault. I'm the curse … always.

Lian fussed briefly over Callan, who waved her off.

Then her brown eyes zeroed in on Tammy. "What in the Everdark were you thinking?"

Callan watched her as well, and Tammy turned away, staring down at her bare, mud-caked toes. "I'm sorry. I just … I thought if I could make a wish to bring Blaise back, I could make everything right again. I could fix all the mistakes, not steal the artifact, not try that stupid ritual, not lose him. Then maybe they could forgive me. All three of them. Vonny, Kole, even Blaise …"

Callan shook his head and turned away from her.

Rushelle appeared by her side and wrapped her in a blanket, adding a warm hug over the top. "Glad you swam back to us, little duck."

Tammy clung to the blanket, but it did nothing to warm the frost in her heart.

Lian's gaze narrowed. "Wait, what artifact? Something from Darkfrey Estate?"

Tammy shook her head, her heart fluttering from Lian's intense gaze. "It belonged to the Mesmans. Blaise took it from their home the night of the … the night he died."

Lian cocked her head. "You're telling me Vonny Mesman had a shadyr relic?"

"Blaise said they had a few. I sort of always thought he was just lying to seem special, until he actually brought that one with him, that night."

Lian exchanged glances with Callan. "That seems a bit strange."

"It does."

Harper stepped up beside them but seemed to ignore their conversation. Her gaze was fixed out over the water, and her forehead crinkled.

When she opened her mouth, Tammy didn't expect her to start singing. Her voice was strong and rich against the wind cutting over the lake.

"Hungry light shines over the waves and my mermaid she yearns, when will I return, when will I return?" She paused, then turned to her gaping audience. "Hungry light shining over the waves. That's what we just saw, wasn't it?"

"I suppose?" Callan said. "But it's just a song."

Harper shook her head, her bright green eyes flashing. "There's also the last verse that references a star: My star shining bright, in love under the light. It's very teeth-and-stars-ish, don't you think? It has to mean something."

Rushelle, who had applied a blanket and hug to Callan, perked up. "I've never thought about the lighthouse that way, but it does sound a bit like that, what with how it works."

"How do you mean?" Lian asked.

"Oh, I sometimes forget I'm not with the Crybel's Cove crew anymore. Most shadyrs assume they keep the lighthouse going, right?"

Tammy, Lian, and Callan nodded.

"Nope!" Rushelle grinned. "The lighthouse has no keeper, isn't even hooked up to electricity. It just does its own thing. Has for a long, long time. Maybe fifty years. The bulb, if that's what it is, is powered by some kind of magic."

Harper spoke up. "Some kind of *light* magic. Like a piece of a hungry star!"

Lian frowned. "Maybe. What else do you know about it?"

Rushelle shrugged. "Not much. Don't know if anyone does. It's a kind of a 'if it ain't broke, don't fix it' situation, cos nobody wants to set foot on that island if they don't have to. What's this about, anyway? After more clues about Everly's glowy dealeo?"

Lian chewed at a thumbnail. "Yeah. And we need clues fast. Harper might be onto something. We don't have any other real leads."

"I agree it could be worth following up. Harper's got good instincts." Callan shoved his foot into his boot, despite the fact he was still dripping wet.

Several red marks marred his arms where the beshadowed squids had come for him, and Tammy realized with a terrible sinking feeling that tonight could have been so much worse.

Lian's gaze was heavy with concern as she watched her son. "I'm going to let the rest of you take point on the lighthouse excursion. I have an errand to run myself."

Rushelle stepped over by her side, dangling her car keys in one hand. "What are we doing, ma'am?"

"I've been thinking about the other missing shadyr artifacts since they didn't show up at Gorhanmere. If Vonny and Kole had one, maybe they have more."

Callan's eyebrows lowered. "The question is, why?"

Lian grabbed the keys from Rushelle. "I'd like to find out."

9

Lian yelled into the intercom at Darkfrey Estate's front gate for a solid twenty minutes before deciding that Vonny truly wasn't there. She didn't even consider talking to Kole. He'd been a lost cause for years.

Where could that woman have snuck off too?

She wasn't with her brace, apparently, not on duty, but not at the estate. Sounded shady as the Everdark to Lian.

Back on the road, Lian rubbed her eyes. She was exhausted. In all the turmoil of the last few days, she'd hardly slept a wink. She'd thought last night, with both her sons alive and under her roof again, she'd be able to get the rest she needed.

Then they decided to go out on a hunt. And every raw, motherly nerve ending inside Lian screamed for the duration of their absence. She'd paced the entire time, with Rushelle kindly topping up her teacup and insisting she wasn't tired, either.

Lian had only driven Rushelle's tiny yellow sports car once or twice, but the thrill of having the engine purr beneath her was just as exciting as the last time. Having raised two sons, she'd never had the option of a little two-seater with a speedometer that went all the way up to ludicrous.

Lian had sent Rushelle off with the rest of the team to prepare for the next mission, despite her insistence on sticking together. Rushelle was their only in with the Crybel's Cove crew, the offshoot of the Darkfreys that had jurisdiction over the sea.

And if the Howells were going to need a boat and access to Carnock Island, they needed an in with Crybel's Cove. Lian hated putting Rushelle in that position, but she hated the idea of not doing everything they could to help Everly even more.

Tammy's revelation that the Mesmans once had an artifact in their home crawled underneath Lian's skin. For as long as Mordan's lineage had ruled over Shroudhaven, they'd insisted that any shadyr artifact belonged in the estate's possession. Mordan was especially protective of them, keeping them under lock and key in his special, temperature-controlled storage area.

Although Lian didn't care for Mordan and his fascist ways, she had never truly been bothered by his decree. Most of the relics were either useless or too hazardous

to fall into *anyone's* hands, human or shadyr. As long as they sat in their glass cages at Darkfrey Manor, they weren't in dangerous hands.

Until she found out that they were.

All those empty cases ... The Bane, they'd found. Her sword, she had by her side as always. Tammy had revealed that the Mesmans definitely had one, maybe more.

But ... why?

Only an answer Vonny herself could give.

Shroudhaven was just coming to life when Lian rolled into the downtown area on her way home from the estate. It had been her home forever, and would likely continue to be home up until the day she died and could be buried alongside her husband in Shroudhaven Cemetery.

Pimeys had settled this town since the beginning, and they came from original shadyr stock, though not every Pimey carried the shadyr gene. Lian had happily traded her ancestral name to take her husband's, but she'd always be a Pimey at heart.

She passed Pimey's Diner—owned by one of her cousins—and a few blocks later, she rolled by Pimey's General Store, owned by her great uncle but run by one of her nephews who wasn't much older than Rylan.

She'd wanted a simple, safe life like that for her boys. But the world had other plans.

The sports car hummed along the street where the abandoned Rook's Theater rested. The old movie theater had closed a while back after a tragedy more than likely brought on by an eidolghast. The theater was usually empty, doors boarded and locked, the entire facade covered in graffiti.

Lian was surprised to recognize Harper's campervan parked at the curb in front of it. She slowed and whipped the tiny coupe over to park on the other side. The kids should all be back home, cleaning up from what just passed, and getting packed and prepared for what was next. She had to go check that everything was okay.

Lian moved to leave the car when Harper appeared from around the back of the theater, walking with a bit of a skip in her step as she jingled her keys and rounded the front of the van to the driver's side. She was alone.

But the street wasn't empty.

The moment Harper's van pulled away from the theater, Vonny Mesman appeared from the shadows. She wore her usual uniform of a Darkfrey jacket and tactical wear. Even though the hood was up, Lian easily recognized Vonny's platinum bob swinging freely.

Vonny was also alone.

Lian shoved open the driver's side door and jogged toward the front of the theater, heading Vonny off on the sidewalk. "I want a word with you."

Vonny drew up short, a flash of annoyance crossing her sharp features before she

grinned pleasantly. "Whatever about, Howell?"

"Tammy almost died this morning."

"Only almost? What a shame." Vonny shrugged and attempted to walk around her.

Lian tossed out an arm, nearly clotheslining the shorter woman. "We're not done. You hurt one of my kids. You sent her racing to certain death."

"Your 'kid' deserves whatever is coming to her," Vonny seethed, knocking Lian's arm away. "If some harsh truth sends her over the edge, then she knows it too."

"She's a wounded child!" Lian snapped.

She drew a breath and rubbed the bridge of her nose. She'd come to get info out of Vonny but her anger over Tammy was taking control.

She soothed it away, trying a new tack. "I knew you long before the accident that took Blaise. You weren't like this before. You used to have compassion. You used to care about Tammy. Can't you stop blaming her? Blaise's death was a tragic accident."

Vonny lunged forward, getting in Lian's face. She was several inches shorter than Lian, but no less threatening.

"He's not dead!"

"Either way, he's gone," Lian replied, careful to maintain her composure. "Tammy mourns him every day, just as you do. She carries the weight of her own guilt for not being able to save—"

"I don't give a shit about Tammy's guilt." Vonny sliced her palm through the air as if to cut off Lian's words.

Lian said, "If I hear you've spoken to her again, there will be consequences."

Vonny cocked her head. "It's cute you think I'm scared of your threats."

This time, it was Lian's turn to step closer. She lorded her height over Vonny and tightened her jaw, putting the full force of her 'mother bear' fury into her eyes. "Don't you remember sparring class, Mesman? Or was the way I beat you into a pulp so humiliating you wiped it from your memory?"

Nothing but their breaths fell between them for several long seconds.

Then Vonny took a single step back—relenting.

Dear ghast, miracles do happen.

Vonny glanced away, her eyes on the street rather than on Lian. "Look, I have places to be—"

"One more thing," Lian interrupted.

Vonny sighed, tucking her hands into the pockets of her jacket. "What?"

"I know shadyr artifacts are missing from Darkfrey's private collection."

Vonny's eyebrows drew together. "And how might you know that?"

Lian considered her next words. She didn't want to come out and accuse Vonny of taking them. That wouldn't get them anywhere. Lian had to try another strategy

to get her to drop some clue about where they were and why.

"I was told the Gorhanmere shadyrs had them, but they only had one. Do you have any idea where the rest might be?"

"Apart from the ones you stole, no. Why are you looking for them?"

Lian hedged her bets—how much could she tell Vonny without compromising the situation? She couldn't imagine the Vonny Mesman she'd once known had turned *completely* evil in the interim, even with her son's death tossing her into existential denial.

"Everly's in trouble," Lian said carefully. "We're running out of options to help her, so I'm investigating every possible path."

Vonny blinked, then coughed a short laugh. "Everly? The human?"

"Not *only* human."

"Whatever she is, she's not a shadyr. Quit wasting your time trying to fix a cockroach."

A pang hit Lian straight in the chest. "Is that what you think? Anyone without shadyr blood is nothing more than a bug?"

"We're the superior species, Howell, whether you like it or not."

Lian clenched her hands into fists and carefully took hold of her emotions. There was no getting through to this woman. But Lian would make sure she didn't hurt her kids again.

"We're done here. I'm going to be keeping an eye on you. Because if you're happy to stand by and watch people die, if you're driving kids to their death, who knows what else you're up to."

Vonny bared her teeth.

Lian remained silent, planted to the sidewalk in front of Rook's Theater. Vonny glanced past her, then back, then past her again before grimacing. She whipped her phone from her pocket, the screen glowing to life as she marched away.

Lian glanced at the theater as well, before following Vonny down the street.

Because as little information as she'd gotten out of that discussion, she was now certain of one thing.

Vonny Mesman was up to *something*.

The wind on the docks at Crybel's Cove was furious, as if the ocean was trying to warn them away. Everly gingerly climbed from the back of the Howells' SUV onto the asphalt. Stray strands of hair whipped against her cheeks in the gale. She glanced up at the clouds, nervous at how dark they'd become.

The team had taken an hour at Howell House to pack supplies for the journey. Everly's small daypack held a flashlight, extra clothes, a few tools, some non-perishable food, and a water bottle.

She hooked her arm through the strap and fell into step with the rest of the team. Their packs looked like something elite special forces would carry, filled with survival kits, paracord, flares, and first aid kits—the kind with tourniquets and sutures rather than Band-Aids and cotton balls.

Everly kept pace, determined to prove she could walk and function on her own, no matter how weak she felt. Back at the house, she'd wanted desperately to crawl into bed and stay there, to sleep, to not feel the constant burning pain in her arm and hand, but the whole purpose of this journey was to figure out answers to her affliction.

If she let the Howell team venture into any kind of danger without her, and something bad happened, she'd never be able to live with herself.

So she'd splashed water on her face, double-fisted two energy drinks, and shoved her exhaustion as deep as it could go. The pain from her cracking arms, however, she couldn't do much about. Ibuprofen wasn't even touching it. It had spread all the way up to her shoulder on the side with Rylan's cut. Zozo's spread slower but was still larger than before.

Rylan's boots creaked on the dock's wide planks as he walked nearby. Since Everly had collapsed at the house, he had stayed close, but his expression remained remote.

Now they weren't stuck in a car together, he seemed to be hovering on the edges of her effect on him. Far enough away that he remained in human form, but close enough that holding his form clearly took some effort.

He looks as tired as I feel.

The whole team did. But Everly's condition had already worsened. They didn't have the luxury of waiting. Another reason why she refused for them to make this journey alone.

Everly had learned on the way over that Crybel's Cove—the small township seated between Shroudhaven and the ocean—had a Darkfrey team put in place specifically to keep shroudpools from forming out at sea.

Two members of the team waited at the edge of the pier next to a small fishing boat. Their waders and linen shirts were more suited for deep-sea fishing than ghast hunting, but they wore the standard Darkfrey jackets.

One man was older, closer to Lian's age, with salt and pepper hair and a wind-weathered face. His skin was deeply tanned, and the bronzed color made his icy-blue eyes glow. The younger man was closer to Everly's age with blond hair that hung shaggy over his forehead.

Rushelle took the lead as the team crossed the splintered planks of the pier.

She grinned as she greeted the two men. "Hey, fellas."

"Rush," the older man replied, a hint of sheepishness in his gruff tone. "Been a while."

Rushelle turned her sunny smile back to the Howell team. "This is my uncle, Flint, and my cousin, Layton. They've agreed to take us to Carnock Island. They tried to kill me once, so they owe me a favor."

Everly shot a look at Tammy, who returned the astonishment by mouthing, "*What the …?*"

Flint cleared his throat awkwardly. "It wasn't really like that. It was meant to be a teaching moment."

"And hoo boy did it teach me!" Rushelle said. "Now, we're on a pretty sensitive time crunch. Are we all set to board?"

"All set. And listen, we're sorry about how things went down. But this is a one-time deal. We aren't meant to be running joy rides out to the island. Not for anybody. Including whatever you lot are meant to be." He widened one eye as he took them in.

Rushelle, still in pinup makeup. Rylan, clearly struggling to hold human form. Denny and Cherry squabbled about something over to one side. Tammy was trying to look the shadyr soldier part but seemed to be barely holding it together, and Callan seemed more interested in keeping a worried eye on her than on the conversation.

Everly could only guess how rough she herself looked. She'd already had to take her small pack off and put it at her feet because it was making her tired.

"We're in a hurry, is what we are," Rylan grumbled, heading toward the boat.

Everly spoke up. "Can't leave yet. We're still waiting on Harper."

As if summoned by her statement, the rumble of vintage engine announced the campervan as it pulled in behind them. Harper bounced out of the driver's side seat, shouldered her pack, and locked up. She sashayed along the docks like she'd stepped off a photoshoot. Even Everly did a double-take.

Where did she get rose-gold hiking boots from? Are they new?

Everly didn't see Harper pack, so could only guess what filled the well-stuffed backpack. She could see Harper's personalized axe hanging from her belt holster. She'd also taken the time to freshen her makeup—probably in the car on the way, something she often did that terrorized Everly in the passenger seat.

Callan raised an eyebrow at Harper as she joined them. "All done?"

"Yup, should be safe and sound."

They'd decided it wasn't a good idea for the Bane to sit in the camper while they were gone, or unguarded in one of their homes. They also didn't think keeping it too close to Everly was for the best, either, in case it exacerbated her condition. Harper had ducked away while the others packed to hide it somewhere safe.

She clapped her hands and bobbed on her toes, looking entirely too energized compared to the rest of them. "Is it time? Are we going?"

The dull hum of a vibrating phone came from Cherry, and he fished it out.

"BRB," he said, his brow furrowed as he hurried off to answer the call.

Rushelle checked her own phone, then caught Rylan's eye. "I'm worried about your mom. She's a tough lady, but nobody should be alone in Shroudhaven. Ever."

Callan smirked at his brother. "You would know, wouldn't you, sleeping beauty?"

Rylan made no reply, but color rose in his cheeks. A sensation Everly too was experiencing. Rylan wouldn't have told Callan about what happened in her dreams, would he? No. Everly couldn't see him sharing that particular experience any time soon. But he clearly still remembered it himself.

"What are you thinking?" Rylan asked Rushelle. "You want to go after her?"

She nodded. "Now I've sorted out your passage, you think you kids can handle this without me?"

"Of course." Callan handed over the SUV keys. "We've got Harper's van."

Cherry returned, his face twisted in confusion and his phone dangling from one hand. "You sure? Because you're another shadyr down. That was Jasper asking for my help. It seemed kind of urgent."

Harper stepped closer to him. "Everything okay?"

Cherry ran a hand up through his red hair. "I ... have no idea. I wouldn't leave if it didn't seem important. Rush, can you drop me downtown?"

"Of course, sugar. I'll drive you." She turned back to her cousin and uncle and in a low, dangerous voice, she added, "You're going to take care of my friends, now, aren't you? You're not going to leave them to die like you did me?"

Harper and Everly exchanged wide-eyed glances.

Flint nodded. "We'll get them to the island safely. You have my word."

Rushelle brightened again, did a quick round of hugs, and headed off with Cherry to the SUV.

Rylan glanced around at the remaining team. "Looks like it's just us. Let's get moving."

Everly picked up her backpack of supplies, but before she could toss it over her shoulder, Rylan snatched it and put it on his with his own pack. He shimmered into vampire form through a gust of black mist, then stomped away to the boat without another word.

Everly didn't hate that he was being protective of her, but he acted so put out by having to do so that it only made her feel worse. After the incident at the lake, and her second collapse, Rylan had told her in no uncertain terms that she wasn't to use her powers again. No matter what.

Even she had to admit that the cracking spread much faster when she did.

The fishing trawler swayed on the waves as Everly stepped onto it from the dock. Harper came after her, carrying a bag of her own, and the two of them were directed to go into the cabin by the stoic Layton.

"I'm loving this whole sailor slash shadyr aesthetic," Harper murmured, glancing over her shoulder as she stepped through the narrow door. "But what the heck did Rush mean when she said they left her to die?"

"I'm still wondering that myself." Everly followed her into the claustrophobic aisle.

They passed a small corridor with a pair of bunkbeds on each side and bathroom access, dumped their packs, and headed up front to the cabin.

A bench ran the length of the room and wrapped around one corner where a table was anchored to the floor, walled in by a small kitchenette and bar situation.

The far wall held a bank of windows that looked out over the sea, lined underneath with high-tech screens and controls. Rylan had taken a seat up there beside Flint. Everly eased onto the bench near Tammy and Callan, and Harper plopped down next to her, squeezing in tight.

Denny sauntered in like he owned the boat, heading right for the mini fridge. "What, no beer?"

Harper let out a sound of disgust. "We should've left him behind."

Callan sighed. "As annoying as he is, he's also a relatively capable shadyr. Sometimes. And we need numbers. We don't know what we're walking into."

Denny snatched a soda and popped the top.

"Booyah! 'Capable shadyr.' You hear that? Don't you forget it, either," he said, then tossed back a big swig and climbed into a bunk.

Callan winced. "I should not have said that loud enough for him to hear."

"Yet he didn't seem to hear the 'relatively' or 'sometimes,' did he?" Tammy said.

Layton finished up on the exterior deck as rain began to spatter on the windows, and headed in to join Flint at the steering wheel.

As the boat's engine whirred and they pulled away from the dock, Harper leaned over Everly and said, "Psst. Cal. What's the sitch on Rush and these guys? They tried to *kill* her? Are we safe with them?"

Callan's mouth twisted. "It's no secret that Rush has never been interested in the shadyr mission. All she wants to do is work on those weird fantasy romance satire novels she's always tapping away on her laptop."

Denny snorted from around the corner. "Like a woman could write a *proper* novel."

Tammy, slouched on the bench next to Callan with her black hands shoved into the pockets of her hoodie, leaned up to say, "They're really good, actually."

Harper gasped, her eyes glittering. "You've read them?"

Tammy shrugged bashfully. "I was bored."

"Oh Em Gee! Can we fangirl for a sec? 'Hunted for the Far King' is my absolute fave. How about you?"

Tammy's jaw dropped, as though the idea of interacting with Harper over a shared passion horrified her.

Callan lowered his voice and side-eyed Tammy. "Wait. Aren't they, um, erotic?"

"Kill me now," Tammy groaned and slouched deeper into her hoodie.

"Don't be a child," Harper scolded him. "And yes, they are super hot. The spice, it's just, chef's kiss!"

Everly squinted and shook her head. "And what do her books have to do with these guys?"

"Right, that." Callan dropped his voice to a whisper as Layton trudged by on his way out of the cabin. "Rush was part of the Crybel's Cove team before she came to us. Apparently, they got fed up with her attitude toward her duties and left her alone in a deadly situation. Luckily, Mom saved her."

Harper sighed. "Sounds like Rush got double lucky getting away from these guys. And now she's free to bring her gift of delicious smut to the world."

Callan chuckled. "Yeah, and the irony of it is, Rush has been more than happy to help Mom out with shadyr stuff when needed. And she's a natural, have you seen her fight?"

Everly nodded, remembering her ferocity at Rook's Hotel.

"She just doesn't want to be fighting all the time. Which is fair. Some shadyrs don't understand that, though. For some, there is only the mission, and if you don't stick to it, you're a traitor."

Layton banged through the door into the cabin, swiping water off his face and ruffling his wet hair. "It's getting sketchy out there."

Flint spoke up, though he didn't turn away from the rain-darkened view outside. "Weather turns on a dime out this way. It's not abnormal for a gale to rise up out of the blue, or go away just as fast."

Sleet pelted the window, and Everly could hardly see outside.

Rylan glared at the gray sky. "Should we be worried?"

"Probably not," Flint replied, punctuated by boat-shaking thunder. "Maybe."

Twenty worried minutes later, Carnock Island formed from the stormy darkness ahead, a hulking silhouette that rose from the sea. High above, the lighthouse beam slowly circled like a shooting star, sparkling through the lashing rain.

The wind whipped around the boat, battering at the sides like fists while the waves tossed them about recklessly. Everly sat on the edge of the bench, clinging to the seat beneath her so she wouldn't be thrown to the floor. Her heart had lodged in her throat,

and fear chilled her spine as the storm gained potency.

An anxious atmosphere filled the cabin. Everyone stared ahead of the boat as if they were heading toward certain doom. Flint and Layton stood at the helm, Layton assisting with gadgets Everly didn't understand while Flint's attention remained focused on steering through the rain.

The sense of impending doom only intensified when, as the boat drew ever closer to the dark shore, Flint muttered, "Well. That's not good news."

Rylan stood, one hand latching onto a railing. "What is it?"

Flint and Layton exchanged glances, and Flint met Rylan's gaze. "The lighthouse dock's gone."

Rylan's brow furrowed. "What do you mean, gone?"

"Absent, no longer there, vanished—"

Rylan's growl cut Flint off.

The old man shrugged. "Anyway, we can't set you down here. In this weather, I'd recommend not letting you out anywhere, but if you insist, there's a small bay back along the island that might be calm enough that we don't all get smashed to pieces on rocks."

"That will be a lot farther from where we want to be, won't it?" Everly asked.

"We came prepared to cross the island if we needed to," Rylan said.

"I'm not sure we were quite prepared for this." Callan gestured to the weather. "We could try again tomorrow, bring Cherry, Rush, and Mom along for backup."

A large wave smashed the side of the boat, rocking it violently.

Flint flashed an irritated glare over his shoulder. "We brought you to the island like we promised Rush, but one time only. We can't dock here, and in this weather, it's not safe for us to remain on the sea. So I suggest you make a decision—are you staying or are you coming back with us?"

10

The storm had eased in the shelter of the bay, but the water was still beyond choppy. Everly stared down at the restless surface of the ocean and the dinghy bobbing there. The shore wasn't that far away from Flint's fishing trawler, but the tiny rowboat looked rickety enough to turn into toothpicks the minute a wave slammed into it.

And all six of them were meant to ride the thing through four-foot waves?

Harper and Tammy descended first, keeping their weight low and balanced as they crawled into the rocking boat.

Flint handed Rylan a satellite phone. "I have no idea what it's going to be like on the island, if this will even work. But if you can get a signal to us when your mission is complete, we'll try to come back for you."

A muscle ticked in Rylan's jaw. "That's a lot of ifs."

As they were all standing in a group around the ladder, he was back in vampire form again, making his expression more vicious.

Callan placed a calming hand on his brother's shoulder and addressed Flint with a stoic nod. "We appreciate your help. Hopefully we won't be long."

Layton stared through the rain at the island. "From what we've seen, the established shroudpools are mostly on the north side of the island. If you keep south, hopefully you'll avoid the worst of it."

Callan and Denny headed down next, then Rylan stepped onto the short ladder and reached back for Everly's hand. Biting her lip, she took it. Even though the ladder was only three rungs, both the trawler and the dinghy rocked about wildly, and she didn't trust her arms to have the strength to hold on. They stepped down the ladder together, one of Rylan's arms around her waist to keep her from slipping.

The team piled shoulder to shoulder into the small rowboat, balancing packs between them.

Once everyone was seated, Layton leaned over to toss them the rope. "Try and get to the beach fast. Nyevmers are rare, but still a threat. Best to stay out of the water."

"Nyevmers?" Everly asked, a slight catch in her throat.

She clutched Harper's leg. The seasickness hadn't bothered her much on the larger fishing boat. The smaller dinghy was like a buoy in the middle of a hurricane. The constant up and down was liable to make her vomit before they reached the shore.

Rylan picked up one oar and thrust the other at Denny beside him. "Water-dwelling eidolghasts."

"Oh. Good," Everly replied, blinking fast against the rain. "Sea monsters. Coolcoolcool."

Silence fell over the rowboat, broken only by rumbling thunder that Everly couldn't tell was coming or going. Denny and Rylan paddled with efficiency, gliding the rowboat over the waves. Every few feet, a wave would slap into the prow and send water splashing over the occupants, soaking them more thoroughly than the rain already had.

All the while, high above the mountainous island, the lighthouse beacon rotated. Circling. Circling. Circling.

The rowboat scraped against the sand with a jarring thud. The island stretched ahead and above. Menacing. Ominous. Shrouded in fog, with the illuminated lighthouse up above like the lure on an angler fish.

Lowering his oar, Rylan slid over the side and splashed into water up to his knees. Callan half-stood to join him, but with one hand Rylan grabbed the prow and tugged the boat and its occupants onto the sand.

"You know, I can almost see an upside to being shifted all the time," Callan said as he stood up, shouldered his pack, then hopped out of the dinghy.

Rylan bared his sharp fangs at his brother. "Yeah, means I can beat your smart ass whenever I want."

The rest of the team loaded up and followed, then Rylan finished dragging the boat well out of reach of the ocean.

Rylan halted on the sand in his Goldilocks distance away from Everly and shook off the vampire form as if to make a point. Everly couldn't be sure, but it seemed like he was closer than before. His olive-green eyes roamed the dark wall of trees that covered the steep hill.

"I wonder what we're going to find in there."

Harper pumped her arms in the air like a cheerleader. "Everly's cure! Everly's cure!"

"Jeez, save some optimism for the rest of us," Tammy grumbled. "'Cause I am fresh out."

Callan crunched over the sand to stand beside her. "Come on, let's treat this as an island holiday."

"Ugh, you too?"

Rylan wiped water from his face. "We're going in. Stick close together. Keep your eyes on the dark. The place could be crawling with eidolghasts and who knows what

else. Cal—can you take the lead? Denny, can you handle the rear?"

"Don't say something like that to him!" Harper hissed.

Denny smirked and nodded.

"Tammy, you're up with me," Callan said and marched forward.

She grumbled about babysitting but hustled to catch up. Harper scurried forward, probably realizing she didn't want to be *the rear* directly in front of Denny, which left Everly and Rylan in the middle together, no doubt as he'd intended. As he took his place behind her, he returned to vampire form.

The group set off over the narrow strip of beach toward the woods.

Everly glanced back at Rylan. "I'm sorry. About all of this. About ... what I do to you."

He remained silent for a moment, then in his gravelly voice muttered, "You have no idea ..."

Everly winced. "Is it bad? Hard I mean, transforming involuntarily?"

"Not too bad. I've been able to at least direct my form into something familiar like vampire or werewolf, which means it's not much of a strain. But there are other eidolghast energies coming from you as well. Rare ones. A bit of nyevmer. Some auerdax. Even some I have no idea what they are. Forms I've never experienced before, trying to come out."

Cold wind whipped around Everly, driving raindrops into her eyes. "So, I'm just overflowing with eidolghast energy. Great. Great. Good to know."

Fog drifted in and out of the thick trees like a tide. An overgrown path marked by a weathered wooden sign came into view. A carved impression of a lighthouse sat above a blood-red arrow pointing straight ahead.

The minute the trees closed around them, the howling wind, crashing waves, and steady rain all vanished. The forest was like a vacuum, sucking up all sound so thoroughly that it couldn't be natural. Everly rubbed her ears to make sure she hadn't suddenly gone deaf.

Beyond their footsteps on the ground, there was nothing. No birdsong. No insects. No hint of the storm raging around the island.

Just empty, eerie stillness.

It was also dark. Much darker than it should have been.

One by one, flashlights winked on, dispelling some of the gloom. Outside their bright bubble the darkness was a deeper black than physically possible. Like the shadows were no longer a trick of the light but living, sentient beasts.

As much as Everly wanted to keep her head down and pretend there was nothing to fear, she followed Callan's instructions and eyed the darkness around them, watching for danger.

Which was how she saw the woman.

A tattered white dress trailed around her as the woman paced slow, awkward steps through the trees in the distance. Everly's breath caught in her throat, and she came to a sudden stop.

"Over there," she whispered.

Also hushed, Harper said, "Is that …?"

Callan hissed, "Shh!"

The woman turned toward the sound.

She had no face.

Where her eyes should have been were only smooth, empty sockets covered by dark skin. Her nose and lips protruded slightly but were smoothed away as if someone had stretched an ebony veil over her face. Long, dark hair tangled in strands around her, soaking wet.

Her head angled and twisted toward them in jerky movements.

Callan kept his hands up, signaling them all to stay still, stay silent. The whole team froze, mouths closed, barely breathing. Long moments later, the ghostly woman turned and walked away. Where her feet touched the ground, glowing spots sizzled. Dark shapes shifted around her like a crowd of transparent people, rippling and darting, as if she were tiptoeing among an army of shadows.

Then, just like that, she vanished.

The Howell shadyrs relaxed and turned back to the path, but Harper and Everly remained wide-eyed.

"Was that a ghost?" Everly said.

Harper let out a long, shaky breath. "And more importantly, where was her *face*?"

Callan replied, "You never know what you're going to find in a beshadowing. Ghostly, undead, twisted remains of human victims aren't uncommon. You're lucky she had no face and didn't see us. For all we know, she could hurt us. Stay vigilant if she returns."

Harper made a puppy-dog expression. "Human victims? I wonder what her story was."

Everly matched her pout. "Aw! Are you being sympathetic to a ghost? If I hadn't told you recently, I love you."

Harper reached back for Everly's hand as they returned to their march.

Along their line, heads turned side to side, keeping all angles around them monitored.

Softly, the quiet of the forest changed. Distant at first, a long, low groan broke through the silence. The team exchanged glances, but the source of the sound couldn't be identified.

Another whine started up, this one louder and with an almost human-like resonance behind it. Then a third, higher in tone, joined it, and then another, until a chorus arose within the forest, like a hospital ward filled with pain.

"More ghosts?" Everly asked.

"It sounds like someone being tortured," Harper added.

Tammy grumbled, "It's coming from the trees. The one at Dark Corner does this sometimes."

Denny reached around to his pack and drew out a wicked-looking machete. "As long as they don't start moving."

Harper tapped the axe by her side, as though reassuring herself it was still there. Everly squeezed her hand lightly.

"I'm getting the hint of a weroth stalking around out there somewhere," Tammy muttered.

Callan said, "Yeah, not close though. Hopefully it stays that way."

The ground turned steep beneath Everly's boots. After several moments, she and Harper were forced to release each other and walk single file as the undergrowth crept out of the trees and onto the path. Everly's calves burned from the effort of climbing, and her injured arm throbbed in time with her heartbeat. Her head swam and she focused on the solid ground beneath her feet.

The trees kept up their mournful cries until a sudden rustling cut them off. Callan threw his arms out to stop the team.

Everly clutched her flashlight, ready to turn it into a weapon if required.

She recognized the familiar leaping gait of deer. She let out a sigh of relief, glad it wasn't more creepy faceless ghosts, until one of them passed through the beam of her flashlight.

Tawny body, four spindly legs ...

But where its head should have been, instead there was an octopus.

The cephalopod parts were pale pink and slimy, fading into their fur-covered bodies like some kind of twisted centaur. Long, curling tentacles dangled down the creatures' chests, whipping around as they leaped over the undergrowth, directly toward Everly and the others.

"Move," Rylan yelled.

As one, the team turned, running along the path from the swarm of grotesque chimeras.

The creature at the lead lifted its cephalopod limbs and released an ear-splitting, high-pitched squeal like the cry of a wounded rabbit. The trees joined in, howling dreadfully.

Everly kept her sore arms tucked in tight, and her eyes darted between the pursuing

monsters and the path. Her chest ached, each breath hard to draw. She pushed through the pain, running her fastest.

The crash of bodies through bushes came from ahead as the path narrowed. Denny moved to the front, swinging his machete to clear away plants as he ran.

A protruding root caught Everly's foot, and she stumbled. Rylan grabbed her jacket and hoisted her back to her feet before she could hit the dirt. He moved in front of her, taking her hand and dragging her through the ever-thickening foliage. Small hooves trampled the ground behind them.

The touch of a tentacle brushed the back of Everly's neck.

Then the path disappeared.

Even with Denny going berserk up front, their pace slowed significantly. Rylan swore then put Everly in front of him again, turning to confront the pursuing beasts.

"Look," he called out.

The others slowed, glancing back.

The octopus-headed deer had stopped. They stood eerily still, staring with bulbous white eyes. Then they bounded away in the opposite direction.

"When the monster chasing you gets scared and runs the other way ... That's always a *good* sign, isn't it?" Harper muttered.

"We're for sure going to die here," Tammy agreed.

Harper's flashlight blinked on and off, and she let out a short, sharp curse, then banged the heel of her hand against it. It blinked a few more times, then extinguished entirely.

Callan and Tammy's lights went dark, too. Within seconds, only Everly's was left, and then it sputtered out, plunging them into darkness.

The trees went silent all at once.

Callan cleared his throat. "If this isn't the beshadowing that keeps on giving."

Everly reached for Harper, her heartbeat racing in her throat. She couldn't see anything. Even the shadyrs, who had better dark vision, seemed unsure, unable to tell where to move next.

"I could try to use my powers, give us some light."

"No," Rylan said from somewhere nearby.

"Just a bit, just enough to see."

Harper sighed from her left. "Gotta agree with Rylan on this one. It's not worth it. You keep those powers closed up tight. No matter what. We can't have you shattering to bits before we even get to the lighthouse."

A bright beam flashed over the canopy, and the team squinted away from it. It turned the forest a dull, eerie gray before it circled away, and everything went dark again.

"Speak of the devil," Harper sang.

"We must be close," Rylan said. "Wait for the next pass, then move."

A long, grim moment later, the lighthouse's strange glow circled back around. As the light fell on Everly, her skin tingled.

"Go," Callan called, and they jogged forward.

The pale illumination gave the whole forest a kind of underwater ambiance. Aiming for the source of the beam, they pressed forward until they lost visibility again.

At least the darkness gives me a chance to catch my breath.

Everly's entire body ached, and even the slower speed at which they pressed through the undergrowth left her gasping. She had all the symptoms of a full-blown panic attack but knew it was the Bane wounds spreading the weakness through her.

Every time the lighthouse beam came around, Everly got an eyeful of the forest around them. The trees were spaced farther apart in this area of the woods and draped in thick vines as large around as Everly's thighs. And each time the beam washed across Everly, it roused the dragon.

It liked that light. It *wanted* that light. Everly shivered.

In darkness once more, Tammy whispered, "What's that?"

"What's what?" Callan replied.

"Look off to the right and upward when the light comes back around."

Everly trained her gaze on the area Tammy had indicated and waited. The light returned.

A huge, oval shadow hung from the vines in the trees.

"What *is* that?" Callan squinted at the shape.

Nobody moved, too busy taking in the looming silhouette and trying to determine its risk.

Everly was able to make out a rounded, canoe-like shape, longer than a train carriage, but little else.

Denny, on the other hand, gasped. "Well, I'll be an eidolghasts uncle. It's a submarine."

He took off into the underbrush, crashing over the forest floor.

"Dude! What are you doing?" Callan called, lurching around the women and leaping over a fallen tree trunk to snatch at Denny's arm.

He missed.

Rylan hissed, "Get back here, you idiot!"

Denny ignored them both. The lighthouse beam illuminated him trampling through the forest on a trajectory for the hanging submarine.

Callan sighed. "We have to stick together."

"Do we though? We could just leave him," Harper suggested.

"Dark," Tammy said. "I like it."

"Come on." Callan moved off after Denny, the others falling in behind.

Everly watched the canopy for glimpses of the sub, surprised at how large it was, and how delicately it hung from the thick vines.

As they joined Denny beneath the craft, he said, "Son of a ghast. It's a U-boat."

The lighthouse beam left and Everly blinked at the darkness overhead. Even without the glow to silhouette the monstrosity, she could sense it there. Heavy. Choking.

"Those bastards tore up the Atlantic Seaboard. They hunted Allied shipping vessels in packs. A heap of 'em went missing after World War II."

"But how did it end up here? Up *there*?" Harper asked.

The light came back around as Denny shrugged, his gaze still on the craft. He pointed at a gaping hole in the vessel.

"See that? Bet an Allied sub took it down, Nazis and all. Otherwise, it looks untouched. Can you imagine what treasures are inside that thing?" Denny let out a whistle. "I'm going in."

"Are you kidding?" Rylan grabbed the back of Denny's jacket. "We're in the middle of a beshadowed forest. You are *not* climbing into the ruins of a Nazi submarine."

Denny groaned, trying to shake Rylan's grip. "Aw, come on. You never know what we'll find. Those guys were up to all kinds of wild stuff. The Holy Grail could be in there for all we know. That'd be a way to fix up your girlfriend."

Rylan pulled Denny in close, the light flashing on his stone-cold vampire face. "We've been here too long already."

"Let's keep moving," Callan said.

Something pungent hit Everly's nose and she gagged.

Beside her, Harper said, "Oh my ghast, *warn* a girl before you let one rip, you neanderthal."

"It wasn't me!" Denny replied.

"That's not gas," Rylan said. "That's death."

The smell grew stronger.

Metal groaned like a whale's song, and in the eerie gray light, a horde of humanoid figures poured from the cavernous hole in the side of the U-boat.

Then the light left them again.

11

The inky black between rotations of the lighthouse beam held no ambient light at all.

Just chilling darkness, filled with rustling and stomping, strange grunts, hissing sounds, and the squelch of wet fabric.

"Everly?" Rylan called out.

"I'm over here," she yelled back.

Footsteps pounded her way.

Callan's voice covered the sound. "Tammy, to your left!"

"I know!"

Disturbing, gurgling growls filled the air.

Denny shouted, "At least a dozen of 'em! More still coming!"

A dozen of *what?*

The shadyrs could see at least something in the low light. Everly blinked, trying to take anything in.

I might as well be blind.

She still held her flashlight, so she whipped it up and shook it, desperately hoping the bulb would come back on. When that didn't work, she beat it against her thigh.

Come on, come on!

Nothing. It was dead.

A pained cry came from across the space, sounding like either Tammy or Harper. Rylan grunted and a hailstorm of fist-meeting-flesh sounds came from nearby.

I need to see what's going on. I need to help.

Holding her least shattered arm up in front of her blind eyes, she focused on the dragon inside her. It was wounded, angry, hungry, but she felt almost like she was getting a grip on it and its powers. The sulking state of the being inside her seemed to make it easier to control.

A bright glow emanated from her fingertips, and agony shot along the length of her arm, right up to the base of her skull. Everly cried out.

"Stop it!" Rylan barked at her.

The pain in her hand and the fury in his eyes made her pull the dragon's power back inside herself. Before the light faded out again, she could see at least five human figures encircling him, limbs thrashing. Then darkness again.

"I have to do something!" Everly yelled back.

"Just stay safe." Harper's words were punctuated with a loud *oof* and the chop of her axe. "We've got this."

The lighthouse beacon circled around again, casting a pale beam across the scene as the light filtered in between the twisted trees. Everly's eyes widened.

When the things had come out of the U-boat, they'd appeared humanoid. Now Everly could see that they weren't *living* humans, and they weren't *entirely* human either.

They had dripping, bloated bodies covered in barnacles, and eyes cloudy from death ... where they hadn't rotted away entirely.

Rather than normal noses and mouths, they had sloping, fish-like snouts of scaly, pallid skin. Several had missing limbs, or limbs where the skin had been torn away to the bone. Some of their uniforms had remained eerily intact, though. Light passed over familiar red armbands, and Everly froze, shocked to see something in real life that she'd only ever seen in historical photographs.

The crew of the U-boat, beshadowed back to a twisted semblance of life, undead and murderous.

There were so many of them.

Callan, Tammy, and Denny remained in human form, with no eidolghasts nearby to trigger a change that could give them an advantage. Denny hacked into the zombies with his machete. Callan and Tammy stood back-to-back, large hunting knives in hand as the horde edged in on them. Harper had her axe out, charging toward the heart of the fray.

"Harper!" *What is she doing?*

Everly wanted to run in and drag her human friend back to relative safety.

But Rylan created a barrier between the chaos and Everly. The soggy creatures swarmed him, pummeling at his pale, vampire-form skin, trying to get their jagged teeth into him. Any time one attempted to shamble past him toward Everly, he wrenched it back into melee with him.

A zombie swiped a thick, meaty arm at Rylan's face, and it hit with a terrible crack. Rylan bared his vampire teeth, covered in blood, swinging to strike back.

Darkness came again.

Everly was sorely tempted to bring out the dragon, to let it feed on these long-dead corpses—if they even still had souls. But her arms throbbed mercilessly.

She hadn't liked making the choice, but she'd let the dragon eat at Myrkur Lake, taking the lives of several of the strange, beshadowed marine creatures there. She'd

hoped that would somehow help it heal, but it only made things worse.

Even what little she'd done there had taken the cracks from her forearm right up to her shoulder. She didn't like the idea of them spreading into her chest, up her neck, to her head. One more use of her powers might be enough to rip her to pieces.

As the lighthouse beam came back around, Harper swung her axe in a wide arc, disemboweling three zombies in a row. Wriggling masses of fish and worms tumbled to the ground beneath them with a wet squish.

Squealing in disgust, Harper dodged back. Even with stomachs hanging open, the fish-men didn't slow. With a wicked grin, Harper hoisted her axe again.

She twirled, and the axe sliced through one zombie's neck with such power that its head flew face-first into the living corpse next to it, crushing its skull. Their two bodies collapsed onto the third and pinned it down, letting Harper take an easy coup de grâce.

Wow. Everly had seen glimpses of Harper's warrior side, but this was something else.

They'd fought over Harper's inclusion in the dangers of Shroudhaven. Everly knew Harper had done combat and self-defense training since the doxing. She knew she was a strong woman. She knew Harper always pushed herself to do everything at the highest standards. Maybe she should never have doubted her friend.

Maybe I'm the one holding her back.

Closer to her, Rylan had incapacitated all but one of the zombies on him. He grabbed the last with both hands and lifted its full body above his head. With a rough growl, he threw the thing at a thick tree trunk where it splattered, gray chunks dripping down the bark.

Denny joined Callan and Tammy, the trio back-to-back, surrounded in a close circle. All the zombies seemed drawn there like a feeding frenzy, very few straying from the mob. Harper hacked into the edges from the outside. Everly could barely see the three in the center or the flash of their blades through the horde as it jostled them within the crush of their stinking bodies.

"Rylan, they're being overwhelmed," she gasped. "They can't change like you can. They need you."

He followed her gaze, swearing under his breath.

"I'm fine, go!"

"I'll be right back." Rylan charged, hitting the crowd like a cannonball.

There were no fish-Nazis close to Everly then, but they churned and swarmed in the mass nearby. More still fell from the U-boat. No longer a flood of bodies, just the odd straggler, tumbling down and seeking the closest prey.

Everly stepped backward, trying to distance herself from the danger so Rylan could focus on the others, as the lighthouse beam dimmed then passed away again, dropping Everly into darkness.

Something crunched through the underbrush nearby.

"Harper?" Everly whispered.

No reply.

Everly scrambled the other way, feeling her way through the dark with her hands. A branch whipped her cheek, stinging. A stomach-churning, slurping hiss chased behind her.

She moved quickly, breaking away from the sounds of the larger battle, but her pursuer remained close at her back. Her arms felt so weak, but she grasped her long flashlight tight, ready to swing it if she had to. Damp trunks and thorny bushes blocked her path and she stumbled between them, heart racing.

Slimy hands grabbed at her, fumbling for purchase as they scraped over her back. Everly gagged as a strong, low-tide stench hit her.

"Get off me!"

She swung the flashlight like a bat, missing her target in the dark. The fish-zombie lunged. Wet, slippery hands covered in scales slapped into her chest and she went flying onto her back. Pain shot through her, and she gasped a soundless scream. The zombie didn't slow down, throwing itself upon her.

She bunched her body up, getting her legs between them before the monster could land on top of her. Her arms were weak, but she could still kick. Growling, hissing sounds helped her zero in on the thing's head. She reared back and kicked both legs up with everything she had.

Bones cracked—its neck, she hoped—and the zombie collapsed into a heap at her side. He moaned a strange, gurgling sound, and the leaves rustled beneath him as he twitched sickeningly before he stilled.

Everly lay there gasping, trying to catch her breath as the lighthouse beam returned.

A shadow fell over her face. Everly almost sobbed as she looked up, hoping to see Rylan there, or any friendly face.

Instead, another twisted fish zombie growled down at her.

Everly tried to shove up off her back, to scramble away, but pain lanced through her arms, her elbows buckling.

The zombie slammed down on top of her, crushing her back onto the muddy ground. Her head bounced off the dirt, sending brilliant lights bursting in her vision.

She kicked her legs but didn't have the right angle between them to do more than squirm beneath the fish-man's weight. Grasping her flashlight with her good arm she thrust it up at the monster. It hit soft and squelchy flesh. The impact seemed to kick the light back to life, the bulb illuminating as it sank abnormally deep into the monster's bloated, decomposing belly.

Teeth bared in disgust, Everly tried to wrench the flashlight back out again, but it

had suctioned into the zombie's middle, disappearing under the torn fabric and rotting flesh, making the creature glow dull red from within.

The creature's scaly, dripping hands slid all over her, grabbing and swatting at her weak swings as she fought to ward it away. Her legs were stuck, her arms basically useless, her only weapon gone.

"Help—"

One heavy, soggy arm pressed down over her neck, pinning her in place and cutting off her cry. She writhed and kicked, but its mushy, wet chest, glowing red, sagged down, molding over her body.

Horror and the overwhelming stench of death sent panic cutting through Everly like knives.

"Everly? Evie? Where are you?" Rylan called out in the distance.

She tried to call back, choked to silence by the weight on her throat. Tears stung her eyes as she could barely draw breath. The zombie leaned its face close to hers, jagged teeth bared. Gas puffed from its mouth, smelling of wet, decaying fish.

Everly groaned with effort, pressing her hands up against the zombie's ribcage. She shoved with all her might, her injured arms radiating agony.

The fish-Nazi snapped at her from only a hair's breadth away, trying to bite the flesh clean from her face. Slimy ichor dripped from its mouth onto her cheek. She choked on the cloying death smell as his skin sloughed away beneath her fingertips, sinking in the way the flashlight had.

But her strength held. She kept the living corpse and its gnashing mouth propped up away from her body. She just had to hold on, keep it from biting her until Rylan got back. She just had to keep the overwhelming pain coursing through her arms from breaking her.

He'll come for me. Rylan will come and help me.

Only, she couldn't even see the battle anymore, hidden down in the thick undergrowth as she was. She didn't know how far away she'd gotten, or what was happening to the others.

The zombie shivered, moving strangely. Its mouth opened wider, then wider again, gaping open larger than humanly possible as it made horrifying gagging sounds.

For a desperate, panic-filled moment, Everly thought it was going to vomit on her face.

Then something else emerged.

Everly couldn't even scream.

A sharp, snake-like face appeared down the zombie's throat. Beady, white eyes stared at her from behind the zombie's teeth. A huge, ghostly-pale moray eel. Needle-sharp teeth snapped as it slithered out over the zombie's tongue, straight for Everly.

12

J asper had been irritatingly vague on the phone.

"I need assistance with something," he'd said.

"I don't know from whom else to request support," he'd said.

"I don't want to be alone ... on this."

That was what decided Cherry to go to him. There was the smallest hint of vulnerability in those words, like an opening in Jasper's cool demeanor, a hint that maybe something had changed.

Just don't get your hopes up, he reminded himself.

The Crow's Nest was dead at that time of midmorning. Most shadyrs who stopped in for a post-patrol drink had headed home by then. Crowea herself, the old, wild-haired witch who ran the establishment, had long since turned in for the night, and her third shift bartender—a bookish woman in floral overalls—sat on a stool at the bar, paging through a fancy hardcover.

The bar remained open twenty-four seven, as a sort of haven for shadyrs, but with bare-bones staff and little service actually offered. The woman glanced up as Cherry passed into the building, eyed him as if checking he wasn't going to cause trouble or interrupt her reading, then returned to her book.

The Crow's Nest was a kitschy place of mismatched armchairs arranged around low tables. Each cluster of seating was separated from the rest by low bookshelves loaded with treasures and trinkets related to witchcraft, or that had simply caught Crowea's eye, from sparkling crystals to fairy figurines.

Antique lamps draped in colorful scarves gave the place a soft glow, and the walls and ceilings were covered in tapestries, posters of unicorns, and signs saying things like 'Witch, please.'

Cherry liked the bar, though he liked it a lot more when it was a place he could hang out with his secret boyfriend. They'd spent hours sitting in those plush armchairs, across the room but within sight of each other, chatting via text. Then they'd slip away into the shelter of the curtained back areas when the desire to be closer became overwhelming.

Seeing Jasper there now, chewing his nails as he sat waiting, brought all those

memories back like a slap to the cheek.

He only chews his nails like that when he's really worried.

"Hey," Cherry said, stopping at the entrance to the two-armchair nook.

He was going for nonchalance, but the word came out semi-strangled. Loaded with unspoken regrets. His heart rate kicked up a notch and his stomach fluttered as it always did in Jasper's presence. Cherry found Jasper gorgeous, but in an understated way.

His tan cardigan gave him a sort of gentle sophistication, which perfectly matched his uptight personality and his beautiful dark skin. His ebony hair was styled back in its usual perfection. He didn't like a hair out of place, which became something of a game between them when Cherry liked to muss it up.

Jasper stood, patting at his clothes to smooth them. "Hi. Um, I really appreciate you coming. I know it's late ..."

Cherry shrugged. It was the hour most shadyrs would be getting a morning nap in. He'd been up half the night already and would have continued to the island with the others if he wasn't here. Luckily, shadyrs didn't seem to need as much sleep as regular humans.

Cherry stepped forward, sliding into the armchair directly across from Jasper. "It sounded important."

Jasper returned to his seat, rubbing his hands over his knees.

On the table between them, Cherry noticed a glass waiting for him, dark cola with a maraschino cherry dangling on the side. His lip twitched at that in-joke between the two of them. It didn't seem fair that a relationship could end but all the little details remained, left behind to hurt at inopportune moments.

He glared at the drink. "Was it actually important? This isn't some ... ploy, or—"

"No! No, I mean, it is important," Jasper said.

A zing of disappointment stabbed through Cherry's chest. "Good. Because I had to abandon *my team* on a critical mission for this."

Jasper raised his thick eyebrows. "What's happening, are they okay? I observed that Everly wasn't with you earlier, is it about her?"

"That's precisely none of your business."

Jasper's eyebrows lowered again. "Oh. Yes. Of course."

Silence fell between them. The bartender turned a page in her book and somewhere behind her, a refrigeration unit kicked on with a mechanical hum.

"Before we proceed, I wanted to be sure there wasn't too much animosity between us."

"You want to know if I'll have your back? Oh, I'm still angry at you. But I don't want you dead. Most days."

Jasper waved his long fingers at the drink. "I guess that was my misplaced attempt at a peace offering."

Cherry picked up the cola and had a sip. He needed the caffeine and the sugar, and to hide the smile that touched the corner of his lips. He wanted to hide every ounce of emotion he still felt for this man because it was a weakness. Like the longer he spent in his company, the more likely it would be that Cherry would forgive him and fall back into old habits.

Fall back into Jasper.

But that couldn't happen. They were too different. Too opposed. Howell versus Darkfrey. Jasper had proven where his real loyalties lay, and Cherry didn't want to be the runner-up, the hidden trophy, any longer.

Jasper cleared his throat. "It is good to see you."

Cherry recognized the affection glinting in Jasper's eyes, the way he leaned toward Cherry like a moth drawn to the flame.

"Don't," Cherry said, dropping the drink roughly back onto the table.

Jasper blinked. "Don't what?"

"Don't ... be like that. Don't act like you still care about me."

Jasper glanced down at his shoes. "I do, though."

"Just not more than you care about keeping up appearances," Cherry scoffed, irritation and betrayal turning the cola bitter in his mouth.

The skin around Jasper's eyes tightened. "That's not fair."

"You're right, it's not." Cherry shrugged. "But it's true."

Muscles twitched in Jasper's jaw, as though working through his reply. But nothing came. He couldn't even deny it.

Cherry sighed. "Forget about it. What did you need help with?"

Jasper chewed over his words for a moment longer, then said, "It's a mission. Something Vonny has asked me to do."

Cherry scowled. "And you need me for what?"

"She told me to keep it quiet, that I couldn't tell anyone at the estate. But she didn't expressly say I had to go on my own."

"What's the job?"

"Can't say." Jasper averted his eyes.

Cherry leaned back, folding his arms. Of course, Jasper had to follow the rules to the letter.

"Why'd she pick you for this super-secret squirrel mission? Why not go as a brace?"

Jasper's eyebrows dipped, his dark eyes flashing, troubled. "I don't know."

"And that didn't raise a red flag? Did it occur to you she might have sent you on a mission *alone* to get you killed?"

Jasper said warningly, "She's one of my brace. I trust her."

"Yeah, I suppose you're right," Cherry said, laying on the snark. "If she wanted, she'd probably kill you herself."

Jasper snorted a soft laugh, then shook his head. "I trust her ... but I am also acutely aware of what happened to our last brace member who went off on his own. That's why I asked for your help. I didn't want to be alone."

Their gazes met, and Cherry's heart constricted. Their relationship hadn't lasted long, but it had burned bright, and Cherry would have given Jasper anything if he only asked.

"Fine," Cherry said, channeling irritation into his tone so Jasper wouldn't hear the pain he felt just sitting there, looking into his eyes, wishing things were different. "You're right that you need backup. It's the smart thing to do. I'll go to make sure you stay safe while you do whatever secret thing you need to do."

Jasper's expression smoothed into a relieved smile. "Thank you."

"Nobody should be alone in Shroudhaven." Cherry took another large gulp of the cola to try to wash away the lump in his throat. "So where are we headed?"

Jasper stood up, straightening his cardigan. "Rook's Theater."

The eel snapped.

Everly whipped her head to the side. Sharp teeth grazed her ear.

Tears spilled from her eyes as she strained to keep the undead fish-Nazi away from her face. Its arm still pressed against her throat. She couldn't catch her breath and her arms felt like they were about to splinter into a million pieces.

I should use the dragon. She could feel it, squirming inside her. Hungry, always hungry ... but weak.

Possibly still strong enough to throw the monsters on her clear away, though. But what if that shattered her entirely? What did it matter if she was going to die there anyway?

With a gurgling hiss, the eel coiled its body and retracted back into the zombie's gaping maw, tensing for another strike.

Gasping for breath, dizziness overwhelmed Everly. Blind panic pulled her in like an icy embrace.

No, don't lose control.

The eel lunged again. She turned her face the other way, and its teeth tangled in her hair.

Facing that new direction, she stared almost directly into the beam of the lighthouse, and within it, saw the silhouette of something charging her way. Bounding, speeding,

growling.

"Everly!" the strange shape boomed with Rylan's voice.

Sparks crackled and black mist swirled.

He slammed into the zombie that had her pinned, taking it and the eel with him as he dove over the top of her.

The lighthouse beam drifted away again, leaving them in darkness. The flashlight still glowed from within the zombie's stomach, casting a red aura over it and what must be Rylan. But Rylan was in a form Everly had never seen before.

He'd been fighting the shadyr transformation that Everly's presence forced on him since he woke up. Trying to keep it to a familiar vampire form. But his guard must have been down due to the fight.

Now, he was ... *everything.*

He shifted rapidly and uncontrollably as he rolled across the forest floor, grappling with the dead Nazi.

He sprouted fur as he tore the protruding eel free and flung it away, and fangs burst from between his lips as he took the full brunt of the soldier's uppercut. Then fur became scales, first shimmering iridescent, then sharp and metallic. A ripple of a translucent glow passed over his face—the shadyr's ghostly form she'd witnessed back in Gorhanmere.

Then *wings* burst from his back, bony and leathery. His shifting settled into one solid form. His body mass was twice normal. In the red glow, his eyes shone. He looked like some kind of demon, or dragon.

Without pausing, Rylan launched off the ground, taking the zombie with him. The fish man struggled sloppily in Rylan's grip, then was swiftly torn in two. Three *thunks* hit the forest floor. Top half. Bottom half. Flashlight.

Baring monstrous teeth, Rylan swooped down from the sky and flew back the way he came, leaving a gust of air across Everly's body in his wake.

She gasped that oxygen in. Shaking off the paralysis from the shock of Rylan's form, she could breathe again. With the waterlogged zombie no longer crushing every part of her, she could breathe again.

She was left lying on her back, panting, wondering what the fuck just happened.

"Hey! There you are." Harper burst through a bush in front of Everly. "Are you okay?"

Everly shook her head, then took the hand that was extended to help her up. It was covered in gray slime. The flashlight offered some illumination from where it lay on the ground but didn't extend to where roars and hideous tearing sounds came from the distance.

Everly stared wide-eyed into the darkness. "What is happening?"

Harper rested her gore-covered axe on her shoulder. "Rylan's gone full beast mode. He's mopping up everything out there."

The lighthouse beam returned, and now Everly was standing again, the area beneath the U-boat was visible. Rylan flew low, snatching zombies from the ground like an oversized bird of prey. Rotting heads were removed. Zombie bodies were flung like torpedoes, bowling over more. Dismembered legs were used as makeshift clubs.

Everly stared, eyes and mouth stuck open. Darkness came again, and when the next beam returned, it fell over a graveyard of mutilated carcasses.

Air swirled around Everly as Rylan landed in front of her. His shirt was gone, the flexible body armor beneath stretched to its limits. His chest rose and fell in huge breaths. His skin was a deep red, covered in thick, metallic scales.

With glowing red eyes, darkened by lowered brows, he stared at Everly, then tilted his head away from her.

"Everyone good?" His gravelly voice seemed an octave lower than usual.

Through the trees, Callan called back, "I think so."

"Unbelievably, yes," said Tammy.

"Right?" drawled Denny. "Didn't think we were walking out of that one."

Everly clasped both arms to her chest, shaking. Rylan eyed her for a moment, then bent down and snatched up her flashlight. He wiped it twice on his pants before handing it to her without a word.

"Um. Thanks." She shivered harder.

Callan, Tammy, and Denny picked their way through the undergrowth to join them.

Tammy's hooded sweatshirt had been ripped along the shoulder seam, exposing her body armor beneath, and the hint of red. Denny had zombie goop on his face and neck, and a nasty gash tore the thigh of Callan's pants, stained with blood around the edges. Rylan stood taller than everyone by at least three feet, and his pointed wings soared even higher.

Callan said, "So ... that's new."

"Yeah, man," Denny agreed. "*I* want to be a dragon!"

Rylan growled back.

"What even is that form?" Tammy said.

"Herrelspurn?" Callan said. "I've never come up against one before but from the descriptions we learned back with the Darkfreys, it doesn't seem quite right."

"The wings are from that form, but not the rest. This feels strange, almost like more than one form." Rylan took several steps back from Everly and shook himself.

Black smoke and sparking light swirled around him, and the wings vanished. His body shrank. Then the red skin tone and scales faded, leaving only unmarred, human skin behind.

Callan smirked and poked at his brother's shredded shirt and the split seams on his pants. "Whatever it is, we can mark it down as another 'not friendly to clothing' form."

Rylan smacked his hand away, clearly not sharing the humor.

Everly tried hard not to stare at the holes. Shadyrs seemed to struggle with clothing for anything other than vasmire/vampire form, which didn't make them significantly different from their normal body shapes. And auerdax/ghost form, for which they seemed to take whatever they were touching with them onto the ghostly plane.

Their flexible Darkfrey body armor was designed for shifting, but normal clothing not so much.

Everly was surprised to see Rylan switch back to human form now, rather than vampire, given his proximity. Then, with a slight groan hidden under a cleared throat, he took a few more steps away. He seemed to be attempting nonchalance in distancing himself from her.

It didn't work.

It was painfully obvious to Everly that he neither could nor wanted to remain near her.

Harper rubbed at the side of her waist where her clothing was damp and ripped. "Do we need to be worried about zombie bites? Asking for a friend."

"Harper!" Everly gasped, reaching for her.

She lifted the bottom hem of Harper's pink hunting jacket, peeling back layers of clothing beneath.

"I don't think so," Callan said, moving forward to inspect her wound as well. "They were beshadowed corpses, not movie-style virus-based. I mean, you'll want to disinfect it for sure, though. Short course of antibiotics couldn't hurt."

He got his flashlight back out, and after a few hits, it started working again. He shined it on Harper's skin

Everly ran a finger gently over the area to clear the gunk away. "Looks like it didn't even break the skin. Is that a scar?"

"Oh. It's nothing," Harper said, covering up again. "I'm fine."

"Yeah you are," Denny leered, eyes still on her waist as though he had x-ray vision.

"No thanks to you."

"Come on, who could resist that tempting lure?" Denny wistfully looked over his shoulder at the U-boat they'd left behind.

"Literally *everyone* except for you," Tammy replied.

Callan looked ready to tackle Denny if needed. "You're not still wanting to go in there."

"I mean ... the booty we could be leaving behind ..." Denny turned back with a sigh. "Nah man, I think I learned my lesson on that one."

"As if that's possible," Tammy muttered.

"Let's move on then," Callan said, adjusting the straps on his backpack.

Rylan took a few steps toward the U-boat and retrieved his and Everly's packs that he must have shed earlier.

Exhaustion, both physical and emotional, washed over Everly. She wobbled, and Harper caught her by the elbow with one hand, balancing her before she could fall.

Rylan's eyes flashed. "We should rest."

"We're almost there," Denny argued, pointing at the rotating light beyond the canopy.

"You can't even see that your idiocy got some of us injured, can you?" Tammy said, her eyes on Callan's still-bleeding leg. "Not that I care if I turn into a zombie. Then I could eat your brains. No wait, you don't have any."

"I was also going to suggest a bit of T and T time—triage and treatment," Callan clarified to Everly and Harper, then turned back to Rylan. "I thought you'd be keen to push on though."

Rylan's gaze flickered once more over Everly. "We should *rest*. Just for a couple of hours."

Everly nodded slowly. She wanted to keep going, wanted this done as quickly and safely as possible, but she literally couldn't move. She was frozen in place, all energy going toward reducing her interior turmoil and nothing left for external motion.

Tammy and Callan both needed first aid, and Denny, for all his brazen arrogance, looked exhausted. Harper somehow continued to buzz around, full of energy, but Everly worried she might have other wounds she wasn't bringing to anyone's attention. Rylan's expression had grown stony. Physically, he showed no wear and tear, but his jaw twitched and he rubbed at his temples.

Rylan shook his head, the hint of a snarl on his lips. "We're all dead on our feet. And we have no idea what we're going to walk into when we reach the lighthouse."

13

They moved far enough away that the stench of zombie parts wasn't overwhelming, but there wasn't anywhere to take shelter. No cave or clearing, and no way they were using the U-boat.

They simply picked a patch of ground between twisted trees where there was enough flat dirt to sit down.

It was probably as good a place as any. If the octo-deer didn't come in there, maybe the area was safe from other beshadowed threats too, now that they'd cleared out the zombies.

The Howell team got moving quickly. Denny cleared some of the brush away with his machete and Rylan pulled a lightweight tarp from his pack and spread it out before putting Everly's blanket on top, then immediately directed Everly herself to sit down.

He quickly turned away and pulled white blocks and metal tools from his pack, which turned out to be for fire-starting.

Callan and Tammy had opened the first aid kits and were arguing over what triage meant and who got treatment first. Tammy's shoulder wound was a nasty graze, which Callan quickly cleaned and taped over with gauze as she grumbled the entire time.

Everly heard snatches of *not even worth it* and *don't bother* and *that's enough, we need to work on your leg.*

When they ripped back the fabric of Callan's pants, Everly had to agree with Tammy. His wound was far worse. Everly was surprised he was walking around the way he was. The Howell boys were tough.

But they shouldn't need to be. They are only here, getting hurt, because of me.

Rylan turned from the fire and offered to do the suturing.

"I've got it," Tammy snapped, dousing the wound with a pungent fluid.

Callan winced and mouthed to his brother, "Help."

"She's got it." Rylan grinned back.

Everly settled against the tree trunk behind her. The bark was sodden and soaked into her clothes, but as she was still wet from the storm, it made little difference. She pulled her blanket up around her, trying to fight the incessant shaking of her body.

The warm glow of Rylan's fire chased away some of the chill. Everly tipped her head back against the trunk and watched him feed sticks into the flames. She couldn't stop picturing the zombies. Their red armbands.

The way they'd swarmed her friends, almost overwhelmed them. The eel, with its dead, white eyes, snapping at her face. The ghosts, the hybrid creatures, the trees with minds of their own ... This place was a nightmare.

Her heart turned into a hummingbird in her chest.

They're only here because of me.

Tammy had her face close to Callan's thigh, moving her black hands in small, careful motions as she sutured the gash.

Callan stared at her with his eyebrows raised, wincing at each tug of thread. "You're really good at that."

She didn't look up. "And I bet that surprises you, 'cause you expect me to be a child about everything."

His lips twisted upward. "That's not it. I just thought you were going to enact vengeance on me for making you get treated first."

She paused and looked up then, completely deadpan. "You mean like a child would?"

Callan rubbed the back of his head. "Okay, got me there. Honestly, I think you're more mature than me most of the time."

Tammy only grunted in reply.

Harper warmed herself near the fire, stretching her back. "Any idea what time it is? I've completely lost track in this place."

Rylan scowled at his watch as though it had insulted him. "Later than it should be. We're moving too slowly."

Apparently finished hacking into bushes, Denny sheathed his machete and took a seat near the fire. "You're the one who called a break."

"And why do you think that was? Whose screwup wasted our time and left us in this position?" Rylan stuffed his fire striker violently into his pack. He glared Denny down as though he wanted to shove it into him instead.

Harper sighed and dropped onto the tarp beside Everly. She placed her axe on her lap like a pet.

"I told you we should have left him behind. But *no*, he's 'capable.' Isn't that what you said, Callan?"

Callan half-smiled, half-winced as he watched Tammy tie off a stitch. "I did. Can I take it back now?"

Denny huffed and reached into his pack.

"So help me, if you pull a beer can from there, you're a dead man," Rylan growled.

He rolled a log over a bit closer to the fire and sat down, keeping his gaze fixed on

the man.

Denny let go of whatever he'd been holding and pulled back out empty-handed.

"Look, so what if I make mistakes sometimes? Everyone does. Even golden boy here," he added, motioning to Rylan. "He ran off alone and got himself got by a vasmire, didn't he?"

"At least he didn't get anyone else hurt in the process," Tammy said.

Rylan's jaw clenched and he turned away.

Callan pointed at Denny. "Dude, you're a human wrecking ball. You saw a Nazi submarine hanging from vines in a beshadowed forest and literally thought *I want to be in there*. Nobody in their right mind would do that."

"Yeah, well maybe you're right about that. Because nobody in their right mind would put up with this disrespect." Denny picked up a stick and threw it into the fire, shooting sparks into the sky. "I'm a damn capable shadyr, and ya'll are on my case non-stop. Denny, don't say that. Denny, don't do that. Denny, ew."

Harper squinted at him. "Have you even heard what comes out of your mouth?"

"You know, sure, I say the wrong things or do the wrong things sometimes. I'm not gonna pretend I don't. This world is hard for people like me." Denny folded his arms, frowning like a kid no one picked for their team. "I didn't grow up all woke and LGBQRTAV whatever like you kids."

Tammy groaned. "Oh my ghast, you're such a bigot."

"But you know what?" Denny snapped irritably. "I also show up. I didn't have to come to this cursed island, but I did because we're a damned team."

Harper scoffed. "Do you even know what a 'team' is? All you ever think about is yourself."

"That's not true at all, I also think about you, a lot. You and me. Together. You know what I mean."

Harper wrapped her hands around the axe on her lap and looked ready for murder.

Callan rubbed his forehead. "For ghast's sake, dude, shut your mouth before you dig your own grave."

Rylan glared at Denny from across the flames. "Seriously, how do you sleep at night?"

"Face down and naked, so ya'll can kiss my ass."

As they continued to argue, Everly squeezed her eyes shut and swallowed the pulse pounding in her throat. It didn't matter what Denny did. They were surrounded by danger. If it wasn't that fight with the zombies, it could have easily been something else. Her friends could have died, could still die, all because of her.

Her heart beat so hard it hurt, and she put her trembling fingertips to her solar plexus to massage away the knot of anxiety. Her breaths came short and fast, then shorter and faster as the group continued to argue around her.

All my fault.
It's all my fault.

She couldn't chase away memories of the skirmish, but they became twisted *what-if* versions. What if Rylan hadn't pulled that zombie and eel off her? What if Harper had been bitten? What if Callan and Tammy were crushed within that mass of dead flesh?

Every bit of fear that she'd fought back rose to the surface and overflowed. Panic consumed her in a way the zombie never could have, spiraling her down into darkness.

"Ev? Oh, hey." Harper moved closer, and she wrapped an arm around Everly. "It's okay. Remember your toolkit."

"What's happening?" Rylan said. "Is she hurt?"

"Panic attack, I think," Harper replied.

Their voices all sounded muffled behind the pulse in Everly's ears. She struggled to peel her eyes open again, trying to bring herself back into the here and now, then wished she hadn't. All the catastrophizing happening in her head was better than the look Rylan gave her. He got to his feet and stared down at her as her body rebelled against itself.

He's watching, he can see me falling apart.

She'd had panic attacks as a kid too, back when they'd been friends, but then she could disguise them. Blame it on a tantrum or simply run away and hide. She had nowhere to hide now. He could see every bit of how broken she was.

Shame screamed inside her almost as loud as the panic.

Pull it together.

She dealt with this all the time. She had her toolkit; all the breathing and grounding techniques years of therapy had given her. But everything felt so out of control right now. Everything had changed irrevocably. Even her old methods of calling her anxiety the "dragon" no longer worked because she knew now that the "dragon" wasn't just anxiety. It was the monster inside her, the light that consumed souls.

That being would escape if she lost control. And if it did, it might kill her, or kill her friends.

Everly focused on Harper's arm around her shoulders. She set her mind to controlling her breaths, counting them out. At first, they remained ragged, and she was barely able to count before it felt like her lungs would explode. But she kept going, kept counting, found a rhythm in time to how the lighthouse beam swept around them.

The rushing in her ears faded and the tightness in her chest released. Her exhalations were slow and calm, and her vision cleared to see everyone staring at her.

Shame heated her cheeks and neck, strong enough that her flight impulses almost kicked her into panic mode again.

Her voice was a harsh whisper. "I'm sorry."

Rylan's expression changed. No longer dark and brooding, it was something else, something like awe.

"Wow," he said softly. "I think I get it now."

"Get what?" Everly felt completely confused.

"How you can control that thing inside you, the dragon."

Everly shook her head. Control was the furthest from what she felt.

"You just navigated out of a panic attack in less than thirty seconds," Rylan pointed out, as though that explained things.

Callan's eyes widened. "Wow, yeah. Most people would have been knocked down for way longer. What? You think none of the shadyr kids at Darkfrey Estate dealt with anxiety issues?"

Everly's face remained scorching. "No, but, it's just ... I can't ..."

Callan shrugged. "It's nothing to be ashamed of. Not for anyone."

"Especially not you." Rylan didn't need to say why.

He knew everything she'd been through as a kid and was intimately acquainted with her nightmares.

"What you did just now, that is seriously impressive self-control. No wonder you've been able to keep the dragon locked away for so long. Why you can keep it under control. I doubt anyone else would be able to manage it like you do."

Everly gaped, close to tears.

Harper reached down to take Everly's hand and squeezed it gently. "You're a badass, and I'm not the only one who can see it."

Everly dropped her head onto Harper's shoulder.

"Thank you," she said to everyone.

As her friend's hand rested on hers, Everly realized she was shaking. "Are you all right?"

Harper shrugged, a slight crease across her forehead. "Tired. More than I thought I'd be."

"You sure you didn't get hurt? Those scars on your waist, I've never seen them before. They looked new."

Harper shifted, bringing her arms back off Everly. "Well, they're not, and shut it before Denny starts picturing us naked together."

"Too late," he jeered.

Callan and Rylan also turned from the conversation as though there was something more important to see on the other side of the fire.

Tammy, however, eyed Harper. "Huh, I didn't think princesses were the cutting type."

Harper tensed. "What?"

"Scars? On places like thighs, waist, arms, where you think people won't notice? Classic cutting behavior. Not that I'd know."

Callan flashed a sharp look at her.

"You're right, you don't know. You don't know anything about me. I'm not a cutter, and I'm not a damned princess, either," Harper snarled, inordinately furious. "You all look at me and expect me to be a certain way. You don't even consider who I really am. That maybe I'm sick of those expectations."

Her anger exacerbated the shaking, and Everly sat up, turning to look at her best friend. Her hands were claw-like, wrapped around the handle of her axe and squeezing tight.

Before Everly could try to calm her, Harper surged on. "I've been expected to be perfect in every way my entire life."

Firelight sparkled in her eyes and along with her battle tangled hair it made her look like a goddess of vengeance.

"Expected to act just right and be top the class and win the pageant and marry rich but be a girl boss and be attractive but don't look like you try too hard and don't be a whore but make men want you and be smart but not so clever its off-putting and don't ever put a foot out of line or it won't matter if you did *everything else* right, it will all be over."

"You know what it's like," she flicked her chin toward Tammy and Everly. "How hard we have to work *every moment* of our lives while watching white men succeed when being entirely mediocre, or worse."

She turned her tirade toward Denny.

Then she turned her head upward, as though yelling at the universe. "How are we even supposed to know what we want, who we are, when every second of our lives we're told what to be based on how others see us?"

Nobody answered, only stared.

Harper's face changed from pure fury to confusion to shock. She covered her mouth with her shaking hand. "I don't know where all of that came from. I mean ... I do. But I don't ... This isn't the time. I just ... I'm tired."

"Hey." Everly reached for her, and Harper tensed, then relaxed into Everly's embrace. "You can be whoever you want to be. I'll still love you. I'm sorry if I ever made you feel otherwise."

Harper squeezed Everly tight enough to make her wince.

Everly looked over Harper's shoulder toward Rylan, and he turned away as though caught staring.

He grumbled, "Come on, let's get a few hours' rest. We all need it."

It was clear they did. Nerves were raw all around. It was also clear to Everly that she'd been too deep in her own mind lately to realize that Harper was going through something, too. Down in her lap, the handle of her axe had splintered where she'd been gripping it tight.

The strength she'd shown while fighting earlier ... Everly didn't want to question her friend's skill, but it wasn't normal.

What secrets was Harper keeping?

14

Tammy tried to sleep, but every time she closed her eyes, visions of beshadowed fish and squid swirling in murky water surrounded her. Within those creatures was a face, pleading and scared, and hands reaching out for her as they were drawn down into the dark. It was Blaise, then it was Callan, then it was Blaise again.

She tried so hard to rest. She didn't want to be a liability to the team. So she lay there, as still as possible, mind twisting in knots.

Maybe I need Everly to teach me some of her breathing techniques.

The few times Tammy opened her eyes over the couple of hours they rested, she checked on Callan first, who slept as easily as he did everything else. Rylan would always be there, standing alert as he kept watch over everyone, but especially Everly. She seemed to be in a troubled sleep. Harper cuddled up against her. Denny snored.

Tammy was still wide awake when Callan gently shook her shoulder. "We're moving on again. Eat and pack."

Even though her phone indicated it was early afternoon, the forest was dark as night. Even her shadyr night vision couldn't see into the deepest shadows. A symptom of the beshadowing, she guessed.

A few others had their flashlights on already, but Tammy figured more light couldn't hurt. She slapped her flashlight against her palm. The bulb flickered in and out for several seconds before it finally caught and held steady.

The fire was buried, and tarps and blankets were packed. They ate ravenously, tearing into granola bars, trail mix, and jerky. Everly nibbled at hers before she tucked the bar back into the wrapper and hid it away in her backpack. In the ambient glow of the flashlights, there were dark circles beneath her eyes.

Callan offered Tammy some of his jerky. "Did you get any sleep?"

"Yeah. Some," she lied, and waved away the offering, indicating the half-eaten nut bar she had in her hand.

"You still got water?" he asked.

Tammy's eye twitched. "Yes, I'm sleeping. I'm eating. I'm staying hydrated. I am

capable of being a functional human, thanks for checking."

Callan grinned around a piece of jerky. "Sorry, I know. You're more than competent. I just wanted to make sure you're okay."

Tammy closed her eyes and turned her face away until she could return it to a comfortably blank expression.

Callan had been hovering over her every moment since they'd crawled out of Myrkur Lake. She deserved it. She'd done a crazy, self-destructive thing and nearly died for it. Almost took him with her.

And now he was treating her like she was a pet that was so pathetic it might strangle itself on its own leash.

Imagining what his attentiveness would feel like if it came from adoration or respect for her left a painful hollow in her chest for how much she wanted it. But she knew it was only pity. Poor little Tammy, disowned by friends and family, cursed, living with the guilt of accidentally killing her best friend.

She knew Callan would never have real feelings for her. But the fact that he pitied her hurt even more.

I'm nothing but a burden. Why would anyone ever want me?

With her face schooled back into its normal cool, sardonic glare, she turned back to Callan. "I'd be a whole lot better if you stopped treating me like a baby."

"Sorry, I know ..." Callan repeated.

She stood up, hefted her pack on, and walked away from Callan's under-his-breath cursing.

With everyone ready, Rylan took the lead and they headed in the direction of the lighthouse.

Tammy expected more trouble before they reached the end of the forest, but the rest of the journey—a mere ten-minute hike—passed uneventfully.

As the trees thinned out, the lighthouse beam grew stronger and brighter. They left the thick undergrowth behind for a rocky clearing backed by a cliff, upon which the lighthouse sat perched high above. The land narrowed ahead of them, dropping off on each side into a roaring sea.

The rain had ceased. It was no longer as dark as night now that they were out from under the canopy, but bulbous, low clouds the color of ash still hung across the sky.

Tammy's steps faltered as she looked up at the lighthouse, trying to make sense of what she was seeing. It leaned out over the ocean at an angle that didn't seem possible, though the topmost portion where the light circled endlessly was still upright, balanced like a hat.

A jagged gash ran the full height of the building. It could split in half at any moment and tumble into the ocean.

The light reflected off the stormy clouds, casting an aura around the structure. Lightning branched and forked, brightening the sky and striking the highest part of the lighthouse every few seconds.

"I guess popping your wings back out and flying up there isn't an option," Harper said to Rylan.

"I'm not particularly keen on testing whether that form is lightning proof, no."

Nothing grew in the small clearing between the trees and the high cliff where the lighthouse sat. They moved closer, and Tammy dodged large boulders and fallen rocks that had sheared off the bluff.

At first, she worried they'd have to climb, but a narrow, nearly invisible staircase came into view. It zigzagged up the cliff and opened onto a surface out of sight.

The staircase was cut directly into the gray rock, with the cliff face on one side and a sheer drop on the other. Each step was carved at abnormally deep levels and covered in moss and algae, so ascending was a study in danger.

Rylan shuffled positions to be behind Everly again, leaving Callan and Tammy up front.

Callan took a step forward, then turned back. "Want to take point?"

Tammy's eyes opened wide for a moment. But then she looked back at Everly, how woozy she seemed, and Rylan on guard behind her.

Callan's probably just putting me somewhere he can keep an eye on me.

"Whatever." With a huff, she took the lead.

Tammy kept one hand against the wet wall to stay balanced. She moved slowly and surely, testing out each slippery step for the best purchase before she shifted her weight forward. She wouldn't slip. She would show confidence. She would keep up a good speed. She would stop being a liability, a burden.

She was halfway up when she felt the first hint of an eidolghast.

Its energy pressed against her senses, and her body wavered and grew hot.

Oh no. No no no.

Tammy halted, turned her face to the wall, and clung on with both hands. She squeezed her eyes shut and focused on the sound of the waves crashing against the cliff.

Callan put a hand on her shoulder. "I feel it too."

His calm, sympathetic tone infuriated her. Every shadyr there could no doubt feel it. But she was the only one who couldn't refuse her transformation.

Don't change, Tammy snarled inwardly, fighting against the wave of magic rippling through her.

Cherry wasn't even there to make her feel better by changing as well. She'd be the center of attention. The sole person incapable of being strong.

The ghast's presence overwhelmed her senses and inky, shadyr magic burst around

her, bringing the change. It wasn't a weroth or a vasmire or any familiar presence she'd experienced before. If they were out on the sea, it could have been a nyevmer, but here, up on a rocky bluff?

She'd studied all the known eidolghasts, the forms shadyrs took for each. If it was a nyevmer, she knew what was coming.

Tammy still yelped as her legs fused. The seams on her pants burst, dropping to the ground. She sagged against the wall, struggling to remain on her feet, but they vanished too, replaced by a wide, midnight-blue fin.

Her boots fell right off, dropping onto the step. She slipped, her new tail sliding out from underneath her. She wobbled, about to tumble right over the edge of the stairs, and her eyes filled with the view of the sharp rocks far below.

Callan caught her with both arms, gathering her against his chest. "Whoa. Got you."

Tammy's breath hitched in her throat. She clung to his shoulders, her skin heating from his proximity and the transformation still taking place. She hoped her top half wasn't going to change much. Her armor and hoodie still thankfully remained in place.

Her hands prickled and morphed until they were covered in delicate scales, webbed with a translucent membrane. Her nails grew sharp. But to her disappointment, her hands remained stained, shroudpool-black.

"Wow," Callan said, taking her new appearance in. "I mean, I've never seen a shadyr in nyevmer form before. You have gills."

Startled, Tammy released one of his shoulders and touched her neck. Four raised slits had formed above her collar bones. Her studies had told her that this form let shadyrs breathe underwater, but that would be something else to actually experience.

"You guys turn into frickin' mermaids?" Harper squealed from farther back. "Are we still completely certain shadyr bites don't transfer powers?"

"Yeah, this is nyevmer form. But why here? They're water-based and we're not that close to the shoreline." Callan frowned at the ocean in the distance.

"Wherever it is, we need to keep moving."

Right. Moving. Upstairs. With a tail.

"I can ... wait here. You guys keep going." *I couldn't even lead the team up some stairs without screwing up.*

"Don't be like that," Callan said. "Come on, hold tight."

Tammy flushed even hotter. "What?"

He bent down and looped his arm beneath her tail. Tammy gasped, fumbling for his neck as he lifted her into his arms.

He settled one beneath the part of her fin where her knees would have been, then wrapped his other carefully around her back beneath her backpack so she was sitting in his grasp, fin dangling.

Callan glanced at the pants on the ground. "You got spare clothes in your pack?"

She bobbed a small nod.

He called back down the line, "Can someone grab her boots?"

Then he straightened his shoulders and resumed the climb.

Utter shame left her speechless. Every point of contact between the two of them left a lump in her throat. The combination left her eyes hot and head spinning, but surprisingly, the touch of his skin on hers didn't send her wildly teleporting away to Dark Corner.

That was progress, at least. That was one small blessing in a world of humiliation.

He has to carry me. I have graduated to a literal burden.

It didn't help that the two human women were ogling her with barely concealed fascination. They reached the top of the stairs and stepped onto flat ground again, and Harper dashed over for a closer look. "A mermaid in a hoodie. Omigosh you're too adorable."

Everly asked, "Was the song written by a shadyr, do you think?"

Rylan shrugged. "After Harper noticed the connection, I did a bit of research into the song, but no one really knows where it came from. We're still going on pure speculation that the lyrics actually mean something and aren't entirely made up."

Everly paled.

"I mean, it's still worth checking out. Obviously."

"Okay, but we know from Rush that the lighthouse lamp is something magical, and now I know mermaids are a thing too, I think we're on the right track," Harper said, putting a hand on Everly's shoulder.

Everly half-smiled. "I can't believe mermaids were also shadyrs all along. Are there any mythological creatures you guys didn't inspire?"

Harper gasped so loudly everyone turned toward her. "Rush was a Crybel's Cove shadyr, right? She must have done this all the time, back then. Can you imagine her in mermaid form?"

She fanned her face. "I'm picturing a sunny yellow tail and all the pinup vibes."

Denny smacked his lips. "A yellow tail would be unlikely. Shadyrs take on darker colors to camouflage in the water. The scales also provide natural armor. What? I know things. Capable shadyr, remember?"

"For some reason, I keep forgetting," Harper said flatly.

Staring up at the lighthouse, Everly swayed, bumping into Tammy's tail.

"Sorry." She straightened herself up.

"Are you okay?" Tammy asked.

Everly nodded, a disoriented vagueness in her gaze

Rylan said softly, "Do you need another break?"

Everly took a few wobbly steps forward. "No. Let's keep going."

Callan readjusted his grip on Tammy and followed. The full lighthouse was within view now, and the base was surrounded by a strange growth, part smoky crystal and part slimy coral. Dark shapes reflected off the sharp edges, flitting unnaturally.

The group came to a stop. Three shallow steps with rusted metal railings led up to the front door, but the entire entrance was encased in the crystalline growth, at least three feet thick.

Rylan took a few deep breaths and shifted into the hulking, draconic form he'd taken before. Tammy's cheeks heated. There he was, able to pick and choose his shifts from Everly's interior ghast library—or however that worked—and she was stuck as the most useless possible form.

They should have left her behind.

In two giant leaps, Rylan charged at the door and the growth in front of it. The collision shook the conglomeration of coral, crystal, and shadows, but made no dent. He pushed again with his shoulder, then kicked at it, before shaking his head.

"No way we're getting in here. Not without a bulldozer."

Callan glanced at Denny. "You didn't bring any C-4, did you?"

"I wish! Lian went and confiscated my stash."

"Smart woman," Rylan said.

Harper motioned around the structure where the clearing stretched behind the building. "Maybe there's another entrance?"

The team fanned out to search, minus Tammy and Callan.

He's stuck here looking after me.

"You can put me down," Tammy told him.

"I'm not going to dump you on the ground."

"I am capable of sitting down. I can just, you know, sit down for a bit."

Or maybe commando-crawl away into a dark hole where I can hide for the rest of my life.

"I know." He flashed an amused grin. "But this isn't so bad, is it?"

Tammy's eyes widened and her cheeks heated, making him smile even more. It wasn't bad. It was nice. It was so nice but admitting that was the most horrifying part of the whole experience. That a part of her adored his attention. And that maybe, he knew.

No matter how many walls she'd put up or how rude she'd been to him, somehow, he'd seen the humiliating truth hidden deep inside. That she liked him. How dare she? Her, the burden, the cursed. How dare she want someone like him?

Something inside her was about to break and she had no idea if that was bad or good.

Rylan continued pacing around the front door, kicking at the concrete stoop and the walls around it like he might be able to break his way in. Denny wandered about aimlessly, moving to look over the ocean-side cliff as though enjoying the view.

Everly and Harper circled the entire base, returning around the other side.

"Any luck?" Callan asked.

Everly shook her head, and Harper put an arm over her shoulder.

A gust of wind came off the sea, drowning out Denny's voice.

He put both hands around his mouth and hollered again, "Hey, didn't the Crybel's Cove shadyrs say no one comes out here?"

Rylan looked up from his study of the blocked entrance. "Yeah. They did."

Denny pointed over the edge of the cliff. "Then who's that guy?"

15

"There's a shifty-looking man scampering around on the rocks down there," Denny clarified, waving a hand into the wind that howled up from the shore below.

Skeptical expressions were shared, but the group joined him at the cliff's edge.

Everly moved slowly, fogged by pain and the effort of hiding it. By the time she'd caught up with the others, the elusive figure climbing on the rough coastline below had vanished.

"He went right into the cliff," Denny told Rylan, pointing down beneath them.

"Like a ghost?" Rylan asked.

Given the beshadowing, there was a possibility that what Denny had seen wasn't a real man at all.

Denny shook his head. "Definitely a solid dude."

"And he didn't take a nosedive into the waves?" Callan asked.

"Nah. Look, he came in that way." He aimed his finger at a small patch of dry stone on the shore, marked with wet footprints.

Rylan squinted into the gale. "Caves, maybe. Won't know till we get down there. Worth a look though."

Everly stood watch on the cliff's edge while the rest of the team attempted to find an easy way down the precarious cliffside. The one they found was a narrow goat track, far more treacherous than easy.

Callan eyed the path with Tammy still held in a princess carry. "This is going to be tricky. Can someone hold her for a second?"

Denny reached out first, and Tammy recoiled. Rylan accepted the mermaid-tailed girl.

"Here man, you can take this for me instead." Callan took off his pack and chucked it to Denny, who strapped it to his front with minimal grumbling.

Harper took Tammy's pack off her as well, and Tammy was passed back to Callan to be slung over into a piggy-back position. She clung to his shoulders, and he looped one arm around the bend in her tail to support her.

The entire process left her red-faced and scowling, but she said nothing.

Everly had some idea of how Tammy felt about Callan, no matter how much she'd tried to deny it when they'd talked at Gorhanmere. She'd joked about the two of them being hopelessly in love with Howell boys who weren't interested in them.

But from her point of view now, Callan seemed to be enjoying his mermaid-carrying role. There was a depth in his gaze and pleasure on his lips that went beyond a leader's responsibility or brotherly concern. Completely different to the growing disgust Everly saw in Rylan's frown each time he looked her way.

Callan stepped onto the rocky ribbon of path that curved down the cliff face toward the crashing waves, then slowly worked his way forward. Denny fell in line behind him, then Harper, and then it was Everly's turn to step out into empty space.

Everly leaned against the rough wall, ignoring the way the sharp, wet rocks scratched at her clothes. At least if she was tilted that way, she'd be less likely to go sailing off into the dark, white-capped waves below.

Her knees shook as she turned her attention away from the open air to her right and shuffled down the path behind Harper. On the bright side, the sheer burst of adrenaline racing through her limbs had gone a long way toward numbing the agony in her cracking arms.

Rylan was right behind her, close enough that he'd taken on vampire form again, unable to fight it. The back of her neck tingled with the weight of his eyes on her, waiting to see the next sign of her weakness, her pain, the next sign that he was right all along telling her to leave this dangerous place.

Everyone had been overly worried about her since seeing the damage from the Bane. She wanted to be okay, to have left like Rylan wanted before anyone found out, but now she was starting to get overly worried, too. She wasn't okay. The cracks inside her were spreading across her collar bone. She zipped her bomber jacket right up.

Just keep moving forward. Don't fall.

Rain spit from the roiling sky and lightning flashed all around them. Every crack of thunder sent another wave of guilt through her, especially when the ground rumbled in return.

Don't let anybody fall.

They drew closer to the jagged black rocks that poked out of the unsettled waves, carved from the cliff by eons of saltwater erosion. Every time a wave splashed against them, salt spray misted over Everly, leaving a tangy taste in her mouth.

When they reached sea level, Callan came to a stop, raising his hand to be seen in the gloom.

"Looks like something up ahead," he called back, his voice almost lost to the constant roar of waves and wind.

Everly eased up behind Harper, peering around her tall double-backpacked frame to see Callan disappearing into the cliff face. She shuffled forward over slick, uneven rocks toward a slim opening, leading into inky blackness. The narrow entryway was a path of craggy steppingstones spread between water that churned so violently it could strip skin from bones.

"This is right about where that dude disappeared. Told you!" Denny called out.

Callan had already gone in, taking Tammy with him. "It's big in here, goes way into the island."

Denny and Harper followed next, carefully hopscotching from rock to rock.

"Careful," Harper called, pointing. "Stay to the left. That one wobbles."

Everly hesitated. Taking one step at a time was one thing. Leaping over slippery rocks was another.

Rylan moved up beside her and wrapped an arm across her back, holding tight around her ribcage and pressing her into his side.

Through vampire fangs, he said, "We'll go together."

He counted down before she could argue. Three, two, one, she jumped. He lifted. They landed and he steadied her when her knees buckled. His skin felt hard and cold.

"Again," he said, and they leaped.

The impact of landing shot pain through her arms and she cried out, biting it off too late.

"One more," Rylan said softly.

She nodded, vision blurring. She forced her eyes open as the final jump took them across to a larger ledge where the others stood. They hit the ground, and it held firm under her boots. She closed her eyes then, screwing them up against the pain. Rylan guided her a few steps and pressed down on her shoulders, seating her on a boulder.

"You're doing great. You're stronger than I ever realized." His voice was so hushed, so gravelly it could have been a crash of the waves echoing from outside.

Everly's eyes popped open at the words, but his back was already turned to her, facing the others.

Packs had been put down and flashlights were on, sweeping through the space to show a floor of choppy water that reached farther than their light sources could illuminate. Occasional miniature islands and pillars of rough stone covered in seaweed broke through.

The low cavern ceiling was smooth except for wavy lines where water had worn away at the rock over millennia.

Rylan turned to the slim crack and the ocean outside. "Is it low tide now?"

Denny reached up to the wet cave ceiling, ran his fingers across, and then popped one in his mouth. "Must be. That's not fresh water leaking in."

Everly eyed the underground lake, the way the ocean pushed in through the entrance, eddying through the deep pool in front of them.

"We should get out of here before the tide rises. This doesn't seem safe," she said. "Who knows who that guy was. Could be another zombie or something."

Rylan shook his head, pointing out into what was only darkness to Everly. "I think I can see something that way. Looks like the cave goes up, and we're right beneath the lighthouse. We need a way in."

Callan eyed the dark water. "I guess we're swimming in. We should check for underwater hazards first. I'll go."

Tammy, still clinging to Callan's shoulders, shook her head. "No, I'll do it. I'm already, you know, ready."

Callan twisted his neck to try to face her. "Yeah, but—"

"I can do it," she growled.

He nodded once. "Okay."

He carried her to the water and sat her at the edge. She unzipped her hoodie and tossed it onto the rock. In just her body armor and T-shirt, a visible shiver ran through her.

"This feels so weird," she said, then, clutching her flashlight, she slipped into the pool with hardly a sound.

Tammy swam away from the shore, slow at first until she seemed to get the hang of the tail. After several yards, she paused, took a deep breath she didn't need, then submerged.

Thunder rumbled outside, echoing through the cave like they were caught in the belly of a hungry beast. Tammy was taking a long time. Longer than a human breath. They said shadyrs in nyevmer form could breathe underwater, but Everly found herself holding her breath, too.

She got to her feet to watch for Tammy's return. Harper pressed close to Everly's side, her left hand resting on her axe and her right hand tucked around Everly's arm. The group waited in silence.

Tammy popped out of the water a few moments later, way out in the pool and almost beyond the beam of Everly's flashlight. Water glistened on her shaved head.

"It's deep," she called, her voice reverberating off the stones. "Really deep. Disturbing lack of ocean life, but ... there are bones down there."

Lightning illuminated the cavern, and Callan grimaced. "What kind of bones?"

"I don't know. Big ones and small ones. I didn't get close enough to see." Tammy's voice came through chattering teeth as she swam back to them. "And I feel like, I don't know, I can sense a shroudpool down there, too. I didn't want to get any closer."

"Yeah, best if we don't," Callan said.

"Understatement," Denny guffawed.

Tammy tipped her head backward. "And Rylan's right, there's a path going upward a bit farther ahead."

"Then we follow it," Rylan said, but he didn't move.

His gaze was locked on Everly, and he shook his head. She could almost read his mind. He didn't want her going any farther but knew they couldn't leave her behind alone.

She carefully put on a mask of 'I'm really okay and not in pain at all.' She had no intention of remaining behind, even if it was safe. They'd come to this cursed island, to this dangerous lighthouse, to this abyss of a cave, because of her. Whatever they were facing next, she'd face it too.

Callan squatted down, grabbed Tammy's hoodie, and re-arranged things in his pack. Pulling out a waterproof pouch, he put his phone, the satellite phone the Crybel's Cove shadyrs had given them, and a change of dry clothes inside.

"Sort your gear and get ready for a swim. Keep something dry for the other side." He made sure it was sealed properly, then did the same for Tammy's belongings.

Tammy had returned to the edge beside them and took her pack from Callan. It floated on her back, tipping her forward as she swam.

Rylan still hadn't moved. He stared out over the underground lake. "The nyevmer is close. Can you feel it?"

Callan and Denny both nodded.

Harper paused from taking off her outer layers. "You think it's in here with us, rather than out there at sea?"

Rylan's eyebrows drew together as a response.

"That's comforting," she said, stuffing her jacket, shirt, and boots into her pack. She seemed to consider taking off more, then stayed in her tank top and jeans.

Callan squinted into the distance.

"It's farther inside the island. These caves must go deep, which is why we were feeling the ghost's presence up on the bluff. I don't think it knows we're here. We'll try and get across the water fast. Shouldn't be a problem once we shift. You two are going to have to swim the old-fashioned way, though," Callan said to Everly and Harper.

"Leave my tail jealousy out of this," Harper said.

"We can help you both swim faster. Cal, can you take Harper's pack as well as yours?"

Callan nodded as he stripped down to his body armor and pants. He lowered himself into the water, and after a moment, flung his soaking-wet pants back onto the shore before reaching for his and Harper's bags.

Denny didn't seem to have the same qualms, taking off all bottoms and packing them away before walking into the lake and shifting.

Everly's eyes popped wide open in pure horror.

Rylan actually chuckled. "What with changing form all the time, shadyrs have different standards of modesty."

Everly grew even more concerned as Rylan started stripping off his own clothes. *This time it's him who's going to put me into a coma.*

He stopped removing clothes at body armor and pants. He squatted down and packed the rest away, compressed Everly's smaller backpack into a tight bundle, then squeezed it into the top of his.

His starry eyes shined up at her and he reached a hand out. "Boots, jacket."

Everly stripped as quickly and un-awkwardly as she could. She had another layer under the long-sleeved top she wore, but didn't want her arms showing, so left it on. She followed Harper into the water.

It was *frigid*. Much colder than the ocean had been when they'd climbed from the rowboat onto the beach. Even the rain wasn't as cold as the cave's water. Everly sucked in a breath, holding it deep in her chest as she waded into the water, her jeans and shirt soaking through immediately.

She gritted her teeth as the cold spread over her injured arm. She'd managed to ignore the pain while investigating around the lighthouse and climbing down the cliff because she'd had other things to focus on, like fear of a short, deadly drop onto pointy rocks.

But the salty water burned like fire on her wounds, and when she left the ground behind for deeper depths, swimming with her injured arms forced out a whimper.

She heard Rylan enter the water behind them, and carefully avoided looking back as he removed his pants and shifted.

A moment later, Rylan's strong shoulders broke the surface of the water beside her. He brushed his hands back over his shorn hair, shaking water off his face and out of his eyes. In the glow of Everly's flashlight, his dark scales shimmered like an oil slick—one moment blue, the next vivid green.

Of course Rylan's mer form would be insanely beautiful. She shouldn't have expected anything less. But it still sent a pang of yearning through her. His pack wasn't strapped on his back but held under one arm to the side, the side closest to her.

"Lean on this, and hold on," he said.

Gratefully, she did, resting her arm that held the flashlight over the semi-buoyant bag, so she could at least pretend to assist the swimming with her other hand.

Harper moved ahead of them with ease, but Rylan quickly caught up, gliding through the water even with Everly in tow.

As they reached the rest of the group, Callan said to Tammy, "Show me the bones."

Tammy nodded. She dipped beneath the surface, Callan right at her tail. Harper and Denny treaded water nearby, with Denny apparently trying to show off his tail to her, without the hoped-for response. Rylan kept him and Everly moving on.

After several moments, Tammy popped back above the water, followed by Callan.

His expression was grim. "The bones are strange, eidolghasts mostly, I'd guess. But some are human. And even worse ... Infants. Counted at least three skulls."

Harper gasped. "Oh no. *Babies*?"

A strange rumble echoed through the cave from far ahead, and the water around Everly's torso rippled from the force of it. Her heart jerked in her chest.

"Was that thunder?" Harper asked.

Her hair, which had been shiny and straight before leaping into the water, had turned dark and wavy, clinging to her skin. However, her mascara wasn't even running, despite the waves splashing against her face.

"No," Callan replied. "That was the nyevmer."

Harper gulped. "Do they ... eat children?"

"Not as far as our knowledge of them goes, but who can tell with eidolghasts?"

Everly's blood ran cold. She'd seen vasmires, weroths, and an auerdax. She didn't want to imagine the horror of what a water-dwelling eidolghast looked like. "How close is it?"

Rylan responded, "Close. But our exit is closer."

Even Everly could see it now, her flashlight beam reaching a small shore that led to a dark passageway.

They swam toward it. The current moved quickly around them, water flowing in the same direction as they swam.

It was definitely rising.

Tammy called out, "Hey. Do you guys see that? There's a light in there, up the tunnel."

They reached the shore, Harper and Everly pulling themselves out of the water first while the shadyrs who were able to shifted back to human form. The reverse process was a bit trickier than entering the water, and the three women turned their backs as Rylan, Callan, and Denny stepped out of the pool, retrieved dry pants, and put them on.

"Check it out!" Denny said.

Still at the water's edge, Tammy grumbled, "I don't think anybody here wants that."

"Not *that*. Footprints. Old fellow came this way." He wandered over beside Harper and Everly, still doing up his fly.

He pointed, and Everly shined her flashlight at the wet trail leading from the water, up into the passage in the cave wall. The marks were wide apart and too splashy to make out clear human prints from.

Harper blinked rapidly. "Oh no!"

"What's wrong?" Everly turned her light to check her over.

Harper looked her way with one bright green eye, and one brown eye, pouting.

"I lost a contact." She groaned, fishing the other one out.

Fully dressed, Callan joined them, handing Harper her pack. "Wait, your eyes aren't green?"

"Secret's out, I guess. It's like, a whole Bellsy thing. The bright-green eyes. But no, sorry to disappoint. Just another bit of me that isn't me."

Even Everly hadn't known that. She shivered, still chilled through and unable to produce any body heat.

"You wear them every single day?"

"I wear a lot every single day." Harper shrugged.

Her face had lost the sparkle and energy she'd had that morning, and her forehead was creased. She hadn't bothered changing or putting any dry layers back on but didn't shiver like Everly.

Callan scooped Tammy out of the water like a fisherman with a big catch. He kept her at the front for the upward climb, balanced by their backpacks behind him.

Rylan had pants back on, but left his top half in body armor only, as though expecting trouble. He'd changed not to human, but vampire form, and his fingers were cold as he draped Everly's jacket over her shoulders and handed her boots back.

He didn't say anything to her, instead heading to the passage entrance where his brother waited.

Callan nodded to him. "It's a stairwell, and there's light at the top."

Rylan's galaxy gaze turned skyward. "It's got to go into the lighthouse. We're going up."

Callan smirked at Tammy. "Looks like there's going to be a mermaid in the lighthouse, after all."

Harper hummed a bar of the song. "The question is, will she be the only one?"

16

ater weighed Everly's clothes down as she trudged upward, her body growing weaker by the second.

The stairs curved out of sight, toward a blue glow that ebbed softly like the sun shining through water. The dragon stirred weakly inside Everly, and its need for the light above them seeped through her being. She struggled to tell where the soul-eater's wants ended and her desire to be whole again began.

Everly trailed her fingers along stone walls covered in green algae. The cool dampness eased some of the pain crackling beneath her skin. The walls seemed to hum and pulse beneath her fingertips in time with the blue glow that illuminated the stairwell.

My love flows as deep as the ocean's black heart,
It beats in the night, it beats in the night.

The song was well and truly stuck in her head. It had always seemed so innocent when she was a kid, almost romantic. But now, the lyrics made her shiver.

As they ascended, the complete lack of sea life down in the cave transformed into an abundance of creatures moving around them. Small crabs skittered, sea snails climbed the walls, and a brightly patterned baby octopus glided away across the slick stairs to hide from their approach.

Finally, the stairwell curved one more time, and they spilled out onto the ground floor of the lighthouse.

"We made it." Denny puffed out his chest. "And we never would have found our way in if not for me. How about that?"

Nobody bothered replying to his ego.

"Everyone keep quiet," Callan ordered in a whisper. "We know we're not alone in here."

The blue glow lit the entire space, shimmering like they were underwater. Everly tucked her flashlight away in a pocket and padded softly over slick, wet floors carpeted in ribbon seaweed.

A third of the room was overtaken by the same coral and crystalline growths that had obscured the front door. An old-fashioned piano sagged against one section of wall, pouring water from its keys like a fountain, while more living coral grew out of its boxy top, covered in a horde of fingernail-sized crabs. The ceiling dripped constantly in a pitter-patter song.

No mermaids, strange men, or zombies appeared. Rylan waved them over to the curving stairwell that hugged the inside of the round wall.

"Up we go," Harper whispered cheerfully, linking her arm through Everly's.

"A million stairs is exactly what I wanted right now." Everly replied with a weak smile, grateful to have someone to lean on as the upward hike continued. Barely any warmth had returned to her body after the swim and her entire skeleton rattled with uncontrollable shivering.

Despite the bizarre angle that the lighthouse appeared to have from the outside, the interior thankfully seemed to be flat and level. Halfway to the first landing, they passed a square frame on the wall.

Everly paused with her foot on the next step, her gaze sweeping across the portrait. The walls were covered in barnacles and creeping seaweed, but the portrait remained as clean and bright as the day it was painted. It depicted a young woman close to Everly's age with midnight-dark skin and ebony hair that hung in wet ringlets around her shoulders.

Her coloring was so similar to the faceless ghost that had greeted them when they first ventured onto the island that it made Everly shiver.

The woman in the portrait sat on a lush velvet chair. Water puddled all around her, and her long mermaid tail curved around, tucked around the claw-foot leg of the furniture. She had huge sad eyes and a strangely off-putting smile that didn't sit right on her face.

Harper leaned over Everly's shoulder to peer at the girl. "Is that her? *The* mermaid?"

Callan turned back from in front of them as though noticing the painting for the first time.

He shifted Tammy in his arms to show off her tail. "Are we thinking she was a shadyr?"

"That's more likely than a true mermaid. But neither Crybel's Cove nor the Darkfreys have any knowledge of a shadyr in residence out here," Rylan said softly from a few steps down.

"Why would they? Why would anyone want to stay in this place?" Everly whispered.

"Maybe she couldn't leave." Tammy replied, her voice flat and dark.

Even in death? Everly wondered whether Tammy saw the similarity to the ghost woman too.

"Keep moving," Rylan urged softly.

They tiptoed by the portrait as though it might come to life. As the stairwell curved around, another frame loomed out of the blue gloom.

"Same girl," Callan said. "But she's just a kid in this one, like, maybe ten years old?"

Everly stepped past it, eying it as she went. The mermaid girl was depicted lying on a wet stone floor with her tail flipped up stylistically behind her. A window overhead opened onto a stormy sea. Every brushstroke was so precise and realistic.

"She looks so sad. I mean, apart from that terrifying smile."

"Creepy, right? What's going on with that," Harper replied.

A landing beneath a tiny porthole window indicated they'd reached the first floor, where a door hung open to an empty room that was drier than the rest. A workbench lined one wall, weighed down by bent tubes of paint, ratty canvases, and multiple easels holding a variety of artworks in progress. The harsh scent of turpentine stung Everly's nose.

There was no natural light to illuminate the paintings, though Everly thought she could make out the blobby beginnings of yet another portrait of the same mermaid, rougher and more twisted than the others.

"Who do we think has been doing the painting? Self-portraits?" Everly asked.

"Or the dude we followed in here?" Denny added.

"Keep moving," Rylan said again from the back. "Our target is right up top. We don't stop unless someone or something makes us. This isn't a sight-seeing trip."

Between the first- and second-floor landings, they passed a growing collection of mermaid paintings. Her age varied from hardly old enough to be considered a teenager to possible thirties, always with those sad eyes and side-show clown smile.

Each of the portraits was eerily clean and well-maintained, while the walls around them looked as if they'd been soaking in ocean water for years.

The second-floor landing had no room attached. The wall where the entrance should have been seemed somehow melted. Streaky fingerprints of rust-red marred the surface.

The third floor did have a doorway, though if there'd ever been a door hanging in the frame, it was long gone. The round room inside was filled with narrow rows of floor-to-ceiling shelves that held glass jars in a variety of shapes and sizes.

Each was filled with cloudy, yellow liquid. In the closest jars, dead, pale fish, bleached urchins, and tangled squid pressed against the glass. There were hundreds of preserved specimens in there, maybe thousands.

"Wow. Just when I thought this place couldn't get creepier," Callan whispered.

From his arms, Tammy replied, "I don't know, I think it's kind of cool. I'm keeping a list of decorating ideas."

Callan huffed. "But in black?"

"Of course."

The whiff of chemicals followed the team as they hurried by.

Two more landings up, Callan halted at yet another portrait. "I think it's safe to say the mermaid and lighthouse connection is real, one way or another."

"And if that part of the song is true, hopefully the rest is on track to get us what we need for Ev," Harper agreed. "But if the mermaid is real, where is she?"

"With how ghast-twisted this place is, I think it might be best if we don't find her," Denny muttered.

Harper pouted like she'd been told she couldn't go see a rockstar backstage.

"Denny's right," Rylan said. "Which is something I never thought I'd say. But from the look of the portraits, this mermaid could have been here her whole life. Just look at this place. It's not a healthy environment. Beshadowings corrupt things and people."

"Speaking of, have you guys noticed the water?" Tammy said, pointing to the floor. "It's flowing up now."

Everly looked down to see the trickle of water, which shimmered in the blue glow, flowing up the stairs. She wished that same, distorted gravity would also work on her. Her breath hitched in her throat; her lungs felt like the remains of a bonfire had been shoveled inside them.

They had to be at least halfway up by now, but when she pressed her face close to the small portal window to peer up toward the rotating light, her heart compressed. "It feels like we haven't gotten any closer to the top."

"You need a break?" Rylan asked.

"No."

His gaze pierced straight through her obvious lie.

"Maybe soon," she amended.

He leaned toward her as though ready to scoop her up into his arms like a mermaid, so she turned and put one foot in front of the other again, to prove she could keep going.

But the lighthouse was the thing that kept going, and going, and going.

Everly lost count after the eighth floor. Every landing had a new room, some of them empty, some of them bizarre enough to have them questioning their sanity. They passed a room where gravity had been turned upside down. Water covered the ceiling, waving lazily as it cast aqua refractions over the surprisingly dry floor.

Another room was missing entirely, opening directly onto a perilous drop into the ocean, as though all the other parts of the lighthouse around the hole didn't exist.

Small creatures continued to dart around them as they climbed. At first sight, most of the animals were recognizable as crabs, octopuses, or starfish, but upon closer inspection, they weren't quite ... right.

Starfish scuttled around at a much faster pace than should have been physically possible. A few times they had to dodge plate-sized fish flopping their way down the stairs, screaming like goats. The crabs had eyes on their backs that were too human.

On the next landing, Everly paused to catch her breath by another room as lightning

flashed through two windows that had no glass. A collection of fishing rods in different shapes and sizes leaned beside the openings.

Water rained from the ceiling in patches, splashing on the floor and weaving streams among the furniture. Piles of strange objects, from empty cans to ship anchors cluttered every part of the round room, creating a hoarder's labyrinth.

The furniture, however, was what caught Everly's attention.

"Look," she murmured. "Is that the armchair from the first portrait?"

It was hard to tell, as seaweed sprouted in patches and barnacles covered the legs. The armchair was one of two situated on a sodden Oriental rug that was barely visible beneath drifts of fine fishbones and large, pale-blue scales glistening like mother-of-pearl. A badly water-damaged picture book lay open on one of the chairs.

Harper moved in for a closer look.

"Come on, we've got to keep moving," Rylan grunted.

Harper ignored him and traced her fingertips over the soggy velvet. "I think you're right, Ev."

With a clatter, one of the fishing rods fell into the surrounding pile of detritus.

Everly's eyes widened. "Harper, get out of there!"

Her friend didn't move. She stared, fixated on the shadow behind one of the armchairs. Everly rushed to Harper's side to drag her out if necessary.

"Evie!" Rylan called out after her.

Harper raised a hand, waving the warnings away. "I thought I saw ..."

Lightning flashed, and behind the armchair, something coiled and shifted.

And then it screamed.

17

Harper's hand tightened on the axe at her hip.

Rylan and Denny charged in behind her and Everly, and the thing on the floor whimpered. Harper's throat grew tight. The *shnickt* of Denny drawing his machete swung her head around.

"Woah, woah, woah, back off," Harper hissed. "Can't you see she's terrified?"

The figure tucked into herself, folding smaller into the shadow of the armchair. She slipped on the wet floor and a pale-blue fin flopped into the light before being pulled swiftly back into the shadow with a soft squeal.

"Harper? Be careful," Everly called from behind Rylan, her voice desperate as Harper stepped forward.

"Shh, it's okay. We're not going to hurt you," Harper murmured.

She slowly took off her backpack and left it behind, then moved onto hands and knees on the seaweed-slick floor.

"We don't know that it won't hurt us," Rylan growled.

He was clearly annoyed that the human had knelt to engage the strange lighthouse inhabitant, but to his credit, he remained just inside the doorway, waiting to see what happened before he decided on a course of action.

One fretful eye appeared around the chair back, framed by dark, tangled hair. Harper recognized the starry-sky of a shadyr's eyes. They gleamed with reflected blue glow and internal sparks.

With a squeak, the face vanished again.

"Who are you? Are you here to kill me?" The small, shaky voice drifted from the darkness beyond the chair.

Harper waved a hand at the others. They sheathed their weapons and stepped backward.

Everly mouthed again, *be careful*, and Harper mouthed in reply, *I know*.

"Kill you? Of course not. We won't hurt you." Harper shuffled forward on her knees, water sloshing around her jeans.

"Hey," she said softly. "My name's Harper. Who are you?"

Four scaled and clawed fingers appeared, clutching the leg of the armchair.

"Daddy said humans ... humans would try to kill me." She had a surprisingly deep voice, soft and velvety, with a tremor like water bubbling over rocks.

Harper angled her legs to the side and went down on her hip, peeking around the edge of the chair. "Why would we do that? Some of us are just like you."

The girl's face appeared again, eyes round, showing a war between fear and curiosity. Lightning lit up the room, brightening the shadow she hid within. She wasn't as young as Harper had initially thought. She looked wild—like a girl raised in the wilderness by wolves if those wolves were from the ocean.

Her curls hung to her waist, damp and matted, intertwined with seaweed, netting, and bits of coral. Her hair and skin were both a warm, russet brown, playing off her sky-blue scales.

Despite the wildness—or maybe because of it—she was one of the most beautiful women Harper had ever seen.

Careful to avoid her voice being too loud or jarring, Harper called back to the others, "Shadyr, late teens maybe. Not the same one as in the paintings."

Everly looked to Rylan. "There's more than one?"

"What's she doing hanging out in this place?" Denny yelled back.

The girl cringed into the shadows again.

Harper hushed and murmured soothing sounds. "Don't worry about him. He's just loud, but he won't hurt you, but more importantly, *I* won't let anything hurt you, okay? Do you have a name?"

She was rewarded with a timid, "Neri."

"Neri. Nice to meet you." Harper's gaze flicked over her pale-blue tail which had unfurled a little into the light. The scales were ragged and patchy, some missing entirely. "Why don't you change back to your human form? There's not enough water for you to swim in here."

Neri blinked. "Change? I can't change, I'm a mermaid."

Callan, still holding Tammy out of sight on the landing, said, aghast, "You don't think she's been in mermaid form her whole life?"

Harper turned back to the others. Rylan had tensed up, and even Denny seemed disturbed.

"Callan," she called. "Can you bring Tammy in here?"

Rylan and Denny stepped aside and let Callan through the doorway, with Tammy still in a princess carry. She waved awkwardly, gave her tail a little wiggle, and offered Neri a rare smile.

Neri's shiny gaze took her in. Her cupid's bow lips parted, and she planted her palms on the floor, abruptly sliding out from behind the chair for a better look.

As she came into clear view, Everly covered her mouth with her hands. "Oh my."

Neri wasn't wearing a thing. Her tangled hair only partly obscured her slim, bare chest and ribcage, visible through a thin layer of skin. Rylan and Callan averted their eyes. Everly smacked Denny until he turned around.

"Another mermaid!" Neri exclaimed with a childish kind of excitement, crawling on her stomach closer to Tammy, her smile widening.

"Umm, I'm not *really* a mermaid. Like you aren't really a mermaid. We can just change to look like this sometimes."

Neri shook her head. "No. My mom was a mermaid, and so am I."

"The paintings up the stairwell, are they your mom?" Harper asked.

Neri's smile faded. "Mm-hm"

"Why didn't they tell her what she is?" Rylan asked softly. "Her mom was clearly a shadyr too, and sounds like the dad is around, warning her off humans. Why have they let her stay here, without training? Why let her think she's a mermaid?"

Neri's eyes widened as she took in Rylan's ghostly-white skin and sharp fangs. "You're not like me, what are you?"

Harper smiled and waved it off as though having a vampire around was normal. She didn't want to go too deeply into shadyr lore and how they worked. Too much information would probably overload the girl.

"Don't worry about him, it's just a ... condition he has. All of them, and you, you sort of change to look different when monsters are near."

"Like the monster that lives in the caves beneath the lighthouse?" Neri wrinkled her nose. "Daddy told me about it. That's why I'm not allowed down there."

Harper inhaled slowly, keeping her voice even. "Where can you go? Have you ever been out of the lighthouse?"

"Not yet. Daddy said he might take me out soon. There's something he wants to do that I need to be away from the lighthouse for. I don't know what it is."

Neri turned herself over onto her back so she could face Harper again, her arms displaying wiry muscles on a tiny frame. Bruises and scrapes marred her elbows, waist, and stomach. "I mostly just stay in here. Daddy says it's not safe outside my room."

Harper looked at Everly to find an identical expression of horror.

There's a mermaid in my lighthouse, and her heart belongs to me.

There's a mermaid in my lighthouse, to her I own the key.

A shudder ran up Harper's entire body. "Show her. Tammy, can you show her that you can change into a human?"

"Um, maybe? The nyevmer is farther away now, but I'm still not very good at controlling the change."

"Try," Harper growled.

She'd ask one of the guys to switch from human to mermaid but didn't want any men stripping down in front of Neri.

Callan helped hold Tammy upright and Everly extracted a blanket from Harper's pack and wrapped it around the waist section of Tammy's tail. With a look of intense concentration, Tammy brought up the shadyr transformation mist, which slowly swirled around her.

Neri gasped and reached up to take hold of the arm of the chair. She hauled herself into the seat, presumably for a better look. As Neri's hips passed over the edge of the chair, Harper glimpsed more red welts and open sores from dragging herself around on the rough floor.

Fury made her see red.

Within a few moments, Tammy's flipper vanished and pale, human toes poked out. She stood there on two, obviously-human legs. But the mist still swirled, and she wobbled.

Tammy grunted. "I can't hold it. I'm sorry."

With a flop of a tail fin, she fell backward into Callan's arms again.

"You're doing much better. You almost had it," he said.

She rolled her eyes.

"Is this ... some kind of trick?" Neri asked in a tiny, deep voice. "Is this a dream?"

Her whole body had gone rigid, and a green tinge crept up her face. She tugged at her hair with her webbed fingers.

Harper knelt beside the chair, determination burning in her veins. "Your dad, where is he now?"

If they were going to act, she needed the info, and fast.

Neri stared at the floor, blinked, then looked at Harper with a frown. "He just got home but went up to check the light. I thought you were him at first, coming back."

"He has to be the man Denny saw," Everly said.

Harper pushed on. "What about your mother? Where is she?"

Sadness passed over Neri's shining eyes.

"She died when I was really little. I only know what Daddy told me ..." She froze, then shook her head, eyes drawn to a jumble of trash over to the side. "About her. But she sounded brave. She survived a shipwreck at only ten years old. Daddy pulled her from the sea and brought her here. To safety. Where mermaid hunters wouldn't find her. He looked after her for twenty years before I came along."

Heavy sickness settled in the pit of Harper's stomach.

He *looked after* her. A child, then a woman, who gave birth to Neri.

More thunder rumbled through the structure. Harper cringed as the whole lighthouse swayed in the stormy winds.

A knot of anger and anxiety hardened in her chest. Harper stood and moved over to Everly and Rylan, leaning in close.

"We've got to get her out of here," Harper murmured. "She's been held captive and lied to about everything."

Everly's mouth was pinched. "Nobody's out there hunting mermaids. She wouldn't even be a mermaid if she wasn't here."

Rylan shook his head. "Doesn't mean she's safe to trust. She could be unhinged, beshadowed, dangerous."

"She's a *victim*. Plus, this Daddy guy was clearly helping himself to Neri's mom." The thought made Harper sick to her stomach. "Maybe even when she was still *a child*. He could be doing the same thing to Neri. Or if he hasn't yet, the threat is still there."

Callan leaned in, his forehead a twisted mess. "I think ... I think it could be even worse than that."

"What could be worse than that?" Harper snapped.

Callan's jaw clenched and he stared at the floor.

Rylan sighed and brushed his hand over his hair, glancing up at where the lighthouse lamp would be. "Fine. But we have to get to the top first, past that guy by the sounds of it, and figure out if the artifact powering this place can help Everly. Then we'll deal with saving the little mermaid."

Harper folded her arms. "We're not leaving her here, not for another moment. I'll carry her if I have to."

Rylan said, "We don't even know if she wants to leave, if she will leave."

"Neri?" Harper turned back to her suddenly. "Will you come with us, out of the lighthouse?"

Neri pulled her tail up, cuddling it to her chest. "Out?"

Harper put on her best and friendliest camera-ready smile, moved closer, and crouched beside the chair. "Yeah, outside. We can show you what it's like out there."

Neri's head whipped from side to side. "It's dangerous."

Harper chewed her bottom lip. She couldn't lie to this girl.

"It can be. But I'll protect you. I promise."

Neri shifted forward, and after a few false starts, reached a hand toward Harper. Harper held her breath as the girl's fingertips lightly brushed her knee and then pulled back.

She whispered. "You really think ... I could have legs?"

Harper gave her a sparkling smile and a nod.

But Neri's gaze had slipped over Harper's shoulder, and her eyes widened.

A new voice roared through the room over the noise from the storm. "Get away from my mermaid!"

18

Harper whirled around and threw herself in front of Neri. At one point in the distant past, the ... *thing* ... in the doorway might have been a man.

He hunched there, bigger than seemed natural with shoulders that curved smoothly into a wide, scaly neck. If his head, neck, and shoulders had ever been separate body parts, they weren't now, as though someone had remolded his upper body into a hideous, humanoid fish, like the zombies. But he stared at them with piercing clarity.

He had the face of an anglerfish—beady eyes, uncovered nostrils, and far too many sharp teeth. What human features remained on his face were aged, lined by carved valleys and folds of dripping, gray skin. His lower appendages stuck out from the wet, fraying hems of his shorts, white and bloated with water retention.

They were less leg and more a cluster of tangled tentacles. His thick arms were covered in barnacles, his hands like meaty seal fins.

He was a walking nightmare.

"It's okay, it's just Daddy," Neri said from behind.

Harper tasted bile. She pulled her axe from its holster and held it steady in front of her. The heavy lump of metal had made swimming through the caves difficult but now, staring down the hideous monster blocking the doorway, she was very, *very* glad to have a weapon. She just wished her strength hadn't waned so much.

It runs out so fast. I should have brought the Bane with me for a top-up. But then Everly would have known, had felt it, had suffered from its presence. Hopefully she had enough power left.

"Don't come any closer!" she ordered the fish-man.

The rest of the team cleared away from the door, giving the man space.

"Who are you?" he hollered through a gurgling throat. "Did you come to steal my mermaid?"

Rylan held out a calming hand. "That's not what we came for."

Technically, Harper thought, *but it will be what we do.*

This monster had held Neri captive for years. For her *entire* life.

That stopped now.

"She's not yours," Harper spat back, disgusted. "She only belongs to herself!"

His beady eyes bulged wildly, and he stomped closer. Tiny creatures climbed and clawed around the bundle of tentacles that formed his feet.

"No, Daddy, don't hurt them. They said they're like me, look." Neri pointed across to where Callan held Tammy behind the door.

Her iridescent, dark-rainbow tail sparkled in the intermittent bursts of lightning. The man zeroed in on her with ruthless excitement, breathing audibly.

"Another mermaid?" He sloshed forward, flipper hands squeezing and releasing as he reached for Tammy.

Callan took a long stride away from him.

"Back off," he snarled, holding Tammy tight to his chest with one arm.

His other hand drew the wickedly large hunting knife from a sheath strapped to his thigh. His nebulous shadyr eyes flashed dangerously.

The old man doubled over, gasping despite being completely untouched. His wet, scaled upper body shook as he straightened, arms flailing.

"Mermaid hunters, mermaid hunters!" he screeched at Neri. "They have one already. They want you, too."

Neri curled back into the armchair, shivering all over. "They said they wanted to take me away."

"There's no such thing as mermaid hunters," Harper snarled in frustration.

This man is completely mad.

He didn't seem to know what shadyrs were and wasn't one himself, or he'd be stuck as a mermaid, too. He was just a man, twisted by the beshadowing and his obsession with mermaids. Disgust filled every part of Harper's being. She had no idea if he had ever once been any kind of good person.

Maybe when he'd saved Neri's mother's life, it had been out of the goodness of his heart. Maybe his initial intentions had been heroic.

Then why did he keep her locked up here?

No. Harper couldn't imagine that he was ever a good person.

She didn't dare imagine what Neri had been through, or her poor mother before that. They were both trapped here for ages, unable to leave this beshadowed, forsaken place.

He'd imprisoned them. Given them no other option but to be his pets.

It was too late for Neri's mother, but Harper would be damned if she didn't get Neri out of there.

But now Neri stared at *her* with the eyes of cornered prey.

The rest of the team remained where they stood around the room. Everyone was on alert but in a holding pattern, waiting to see whether this could be talked out before resorting to violence.

They slowly lowered their backpacks to the ground, preparing for the need for action.

When the man had his back to them, the Howell team signaled to each other with hands and mouthed words. Rylan pointed to Everly, then upstairs, and she shook her head. Denny pointed to Rylan and made a flappy bat shape with his hands, and Callan put Tammy down on a wooden crate against the wall behind him, gesturing for her to stay. She gave him two middle fingers in return.

Harper knew if it came to a fight, Rylan might be the only useful shadyr since their mermaid forms were useless out of the water. She still had some strength from the Bane, but nothing near what it was like when the cuts were fresh. Better if they could talk their way, and Neri's way, out of this.

Harper also couldn't see Neri being happy going with them if the first thing they did was murder her father.

Readjusting her grip on the axe, Harper lowered it into one hand and raised the other. "Okay, slow down. We're not mermaid hunters. We all want what's best for Neri. If you're her father, that's what you want too, right?"

The man's bloodshot gaze swung between Neri and Tammy, his hands still making strange grabby motions.

He sang in a low, surprisingly clear warble, *"There's a mermaid in my lighthouse, and her heart belongs to me."*

Since coming to Shroudhaven with Everly, Harper had gotten to know the casually-called "mermaid song" that played nearly constantly around town. She could sing it word-for-word without issue now. But listening to the words spill from the fish man's mouth sent a chill through her. The words landed differently now. More haunting. More disturbing.

Not a love story, but one of horrific captivity.

There was a familiarity to his voice that stung Harper right through the heart.

"You ... Did you write the song?" Harper asked.

"There's a mermaid in my lighthouse, to her I own the key," the old man continued as if she hadn't spoken.

Everly caught Harper's eye, shaking her head. "And those portraits. I bet he painted the portraits of Neri's mom. From the time she was a child until ..."

She trailed off, letting the shadyr's death settle in silence between them.

"My muse, my muse. The greatest of muses." The man broke out of the song, his teeth gnashing wetly with every word.

His voice gargled, as though the water that soaked everything else here had taken root in his throat.

"My lighthouse. My muses. My mermaids. You will leave. All leave. Except her."

He pointed at Tammy with fused-together fingers that ended in sharp nails.

Callan raised his hunting knife in response.

From across the room, Denny spoke up. "Dude's mad. We can't negotiate with him. His mind is too broken."

"I don't think he's just going to let us leave, either. He wants Tammy now, too," Callan said.

"And we're not leaving Neri!" Harper hissed.

Everly nodded back to her in solidarity.

Neri's father shuffled sideways, sending up little swirls and eddies in the water on the floor as he skirted around Harper.

"Neri? You hear that? They want to steal you. They do. Tell them. Tell them this is your home, and no one will take you from me. This is where mermaids belong. This is where you're safe."

Harper glanced back and could see a sickening doubt in Neri's eyes. "Can't you see, he's your captor. He's lied to you your whole life. He's kept you here, like a possession, no matter how it's hurt you. He's a monster."

Neri's head turned rhythmically from side to side, tears bursting from her eyes. When Harper reached for her, she cowered back into the chair.

Harper turned to Everly and the others, desperate. "How can we make her see?"

The fish man cocked his head. His graying eyes locked onto Harper's face and a wide, sneering grin displayed his disturbingly sharp teeth.

Callan took a step forward, glaring the man down. "The human bones in the cave, where are they from?"

"Bones?" Neri asked, her husky voice broken by a shiver.

"There's no bones," the man barked, waving an arm through the air.

"Underwater, in the cave," Callan explained to Neri in slow, hard words. "We found bones, of babies."

Neri's face crumpled. "There are *baby* bones in the caves?"

"No such thing!" the fish man howled.

He barreled across the room, shouldering Harper aside, then grasped onto each side of Neri's head. His thick, fingery fins pressed over her ears, squeezing so hard that he lifted her from the chair by her head. He bounced her up and down against the cushions with the anger of his words.

"Don't listen to them, don't listen, they lie, they want to steal my mermaid. Don't listen, don't listen."

Neri shrieked, her tail whipping underneath her for some leverage against the assault.

Fury turned Harper's entire body to flame. She lunged forward and raised the axe high over her head before she brought it down with all her strength.

The man was beyond saving at this point, anyway. The power of the Bane reignited, pulsed, imagining the deadly sharp metal slicing into the monster's skull. Craving it.

"No!" Neri cried.

At the last moment, Harper turned the axe broadside so that the flat portion slammed into the old man's head instead of the sharp edge.

He let go of his daughter and tipped sideways with a small, pained grunt, stumbling several steps through the pooling water, then splashed down on his back. Thunder rumbled outside the lighthouse, and the walls shivered and creaked.

Neri screamed in horror and pitched herself off the armchair, scuttling away behind piles of clutter.

Harper strode to the man, kicking water in his face. "Why are there bones of children down there?"

The fish man lashed out with his strangely bloated tentacle legs. When she dodged them, he glared up at her, remaining mute.

Callan answered, "I suspect they're Neri's siblings. With Neri's mother being shadyr and this asshole being human—at least in the past—there's only a fifty-fifty chance that the infants will carry the shadyr gene."

Acid rose in Harper's throat. They could have died in childbirth, or during infancy. They *could* have. This clearly wasn't a safe environment for having or raising babies. That Neri survived to this age was a miracle. It could have easily been natural deaths … and if that were the truth, it would still have been horrifying cruelty at the hands of this man.

But Callan's theory rang too true. It wasn't that, or only that.

Harper sneered down at the monster as she said, "You *killed* your children because they weren't born with *tails*?"

Neri's tiny, scared voice arose again over the constant fall of water in the room. "You're lying, stop lying. Why did you come here? Why are you saying these things?"

Neri's father huffed like a rabid beast, then rolled to his hands and knees. With effort, the awkwardly-shaped fish-man hauled his bulk to his feet and lifted his malformed head to glare at Harper.

"There's nothing down there, Neri, only the monster," he gurgled, though he didn't look away from Harper. "They're trying to steal you from me."

Harper's lips curled away from her teeth. "Liar! You forced yourself on Neri's mother over and over, turning her into a baby factory until she gave you the offspring you wanted."

A new horror flowed ice into her veins. "Then what did you do? What did you do to her once you had a fresh new mermaid for yourself? You couldn't let her stay and tell Neri what you've done, could you?"

Neri wailed wordlessly.

Something switched in the old man's unfocused gaze.

With a wild, inhuman sound like a cow being slaughtered, he lunged at Harper, his long nails curved into vicious claws.

19

Jasper stared up at Rook's Theater, hoping he wasn't leading Cherry to his death.

He rocked back on his heels as he noted all the new graffiti that had popped up in the weeks since he'd last walked past the place. The back wall was so smothered in impressive street art and illegible spray tags that it looked like an abstract art exposé on the declining modern world.

"If the thing you're after is the weird bone sculpture Callan saw, it's not there anymore." Cherry stood with his hands in his jacket pockets, eying the theater warily as though he suspected it might try to steal his wallet. "We came back and checked the next day."

Jasper knew that. They'd still been communicating back then, still been together. "No, that's not my mission target."

Cherry took one long step toward him, hovering close to his personal space. "Don't suppose you know what that thing was?"

Jasper tilted his head. Was Cherry grilling him? Was that the only reason he'd agreed to come along?

The idea brought half a smile to Jasper's lips. He always did admire Cherry's audacity.

"No, I have no knowledge of bone statues."

A deep chill rolled off the nearby river, and cold wind cut past Jasper, sending a shiver through him despite his Darkfrey armor, two layers of shirts, and cardigan. Shadows lay like a cloak over the theater, and there was a sense of despair in the air. He was glad Cherry was here beside him, whatever the reason behind it.

But there was a heaviness to Jasper's shoulders tonight that even Cherry's closeness couldn't banish.

He should have been gratified to have been given such an important mission by a superior. On any given day, he attempted to stay low-key so that nobody would suspect that he didn't exactly fit the traditional Darkfrey lifestyle, but that also meant he often felt unseen and unneeded.

More a ghost in the system than an active participant. Vonny picking him for something she considered important should have pleased him.

But Cherry's words from back at The Crow's Nest hung over him, deeper than the shadows over the theater.

Did it occur to you she might have sent you on a mission alone to get you killed?

The statement had rooted in his gut like a poisonous plant.

Was there an ulterior motive to Vonny's actions? Why had she given him so few details and demanded he go alone? Was this a real mission at all? Did she know his secret?

The possibility that this was some sort of trap, some way of ridding the Darkfreys of an unwanted member, left Jasper shaken. The possibility that he'd brought Cherry into that trap almost had him turning tail right then.

He hated that his faith in the Darkfreys had been broken enough to let those doubts in. It was ridiculous. Even if they knew he was gay, they wouldn't send him to die, surely. At worst, he'd be kicked out like Cherry.

Except Cherry had told him what Rushelle's brace did to her. Sent her into a deadly situation, alone, and left her there. Just because she wanted to write some damned books instead of hunt monsters. Cherry probably got off lightly because he hadn't reached brace duty yet. Jasper could imagine Vonny and Nilson taking his deceit as a personal insult to their brace, their status.

Despite the brisk chill, Jasper found himself sweating.

"Are we getting into this spooky joint or what?" Cherry flashed a wide, cheeky grin his way, although it didn't reach his eyes.

Jasper's heart fluttered uncomfortably. He could smell Cherry's lip gloss on the air, and the gloomy, overcast light made his red hair glow brighter than normal. He was so effortlessly, inordinately beautiful. So perfectly comfortable with who he was and what he stood for, while Jasper's own skin was ill-fitting and strangling.

This was a bad idea. Being here. With him.

But the sad truth was, he couldn't do this alone. He felt stronger and safer with Cherry at his side. Cherry's presence made him a better version of himself.

Jasper walked up to the back door and examined the rusty chains that had been wrapped through the scratched handle. A combination lock dangled from the chains, and a cursory check proved it was locked tight.

"Von didn't give me a key. Guess we're going to have to break in," Jasper said, backing up to study the building.

Most lower windows had been boarded up with plywood that had been painted like movie poster art.

Why hadn't Vonny gotten access to this place on record so she could give him a key? We should leave.

Cherry scoffed. "It's a decoy."

Jasper raised an eyebrow. "Sorry, decoy?"

Cherry's thick combat boots scuffled across the alley as he stomped up to the back door. He grabbed two dangling edges of the chain and shifted them around, then a split second later, the chains peeled away from the handle.

"The lock was already busted last time we went in. We just hung the chain up again to look like it's doing something. The place is wide open." He tossed the chain aside, then motioned for Jasper to follow him. "Come on. Let's get your mystery job done."

Beneath Cherry's fingertips, the theater door creaked like the cry of a pterodactyl. Jasper hurried in behind him as they traded the cold morning air for the dark, musty interior.

Jasper's vision adjusted immediately, and his underlying shadyr night vision kicked into gear so that he could see his path through the crowded hallway. The place was a horrendous mess, like a wave of furniture and refuse had crashed through the area.

The two of them picked their way around broken chairs, rolled-up backdrops, and dress mannequins that lay haphazardly in the shadows. A hideous jumble of life-sized doll children had been piled to one side.

"I did not notice them last time." Cherry whistled low under his breath. "I know I said I had your back, but if those things come to life, I'm out."

Jasper couldn't argue with that sentiment. Fighting ghasts was one thing; coming up against creepy black-eyed demon children was quite another. They didn't have a shadyr form for that.

"I can't sense anything, can you?" Jasper asked, then bit his tongue.

Proximity to eidolghasts was a sensitive topic for Cherry. It didn't help that he'd been kicked out of training before he'd had the chance to master control of his shifting.

With a sigh, Cherry gestured to his still-human self. "We're obviously free from beasts of the Everdark. This place is eerie as, but I don't think it's beshadowed. Just, you know, naturally creepy."

The corridor spilled past musty bathrooms and more junk piled up along the walls on either side. Old clothing racks, strange statues—including several plaster gargoyles and creepy robed angels—plus boxes and boxes of props that exploded with feathers, rope, and gold chains. Everything that had once had a place on the stage had found a new home in the halls, giving the place an overcrowded, menacing feel.

"So ..." Cherry said, his low voice breaking the silence. "You gonna give me a clue what we're looking for?"

"A shadyr artifact," Jasper replied distractedly, his gaze sweeping the darkest shadows behind the debris. "One that's been missing from the estate for a while."

Cherry looked skeptical. "Why do they think one is here?"

Jasper shrugged. He didn't have an answer to that. But Vonny thought it was there. A number of relics had been missing from the estate for years, and the Howells' trip to

Gorhanmere had only turned out one.

Maybe the estate had decided it was time to start hunting down the others, and Vonny had info that one was at the theater. Why Jasper had to come for it alone, though, was the bigger mystery.

She'd given him a rough description of what to look for, but this place was a treasure hunter's nightmare. The clutter could take decades to search thoroughly. Jasper had to hope that if he was close, he'd *sense* the artifact.

When he'd followed Lian and Everly into the forbidden chamber at the estate that housed other shadyr treasures, he'd felt them then, a soft, thrumming magic that warmed his veins. He hoped this relic would be the same, and he wouldn't be stuck seeking a needle in a costume stack forever. Jasper pulled ahead of Cherry, sweeping the quiet building with his honed senses. Nothing. Lacking any other clue, he headed toward the center of the building.

They passed through broken doors, then through two rows of trumpeting angels that glowed demonically in his night vision. Every step he took made them move and shake, and their smooth, sightless eyes appeared a little too knowing. Too seeing. He forced his gaze to remain firmly on the path ahead, even as his skin crawled.

Cherry spoke again, breaking the loaded silence. "This place must have been beautiful once, don't you think?"

Trust Cherry to see the beauty in anything.

Jasper offered a soft grunt in reply. The ground sloped down as they left the entrance hall for the theater. The ceiling soared overhead, stretching out around them in a dusky dome, while old, broken seats stepped toward a decimated stage.

Jasper eyed the damage, noting that it looked a little too new to have rotted over time.

Cherry followed his gaze. "Yeah, the Howell boys really ripped this place up. This is where Rylan took down a vasmire, solo. When Callan, myself, and the ladies came to check it out, we also got hit by a weroth. Weird, don't you think? Two eidolghasts of different types wanting to hole up here so soon after each other?"

"We can't attribute logic to those creatures," Jasper said distractedly. "And two points of data alone can't conclude anything."

"I love it when you talk statistics to me."

A hot blush hit Jasper's cheeks and he turned away. "Let's, uh, investigate down there."

The wide path through the seats turned into a steeper decline. Jasper kept half his attention on his feet and the other half on bottling up his feelings until they reached the orchestra pit.

Cherry *tsked*. "Well, at least we know that weroth isn't still here. Otherwise, I'd be furry by now."

"Are you still training with Callan?"

Cherry took a moment before replying, "Yeah. And he's a good teacher. I guess I'm just finding it hard to focus lately. Everything has been feeling hard since ... you know."

Pop. The bottle opened again.

For one overwhelming moment, Jasper wasn't sure why his chest seemed to be heating from within and thought maybe he'd suffered some form of literal heartbreak.

Then he remembered what he'd come looking for.

Down below, where the orchestra used to play, the destruction was massive. Everything once housed there was shattered to pieces. Jasper couldn't even make out what anything had originally been. Chairs, tables, ghast knew what else, all now nothing but blackened splinters.

"Do you feel that?" he asked.

Cherry screwed up his nose. "Maybe, a little. Shadyr senses tingling, right? Not an eidolghast?"

"No, something down there. I think it's what we're after."

Jasper hopped over the wall and dropped into the pit, focusing on a far corner of the room.

Cherry landed lightly behind him. "Where's it coming from?"

"Over here." A narrow, closed door peeked out of the shadows, and Jasper could feel the artifact pulsing from within.

Cherry laughed out his nose. "You've always been better at all this stuff than me."

Jasper strode to the door and pulled it open. The closet was empty except for a bundle of rags on the floor, but that low hum was obviously coming from beneath the tattered fabric.

Jasper knelt and peeled back the material, revealing a strange, diamond-shaped blade with no hilt. A fine filigree pattern covered its surface, and blood seemed to ooze up through the ornate shapes.

"Wrap it back up." All humor had left Cherry's face, and he stared coldly. "That's what you came here for?"

Jasper bundled the odd blade in its wrapping again and stood to face Cherry. "Fits the description Vonny gave me, yes."

"It doesn't belong to the Darkfreys. Give it to me." Cherry's hand shot out, waiting.

Jasper didn't release the bundle. "Of course it belongs to the Darkfreys. It's a shadyr artifact. I can feel the power in it."

Cherry shifted uncomfortably. "That's the Bane of Teeth and Stars. That's what we found in Gorhanmere. It belongs to us now."

"What's it doing here, then?"

"I don't know! Harper was looking after it. She must have hid it here for safekeeping

because it makes Everly sick when it's near her." His dark eyes lifted accusingly to Jasper's. "Did you know the artifact you were sent to get was the one we found?"

"No, I didn't know. I only knew it was a missing artifact." Jasper swallowed the pleading tone from his voice. "But that's all I need to know. All shadyr artifacts belong at the estate."

Cherry's open hand sped out and wrapped around the parchment-covered bundle. "Not this one. We earned this. The Darkfreys were too scared to deal with their crazy renegade brethren. We almost died to get this, and you're just going to come in and steal it from us? No wonder Vonny kept this quiet. She didn't want anyone knowing what cowards you all are."

Jasper tightened his long fingers on the bundle and yanked against Cherry's hold. "There has to be more to it than that. This must be important, or Vonny wouldn't have sent me—"

"You really think she respects you?" Cherry narrowed his eyes viciously, fingers digging in as he strengthened his attempt to snatch the artifact. "That thing is important. To us. This is what brought Rylan back, and it's our only solid lead into what is inside Everly. I can't believe you dragged me here as 'backup' to help you *steal it*."

Breath snorted hard and fast from Jasper's nose as the artifact was wrestled between them. Each of Cherry's words struck him like a blow. But he had to complete his mission. He had to take claim over what was rightfully Darkfrey property. He wrenched back, wresting the parcel free from Cherry's grip, leaving his ex staggering.

Cherry grunted and stepped away from Jasper, shoulders slumped. "So, that's where we are? Yet again, you choose the Darkfreys over me, when I ..."

Jasper stared between him and the bundle in his grip. "I didn't know anything about this artifact, or where it came from, or its connections to your team."

"But you do now." Cherry glared up from beneath a veil of bright red hair. "Are you going to do the right thing and hand it over?"

Jasper sighed, his breath coming out shakily. "You know I can't do that. This is a shadyr artifact, and they all belong to—"

"You sound like a fucking robot," Cherry cut in, hands balled into fists.

Bristling, Jasper tucked the tattered bundle into his cardigan as he replied, "My mission was to retrieve this artifact, and now I have it."

"Yeah." Cherry laughed scathingly. "Yeah, you have your artifact. And your brace. And your precious Darkfrey status. How does it feel to sacrifice everything to an institution that doesn't give a crap about the real you, who will never truly accept you or love you?"

Jasper gritted his teeth as pain billowed through his chest like Cherry had ripped him open with his fingernails. "Move out of my way. You know you can't best me in

a fight."

Cherry huffed, shaking his head. "You would, wouldn't you? You would beat me."

He backed away a couple more steps, swallowing visibly. For the first time since the argument began, Jasper caught a glimpse of Cherry's emotions bald on his face. Then his expression walled back up and he turned a penetrating glare on Jasper.

"Don't ever call me again, even in an emergency," Cherry said. "Don't expect me to ever have your back again, or care if that means you die."

As their eyes met one last time, Jasper's insides turned cold at the lack of emotion in Cherry's usually bright, expressive gaze.

Then Cherry whirled on his heel and stalked away. He clambered easily up the orchestra pit's tumble-down wall, then stomped up the aisle.

Leaving Jasper frozen on the dusty parquet. He stared into the quiet darkness for some time after the sharp finality of the theater's door slamming shut. Jasper pressed his hand against the bundle at his chest and found himself disappointed that this hadn't been an attempt by Vonny to kill him.

It would have hurt less.

20

N eri's father's gnarled flippers latched onto Harper before she could get her axe up between them. She had no room to move, not even an instant to try to throw up a block before his claws sank in.

He squeezed with unbelievable strength, nails digging into her arms as he threw his entire deformed bulk against her body. They went down in a tangle of cold, wet limbs. Sharp scales and seashells crunched under Harper's back. Her axe fell out of her hands.

The Howell team was yelling, and Neri continued screaming. Harper couldn't make out any words over the fish man's roars.

Harper struggled to get her hands between her and the madman. Water sloshed like a miniature ocean around them, and the waves passed over her face and head, leaving her sightless and sputtering. She flailed blindly at the fish man even as his weight pressed her deeper into the ocean-floor carpet, deeper beneath the water.

Neri's father had appeared ancient and run-down only moments before, but he was supernaturally strong in his twisted, fishy, beshadowed form. More than human. More than superhuman.

Harper knew something of supernatural strength, though. With a final slip of an elbow, she got her arms into position, leveraging against the man's chest. With a howling war cry, she thrust upward, throwing the fish man off her.

He rolled sideward, tumbling into a pile of junk.

Harper lifted her soaking head from the water for a deep, thankful breath. In the clear gap the man left behind were Denny and Callan, staring back, arms out and baffled.

"Gotta be faster than that," she told them, kipping up to her feet.

Her attempt to show her strength and capability was ruined when her legs wobbled, knees landing in a splash.

The Bane's power was fading so fast. And she was capable, she knew it, even without the Bane. At least normally.

But right now, she was a human who hadn't had a proper night's sleep in days and had pushed her body to the limits every moment between.

I've screwed up. I should have been more careful to rest even when I didn't feel like

I needed it. I shouldn't have relied on the Bane to keep me going when I couldn't bring it with me.

But the desire to use that power, to draw it into her and revel in the strength it gave was so alluring, so irresistible. She already craved the feel of it slicing her skin again. The rush of pure, condensed energy flowing in. But that couldn't happen, not anytime soon.

Whatever was left in her would have to be enough. For Neri, and for Everly.

Harper shoved her mass of wet dark hair away from her face, grabbing her axe from the roiling water before she straightened.

Across the room, Rylan faced the fishy monstrosity, fists clenched, ready for a fight. The man didn't let them down.

Neri's father laid into him with those heavy, clawed flippers. A windmill of blows smashed against Rylan's body. Rylan kept his forearms up to guard his head, taking the blows without fighting back. Waiting for an opening, or the man to tire.

His shadyr form gave him some protection, but even still, skin broke, then regenerated, broke, then regenerated as Rylan glared the man down with bared vampire teeth.

Callan and Denny ran to join him, but they only had their blades and their human forms to help. They sliced at the man's back, but the knives glanced off his thick, leathery skin.

Harper checked for Neri, Tammy, and Everly.

Tammy was down on hands and scaly hip, crawling herself toward the fight with a look of determination in her kohl-rimmed eyes.

Everly crouched on the floor, staring into a dark corner between a broken cabinet and a stack of old tires. A hint of sky-blue tail flicked her way.

Harper passed beneath a waterfall coming down from a split in the ceiling and swiped her eyes clear as she stumbled to Everly's side.

Everly had Neri by both arms.

"I can't hold her back much longer," she panted, her face pale and scrunched.

Harper lowered to one knee next to her, looking at the scared girl.

Neri clawed at the wet floor, tears streaming down her face. When Harper got close enough, Neri's cold, trembling hands caught hers.

"Make it stop. Please! You made him angry."

She whispered the word *angry* as though it were the worst thing in her tiny world.

Harper knew anger, too, and did everything she could to contain it.

She made her voice as gentle as possible. "He's the one that has to be stopped. What he's done, what he's doing to you, imprisoning you here, has to end."

"Please don't hurt him!" Neri's scaled hand squeezed, her eyes widening fearfully.

"If he backs down, right now, and lets us take you to safety, we won't hurt him.

But do you think he'd allow that? Do you really think he'll ever let you go?" Harper begged the shadyr with her eyes to *listen* and understand what she was saying.

Neri released Harper, bringing her arms into herself. She clutched at her hair, wringing it fretfully in front of her chin. Her head shook in tiny side-to-side motions but deep, knowing despair filled her eyes.

Harper wanted to pull the traumatized girl into an embrace and hold her until everything was okay again.

She settled with placing just the tips of her fingers onto her shoulder. "Please, stay with Everly. Stay out of the way, until ... your father isn't angry anymore."

Neri didn't respond but made no further attempts to move.

"Thanks," Everly said, leaning back on the broken cabinet with a tired sigh. "I'll keep an eye on her. Are you okay?"

Harper gave her a tentative smile that probably wasn't reassuring at all. "Yeah, I've got this."

She sloshed away, unsure if she was more unsettled by what they might have to do to Neri's father, or how hard she found it to stand back up again.

She hefted her axe and raced toward the fight.

Rylan and Denny grabbed the fish man by both arms and threw him against the wall. The whole room shook, and jets of water spurted from the ceiling. The movement barely stunned the man, and he spun away from the cracked concrete on light feet, racing back toward the team with a mighty, gurgling roar.

Whip-like, Tammy's tail lashed out at his tentacle-ankles, skittling him.

Neri's father barrel-rolled, knocking Denny down on his way, then disappeared behind the chaos of waterfalls pouring from the ceiling.

Rylan growled and swiped at the blood-tinted water rushing down his white-skinned face. "We're barely touching this guy. I can hold him for a while, but he just won't stop."

Denny righted himself with a groan. "Not our fault our only options right now are being human or mermaid."

"Lucky you, you have a choice," Tammy muttered from the floor.

"They aren't your only options though," Harper said, pointing her axe at Rylan. "You annihilated the Nazi zombies in that crazy dragon-man form. Didn't you make that work because of Everly's presence?"

"Wings would only get in the way here." His starry-eyed gaze swept across the room to where Everly hunched beside Neri.

The two of them locked eyes, and strain tightened Everly's expression. She carried so much guilt and despair over what had happened between the two of them, even though it wasn't her fault. Everly never meant to drag Rylan into her dream world, and the way he'd been treating her since she risked her own life to save his grated on

Harper's nerves.

Her best friend deserved better.

"Then work something else out, and maybe be grateful about what she's done for you, and continues to do for you, for once!" Harper turned to face the direction that the old man had rolled toward.

Through the film of falling water, his silhouette approached.

"All of you, pull it together. Or do you want your asses kicked by a fish?" Without waiting for a reply, Harper raised her axe and leaped at the man.

He blocked her first blow with one flippered arm. Strange black blood spurted where the blade sank into his slimy skin, but he didn't react with pain. He whirled like a waterspout and slammed into Harper.

The Bane's remnant energy flared inside her, and she held her ground. She redirected the momentum into another slash of her axe, taking several claws off the end of one flipper with a well-placed strike.

The fish man screamed, eyes rolling wildly. He darted away, trailing more black blood on the water.

Harper raced in pursuit, but a larger figure leaped in front of her. A massive shape like a werewolf, but instead of fur, the skin was covered in glistening, dark-blue scales.

It had to be Rylan. What was that? Was he drawing from part weroth and part nyevmer? Whatever it was, it was strong, and fast. He sped for the man, tearing across the room on all fours.

Rylan swiped out with claws much longer and sharper than the lighthouse keeper's ugly nails. He caught Neri's father across his deformed face and sent the old man flying into the wall with a dull *thwack*. At the same moment, a vicious crack of thunder broke over the lighthouse, and the floor shuddered under Harper's feet.

Her knees buckled and she sank quickly into the water, shooting one hand out to catch herself before she could fall in face first. A wave of exhaustion washed through her. The initial adrenaline of finding Neri and then being caught off guard by her grotesque father had begun to wear off, and fatigue was overwhelming her.

Clutching her axe with white-knuckled fingers, Harper shoved aside the woozy, pale feeling in her head. *I don't have time for being weak.*

Rylan and the fish man were in full savage mode as Harper hefted her suddenly too-heavy axe and straightened back up onto too-heavy legs—right as Rylan slammed Neri's father into the wall again.

The lighthouse shook, and a deluge of fresh water poured from overhead as if the ceiling had yawned open and dumped the storm inside.

"*Ah!*" Harper squealed embarrassingly and was thrown backward by the heavy downpour.

She hit the floor and was washed across it by the rising water. Her axe disappeared under the surge.

The wave crashed around the room. One of the piles of random objects toppled over. Broken mugs, moldy action figures, and empty cans splashed down. One bright-yellow object caught Harper's eye as it burst free of the clutter and skidded through the water—a wind-up emergency radio.

"No!" Neri gasped.

She pushed past Everly, knocking her against the tires. Everly grimaced, holding her arms into her chest. Neri threw herself belly first over the wet floor toward the radio.

Her cry caught her father's attention and his eyes bulged as she scooped the radio into her hands. "What is that? Where'd you get that?"

He swiped away Rylan's blows and stomped toward his daughter. Neri backed into shelter behind a small cupboard, tail flopping as she hopped on her hands.

Rylan threw himself onto the man, drawing the attention back to him. A flash filled the frame of the window behind them, and Harper caught sight of a huge crack in the wall she hadn't noticed before.

The lighthouse shuddered and groaned like a dying dragon. Rylan and the fish man battled like wild animals, growing closer and closer to Neri.

Harper's heart lodged in her throat, and she splashed her way through the deepening pool toward the terrified mermaid. It was like being on a sinking ship that was taking on water from every angle.

More ceiling fell away on the other side of the room. A wave of saltwater sent Harper slamming into Neri.

Harper clung to the girl and yelled over the roar of rushing water, "Neri, get back, it's not—"

She didn't get a chance to finish her sentence.

Rylan and the man slammed into the wall again. Their combined weight hit the crack, and with a terrifying crunch, the side of the room fell away.

The whole building tipped, as though the interior was finally catching up to the crooked angle of the lighthouse exterior.

Water swept around Harper. It lifted her like driftwood and sent her spinning.

Neri's cold fingers tightened on her own, and the two of them clung to each other as they washed toward the hole in the wall.

Harper gasped for air, thinking fast as the exit rushed at them.

A large, dark silhouette clung to one side of the ruined bricks as water washed out around his bent knees. Rylan. But he was out of reach.

Harper extracted one hand from Neri's grasp, threw her arm out, and grabbed for anything she could.

She snatched at the sharp, broken concrete, catching the edge of the floor with the very tips of her manicured nails.

As her nails scraped and broke along the stones, she managed to latch one leg around the wall right before the water sent her spilling into open air.

Their tumble ceased with a jarring snap of her muscles. She clasped Neri's wrist in her hand, and Neri held on. They hung far above the white-capped waves that tore at the jagged rocks below with deadly ferocity.

Neri shrieked, a raw, ragged sound that was surprisingly loud over the booming thunder and crashing waves. Her slippery fingers slid down.

Harper tightened her grip, confused over why Neri felt so heavy …

Until she saw the old man clinging to her tail far below.

"No!" Harper groaned hoarsely.

Neri's fingers dug into Harper's skin, and she squeezed her terrified, starry eyes shut. Water poured around them, obscuring Harper's vision and making it that much harder to maintain her grip. Her ankle and knee screamed from the way she clutched the wall while her arm ripped from its socket under the weight of Neri and her father.

"Let go! Let go, you're going to kill her!" Harper yelled at the man, sputtering as salty water filled her mouth.

The man howled, wrapping his arms tighter around Neri's tail. He writhed about, and Harper couldn't tell if he was trying to climb or trying to get her to let go of his mermaid.

He slipped, flopping against the wall and taking Neri with him, smashing her side into the concrete. She cried out, whimpering.

He'll never let Neri go, even if it means tearing her in half.

Harper gritted her teeth and pulled. She grabbed an exposed metal rod with her other hand, leveraging against it. She hauled with all her strength, pulling Neri and the man back to the lighthouse floor, inch by painful inch.

Over her shoulder, she sensed Rylan trying to reach her, to help her from where he'd wedged his own body safely, but he was too far back.

"Hold on, Neri!" Harper screamed.

Neri nodded, her eyes huge and sad. Her body rocked against the concrete as her father struggled to climb her like a rope, roaring madly at Harper.

Harper yanked harder, angling her body back. Her muscles screamed and burned but she didn't give up. She could do this. She still had the Bane's power inside her, however much it had faded. It would make her strong enough.

I need to be strong enough.

She wasn't.

The old man thrashed again with a gurgling shriek, sending Neri's tail swaying

wildly. In a split second, Neri's fingertips slipped away.

Then both the beautiful mermaid and her hideous captor fell down, down, down.

And the man kept hold of Neri until they hit the wild, deadly waves far below.

Then Harper lost her grip on the lighthouse as well.

21

E verly's breath caught in her throat as Harper washed through the water and over the edge of the destroyed wall. She seized, terror turning her insides to ice-water as she imagined her best friend crashing down onto the ferocious rocks below.

In the blasting wind and backwash of rain, Everly caught sight of Harper's fingers digging painfully into the shattered concrete, one leg hooked around the wall. She was alive, but barely holding on, pelted with debris from the sloping room as the beshadowed lighthouse tilted precariously into open space.

Pull yourself up, Everly pleaded silently. *Why isn't she pulling herself up?*

The rush of water that had washed Harper and Neri through the break in the wall had tumbled Everly across the floor alongside the fallen armchair.

She'd been thrown sideways against an unbroken portion of the wall and found herself pinned by the armchair while the water continued to cascade around her. The initial flood that poured from the ceiling had eased to a consistent stream. It rushed over the chair, strong enough that Everly couldn't get free to even attempt to help her best friend.

But the truth was, she wasn't in any position to help *anyone*. Not with her arms breaking apart from the inside. Every time she even moved her fingertips, debilitating pain tore through her and more shards broke below her skin, spreading over her shoulders.

Rylan—the strange, scaley werewolf version of him—hunched against the very edge of the broken wall, too close to falling for Everly's comfort. Callan and Tammy were tangled up on what was now the top side of the room. Tammy's arm wrapped around one side of the doorframe, securing her and Callan to the forty-five-degree angled floor while water flowed around them.

From Everly's sideways position, the whole lighthouse felt turned inside out. Down seemed up, up seemed down, and simply staring out upon the tableau disoriented her.

The old man was nowhere in sight, and Everly had lost track of Denny too until he appeared by her feet, balancing between wall and floor.

"You good, kid?" he asked around panting breaths.

Everly gestured to the chair across her midsection. "Not going anywhere. Help Harper, please. She went over."

He pressed both palms to the wall and lifted his leg to step over her and the fallen chair. "Those curves aren't getting wasted on the rocks on my watch."

Everly stared at his back, aghast. He couldn't be Harper's only hope. Her mind went into overdrive, trying to find some other solution. She couldn't take the risk to use her dragon's powers to reach out for Harper, because it liked to eat the things it reached out for.

Harper's screaming voice cut through the storm. What was she shouting—Neri's name? Was she still there, too?

Rylan leaned forward, one taloned hand reaching toward Harper's leg. He slipped, his clawed feet scrabbling against the slick stones and rushing water. He latched back onto the wall, readjusting to try again.

More screaming, three voices piercing through the waves and storm.

Denny leaped forward in a rush, landing on his chest, and threw his arms out into open space.

The screams grew quieter, rushing away into nothing.

Please, please, please have her.

"Oof! Gotcha!" Denny grunted, shuffling sideways to avoid sliding through the hole.

Once he'd anchored himself, he dragged a limp body up over the edge. Like a ragdoll, he yanked Harper away from the hole and propped her against the wall next to Everly and the armchair. "Bout learned how to fly, didn't you?"

Harper said nothing.

"That's okay, maybe you can thank me later," he added with a wink.

Harper didn't even react. Didn't even cringe. She just stared, silently, her expression one of complete desolation.

Everly made an angry sound of disgust and shoved against the chair on top of her. "Thank you for saving her. Now could you shut your gross mouth before you spoil the one good thing you've done even more?"

Denny pulled a rude face and leaned to free Everly from the armchair, but Rylan reached her first. He lifted it gently and pushed it aside into the trickling water.

"You okay?" he asked, offering her a hand.

He'd shifted back to a more manageable vampire form. His body armor held together but was scraped and dinted, and his pants hung in tatters.

Everly nodded and moved into a seated position against the angled wall.

Harper trembled. Blood speckled her fingernails on one hand, and her knees visibly shook as she lay back against the cold concrete.

"I dropped her."

Everly gasped out a sob. *The poor girl.*

Like a nightmare, she could imagine the emaciated mermaid tumbling through the air. And her best friend didn't have to imagine; she'd seen it with her own eyes.

"What happened ... it wasn't your fault. You tried to save her."

Ignoring the agony in her arms, Everly reached out for Harper's mangled hands, sweeping her gaze over the wounds. Most were superficial from where she'd clung to the stones—lacerations on her fingertips and broken, bleeding nails.

Half-moon fingernail marks had formed bloody pools on her opposite wrist, bruises already blooming under her brown skin.

Harper still didn't move beyond the shudders that railroaded through her, as though too exhausted, too traumatized, to even cry.

Enough tears ran down Everly's face for both of them. "You're okay. I'm so glad you're okay."

Harper's head shook in a small twitch. "It ran out too quick."

"What ran out?"

Harper's dazed stare lifted from her hands to Everly, then she turned away, her gaze seeking out the hole in the wall. "I should have brought it with me. I should have been stronger."

"Brought what?" Everly asked, exasperated. "Harper, you're not making any sense."

"I promised her ..." Harper's voice caught, and a sob broke like a dam from her throat. "I couldn't save her."

"You did your best," Everly assured her, reaching up to cup Harper's cold cheeks in her hands. "You always do your best."

"Look, that all went sideways, in more ways than one," Denny offered. "Blame the old bloke, not yourself."

Everly pulled Harper into her arms and looked at the others over her shoulder. "Speaking of, where is he?"

"Went down as well," Rylan confirmed.

Harper shuddered harder in Everly's arms.

Rylan stalked across the tilted floor, pushing wreckage and clutter back to clear a path up to where Tammy and Callan waited near the door. "I appreciate that we've just witnessed a tragedy, but we're on a time limit here. We've already taken way too long."

Everly shot him a warning look.

Rylan returned one as equally intense. "None of us want a second tragedy to mourn. It's time to keep moving. For Everly."

Harper nodded against Everly's shoulder and pulled away.

Everly slid an arm around her friend's waist and ducked her head, uncomfortable with Rylan's pointed gaze.

Harper let herself be guided forward as she stared at the water running over their feet. Denny and Rylan helped them crawl up the steep incline of the slippery, seaweed-covered floor, and Callan and Tammy caught them at the top, pulling them out of the broken room and into the stairwell.

A while later, Rylan and Denny joined them, dragging the few packs that could be salvaged behind them—Rylan's, with Everly's inside, and Callan's. The others were gone. Harper didn't seem to care. Denny muttered something about how he could have done with a beer. Callan took his, then lifted Tammy as well.

Glancing back into that room filled with tragedy, Everly noticed the hole in the wall already closing over. That strange growth of coral and crystal crackled its way like a timelapse across the gap.

Everly, waterlogged and weighed down by her clothes and shoes, found every step, every movement, utterly exhausting. Coupled with the pain in her arm and the heavy atmosphere, she wanted to curl onto the floor and give up.

Rylan was right, however. They were close to their goal. Too close to give up now. *It had better be worth it.*

Sparkling blue light beamed down from high above, and the stairs continued to circle toward the sky beneath that hypnotic, underwater kaleidoscope. The crooked angle of the lighthouse affected the stairs now, too, leaning them up and down, up and down as they spiraled around.

But the light they'd been following for some time finally got closer. As they reached the final level, the lighthouse straightened up again.

When they arrived at the top, there should have been more fanfare, more celebration, more relief after the disaster they'd been through. But Everly just stepped off the final stair with a long, low sigh and trudged into the room.

The stairwell spilled onto a wide landing that took up the entire topmost floor of the lighthouse.

Windows lined the dome, revealing the gunmetal sky and the lashing storm outside.

A metal floor encircled the all-glass container that held the magical light source, while a silver surface rotated and evenly dispersed the light into the wild, stormy night.

Everly released Harper's waist, drawn by the vivid glow of the object inside the rotating tube.

It called to her. She felt the hum of it in her core and pure glee from the dragon. She recognized the magic of it as something that had always been a part of her, even when she hadn't understood what it meant.

Moving slowly, boots squelching on the landing, Everly chased the rotating light for a better look.

The twirling mechanism rolled around, coming back toward her. Light flashed,

power bloomed around Everly, and she caught sight of the source.

She stumbled backward, blood draining from her face.

It was so beautiful. It was so pretty she just wanted to touch it.

She ran into Rylan, who steadied her with his hands on her shoulders. "Hey, what's wrong?"

She winced at his touch, her head shaking.

Abstract, spiraling fractals of the most delicate crystal, glittering from within.

Tantalizing, tempting. It fell from her tiny fingertips and shattered into a million shards on the hardwood floor.

It all came back to her so clearly, the memory she'd locked away, shoved deep down in an attempt to forget.

She had broken the crystal sculpture. Blinding light had brightened the room like the birth of a sun. Pure, raw energy filtering into her tiny body, coiled up within her, dug in tight.

She'd felt hungry, so hungry. And then she didn't.

And her father collapsed, eyes glazed and unmoving.

Everly gasped, choking on her forgotten need to breathe.

It was the dragon. Trapped in that crystal. That was the moment she'd taken the being into her, unbidden. And in the process, it had killed her father.

The revelation was bittersweet. She'd carried the guilt of his death for her entire life, thinking herself the terrible daughter that made her dad so angry that he had a heart attack and died.

Instead, the piece of the Beast of Teeth and Stars within her had killed him. And it was still her childish selfishness to touch and break what wasn't hers that had freed it.

Now, another piece of that thing was the only option she had for healing the damage the Bane had done to her.

The thought of allowing *more* of the soul-eating monster into her body, even if it could save her, terrified her. How much the creature inside her wanted that scared her more. Her insides howled with longing.

"Hey, is that ..." Tammy stared at the crystal, her head tilting as it spun past them.

"Looks just like the one in Barry's maze," Callan agreed, shifting her in his arms.

She looked comfortable hanging against him now, as if the two of them had become one entity, reliant on each other and preferring it that way.

Denny barked a laugh. "Well, ain't that our ghast-twisted luck. We come all this way when there was one right there back home."

Rylan let Everly go and moved toward the rotating housing, wrenching it to a stop with a pale hand. The crystal hung there before them, scintillating as it floated, suspended in mid-air behind a shield of glass.

He caught Everly's gaze. "Is it even the right thing?"

She blinked, still lost in the memory that played on repeat in her head.

Swallowing hard, she said, "That's it. It's the same as the one ... When I was a kid. That's like what I broke when my dad died."

Harper's eyes lifted from the floor, and she stepped beside Everly, gently touching her shoulder. "The dragon has been in you since you were three?"

"Why didn't we know about it until now?" Callan asked.

Rylan answered for her, "You must have been fighting it this whole time. After seeing your dad die, you've been holding it back ever since."

"Except when I couldn't." She could see them now, the times she'd been weak and it had escaped her control.

When she was lost in the woods as a child, after the car accident, and the night Rylan was apparently killed, she'd seen its light then, before the first time she'd fully let it free at the theater.

Everly stared at her hands, at the jagged red cracks running under her skin.

Rylan snapped the latches and opened the housing. He reached in and grasped the crystal. It glowed brighter for a moment, then faded until it sparkled only from the flashes of lightning around them.

"So we break it, right? That's how we release more of the dragon into you? Help it heal itself?" He looked ready to dash the thing across the metal floor.

"No!" Everly cried.

If it worked, if it made the beast stronger, if it took control in this small space surrounded by her friends, who knew what the consequences could be.

Before it had been wounded, she'd barely kept it under control. Her whole life, she'd locked it up, starved it, leashed it, and then broke it, stole its playthings. What would it do if it were stronger?

"I, I don't think ..." Everly grit her teeth and forced her words out clearly. "I don't want more of it in me."

"Are you kidding? It could be the only way to save you," Rylan growled. "There are crack marks *on your neck*."

Everly raised her head to him, her voice hard. "And I'm still here. I'm surviving. And I'm saying I don't want any more of that thing in me. I just want to leave and forget this whole beshadowed town. Isn't that what you want?"

Rylan's chest swelled up and down with each seething breath.

The walls groaned, and another booming percussion of thunder shook the lighthouse.

Harper stepped between them. "Let's go. I want to get out of this place. We have what we came for. Can we just go now?"

"Yes," Everly said without hesitation.

She turned to lead the way down the stairs, body aching to the bone and heart stinging more. They got what they came for, had paid too high a price, and it all came to nothing.

All she wanted was to escape that cursed place without any more lives lost.

22

The blue glow of the lighthouse had been extinguished with the removal of the crystal, leading to a dark stumble back down the crooked stairwell. The few flashlights they had from the remaining packs offered a little light but didn't do enough to cut through the gloom.

As they went by the doorway to Neri's room, Everly noticed the growth that had so quickly formed over the hole was cracking apart.

From somewhere far below, a strange, mournful wail arose.

The desperate sound cut through Everly's thoughts and banished the agony in her arms. The team drew up short as the wails intensified. They echoed up through the stairwell, each warble repeating like a whale song of doom.

Several feet away, Denny barked, "What the ghast is that?"

Callan replied, "The nyevmer?"

In a boom of thunder, the lighthouse lurched beneath their feet, shifting again, tipping them against the opposite wall.

"Hurry," Rylan commanded. "I don't trust this place to stay together much longer."

"Right, so let me get the plan straight. We just have to escape this collapsing lighthouse, get through the underwater caves where something is howling at existence, and then hope someone comes to take us off this forsaken island," Tammy muttered from Callan's back.

"We deal as we go, now move."

Callan took the lead. "Someone will come and get us. I've still got the sat phone. Besides, we just turned off a lighthouse that's been going for decades. If the Crybel's Cove shadyrs were expecting a signal, I don't know what more we could do."

Some logic in Everly told her that lighthouses weren't really necessary anymore, that they were mostly a backup for other navigational technology. But she hated to think of anybody who might be out there on the waves in this weather, especially knowing that if they crashed to the rocks, their blood would be on her hands.

Rylan kept the crystal carefully in his hands, watching for her to pick up pace before falling in behind her.

They circled down the lighthouse stairs, splashing and slipping as horrifying cracks and crunching noises overwhelmed the thunder. Through a portal window, a chunk of wall fell past them.

They spilled onto the ground floor, where the crystalline coral growths were changing into crumbling sand, blocking the main entrance like a sludgy dune.

The ceiling cracked and shifted.

"Run!" Callan yelled.

They bolted as one for the narrow passage that led to the caves. Callan and Tammy disappeared into the darkness, a sloshing sound rising behind them. Denny and Harper followed, and Everly hit the top of the stairs and almost tumbled face-first down them from momentum.

Rylan grabbed the back of her jacket and shoved her against the stone wall. She cried out as her shoulders stabbed with pain but was muffled by Rylan's cold chest as he pressed against her.

In a deafening smash, the thick slab of ceiling slammed against the passage entrance. Lumps of plaster and concrete sprayed through the air, pattering against Rylan's back.

Everly wiped a spatter of sand from her face, and Rylan wrapped an arm around her waist, pushing her down the stairs. "Keep going!"

The rubble above them groaned, twisting on itself under the pressure. Then it exploded outward, filling the space they previously stood with crushing sections of floor and bone-breaking wreckage.

Rylan sped Everly onwards, faster than she could comprehend, until water splashed up around them.

The cold cave water swallowed Everly whole. She broke the surface, sucking in a breath as the chill penetrated her clothes. It hurt as much as it helped, numbing the pain but inflating it all the same.

The small beach at the base of the stairs had gone. Waves washed up into the stairwell, and Everly and Rylan swam out to meet the others around the glow of two remaining flashlights.

Tammy bobbed in the water, her tail swaying beneath her. Denny and Callan finished shifting and rolled wet pants into a bundle, putting them into Callan's pack.

The tide had risen significantly. Everly looked up, and if she had the strength to raise her arms above her head, she was sure she'd be able to touch the cavern ceiling.

"Well, we're not getting back out that way," Rylan said, tipping his head toward where the lighthouse must now be a pile of wreckage, smothering the ground above.

Another haunting howl pierced the air around them. It was strangely musical, like a hurricane trying to sing, broken by sobs.

It came from between them and their only exit.

"What *is* that?" Harper whispered.

Rylan shifted into mermaid form, then turned his galaxy eyes toward the sound. "We'll find out soon."

Everly slid closer to Harper, and shadyrs placed themselves two on either side, pulling them through the water. Everly focused on the burning in her arms to ground herself to the world. If she was hurting, she couldn't pass out. If she didn't pass out, she'd be less of a problem for the shadyrs to deal with.

Harper made little effort to swim, letting herself be towed along. Everly reached out to hold her hand, and while Harper took hers in return, there was no strength in her grasp.

Out of the narrower cave and into the larger underground lake near the entrance, the wailing was deafening, and it echoed off the rocks like a sonic weapon. The entire cavern had filled with water, the few rocky islands completely submerged except for those that rose like pillars all the way to the ceiling.

"Go, straight through and out," Callan ordered.

Harper let go of Everly's hand and broke away from the group, lurching through the water in uneven strokes toward one of the pillars where the howling sounded loudest.

"What is she doing?" Rylan muttered.

"You don't swim toward the spooky sounds!" Denny hissed.

Callan swam after her. He caught up easily, but she swiped away his efforts to pull her back.

"Look!" She splashed an arm out, pointing into the shadows.

Tammy turned her flashlight that way, and sky-blue scales reflected the beam.

Neri perched, half out of the water, clinging to the pillar like a child to a parent's leg. Her long tail trailed in the chopping waves below. She hunched over like an abused animal, cupping something small and white in one hand.

Harper picked up her pace, splashing toward her. "You're alive. You survived."

The crying ceased for a moment. Neri turned toward them but didn't seem to register what she saw. Her head shook and she screamed again.

Rylan huffed, pulling Everly at his side as he followed the others toward the girl.

Tammy's flashlight shone onto Neri again as they got closer. She held a tiny skull in her shaking fingers.

Denny grunted. "Can you shut her up? She's going to attract trouble."

After a flash of anger his way, Harper wrapped her arms around the rocky pillar beside Neri, pulling herself up to catch the girl's gaze. "Hey, shh. It's going to be okay."

Neri's wailing stuttered out between sobs. "It hurts. I can't ... I'm trying to heal my heart but it's not working."

"I'm sorry. I'm so sorry." Harper reached out a hand but hesitated to touch her.

Neri looked up, her eyes red-rimmed and wide, tears soaking her thick, dark lashes. "You weren't lying."

"No ... we weren't."

Neri's face scrunched in on itself, and her mouth opened wide, but no sound came out. She clutched the skull to her chest with white-knuckled fingers.

Harper's hand hovered in the space between them. "Hey, hey. I'm so, so happy you're okay. How did you survive that fall?"

"I missed the rocks. It hurt. The waves, the water hurt, but it's my heart that won't heal."

"Your father?" Rylan asked cautiously.

"He didn't miss the rocks." Neri's eyes welled with more thick tears. "I didn't know where else to go. I swam around and found my way in. I just wanted to go home. And I found them. I found them."

A sob racked Neri's entire body and the skull tumbled from her fingertips, sinking like a ghost back into the depths.

Neri sucked in a deep, agonized breath, and a loud howl reverberated from her mouth again. Everly had to put her hands over her ears. There was a musical quality to Neri's mourning screams—a cross between humming and crying, with a strange mix of familiar tunes, snippets of pop songs and classics from across decades, but it was too broken by pain to be a song.

In gasping sobs, Neri choked out, "What do I do? What can I do?"

Harper bent in closer. "Come with us. I know I wasn't strong enough to hold onto you, but I still want to try to keep my promise."

Neri squeezed her eyes shut, her expression twisted into one of abject despair, then she tossed herself into Harper's arms. They slipped, together, off the rock and down into the water, as Neri clung to Harper's shoulders with her bony arms.

As her wails dissolved into hushed whimpers, a new sound echoed through the tunnels, this one much less hauntingly sad.

A wicked and harrowing roar.

Where is it?

Rylan turned in the choppy water and looked back toward the tunnels they'd just left behind for the incoming eidolghast.

Only inky blackness met his searching gaze. Deep, warbling rumbles echoed all around them, and the waves against his shoulders splashed harder.

"Get ready for a fight." His shadyr senses told him the monster was close now.

But where? Rylan's gaze turned downward, toward the void-like depths of the water beneath them.

He'd never seen a nyevmer beyond sketches during Darkfrey training. He expected something the size of a weroth or auerdax. But the shape that formed from the darkness, birthed from the abyss beneath his tail, was enormous.

"Split!" he roared.

The Howell shadyrs in mermaid form dove to the sides. Everly, Harper, and Neri clung for shelter against the rocky pillar.

The water where they had just floated opened into the pit of the creature's maw. It breached.

Whip-like tentacles lined both sides of a mouth like a bear trap, each tendril ending in sharp, three-pointed claws. Its elongated skull led to a pointed crown of bone, ringed in tiny, glowing eyes.

Its head cracked into the ceiling and shook the cavern before it turned, slithering back down into the deep again. The curve of its ridged, sea-serpent body was massive and went on, and on, until a tail of bony-points flicked the surface, then disappeared.

The ghast's sheer size was enough to kill them all.

Rylan struggled to remain upright as the creature's passing displaced tons of water. He was tossed in the waves, and his head bumped the roof of the cave.

Denny sputtered, "That thing is massive!"

"Yeah, I don't think we're taking it down." Tammy's shorn black hair speckled with droplets that dripped down her terrified goth-doll face.

They were right. It was bigger than any eidolghast Rylan had ever seen, bigger than the diagrams shown in training, bigger than a damned train.

"It must have ended up in here when it was smaller and couldn't get out again. Could have been here decades. That's why Crybel's haven't dealt with it, how it got so big. It can only be sensed on the island, and they don't go there."

Rylan thought of the shroudpool and eidolghast bones deep in the water. The nyevmer's presence here over so long would have formed the shroudpool, and the beast was big enough that it probably fed on any other ghast that came through from the Everdark. That was probably *how* it got so big.

"If it's stuck, I say we leave it and get the Everdark out of here." Denny flicked his head to indicate the opening in the cliff face.

Rain poured sideways in the show of lightning.

"The smartest thing you've ever said," Callan replied. "Go. And go fast."

Rylan swam up beside Everly and wrapped an arm around her waist without slowing down. Harper and Neri were similarly collected by Callan and Tammy, while

Denny took the lead, speeding through the water toward the narrow channel between the cave and the sea.

Rylan eyed the passage. Where they had jumped over stones to enter before, now there was only a treacherous sliver of space between the cavern roof and the waves. He tightened his grip on the crystal in his left hand, reassuring himself that he still had it.

Beyond that small hole, the storm continued to rage. Lightning flared in the cavern and thunder tore around the Howell team like a scream. The walls growled along with the nyevmer so that the whole cave was like the mouth of a gargantuan beast, about to snap closed.

The water roiled and sloshed around them, and Everly gasped for breath as it splashed continuously over her face.

Rylan had to remind himself she didn't have the luxury of breathing water like he could right now. But they also didn't have the luxury of slowing down. The nyevmer circled back like a tsunami barreling through the deep. It spiraled around them, toying with them, creating a whirlpool as it edged in closer, and closer.

They still had a long swim to the exit. Rylan took in the team.

Harper's crazy energy and bloodlust seemed to have leeched out of her system completely, but she still held Neri tightly in both arms, a fierce, protective set to her jaw.

The mermaid girl was a shadyr, but untrained and utterly traumatized.

And under no circumstances was Everly to use her powers. She looked like she couldn't even lift a finger without agonizing pain.

Denny was an asshole but had been surprisingly capable. Tammy as well had shown mettle beyond what Rylan would have guessed, and he knew Callan was up to the task. That gave him a complete brace. It would have to do.

He let go of Everly and removed his pack, letting it float over to her, semi-buoyant. She rested her arms over it like a lifebuoy.

Then he pushed the crystal from his hands into hers, indicating Harper and Neri as well. "You three keep swimming. Don't stop. We'll try and buy some time."

"What? No." Everly glared, her face white and pained, her teeth chattering.

Rylan pointed at the cliffside opening. "You're not doing *anything* except getting the hell out of here. Take Harper and Neri and get out before the water rises too high. We'll hold off the ghast."

"It's too big. The dragon could help."

"No. No way," Rylan snarled, his expression twisting with irritation. "You're in no position to use your powers right now. Don't you dare even try. Leave it to us and get the Everdark out of here!"

Her jaw set and eyes hardened. "I'm not leaving while the rest of you get yourselves killed! The dragon could stop it."

The nyevmer's head crested, then dipped back under water right behind Everly. Rylan grasped at her jacket, pulling her closer.

Fury curdled his voice, and he yelled, "And then you die instead? After all we've been through? No one wants you here, just trust me for once and leave!"

He pushed her roughly back out of his grip, toward the exit. She turned away from him, shoulders shivering. Harper, who had taken Callan's pack, reached out and grabbed Everly's shoulder, pushing her along as Neri swam at their side.

Callan caught Rylan's eye. His features were hard and judgmental, but he didn't say anything, just nodded and turned toward the eidolghast. Tammy stayed at his side. Denny swore, eyed the exit, but remained with them.

Rylan threw one more look at Everly's departing back, then he dove. He sliced through the water toward the deep, inky bottom of the pool as the nyevmer raced up toward them.

Callan, Denny, and Tammy drew up nearby, bodies arcing through the deep blue. Callan signaled and they went for the thing's head.

The closer they got to the ghast, the chillier the water became, as though it were made of living ice, or something far colder.

Its sharp-edged mouth opened, bigger than a doorway, inviting them in. The current suctioned down toward it. The water whipped, and flailing tentacles reached up for them. Rylan darted sideways as the clawed tips snipped at the water around him.

Denny and Tammy went low to avoid the whirlpool maw, tumbling into darkness beneath the beast.

Rylan waved to Callan, then the two of them fell into a dive, heading for the top of the ghast's bony head. It continued its rush toward the surface where three silhouettes swam huddled together.

Rylan latched onto the bony skull with his claws, his brother anchoring himself on the other side. Tentacles curled back at them.

The razor-tipped ends bit into Rylan's tail. He felt the crushing pressure, but they didn't penetrate his scales. He struck back with his own hands, grasping the end of the whipping limb, and tore the talons from the end. Blood spurted like a fog in the water, and the tentacle thrashed wildly, pulling Rylan off the nyevmer's head before he could let go.

Callan tumbled sideways as a clawed tentacle whipped against his chest.

Rylan wrapped the torn tentacle in both hands, pulling roughly to the side. He beat his tail against the water with all his might in an attempt to drag the creature in a different direction, but he may as well have been a flea on a dog.

They were almost at the surface, a tail and two sets of human feet right above them. Changing tactics, he went back for the head. He pushed out, raking his claws over the skull as he clung for purchase. The ring of eyes looked everywhere and nowhere, glowing faintly in the blue.

Rylan thrust a clawed hand into the closest, digging into the eye socket in a pop of inky fluid. The creature roared, twisted, and sped upward through the water. Rylan tossed his body weight aside to avoid being sandwiched between the creature and a mountain of stone.

They breached into air. The nyevmer smashed into the side of the cavern, mouth-first. The rock crumpled as if it were nothing more than Styrofoam. Then the beast pitched sideways, thrashing the entire length of its body against the cave wall.

Debris exploded outward. Brick-sized rocks lashed Rylan's body and arms, and a larger stone slammed into the side of his head, momentarily stunning him. The nyevmer crashed back down into the water.

Caught in the twirling currents, Rylan was thrown around wildly, and he couldn't figure out which way was down or up. He slammed into the ghast's slimy, long torso, then rolled out of control into the dark depths.

A giant rumbling filled the soft silence of the underwater.

Huge boulders plunged down everywhere like torpedoes, sending waves careening through the pool. Rylan swam in the opposite direction, aiming for the surface as he dodged the avalanche before it could pin him to the bottom. He fought the pull of the falling boulders all the way to the surface, where he burst through to madness.

Denny and Tammy yelled over the splashing rubble, and Callan floated between them. There was barely any light, just the dim glow of a flashlight lost somewhere deep in the water below.

Debris covered the entire side of the cavern, blocking off the tunnel to the sea. Boulders were scattered like giant knucklebones, while the tide continued to pour through the cracks.

Rylan searched for Everly, spinning a three-sixty as he surveyed the churning waves.

The nyevmer's tail flicked through the water in the far end of the pool. Everly, Harper, and Neri washed together in the new shallows created by the rockfall, gasping in the small gap between there and the cavern ceiling.

Rylan's breath caught at the sight of them. The nyevmer hadn't swallowed them whole. It hadn't smashed them against the stone.

But they hadn't made it out of the cave.

The whole team was hopelessly trapped, in that shrinking gap of air, with the nyevmer.

23

Rylan wanted to go to Everly, was drawn there with every fiber of his being. He wanted to hold off the rising water and destroy the gargantuan eidolghast and make everyone safe, but how could he possibly do any of those things?

Just deal. One problem at a time.

The nyevmer didn't give him a choice of what action to take next. It roared and sliced across the surface of the pool toward him.

Crashing head-on into the cave hard enough to collapse the roof around them hadn't slowed the beast down. Its bony, plated head seemed impervious. The thing was unrelenting.

Denny worked with Harper and Neri, clawing around the rocks in an attempt to reclaim an exit. Tammy supported Callan in the water, who was worryingly still. Rylan couldn't allow Everly even an inch of time to consider using her powers.

He had to deal with the nyevmer alone.

Rylan swore at the icy water and squared himself up against the oncoming giant.

It reached him fast in a surge of fluid. Rylan ducked under, slamming and rolling painfully along the creature's sharp, scaled belly. Like grappling hooks, he flung out both clawed hands, seeking purchase.

At the skeletal tail, they finally caught. He was dragged behind as the ghast spiraled down into the depths. Then it jack-knifed its long body without warning, bringing its toothy maw and talon-ended tentacles straight for Rylan.

Three tentacles wrapped around Rylan's mer-form body. His arms were pinned, and the claws nipped at his tail, slicing clear through one fin. A roar of bubbles escaped Rylan's mouth.

The nyevmer drew him through the deep blue water on a trajectory for its tooth-ringed mouth. He fought back, swimming the other way with all his remaining strength. His damaged fin curled and flopped uselessly.

Rylan needed a plan, fast. He didn't have a weapon beyond his claws, and this ghast was simply too big.

Then a thought struck him.

He wasn't stuck with just this form. He was against a nyevmer, and shadyr forms were meant to be a match for what they fought. But what if they weren't the best option?

Could he even control the shift enough to use a different form, with the massive nyevmer so close, overpowering his senses?

Closing his eyes, he thought of Everly.

He could sense her high above at the surface like the warm glow of a campfire. Since waking up, her presence had been nearly overwhelming to him. The sheer energy—multiple energies—radiating out of her left him reeling.

He couldn't even name half of the ghast signatures he felt coming from her. He imagined that they were somehow the essences of any eidolghast the soul-eater had once consumed. Everly herself had only been around for a handful of destroyed ghasts, but at some time before that, the creature in her must have glutted itself.

Having stayed as close as he could to her over the course of that long day, he'd found some sense of balance, been able to wrangle control over which ghast energies he took in, which forms he was forced into.

He'd been able to push himself into chosen forms, even partial forms, which would give him the best tools he needed for a fight. Or been able to close himself off to her influence, which is what he'd been doing to stay in nyevmer form.

That mermaid shape wasn't going to help him in the creature's mouth, though. He had to change.

The moment he opened his senses to Everly, her power fully overshadowed the nyevmer.

Rylan cataloged the ghast essences he could feel, making a rough plan. He only hoped he could control the change. The timing would have to be perfect. If he changed to the wrong form at the wrong time, it would all be over.

Black mist swirled around Rylan's body, unaffected by the water. He no longer fought against the tentacles. He let them pull him directly into the vacuum of the massive mouth. His tail vanished.

The nyevmer's teeth snapped shut like a trap.

Rylan cringed as they went right through his body. He didn't feel a thing. They passed into his ghost-like form, mashing and gnawing in vain around his incorporeal body.

He wanted to sigh in relief but had to keep his breath held carefully. He was still underwater, inside the creature, and no longer had the amphibious features of mer form.

Darkness disoriented Rylan, and he turned, trying to gain his bearings. He caught a glimpse of light and saw teeth leading out to waving tentacles and ice-blue water. He swam in the opposite direction, straight into the solid mass of the nyevmer's head.

Eidolghast didn't always have brains or spines or hearts the way living things of

Earth did. It could be hard to find a vulnerable target. Still, if this nyevmer had a skull like a steel vault, it must be protecting some vital organ within.

Using Everly as his focal point, Rylan allowed the shift to ripple over his body. His skin grew hard and red and his size doubled, expanding outward as it became whole, solid, and on the physical plane once again.

Pressure met him on all sides. Dark, gooey, heavy organs crushed against him. Rylan twisted and slammed his arms and wings outward, tearing through the vulnerable, fleshy insides of the nyevmer.

The incredible strength of this demon-dragon form shocked Rylan anew as he tore through the ghast's soft viscera. Sparks of bioelectric connections fizzing out went off around him. He held his breath and ricocheted throughout the insides of the beast's skull, still unable to break through.

But being trapped inside made the damage he dealt all the more devastating. He could feel the ghast roaring, screaming, the sound vibrating all around him as his lungs burned. He slashed and sliced the inside of the ghast to ribbons.

Finally, the nyevmer fell silent and still.

From inside the monster's skull, Rylan felt the hum of life fade away, and the draw of water and gravity pulling them down. He thrust his hands about, latching onto raw meat, slippery and cold between his fingers.

He kept pushing, kept tearing, wanting to be sure the creature couldn't survive. He hit a wall of thin cartilage and ripped through. More meat, then an armored barrier, and then the relative softness of water rushed against his face.

He burst free through the back of the nyevmer's neck.

Everything was black. They were deep, so deep. The pale glow of the creature's eyes had extinguished, and even Rylan's shadyr night vision couldn't penetrate the dark.

His dragon form sent him tumbling toward the abyssal depths as if he weighed more than a boulder. Wings tangled like sheets around him. He tried to swim for the surface but couldn't, nor could he breathe without the nyevmer gills.

His head grew cloudy and confused. Tired, more than anything, as bubbles rushed free from his mouth. He closed his eyes. The water seemed to cradle him. Maybe he could breathe it, after all. He just had to inhale.

He slammed into thick silt and sharp bones beside the nyevmer's still body. The impact brought back just enough alertness to realize that inhaling would be a very bad idea. He flailed both arms and latched onto the dead beast.

Even as a corpse, the sheer size of the thing and the physical contact forced the shadyr shift through Rylan's body on instinct. Chilled water rushed through his newly formed gills like life itself, and his eyes snapped open.

He burst to the surface, breaking into the air with a gasp. Every inch of him was

battered and bruised, and it took him several moments to gather his wits. He blinked blearily around the cavern.

There was barely enough room to move without bumping and scraping against the rough ceiling at the top of his head. Water continued to rush in, rising with every passing moment. Everly, Harper, and Neri treaded water near the cave-in, tugging at the fallen stones. For every rock they moved, more crumbled into place.

At some point, Denny must have reclaimed their last flashlight from the pool's depths, but it was dim and flickering in his hands as he swam about, collecting their two remaining backpacks that bobbed on the water's surface.

He spotted Rylan, shining the light his way. "Where's the nyevmer? I lost track of it."

"Dead," Rylan coughed out.

"Yeah, good one. Where is it?" Denny laughed, then stopped. "No way you took that thing down solo."

The others turned Rylan's way, questioning.

"Except I did." His and Everly's eyes met.

Maybe not entirely solo. He couldn't have done it without her.

"Having access to multiple forms helped."

"Rylan!" Tammy called.

Her normally dry and dull tone was high and hysterical. She treaded water nearby with Callan supported against her. He was hunched-over, gasping painfully.

Fear pulsed in Rylan's gut. He dove under and swam quickly toward his brother. He came up beside them and hovered next to Tammy in the water.

Callan was conscious but grimacing as he pressed his hand against a gaping slash in his chest armor.

Rylan swore, lifting Callan's fingers for a better look. His body armor was torn right through to the skin beneath. The wound stretched from his collar bone to his solar plexus, the edges raw and red.

For a moment, he wanted to tell his brother to shift into vampire form so he could regenerate. But the other shadyrs didn't have that connection to Everly like he did. He grunted, hands balling into fists so tight his claws dug into his palms. They couldn't offer any first aid in there, being almost completely submerged.

"We need to get out of here. Try ... try and keep some pressure on it."

Tammy shivered. She probably knew just as he did how futile that would be, with the length of the wound and the saltwater smashing around them. But after a brief hesitation, she pressed one black, webbed hand there, shifting her other arm around Callan's back.

"What are we going to do?" Water splashed over Tammy's chin. "This place is filling up fast."

Callan hissed and jerked against her touch. His long dark hair clung over a face that was turning white.

He stared at his Rylan with red-rimmed eyes. "With the nyevmer dead, we can hold these forms for maybe twenty minutes, max."

Tammy's mouth moved but said nothing. She was probably doing the math in her head like Rylan was, and realized that nothing added up.

She shook her head in denial. "No. Longer if we get close to the corpse. Like we did for you with the vasmire bits. We could swim down and stay near it."

"Yeah, but what are they going to do?" Rylan turned and flicked his head toward Everly and Harper.

They still fumbled madly at the stones. Whitecaps splashed around them, and the humans tilted their heads back for clear breaths of air. Denny and Neri resurfaced beside them, shaking their heads. There must have been no other way through below, either.

"Keep him afloat," Rylan told Tammy.

He saw tears rush into her eyes as he turned away. He left them, streaking across the water as fast as possible toward the cave-in.

Rylan came to a halt behind Everly and gripped her by both shoulders. "Enough. You're going to hurt yourself."

He pulled her away from the rubble. He would take her place digging, although he had little hope that it would help.

Before he could get a grip on the rocks, Everly splashed back up against him and shoved him with all her might, crying out painfully.

Her shove barely did anything at all beyond making him aware that she was *very* angry.

"You ... jerk!" she hissed, swiping an arm feebly through the water. "If you'd let me use my powers to kill the nyevmer, maybe we'd have gotten out of here before the whole cave collapsed!"

She lashed out again and Rylan caught her hands in his, careful not to squeeze. Her fingers were too pale, with bright red crack-lines mosaiced all over.

Rylan growled, "If you had, you might be dead already."

"And now we're going to die anyway! All of us!" Everly jerked away from his grasp and sank beneath the rising water momentarily.

He grabbed her by the waist and hauled her sputtering back to the surface.

"You're going to hurt yourself," Rylan said evenly, but his heart raged painfully in his chest.

This, all of this, was a nightmare.

"Better that than everyone dying for me." Her features hardened and she pushed herself out of his arms, turning to face the collapsed exit.

A chill ran up Rylan's back as her energy surged. "Evie, no!"

Pale light burst through the cavern, glittering over the waves. Rylan threw up an arm to shield his dilated eyes, too late.

"Stop, no!" Harper screamed.

Bodies splashed around in the water. More cries.

The light sputtered and strobed, and with a gurgling crackle, it went out instantly. Everly screamed. Her agonized shriek ended with a gurgle.

Terror overwhelmed Rylan. His vision swam with bright-colored globs, burned into his retina. He blindly swam forward, sweeping the water with both arms. Everly had been right there in front of him, hardly an arm's length away, but now, she was nowhere to be found.

Rylan dove underwater, silently begging his eyesight to right itself. Purple flares painted the focal point of his vision, and beneath the surface, he couldn't see any form or substance through the imprinted light.

Hair tangled into his fingers, and he swam to meet it. His hands found Everly's jacket, her curves. Looping an arm around her waist, he dragged her to the surface with his heart beating out a wild rhythm in his throat.

They burst through into the steadily dwindling air. She sank into his arms, her face dipping toward the surface. Rylan's vision cleared to just a couple of stars floating across his sight. Nearby, Harper surfaced. She must have gone under for Everly, too.

"Is she okay?" Harper said from behind her fingers.

"I don't know," Rylan replied.

Everly's head rolled limply against his chest, but she gasped a breath.

Harper cried, "You idiot. You could have killed yourself."

Everly's shoulders convulsed, and Rylan pulled her closer.

"Bring her over here." Harper waved a hand in the water, showing a shelf near where a flat boulder had fallen just below the water's surface.

Rylan swam over, lifted Everly, and floated her onto the shelf like it was a bed.

He supported her head so that her face remained above water.

Everly squinted her eyes shut.

"I can't feel my arms," she said, her voice high and frightened.

Rylan swallowed hard. Her arms were the least of his concerns. The cracks had spread right up onto her face and across her chest, meeting between her collar bones. Her breaths were shallow and uneven.

"We can't wait any longer," Rylan said firmly, trying to keep his voice calm and even so his own fear wouldn't exacerbate her terror. "Where's the crystal?"

"I have it," Harper said.

She reached down to where her axe used to hang at her hips, bringing the crystal

back up. Rylan took it carefully.

Everly jerked, trying to back away from him, but the cave ceiling was at her nose and the wall blocked her other side. "No! We can't."

"We don't have a choice." A wave of water washed around Rylan, and his scalp bumped into the ceiling.

Everly shook her head, struggling to keep her eyes open. "I can't ... risk it. I need to be somewhere ... Somewhere alone, away from you. All of you. It might hurt you the way it hurt my dad ..."

Rylan held the crystal up, prepared to smash it anyway.

Everly turned her face toward him, panting hard. "Don't you dare. If you try to force that on me, I will burn through every last bit of the dragon's light before you have a chance to smash that thing."

Rylan's arm stayed, his teeth bared. Harper stared at him with eyes showing white all around the unfamiliar brown irises. Neri cowered behind her, clinging to her shoulders.

Tammy moved closer, swimming slowly with Callan supported in her arms, her hand still pressed into his chest as though she could hold him together.

Rylan's fingers shook around the crystal. What if Everly was right? What if saving her meant losing Callan, his own brother? And Tammy, Harper, Neri ... even Denny?

Could he live with that? Maybe he wouldn't have to. He could be gone as well. The whole mess ate at his heart.

Either way, Everly wasn't giving him a choice.

Rylan lowered the crystal but kept it tight in his hand.

Harper shook her head and whimpered, moving away, closer to Neri. Denny continued to dig against the rocks. His movements were slow, his face resigned, but he kept going.

Even if they could keep up their mer forms until the high tide passed, they couldn't get out without help. They were buried. They might survive this high tide, but the next? And the next? No one would know where to look for them. They might start the search at the collapsed lighthouse, but they were a long way down.

Rylan's shoulders slumped. This really was it. On some undeniable instinct, he looped an arm under Everly's neck and pulled her closer. Their eyes met.

Warmth flushed through Rylan's body. Every inch of him wanted to protect her. He wanted to take away the pain in her shattering body. He wanted to take back what she'd done to herself in order to save his life. He wanted nothing more than to make sure she walked out of there intact and unharmed with the lighthouse crystal in hand.

He clutched Everly to his chest, racking his mind for any solution to this problem. The stones were immovable, the cavern filling up fast. Everly's powers were out of the question, and Rylan had nothing. No answers.

They'd come this far only to die. All of them.

Cold water closed around his neck and pinned his head to the ceiling.

"It won't be much longer," Everly whispered calmly. "When I'm gone, when Harper and I are gone"—her face wrinkled with emotion— "swim down with the nyevmer and wait for the tide to go out again."

He pressed his forehead against hers, words hard to force out of his throat. "Don't say that."

She turned her face away weakly. "That's what you want, isn't it? You want me out of your life, and soon I will be."

"That's not ... this isn't how I wanted it."

"You hate me. You didn't even want the poster." Her voice was flat, eyes delirious. Rylan frowned. "The what?"

"You took it down. You don't want anything that even reminds you of me."

The one in my old room? Three thousand years ago, he had taken the poster down last night. He shook his head, forehead wrinkled.

"No, that's not ... The ... the silverfish were getting to it. I put it away to keep it safe."

When he had walked back into his childhood room after so long away, that poster more than anything reminded him of her, and their time together as kids. That time— their entire relationship—was so special to him. He didn't want to see it get destroyed, so he packed it away, out of sight.

Just like he did to Everly.

He'd forced her away when he joined the Darkfreys. He'd been sure he was making the right choice. Keeping her safe. But in doing so, he was the one who destroyed what they had. Or could have had.

Now, facing the end, he knew that it hadn't been worth it.

All those years they'd been apart when he'd wanted her near. All those times he'd thought of her and refused his feelings. It all felt wasted.

She shivered in his arms, and he turned her face gently back toward his. "I just wanted you to be safe. And I thought I could do that by keeping you away. But I have missed you, every single second. Keeping you safe wasn't all I ever wanted. I wanted *you*. I don't want to push you away any longer."

Everly blinked hazily at him. "I see how you look at me, you hate me."

"Not you." He had stared at her with growing disgust, but it was at himself. "Every moment you remained here, every time you were hurt, or put in danger, that was my failure, that was me I hated."

He hadn't been able to stop it or fix it.

"You can't keep me safe, not from everything. That's not your fault."

Rylan knew she was right. He'd thought he couldn't be with her if he wanted her to be safe. But if he couldn't keep her safe, why couldn't he be with her? Even if for only their very last moments.

The water slipped higher, cresting over his chin.

Rylan cupped her face in his hands. "Don't think that I hate you. Don't ever think that. How could I hate you? I love you."

Her mouth opened in a shaky O. "You love me?"

He leaned in, whispering against her ear. "I've always loved you. All I've known my entire life is loving you. I never wanted to lose you, Everly. The dumbest thing I've ever done in my life was pushing you away."

Everly turned to face him. Her eyes closed and she pressed trembling, deathly-cold lips to his.

24

J asper stomped toward the Darkfrey Estate entrance, glowering at his surroundings as though they were to blame for all his pain inside. The gates opened with an electric hum and the driveway ahead was gloomy and foreboding.

The perfect atmosphere to match his emotions.

A blood-red sun sank behind the wooded hills. Storm clouds crowded in the distance and a harsh wind blew dust and leaves around.

Jasper had taken the long way home from the theatre, meandering through Shroudhaven to buy enough time to drown his thoughts and worries. Along with trying desperately to wipe the visage of Cherry's betrayed features from his mind.

Have I lost him for good now?

The artifact—the "Bane," Cherry had called it—was wrapped in its tattered parchment and shoved beneath his right arm, bulky and pulsing with that low energy.

Jasper couldn't wait to dump it on Mordan's desk and be done with it. The thing had ruined everything and chased Cherry even further away.

In actuality, though, Jasper knew *he* had done that. Not the Bane. His choices. His mistakes.

The sports complexes surrounding the estate buildings were all quiet beneath their floodlights at this time of evening. Training was done for the day and shadyrs who were part of braces generally took some downtime around sunset before patrols started. He walked the grounds undisturbed and then took the stairs to the main building two at a time.

One of the admin staff clicked off lights to a room on the side as she stepped out, then jumped, caught off guard by Jasper's passing. She took in who he was and gave him a respectful nod.

That was what being part of a brace meant at Darkfrey Estate. They were the top of the pecking order. Every other service and role at the estate, from paperwork to cleaning, existed to serve them and their mission. He could see even in this staffer's eyes that he was important. What he did meant something.

But did that mean that everyone else *wasn't* important? That's how many Darkfrey

shadyrs behaved.

It was something Cherry always hated about this place.

Jasper returned a nod to the woman, imbuing it with his thanks for everything she did. She seemed taken aback by his acknowledgment of her existence. She gave a shy smile, then clicked away in her heels with a bundle of paperwork clutched in her arms. Her footsteps echoed into nothing, leaving a hush over the building.

What am I doing? What do I want? Jasper rubbed his forehead, his mind a noisy mess.

The answer was easy in the past. To be a Darkfrey. To be the best shadyr he could be, to give everything he could to the cause, and receive the respect that came with that role.

Now, those goals felt hollow.

He let his feet lead him blindly forward. He was still down the hall from Mordan's office when a voice broke the silence.

"You sure took your time."

Jasper whipped his head up, unease snaking through him. Vonny leaned against a doorframe between a suit of armor and a gilded painting.

Jasper blinked at her and brought himself into a pose of attention. Although she never was his brace leader, she always held superiority over him.

Jasper delivered his half-truth with the ease of everyday practice. "The mission was more complicated than anticipated."

Vonny muttered under her breath. "Did you even get what I sent you for?"

"Of course I did. I was heading to Mordan's office to return the retrieved artifact now." He tugged the bundled-up Bane from beneath his arm and held it up as evidence.

"Why would you do that? He didn't give you the mission, I did."

He hesitated, grip tight around the ancient parchment. "Because the relics belong with the estate, that is how it should be."

Ghast damn it, Cherry is right. I do sound like a brain-washed robot.

Vonny straightened and traipsed his way. Something about standing in the empty hallway with Vonny Mesman staring him down left Jasper cold inside. That chill grew when another form loomed through the shadowy doorway behind her.

Kole Mesman. Vonny's husband.

Like most at the estate, Jasper typically gave the man a wide berth. He was ... strange. Possibly unhinged. The loss of their son affected them both, but it had twisted Kole beyond recognition of his former self. He was prone to violent outbursts, which were terrifying given the bulked-up state he'd built his body into. A brick wall of corded muscle, barely contained beneath his clothes.

The couple stopped in front of Jasper as a single unit. Kole reached over his wife's shoulder, holding out a meaty hand.

"We'll take it from here."

Were they trying to take the credit for the find? That explained the secrecy to some extent, but something else felt off.

Jasper eyed the older man's palm. It was scarred and covered in a sheen of sweat. His own hand, which held the Bane, twitched and withdrew back toward himself.

"I don't mind conveying the artifact to Mordan. I'd like to know the relic reaches the place it belongs."

Kole's eyes narrowed dangerously, and Jasper worried he'd overstepped.

Vonny tilted her head, blond bob swinging. "Of course it will go where it belongs. Don't you trust us? Or do you just want to go and get your pat on the head from your master for a job well done?"

Jasper blanked his features and spoke evenly. "I'm sure Master Darkfrey will give credit where it is deserved. I simply thought delivery jobs were a duty below your standing."

Clearly tired of waiting, Kole reached out and snatched at the bundle. He yanked it from Jasper's fingers, then sneered at him. "You haven't got the faintest understanding of my duties."

The couple turned their backs on him, marching away.

"What does that thing do?" The words fell from Jasper's lips before he could silence himself.

They kept walking, and Vonny called back, "You don't typically make a habit of asking questions. One of your very few qualities."

"Cherry said it was related in some way to Everly, that it makes her sick, or—"

Damn it, shut your mouth.

They didn't need to know what he knew. He wanted to know what *they* knew.

Vonny stopped and turned back with a raised, pale eyebrow. "*Cherry* said?"

Ghast damn it, get it together!

Jasper's thoughts swirled and he couldn't grasp onto the point he was trying to make, why he was daring to rile up the Mesmans. The mission was done, what did it matter? But it all felt wrong. He wanted answers. And he wanted those answers from a superior he should be able to trust.

Jasper lifted his chin. "That artefact belonged to the Howells. It was the one they reclaimed from Gorhanmere. You didn't give me that information when you sent me on the mission. Why not?"

Vonny stalked toward him and shoved the point of her fingernail into Jasper's chest so hard it bruised. The action was at odds with the sweet smile on her face.

"Listen to me carefully because you seem to be extremely confused right now. Your job isn't to ask questions, and certainly isn't to question me. Your job is to keep your mouth shut and do as you're told. Do you hear me?"

Jasper swallowed against his heart in his throat, but he didn't lower his gaze. He tried to channel Cherry's bravery, even as he knew he fell short.

"I want to know why you sent me for it, why alone, and what you're going to do with it."

His heart stopped beating as Vonny's faux good-natured expression faded away, replaced by fury. "The last time someone didn't keep their mouth shut and do as they were told, they found themselves alone and afoul of an eidolghast. The same could easily happen to you. Except this time, hopefully *you* would stay dead."

Jasper's carefully-crafted blank expression vanished.

"Rylan?" He choked the name out, shock making his fingertips numb.

Vonny's expression didn't change. She stared him down, while Kole looked on with cold, hard eyes.

"I'll go to Mordan," Jasper stuttered.

Vonny and Kole exchanged amused glances. Vonny pushed her nail into him one last time before pulling it back like a gun.

"Go ahead," she said, shrugging. "Do you think I care what happens to you if you go down that path? Think what you want, say what you want, but at the end of the day, you're just another replaceable nobody. Raise your voice and find out how quickly you'll be on the other side of the fence, sleeping on the streets."

Jasper gaped, unable to form words.

She reached out and patted him on the cheek. "Poor thing is so confused."

"Then let me clarify for him," Kole growled, face lowered in shadow. "Get your act together. The cause is what matters, all that matters. We would do anything for the cause. Anything. You would too if you were truly loyal."

Anything? Jasper barely heard his own voice over the hum building in his skull. "I am loyal, I've done everything, given up everything for the Darkfreys."

"Prove it." Kole rolled his head, cracking his neck.

Vonny smiled at him sweetly. "The way you 'associate' with that queer is a black mark on your record, Jasper. You'd be better off if he were out of the picture, permanently, don't you think? To avoid any … temptation, or the spread of rumors. Prove you are loyal."

The blood drained from Jasper's face.

Do they know? What do they know?

Vonny and her husband turned away and left him paralyzed there, as lifeless as the empty suit of armor beside him.

Nausea bubbled in his stomach as Jasper watched the two of them fade down the hallway. Once they were out of sight, his body gave in, buckled over, and he dry-retched.

They had been involved somehow in what happened to Rylan. And Mordan Darkfrey as well, he had to know. They were too unconcerned about Jasper going to the estate's leader. They were too unbothered by his questions. They didn't even need the silence they could buy with what they clearly knew about him.

They had everything they needed against him, and what evidence did he have? Guesses? Worries? Vague admissions of guilt witnessed by no one but him?

Nearby, doors opened and closed, and voices penetrated the stone-cold silence of the hallways. Braces prepared to leave for their night patrols, as they had done every night of his life at the estate.

But now ... everything had changed.

He had believed in their mission. He had been loyal. He had worked so hard and sacrificed ...

But now, he couldn't look at the Darkfrey crest or his fellow brace members without questioning everything about *how* they achieved their goals. It was wrong, it was all wrong.

Cherry had been right. The one right thing in his life. He should have listened earlier. He shouldn't have been so scared to lose something that never belonged to him anyway—the acceptance of this place.

Darkfrey Estate was broken, and it broke him, and his friends had been hurt in the process. Even worse, Jasper himself was complicit in the betrayal.

He clenched his hands into fists and whirled on his heel. Regardless of what he'd done before this moment, he knew now what he had to do. What he would have to find before his time at Darkfrey Estate ended forever.

Evidence. Even just a scrap of evidence. That was what he needed.

Those nights that Rylan had spent sneaking about alone before he went missing, is that what he'd been searching for too? Is that what got him almost killed? And if one of the best shadyrs Darkfrey estate had ever seen had failed on that mission, what chance did he have?

25

The water rose shockingly around the gills in Tammy's neck as she tried to keep Callan afloat. Every particle of her energy was focused on him and her screaming thoughts of oh-ghast-what-are-we-going-to-do-with-his-wound-if-we-even-survive-the-incoming-tide, which was how she found herself inhaling a lungful of water through her nose.

Her brain confused the signals between her human side and her shadyr side, and she didn't know whether to breathe the quickly diminishing oxygen or the water.

She attempted both at once, nose and gills gulping.

Tammy slipped beneath the surface as icy saltwater filled her lungs. She choked and gagged, eyes stinging. Her body flickered unstably and the fear of vanishing to Dark Corner beat out her fear of drowning.

Don't go, don't go. You can't leave them like this. She flailed for the surface, slamming into Callan's tail in her desperate bid to find air.

Callan's hands found hers and he pulled her up. He latched an arm around her waist and held her head above the water as she coughed in a way that felt like vomiting directly from her lungs. She spat out the excess water and wheezed painfully at the air.

"I'm sorry," Tammy gasped the words out, beating her tail against the water to back away from him. "Are you okay?"

"You're choking on water, and you're worried about me?" Callan's eyes moved lazily, unlike his normally alert gaze, but he still managed a smile.

Somehow, he always managed to smile. Tammy's heart ached.

She moved quickly back to his side to help support him. He wasn't yet incapable of swimming on his own, but she could tell too much motion would put dangerous strain on his wound. Her breathing screwup had already hurt him too much.

Tammy focused on her shadyr form and dragged in a deep breath through her gills. She could taste Callan's blood in the water. For the fiftieth time, she blinked away tears. For all her nihilistic talk of looking forward to the moment when she was freed from the burden of life, Tammy was shaken to her core in the face of death.

The thought of leaving scared her. The thought of Callan leaving her terrified her

more. He couldn't die. She couldn't lose someone else she cared for.

A sob escaped, and her body flickered again, trying to drag her away to the place of her nightmares, her personal hell. She set her jaw and held on with everything she could to existing in this place only, there beside Callan.

He looked back at her with widened eyes. "I'm an idiot. Of course ... You can go."

"What? No."

His head lolled in the waves that beat against his ears. He tipped his face upward to speak above the water.

"You can get out of here. You can live. Tell Mom where to find us."

"You *are* an idiot. You know we wouldn't get back out here and break through into the cave in time. You're bleeding out! Everly and Harper, they can't ..."

Callan's eyes closed in a slow blink. "The other shadyrs might be able to hold nyevmer form until the tide goes down."

"Great, so I can save fucking *Denny*."

"And my brother. And Neri. They must almost balance out having to save Denny."

Tammy half laughed, half sobbed against Callan's cheek. "I'm not going anywhere. If this is it, if this is the end, I deserve front row tickets more than the rest of you."

Wincing, Callan turned in the water and wrapped his hands around her upper arms. "You *have* to let go of this guilt!"

Surprised by the vehemence in his tone, Tammy stiffened. She wanted to back away from him, but she couldn't leave him swimming without her support.

Since they'd arrived at the lighthouse and she'd been trapped in mermaid form, he carried her, never once complaining. She had to stay and carry him now. She would stay and look him in the eye, no matter how his hands on her muddled her mind so that she couldn't think straight. No matter how she wanted to hide, and scoff, and roll her eyes.

She carefully wiped the emotions off her face. "You don't know what you're talking about."

"You think I don't know anything about survivor's guilt? I know you're suffering. I know how much it hurts. I know how it makes you blame yourself. You internalize *everything* that goes wrong around you. You blame yourself even when a situation has nothing to do with you."

"I do not," Tammy said hotly, her cheeks burning with shame. "I blame myself exactly the right amount!"

"Remember when you and Everly set off that weird mini-beshadowing at The Crow's Nest?"

Tammy flushed hotter, despite the cold water creeping up her cheeks.

"You blamed yourself for that, entirely."

She lifted one blackened hand up between them. "Of course it was my fault."

"No," Callan said firmly. "It was some kind of reaction between you *and* Everly, that no one could have predicted, that you didn't choose to do, or choose to have happen to you. You do this *every* time. You're so absolutely certain that your existence causes everything around us to go wrong."

Tammy wanted to cover her ears with her cursed hands. She hated that he could see all her failings so clearly.

"Because it does."

"It doesn't. Life just fucking sucks sometimes but you're not some omnipotent deity making that happen! It just ... happens. It's not your fault." His thumb brushed over her cheek, then he locked gazes with her. "Transport yourself out of here. You can leave and save yourself. And even if it's only yourself that you save, *it's worth it*."

"I don't deserve to get out of here while you die," Tammy said hotly, the words thick with withheld tears.

"You think being here to *watch* us die, and die alongside us when you don't have to, is what you deserve?" Callan pulled her closer, enveloping her in an embrace. "No one deserves that."

Their tails bumped beneath the water. Their chests pressed together, and Tammy tried to pull away, worried she was hurting him more. He held her still with surprising strength. But his hands were shockingly cold.

Callen pulled back enough to lock eyes with her. "Blaise fell through the shroudpool, and you couldn't save him."

Tammy flinched as though he struck her physically.

"Do you know why that hurts so much? Because you care, so deeply." He kept holding her tight. "You carry such immense guilt *because* you love so strongly. You love with your whole heart and soul. That's something that takes great courage. It's something to be admired. You have to stop trying to hide from that. You have to let yourself live."

Sobs rushed from Tammy's chest so thick she couldn't breathe.

The water pressed them higher, ducking them under, but Callan didn't let her go.

They surfaced again, and Callan dropped his voice to a whisper at her ear. "Don't argue. Just go. I want you to live. Mom would want you to live. You are loved. You're worthy of being loved the same way you love your friends and family."

"No, I'm not," she gasped, voice small and lost beneath the waves.

"You are. Nothing will ever make me believe otherwise." Callan grunted as his upturned cheek hit the ceiling.

"Have we reached the point we're all doing declarations of love?" Harper sniffed and sobbed out a giggle from close by. "Because I love you, I love all of you. I know I've only known you a while, but I do. Except maybe Denny."

"That hurts like you punched my heart in the dick," Denny replied, nose pressed

against the stone above them.

The water lapped at the side of Tammy's face, obscuring her vision and washing away tears. Part of her was mortified that the others no doubt heard everything she and Callan had said to each other, but that part was drowning beneath the fear of losing any of them.

She felt Rylan reach out and wrap one arm around his brother, drawing him close and bringing Tammy with him.

"You still hanging in there?" he asked.

"Pssh, it's just a scratch." Callan still smiled.

Rylan frowned deeply as he took in his brother's wound and pallid skin. Everly was cradled tight at his other side, eyes bloodshot and unfocused. Harper and Neri bumped up behind them, bobbing in the water. Even Denny moved in. They'd all floated closer, coming together in their final moments.

The water had officially reached the top of the cavern.

Time was up.

Mere seconds later, the waves closed over Tammy's head.

When she had been thrown out of the Darkfreys, all she had were the clothes on her back, a dead best friend, and fresh enemies of his parents who had once treated her like their own daughter.

Lian had taken her in with open arms when nobody should have wanted her. It was her, Lian, and Rushelle at first, then the family grew with Denny, Cherry, and Callan. She didn't think they could love her, that they did anything other than tolerate the burden of her, her curse, and her attempts to push them away.

But she did love them. Quickly and completely. They became her family. She loved them. All of them. And if she could dig past her issues and trauma and yes, survivor's guilt, and trust that Callan had spoken the truth—they loved her, too.

She floated under the water, cut off from the surface. Cut off from safety.

She could breathe, for now. But she couldn't watch anyone else die.

Tammy opened her arms and grabbed for her teammates.

Her friends must have thought she was going for one last embrace. One last goodbye beneath the waves. Because all of them drew in, arms looping around one another. One tug from her brought the whole team into a group hug.

Then Tammy pictured Dark Corner.

The place had haunted her nightmares. Every time her "ability" had dragged her back to Dark Corner, she'd hated it more and more. Now, though, she needed the shroudpool to be their salvation.

I can do this.

I have to do this.

She closed her eyes, concentrating so hard it hurt as she opened herself to the pull of her curse and its destination. This had to work. Everly and Harper had already taken their last breath and wouldn't last much longer.

Tammy clenched her hands tight, crushing her friends, her family, close to her. She wasn't going to let them go. She wasn't going to lose them like she lost Blaise.

Opening her eyes, Tammy zeroed in on Callan's face.

He stared at her through the water, his eyes wide open, a small smile on his lips as they shaped the word, "Go."

"I will." She nodded and mouthed back, "And I'm taking you with me."

The world changed in an instant.

The cold press of water vanished, and her body slammed into solid ground, feeling much, much heavier than it had been while floating. Splashing water pattered down all around.

Tammy groaned as dried grass and twigs crackled beneath her back. Her eyes scrunched closed with the pain and shock of the impact. The familiar sulfurous stench, laced with several layers of decaying leaves and undergrowth, met Tammy's nose.

She was back at Dark Corner.

She was terrified of opening her eyes, to find out whether she was back at Dark Corner alone. She'd lost her grip on her friends somewhere before or after the impact with solid ground, and felt no one in her hands.

Please, please. They have to be here too.

26

Everly's blurred vision tried to take in the change of surroundings. For a few moments, she thought maybe she had died or fallen into delirium.

She wondered when that delirium had begun, whether Rylan had really told her he loved her, whether they had shared that kiss tasting of salt and long years of yearning.

The pressure on her lungs eased, and she coughed up a splattering of seawater before taking a deep breath.

Bodies slammed against her in a tangle of tails and limbs, followed by grunts and sighs and giant, gaping breaths of air. Salt water spattered around them like rain. Confused voices surrounded her.

"What happened?"

"What is this place?"

"Is this Dark Corner?"

"How in the Everdark did we get here?"

"Tammy? You're incredible."

"Did everyone make it? Is everyone okay?"

Everly counted out each voice in turn. Rylan, Neri, Harper, Denny, Callan, and Tammy. Everyone was there. Everyone was okay.

Then the pain hit her, and Everly knew she had to still be alive because she experienced the blazing agony through every fiber of her being. Breathing hard and fast, she curled on her side, screaming silently. Her vision blanked out completely for a moment, then wobbled back.

Rylan leaned over her with his expression set like stone. "Evie? Hey, it's all right. Just breath."

"Is she okay?" Tammy crawled closer, her mermaid tail flopping behind heavily in the dirt.

Tammy. They were at Dark Corner.

She'd done this. Somehow, for the first time, she'd carried other people with her to the shroudpool.

Vaguely, Everly wondered if Tammy had that power in her all along. She knew the

kid didn't like being touched, that she generally kept her blackened hands out of reach.

She'd probably never transported while touching anyone else before. But the way Tammy had pulled them all in when Everly had thought it was the end, the way she'd clung on so tight, she must have been attempting to do exactly this, and she'd succeeded. She'd saved them. Turning her head, Everly took in the entire team, dazed, drenched, but alive. A mess of mostly mermaids scattered across the ground, far from the sea.

"You did it. We're all here." Everly wriggled her fingertips closer to Tammy.

She had been so scared for Harper's life just moments before, but they were all safe. "Thank you."

Tammy frowned at Everly's hand, eyes roaming to Everly's face with naked concern. "Please tell me that we still have what we went to that ghast-forsaken island for, that it came with us too."

"The crystal? I've got it," Rylan said.

Tammy's eyes glistened, red-rimmed. "Good, because she's not looking so good. Those cracks ..."

Everly attempted a smile, and her lips ached like they could split into a thousand pieces. Everything about her body felt heavy and brittle.

"I'm okay."

"You're not." Rylan leaned close to her on his stomach, raising the crystal for her to see. "But you will be."

Everly swallowed, unsure whether she was more scared of having another portion of the soul-eater inside her, or of the death she felt herself teetering on the edge of.

Rylan's face twisted, and he grunted in frustration as a dark mist enveloped him. The influence of the nyevmer over him and the others must have run out. All around, shadyrs were swapping tails for bare legs. Rylan put the crystal down beside Everly, then rolled away in a haze of dark magic.

Tammy squealed, "Pants! We need pants!"

Denny had the remaining packs—Callan's, and Rylan's, with Everly's inside it—hanging from straps on one arm. "Bet you're all glad I hung on to these. While ya'll were being all sappy and sentimental, who was being the capable shadyr? This dude! You might even say that I *saved your asses*."

Rylan jumped to his returned feet and snatched the bags. He tore through the contents, hauling out the shredded pants he'd worn earlier, and pulling them on still soaking wet, before the black swirls faded. Everly blushed, the rush of blood painful in her cheeks, and turned away.

"How many pairs have we got left?" Denny asked.

"You can have my spare set," Rylan said. "Callan, here are yours."

"I had an extra pair in my bag," Everly croaked. She heard more rummaging, and

Tammy called out a thank you.

"Do we have something for Neri? She's not changing yet, but, you know," Harper said.

"Here."

As flies were zipped up, Everly turned back. Harper helped direct Neri into a man-sized T-shirt. The girl poked at it curiously like it was the first piece of clothing she'd ever worn.

As soon as it was on, she clung back onto Harper like she was drowning. She stared at the foreign world around her as though gigantic mermaid hunters were about to crash through the trees and crush her under their heel. But there was no sign of change on the girl, no sparks or dark clouds of magic.

Denny buttoned up his pants and eyed Rylan strangely, a smirk forming on his wide mouth. "So, when you changed from mermaid to dragon form to beat the nyevmer, you were going pants-less that whole time, right? Nice one, taking out an eidolghast with your—"

"Denny!" Harper scolded.

"—dick out," Denny finished with a grin.

"Rylan? Chuck me a first aid kit, too, if it's still any good," Tammy said.

Everly's pants swam on the goth girl's tiny frame. She took off her hoodie to tie around her waist like a belt, then knelt back down beside Callan. He had the pants draped over his lap but hadn't been able to get up to put them on.

"How's he doing?" Rylan's gaze cut between where his brother lay and Everly.

"I can hold on a bit longer," Callan said, weakly flopping a hand at him.

Rylan turned the pack upside down and dumped the contents at his feet. The first aid kit tumbled out and he unzipped the rubber cover.

"Damp, but not too bad." He under-armed the kit and Tammy caught it neatly, quickly laying out dressings, sutures, and shears.

Rylan nodded to her in thanks, then snatched up a waterproof pouch and stuck his hand inside. He swore as he removed a phone that had been snapped nearly in two.

"Try mine," Callan said, as Tammy cut the flexible straps of his broken body armor with the shears and removed the pieces.

"No luck." Rylan held up the other pouch to reveal a gash down the side, water pouring out. "Did anyone's phone survive?"

In Everly's periphery, she could see Harper lean back to fumble in her jeans pocket. She tugged her cell from her pants and tapped at the screen. "Mine's good. Better be, considering how much I paid for the waterproof model."

"See if you can get a signal and get in touch with Lian. We need assistance, fast," Rylan told her.

Harper got to her feet and said to Neri, "I need to move around to try to find a good spot for this to work. I'll be right back."

Neri stared up at her with dinner-plate eyes, her head shaking and tail hugged to her chest.

Pouting, Harper bent down and scooped her into her arms. "Fine, you can come with me. It's okay, you don't weigh a thing."

Rylan came and knelt beside where Everly lay on her back, staring up at the sunset. She had been trying to slow her breathing, gain some control over her body, but her inhalations remained short, sharp shivers. A dimness clung to her thoughts, and her body was going blessedly, horrifyingly numb.

"You're ... yourself," Everly mumbled, staring up into Rylan's face.

There was no monster there, not vampire or werewolf or any combination of forms. Just human. Just Rylan, as beautiful as he ever was.

He grunted softly. "It's taking a bit of effort, but today has been like one seriously intensive training program. I'm getting a handle on how you ... affect me."

"Show off," Tammy muttered.

Harper wandered in an ever-widening circle, staring at her phone that was held in the same arm that Neri's tail hung over. "I'm not getting any bars here."

"I don't normally get any reception until I'm near the gate. It's a bit of a walk, out that way." Tammy pointed.

Harper's face scrunched up. "How long do we have?"

Rylan brushed a finger through Everly's hair. "Not long enough. I don't think we can wait for anyone else to get here and help. Everly needs the crystal *now*."

She tried to shake her head, but that made the whole world slosh around her.

Rylan picked up the crystal and placed it with infinite gentleness onto her chest, then lifted her hands, draping them over the top. "No excuses. We don't know what will happen if you use the crystal, but we know what will happen if you don't."

I won't last much longer. I'm fading fast.

Rylan's voice was low and rough, reminding her of the waves that still echoed in her ears. "And I'm not strong enough to lose you. I never have been—that's why I pushed you away. I suffered being separated from you because I could survive that. I could survive, as long as you lived. So please, you have to survive now, for me."

Everly swallowed a lump of pain. The last time she had broken a crystal containing part of the Beast of Teeth and Stars, it had killed her father. But she'd also been a child. She knew what she was dealing with now and had learned to control it—mostly. She could only hope she would maintain that control.

Everly took a deep breath and forced out scratchy words. "Move everyone away, *far* away."

Rylan turned, signaling to the others. "Everyone get clear. You've seen the dragon's light in action—double that reach and take up position."

Denny helped Tammy lift Callan and their makeshift med station back to the farthest boundaries of the clearing.

"Good luck. I'll see you again, strong and healthy soon, okay?" Harper hovered on the spot for a moment, biting her lip, then backed away with Neri.

Rylan put his hand against Everly's cheek. His touch was soft, and the hard look on his face had fallen away to concern.

"Do you want me to stay close? I will, if you need me."

Everly stared down at the gently glowing, deadly shard under her chin. "No. Get safe."

Rylan kissed her forehead, leaving behind a hot brand on her skin, then stood. She listened to his footsteps fade away across the cracked dirt, then shivered as a cool breeze passed over her. Above, swathes of scarlet slashed through the parting storm clouds, tinting the thin mist on the ground around her with a bloody cast.

The forest fell silent. She tilted her heavy head and glanced around for a glimpse of her friends, but her eyesight had grown too blurry, showing only faded smudges of gray.

Hopefully, the others were all far enough away to be safe.

She wrapped numb fingers around the crystal, and her head swam as she forced her remaining energy into raising the sparkling item. Her shattered arm turned to an inferno. It was too heavy, the crystal, her own arm. A strange, crunching, chinking sound echoed up through her body, bringing a raging pain along with it.

But she didn't have to lift far. She cried out as she pushed her arm up straight above her head, and then with a rush of exhalation, let her arm drop to the side like a dead weight.

Pain exploded across her every nerve ending. The crystal hit the rocky ground beside her. And the world was engulfed in light.

27

Harper shifted Neri in her arms, holding her phone out as high as she could and glaring at the wavering lack of reception.

"Come on, come on!"

Everly was hurt and exploding with light and everyone was wrecked, and Harper loathed the thought that Shroudhaven's awful phone network would be the reason someone didn't survive.

She'd walked all the way to a boundary fence before even the hint of a bar showed up. A text requesting help was already locked and loaded, just waiting for the magic of technology to whisk it away. She'd tapped the details out fast as Neri watched the bright screen in awe.

Whole team at Dark Corner. Need med assistance and transport ASAP.

"What is it doing now?" Neri asked.

"I just need … no, it's too complicated and I don't even really understand it myself. See those little bars? We want more of them."

Neri nodded under twisted brows, but glared hard at the screen as though doing so would make it work better.

An icon spun, and a little green tick appeared. Harper let out a whoop.

"We did it," Neri said, wide eyed.

A second later, the phone buzzed in her hand. Lian calling back.

"How—get—*shhchshh*." Lian's staticky voice cut in and out on the line.

"We're at Dark Corner," Harper enunciated as loudly and clearly as she could, even though she'd shared it in the text already.

Any other details were almost impossible to convey over the dodgy network. Harper winced as she tried repeating herself the third time, and kept glancing anxiously over her shoulder, back to where her best friend lay close to death.

"I—" *screech*. "—my way." *Shh. Shh. Screech.* "—the road."

"See you soon. Hurry," Harper said, though the line cut out before she finished her sentence.

She turned around to see the spot where Everly lay lit up like a fireworks factory that had caught ablaze.

Oh, Ev. Please be okay.

Neri stared wide-eyed at the light and clung tighter around Harper's shoulders.

"Hey, it's okay. It's just something Everly does sometimes. All good ... as long as you don't get too close." Harper readjusted her hold around Neri and headed back to the others.

All the energy from the Bane had now faded from her system but carrying the mermaid girl was still something she could do with her tired, human arms. Neri really was tiny, and bony. Harper shuddered to think what kind of diet the poor thing had in the lighthouse.

She shuddered to think of *anything* that had happened in the young woman's life until that point. Including the violence of that day. Neri seemed to have calmed down slightly, progressing from near-catatonic to trapped-rabbit. But she hadn't shown any violence, hadn't shown any signs of the beshadowed madness her father had succumbed to.

Maybe he'd always been mad.

If anything, Neri seemed to have decided she could trust Harper, and Harper's suddenly fierce, vengefully protective heart was okay with that.

Rylan, Denny, and Tammy were all bent over Callan. Everly's light cast harsh shadows around them through the trees. Denny stood to the side and kept a watch over the bright tendrils that drifted and whipped around Everly, but none could reach far enough to touch them. He also turned his gaze to the woods, which Harper knew could be equally dangerous.

Rylan's attention was all for his brother now. Considering how he'd shadowed Everly incessantly all day, that made Harper concerned for several reasons. She picked up her pace.

"Lian's on her way," Harper informed the team.

She moved closer, kneeling near the others and settling Neri in her lap.

"Oh thank ghast." Tammy's shoulders slumped.

She crouched on a bed of dead leaves next to Callan, who was on his back, face pale and eyes closed. She had the suture needle in her trembling hand and had managed to close half of the wound. But it had gaped wide open in the time since the flesh was torn, the edges white and ragged from saltwater.

"He needs a hospital. He needs ... I don't know. More than this. He's lost so much blood, and he's barely responding."

"I can help."

The voice was so small, Harper thought she'd imagined it.

Neri's grip around her shoulders tightened just enough to gain her attention, and again she said, "I can help. Maybe. I want to try."

Tammy and Rylan shared a skeptical look as though the wild girl had proposed she perform surgery.

"Umm, how?" was all Harper could say.

"I'm a mermaid," Neri said as an explanation, letting go of Harper and sliding down off her lap to be closer to Callan.

"You're not a mermaid," Harper corrected, but her tone was weak.

She tried to come up with a valid argument, but the truth was, she didn't know why Neri hadn't transformed back into human form yet. Even though the rest of the shadyrs had regained their legs when they crash-landed at Dark Corner, Neri had not. She looked entirely out of place in the spooky forest with her limp, sky-blue tail and ill-fitting T-shirt.

Rylan took a hesitant step forward, as though ready to protect his brother from the tiny girl, but she didn't attempt to touch him. Instead, she inhaled and opened her mouth wide.

Neri sang.

Harper exchanged glances with Tammy at the first few notes. Harper shrugged. If this was all Neri was going to do, at least it wouldn't harm Callan further. Tammy frowned and returned with a sniff to her stitching.

"She's going to draw in trouble again," Denny muttered.

"Like Everly's light show isn't already a beacon the entirety of Shroudhaven could see," Tammy said back. "Let her sing. It's steadying my hands."

Rylan frowned and clutched his brother's wrist, keeping fingers on his pulse point and eyes on his watch.

And Neri sang.

Harper recognized the strange, haunting tones that had filled the cave when they'd found Neri crying over the infant skull, but this was clearer, less shaken by anguish.

The tune was familiar, a strange combination of a few popular nineties songs.

Without the cave echoing Neri's voice into a disembodied cacophony, it was beautiful. Goose bumps rose on Harper's skin as she knelt behind Neri and listened.

The song filtered through her senses, down into her bones, and had a strangely calming effect on her. She closed her eyes and swayed to the music, growing lighter and less achy as Neri went on.

"What in the ghast-blighted Everdark?" Tammy hissed.

Neri's voice faded away.

Harper's eyelids flew open.

Callan looked up, bright and alert. His bloodless pallor had turned back to its normal light tan, and the wound on his chest was gone. Flecks of blood still marked his skin, and a fresh pink scar lay where the injury had cut across his pectoral muscle and collar bone.

But it had closed completely. The stitches lay loose on the surface, as though expelled by his body.

Tammy's jaw hung open comically as she gaped at Neri. "*How?*"

Neri flinched as everyone stared at her, then covered her face in her hands. "I ... I'm a mermaid."

"That's not an explanation!" Tammy snorted. "And you're not a mermaid!"

Harper pulled Neri in close. "Shh, you're scaring her."

"I ... I am. I didn't get legs. You said I would, and I didn't."

"What if she really is a mermaid?" Harper asked. "Weirder things have happened, right? And can any of you shadyrs siren-song away a bloody gash?"

"I've never really considered trying," Tammy deadpanned, paired with an eye roll.

"She's not a mermaid," Rylan said, although he didn't sound certain. "But she has lived as one her whole life, in a beshadowing. I'm not surprised there are some side effects. I'm more surprised she's not completely insane."

Callan probed his chest with his fingers in awe, then sat up.

"Maybe she kept herself sane with her singing. I certainly feel refreshed." He reached out a hand toward Neri but didn't touch her. "Hey, thank you. I feel so much better now."

Neri peeked out from behind her fingers.

"Mermaid songs heal. Well, they're supposed to," she added as she touched her fingers to her own chest. "It still hasn't helped my heart hurt less."

The odd, mashed-up tune still filled Harper's head. Neri had grown up so isolated, with just a madman to learn from. But there had been a few picture books in the room, and for one moment during the fight, Harper thought she saw a radio.

When it got knocked on the floor, Neri had rushed out of safety to reclaim it. Maybe it was more than singing that kept the girl sane. Maybe she'd had a secret connection to the rest of the world.

Harper spoke softly, "Where did you learn those songs? I thought I saw a radio in your room. Have you been listening to it?"

Neri shook her head fearfully. "I wasn't supposed to have it. I wasn't supposed to hear anyone else. Daddy only liked that one song. I wasn't supposed to sing anything else."

"It's okay, you won't get in trouble from us."

Neri's mouth clammed shut.

"I really liked the way you combined songs together, it was beautiful. And I'm glad you had something to listen to. It must have been lonely for you."

Neri emerged from behind her hands and checked each of the faces around her, as

though looking for signs they were about to pounce. Her voice was confessional quiet.

"It came up to me one day from the sea when I was fishing. I liked the songs it played. So many beautiful songs. I wanted to sing them all at once. But sometimes the people talked about *news* and *traffic* and *sports* and the world outside seemed so scary. I knew I wasn't supposed to listen. I knew I wasn't supposed to have it. But I couldn't throw it back to the sea. I knew that's what Daddy would make me do, would have …"

Her tiny frame was racked with sobs.

Harper's mouth twisted. That man was a monster, inside and out. There was little doubt he killed his offspring, and probably Neri's mother, too. But he was the only living company Neri had her whole life.

"I'm so sorry. I'm sorry you lost him. I'm sorry everything has changed so quickly, how scary that must be."

Neri curled herself tighter against Harper's chest and Harper wrapped her arms around her. The girl's wet hair shimmered in the flickering glow cast by Everly, who still shone too bright to look at. Harper stared anyway, her vision swimming with globs of color. The brightest point was a few feet off the ground, hovering as Everly often did when the dragon emerged.

The others had also turned back to watch. After Callan got his pants back on, Rylan put his arm over his brother's shoulder and faced the light, muscles around his jaw twitching and his eyes desperate. There was nothing they could do.

They couldn't risk getting any closer until the scintillating tendrils receded. The tendrils whipped out and were drawn back, over and over, as though some great internal battle was being fought. Everly spoke often about how she had to fight so hard to control the Beast of Teeth and Stars. And now, it looked so much stronger.

"Is your friend going to be okay?" Neri asked. "I can try to heal her, too."

Harper swallowed. "I think Everly's alone on this one."

28

The flash was blinding in its intensity. Everly didn't have a chance to cry out or close her eyes before a shockwave of energy slammed into her. Pure white power surged through her body, searing her veins. It filled her senses, erasing her ability to see, hear, or feel anything exterior to her own thoughts.

She floated in total sensory deprivation for several seconds, too shocked by the sudden absence of *everything* to react.

Her senses returned slowly. First, the sound of dripping met her ears. Not like water, but thicker. More of a *pat, pat, pat* sound, like something thick and viscous.

Then goose bumps rose on her skin as a chilled wind rushed around her. Not the same breeze she'd felt sitting on the ground next to the shroudpool in the woods. This wasn't natural. It tasted like power, control, and blood.

Something gleamed and roiled far ahead, a star in an empty sky. She focused on the light as if it were a life raft in a void-like sea. It bobbed and wove, moving closer.

Everly could feel her body, but she couldn't seem to *move* it. Her limbs felt like phantoms, as invisible as the air she was suspended in. The effect of being indistinguishable from the void around her sent a sharp thrill of terror through her.

"I'm dreaming, this isn't real."

She said the words like a prayer—that this wasn't death, that she could reclaim control. A shiver ran through her, opening her senses back up through her body. She had toes and fingers she could feel again, arms and legs she could move.

A breezy weightlessness filled her. All the pain that had saturated her being was gone. The agony of her body cracking to pieces had ended.

The light grew closer, moving with incredible speed. A scintillating, rippling body of complex, fine-boned patterns spiraling into each other swam through the air like a ribbon.

Her dragon.

It was larger than she'd ever seen it. It had eyes now, sparkling like stars, and a long, treacherous mouth, forming a face so alien, it hurt Everly's mind to gaze upon it. It came to a stop several feet away, turning in circles in the void as though gravity were a concept it despised.

"The Beast of Teeth and Stars," Everly murmured.

"Not that. Not that," the dragon returned in an echoing whisper.

Everly tensed. *It spoke.* It had never communicated before, not in words. Only in urges, hunger, or wrath.

"What are you? Soul-eater?"

"Not Beast of Teeth and Stars. Not soul-eater." Its voice was the crackle of fire, the burst of a supernova. It made Everly's ears ache and left them ringing.

"But you do eat souls," Everly shot back warily. She'd experienced it. She counted them like tally marks scratched in her heart. Starting with her father.

"Souls equate sustenance. Take you *your* name from what is consumed? Beast of Teeth and Stars. Soul-eater. Simple names. Gifted by quarry in fear. I am so much more."

Everly winced, trying to make sense of the being's words. "Then what are you?"

Its long body undulated as it hissed, "The Coruscare."

The dragon, the *Coruscare*, seemed strong, too strong. Between that and the absence of pain in Everly's body, she had to hope that breaking the crystal had worked. That this dreamlike void was her way of processing those new powers flooding through her.

Pressure clouded her senses, as though her mind and body were trapped in a vice. One of contested power. She could feel the dragon needling her will, testing for weaknesses, pushing for control. Whoever won the battle in this space would decide which of them would emerge back into the real world in command.

She could sense its tendrils seeking hungrily all around out there. They had not yet been satiated by the soul of one of her friends, which comforted Everly. She used that relief to strengthen her resolve, to pull back against the dragon's reach, to try to contain it, lock it back away. She had to emerge the victor.

"That name means nothing to me. But I know what you are, soul-eater, and I won't let you control me."

The void shivered and the creature's words dripped venom. "Nothing? You know nothing!"

It rushed at her, straight through her, blinding her with its light.

Everly fell. Not physically—there was no sensation of falling, no dip to her stomach. But the void around her flashed by as if she were falling down a star-filled tunnel, straight into another world.

Her surroundings stopped abruptly, and she shook her head to clear away the disorientation.

Everything around her was bright, glaring white.

A vast realm of pillar-shaped mountains and rippling plains stretched out under an egg yolk-colored sky. Alien, crystalline plants grew in geometric patterns, and directly

ahead, a transparent pyramid soared over the land.

My realm.

Time and space passed with a fast-forward sensation. Everly was inside a vast room that cradled a throne within a kaleidoscope of diamond-cut ornamentation.

The throne was mammoth in size, a sharp-cut circle, hollow through the center. Within that gap, the Coruscare floated, its glow setting every surface in that gleaming space ablaze.

Other creatures moved nearby. Much smaller, humanoid but unlike anything Everly had ever seen. Except for their eyes. They had shadyr eyes. A line of them trailing into the distance, dragging in squirming bodies of eidolghasts, and sometimes their own kind, injured and chained shadyrs, all brought toward the Coruscare.

My servants.

The Coruscare lashed out with a white tendril and consumed the prisoners. All other shadyrs fell forward in supplication.

The throne room vanished.

Something large, hulking, and dark flashed by. A black void, smoky and oozing malice. Everly shuddered.

She had dreamed of that thing before. Everything it touched turned into *nothing*. It rushed for the Coruscare.

The Bane appeared, flew through the darkness, and slammed into the light. Tremendous, overwhelming power split the dragon into pieces. Agony burst through Everly like a thousand dying worlds.

My enemy.

Her surroundings went into hyper-speed again. Images of war, eidolghasts and shadyrs fighting as they fled that dimension and found a balance in the human realm. Three shining crystal pieces were separated, swallowed by the chaos. Vanished. Lost.

Then her father's face. He opened a cabinet, smiled as he placed a crystal on the shelf. A moment later, Everly saw herself as a small, brown-haired child, hand grabbing at the latch to the cabinet. Standing on tiptoes, the very edges of her fingers shoving against the pretty crystal. Her dad loomed behind her, she dropped the crystal, the Coruscare emerged.

Sensations of freedom and confusion washed over Everly. The thing of light did not know this realm, could not exist in this new dimension in its true form. So it took shelter in the closest being.

Hunger.

The Coruscare's fractured piece entered Everly's tiny body, merging with her like a parasite, and then eased a hunger of thousands of years by consuming her father.

It didn't expect this new beast it inhabited to lock it away again. That it would

tangle in the small creature's thoughts and become trapped by them.

Fast forward again. Familiar woods. Everly, pale-haired, still small, angry, crying. Lost.

Weak. Weak enough for the Coruscare to taste freedom.

Everly felt the Coruscare's fear that its human host would die in those woods, and it would be lost entirely.

Then Rylan found them.

Confusing dream and reality, Everly tried to cry out to the young boy, tell him to run, before his soul was consumed.

No. The Coruscare didn't consume Rylan that day.

But something happened.

The thought snapped Everly out of the barrage of flashbacks.

She fell violently back into the present moment. Her limbs flailed as if she'd left her body and returned.

The Coruscare stared at her with twinkling, ageless eyes, satisfied at the utter terror on her face.

"What did you do to Rylan?" Everly said. "That day in the woods, when I was lost."

The dragon bristled and hissed. "Sought subordination, succor, from descendant of my changelings."

Subordination? Succor?

"What did you *do to him*?" Everly snarled.

The Coruscare's light strobed like a heartbeat. "Partial consumption. Connective tether forged. Bondage to create a guardian. Protection was required more than sustenance. My being was held captive to your fragile form ... Couldn't allow host to perish. Could not lose any piece of resplendent self."

Everly's hand fluttered to her lips. Nausea bubbled in her stomach. All those years they'd been close. All the times he'd watched over her, stood up for her, took care of her ... He'd only done so because the Coruscare had forced him against his will. He'd been tethered to her like a *pet*, against his will.

Her voice broke as she said, "You *enslaved* Rylan to me?"

The dragon's expression remained stoic and unmoved. "To *me*."

That's why Rylan had been in her dreams since they'd met. A literal piece of him had been within her that entire time. It was never fate. It was never love. It was this creature, this hateful, emotionless alien's enthrallment.

Almost unable to breathe, Everly whispered, "Zozo too?"

"The four-legged beast? Accident. Desired sustenance. Host regained control too soon. Only partial consumption achieved."

Everly exhaled sharply. She'd made no emotional bond with the big cat. It had

only been protective of the thing inside her, lashed to it in servitude.

The flashbacks she'd witnessed churned like curdled food through her mind. *My realm. My servants.*

"And the shadyrs ... their ancestors in the Everdark. They weren't feeding you their own kind because they wanted to. You forced them to."

The Coruscare made no reply. The pressure on Everly's mind built, crushing her thoughts and feelings.

Everly pushed back.

"They're free now. They're all free of you now!"

She'd seen to that. She'd almost died for it.

"You have no more servants. You have no realm."

"This realm. Eidolghasts should rule instead? No. They stole my last. This realm will be mine."

Everly gritted her teeth against the waves of power washing over her, trying to drown her. "You'll have *nothing* that I don't allow."

"Resplendent self is stronger. Two of my thirds exist here now. Find my third. Give it to me. Make us all." The Coruscare moved close to Everly's face, swirling before her eyes in a mess of sparkles and teeth. "*Our* realm."

"No. I don't want that. And I don't want any more of you." Everly extended her senses, feeling out into the real world for her body, for consciousness, for the tendrils that lashed around her. She focused on bringing everything back.

The dragon reared up, body snapping in violent motions. "Still strive to control? I ruled realms. I am god. How does fragile form hope to dominate?"

Everly took a long, solid breath. "I have so far."

With a great heave against the boundaries of her dreamscape, Everly broke through to consciousness. She opened her eyes to the arching limbs of the twisted, dead tree beside the Dark Corner shroudpool.

There was no longer any pain, although her fingertips tingled slightly. All the agony and dizziness she'd known were gone. Other than a faint bleariness from having just awoken, she felt good. Healed.

But at what cost?

Pale beams of light shone down over her, rushing back into her. The dragon—the *Coruscare*—growled from within its cage. She was holding it back for now, but she could feel the bend and push of its will against her own, wrestling for control.

How long will I be able to keep that thing at bay?

Singing flowed to her from nearby, and then sounds of a discussion. Everly lay there for a moment listening, counting the voices of her friends, too afraid to open her eyes and see one of them gone.

She smiled as she heard Tammy, Denny, Harper, and Neri. Then Callan spoke, too. Her smile faded as Rylan's voice reached her.

He said he loved me.

It had meant everything to her, that moment between them in the caves. Now she worried that it meant nothing. Rylan had been freed from the Coruscare's enslavement, but he'd lived with that forced need to protect her his whole life. He'd barely known freedom. How could she accept that the love he professed was real?

Sighing, Everly opened her eyes and lifted her hands before her face. The skin was smooth and clear, completely unmarred by the cracks that had spread there before. She was whole again, but the Coruscare was also stronger. She hoped it would be worth it.

"Hey, Ev's moving!" Harper called out.

Rylan was the first to reach her side, kneeling to check over her. "How do you feel?"

He'd protected her for so long, Everly imagined that it would be a hard habit to break. She shifted to sit up, withdrawing from his efforts to help.

"I feel good," Everly said, brushing back her pale gray hair.

Her clothes were still wet, and the sunset had only a small tint of red remaining as it faded into night.

"How long was I out?"

"A minute, maybe two." Rylan reached a hand for her as she prepared to stand.

She ignored it, leaving him frowning.

Footsteps crunched as Harper trotted over to her side, Neri in her arms.

She made a couple of abortive attempts to hug Everly without dropping the mermaid girl.

"Screw it!" Harper huffed and pressed herself toward Everly with Neri in between them.

Neri squeaked.

"I was so worried about you!" Harper cooed, pressing her cheek to Everly's. She shuffled back to give everyone more room as they gathered around.

Tammy's lips turned up in a rare smile. "You look so much better!"

Everly pulled up the sleeve of her jacket, revealing smooth, unbroken skin.

"Yeah. My arms are back to normal, cracks all gone. Even all the little scrapes and bruises I got in the lighthouse are gone."

"Did Neri heal you, too?" Callan asked.

"Huh?"

Harper chimed, "Neri has healing powers! With her voice!"

"Yeah, check this out," Callan said, showing off the fresh pink scar where his open wound had been.

Tammy tsked. "All that excellent stitching I did, wasted."

"I still appreciated it," Callan said, beaming.

Everly blinked. "Wow. Okay. Um, I don't think it was her that fixed all this, though. I heard her singing, but it only started after I woke up. I was already better by then."

Rylan had shoved his hands into his pockets, glowering. "You think it came from the crystal? That it healed you?"

Everly nodded.

Harper said, "I mean, we were hoping for a power-up. But more like it would fix the dragon so the cracking stopped spreading and you could heal normally. You got the full regen package. So cool! If you got that from the crystal, do you think Neri's healing could have something to do with her living near it for so long?"

"I have no idea," Everly replied. "But anything is possible at this point. The dragon powered up in a few ways. It talks to me now. And it has a name."

Harper gave her a questioning look. "A name?"

"The Coruscare."

Harper's expression remained the same, but a sharp inhale came collectively from the shadyrs.

Rylan's eyes sparked like lightning. "The WHAT?"

29

"The thing ... the thing inside you is the Coruscare?" Rylan growled, rubbing the remnants of seawater off his chin with the back of his hand.

Every shadyr stared wide eyed at Everly in a way that made her want to shrink away and vanish.

"No way!" Denny said.

Tammy's dark hands covered her mouth. "Oh my ghast. *The* Coruscare?"

Everly winced. "You know it?"

"It's literally a class at the Darkfreys," Callan said. "The Coruscare and Pre-Transition Mythology."

Everly's memories itched, taking her back to sneaking through the estate grounds with Lian. She'd seen that on a projector screen as she peeked into classrooms. They studied the thing inside her as though it were a myth?

Rylan's gaze grew intense. "Shadyrs have a rich history, but myths from before coming to this world are pretty sparse. We know the Coruscare was worshipped as a god and some histories speak of the gods being literal. Like they actually existed as tangible entities. But when early shadyrs came to the human realm, the gods didn't come with them."

He shook his head at some inner thought. "After a while, shadyrs questioned their existence, gave up their worship, and they kind of faded into obscurity. They're no more part of current shadyr culture than, say, Babylonian gods are to modern humans."

"The Coruscare is real," Everly said softly.

She tapped her chest and raised her gaze to his again.

"It's the Beast of Teeth and Stars."

It only took a couple of minutes for Everly to relate everything she'd learned while unconscious. The shadyrs listened raptly.

When Everly was done with her tale, Callan shook his head and let out an astonished laugh. "Wow. It never occurred to me to connect the Coruscare to 'the light' in the Everdark."

"I don't even get how you're making that connection now," Denny shrugged.

"The Everdark wasn't always dark," Callan explained. "We were always told that it was when the eidolghasts took over, destroying the light, that the entire realm became beshadowed and the shadyr ancestors had to leave."

Everly grimaced. "The Coruscare ate eidolghasts. It held them back from taking over the realm until it was broken by the Bane. The Coruscare was the light that was destroyed."

"Huh, I always assumed the light was like, daylight, and the eidolghasts took over. No wonder our 'god' didn't come over to this world with us." Denny made a *squicky* noise and dragged a finger across his neck.

Everly kicked at the remaining crystalline shell that had shattered on the ground beneath them. "Well, it did come to this realm, just broken and trapped in three pieces."

"Two of which now exist inside you." Rylan shook his head, laughing breathily. "The god of the shadyrs."

Tammy, Callan, and Denny also stared at Everly, each of them with expressions that were borderline awed.

She turned away and stared at the ground, crushing one of the broken shards beneath her boot. "Yeah, well, I can guarantee you it wasn't a benevolent god."

"This is still huge news. Like, huge." Callan squatted down and picked up a few of the larger pieces of crystal, putting them in his pocket.

Tammy glanced over her shoulder. "Hey, we should get moving. Lian's going to beat us to the pickup point."

Everly nodded and strode forward quickly, avoiding Rylan. She didn't like the new way he looked at her, how they all looked at her. None of them seemed willing to believe her whenever she tried to explain that the thing inside her was. Not. Good.

They passed out of the clearing and through the chain-link fence, then waited on the dirt road until headlights appeared in the distance.

Harper bumped a shoulder into Everly's, offering a kind smile. "You're the real goddess here, don't ever forget that."

E verly rested her forehead against the cool glass window and watched Howell House grow closer.

The sight of the homestead chased away the pain and horror of the last day. There were times while on the island when she'd been certain she wouldn't make it out alive, that maybe none of them would. Seeing the welcoming lights that lined the wide veranda was like the best kind of victory prize. This place was more her home than the house she'd grown up in.

She wasn't sure she'd *actually* won. Not while the Coruscare was still a part of her.

But she'd come home intact, with all her friends—and a new addition—and for now the world felt whole.

Lian put her SUV into park, then glanced back at the team. "Rush will no doubt have a big dinner laid out for you. Our stakeout on Vonny didn't get far. She holed herself up at the estate and wouldn't come out. We can debrief after you're all fed and recuperated."

"I don't know what any of that meant," Neri whispered, eyes wide.

Everything was new to Neri, and her learning curve was going to be steep. Getting her into the car had been a struggle and required a lot of coaxing. The poor girl was terrified of *traffic* from her radio-only education.

"That's going to happen a lot. I'll catch you up as we go." Harper reached over and opened the car door.

At the same instant, Neri screamed.

Everly jumped in her seat and whipped her head toward the young woman, who was sitting between her and Harper.

Neri stared down at her legs, her eyes so wide the whites were visible all the way around.

She had legs.

Naked legs.

Rylan, who was in the front passenger seat, had turned around at the first scream. He whipped back to the front with a "Shit! Sorry!"

"Woah!" Harper squeaked, throwing both hands to grab the hem of Neri's T-shirt and pull it over her lap.

Everly leaned forward and tugged her bomber jacket off, laying it over Neri's thighs. Harper grabbed the sleeves and tied them around Neri's waist to create a makeshift skirt.

"What is *happening*?" Neri screeched.

Harper took her hands. "Looks like you are human, or shadyr, after all."

There was a scuffle in the backseat, and Everly glanced around to see Callan holding Denny in a headlock.

Tammy cringed away from the wrestling men beside her. "One minute, he's saving our lives. The next, he's trying to sneak looks at naked girls."

"Sounds about right," Everly said wryly.

"I was just ... reaching ... for the seat release ... thingy." Denny wrestled himself free from Callan, brushing off his disheveled clothing indignantly.

"Nobody believes you," Tammy said.

Denny huffed. "I know you all think I'm the world's biggest asshole, but at least *I* didn't enslave multiple generations of women to be my mermaid harem."

Callan scoffed. "Wow, talk about setting a low bar."

Lian hummed and eyed Neri with interest. "You said she lived above a nyevmer her whole life?"

Rylan nodded. "Yeah, a big one. It was trapped in the caves beneath the lighthouse."

"She must have had one heck of a shadyr hangover," Lian explained. "Almost two decades in contact with the ghast and completely untrained? Took her body a while to catch up."

Neri clawed at her thighs and twitched her toes. "I don't know what to do with these. They feel so *strange*."

"It's okay. I'll help you. Don't worry." Harper leaped out onto the gravel driveway, then turned to help Neri from the seat.

Neri moved her legs weakly, and even with Harper supporting her, she collapsed the moment she tried to stand.

While Harper held Neri up, Everly hopped out behind and adjusted the jacket-skirt. Then she took one side, tucking Neri's arm around her shoulders, and Harper took the other. Together, they coached Neri on how to move her brand-new legs, while keeping the majority of her body weight on their shoulders.

Denny flipped the car seat forward and the rest of the team piled out after them, groans of relief and exhaustion all around.

Callan asked, "Is Cherry back yet?"

Lian shrugged, casting her eyes toward the lights of the town. "Got a message a while ago saying he was on his way. Taking his time though."

Halfway to the door, the excitement on Neri's face became contagious. She didn't really get the hang of it—Everly and Harper were doing most of the work. But she marveled at her newfound ability like a child discovering how to walk for the first time.

With a little practice, Everly figured she'd be ready to go at it alone. Both girls found themselves grinning as they carried Neri up the porch steps and into the house, where she declared, "It's so *dry* here."

Lian ducked up the stairs ahead of them and returned with a long cotton dress that she offered to Neri. "It might be a little big. But it'll keep you warm until we can get you some clothes of your own."

Neri ran her fingertips over the fabric like a pet.

"It's for me?" She pressed it against her cheek. "It's so soft."

Lian's stoic face melted, and she blinked glossy eyes at the young shadyr before waving her and Harper off to help her get changed.

Lian held Everly back in the hall as the others passed them toward the kitchen.

"You did good, saving that poor thing."

Everly shivered. They almost hadn't.

Lian nodded solemnly as though she could read minds. "All of you are going to need recovery time after this, not only Neri. I hope you're not still planning on packing up and leaving."

"I ... hadn't really had time to think about it."

"Forget what my blockhead of a son has said," Lian muttered, flicking her head in the direction Rylan had gone.

Everly inhaled a wobbly breath. What he'd said to her in the caves was *All I've known my entire life is loving you. The dumbest thing I've ever done in my life was pushing you away.*

Lian reached out and took her hands, squeezing them. "You're wanted here. I can support you if you're here. Neri can recover here. And if that thing inside you is the Coruscare, that's of huge significance to shadyrs."

Rylan's words, what she'd seen the Coruscare do, to others, to him, left Everly's heart cold. "Maybe having the Coruscare inside me is exactly the reason why I shouldn't be around. What it's capable of ..."

"Just ... think about it. This old woman isn't fond of saying goodbye to family. Okay?" Lian pressed her fingers, then left toward the kitchen.

Harper and Neri returned from a side room, and Harper handed Everly back her jacket. It was still damp from their underwater adventures, like the rest of Everly's clothes. She longed for a hot shower and bed, and Harper looked equally tired.

But Harper's grin glowed as she said, "I smell bacon! Wow, Neri gets to eat bacon for the first time. Are you okay with eating animals?"

"Like fish?"

They followed their noses down the corridor.

As Lian had promised, Rushelle stood in the warm kitchen, flipping bacon in a cast-iron skillet. She glanced over at the three of them as they entered, and when her gaze found Neri, her eyes lit up.

"Oh, you brought home a new friend! Omigosh, omigosh, look at you! Oh honey, let's get some food into you!"

The rest of the team was at the table already. There was an empty space beside Rylan, and the vulnerable look in his eyes almost broke Everly. She turned from him and sat on the other side, keeping her gaze down.

Tammy hovered for a moment. She often didn't join them at the table, instead perching on a nearby cabinet or lurking in a corner. But she shuffled forward, taking a spot beside Callan with inaudible mumbles and a halfhearted eye roll.

Harper helped Neri into a chair at the table and set to work making a plate of food

from the various platters awaiting them, doing her best to explain what went on it.

Bacon (Neri knew pigs from her picture books), chips, quiche, cauliflower gratin (white vegetables were an obvious novelty). One of the more surprising things that amazed Neri were the simple bread rolls. She'd heard of bread, but the way her eyes lit up at the first nibble made Everly's heart ache and swell simultaneously.

Lian said, "Just go slow, kid, your stomach won't be used to all this."

Rushelle bustled around on sunshine-yellow stilettos, taking orders for hot drinks. She reached Neri.

"Hmm. No coffee for you, yet, but I'd love to see if you like a chamomile tea with plenty of milk and honey." As she returned to the kitchen, she asked Lian, "Is little duck going to be joining us here long-term?"

Lian leaned back in her chair and addressed Neri. "We've got plenty of room. You're more than welcome."

Neri shot a wide-eyed gaze at Harper. "Is this where you live?"

Harper shook her head. "No. Me and Everly have been staying at another house nearby. But ... we don't technically live around here, in Shroudhaven."

Neri listened intently, fiddling with the sleeves on her borrowed dress, and frowning at every other word. Even when other people spoke, she looked almost exclusively to Harper, leaning toward her in her chair as though her presence was a protective bubble.

"She can stay with us," Everly said. "I think she should stay with us."

Harper pouted. "And where are we staying?"

Everly kept her gaze carefully away from Rylan. "We can stay here, at the Boderleth house. However long is needed for Neri."

"Wonderful," Lian said like a sigh. "Whatever support she needs, whatever support you need, I'm here for you."

As Everly looked up to offer her a smile, her gaze flickered over Rylan. His face was set like stone, cracked down the middle with a line of confusion. She turned away again.

Harper beamed and mouthed *thank you*.

"Yeah, it's better if she doesn't stay here," Tammy scoffed, then smirked. "I mean, we want her as far away from Denny's influence as possible."

"Hey, I was a damned hero today!" He threw a chip at her across the table.

Tammy snatched it, popped it in her mouth, and crunched it between her teeth. "Okay, I'll admit, you saved a life or two. Let's balance that against how often you've endangered lives, and *whomp whomp*, still in the negative."

"I think Tammy here is winning the hero game at the moment." Callan chuckled.

"Maybe we shouldn't be keeping score," Tammy groaned.

She flicked her hood up over her head and sunk into her chair.

The team ate, and laughed, and took turns relaying every perilous moment on the island. By the time all the details of their harrowing journey had been told, their plates and glasses were empty and most of the eyes around the table had begun to droop.

Everly got up to take her plate over to the kitchen, and when she turned from the sink, Rylan was right behind her.

He leaned in and spoke under his breath. "Can I talk to you? Alone?"

His piercing warm-green eyes held a painful vulnerability.

All I've known my entire life is loving you.

The world seemed to stop turning. She'd dreamed for so long that Rylan would admit that he wanted to be with her. As a girl, she'd been *convinced* that Rylan was her soulmate, that they were fated to be together.

She knew better now. But how could she tell him? How could she explain that the feelings he'd confessed weren't his own? That they were a leftover symptom of having been enslaved to the malevolent deity within her?

Once Rylan shook off the remnants of protective nature he'd been conditioned to feel, he'd figure out that he didn't want to be with her. She just had to wait for that to happen.

"I ... I'm not ready."

She turned to rejoin the others in the kitchen.

He grabbed her arm, gently pulling her back toward him.

"What's going on? You've been avoiding me since we got back."

Everly shook her head. She couldn't speak. She desperately longed to forget what she'd seen, what she'd learned, and just *be* with him. Being with him would have been proof that fate existed, love existed, that this dark, difficult life had meaning.

But none of that was real.

She took a slow step back, releasing herself from his grip.

His jaw worked, twitching as he swallowed. "Please talk to me. I—"

The screen door slammed, and footsteps stalked down the hall.

Callan got to his feet. "Cherry, you okay?"

Cherry stopped at the entrance to the kitchen, blinking as he took everyone in. His cheeks were streaked with dried tears and his eyes were a red that matched his hair.

"You're all back." Eyeing Neri, the torn, damp clothing, and Everly standing upright and looking healthy, he sniffed. "Looks like I missed out on a lot."

"Adventure of a lifetime," Denny crowed. "There was a fucking U-boat full of Nazi zombies, dude!"

"You say that like it was a good thing," said Tammy.

Callan frowned, moving to Cherry's side. "Are you okay? What did Jasper want?"

Cherry laughed bitterly. "The Bane. He wanted the Bane."

Harper rose to her feet, knocking the chair over behind her. "He what?"

Neri squeaked and put her hands over her ears.

"Vonny sent him on a mission to find it. He took me as backup, to Rook's Theater," Cherry explained, giving Harper an apologetic grimace.

"Vonny wanted it? What is she up to?" Lian asked.

Harper groaned and grabbed fistfuls of hair at her scalp. "Ugh, I thought it would be safe there!"

Everly stepped beside Harper, placing a hand on her shoulder. "Hey, it's okay! It might be better if it's not near me, anyway. We'll work something out if we need it again."

Harper smacked Everly's hand away. "It's not okay! You have no idea ..."

Everly's mouth hung open at the alarming look in her friend's eyes. Brown eyes she was so unfamiliar with. She'd thought the two of them shared everything, but she hadn't even known her true eye color. Her best friend, who'd scolded her for keeping secrets, clearly had some of her own.

Cherry shook his head and slumped into a seat at the table. "I'm sorry, once I knew what he was after, I tried to stop him."

"Did you really?" Harper spat. "Or did you just let him walk away with my blade?"

"Your blade?" Everly asked.

"What, you think I gift-wrapped it for him?" Cherry's dark eyes grew glossier.

"I have to get it back." Harper started pacing, glancing at Neri, then toward the front door, back and forth, over and over. "I need it back."

"I told you, it's okay, we—"

"I NEED IT!" Harper roared. "I can't be strong enough without it!"

Neri whimpered and Lian rose to her feet to comfort her.

Harper clutched at her head again. "I'm sorry. I'm sorry. I ..."

"What's going on, what do you mean you need it?"

Strong. The word echoed in Everly's mind.

What was it, the shadyrs in Gorhanmere said? *Our family is strong.*

And they had been. Unnaturally strong. And covered in scars. Like the ones on Harper's waist that Everly knew hadn't been there up until recently. Harper was too fond of mid-riff tops to deny that.

She had cut herself with the Bane the night Rylan was freed. She must have discovered then what the Gorhanmere shadyrs knew. The way she'd been so full of energy ever since ... Everly felt like a fool for not having realized earlier.

"You've been cutting yourself with the Bane," Everly accused, her voice hushed.

Harper scoffed. "That's ridiculous. Why would I do that?"

"Because it makes you strong."

Harper's eyes flashed.

Everly took a step back. "It's true? Why would you do something so dangerous?"

All eyes in the room were focused on Harper, and she turned a slow circle like a cornered animal. "You have no idea what you're talking about."

"And you have no idea what consequences there could have been. You could have ended up like the shadyrs up in Gorhanmere. All so you could be stronger? You didn't *need* that."

Harper snarled. "Of course I did! None of you know what it's like to be the only human in the group of superheroes. I know you don't think I can keep up, that I'm not good enough, never good enough. None of you would understand why it's necessary."

"Because it's not!" Everly shot back.

"What does it matter now? It's gone!" Harper glared at her. "It's gone, and you're not going to help me get it back, are you?"

Everly's lips tightened into a thin line.

Harper's shoulder slumped and she turned to where Neri watched from Lian's arms with wide eyes. "I'm sorry. I'm ... tired. I'm going home now. You don't have to come with me ..."

Neri reached a hand out and said, "I have ... big feelings sometimes, too."

Harper just nodded slowly and walked them toward the front door.

"I'll drive you." Lian grabbed her keys, though her expression told Everly in no uncertain terms that she wasn't happy with this new revelation, either.

Everly brushed past Rylan and followed them out, feeling like even though her body was no longer shattering into pieces ... her heart was.

30

Harper's campervan, which contained most of their belongings, was still parked at Crybel's Cove docks. Rushelle and Lian returned it to the Boderleth house the next day.

Unpacking into the house Everly thought she'd said her final goodbye to wasn't as hard as she thought it would be. They had cleaned and banished so many of its ghosts that Everly was able to treat it as a simple roof over her head, nothing more.

It hadn't yet started to feel like her home, though.

Harper barely spoke to her. She took to helping Neri acclimate to her new life like a project to perfect. That hyper-focus also doubled as a great way to block Everly out.

Neri woke up screaming every night for her first week.

She would dream of the "monster below" coming up through the ground and swallowing her. Taught her whole life to stay up high for fear of the nyevmer in the caves beneath, even sleeping in a bed on the first floor left her terrified.

Everly dreamed most nights of the Coruscare. Of it telling her its desires, wanting to be made whole, trying to seize control. Being woken from that wasn't so bad.

Harper tried to hide it, but Everly could see she was drawn, pale, and shaky. Whatever withdrawal she suffered from the absence of the Bane, she pushed through it, for Neri.

Everly wondered whether her disconnection from the Bane would have been different without the responsibility of the new shadyr there with them. She wondered a lot of things about Harper's use of the Bane. But Harper didn't give Everly an opportunity to ask, or to apologize.

After another sleepless night of Neri screaming, they decided that being higher up would make Neri feel safer. There would no doubt be more screaming, more trauma to heal, but they wanted to work with what they had, and they knew Neri wanted a space for herself farther from the ground.

Everly thought back to her vague, dusty memories of the house. She didn't like the attic or the basement here in her childhood home. But she recalled the attic being a fairly large-sized room tucked under the roof beams.

As morning fog drifted like a pale tide outside the windows, Everly descended to the kitchen. She set some coffee to brew, then gathered some necessities for cleaning—multiple trash bags, a basket of sprays and wipes, a broom and mop. While she was waiting for the coffee machine, she stared out the window into the early morning air, lost in her thoughts.

Movement drew her attention, and she moved closer to the window, staring out wide-eyed, hoping to catch a glimpse to prove it was Zozo. But whatever had been there had already vanished.

Everly didn't really expect the cougar to stick around as close as he had. For two days now, the meat she placed out in the backyard hadn't been eaten.

Maybe the cougar had fully recovered from its forced attachment to her. Maybe that meant Rylan would recover soon, too. Maybe he already had. He'd stopped trying to call a few days back, after several attempts that Everly didn't answer.

Harper appeared at the kitchen door wearing hot pink yoga pants and a man's-sized T-shirt with the sleeves cut off. She'd taken to only wearing her green contacts when doing photoshoots because the change had confused Neri, so her brown eyes took in the supplies Everly had gathered but didn't make contact with Everly herself.

Lian and Tammy had picked up Neri a few moments earlier. They were taking her shopping to continue filling out her wardrobe and personal belongings, and to keep her out of the way while Everly and Harper prepared the attic for her as a surprise.

"I'll take these up." Harper hefted the basket of cleaning supplies to her hip.

She left the room before Everly could offer her a coffee.

With a sigh, Everly poured hers into a travel cup and followed with the rest of the gear.

Harper had the attic stairs pulled down, and she vanished through the hole in the ceiling.

"Not much room up here. There's a load of stuff right at the top of the stairs," Harper called down.

Everly climbed and once her head and shoulders were through, saw what Harper meant. It looked like her dad had received a shipment of boxes and left them all there, half-opened, spread over the floor. She vaguely remembered that he was always up and down between the attic and antique store. He must have kept overstock and new purchases up there.

Harper shimmied between the boxes to make more room for Everly. There were two windows at either end of the oblong room, but they were covered in dust, only letting a weak yellow illumination filter through.

"Light switch is over there, I think." Everly pointed and climbed the rest of the way.

Harper found the old-fashioned toggle and flicked it. With a low hum, two bare bulbs popped to life. Evenly spaced through the center of the room, they revealed

mountains of dusty boxes, wooden crates, old suitcases, and smaller items of furniture.

Harper set the basket of cleaning supplies on top of one pile and whistled. "We might need to call in for backup."

Everly analyzed the space as she took a slow sip of coffee. The room was dusty, but dry, with no scent of mold or mildew to worry about. There was a lot up there, but they didn't have to deal with it all right away. Most were stacked neatly to the sides.

The main issue was the boxes scattered on the floor. If they could be sorted and stacked somewhere else, there would be more than enough space to get a single bed in and lay out a small bedroom.

"I can hang some curtains across the middle beam there to section off this end for Neri, and we can clear the rest out later if she wants to expand. I think we can manage to clean up half the attic ourselves. We managed with the rest of this sty of a house." Everly offered a small smile, which Harper returned briefly before she seemed to remember herself, returning her expression to carefully neutral.

Harper squatted beside one of the opened boxes that cluttered the floor to inspect its contents. Everly frowned and set her coffee down on the floor as she checked the box closest to her. She was glad it was just her and Harper. But Harper didn't seem quite ready to talk yet.

They worked in silence as they checked the boxes, taped them back up, and stacked them on the other end of the attic. Most had what appeared to be the contents of an elderly woman's home.

Pretty lamps and teapots, ornamental plates, and a teaspoon collection. Then Everly opened one that had some kind of body armor, similar to what the Darkfreys wore, but a much more old-fashioned design. It was made of steel and rubber strapping rather than carbon fiber and high-tech elastics.

Everly dug deeper, sifting through Darkfrey uniforms and binders until she found something black, sharp, and shiny at the bottom.

"Woah!" Harper exclaimed, robbing the word from Everly's mouth. She sat across the floor, shuffling papers that she'd pulled from one of the boxes.

"What is it?" Everly replied.

"I think I found something you'll be interested in." She turned the sheets outward for Everly to see.

"An invoice, for all of these boxes, purchased at the estate sale of Portia Darkfrey." Harper flipped over to another document, a long list stapled together.

She jabbed her finger at a line, shuffling closer so Everly could read.

It seemed to be a catalog, and Harper's manicured fingernail underlined the words "Starry crystal."

"Do you think that's the Coruscare crystal? Where he got it from?" Everly exhaled

the words. "From a Darkfrey, but how? Why would they be selling things like that at an estate sale?"

Harper's lips drew thin, and she flipped another sheet of paper to the front again. This one was a yellowed sheet of newspaper, torn rough down one side—*The Shroudhaven Post*, classifieds section, with an ad circled.

"Your dad kept good records. He found all this through her estate sale and has her obituary circled here. It says here she had no surviving next of kin and was given a state burial."

Everly raised an eyebrow. "But ... she was a Darkfrey. I mean, there's only *one* Darkfrey family in the area."

Harper handed Everly the papers to inspect herself. "My best guess is that Miss Portia was disowned by her family, the same way they cast out anyone who doesn't fit their definition of good soldier material."

"I wouldn't be surprised. Maybe Lian wasn't the first to start the tradition of absconding with precious relics." Everly smirked, shaking her head as she flicked through the documents.

It was just conjecture, but it made a weird kind of sense. Portia Darkfrey had died, separated from her kind, and Everly's father had bought up a large portion of her belongings after the fact.

Including the crystal. Everly breaking the crystal, her father dying, her life falling apart so that she ran away and met Rylan, the Coruscare bonding them ... all happened because the Darkfreys didn't care enough about that one family member to deal with her estate after her death. Even Everly had given her mother that courtesy.

Everly shook her head and let the papers fall to her lap. "Maybe if the Darkfreys weren't so keen on kicking people out for being different, none of this would have happened."

"Maybe we can ask Lian if she knows any more about it, but I would bet my top social account that Darkfrey bigotry is behind this." Harper's eyes sparkled at the prospect of gossip.

Everly smiled back, and for a moment, things felt good. Sitting there talking with her friend had felt almost normal again.

They stared at each other for several moments as the house creaked and settled around them, and their expressions dulled.

As one, they both gasped out, "I'm sorry."

"No, what are you sorry for?" Harper asked.

Everly took a deep breath, then expelled her thoughts. "I feel like, I've been so worried about your safety that I must have seemed like I doubted you, that I made you feel like you were somehow lesser. That I pushed you into wanting to use the Bane."

Harper's eyes turned down to the dusty floorboards. "No. It wasn't you. It wasn't even the Howell team. Honestly, they accepted me as much as could be expected. It was always me. It was my own insecurities."

Everly pulled her plait of pale gray hair over her shoulder and worried it between her fingers. "I can totally see how hard it must be though, being the sole human. I understand—"

Harper shook her head. "It's not just being a human in Shroudhaven. It's something I've dealt with my whole life."

She lifted her brown hands up on display. "The standards I live by aren't what the majority has to live by. I always feel like I have to push the limits and fight to be *the best*. Be more, do more, be better. If I'm not excelling, I'm falling short, and the world will be ready to point it out and crush me back to where it thinks I belong."

"I hate that you've experienced that," Everly said softly. "They're the problem, not you. You're enough, exactly as you are."

Harper's long lashes fluttered as she met Everly's eyes. "I'm working on accepting that. That other people's biases are *their* flaws, not mine."

Tears flooded Everly's eyes, and her heart swelled. "You're kind of my hero."

"Oh, you've got that *way* backwards," Harper said, her voice cracking.

She leaned in and pulled Everly into a tight hug.

"You're *my* hero." Her voice was small and muffled against Everly's shoulder. "I'm sorry that I took such a risk trying to be stronger. I'd used the Bane for barely twenty-four hours, and this week without it ... Ev, I can hardly explain what it's been like. I feel like I'm barely clawing free of the cravings now. I think about what things might have been like if I still had it around, and it terrifies me."

Everly squeezed Harper tighter. It scared her, too.

Harper leaned back out of the embrace. "My drive to be perfect, and everything it's rooted in, it's something I'm working on, and will keep working on."

Everly smiled. "Seems to me having Neri around will be good for that."

Harper quirked an eyebrow.

"I mean, you saved her when you'd lost your green contacts, your hair was tangled from swimming, the strength from the Bane had worn out—although *somehow* you still had some makeup clinging on."

Harper chuckled. "I have the best cosmetics sponsors."

"Still, you didn't need any of those things, or shadyr abilities, or superpowers, to save Neri. You just needed your amazing heart. And Neri needs that. She's clearly attached especially to you. She doesn't need perfection from you, she just needs you."

"Yeah, she is helping." A pink flush tinged Harper's cheekbones.

She avoided Everly's eye as she admitted, "She's helped me in other ways too."

"Other ways?"

"Finding myself again? Finding ... who I am and what I want." Harper bit her lower lip. "I haven't felt a lick of attraction to anybody since the absolute circus of my last relationship. But I feel things ... *romantic* things. For Neri."

Everly laid her hand on Harper's knee, palm up.

She waited until Harper took it and entwined their fingers before she said, "Is this new?"

"Liking girls? I don't know ... I've wondered recently if I was only dating guys because it was the thing I was expected to do—get the man, get the ring, get the house, get the kids. Like I had to follow that path to uphold an image of perfection, and I never even questioned that path until recently."

"Hey, whatever path you want to take, I'm here for you. Thank you for telling me."

"Just ... don't tell anybody else yet, okay? I'm not ready to ... I'm just not sure who I am right now. I don't want word to get out to my followers and then I'm caught up in some scandal accusing me of trend jumping or attention seeking."

A soft smile formed on Harper's lips, steeped in sadness. "I like Neri *a lot*, but ... she's been through so much. Obviously, I can't, and won't pursue more from her. It's just nice to feel something real again. I want that to just be for me, for now."

Everly placed another hand over Harper's. "You don't owe me or anyone else an explanation. Your secret is safe."

Harper took a deep breath and squeezed Everly's hand in return.

Everly wiped her eyes but couldn't wipe the smile from her face. She leaned in and gave Harper another crushing hug.

"You know, I found something I think you might be interested in, too."

Turning around, she dug down into the bottom of the box with the Darkfrey paraphernalia. She wasn't entirely sure what to expect when she drew the shiny black object from the depths, but knew it had to be some kind of weapon.

An ornate hilt of silver and obsidian-like material led down to a long, flexible, whip-like sword. The segmented pieces of the blade were also of dark, smoky crystal, and wickedly jagged.

Harper gasped audibly. She took the grip carefully from Everly, inspecting it as the length lay on the floor. She frowned and twisted something near the pommel.

"I think this might—" *shnickt*, the length retracted, locking back together as one solid blade. Harper's eyes glittered.

"Whip sword," she whispered in awe.

She got to her feet, giving the sword a few slow twirls. "Hot damn, I'm in love!"

"I can't wait to see you kick some ass with that." Everly chuckled, then added, "Just be careful not to cut yourself with it."

"Oh, hardee har har," Harper mocked back. "Like we've learned nothing from playing with ancient dark magics. Don't worry, I will report any and all weirdness that may result from my new toy and suspend use of it if needed."

Everly's eyebrows knit. She hoped that having found the weapon in the same box as other Darkfrey armor and gear meant it had been one that was used by Portia, safely, in the past.

"Lian seems to get along well enough with her blade. We can get some shadyr eyes on it soon too, just in case. But yeah, we'll be careful, and we'll work it all out together."

"Together," Harper echoed with a glowing smile.

Everly glanced back down at the invoice for the "starry crystal," hoping this new weapon would bring no drama with it.

Whoever cataloged the estate must have known nothing about what they'd sold but had gotten the starry part right. The crystal had belonged to the Beast of Teeth and Stars.

And there was another crystal out there, powering Cardboard Box Barry's magical box maze. The Coruscare had told her it expected her to retrieve the final piece, but she knew she couldn't do that. What Barry did for Shroudhaven was way too important to take the crystal away from him.

Not to mention, what would happen to her if the Coruscare was whole again? Anytime she'd allowed the light to take control, she'd barely managed to rein it in before killing anybody around her. She was already struggling to maintain control.

A fully intact Coruscare might be more of a danger to Shroudhaven than anything else they'd faced.

"It's mine?" Neri stared wide-eyed at the space.

The front half of the attic was transformed. Cleaned glass let bright afternoon light in through white lace curtains. The golden sunshine landed on a simple bed that Harper and Everly had bought flat-packed, hauled up the ladder together, assembled, and made with fresh sheets and a fluffy comforter.

Harper arranged a scattering of plush cushions, rug, and nightstand, while Everly hung drapes to separate off the rest of the storage area. They'd found a couple of smaller cabinets and tallboys in the antique store, and slowly but surely carried them to the top of the house, together. They moved Neri's few belongings in, ready for her to add more.

"Do you like it?" Harper asked. "It's okay if you don't, or if the ladder is a problem."

Neri did a slow turn all the way around, then sat on the bed. Her eyes widened

and she bounced up and down a few times, smile widening. "It's like from a picture book. All soft and warm."

Everly grinned. "I think she likes it."

"You two did good work here today." Lian carried in shopping bags full of clothing.

She was followed up by Tammy, who placed a plush pink seahorse toy next to Neri on the bed.

"Did you buy that for her?" Harper pried cheekily.

"Maybe? So what if I did? It was cute. Whatever. Ugh."

"The shops were fun, like seeing friends you only know from sounds." Neri hummed a few bars of the nearby mall's radio ad jingle.

"My legs are very tired now though." She leaned over and touched a hand against Harper's thigh. "How do I get legs like *yours*? They're so strong and perfect."

Everly bit her lips together to avoid giggling at Harper's deer-in-headlights expression.

"Okay, come along everyone. You're all coming over for dinner tonight," Lian said, taking the lead down the stairs. "No excuses this time."

Harper grinned. "Ooh, sounds good! I can show off ... I mean, get my new sword checked over."

Everly smiled wryly. She had been avoiding the daily dinner invites, often using Neri as a reason, that she wasn't ready, needed quiet time. But it was Everly who wasn't ready to see Rylan again so soon. She wasn't ready to know if he'd realized how he really felt about her yet, or if he hadn't.

"I'll give you all a lift over now," Lian called back to them like an order.

Given no other option, they loaded into Lian's SUV, and she drove them around the block toward her home. The sunlight was warm with sunset shades, breaking the sky into a thousand shades of pink and orange as they coasted slowly up the long, tree-lined drive. Dust motes chased the light like sparks of gold in the cool air.

Everly was staring into the nearby overgrown field, lost in daydreams of her childhood spent out there, when Lian slammed on the brakes.

From the briars beside the road, a figure stumbled onto the laneway, right in front of them.

"Jasper?" Harper said from the front passenger seat as the figure collapsed in the dirt.

The women were out of the car in an instant, hurrying to his side.

Lian put a hand on him, and he opened bruised eyes, cringing away from them.

"It's us, we won't hurt you," Harper said.

"What happened to him?" Everly asked, kneeling.

His lips were split and knuckles raw. He looked up with wild eyes and clutched at his cardigan-covered chest. Something crinkled beneath.

Neri clung to the car door, peeking around it. "Can I help?"

"Let's get him to the house first, we don't know what's out there," Lian said.

She nodded to Everly, and the two of them got their arms under his shoulders and lifted.

Back on his feet, Jasper groaned and coughed. "It's the Mesmans."

"They did this to you?" Lian hissed.

He shook his head weakly. "At Darkfrey Estate, they ... they're trying to create their own ... They're trying to open a shroudpool."

EVERDARK CURSED

1

How do you tell somebody that you enslaved their soul for the better part of fourteen years?

Everly had been mulling over that since she'd taken in the second piece of the Coruscare and learned more about the ancient god-like being inside her. About what it had done to Rylan. How it had influenced his feelings for her.

Dragging a bloodied and beaten-up man into Rylan's home probably wasn't the best way to lead into that discussion.

Everly had been making excuses all week, but this one felt legitimate. She adjusted her grip under Jasper's shoulder as she helped support him toward Howell House.

"Can we get some help out here?" Lian called from Jasper's other side.

The screen door swung open, and Rylan burst through. His gaze went straight to Everly, passing over her body then up to her face.

His gravelly voice sounded dangerous. "What's happened?"

Cherry followed quickly after him, attention drawn straight to Jasper. His mouth dropped open, then his face closed into a cool glare.

He flicked his bright-red hair away from his eyes. "Did you guys do this for me ... because he betrayed me for the Bane? I mean, you didn't have to go to this extreme on my behalf, but I appreciate the gesture."

"It wasn't us," Tammy said from a couple steps back. "If it was, we'd have done a more thorough job. Maybe taken an ear as payback for stealing our property."

"She's just joking." Harper turned around to reassure Neri, who trailed at the back of the group. "We all know Tams is a sweetheart under all that black and nihilism."

Lian tsked. "We found him like this just down the lane."

She beckoned to Rylan, and he came over to take her place supporting Jasper. His arm brushed against Everly's where it looped around the injured man's back, and awkward emotions settled like bad yogurt in Everly's belly.

She wanted to tell him it was fine, that she could manage Jasper on her own. She wasn't the weakling she'd been when the Bane's influence had her cracking to pieces.

Rylan had only seen that side of her since he woke up, and he hadn't known her before that for years. She hated the idea that he thought her weak, or that he still needed to protect her—the way the Coruscare forced him to feel.

She felt strong now. Powerful. More energized than ever with twice as much of the Coruscare within her. It was a new kind of strength, in body and mind. As though she'd finally wrestled her dragon into submission.

But the words wouldn't come. As though she'd taken so long to work out how to talk to Rylan again that she'd forgotten how, and even simple words couldn't be forced through her lips. So they supported Jasper up the front steps together in silence.

Cherry's forehead creased as he held the door open and stepped out of their way.

The combined scents of lamb roast and childhood memories hit Everly as she stepped inside, covering the faint odor of blood and old sweat wafting from Jasper.

Birdie yapped madly up ahead. The old dog was nearly blind and deaf, but clearly had a good enough sense of smell to sniff out a stranger.

Rushelle's voice came from the kitchen. "What's going on, do we have a guest for dinner?"

"Med kit first, then we'll see about another plate," Lian replied, taking the lead.

Everly and Rylan helped Jasper to the kitchen, with Harper, Neri, and Tammy following. Cherry closed the front door after them, then hovered at a distance.

Jasper hissed in a sharp breath as Everly and Rylan lowered him into a chair at the long dinner table. The action brought their faces close together.

Everly turned away from Rylan's gaze and the hint of vulnerability there that jabbed at her heart. Avoiding him wasn't fair. She had to talk to him and explain, but that couldn't be now.

Birdie skittered around on tappy paws, growling near Jasper's feet until Lian scooped her up and shooshed her. The table had been laid out in preparation for their arrival, and Rushelle hovered in the kitchen, holding a full baking tray with bright-yellow oven mitts.

"Oh dear, we got a little lost duck? We'll sort you out." She put the dish onto the counter and strode over to dig around in a large drawer.

Neri, who clung to Harper's back as though she were a human shield, poked her head around to take a wide-eyed look at Jasper. "Do you want me to—"

"Nah-uh," Everly hushed her gently.

She stepped closer and spoke softly, smiling to comfort Neri. "I think he just needs a bit of a cleanup. He'll be okay. Better if we keep your *talents* for later, just in case."

Everly directed the last bit to Harper, who replied with a knowing nod.

Harper took Birdie from Lian and transferred the tiny dog into Neri's arms. "Come on, let's go to the loungeroom, give them all some space."

Neri's eyes remained round as Birdie licked her chin and cheeks.

The mermaid girl had met the dog previously but her sheer awe of the creature remained. "Am I holding her right? Are all dogs so small? I just want to bundle her up and squeeze her. I won't. I won't squeeze her. But I want to."

Harper chuckled as they wandered away. "If you like little puppers so much, just wait until you see your first cat."

Rushelle strutted over with a first aid kit. She held her cleavage into her tank top as she bent over to inspect Jasper.

"Boy, someone did a number on you! Hold still, love, this might sting."

She tore open packets of gauze, tipped liberal amounts of antiseptic onto them, and cleaned the split skin on his curved nose.

Denny and Callan arrived, and Tammy kept throwing Callan confused looks until she hissed, "With all the drama going on, I'm shocked you haven't asked yet if I'm okay."

Callan shrugged, and his lips pulled into a half-smile. "I mean, clearly you're fine. I know you don't like me treating you like a kid and checking up all the time. See? I can learn."

"She sure is fine," Denny added with a leer, scratching at his blond beard.

"For ghast's sake, dude, she's half your age! And also, no, just no," Callan growled. "Go and sit in your corner until *you* can learn something for once."

"Mo mand mit min mour morner," Denny mocked back, but slouched away to a chair across the room.

Rylan remained standing, looming over Jasper as he cast questioning glances between him and Everly. "Anyone going to explain what happened?"

"We found him on our way here. He said it was the Mesmans who did this." Everly grabbed some gauze as well and wiped at a spot of blood on her jacket.

Jasper's normally neat, dark hair hung bedraggled over his bruised face. "No, I said they ... they're doing worse. This was Nilson's handiwork. He caught me acting suspicious, which I suppose I was, but he took it the wrong way. He confronted me, and I provoked him."

Rushelle gasped. "Why in the Everdark would you provoke that badly stuffed sausage?"

"I needed an out because the Mesmans were beginning to suspect my espionage. Fleeing Nilson's wrath was the excuse I needed to get out of the estate with these." Jasper leaned away from Rushelle's wound cleaning and reached into his cardigan.

He pulled out a few sheets of crumpled paper and aged parchment, covered in notes and sketches.

Rylan took them, leafing through. "I've seen stuff like this before. I found notes like this when I was looking into the missing bodies—before someone took me out."

"And you think it's Vonny and Kole? I mean, they are fanatical nutjobs, but would they really have attacked their own?" Lian said as she reached for the papers to check them over.

"I can believe it." Tammy folded her arms tightly, tucking her shroudpool-stained hands out of sight.

Everly still felt chills when she remembered the madness in Kole's voice when he'd confronted her and Lian at the estate.

I can believe it too.

Jasper winced as Rushelle wiped around his blackened eye. "After they used me to get that Bane artifact, I realized something more was going on. So I've been watching them all week, trying to ascertain what they are doing. They've taken over a whole ballroom in the old part of the estate, plus a couple of other smaller rooms here and there, all kept secret, locked up."

"And you managed to get a look?" Rylan asked.

Jasper nodded. "I was lucky one day when Mordan called them away on short notice and I got in to see what they were working on. I had planned to simply retrieve some evidence. But after seeing what they were doing, I was worried about going to Mordan on my own, so I came here. I'm sorry to burden you all with this."

"Formal little chap, aren't you?" Rushelle beamed from him to Cherry. "I can see why you liked him."

Everly's eyes widened.

I thought Harper and I were the only ones in on that secret? Cherry flashed a hard look at Rushelle.

I guess not.

"Oops, sorry. Sorry. Don't know what came over me. I know *nothing.*" She winked dramatically, then patted Jasper on the shoulder. "But don't worry about us, we're used to being on the Darkfreys' bad side."

"And what exactly are the Mesmans doing?" Rylan asked.

"Trying to open a shroudpool." Jasper pointed at where Lian had pushed aside the dinnerware and spread out the pages. "There are mentions of it here and here, mostly to do with the original crossing of shadyrs from the Everdark to this dimension, and Kole's notes all around that for his own plans. And see this sketch here? They are building that, now, in that ballroom."

"That's feels like a really bad idea," Everly said, leaning in to get a look at the notes. "A shroudpool at the estate? It sounds like a recipe for a nasty monster infestation. Why would they do that?"

"They want to go after Blaise. They want to get their son back." Tammy's voice was quiet and rough.

Her body flickered, like lights in a brownout. She wrinkled her nose and squeezed her eyes shut but didn't vanish entirely.

Silence fell over the room.

Callan broke it, murmuring softly to Tammy, "It wasn't your fault."

"Ugh!" She dodged away from his comforting hand.

"Couldn't they go through one of the other shroudpools around town if that's what they wanted to do?" Everly asked.

Callan still had his eyes on Tammy as he replied, "I'm guessing the Everdark isn't exactly a small place. A random shroudpool could take them who knows where in relation to where Blaise could be, and the Dark Corner shroudpool has been dormant since then, so it's not an option. If getting Blaise back is their goal, they would have to do … *something* more. Ghast knows what though."

"No one actually thinks the kid could still be alive but, right?" Denny pitched in from over in the corner. "No one comes back from the Everdark alive."

With a sigh, Lian shook her head and lowered herself into her chair. "The Mesmans are in denial. They still talk about Blaise as though he's alive and waiting for them. But there's no chance. I'm sorry, Tammy."

"You think I don't know that already?" the goth-girl hissed.

Everly focused back on the papers, shifting them for a clearer view of another sketch that caught her eye. "I've seen these before. This is the sculpture thing that was at my house on my first night back."

That weird, skeletal effigy made of pitch-black bones had been destroyed and removed before anyone else could see it, but it wasn't the only time she'd seen something like it.

"There was one at the theater too," she added.

Callan nodded. "I think they are lures. Eidolghast lures. Set them up, and the ghasts are drawn to them. It was too strange, having a vasmire then a weroth show up at the theater so quickly after each other. And I'm sure I've seen one of these before. The night Dad died."

Lian inhaled audibly from across the table, and Rylan straightened, tense as a tightrope.

Callan cleared his throat. "I was so young then, and it was all so … I never really thought much of it until I saw it again at the theater."

"So, the Mesmans are making these too? How? Why?" Lian's tone was icy cold.

"I'm guessing they set the one at the theater to get me out of the picture." Rylan rubbed his forehead, eyebrows low and head shaking. "They knew I'd been getting my nose into their business. They didn't want to take me out at the estate—"

"Not Mordan's golden soldier boy," Denny scoffed.

"—so they left clues for me to check out Rook's, and knew I'd be on my own. I'm guessing they set the lure and hoped an eidolghast would finish me off for them."

And it almost did. Or at least, left him so weakened that the second ghast he faced that night practically killed him.

The vivid memory of Rylan's torn body bleeding out on the street still made ice crystals grow through Everly's chest. "Okay, so it might have been them who were after Rylan, but why set a lure at my place that night, too? They didn't know me. I'd only just come back to town."

"Maybe they aren't lures. We're just guessing here. I might not be remembering right from when I was a kid, either," Callan offered. "It was a long time ago."

Lian leaned back in her chair and closed her eyes. "I wasn't on the Darkfreys' good side, but there was no reason for the Mesmans to go after us back then. It doesn't make sense."

"That was well before they lost Blaise, too," Rylan added. "They've been messing with this stuff for ages."

"And how? How are they actually doing magic? Shadyrs haven't been able to since interbreeding with humans after the crossover," Tammy said.

Jasper tilted his head. "It was ten years ago that a number of relics went missing, blamed on the Gorhanmere shadyrs."

"Who only actually had the Bane," Everly squeezed in.

Jasper nodded. "And that wasn't long before Rylan and Callan joined the estate."

"Blaise said they had more artifacts than just the one we tried to close a shroudpool with," Tammy said. "So they've had them all this time, and are somehow using them to do old shadyr magic?"

"And they have one more artifact now too—the Bane." Cherry's voice cut across the room after staying quiet for so long.

He kept his head turned away from Jasper, refusing to even look in his direction.

Jasper gulped visibly. "Vonny sought it out especially. I don't know what for."

"Do they know its connection to the dragon?" Rylan's gaze went straight to Everly.

Everly shrugged. "Maybe they're going to use it for a power boost, like the Gorhanmere shadyrs did."

And Harper.

The strength and energy boost the Bane had given Harper for the short time she'd used it was impressive, but had also changed her. She'd been that much more wild, hectic, edging on bloodlust under its influence. And since the Bane had been taken from her, the withdrawals were equally powerful.

Harper excelled in hiding her weaknesses as she excelled in so many things, but Everly could tell she was tired and drawn lately. Whether that was simply the effects wearing off, or from the effort of fighting the intense desire to have it again, Everly didn't know.

But she did clearly recall the wild gleam in Kole Mesman's eyes, the knots of muscle barely restrained beneath the massive man's shirt. She wouldn't be surprised if power was what he wanted.

He might already look powerful, but there was never enough for men like him.

"It could also simply be to add into their collection. I'm unsure." Jasper's shoulders lifted then slumped. He stilled Rushelle's hands as she applied a butterfly bandage over a tear on his cheek, nodding to her.

"I've told you everything I know. Thank you for your hospitality, but I won't intrude any longer. I understand my presence isn't wanted."

He couldn't be going back to the estate. That sounded to Everly like a death sentence if he got this roughed up before he'd even delivered stolen intel to the other side.

But she didn't really know much about Jasper beyond what Cherry had shared. "Do you have somewhere to stay?"

"Well ... no. But I'll find my way." Jasper's groaned as he stood.

Lian pushed her chair out to stand as well. "We have plenty—"

"No," Cherry cut in.

Rushelle paused midway packing up the med kit. "At least for dinner?"

"No." Cherry finally turned to stare at Jasper, his dark eyes blank. "He said he'll find his way. That's what he needs to do."

2

Stepping out of Howell House felt like stepping out into a lonely tundra. The night wasn't especially cold, but the warmth Jasper felt inside the home had seeped through to his bones.

The smell of the meal cooking, the long farmhouse table set for everyone to eat together, the kindness they'd shown in patching up his wounds—that warmth of family was so distant to the cold, industrial cafeteria, and toughen-up-it's-just-a-scratch culture of Darkfrey Estate.

Howell House wasn't only a halfway stop for outcast shadyrs. It was a home, one filled with love and acceptance. Jasper could feel it to his core, and having to step away from that, from Cherry, wrenched the warmth from his body, leaving nothing but a bitter chill.

One he was sure he deserved.

Jasper carefully closed the front screen door so it wouldn't slam, not wanting to disturb the family inside any more than he already had. The news he had brought would have been hard for them to hear.

He stood there on the porch, staring at the star-spotted sky for a long moment as he pushed his emotions away, and tried, tried desperately, to stop thinking about what life would have been like if he'd left the Darkfreys back when Cherry did. Left *with* him. Stayed by his side, instead of putting his career and goals as a shadyr first.

We could be in there now, together, and happy in that warmth.

We could still be in love.

Instead, Jasper straightened his cardigan against the cold, and wondered where on this plane of existence he was going to spend the night.

There were a few Darkfrey safe houses around town. Maybe he could find one that wasn't occupied, at least until morning. Then he could think about where to go longer term. Staying in Shroudhaven could be risky now that he was on the wrong side of the Mesmans and alone, but what was life for a shadyr outside of this town?

There were the odd few shroudpools out in the world, in other cities, even other countries, that had small bands of shadyrs guarding them. Maybe he could make his way to one of those and hope he'd be accepted.

He also hoped that the Howell team could do something with the evidence he'd provided. Maybe they could fix things. Maybe he'd be able to come back, one day.

Laying the burden of action on the Howells left him feeling guilty, but there wasn't anything he could do with it alone.

And he was alone now. Utterly. Not a Darkfrey, not a Howell, not someone who was loved by Cherry. He wasn't sure what he was anymore.

His chest ached like his ribs were cracked. They probably were. Nilson Darkfrey was a beast. The pain made standing upright a struggle, and imagining scouting the streets of Shroudhaven for a refuge on foot made Jasper's eyes water.

It's going to be a long night.

The old wood of the porch steps sighed as though in sympathy as Jasper walked away. The gravel crunching under his feet almost covered the low whine of the screen door opening behind him.

"I've got to say, I really didn't think you had it in you."

At the sound of Cherry's voice, Jasper's throat tightened. He cleared it, and turned around, trying to hide how his heart was racing. Trying to push down any hope that tried to rise within him.

He came out after me? Why?

Cherry's expression remained stony. Dark, nebulous eyes assessed Jasper from under strands of bright-red hair.

Jasper cleared his throat again, but it had gone dry. "That I had ... what in me?"

"The guts to turn on the Darkfreys, finally. I'd come to accept that would never happen, and then you go and surprise me. And all it took was discovering that your brace buddies were psychopaths trying to bust their own personal hole into a hellish dimension of monsters."

"I should have left them for less."

Cherry raised his eyebrows.

"I mean ... not that you're less. I mean—" Jasper winced and ran a hand through his hair, trying to pull himself together.

One corner of Cherry's lips twisted. "I know it was hard for you. I know how much you wanted their acceptance, and when you thought you had it, you didn't want to lose it. Not for anything, or anyone."

He leaned against one of the porch posts and folded his arms. "But did you ever think you were looking for acceptance in the wrong place all along? You'll never truly belong with people who treat you as ... *less* ... just for being who you are."

"I don't think of you as less. Never. That wasn't my intention." Jasper's voice dropped away under Cherry's cool glare.

It dared him to answer all the unspoken questions. If he didn't think that, then why? Why didn't he leave with Cherry? Why couldn't he be himself? He didn't think of Cherry as lesser. Cherry was truth and bravery and sincerity bundled in human form.

It's me. I'm the one I've always thought was lesser.

Before the sting of that realization could fully pierce Jasper's heart, Cherry spoke again. "Growing up with the Darkfreys and their hateful culture, it's easy to think that's how the whole world is. That everyone's out to get you, so you better stick with those you've got. But it's not like that."

Cherry turned, staring up at Howell house. "You've told me many times how brave I was for coming out and then leaving the Darkfreys, but it was only hard *because* of the Darkfreys. It was easy to be myself once I left. I'm with good people now, where acceptance is *normal*, not some impossible dream."

Jasper nodded once, but he didn't really understand. He couldn't fathom the concept of acceptance, of not having to hide major parts of himself from those he considered family until he had forgotten how to even accept himself.

His head hung heavy, a dull throb behind the growing bruises around one eye. He nodded again, more to himself this time, relating to the words *impossible dream.*

That was what he saw in front of him. Cherry, silhouetted by the warm glow coming from the home behind him. "I'm sorry. I can't apologize enough for taking so long ... too long. I don't expect forgiveness."

"Good, because I have none for you." Cherry's shoulders lifted then fell. "Still ... there's a place for you here, if you need it. You don't have to be alone."

A pinprick of warmth burst inside Jasper's chest and his dry lips parted but couldn't form words.

Cherry fixed a firm stare his way. "But before I let you back inside, I need to know that this isn't some setup for more betrayal, that you aren't going to hurt us ... the good people here, again."

It was the last thing Jasper wanted. If he could go back in time and rewrite every instance he'd hurt Cherry to wipe it from history, he would.

It was a hard promise to make, because life was unpredictable, and sometimes people got hurt no matter how hard you worked to avoid it, but he wanted to try. He wanted to be as brave as Cherry and do his best to make things right. His body ached as he straightened himself up, and his heart ached as he held Cherry's gaze.

He didn't get a word out before Cherry's eyes widened and he leaned to look over Jasper's shoulder. "Or is this some kind of ambush already?"

"What?" Jasper spun around to see where Cherry was looking.

Out in one of the overgrown fields that surrounded the homestead, only a stone's throw from the front porch, a shadowy figure stood still.

"I came alone, I swear." Jasper squinted at it, urging his shadyr night vision to gather more details.

The silhouetted form didn't move, and Jasper scanned around, spotting another close to the other corner of the property.

Did I bring trouble here? Have the Mesmans sent people after me, or come after me themselves?

He was their enemy now, and he knew how they dealt with their enemies based on what they attempted to do to Rylan. Jasper shuddered at the thought that he might have brought danger to the Howell House doorstep.

Cherry eyed him skeptically.

Jasper set his jaw, refusing to be the cause of more pain for him. "I promise, I will do everything I can to keep you all from harm."

He set off at a disjointed jog toward the closest figure.

"Don't go out there alone, you idiot!" Cherry's footsteps hurried behind his.

"Get back into the house," Jasper called over his shoulder.

He knew it wasn't smart, but the sting of too many regrets had skewered his chest and he wanted to be reckless, and brave, and take any action he could to keep that warm home behind him safe.

He picked up his pace, stomping through knee-high dry grass and dodging clumps of berry brambles. The figure stood in the shadow of an old, half-dead oak tree. As he grew closer, and his vision pierced the darkness, it became clear his target was not a human.

He hadn't seen one of the bone lures in person before but recognized it now from the sketches he'd stolen.

Obsidian-shaded bones of human appearance had been melded together into a horrific effigy. A tangle of spines swirled up the middle, forming the figure's base. Ribs fanned out with fingerbones studded along the edges.

More than one jawbone created a mockery of a crown at the top. Worst of all, it *moved*. A shimmer and a sense of dripping, like looking through an intense heatwave that affected only those blighted, blackened bones.

"Is that what I think it is?" Cherry gasped.

Jasper spun around, scanning the fields and the view down the lane to the rest of the town, then back up behind the house to the forest in the distance.

"There's at least one more over there. I can't see or sense a ghost nearby yet. They may have only just been set up."

Looking at the bone lure made him feel ill, a nausea that burrowed through his skull. He reached for one of the dry branches overhead and snapped it off, then swung it at the effigy like a baseball bat. A hail of broken wood and bones sprayed out from his blow.

"Go back and let the others know. I'll get rid of these and check for more."

Cherry hovered for a moment, face tinted green as his gaze locked on the half-smashed statue. Then he gave a single nod and ran back to the house.

Jasper watched him go before letting the wince of pain reach his face. Nilson's beating left him sore in a way that didn't agree with being part of the sharp impact between wood and bone.

He dropped the makeshift club and kicked the effigy, taking it out at the base so that it fell backward into the weeds and scattered acorns.

He stomped the remaining pieces with a satisfying crack, over and over until they stopped moving. Jasper hoped that meant it was no longer working its dark magic.

He only hoped he stopped it soon enough.

Breaking the effigy apart left his battered body aching and sweat beaded on his forehead.

He turned to where he'd seen the other lure, as the deep, churning heat of his shadyr shift warned him an eidolghast was nearby.

He stepped out from under the cover of the oak tree but still couldn't see anything moving within the field around him. Even the tugging magic of the shift felt different, unlike the usual vasmire or weroth changes.

Where was the eidolghast?

What was the eidolghast?

The world grew darker, as something above Jasper blocked the dim moonlight. He turned his face up as a massive shape swooped in a dive directly for him.

3

The news Jasper brought about the lures, and their purpose, caused Everly's anxiety to spiral, and set a low rage simmering. All that suffering, all those families torn apart, made a desire for vengeance rise within Everly. She locked it down before her rampant emotions could let loose the creature inside her.

She could feel that the Coruscare liked the concept of revenge, could feel its encouragement, like a warm hand on her back, pushing her toward an edge she might never come back from. She could be a wrathful god of vengeance. She could rip the lives and souls from all those who had done them wrong. She had the power ... she just had to set it free.

No. That's not me. And you are not in control, dragon.

Everly collected Harper and Neri from the loungeroom once Jasper had gone. She caught them up on the new information about the plot to open a shroudpool as they headed back for dinner. Neri didn't understand, and that was probably for the best. Everly wished she didn't either.

Birdie had fallen asleep on her well-worn spot on the old lounge, and Neri threw besotted glances back to the little dog as they left.

Everly had noticed Jasper eye the newest member of their group curiously, and it was safer to keep Neri away from too much attention until they were certain Jasper could be trusted. Cherry clearly wasn't happy about the Darkfrey loyalist being around, although he did slouch past them in the hall, heading outside after his ex.

Rylan and Callan were still pouring over the Mesmans' notes and diagrams, speaking together in low voices. Tammy had excused herself as no longer hungry, despite Rushelle's pleas to stay as she fixed place settings and returned to bringing out the meal.

Everly took a seat beside Lian, who was staring dully into the distance. Learning that her husband may have died in a purposeful attack would need some processing, and there were still so many questions unanswered.

Everly attempted to focus on what she could do to keep her friends and family safe in the here and now.

She leaned a little closer to Lian and asked gently, "Do you know anything about

619

a Portia Darkfrey?”

Lian blinked a couple of times. “Hrm?”

Harper and Neri moved into seats across from them, and Harper placed her rose-gold tote bag onto the table. “We found a lot of belongings of Portia Darkfrey’s in Ev’s attic. A bunch of shadyr and Darkfrey gear. Including this gorgeous darling.”

She reached into the bag and pulled out the segmented weapon that had been coiled inside like a rope. “We were hoping you could tell us that it’s safe to use and mine all mine.”

“Portia Darkfrey?” Lian reached for the glossy, dark weapon and held it to her face for inspection. “Yeah, I knew of her. As a shadyr you tend to know everyone from the Darkfrey family line, high and mighties as they are.”

Everly waited, expectantly.

“Didn’t know her personally though. She was an older woman when I was a kid back in my days at the estate. I remember the fuss when she left. I don’t know why she did though. Some said she was kicked out, some said she deserted. Either way, it was clear she was someone who didn’t fit into the Darkfrey mold. Gossip wasn’t tolerated though, so before long, it was like she never existed.”

“You ever see her around town?” Everly asked.

“Maybe once? She kept very much to herself, and we were instructed to consider her invisible, too. It’s funny, after I left the Darkfreys, I started thinking about her again, feeling like I understood more about the many reasons one might leave. I considered trying to find her, reach out in solidarity and all. Never did though. What was her stuff doing at your place?”

“Dad bought it. We found invoices from her estate sale and a clipping of her obituary. She died sixteen years ago.”

Then not long after that I broke the crystal that was part of Portia’s estate and let the Coruscare into me. And it killed my father.

Such a powerful object, lost into obscurity until it ended up sold off with a bunch of bric-a-brac, as though it had just been a household decoration for Portia. Even the piece of Coruscare from the lighthouse, and the one in Barry’s maze, they were used for the residual powers they exuded, but no one had any idea what they truly were.

Everly wished someone had worked it out, had kept the fragile shard that held a third of a malevolent deity locked away, out of reach of a curious toddler. Her life could have been so different.

“Whatever the reason was that Portia left, there must have still been bad blood there, since she seems to have died very much alone.” Harper pouted in disgust. “Which doesn’t surprise me from what I know about the Darkfreys. But what does surprise me is that they didn’t swoop in to reclaim her gear when she was gone.”

"Well, that was back before Mordan was in charge. He's kept a tighter hold on anything deemed valuable than his predecessors did. A lot of those who leave the Darkfreys do so with just the shirts on their backs, which sometimes includes the body armor. The Darkfreys have enough resources that they don't really care about a few basics going missing. Portia must have taken more of her own valuable collection with her though, because this beauty ..."

Lian let out a low whistle, brushing her finger carefully along the sharp edge. "This is something else. There's old magic in this one for sure."

"*Safe* old magic?" Everly pressed.

Harper pulled a pinched face that threatened getting a tongue poked out.

Lian tilted her head from side to side. "Hard to say. If Portia was actively using it, and she died when you say she did, she led a decent, long life—for a shadyr at least—so I doubt it was doing her harm. From the looks of it, this is an early shadyr weapon, possibly pre-crossover considering the materials it's made from. Materials not of this realm."

"So, it's safe?" Harper bounced a little in her chair.

"I'm not sure that's exactly what she was saying," Everly sighed.

Lian smirked and handed the whip sword back to Harper. "I'm saying it's made by shadyrs, *for* shadyrs. Like my sword. Which is the big difference between this, and something like the Bane which was made by who knows what for entirely dark purposes."

Harper's smile faded as she took the weapon. "But I'm not a shadyr."

Everly struggled against the negative words trying to force themselves out, against the idea that her best friend running around with even a *mundane* whip sword didn't sound like a safe prospect.

But she knew how much Harper wanted this, and Harper had never been less than completely supportive of her.

Everly took a deep breath to still her anxiety and smiled. "Shadyr or not, it's yours now, and if any human can make it work, it's you."

Lian patted the back of Harper's hand. "And if something goes wrong, you've got a bunch of shadyrs at your back."

"And a shadyr god," Harper added, grinning at Everly.

Everly's smile strained. She still had very complicated feelings about the being of light inside her.

Her dragon. The Coruscare. The others only saw its sheer power, and how that could be used. They didn't feel how malevolent, hungry, and self-obsessed the being was. As though it would consume the whole world if it were allowed.

It had been quiet since rejoining with the second piece of itself. In a way that brought Everly no comfort. As though it were simply biding its time.

Its power had grown, but so had her own. She understood that being, and herself,

so much more now. There hadn't been opportunity to really test the limits of her control since then, and she wondered whether her confidence was justified.

Whether she was still a threat to her friends' very souls.

A light tingling in her hands signaled to Everly that a panic attack was on its way, so she pushed her chair back, looking for a distraction. Rushelle was still bustling around in the kitchen, so Everly headed that way.

"Anything I can help out with?"

Rushelle smiled sunnily, tucking a blond curl back up into her fifty's pinup-style hair. "All done, love, just can't find the bottle opener. I betcha Denny's left it in the living room again."

"I'll go have a look." As she walked away, Everly ran a finger up and down the digits of her other hand, breathing in and out in time with the action, bringing herself back from the edge of unnecessary panic.

She'd never get used to how her attacks could come at any time, for no apparent reason, but she'd gotten used to the warning signs, and as long as she acted fast, she could normally ward them off.

She spotted the bottle opener on a side table, and when she turned back, she ran face-first into Rylan.

Oookay and back comes all that anxiety again.

His warm, green eyes, sprinkled with the faint hint of stars that shadyr eyes took on at night, searched her face. "Hey, can we talk for a bit?"

Everly fidgeted with the bottle opener. "We can. We should."

I have to tell him.

She still wasn't sure how to let him know that the entity inside her had held just enough of his soul captive to make him feel protective of the being, and her, for most of his life. That the things he felt for her, the words he'd said in her dreams, in the flooding sea cave, came from that forced bond.

She could *never* tell him how much she wished his profession of love was real, how she felt about him in return.

How could she after what she and the Coruscare had done? She wasn't sure she could even trust her own feelings. But that was why Rylan needed to know the truth. He needed the information to know which of his feelings he could trust, too.

Rylan wet his lips and opened his mouth, but Everly held up a hand.

"No, let me go first. I—I have to tell you something. And you're not going to like it. And I hardly even know how to ... but—"

The front door to the house slammed open, and Cherry yelled breathlessly, "There are ghast lures, all around the house!"

"What?" Rylan burst into action, dashing down the hall.

Everly hurried close behind. "Where's Jasper? Was this him? Did he set us up?"

Cherry held the front door open as they went through, with more footsteps coming behind them. "No, I don't think so. He's out there trying to take the lures down."

"Any sign of eidolghasts yet?" Rylan paused on the front porch, scanning the area as Cherry pointed.

A sound somewhere between a foghorn and nails on a chalkboard came as a reply. Out in the field, a pointed, dark shape plummeted from the sky toward Jasper.

"Look out!" Cherry shouted, sprinting down the steps.

Black mist swirled around him as he ran for the field. Jasper ducked and rolled, disappearing in a similar puff of dark smoke as Cherry reached him.

The huge, winged creature crashed down over them both.

4

Everly held her breath, staring at the spot where Jasper and Cherry had stood a moment before. The eidolghast screeched again, turning on the spot. From a distance, in the low light, it seemed like an oversized bat, but its body was unnaturally slim between the wings.

Harper, Neri, Lian, Rushelle, Callan, Denny, and Tammy all pushed out onto the porch, trying to gather what was happening. Seeing what they were facing, jackets and shirts were hastily shed.

"There. They're all right!" Rylan pointed to the side of the monster, where Jasper and Cherry popped up behind a patch of brambles. "Come on, we need to get out there and help them."

"*Flying* monsters now?" Harper sounded half annoyed, half excited at the concept.

"Herrelspurn," Lian said, dropping her gray cardigan on the porch. "Uncommon, but I've faced a few. Watch out for its fire."

All the shadyrs apart from Neri nodded in understanding and headed toward the monster.

Neri's shadyr change had already engulfed her, bright sparks shimmering in the misty magic around her.

As it faded away, Neri stared over her own shoulder in horror. "Wings? I'm still having problems with *legs*."

The leathery membranes had sharp hooks at the end and had torn out through the back of Neri's dress. Her skin had changed too, from a warm brown to a rich, deep red. It wasn't quite the same as the dragon form Rylan had taken fighting the drowned zombies, but it clearly had some part in it.

Harper stepped closer to Neri as though she were about to embrace her. Instead, she pursed her lips into a small smile. "Stay here and take cover. There are plenty of us to deal with this flappy beast. Don't worry at all, okay?"

Neri glanced from Harper to the house and back again. She nodded and stepped inside behind the screen door, wings bumping against the walls.

Everly put a hand on Harper's shoulder. "Ready?"

"Am I ever." Harper grinned back and thrust out her whip sword. It clicked back into a rigid blade with a *shnnnkk*.

Out in the field, the shadyrs all took on the red, winged form. Rylan, Callan, and Denny had shed their shirts entirely to save them from being shredded. They looked like classical demons, emerged from the fires of hell. Cherry and Jasper didn't have time to consider their clothing, and their wings poked out through ragged holes at their backs.

The shadyrs swarmed around the herrelspurn, catching at its wings with their hands. The beast moved fast, twisting away and taking flight.

As it lifted from the overgrown field, Everly got a clear look at it in the dim moonlight. Its flesh was like smoky glass, lit red from within along its narrow, spindle-like torso.

The bat-like wings were tipped with overlong wriggling fingers, but the most disturbing part of the creature was its face.

Atop a mess of dozens of thin necks that twined together between the body and head, there was a face that seemed far too human, and yet not. It was smooth, with no eyes, but all the right proportions and shape of a person, like a porcelain mask. Its nose sniffed, and the human-lipped mouth opened to reveal rows of needle-sharp teeth. It released another bone-chilling scream.

"Oh my ghast," Harper gasped as they ran to join the others.

She held up the whip sword. An aura of golden light shone around the edges of the blade. Looking from it to Everly, her eyes were glossy.

"This is the best present anyone's ever given me."

"Eye's up, kiddos!" Rushelle's voice came from above them.

She, Tammy, and Lian had one of the creature's wings pinned in midair, and it was tumbling out of the sky above them.

Harper dove left and Everly dove right. The shadyrs leaped off the herrelspurn a moment before it hit the ground, letting their wings catch them.

Dry blackberry canes snapped and crunched as the ghast rolled over, swinging its head to where Everly was getting back to her feet. It hissed and flung out a wing toward her, its vast wingspan reaching farther than Everly expected. She dropped herself onto her back again, but the long-fingered tips scraped across her face and neck like razor blades.

She inhaled sharply at the sting, shocked for a moment as the herrelspurn reared back and glowed brighter.

"Evie!" Rylan dropped from the sky on top of her.

The following burst of air stirred up dust and dried grass. He grabbed her, holding her close. One of his deep-red wings fanned out around them like a shield as the roar of fire filled Everly's ears.

Flames tumbled and danced around the edges of Rylan's wing, the translucent

skin shining bright as the sun. Everly turned her eyes to Rylan's face, terrified for the pain he must be in. She found him looking back at her, concern writing lines across his forehead.

"It's okay, it can't burn our wings in this form," he said, and his breath blew hot against her cheek. He reached a hand to her neck, and she saw him swallow. "You're already healing."

Everly blinked, confused. The distraction of nearly being burned alive in Rylan's embrace made her forget that the creature had sliced her skin.

The pain had already passed, and the buffed-up Coruscare seemed to have come with the perk of rapid healing, similar to what it had given Neri from living near it her whole life.

"Yeah, yeah I'm okay."

Rylan had one arm wrapped around her waist, and his face bent close to hers. His eyes glittered like a god's view of a galaxy. The scent of burned grass filled Everly's nose and she coughed on the smoke. The crackle of flame ceased, and Rylan unwrapped his hold.

He stared at her for a long second, and she was sure he was going to tell her to run, to hide, to stay safe. Instead, he nodded to her once, and launched himself at the monster.

Okay?

Before she let her mind spiral by over-analyzing Rylan's behavior, Everly did a situation check. Rushelle's bright-yellow tank top was like a beacon in the dim light, stark against her now red skin. She and Lian had backed off, destroying something in the distance—probably one of the other lures.

Rylan, Callan, Denny, and Tammy were trying to keep the ghast grounded, but it kept slipping free of their hold. Harper stood back from the fight, cursing about it being her first fight with the sword, and it had to be against something that could *fly*.

Cherry had Jasper back on his feet, and they seemed to be arguing, with Jasper hobbling toward the fight as Cherry gestured angrily at his side.

None of the shadyrs were dressed for battle that night. But Jasper looked the strangest—an incubus in a beige knit cardigan.

The herrelspurn was in line with the roof and gaining height. Everly tentatively let the Coruscare's powers out. Starlight glowed around her, and her feet lifted from the ground, hovering above the scorched dirt.

The glowing tendrils emerged, but the sense of hunger, of control being taken from her, didn't come with them. The Coruscare remained quiet, compliant, as she directed those lashing strands of light at the flying monster.

We're just going to hold it. Just hold it. This isn't a meal.

She caught it around one wing, carefully avoiding the surrounding shadyrs. The

herrelspurn shrieked again, a sound that drilled up Everly's spine and into her teeth. She winced.

The creature flailed its other wing, knocking Tammy out of the air. She spiraled, her wings tangled uselessly around her. The herrelspurn breathed fire again, jets of red flame shooting from its throat.

Jasper launched into the air and snatched Tammy before she hit the ground. He wrapped them both in his wings as the flames spread over them.

One shoulder of his cardigan caught alight, and as he reached the ground, Tammy gave him an awkward smile and patted the flames out for him. Rylan, Denny, and Callan landed beside them, not far from Everly.

Rylan's gaze traced the shimmering strands from the herrelspurn all the way to where Everly floated. "Can you bring it down?"

"Maybe. But I don't want to ... I *won't* let the Coruscare eat it. And I don't know if I can control that fine line between kill and consume." Everly's top lip curled with effort as she lassoed the beast with another scintillating string.

She could feel the Coruscare's hunger again now. It would eat everything they touched if it could. But it wasn't pushing back against her control the way it used to. She told it no, and it recoiled, allowing her to guide their actions.

"You don't have to kill. That's our job," Rylan growled. "Just hold it still for us."

Tammy shook out and stretched a shoulder. "So how do we kill this thing?"

She'd left her black hooded jacket behind, but had sacrificed a cobweb-laced shirt to her shift rather than stripping off more. Everly figured she'd choose the same with someone like Denny around, but it sucked Tammy had to deal with ruined clothing because of him.

Callan swiped his long hair back from his face. "The weak point is one of the necks, but there are so many. Seriously, why so many necks and only one head? We could be hacking away for ages before we find the right one."

"It's not the one that's glowing?" Harper stepped beside them, her narrowed eyes locked onto the herrelspurn, which writhed in Everly's snare of light.

It loosed another stream of flames, skimming not far over their heads. They ducked in unison.

"Duh, there isn't one glowing," Denny scoffed. "For someone who looks damn good, you don't *look* very good, do ya?"

"There is, hidden more in the middle, but you can see it sometimes when it twists around." She held up her sword to point, its aura dull compared to Everly.

Callan shrugged. "If I've learned anything in this town, it's to go with the weird. So if you can see it, you can go for it. Worth a shot?"

"I'll try to keep it still, but the fire is a problem for Harper." Everly strained to reel

the monster to the ground.

"I'm on it," Rylan said, and dark magic swirled around him.

He ran toward the herrelspurn as the shift enlarged his body. He emerged from the sparking mist twice his normal size and covered in scales—his combined dragon form. He'd gained so much control over the changes Everly's presence caused him, she'd almost forgotten he could still draw from that to choose any number of shadyr forms.

He tackled the downed creature as another gust of flames blasted free. He caught it in a headlock, trapping its humanoid face between his chest and massive arm, clamping the jaw closed. The large beast reared back, and Rylan lifted from the ground, steadying himself to keep hold.

"Go on, jump in whenever you're ready," Callan urged Harper.

"It's too high up for me," Harper said, her voice strained. "I don't have that strength anymore."

Callan grinned at Tammy. "Let's give her a lift."

The two of them grabbed Harper under her shoulders on each side. Wings pumping, they drew her off her feet.

As they circled over the huge bat-like creature, Callan called, "Dropping the Bellsy bomb in three, two, one."

Harper's hair flew behind her as she fell a few feet onto the back of the creature, Everly's bonds lighting her from below. She grunted fiercely as she thrust her sword deep into the creature's tangle of necks.

With a click, the sword sectioned out again into a flexible whip. Harper kept hold of the hilt as she jumped off the beast's back. The blade wrapped around a portion of the necks, and Harper's momentum sliced through them like a guillotine.

Gurgles of smoky blood spurted from the wound. Rylan let go of the semi-detached head. He snatched Harper and flapped backward in one giant step as the herrelspurn collapsed in an explosion of blood-like lava.

Everly kept the ghast tangled in her light until it stilled completely before she withdrew those tendrils. The glow around her faded and she landed as easily on the ground as if she'd simply taken a step forward.

As the scorching blood sizzled away into the earth, the shadyrs, Harper, and Everly stood together, catching their breaths.

No one spoke, but in the bright-eyed gazes shared between them, a heavy satisfaction was clear. They'd fought as a team and fought well.

"I'd say that confirms the use of those bloody bone effigies as lures," Lian muttered as she and Rushelle rejoined them.

They had already shaken off their demon-like forms, and the other shadyrs joined them, returning to their human shapes.

Across the field, the front door of the house clanged, and Neri jogged awkwardly toward them, still red. Her wings flapped lopsidedly, giving her small boosts of speed that left her stumbling.

"I've never done herrelspurn form before," Tammy said, looking over her shoulders as though she already missed her wings.

"You and your all-black outfit pulled off the look the best, I have to say," Harper grinned.

"Eh, clashes with my hair," Cherry muttered with a smirk. "Why can't we take some kind of cool Coruscare shadyr form?"

"Hrm, that's a good point," Lian said. "The Coruscare is a creature from the Everdark after all. But we don't seem to have any reaction to it."

"Because whatever the Coruscare is, it's not an eidolghast." Rylan's voice was low. "Shadyrs only react to eidolghasts. We don't shift in reaction to creatures from earth, either."

Everly let out a huff of air. She hadn't ever thought of it that way before. She still considered the thing inside her to be a monster, but it was at least a little comforting that it wasn't *that* kind of monster.

She glanced over at Harper who was beaming at her. The sword had stopped glowing once the herrelspurn was defeated. It seemed to react to eidolghasts, too.

Could it be what let Harper see the weak spot?

"I don't suppose you're seeing any glowing weak spots on me?" Even if the sword no longer seemed active, Everly wanted to be sure.

"No weak spots at all." Harper's eyes wrinkled as her smile grew. "Oof!"

Neri stumbled up against her, clinging on to steady herself as her wings kept flapping of their own accord. "Did you get hurt? There was so much fire."

She warily eyed a patch of grass that still smoldered.

Harper's cheeks colored, and she backed away from Neri by a small step but held her arm out to keep the girl from toppling over. "All good here. Thank you."

"I think our newest household member might be feeling a bit rough still." Cherry shrugged toward Jasper, who had slumped over with his hands on his knees.

Jasper straightened up and tried to tidy his hair. "Just ... tired."

As though a strong gust of air had hit only him, he swayed on his feet, then folded onto the ground with a thump.

He shook his head from where he sat. "Okay, very tired. And sore."

"Don't worry, little duck, you're with us now. We'll look after you," Rushelle said, smiling from him to Cherry. "If that's okay with everyone."

There were nods all around. Neri's eyes widened. "Does that mean I can use my ... *talents* now too?"

"If you want to," Harper said.

Neri gave a firm nod.

Jasper shook his head and his nose wrinkled as Cherry helped him up. His voice was a raspy whisper.

"Thank you, for letting me stay. For everything."

Cherry's lips raised in a half-smile, but his gaze remained cool. "Jasper, this is our new friend Neri. Just wait until you hear what she can do."

As Neri began her song, Everly looked out over the field where the lures had been. The haunting strains of the mermaid-girl's voice renewed Everly physically, but she couldn't shake off the worry that had permeated her.

They could bring Jasper in, they could give him their trust, but how long were any of them going to be able to stay safe when their enemy could send monster after monster their way?

5

A hot ember of concern had settled into the pit of Rylan's stomach since Jasper came to them with his information about the Mesmans.

He'd suspected someone had tried to have him killed. He suspected there were dark magics being played with. But having those suspicions confirmed flipped his world over like a rowboat on a wild sea.

It had to be set right.

After the death of his dad, Rylan trusted Mordan Darkfrey to train him so that he'd never feel useless as a loved one died, ever again. He'd put every ounce of his trust into the Darkfreys. He left his home and family. He pushed Everly away.

And now Callan was talking about the possibility that their father's death wasn't simply a tragic ghast attack. That it was one of the Darkfreys' own who caused their father to die.

Mordan had to be told what the Mesmans were doing.

He would deal with them, and the division they had caused could be repaired. He, Callan, and the others could rejoin the Darkfreys.

Is that what I want?

There was a part of him that deeply missed belonging to that institution. He had been part of something bigger. He'd been one of the best. Mordan had treated him like one of his own children.

He only left because he knew someone there wanted him dead, but the others at Howell House left for their own reasons. Reasons that wouldn't change with the end of the Mesmans' plotting.

He doubted any of them would go back if that was all that changed. Maybe Denny, if they'd take him.

Could I go back to the Darkfreys without the others?

Rylan huffed as he slid back his jacket hood, his breath coming out in a white cloud. He was getting ahead of himself. First, they needed to tell Mordan and see how he was going to handle the issue.

They arrived at The Crow's Nest, and Shroudhaven lay in an eerie stillness. Low

clouds created a glary gloom, but no rain fell. The wind that often rushed up the streets like a howling banshee was absent, and the temperature was cold enough that Everly's nose and cheeks turned pink. The rosiness against her white hair had her looking so beautiful that the breath caught in Rylan's throat.

She noticed him staring and averted her eyes. Ever since the cave under the lighthouse, when he opened up to her, shared how he truly felt, she'd been avoiding him.

Is it some kind of twisted revenge for how I pushed her away for so long?

No, that wasn't like her. There had to be something more going on. His lips still tingled with the ghost of their icy kiss in the caves, and the memory of the more heated kiss in Everly's dream.

Since waking up, he felt differently toward Everly than before. Less of a fierce protectiveness, and more a fierce desire to be with her. To feel her lips on his again, and again. But maybe that wasn't what she wanted. He told her he loved her, but did she feel that way about him? He knew they had been good friends, and that pushing her away had hurt her deeply.

But he didn't know whether she felt *more* for him than that. After all the years putting her safety ahead of his feelings, maybe he'd blown his chance with her for good. Misty air huffed from his mouth again, coming out in a shiver.

Lian locked the car, then turned to where they stood on the cracked footpath. "You think he'll show?"

Rylan nodded once. He had Mordan's private number and had set up the meeting away from Darkfrey Estate so the information could be relayed in a neutral location. He didn't want the Mesmans getting wind of things too soon, before Mordan could make his move against them. Mordan had seemed happy to hear from Rylan which was an undeniable relief that he hadn't lost Mordan's favor entirely.

"I still don't get why I have to be here," Tammy mumbled, tucking her blackened hands deep into the pockets of her coat.

Lian pushed the heavy, dungeon-like front door open, leading them inside. "You're part of our evidence. You heard Blaise talk about his parents having a number of stolen artifacts."

Tammy scoffed. "In case them trying to kill us all multiple times isn't enough for Mordan to want to do something about them."

Warm air met Rylan as he stepped inside. The Crow's Nest was always cozy, comforting, and cluttered, with swathes of beaded, multicolored curtains and rainbow light cast through stained-glass lampshades. The smoky remnants of incense and smudge sticks mixed with the scents of alcohol and deep-fried food.

Mismatched tables held groups of people, some in Darkfrey jackets, others looking like average Shroudhaven citizens. But all would have been shadyrs. A few looked up

but quickly returned to their own conversations and drinks with little more than an eyeroll at the presence of the Howell team.

"There he is," Rylan said, tilting his head toward the far end of the bar.

Mordan sat on his own by a small coffee table. His slick, satin lapel jacket contrasted with the frayed corduroy of the old armchair he'd claimed.

On their way there, Crowea swooped over to their side in a jingle of bracelets and swoosh of long skirts.

"Got business with the old man?" She raised her eyebrow over her one good eye. "You know I don't tolerate conflict in my house."

"We won't cause any trouble," Rylan grunted.

Crowea fanned a gloved hand at him almost like shooing a fly. "Trouble follows you like a vengeful ghost, boy."

Lian pursed her lips. "Hopefully this will be the end of some problems."

She nodded to Crowea and turned away.

"One moment." Crowea grabbed Lian's arm. "In case you haven't heard yet, Candace Zathory passed away a couple of nights ago. I know you two were close, many years back."

Rylan recognized the name too. A woman of his mother's age, still active in the Darkfreys' ranks. While she looked like a formidable shadyr, she wasn't in a brace herself anymore, and instead ran some of the classes at the estate.

Lian's shrewd gaze softened. "How'd she go?"

"In her sleep."

"Lucky. Plenty of worse ways for a shadyr to go." Lian patted Crowea's gloved hand. "I'll bring you some drinks, on the house." Crowea jangled away to the bar.

"Are you okay?" Everly asked Lian.

Lian sighed, but her smile returned. "I was friends with Candace back when we were kids but hadn't seen her in decades."

"Loss is still loss though," Everly replied.

"That it is." Lian pulled her ankle-length gray cardigan a little tighter around herself as she led them toward the leader of the Darkfreys.

"Mordan, I'm surprised you came alone." Lian dragged her chair a little farther away from him before sitting down.

Mordan smiled, fine lines creasing around his eyes. "Oh, a Darkfrey is never alone in Shroudhaven."

His grin broadened as his gaze took in Rylan. "Good to see you up and around, my boy."

Rylan took a seat directly across from Mordan, finding himself smiling in return, although he did notice Lian bristling at the term of endearment. Everly and Tammy

shared a small two-seater lounge beside them.

Mordan clapped his hands together. "Now, I know you're not a fan of niceties, Ms. Howell, so would you like to get straight to it?"

"I would." Lian's eyebrows raised, but she reached into her bag and drew out the papers Jasper had brought them as evidence of the Mesmans' activities. "A couple of your shadyrs are messing around with dark magic. Creating lures to draw in eidolghasts. Trying to open their own shroudpool."

Mordan bent forward to look at the loose pages, rubbing his white-and-gray-streaked goatee. "Ah, the Mesmans."

Rylan shifted to the edge of his chair. "You know?"

"Oh, I'm sorry. Did I ruin your big reveal?" Mordan's eyes twinkled.

Rylan shot a look at Lian, who frowned back at him.

"If this is all you've come to see me about, I'm afraid you're wasting your time. They aren't the villains you think they are." Mordan moved to pick up the papers, but Rylan smacked his hand on top of them, pulling them back.

"So, they didn't try to have me killed?" Rylan spoke through gritted teeth, and the ember in his gut seemed to burst into flame.

"Well, yes. They did go a bit off script there. I'm sorry."

"You *knew*?" Everly glared intensely at Mordan and light flared around her. Everyone else stilled, watching her warily. With a shake of her head she muttered something to herself, and the glow flickered and faded.

Rylan swallowed, as though he could put out his own fire burning within but didn't have as much control as Everly had just shown. Swirling thoughts and implications clouded his mind like smoke.

Mordan knew. And he's acting like it was nothing.

Mordan cleared his throat and continued. "They thought they were doing the right thing to keep some important secrets. I did discipline them at the time. But generally, they provide great value to our shadyr mission, so I have to overlook some things."

Lian sneered. "Value? How could luring eidolghasts to innocent family homes be valuable?"

The realization hit Rylan like brass knuckles to the sternum. He wasn't the only shadyr child who ended up with the Darkfreys when one or both of their parents died in an eidolghast attack.

Annabeth had a similar story, and many others over the years since Rylan moved to the estate.

And it wasn't always children. Sometimes those with shadyr blood would be drawn back to Shroudhaven without realizing what they were but would very quickly find out when a ghast showed up at their home.

Rylan's tone was low and gravelly. "You've been using the lures to identify shadyrs. To motivate them to join the Darkfreys."

Mordan's eyes narrowed, but his smile remained. "The Mesmans' magic has proven to be the perfect tool to help bring reluctant shadyrs into the fold. A very successful recruitment method, in fact."

Lian straightened in her chair. Her cardigan opened to the side, revealing her hand resting on the hilt of her sword. "You had my husband killed for *recruitment*?"

Mordan sighed. "I had to do something when it became clear you weren't making any efforts to train your sons. I couldn't very well let two strong shadyr boys of the Pimey line go to waste. I understand it seems cruel, but so is this world and the monsters in it that we are at *war* with. The results have been worth it. We have built the biggest shadyr army in history. I've done what is needed to make us strong enough to fight back the darkness."

Rylan couldn't breathe. He'd left his home, his family ... He had been a child, thinking he was doing the right thing, going somewhere he could learn to be a good fighter, so that he could protect his loved ones from the fate that took his father.

But his father had been killed by the very people he turned to. He spent half his life working for them, being the best soldier he could be, and it had all been built upon a lie.

Rylan couldn't think straight as the ember inside him boiled the blood behind his eyes. His whole body heated, and in such close proximity to Everly and the powerful eidolghast essences she radiated, he almost lost control of his change.

He only had so much control because of what the Darkfreys had taught him. He hated that the parts of him he thought were the strongest were now tainted by their cause.

Who would I be now if the Darkfreys hadn't recruited me? Everything, everything would be different.

His breath came in deep pants that left him dizzy.

A hand rested upon his, squeezing gently. Everly had reached over, locking eyes onto his face. A shiver railroaded up Rylan's spine. He clenched his teeth and made an effort to not explode.

By his other side, Lian sat deadly still. "You are *dripping* with blood. How many have died for your cause?"

"How many would have died without it?" Mordan asked back, sincerely.

"Less, if you weren't busy killing your own." Rylan couldn't look at Mordan.

The sting of shame joined the white-hot fury burning inside him. It wasn't just the betrayal of how he became a Darkfrey that hurt him. It was the fact that they tried to have him killed, and Mordan knew. He *knew* all along and he didn't care. As twisted as they were, the Darkfreys were his family.

He'd felt special there, important. But he was expendable to them.

"I never wanted to lose you," Mordan said. "You really were one of our best. You and your brother would still be welcomed back, if you can put this all behind us."

"You set lures at my home again just last night! You tried to kill us all, and you want them to put it behind them?" Lian's knuckles turned white in their grip around the hilt, but she remained statue-still.

Mordan steepled his fingers and tilted his head almost bashfully. "After Jasper left how he did, there were concerns you all knew things that you shouldn't know. We had to make efforts to stop the spread of sensitive information. But when you reached out for this meeting, I hoped we could come to an understanding."

Rylan's mouth was too dry to speak, and the others simply stared, aghast. Mordan continued, "I've been upfront with you all. I'm hoping that you can understand the logic and honor in our actions. I know your losses have been personal, but we must think beyond ourselves. This is for the greater cause, as is everything I have ever done."

"How is opening a shroudpool part of the greater cause?" Tammy hugged her thin chest tightly, and Rylan could see her shivering despite the warmth of the room.

Mordan flicked his fingers dismissively. "That's just the Mesmans' pet project, and honestly, I doubt anything will ever come of it. Now, I'm sure you realize that the information we've shared can't go any further. Many won't have the capacity to grasp the work the Mesmans and I have done. I'm hoping that you can. Do we have an understanding?"

Rylan tightened a fist around the pages on the table, scrunching them in his hand. He glared at the mad scribblings and sketches, unable to loosen his grip as his fingers shook. Everly still squeezed his other hand, and his mother remained still and pale.

His whole life he'd trained to fight monsters. But he was only now feeling the cost. Life couldn't only be death and loss. And he couldn't be part of an organization that lived that way, that accepted those tragedies as normal. They were no better than the monsters he'd learned to kill.

He whispered, "No. I don't understand."

"Hrm. That's a shame." Mordan shrugged and snapped his fingers.

Every other shadyr in the establishment stood up in a clatter of chairs and downed drinks. They closed in, forming a wall between the Howell team and the exit. From behind curtains toward the back, Rylan's old brace, or what remained of them, stepped out—Nilson, Annabeth, and Vonny Mesman.

Rylan shot to his feet, the others behind him. Lian's sword sang as she unsheathed it halfway in warning. Rylan knew she wouldn't draw it entirely until she needed to strike, because she'd be blinded by its magic the moment it was out of the sheath.

"What is this all about?" Crowea's voice rose from behind the bar. "This is a safe space for all."

"This space, as with every space in Shroudhaven, only exists with my permission," Mordan barked back.

He got to his feet with the slow actions of an old body, but Rylan knew he was as deadly as any shadyr around them. "And traitors to our very race and the safety of our entire dimension won't be tolerated."

"Can you clear a path out for us?" Rylan whispered to Everly.

When she didn't immediately reply, he turned to find her looking green, bent as though punched in the stomach.

Rylan grunted, spinning back to the approaching Darkfreys.

Vonny smirked at him from between her blond bob as she strode forward, unwrapping a bundle of old parchment in her hands to reveal sharp, diamond-shaped metal that oozed dark blood.

"Ghast dammit," Rylan muttered.

Beside her, Nilson held no weapon, and Rylan imagined he'd be pleased to kill them all with his bare hands. Annabeth followed a couple of steps back, eyes red-rimmed but firm.

"Make a break for the front door? Or try for the back?" Lian whispered.

Before Rylan could reply, Tammy stepped in front of him and snatched Lian's hand into hers. *Tammy.*

He guessed what the girl was planning and hoped she could pull it off as she had in the flooding cave. He quickly put a hand on her shoulder, keeping the papers held tight in his other. Vonny watched the way they came together with her teeth bared, pausing for a moment to sneer at them.

Tammy reached across to Everly, and as her black hand touched Everly's skin, the lights flickered and a *whomp* of magical mist burst from them.

Rylan hadn't noticed that reaction when they were in the cave, but he'd also been up to his eyebrows in icy seawater and watching as Everly came far too close to death.

He didn't have long to take it in this time either, as a moment later a tug jarred him, like someone had put a shark hook through his heart and pulled. Sensations of twisting air, being dragged through mist, of *being* only mist overwhelmed him, until they were gone seconds later, and the four of them stood together at the Dark Corner shroudpool.

Everly took a deep breath beside him, the color quickly returning to her now that the Bane wasn't nearby. "How could they? They're evil, all of them."

Rylan's chest hurt, and he squinted his eyes closed. "No. You don't understand how important defending this world against eidolghasts is for shadyrs. Some would do *anything* for that cause. They aren't evil. They're fanatics."

"Same thing, I'd say," Lian muttered. "And no matter what we call them, they now want us dead."

6

Learning that the death of Rylan and Callan's father had been a purposeful attack almost pushed Everly over an edge into a rage she wasn't sure she could come back from.

It had been a strange sensation, similar to a panic attack with the same racing, clenching heart, but with a determined strain deep in her muscles that urged her to take action. Take *revenge*.

She wasn't sure how much of that was her, and how much was her dragon. But for a few moments, the idea of ripping the soul from the man who caused them all so much pain seemed like the most sensible course of action. It would have been good. He deserved it.

Maybe he did, but Everly didn't think she had the right to make that judgment or execute such a punishment. She managed to reel those emotions back in, whether they were her own or the Coruscare's.

Callan picked them up in Lian's SUV, and the return to Howell House was somber and quiet. All in all, attacks on their lives included, they were back home by midafternoon.

Rushelle made everyone hot drinks, and they gathered around the long farmhouse table.

Everly held her chamomile tea under her nose and breathed in the grassy, apple scent, hoping it would help ground her, or bring her some inspiration as to what they could do next. "Do you think Crowea is okay?"

Lian shook her head, but replied, "I doubt they'd hurt her, and as much as she'll be furious about it, I don't know what she can do. Mordan was right in a way. The Darkfreys own this town."

"I'm sure Crow will get back at them in her own way. She must have some witchy hexes up her sleeve," Rushelle said.

"She'll probably close for a week to smudge away all the bad conflict energy." Harper chuckled, but her mirth faded almost instantly. "I can't believe they did that. All of it. I knew the Darkfreys weren't the best people in a lot of ways, but still ..."

Tammy had her head on the table, resting on folded arms, muddling her voice. "What can we do about it?"

There was a resignation in her tone, as though she already knew the answer. *Nothing*.

Trying to come up with a solution to offer, Everly stared at the top of Tammy's head. The goth girl had previously kept her hair trimmed in a soldierly buzz cut, but over the last week or two she hadn't seemed to have cut it, and the black hair had a thicker, shaggy texture. Did she just want a change? Was she giving up on the strict guidelines of being a militant shadyr? Or was she just ... giving up?

Lian leaned her elbows on the table, cupping her mug between her hands so the steam drifted up in front of her face. "We have to think about our safety first. Whether we can stay here."

"I'm staying," Callan said firmly.

Although there were enough seats at the table, he remained on his feet, leaning on a hutch behind Tammy.

Rylan mirrored him on the other side, standing in front of the kitchen counter with arms crossed over his chest. He nodded in agreement, and the motion spread around the others in the room.

Lian sniffed. "You're brave kids, but if I think we have to leave to stay safe, we're going. This is just a building. You are all family."

"We need to stay so we can put a stop to what the Mesmans and Mordan are doing," Rylan growled.

"And how are we going to do that?" Lian shot back. "Frontal assault the entire Darkfrey Estate? If Mordan considers the Mesmans valuable, he's going to keep them protected. Kole never leaves the estate as it is."

"Do we really think they even can open a shroudpool? Is that really a risk?" Everly asked.

The lures were a crime, but they could keep an eye out for them now, put a stop to them when they showed up. Opening another shroudpool right in the middle of Shroudhaven was something else.

Jasper still wore the same clothes he'd arrived in the night before, but had cleaned himself up, and been healed by Neri's singing.

He spoke a lot more confidently than before. "They are building the structure for it now. I'm sure that's what I saw. Whether they can activate it, and how, is the question."

"Eidolghasts open new shroudpools if they stay in one area for long enough," Cherry said. "Maybe they're keeping some ghost pets somehow as part of it?"

"At Darkfrey Estate? All the shadyrs there would sense them if they were," Denny scoffed. "I reckon they can't do it. Even if they've got a bit of old school shadyr magic happening. If they *could* do it, they would have done it already. It's been years since their kid punched a one-way ticket to the Everdark."

A soft groan came from where Tammy had her head down.

"Could you try for once to not be the biggest dick in the room?" Callan snapped at Denny.

"Impossible. And I'll prove it if you like." Denny grabbed at his fly.

"For ghast's sake, that's—"

Tammy raised her head, her mouth open as though in terrible realization. "Do you know why? Why Blaise wanted to try to close a shroudpool?"

Denny opened his mouth again, but Callan slapped the back of his head before he could speak.

Tammy continued, her voice almost a whisper, "Because so many kids were losing their family to eidolghasts. He wanted to find a way to close the shroudpools for good, all of them, so that no more kids would have to lose their parents. So *he* wouldn't lose his parents. He was so scared something would kill them, but it was them! It was them all along ..."

Lian reached across the table for Tammy's hand. Her blackened fingers twitched, but she didn't pull away. "All this time they've been blaming it on you, never knowing it was the price they paid for their own actions."

"It was never your fault," Callan added.

Tammy's face scrunched, and she shook her head. But any reply was cut off by a knock at the front door.

Around the table, eyes scanned about as though doing a head count. They were all there, even Neri, sitting wide-eyed beside Harper, trying to take in as much as she could of all the new information.

Everly frowned. "You think they've come for us again?"

"But why knock?" Harper asked.

Lian got to her feet, striding toward the door with a no-nonsense *humph*. Every other chair scraped against the floor as the rest of them followed.

Through the screen, backed by the fading light outside, a single person stood silhouetted.

"Careful," Rylan hissed as Lian opened the door.

A young red-headed woman gawked back at them all crowded in the entrance.

"Annabeth?" Rylan nearly coughed the word.

"Um ... Hi?" she said, tucking a strand of curling hair behind a freckled ear. Beside her on the grayed timber of the porch was a black rolling suitcase.

Lian stepped out past the woman, her hand on the hilt of her sword and eyes narrowed on the surrounding fields.

She turned back to Annabeth. "You were there today, with Vonny."

Annabeth stood straighter as though at attention and gave a sharp nod. "They told us you were traitors, working to destroy us. I went along with orders even though they didn't make sense."

"Typical Darkfrey," Cherry muttered from the back.

Annabeth's shoulders lifted toward her ears. "I'm sorry. As soon as I got Jasper's message ... Things make sense now. I packed and left right away. I couldn't stay there." She chewed at her bottom lip. "I couldn't stay with the people who killed my parents."

"Jasper's message?" Lian asked.

Jasper winced and directed his explanation to Cherry, despite how everyone looked at him. "When Mordan's recruitment methods were revealed, I believed sharing that intel with Annabeth was the correct thing to do. I'm sorry. I promise I'm not making a habit of divulging secrets to the enemy anymore."

Rylan had kept his eyes on Annabeth. "Annabeth isn't the enemy. She's one of our brace."

Her bottom lip pouted, then she pulled it in, her back straightening even more.

Everly wondered how long the young woman had been trained as a soldier, at what age she'd been 'recruited.' Everly didn't understand brace dynamics, or how long she'd been in Rylan's, but it was clear they had formed a bond. From having both lost parents, and no doubt more.

Everly also knew how Annabeth felt about Rylan. And a dark, mourning place within her heart told her that maybe Rylan would be better off with Annabeth. Someone who truly understood his experience as a shadyr. Someone who hadn't messed with his soul and emotions his entire life. Someone who wasn't capable of doing it again.

We could. We could take him again, make him be ours. Why not have what you want?

Everly shivered at the voice that shared space in her mind. It sounded so much like her own, but the urge behind it was cold and alien.

Or was it? She yearned to be close to Rylan, to have him for herself, to be the soulmates she once dreamed they were. How could she separate those feelings from the urges of the entity that possessed her?

Jasper nodded in agreement with Rylan but continued to look to Cherry with seeking eyes.

Cherry bit his bottom lip. "You were right. She deserves to know. They all do."

"I'm sorry for showing up here unannounced, but Jasper said you were very welcoming, and I hoped ..." Annabeth's hand shot to her neckline and fidgeted with her necklace. "I mean, I understand if you don't want me here. I didn't do enough when Rylan was missing. I haven't been on the right side."

She twitched as though mentally slapping herself, then released the necklace and returned to a rigid stance of attention. Only her round, red-rimmed eyes revealed a

deeper vulnerability.

Everly's heart softened for the girl.

"We all make mistakes. Especially when we put our trust in the wrong people. There are still a couple of spare rooms here, right?" she asked Lian.

Lian nodded slowly, and checked with Rylan, "You vouch for her?"

Rylan gave Annabeth a scrutinizing look but nodded.

"Okay, come on in then," Lian muttered.

Annabeth lifted one foot and seemed to hover for a moment before bringing it over the threshold. She deflated as her tense shoulders released.

"Hey, I like your necklace," Everly offered as she moved to make room.

The pendant had fallen on the outside of Annabeth's button up shirt after she'd played with it. It seemed made of an opalescent crystal, carved in a single, thin point as small as a fingertip. It was a dark, smoky color, with bright highlights like sparks from a fire.

Her hand went to it reflexively again. "Thank you. It's a family heirloom. A piece of true pre-crossover shadyr bone. It's all I have left from my parents."

Everly smirked. "Sweet *and* creepy. I like it."

Rushelle pushed her way in beside them. "Oh, I do like new people! Let me get that for you."

She reached for Annabeth's luggage, grunting as she dragged it toward the stairway. "Wow, did you escape the Darkfreys with a bag full of gold bullion or something?"

Annabeth helped lift the other end as they made their way up the stairs. "I might have, um, stolen a bunch of books."

"Ha!" Rushelle barked. "A reader, huh? I don't suppose you like erotic satire?"

"Rylan, you should show Annabeth around," Everly said.

The words came fast, as though she had to chase them out before they stuck. "You and Jasper, you know her best. Help her feel at home."

"Good idea," Lian said. "And keep an eye on her for a little while too. Just in case."

With the threat of danger passed, most of them had already drifted away, either back to the dining room, or off to their own rooms, in the case of Tammy. Everly took the chance to slip into the living room, feeling the need for space to take some long, deep breaths.

She stood in front of the vintage TV cabinet, staring at photos of the Howell brothers as young boys, when someone cleared their throat behind her.

She turned to find Rylan there, standing close enough to see the warm golden flecks in his olive-green eyes. "Aren't you going to show Annabeth around?"

He shrugged but didn't break eye contact. "Jasper and Rush are on it. Denny also volunteered so I let him take my spot."

"Denny? Nooo, why? Do you hate Annabeth?"

Rylan huffed a laugh.

"Anna can hold her own. Besides," his lips pulled tight, and he licked them, "we need to talk."

Everly took a long, shaking breath. Her body reflexively took a step backward, but she came up against the cabinet, making the frames rattle.

Rylan gently reached for her chin and turned her to face him again. "No excuses. No running away. No interruptions. I just ... want to know why you're avoiding me. I know I probably deserve it, but—"

"You don't. You don't deserve any of it. That isn't why I've been avoiding this. It's just hard. What happened, it's so awful I haven't known how to tell you."

"What's happened?" Rylan's hands moved to her shoulders, his grasp firm through her red bomber jacket. "Are you okay?"

Everly's chest stung like it was wrapped in barbed wire.

He's still so protective. It hasn't faded.

She swallowed away the pain and pressed her feet firmly downward to ground herself.

She had to tell him. Now.

"When the second piece of the Coruscare joined with me, I learned so much, about how it behaves, what it can do. It doesn't just eat souls. Sometimes, it can steal a small fragment of a person's essence, to bind that person to it. It enslaves them, making them want to protect the Coruscare at all costs."

She stared into Rylan's eyes, hoping he would understand. There was a wrinkle between his eyebrows as he stared back, but he didn't speak.

"That night, when the vasmire almost killed you, that wasn't when I first stole your essence into me. It was when we first met, lost in the woods. The Coruscare has bound you too me ever since then."

Rylan's hands dropped and his eyebrows pressed low over his eyes. "What does that mean?"

Everly exhaled slowly, fighting the sting in her nose and her eyes that threatened to burst into sobs. "It means none of your feelings for me are real. It's how the Coruscare has made you feel so that you'd help keep me, its host, safe."

Rylan took a step back. He didn't seem angry, just confused. His eyes roamed the ceiling as though seeking answers, then returned to her.

"Are you sure?"

"It's why I always dreamt of you, every night since we met. Part of you was always with me." Everly winced at how that sounded, almost romantic, so she added, "Stolen, without your consent."

He shook his head fiercely. "But you haven't dreamed of me since you woke me up, since you freed me with the Bane. You must have freed all of me then, right?"

"Yeah, I think so."

"How I feel about you, what I told you in the cave ... That was when I was free. And I've felt that way for a long time. It hasn't changed." He pressed a thumb to his bottom lip thoughtfully. "Not a lot. Feeling protective of you was one thing, but ... I feel so much more than that now."

Everly clenched her teeth in an effort to force back tears. Everything she ever wanted was right in front of her, so close she could see his pulse beating in his neck, and it was all wrong.

"It's not real. The soul bond has been messing with your emotions, our emotions, for fourteen years. It's going to take a while to really know what's real."

"No. I don't need a while. I pushed you away for so long, thinking distance is what would keep you safe. Maybe that was the bond, making me think protecting you should come above how I felt about you. I don't know. Honestly, I don't care. I'm free now and I *know* I want to be with you." Rylan's throat moved as he swallowed, and his eyes locked onto hers. "I just need to know if you want to be with me too."

It felt as though time collapsed around Everly. As though she could stand in that moment for eternity, lost in Rylan's longing eyes, avoiding having to form an answer that would ruin her.

As a child she'd loved him so deeply that she imagined their love would last lifetime after lifetime, soulmates seeking each other out in every new reincarnation, for all of eternity.

He had been everything to her. Her best friend, her savior, her first love.

But she was only a child. Even if she'd carried those foolish romantic dreams into adulthood.

She swallowed her heart, pressing it deep down into a vault of stone. "We don't even know each other. Not really. Not anymore. Not after so many years apart, and everything that has changed."

Rylan's lip twitched and he took a small step closer. "But what do you *want*? How do you really feel?"

I love you. I love you with every heartbeat.

She couldn't say it. She couldn't bind him to her like that again. Not while the *thing* inside her remained. But denying those feelings was a lie she couldn't produce on her stuttering lips.

A stream of light curved in through the living room window and gravel crunched outside.

Lian's voice came from the hallway. "Looks like more visitors."

Rylan groaned and pushed the curtains aside to look out.

Everly peered around his shoulder to see not just one car, but a slow stream of vehicles coming up the drive.

Rylan cursed under his breath. "An attack?"

"Maybe. Maybe not." Lian joined them in the living room, looking out the second window beside them. "Annabeth said she may have told a few others about what's been going on. And word can travel fast."

The first Darkfrey-marked van came to a jolting stop, and a kid that looked too young to be driving hopped out, followed by two even younger children. They hovered near the car in a huddle, looking around as though unsure what to do next. The occupants of the second car were also climbing out, older teens, acting no more threateningly.

Lian sighed. "I guess being worried that Mordan will come after us to keep his secrets is a moot point now."

"Looks like the damage has been done," Everly agreed, as the teens nervously approached the porch, and the younger kids skittered after them.

"Why in the Everdark are they all coming here?" Rylan muttered.

Everly turned to Lian, who stood tall and slim in the beam of a headlight breaking into the living room. Her wrinkled expression was set like a solid wall, but one built from strength and compassion.

Everly smiled. "Because they know this is a place shadyrs can come when they have nowhere else to go. They know they will be accepted here. No matter what."

She just hoped it would remain a place they could all be safe.

7

E verly missed her dreams with Rylan. Even when they were nightmares, they were better than the dreams she'd had since.

Now, she shared her sleeping mind with the Coruscare.

I'm dreaming, she told herself, although it was easy to tell this wasn't real life. The landscape she saw before her wasn't even this *dimension.*

Most of her dreams now took place in the Everdark, before it had become the Everdark, when the Coruscare still ruled over the shadyrs. She seemed to share the entity's memories. And since it had many thousands of years of memories more than her, those were the visions that now dominated her mind.

A swirling, seasick feeling of movement accompanied the dreams, and Everly winced as her body lurched through the yellow-tinted world, the sense of motion disturbingly mismatched to the direction she moved.

She'd seen visions of this dimension from when the Coruscare was at the height of its power, but this was different. The crystalline forests and pillar-shaped mountains burned, blackened and cracking, as eidolghasts swarmed in large mobs.

There were so many of them. Vasmires, weroths, auerdaxes, herrelspurn, and many more that Everly couldn't name. They squabbled and tore at each other, dark gore carpeting the ground.

They did not originate from my realm.

Everly looked for the source of the words, but the Coruscare didn't bring itself before her in visible form. Still, its voice came through as clear as a spike of ice to her eye.

"There are so many of them." Everly shivered. Were there still so many of these creatures in the Everdark? Were there *more?*

My dark mirror, shadow twin, assisted their encroachment. Made them tools to betray and destroy this self. Take this self's power.

Everly's nose twitched. The Coruscare liked to paint itself as the great victim, but she didn't buy it. She'd seen how it used and abused the entire race of shadyrs for its own power. Whatever this shadow twin was, they were probably as bad as each other.

"I thought it was the Bane of Teeth and Stars that broke you?"

A rattling hiss thundered so loud Everly covered her ears.

Forged by the shadow twin. Wielded by. Endless eons we contested but never found triumph, never for either. No comprehension how dark twin destroyed this self, but have seen, since awaking in this vessel.

Vessel was said with a heavy disdain for how it viewed her and her body, but Everly was used to this. She also knew what it meant by having "seen."

Not only did she share the Coruscare's memories, but they also seemed to be able to access the memories of some of the beings it had consumed the life essences of. It made for scattered, confusing dreams, like looking out through the eyes of multiple insects, a kaleidoscope of perspectives patched together.

A tug shifted her untethered consciousness, like a wave pushing her about in the ocean, as the Coruscare took her through the space-time of the dreamscape. The sensation of movement felt so real it left Everly's stomach churning.

The sky darkened, something vast and black shadowing the realm. Beneath the coal-smoke sky, masses of eidolghasts congregated. They moved in wild, hectic motions, as a force dragged them all toward a central point.

"They're terrified," Everly gasped.

This self has seen, from essence consumed since waking. One that saw and survived.

The ghasts clawed and ripped at each other, stampeding desperately to escape the pull, but they were drawn ever inward. There had to be thousands of them. Everly narrowed her eyes, trying to see what was in the middle that they were destined for.

A sickly green orb hovered there, above an immense altar where the Bane lay. The sphere wasn't much larger than a basketball, and it drew eidolghasts to it as though it was a black hole.

And then it would *pulse.*

It enlarged, expanding so much that multiple eidolghasts could fit inside. The crystalline green material that formed it fractured into a web, and eidolghasts were drawn *through* it, shredding them in the process. Then it collapsed in on itself again.

The mass of the victims it had drawn in seemed to vanish, and from the bottom of the sphere, a single drop of thick, dark blood dripped onto the Bane.

The process continued. The sphere expanded and contracted, like a Hoberman sphere toy in the hands of a hyperactive child.

Everly stared, open-mouthed in horror. It was harvesting thousands of eidolghasts, and crushing them into ... what? Some sort of essential oil of monster?

"That's why it hurts you," Everly wondered out aloud. "It's just too much energy. That's why it bleeds constantly. It contains more power than it possibly should."

And the blood was a mix of so many eidolghasts, as Lian had observed in Gorhanmere.

Bane must be destroyed. Have let foes take control of what can end self.

Everly nodded. She could at least agree with that. She didn't like the idea of Vonny being in possession of a weapon that totally incapacitated her. She didn't seem shy about using it either.

Everly couldn't watch the massacre any longer. Even if they were monsters. She turned her eyes away, staring up into the darkened sky.

And the sky stared back at her.

Everly pitched forward on the lounge, gasping into consciousness. Her heart raced and her sleeping bag rustled as she pushed it off, trying to cool her overheated body.

"You all right, duck?" Rushelle leaned in from the hallway.

She had a sparkly toiletries bag in one hand, and a toothbrush sticking out one side of her mouth.

"Yeah, fine. Just a bad dream." Everly gave Rushelle a reassuring smile, thankful for her presence.

After the lures and open conflict with the Darkfreys, Lian had wanted Everly, Harper, and Neri to move into Howell House, at least for a while. But Everly couldn't handle the idea of even more time spent around Rylan.

It was hard enough seeing him at all but living under the same roof would be too much.

She reassured Lian that the three of them would be fine. They were right around the corner, and Everly could deal with almost anything except the Bane.

Still, Rushelle had volunteered to stay over for a while. Just in case. For Lian's peace of mine. Everly was happy with that, even if it meant Rushelle got her old bedroom and she continued sleeping on the couch in the living room. To be honest, she wasn't sure she was ready to move back into her old bedroom anyway. It had never been a happy place.

"Thanks for staying with us," Everly told Rushelle, as she had every day for the last couple of weeks.

Rushelle waved it off, her sunshine-yellow, boa-hemmed nightgown puffing around her fingers.

"It's been no trouble. I mean, I'm not getting to see as much of my boyfriends, but you loves are worth it." She passed Harper in the hall as she stepped back into the bathroom.

"Did she just use the plural?" Harper blinked groggily.

Everly shrugged, still half asleep herself.

Harper yawned and leaned on the ladder-stairs going to Neri's attic room. She'd still been so tired since using the Bane to empower herself. Everly frowned at her friend, wondering whether beneath the already done makeup, she'd find dark circles under her contact-colored green eyes.

"You okay?" she asked.

"Yeah," Harper said through a second yawn. "Neri had a bit of a rough night again. I'm surprised she didn't wake you too."

"I didn't hear a thing. I must have been out hard." Everly pulled her jacket on over the old T-shirt and leggings she wore as makeshift pajamas.

With the four of them sharing one bathroom, she could wait until later in the morning to get in a shower and get dressed properly. "You want me to cover the pack and ship this morning? If you want to get a bit more sleep in, that's okay."

"You're sweet. But I'm okay. Just poke me with a stick if I nod off."

The two of them headed downstairs and Harper made coffee. Everly checked the plate of meat she'd set out for Zozo the night before, but it hadn't been eaten. She still set out food each night, and some nights it would go.

She couldn't be certain it was the undead cougar that ate it. But she felt good on those mornings, and worried on those when the food was left untouched. Then she and Harper went into the antiques store to get a bit of work done.

It felt strange to Everly, acting as though life was normal, going about such mundane motions as printing invoices and packaging antiques for the mail. She could still feel how her dream of the Everdark left her skin crawling, how the eidolghast filled the dimension to overflowing.

And dread burbled in the pit of her stomach at the thought of a doorway to that hellscape being opened in the middle of Darkfrey Estate.

But time passed, and nothing happened.

Life fell into a holding pattern of daily activities, so normal it was disturbing. Although there had been some huge changes as well.

After getting the most urgent customer service work completed for the day, and Everly got her time in the bathroom, the four of them headed over to Howell House where the differences to daily life were more obvious.

The residence was now packed with Darkfrey defectors. Every spare room was full, and the front yard and nearby field looked like a tent city, with shadyrs living out of cars and makeshift shelters. Harper even donated her campervan to the housing efforts.

Although many of the shadyrs had their own homes around Shroudhaven, it quickly became clear that the Darkfreys weren't going to let the defectors live peacefully after leaving. There had been violent attacks, and more use of the bone lures.

There was safety in numbers, and the number of shadyrs making Howell House their home had grown significantly.

How long can this last?

This couldn't be the long-term solution to the divide between shadyrs. There just wasn't enough space or services for everyone there. Everly was suddenly grateful that it

was only the four of them sharing one bathroom at her place. Lian had her come over to fix the plumbing in the old homestead once already.

Darkfrey Estate still held the balance of power—in the shadyr conflict, and the town as a whole. As long as they were retaliating against those they considered traitors, the temporary living arrangements would remain.

Rushelle waved as she headed to the kitchen to help out with the constant work of making meals for everyone, and Harper and Neri split off to join in with a daily training session. Rylan was running a lot of those himself, so Everly went in the other direction.

He hadn't pushed her again for an answer to how she felt about him after they were interrupted last time. She hoped that meant what she'd told him had sunk in, that he'd examined his own feelings and realized they weren't as real as he thought. Even if that left a churning black hole of despair in Everly's chest, it would be the right thing.

Everly adjusted the tool belt slung around her wide waist, and made her way to where Callan was unloading some timber and metal sheeting from a truck. She'd already helped build one temporary shelter, and they'd just brought in supplies for another. It was something she had the skills for, and she liked being useful, even if the shadyrs often watched her with wide eyes and barely concealed whispers.

The information about her possession by the Coruscare had gotten out.

Jasper was a suspect at first, but the trail of gossip led back to Denny bragging about having a god on their side.

It was clear a lot of the Darkfrey defectors weren't entirely sure about this new alliance, and reliance, on the Howells.

Many questioned the existence of the Coruscare, as though Everly were making it up to seek attention, and others still considered Tammy to be a murderer. They acted as though it were beneath them to be cowering together there with these misfits.

And yet, there they were.

Rylan, Callan, and Jasper helped bridge the gap. They had all been well-respected in the Darkfrey ranks, and it was clear some of that respect still held.

"I can take those." Everly looked up to where Callan unstrapped some two-by-fours on the truck bed.

The invoice stapled to the top of the timber with a logo for Pimey's Hardware had been discounted to zero.

It seemed as though Lian was pulling favors from family. Everly knew there had been a divide there too, when Lian left the Darkfreys, married a human, and became a Howell. But with the new revelations of the Darkfreys' actions, some of her relatives in the Pimey line were opening back up to Lian and helping out where they could.

That was the last of the building materials, and Callan jumped down beside Everly. His gaze kept shifting over to the porch, where Tammy stood rigidly in front of an

older couple and two children.

Cherry and Jasper brought over a miter saw and rolled out an extension cable. A few shadyrs close to Tammy's age walked by, chatting in low and gossipy voices.

Everly caught the end of a sentence. "... I wouldn't forgive her, she's cursed."

"Hey!" Callan barked. "We don't act like that here. Tammy's done nothing wrong, and if I hear you giving her a hard time again, you'll be answering to me."

Everly's eyes widened. She'd never heard him speak like that before, sounding like a drill sergeant rather than his usual, cheerful self. He was only a couple years older than the teenagers, but they looked like they were ready to drop and give him a hundred. There were some mumbled apologies, and they bumped into each other in a rush to back away.

"Who is Tammy talking to?" Everly asked.

His expression softened immediately into his usual lopsided grin, tickled at the edges by long, feathery hair. "That's her family."

"Oh. Is that ... is she okay?" Everly examined the people surrounding Tammy, looking for resemblances.

With her dark-rimmed eyes and short hair, it was hard to pick, but one of the kids could have been her brother. He was the first one to step forward and wrap Tammy in a hug. Her eyes went wide, and she almost impossibly became more rigid, straighter and stiffer than the two-by-fours Everly had just unloaded.

When her mother and father joined the embrace, Tammy's face scrunched in on itself. She flickered—there, then not there—but she didn't vanish entirely. Her blackened hands rose ever so slowly up around her parents, and then pulled them in tight.

Callan tilted his head, his eyes glossy. "Yeah, I think she's going to be okay."

Cherry plugged in the saw and stood up to join them. His gaze turned down the long, tree-lined driveway, as Everly had seen him do many times since Darkfrey shadyrs started showing up. There were no new arrivals.

It was obvious what he was looking for, but Everly didn't know how to comfort him without drawing attention to the fact that his parents hadn't joined them, hadn't offered him any apologies, or asked his forgiveness for casting him out.

Jasper watched Cherry for a long moment, as though taking the opportunity to do so while Cherry was distracted. Everly doubted the two were back together, but Jasper often hovered close by Cherry's side.

"Tammy's parents only showed up this morning," Callan addressed Everly, but she figured it wasn't really meant for her. "Some shadyrs are needing a bit longer to change their thinking."

"I thought I saw the brace we met at Gorhanmere on the way in. I didn't know they were here," Everly said.

Callan brightened. "Yeah, Lucas's team. Him, Molly, Benson, and Parker. They arrived a few days back. Lian's old friend, Bob, came with them too. And Jasper's ... parents ..."

The four of them stood in an awkward silence until Jasper cleared his throat. "They're over there."

He pointed along a lane formed between tents to a very clean-cut couple with medium brown skin and silky black hair. The man had a strong Roman nose matching Jasper's.

Cherry sighed and stuffed his hands into his pockets.

Jasper's gaze flickered to him, then he lifted his chin. "You know, it took them that long, and they don't even ... well, I haven't come out to them yet."

His bronze skin warmed across his cheek bones, and he cleared his throat again. "Right then. I think I'd best go and do so."

Cherry's jaw hung open as Jasper marched away. Everly looked from one of them to the other with wide eyes.

Cherry closed his mouth and he flipped his hair nonchalantly. "He can be *such* a weirdo."

As they'd been chatting, Annabeth had moved closer to them, hovering at the edges of their group. When Jasper left, she shuffled into his space, offering a bashful smile as greeting.

"Can I help out?"

Callan turned from checking on Tammy again to greet her. "You're not joining in the training?"

Rylan had taken the group of younger shadyrs, including Neri and Harper, over into the field beside the lane.

"Mm, I'm probably getting a bit rusty, but to be honest I was always more into the academic side of things than active brace duties." Annabeth turned deerlike eyes onto Everly.

"What are they doing down there?" Everly asked, trying to see through the patchy birch trunks.

Callan smirked. "We found a dead vasmire out in the field this morning. Not sure who took it out. We haven't really got any formal patrol rosters and reporting set up yet. Still, we figured we could use the corpse for some of the younger shadyrs to practice their shifting before we clean it up."

Everly made a face. She could still so vividly recall the exact pungent scent of rotting vasmire that filled the Boderleth residence not long ago. "Ew, but I get it."

In the field, Rylan had Neri separated from the others and was crouched in front of her. He seemed to be giving her some kind of pep talk, but his body language came

across as gentle and non-threatening.

Not at all the task master Everly might have expected. Neri was a special case. She was having a hard enough time adjusting to being human. Finding out her body could become all sorts of different shapes and sizes was overwhelming. Everly's chest tightened, and her cheeks warmed as she watched Rylan in his crouched pose, the soft smile on his lips, and head moving in slow, understanding nods.

It had been easy to tell herself he'd changed, that she didn't know him anymore, that he grew up as a soldier under the Darkfrey's influence, and that any of her old feelings made no sense.

But he had taken that same posture, made those same gestures, back when they were kids, to comfort her. It had been one of those times that she first truly realized her feelings for him were more than just friendship.

It didn't matter though. Even if he was still the person she used to love, and still did, that only meant she was less willing to risk the Coruscare hurting him again.

Rylan stood back up, and Harper and Neri split off from the group, wandering along the lane. Everly waved to catch their attention, and they headed her way.

"Do you need to do any special training?" Annabeth asked, wide eyes glued to Everly.

"Oh, not really? There isn't exactly a guidebook for me to follow. I only have dark, whispering urges and disturbing dreams to go by."

Annabeth's eyes managed to widen even rounder. "I saw you at Rook's Hotel that night. It was so amazing. I should have guessed then what it was. Not that it had even seemed a possibility at the time ... I mean, the *Coruscare!* I can't believe I'm standing in front of it, right now."

Her words stumbled rapidly, and she put a hand over her mouth. "I'm sorry, I'm so fangirling."

A chill of anxiety ran down to Everly's fingertips, leaving them numb. There it was again, the Coruscare. For the last couple weeks, that had been the only interest anyone had shown in her. Fair enough, it was something straight out of shadyr mythology. They would be interested. But for those who believed, the reverence that came with the interest made Everly deeply uncomfortable.

"It's okay, just don't think of it as some kind of benevolent deity, all right? The things I've seen from its memories of the Everdark are not—"

"You share its *MEMORIES*?" Annabeth practically yelled. "Oh my ghast. That's huge. HUGE! We have so little in the way of historical records from before the crossover."

Harper and Neri reached them. Neri's skin was silvery, and she pouted over sharp vampire teeth.

"Historical records?" Harper asked.

"Pre-crossover shadyrs didn't even have a written language. A few symbols used for

their magic, but records only really start once they integrated with human culture. By that point, the oral history was fragmented, and often contradictory. Studying shadyr history can be like reading different versions of the Bible from every culture and trying to pick out the facts." Annabeth's eyes glowed.

Everly's stomach lurched. She hadn't really considered how hosting the Coruscare could be important in that way. How the visions and memories she shared with her dragon would be things that shadyrs would want to study.

Which would make her the one to have to break to them exactly how awful the Coruscare had been to their kind. Enslaving their whole race, using them to hunt for its food, or even sacrificing themselves to its never ending hunger.

Everly's chest ached, and she pressed a thumb between her collarbones and took a deep breath. And behind the strain in her lungs, she felt the stirring thoughts of her dragon. It queried why she let this bother her, why she let anything bother her? She could consume, enslave, destroy as she pleased, but she chooses pain.

Take what we want. Take everything. We can.

Annabeth didn't seem to notice how the blood had rushed away from Everly's face. "Do you think we could go over what you know about the Coruscare sometime? Would you mind being recorded? I'd want to keep thorough records of the interview. I wouldn't want to miss *anything*."

"Anna?" Rylan had stepped up behind their group.

His brow was furrowed as his gaze slipped away from Everly toward the redhead. "Can you come and help me out with the training?"

Annabeth paused with her mouth open. "Oh, um, sure."

She cast one more eager glance at Everly before jogging over to join Rylan.

As the two of them walked away together, Everly settled herself with a few more deep breaths. There wasn't much distance between their shoulders, and Everly's rising anxiety distilled into a cool lump in her gut. Maybe Rylan's feelings for Annabeth had changed recently.

It'd be for the best.

Callan watched them leave as well, his small frown softened by a half-smile. "Rylan told me she was into shadyr history, but she is *really* into shadyr history."

Harper chuckled and nudged Everly with her hip. "Aw, and here I thought I was your biggest fan."

"I don't think it's exactly me that she's a fan of." A tremble came out with the words before Everly could hold it in.

Harper tilted her head, assessing Everly. She reached out and tucked a bit of white hair behind her ear. "They're the fools if they can't see the truth though. You may have a god inside you, but you're the woman that *controls* that god."

Everly snorted a laugh. "Well, when you put it that way."

She had felt in control lately. Able to use the Coruscare's powers how she wanted them to be used. No souls consumed. No lives taken. But the urges, the sheer, overwhelming energy inside her burned in a way that made her worry it wasn't sustainable. And somehow the soul-eater felt like it was growing stronger each day, and she didn't know why.

She might be in charge now, but for how long?

She may as well have a leash on lightning.

8

There hadn't been many dinners shared together at the Boderleth house. Certainly not any happy ones.

Even on normal days that weren't interrupted by some hellish new catastrophe, Everly and Harper either snacked on the go while working in the antiques store or had dinner over at the Howells'. Although the kitchen was technically functional, the appliances might as well be in the antiques store themselves.

Sitting with Harper, Neri, and Rushelle around the retro laminate and chrome table brought up a feeling Everly couldn't quite pinpoint. A warmth, but also a deep sadness.

Had her family ever eaten dinner at this table together, before her father died? She couldn't remember. It certainly never happened afterward.

But now, at this time, with these people, it was right. It felt—Everly's eyes washed over with tears—it felt like *home*.

Rushelle had brought some pasta casserole over from the Howells' and Everly managed to get the old oven going well enough to reheat it. Harper insisted on eating together and set the table with mismatched plates and cutlery. Neri picked some miniature roses and dandelions from the front yard to go in an old milk bottle in the center of the table.

Everly scraped up her last forkful and smiled. "We should do this more often. Maybe I could cook something tomorrow?"

Harper raised her eyebrows. "You're a woman of many talents, but cooking isn't one of them. I'm sorry. Unless we all want to eat instant noodles."

"*Instant noodles*?" Neri said with an awe that suggested they were discussing some kind of pasta-manifesting magic.

"I can cook some things," Everly said defensively, knowing entirely well that even when they'd had the time and a full kitchen back at their apartment, Harper had prepared most of the meals.

Healthy, veggie-filled dishes from family recipes she learned cooking with her mom. Everly only ever learned 'fend for yourself' from her mother.

"Okay, fine, I can follow directions on a packet. But that counts."

"I love instant noodles. With a deep, romantic, love," Rushelle said with a grin.

Harper sighed dramatically, scraping up her last mouthful. "I mean ... me too. Who doesn't?"

A knock came from the back door, in a familiar pattern that Everly hadn't heard since she was a kid and Rylan would show up and rescue her from this house.

Everly put her cutlery down on her empty plate. "I'll get it."

She couldn't be sure it was him, but a million scenarios and worries flashed through her head as she went to answer. She opened the door to Rylan wearing a gray hoodie and holding a Pimey's Diner takeaway cake box. His shadyr eyes glittered under the dim light of the candle-shaped fixtures in the hallway.

"Hey," he said.

"Um, hi. You need something?"

"I grabbed this on the way back from town. Thought you might like to share with me." He held up the box, opening the lid a crack.

The scent hit Everly before she saw inside. A toasty caramel and cocoa aroma, rich and buttery, that shot her straight back into her childhood.

"Is that ... Dutch funny cake?"

One of Pimey's Diner's signature desserts, it wasn't really a cake. It was more like a sponge cake and a pie had a baby, with a thick, fudgy layer of chocolate thrown in. It used to be Everly's favorite.

Did he remember?

His satisfied smirk said he did.

Behind Everly, Harper, Neri, and Rushelle came out into the hall to check on her, since they still worried about unwanted visitors.

"We were just finishing dinner. Is there enough for everyone?" Everly asked.

"Oh, I am stuffed," Harper cut in. "Couldn't fit in another thing. We're going to head upstairs and work on Neri's reading."

"She's teaching me fairy tales and how terrible they are," Neri said through a wide grin.

Harper pushed Neri from behind, driving her up the stairs. Neri turned puppy dog eyes back at Rylan as the delicious fragrances hit her, but Harper kept maneuvering her away.

"Me too." Rushelle yawned dramatically and finger waved as she followed them. "Oh boy, just *really* sleepy tonight."

Everly gave them all a deadpan glare before turning back to Rylan.

She sighed. "Come in."

On the way down the hall, Everly's ears tweaked to a scraping sound below her. *Ugh, rats in the basement again.*

"I didn't get any ice cream, so it won't be the complete experience, sorry."

Everly's heart raced.

Exactly what experience is he expecting from this? It could be a peace offering, a way for him to say he wanted to be just friends again and he'd fallen head over heels for Annabeth, because why wouldn't he?

Maybe the funny cake was a way to soften the blow when he told Everly he'd thought about it, and yeah, he could see now that it was the soul enslavement all along. She should tell him to leave, make some excuse now so she didn't have to hear those things. Even if they were good. They would be *good*.

Enough. Everly pressed a palm against her temple to calm her overthinking. Whatever he had to say, he deserved to say it.

Rylan took a seat at the table as she made her way to the freezer.

"Harper was introducing Neri to ice cream yesterday so—" Everly opened the lid to find the tub scraped clean. "Yep, all gone."

"Who puts an empty container back in the freezer?"

"Neri's still learning," Everly said defensively, keeping secret that it was one of Harper's few flaws.

Turning back to see Rylan sitting at her table forced the flutter of butterflies up her throat. The others had already cleared away after dinner, so she couldn't use that as a way to keep busy and delay sitting down with him.

Everly set out some plates, spoons, and cake knife—which she was a little surprised to find considering she had precisely zero memories of cake existing in that house—and lowered herself into her chair with a withheld sigh.

"Sorry about Annabeth the other day." Rylan extracted an entire pie from the box and gestured to the size of slice he should cut, waiting for Everly's approval.

Everly indicated bigger, bigger, enough. "About what?"

"She looked like she was being a bit full on with you. I know she can be a bit ... zealous when it comes to her passion for shadyr history." He served her piece then cut one for himself the same size.

"Is that why you called her away?"

Rylan smirked and shrugged.

He did it for her? Everly held her breath in case she exhaled butterflies. Then she couldn't wait any longer and ate a spoonful of the cake-pie hybrid. A small groan of pure nostalgic pleasure escaped her throat.

Rylan chuckled and took a bite of his.

Her cheeks flushed with heat.

Too busy worrying about imaginary butterflies then I go and make sexy food sounds.

Rylan said, "You remember we used to get slices after school, then go and sit by

the river? You would fight off the ducks so they didn't steal any."

"It would have been bad for them," Everly pointed out. "Also, I did want it all for myself. It's sooo good. I haven't had funny cake since ... around then."

Rylan's smile dimmed and he stabbed at his slice with the tip of the spoon. "I'm really sorry. For pushing you away after Dad died. I don't think I ever properly apologized for that. I thought I was doing the right thing, but I was wrong, and it was cruel."

For a long moment, Everly could only stare at him. It was long enough that Rylan stopped looking at his plate and turned his gaze up, seeking a response from her.

"If you can't forgive me for that, I'd understand," he said.

Everly blinked, snapping herself out of her head. "Oh, no, of course I can. I mean, if you can forgive the whole soul bondage thing in return, I think we're good."

Rylan chuckled. "Pfft, no problem. What's a little bondage between friends?"

Everly choked on a bite of funny cake.

"You all right there, Boderleth?"

He used to call her that when they hung around his other friends, as though going by her last name made her seem more like one of the guys. He'd always been popular, but he had been her only real friend.

She used to wonder why he made time for her, the scrappy kid from the wrecked home. What did he see in her? She knew why now. It had never been about *her*, but the thing inside her. She couldn't quite reconcile whether that was better than her other theory—that he'd just felt sorry for her.

"Yeah, I'm okay." Her voice sounded sad, even to her own ears. "Thank you, for this."

She finished her last bite and stood up, taking the plates to the sink. She hoped this would indicate that it was time for Rylan to leave. She didn't really want him to go, but it was for the best.

Rylan followed her, wandering slowly across the kitchen, hands in his pockets. "Look, I honestly can't say what feelings are my own, or how to make sense of the knowledge that there was something else affecting my behavior for so long. But ..."

He stepped ever closer, moving in a straight line toward her in a way that suggested he wouldn't stop. "I do know that I missed you. When I left for the Darkfreys, then when you left town, I missed you every moment."

He stopped just inches away. "Even now, when you're standing right in front of me, I *miss* you, like you're still too far away."

Everly wished he'd take another step and close that gap. All other worries and doubts were smothered by that same feeling—missing him. He was close enough that a deep breath could bring their chests together, but he might as well be another dimension away for how much she craved him. It would be so easy to close that gap, to have what she always wanted.

Everly's lips opened, her body drawn forward.

And the lights went out.

"Every. Damn. Time," Rylan growled.

Everly could no longer see him, but he was still so close his words gusted over her cheek. "Can't talk to you for five minutes without something coming up."

"We live a hectic and catastrophe-filled life," Everly sighed. "Can you see? There's a flashlight in the drawer near the fridge."

Her night-blindness hadn't improved any with her increase in Coruscare powers. She could feel her way over there but figured Rylan could find his way more easily.

She heard a few steps and some rummaging, then a beam of light flashed on.

Everly glanced out the kitchen window.

That I saw Rylan almost die through.

She shuddered. "There are still lights on down the street. I think it's just us. I'll go and check the fuse box."

"Where is it?" Rylan handed her the flashlight.

"The basement. I thought I heard some rats chewing down there before, maybe they tripped something." She bit her lip, trying not to remember the last time a fuse box put the lights out, at the hotel at Gorhanmere. She hated rats, but hoped it wasn't anything more.

"Rats?" Rylan frowned. "You want me to go?"

Everly shivered, but stepped out into the hall, keeping the flashlight beam steady in front of her. "I'll be okay. I think after everything that's happened recently, I should be able to face some rats. Also, how much do you know about old fuse boxes?"

Rylan followed on her heels. "If something is flicked down, flick it up?"

"Hopefully that will do it, but with how old and dodgy the wiring in this house is, I better check it out too."

As they headed to the basement door, Rushelle, Neri, and Harper appeared on the stairs from above. Everly cast her flashlight over to check on them.

Harper held her sword in one hand and used her phone as a light in her other. "What's going on? Blackout?"

"Yeah, something's tripped. Going downstairs now to try and get the power back on," Everly said, opening the door to the basement.

Harper squealed. "Oh no, this feels like that moment in a horror movie when the killer is hiding under the stairs."

"I'm going with her," Rylan said.

"Ugh, like she needs your protection. She can kick one thousand more asses than you."

"I didn't mean ..." Rylan exhaled roughly, then swore under his breath. "Rush, you feel that?"

Everly turned her light back toward them.

Rushelle's blond curls had been let down for the night and they jiggled as she shook her head. "Oh dear. Yup, I feel the tingle. Something incoming."

"Something?" Everly asked, but she knew they meant eidolghast. "Something that likes to have the lights out?"

Harper's mouth opened, then slammed into a pout. "Another auerdax? I really don't like them. Last time was so much cardio."

Rushelle pulled her phone from her pocket and was speaking to Lian within seconds.

Everly turned to Rylan. He had even more reason to hate that kind of eidolghast. His jaw was set tight, and he pushed passed Everly and down the basement steps. He quickly moved out of the range of her flashlight.

She hurried after him. He might not need the light to see, but if an auerdax was nearby, she didn't want to leave him in complete darkness, where the creature was strongest.

"Ghast dammit. There's a lure down here. The window looks like it's been forced," he said.

He struck out at the bone effigy, snapping it apart and crushing it beneath his boots.

The sound sent a ripple of moving shadows racing across the floor toward the stairs where Everly stood.

Rats. She held her breath, frozen in place, as the critters vanished silently into the clutter under the steps.

Once they were gone, she closed her eyes.

It's okay. It's fine. They're normal, harmless, clever little mammals. They can't hurt you anymore.

When she opened her eyes again, Rylan was right in front of her. "You're okay."

There was no question in his tone. She exhaled through an O-shaped mouth. "I'm okay."

The side of Rylan's lips pulled upward.

Then the house shook like it was hit with a wrecking ball. A thunderous smash echoed down to them, followed by screams.

9

Rylan became a ghost.

His skin and even the clothes he wore turned translucent with a soft, eerie glow. The urge to reach out and touch him, to see if her hand would go right through him, almost overwhelmed Everly, but the crashing upstairs continued.

Rylan's shift confirmed what they were facing. An auerdax, that would be at full strength and solidity in the darkness upstairs. One of the toughest eidolghasts to kill, as it phased in and out of reality depending on the brightness of light around it.

But the last time Everly faced one, she was different. She was too scared then to use the Coruscare's light because she couldn't control it enough to keep it from also consuming her friends. She didn't have that problem anymore.

She sprinted up the stairs, bringing the Coruscare's glow out around her along the way. It lifted her so that by the time she reached the top, her feet didn't land on the steps.

Instead, she floated out into the hall.

"It's coming through. It's smashed in the window, and half the wall!" Harper yelled from near the kitchen doorway.

"Come over here with me," Everly called to her. "I'll keep the lights bright until Lian gets here with her sword."

Rushelle and Neri also appeared to be ghosts now. Neri sat at the back door, with two phones on the floor in front of her creating a small pool of light, staring through her hands in horror. Everly rolled the flashlight to her to add to her shield of illumination.

The Coruscare's glow brightened the hallway more than the dull electric lights would have, but it didn't hurt to have a backup.

Harper dashed away from the kitchen doorway as a chair flew out and smashed against the side of the stairs. The auerdax's twisted, whiplike arm lashed out into the space she'd been standing.

She ran to join the others, and they crowded together in the orb of Everly's brightness. With everyone so close, she kept the scintillating tendrils tucked safely away entirely, just in case.

Beside her, Rylan sneered at the creature with pure hatred.

The auerdax reached through the doorway again, and then pushed the rest of its bulk out, cracking the doorframe as it went. Everly only got a glimpse of the bone-and-slime asymmetrical torso before her light made it fade away.

She hated knowing that it was still *there*, just incorporeal.

"I think I saw something. Like with that flying eidolghast," Harper said in a rush. "A glowing spot."

"A weak spot?" Rylan asked.

Harper nodded confidently. She pointed her blade, currently set rigid, to where the creature was last visible. "I think it's this sword. I think it makes them visible to me. Ev, would you dim the lights, just a bit?"

"Are you sure? We can wait. Lian won't be long."

Harper's bright-green eyes gleamed, reflecting Everly's white glow. "The bone lure is busted. What if that thing decides we're not interesting anymore and wanders over to a neighbor's place? Do we want that on us? We can't even see where it is right now. I think we can take it out. I think we should."

Everly held her gaze then nodded. Concentrating, she closed away the Coruscare's power, the aura around her dimming. Her sock-clad toes brushed the old carpet as she lowered to the floor.

In the half-light, the auerdax materialized before them, much closer than before. No face, no head, just a misshapen torso on clumpy legs, formed from inhuman bones and black ichor.

"Rush? Help me hold it back," Rylan called.

Rushelle rolled up her sleeves and vaulted over the banister. "On it."

The auerdax flung out one of its long, elastic arms, aiming straight for Everly. Rylan snatched it from the air, pinning it between him and the hallway wall.

It was clearly solid enough not to pass through objects with this much light, and the shadyrs seemed to be affected similarly by the illumination level.

From the skulls floating within its chest, it loosed a scream like the keening of eagles.

Soul eater. Star-toothed abomination! It squealed in a language only Everly could understand. Deep within her, she could feel the mocking disdain of the Coruscare in return. And a twinge of hunger.

Harper stood beside her, a narrow glare fixed on the ghast. "It's the shoulder joints! Both of them."

"Righteo!" Rushelle hollered and was down the hallway in three leaping steps.

She grappled the second whip-arm and lifted off her feet as she held tight.

"Keep it still for a few seconds!" Harper raised her sword and moved in.

The massive eidolghast swayed its body, and swung the arm Rylan clung to, smashing him from the wall to the banister and back to the wall again. In his ghostly

form, he passed slightly through, but the way he grunted suggested it didn't cushion the blows entirely. He growled and readjusted his hold.

Harper dodged around him and swung. The sword lodged into the shoulder of the limb Rushelle held, sliding deep between two skulls into the eerie slime. A sickening pop and crackle sounded as the arm detached, and a stream of shadows poured from the wound.

The amputated arm writhed like a headless snake, knocking Harper onto her back and Rushelle into the corner. The detached limb didn't reform and grow back the way injuries to the previous auerdax they had faced did.

As clotted darkness tumbled from the ghast's shoulder, it keened again and launched itself at Everly, dragging Rylan with it.

On instinct, Everly loosed a glittering tendril at the beast, slashing it toward the second shoulder joint. But as it neared, the auerdax faded away, and the Coruscare's powers cut uselessly through the air.

"Harper said both arms!" she yelled.

With a feral snarl, Rylan's shadyr change swirled around him as he pulled from the eidolghast essences within Everly and added the strength of werewolf form into his ghostly visage.

He let go of the end of the creature's limb and pounced onto the monster's back. He thrust sharp claws deep into its shoulder, furred muscles straining as he wrenched.

Slime oozed and coalesced around his hands, trying to reform as the tear grew larger, until the last few strands snapped.

Like ghosts fleeing hell, shadows burst free, rushing from the injury. Rylan leaped back as the auerdax fell. Skulls and bones from all sorts of creatures tumbled loose in a pile.

The back door burst open, and Lian stepped through, hand on the hilt of her sword. She took in the situation before her. "I thought you needed my help?"

Callan peered past her shoulder. "It's already over? What the Everdark?"

Rylan straightened up over the crumbling ghast. "Just 'cause you took days to deal with the last one."

"We had the help of Harper's weak spot vision this time around," Everly explained.

"Unfair advantage!" Callan pointed an accusatory finger at Rylan.

"This isn't a competition," Lian muttered.

"Yes it is," Rylan and Callan said simultaneously.

The sound of crunching debris came from the kitchen, and Lucas's brace stepped through. Lucas sighed at the ghast's body. "Damn. Thought we'd get a second shot at adding an auerdax to our kill score too."

"Thanks for bringing the cavalry." Rushelle climbed to her feet and shifted back

to normal. "It's still appreciated."

"Probably worth it too," Lucas said, thumb-pointing over his shoulder. "We scared off a bunch of Darkfreys that were hanging around, no doubt waiting to pick off any survivors."

"Yeah, this wasn't a random attack. There was a lure. Down in the basement." Rylan forced his change back to human as well.

Harper picked up her sword and winced as she stretched out her arm. She bent to look past the brace of shadyrs.

"The kitchen is trashed. Aw, come on! I just repainted!"

Everly took her flashlight from Neri. Shining it around the hallway, she saw a significant amount of damage in there, too. Several balusters on the stairs were cracked.

The wall where Rylan had hit was also pushed in, and the light fitting dangled freely. Plaster crumbled around the ruined doorframe. There wasn't much kitchen remaining. Despite Harper's Bane energy-fueled paint job, it probably was due to be ripped out and renovated, but it hurt Everly to see it like this just after the happy moments from earlier that night.

The house had been a trash heap when she first came back to town, but at least the bones of it were still good. As Everly surveyed the damage now, her heart sank. Half the front of the house had been smashed in as the auerdax barreled through, drawn in by the lure. It would need a complete rebuild. With that much damage, she wasn't even sure if the second story over the kitchen—Harper's bedroom—was safe.

"I don't think you can stay here anymore," Rylan said near her ear. "I'm sorry."

"I can fix this," Everly said. "I've got some tarps we can put up temporarily and—"

"It's not safe," Lian cut in. "You were targeted, and I know you're strong, all of you, but that's not always enough. That's why you need others at your back."

Everly looked away and into the kitchen again, finding her eyes suddenly stinging and trying to hide them. "Is there even any room still?"

"We'll make room for you one way or another." Lian chucked her under the chin. "It's no problem at all. Go and grab a few things and we'll take you back with us now."

Lian turned and spoke quietly to Lucas for a moment, who then left with his brace.

Neri, still ghostly, skittered over to Harper. "We have to go?"

Harper tilted her head. "Yeah, but we'll still be together."

Everly closed her eyes to the devastation in the kitchen.

We have to go, but we'll still be together. Leaving felt like saying goodbye to that sense of home that had so recently awoken within her. But the people who made it home were going with her.

And you'll be closer to Rylan.

The thought came unbidden, and she gave it an internal groan. It was what she'd

been avoiding for weeks now. She couldn't go down that path. Could she? He did so much for her, considering what she needed, what she wanted, and it was just *him* now. Not the Coruscare's influence. Maybe she could have what she wanted.

Everly opened her eyes and stared at the remains of the funny cake, smashed on the linoleum. She tried not to see it as an omen.

She forced a smile. "Okay. Let's grab what we need for the night. We can come back for more later."

Rylan, Lian, and Callan remained on guard downstairs in case of any fresh attacks, while Everly, Harper, Neri, and Rushelle went to pack bags.

Rushelle had been living out of hers while staying with them, and Everly realized that she'd never really moved beyond living out of her duffel bag either, never thought about setting up more than a sleeping bag on the couch.

She sighed as she collected the few belongings that weren't in her bag already and stuffed them away. The lights were still out, so she spotlighted the flashlight around the room, trying to see anything she'd missed.

"You need a hand?" Rylan moved through the doorway, taking slow steps in, edging closer.

"Almost done." Everly noticed her toiletries case on the coffee table and packed it away. Once she zipped up the bag, Rylan was beside her. She stared up at him, her mouth suddenly dry. "My ... my tool bag is already at your place. So this is it."

There was a scrape across one of his cheekbones from the fight, and Everly reached up, her fingertips hovering above it. "Are you okay?"

He shrugged. "Ribcage got a bit hammered, but I'll survive."

She hated seeing him hurt, acting as though bruised ribs were normal. She wanted him to shift into vampire form so he could heal, but it felt weird to suggest something Rylan would no doubt have done, if he wanted to.

The gray hoodie he wore was a bit too small for him and hugged tightly around his shoulders and biceps. Everly wondered if he'd borrowed it off someone, whether he'd even had time since waking up to sort out the basics of life like his own wardrobe. She wondered what he had left behind at Darkfrey Estate.

She wondered what his lips felt like, when they weren't deathly cold or drenched in seawater.

As close as he was, he took another step closer, and stared down at her with an intensity that left her breathless. "I know you dreamed of me, when we were apart, but did you ever think of me?"

All the time. Everly nodded in a way that was more a tremble.

"I used to think about you, too. When you left town, I used to lie in bed every night and wonder what you were doing with your life, how far you'd gone, whether

you were thinking about me, or if you'd fallen in love with someone."

She'd tried. She had a few relationships in her time away from Shroudhaven. Tried to move on from her feelings for Rylan and find someone else to love. But they never worked out. Her heart was locked in a cage to which only Rylan had the key.

"I thought of you the same way. But we don't know if that was really us."

"I'm completely free now." He put his hands on her rounded shoulders, and she lifted her chin. "And completely in love with *you*."

Their lips were a breath away from each other, and it was Everly who closed the gap. She pushed up on her tiptoes and grabbed the front of his hoodie to pull him down and her whole body shivered in a suppressed sob of emotion as her flesh met Rylan's.

He gasped as he opened his mouth to hers. Her soft body pressed against his firm chest, and he held her with an insatiable strength.

He was warm, and real, and himself, and he *wanted her*. She could feel it through the heated trails his fingertips left on her cheeks, neck, back.

There was nothing else but him. Her world finally felt right, whole, in a way she'd dreamed of her entire life.

Why couldn't she have this? Why shouldn't she? She could no longer think of any excuses. There was no Coruscare, or Everdark, no monsters, or dark plots. No overthinking. No panic. Just the fiery flush of love and desire so long yearned for.

"You need any more light in there, love? I've found another flash—whoops!" Rushelle stepped into the room then pirouetted around on the spot. "Sorry!"

"Every. Ghast. Damned. Time." Rylan breathed, taking a step backward.

His gaze remained locked on Everly's lips, hungry.

Harper and Neri appeared as well. "We're all done. For tonight anyway. I'll do a second round on makeup and camera gear tomorrow. What's going on?"

"Nothing. We're all done too." Everly gave them a thin-lipped smile.

Her heart still hammered in her chest, as though it wanted to burst free and join Rylan's. She hefted her bag onto one shoulder.

"Okay, let's go."

They loaded into Lian's SUV for the short drive back to Howell House. To avoid staring at Rylan and doing nothing but relive that kiss in her head and question the implications, Everly focused on the luggage on her lap along the way.

So weird that I've lived from this bag for weeks now.

She still had some belongings in storage back at their previous apartment. Some clothes, furniture, a few pairs of fancy shoes she'd only ever worn once or twice. Harper had left a lot more behind. This move had been meant to be temporary.

When they hadn't gone back in time, Everly lost her superintendent job.

Harper had her income from views and sponsors and had offered to cover rent

while they worked things out. Luckily, the online sales of antiques had been going so well that Everly had managed her living expenses in Shroudhaven and kept up on the rent of their previous apartment too.

And part of her had always believed they would be going back there, some day. Until Shroudhaven started to feel like home.

Until Rylan had kissed her. Not in her dream. Not when she was dying. He'd kissed her in her mundane living room with a mouth that tasted like dreams coming true.

Maybe it was time to make a decision and settle somewhere permanently. With the Boderleth residence in ruins and still so much going on, it was a hard call to make. She wanted to be here, with all her new friends, and with Rylan, but she didn't know if it was the right choice.

Could she dare make this place her home?

10

When Tammy's family showed up at Howell House, she had so many designs on how she would ignore them, disown them, rage against them in revenge for how they had treated her.

They abandoned me, didn't defend me when the Darkfrey's kicked me out.

She'd considered all the cruel things she could do in return, like tell Lian to turn them away.

Instead, she gave them her room.

Sucks for them, two adults and two kids sharing that closet space. It wasn't really the vengeance she'd once dreamed of, but she found that maybe she didn't really have those dreams anymore.

Tammy folded her futon-style bedding in the living room and stacked it beside Rylan's, Rushelle's, Callan's, and Cherry's.

Cherry let Jasper and his family take his room, and last night, Rylan had given his to Everly, Harper, and Neri. Rushelle had her own place but was happy to join the living room squad for now.

It wasn't too bad sleeping there. The close proximity of the beds reminded Tammy of the dorms at Darkfrey Estate. And it still seemed better than camping out in the front yard. Sure, she'd be surrounded by a lot of shadyrs, but sleeping outside at night in Shroudhaven just didn't sit right with Tammy. There were some brave souls out there.

They had filled the house to bursting before they started telling the defectors they'd have to work something out in the surrounding yard. There had been a few spare rooms in the beginning, which they gave priority to for the underaged orphans, of which there were too many.

That was when Callan moved to the living room. Annabeth got a room as the first comer, but now shared it with two others. Even Lian shared her bedroom to help fit more in.

Only Denny hadn't given up any space in his RV to anyone else. He claimed he was saving it for when Alexis showed up.

As if that's ever going to happen. The creep was delusional.

Tammy had to admit, she'd been feeling delusional herself lately. Sharing sleeping quarters with Callan had been hard at first. She would be so focused on the sound of his breath or every small movement he made that she couldn't sleep.

She found herself staring across the room at him in the dark, trying to force down and crush the romantic notions his high cheekbones and kind, goofy smile raised in her, but was unable to even turn her eyes away. Which was how she caught him looking back at her, more than a few times.

But it's not the same. He wouldn't be thinking anything romantic. Not about me. He's just checking to see if the kid of the team is okay.

But the delusional part of her would remind her that she was only a couple years younger than him. Would remind her how he carried her when she couldn't stave off her mermaid shift at the lighthouse. Would remind her of how his body felt, pressed against hers.

"Last call for breakfast!" Rushelle poked her head around the doorway, her blond curls stacked in a perfect beehive. "Boy, were folk ravenous today. We're almost cleaned out."

"I'm good." Tammy had snagged some coffee and toast earlier.

She was still cringing internally at the guy who joked that her soul was as dark as her espresso. And the other Darkfrey who criticized her lack of discipline for eating before she cleared away her bedding. They all found some way to be on her case.

"Can you go and check on the ladies upstairs? I know they had a rough night, so I don't want them to miss out."

With a nod, Tammy jogged up the staircase, dodging two kids who sat chatting halfway up. They grew silent and stared at her as she passed, whispering in her wake. She was used to it by now. Everyone had their version of gossip about the cursed girl with Everdark-stained hands. None of them really knew the truth. Tammy felt like she was only learning it now herself.

A frustrated squeal greeted her at the door to Rylan's room.

"I know I put them over here last night." Harper searched the bedside table with her brown eyes.

"What's missing?" Tammy asked.

"My contacts. And bronzer. And straightener. And—EUUGH!" Harper screeched and dumped herself onto a messy pile of blankets on the floor.

A rose-gold suitcase was open beside her. Underwear, eyeshadow pans, belts, and shoes tumbled out around it.

Everly checked the surface of the tallboy and on the floor around them. "I can't find them, sorry."

Neri sat on the bed, tugging at her curly brown hair. "It will be okay if your eyes

aren't green today, won't it?"

Harper huffed and resumed her search.

Tammy hovered awkwardly at the door. "Well, they're almost out of breakfast downstairs, so if you want to eat, you've got to get moving."

"You guys go without me. I haven't finished my makeup or even started on my hair. I'm sorry, I'd normally be all done by now, but I don't have a lot of energy lately." Harper slapped her hands on the lid of her suitcase. "And I can't find anything!"

Everly sighed. "Come on, come with us. You look fine."

"Fine?" Harper shot her a withering stare.

Neri dragged fingers down her own cheek and seemed horrified. "Should I be wearing makeup too?"

"No, you're perfect." Harper bit her lip. "I mean, you don't have to wear any if you don't want to. It's okay to not wear makeup. I just … people expect me to be a certain way."

"Fuck people." Tammy's words burst out vehemently.

Fuck them, and their stares, and their whispers, and their gossip.

She couldn't relate exactly to what Miss Princess was going through, but she got the gist. "Seriously, what's going to happen if you went downstairs as is? Would it really be the end of the world?"

"I can't … I don't know *how* to be anything less than flawless. I don't know how to let people see me … like that. Even now, with you three." She tilted her head, hiding behind sleep-crooked hair.

"I think you're already perfect, too," Neri offered, seeming more confused than ever.

Harper's ears went red. Tammy figured her cheeks probably were too but were already covered in layers of foundation.

I bet she contours.

Tammy never thought she could be friends with someone like Harper. She'd stereotyped her as a diva influencer the moment they met, but over time, she saw through the layers.

"I think you should let people see you, however you are. Let them stare. Let them talk. Let them cringe. That's a them problem, not a you problem."

Harper shook her head. "I wish."

"Tammy's right." Everly had a wicked grin growing on her face. "You know what you need? An anti-makeover."

"A what?"

"You're going to let us help get you ready. Don't worry. We're just going to … enhance the real you," Everly said.

She knelt beside the overflowing suitcase and grabbed a bag of makeup removal wipes. Pulling one free, she approached Harper gently, as though she were a wild animal.

"It's going to be okay. It's not going to hurt at all."

Harper cowered. "Can't I just—"

"Come on. This is going to be great. Trust me." Everly reached out and wiped at Harper's cheeks, clearing away the contoured foundation.

Harper whimpered melodramatically, but remained still, letting Everly remove the makeup.

"Great idea." Tammy picked one of a selection of hairbrushes to join in. "You can do this. You're tough as coffin nails."

She grabbed a nearby water bottle and dripped water across the bristles. Stepping forward, she hesitated. Brushing Harper's hair was a step too intimate, so she handed the job over to Neri.

Neri beamed as she pulled the brush through Harper's long black hair, wetting it down. Then she ruffled the damp locks in her fingers like throwing confetti.

Harper sat statue still, eyes round. "You're seriously not going to leave it like that, are you? To dry *naturally*?"

Horror dripped from the word.

"Yup," Everly said.

She leaned close to Harper's face, examining her eyes. She made a pincer motion with her fingers toward the long lashes.

Harper dodged backward. "Oh no, those are firmly attached."

"What else then? Clothes?" Tammy suggested.

Harper had already dressed into leggings and a strawberry-print shirtdress of flouncy soft fabric that puffed around a glittery belt and hung elegantly off one shoulder, but Everly found one of her old T-shirts for her to change into.

They all turned around for a moment, and when they turned back, Harper was trying to tie the excess fabric to one side.

Everly slapped her hand. "No styling!"

"Just a belt maybe? Or ...? Fine." Harper stifled a breathy grunt, her expression indignant. "Do I at least get to see what I look like? The grand reveal in front of the mirror?"

Everly swished her head left to right. "You look like *you*. And you're amazing. That's all you need to know."

Harper stilled, and her face softened.

With a soft pout, she murmured, "Thank you."

Neri played with a strand of Harper's wavy, damp hair. "You look just like when we first met! Messy and wet and beautiful!"

Harper's bare cheeks turned visibly red that time. She covered them with her hands.

"It is kind of nice, taking it all off. It feels ... lighter. I mean, I do still love my

makeup though. I'm not going to give it up. But it's good to be reminded sometimes that I'm worthy without it."

Tammy nodded, and her voice caught as she said, "You are worthy, no matter what anyone else thinks."

Harper's eyes turned shiny, and she wrapped Tammy in a hug before she had a chance to dodge.

She whispered almost silently, "You are too."

Harper thankfully let go before it got weird. "Come on then, let's go see if there's any food left."

"I'm so hungry," Neri said, and hummed the jingle from a local bakery's radio ad. "I hope there's still bread."

Tammy followed them down the stairs as Everly told them all about the funny cake, and that she wished Neri and Harper could have tried some.

"It looked like you and Rylan were getting along pretty well," Harper said with a leer.

Everly shrugged in a way that was clearly meant to seem casual but came across as awkward and mechanical. "Um, yeah, I guess. Just getting to know each other again really."

Harper pretend-coughed out the words, "Getting to know each other's tonsils."

Tammy's eyes widened. That was a development. She remembered how Everly had consoled her at Gorhanmere, about the two of them being in love with the Howell brothers who they could never have.

But if Everly and Rylan were getting together, then maybe …

No. That didn't mean anything about anything. There was no correlation there. *Ghast dammit, why does my brain have to be so dumb about this? About Callan?*

"Okay, maybe things are going *pretty well*," Everly conceded. "But I'm still not sure it's the right thing. I'm still worried about the Coruscare—what it's done, what it could do. It seems to be under control now, but I have such strange dreams … I don't know."

Harper hesitated on the last step. Tammy could see her take a deep breath before nodding to herself and following Everly and Neri to the kitchen.

Tammy smirked without any humor. The woman had charged a weroth with nothing but garden shears, but being out in public without makeup terrified her? The world was so screwed up.

There were some stares and whispers that followed Harper. Tammy hoped she'd be okay.

She split off from them there, since she was meant to be helping Callan with training some of the younger shadyrs that morning. She wasn't sure exactly what value she could add. Maybe it was his way of making her join in for training he thought she still needed too. Or helping her 'make friends' or build her confidence or some other plot to help her out.

Why does he always have to be so ghast-blightedly KIND?

He really had changed lately in how he treated her. Still kind, still caring, but there was a level of respect now that was so sincere it left her questioning everything. Maybe he really did think she could add value to the training. No ulterior motives. Maybe he just believed in her.

At the front door, Lian and Lucas blocked the way out, having a conversation across the threshold. Molly, the youngest of Lucas's brace, stood at attention behind him, her forehead furrowed and a timidness to the set of her shoulders.

Tammy had been jealous of her up at Gorhanmere when Callan had saved her life, but now she just felt sorry for her. Molly was young to be invested into an active brace.

The Darkfreys push too much onto people. Too many expectations. Too much trauma. Tammy found herself for once feeling happy, rather than ashamed, to have gotten kicked out.

"We didn't catch up to those Darkfreys from the Boderleth place last night," Lucas said.

His tone was direct yet polite, the way shadyrs were expected to address superiors at the estate. Tammy raised her eyebrows. Lucas's team hadn't been with them long but was already happily taking orders from Lian.

"Any more bodies?" Lian said.

"Bodies?" Tammy asked.

Lian turned to greet her, nodding solemnly. "The bloody Darkfreys are leaving ghast bodies around town. They aren't even caring about clean up anymore. Almost like a dare, that they are coming out into the public eye in open warfare. Mordan is getting reckless."

"Not just ghasts," Lucas said. "A few shadyrs have been found dead in their homes too. Not defectors, but others living alone. Maybe the Darkfreys thought they were traitors in one way or another or were going to be."

Lian folded her arms. "I can't believe they've gotten so aggressive. They're only going to lose more shadyrs over actions like that."

"Or out us all entirely to the world," Tammy added.

She knew the small local police force was mostly under Mordan's thumb already, and they had influence over the town press too, to clear what was reported and how. Things were different now with social media though. Tammy wondered if Mordan had any idea how that worked. The odd video here and there would be written off as fake, but if they were getting careless with cleanups, that would change things.

Lian muttered, "He could take us back to the good old days of being hunted as monsters."

"Let's hope it doesn't come to that," Lucas said. "Maybe we need to organize some peace talks or something."

Tammy grunted. "Last time we tried that they ambushed us and tried to kill us."

"There are a lot more of us now though," Lian said. "And there are some other older families with a fair bit of influence. If we could get through to them, find some way to get the dangerous individuals under control, maybe you lot could all go back home again."

Tammy shrugged and pushed through to the porch, leaving the two of them talking.

She didn't have a whole lot of interest or hope in peace talks. Sure, her parents had come around, saying a few pretty words and acting apologetic, but things hadn't really changed.

Her heart burned painfully every moment of every day, because at that shroudpool in Dark Corner she'd had the most traumatic experience of her life, thought she'd killed her best friend, and everybody had abandoned her.

Everybody.

Every one of the Darkfreys, with their talk of honor and family and the good of their kind. Her own parents. Blaise's parents. Everybody turned on her.

And it wasn't my fault!

Tammy gasped air in then let it out slowly in a shudder. It wasn't her fault.

Did she actually believe that now? The words had yelled out into her mind before her self-doubt could stop them, coming from some deep, primal place. Already the guilt and shame were making excuses and arguing the blame, but she held tight to those words.

It wasn't my fault.

"Did you see that bliv girl this morning, the influencer chick? She's really let herself go."

Tammy was halfway across the yard and spun around to give the owner of that voice a mouthful. Two guys stood beside a tent, drinking from Lian's coffee mugs.

Tammy was almost upon them when they continued.

"Still hotter than that black-handed freak though," one of them scoffed.

"What did I tell—" Callan's voice behind her got drowned out by her own.

"You want to see what these hands can do?" Her shroudpool-black finger pointed right into the man's face.

"My hands are stained because I almost got dragged into the Everdark trying to save the life of my best friend. They are a mark of *honor*. What have your hands done lately other than jerk off to your Daddy Darkfrey?"

Tammy could feel Callan behind her, right at her shoulder. His presence gave her strength, but mostly in knowing that he believed she had plenty of her own. And in how he'd helped her start to believe that too.

The grins on the guys' mouths twitched and faded. One looked like he was about to talk back, but instead mumbled an apology and walked away.

"That was amazing! You're amazing. That, wow, you." Callan had his hands out in front of him, gesturing as though trying to get words out. "Seeing you so confident lately, just, just, *wow*."

On impulse, Tammy placed her fingers on his, as though it would shush him before he embarrassed her further.

With a halfhearted eyeroll, she muttered, "You helped. You've helped a lot."

He stared at where her midnight skin touched his peachy flesh, then snatched her hand tight in his, dragging her in close.

And he kissed her.

He's kissing me?

Tammy's eyes were wide, staring into the face so close to hers. She was too stunned, too overwhelmed to even consider kissing back.

He's kissing me, he's kissing me, repeated over and over in her head, growing in volume and speed in time with her heartbeat, as though her brain was trying to make her believe that this impossible moment was real.

That she could feel his soft lips on hers, feel his warmth and smell the pepper and hot chocolate scent of him.

Her cheeks flushed and her eyes filled with tears and her nose stung and her lips only wanted more, but her body had frozen and couldn't move, despite how her heart punched against her ribcage.

Callan's lips peeled slowly off hers, and he seemed almost as surprised as she was.

"I'm sorry, I should have asked first if that was okay."

Tammy couldn't reply to tell him it was okay, it was more than okay, because she flickered and vanished.

11

Rylan stood at attention on the porch while Lian grilled him over the incident the night before.

"And you definitely found a lure?"

He nodded.

"Why were you around at Everly's so late?"

"Just ..." Rylan swallowed and sweat beaded on the back of his neck. "Visiting."

"I want more details about how you took that auerdax down so fast."

Rylan nodded briskly again. He was about to speak when Lian turned shrewd eyes upon him.

"Visiting?"

Does she know? How could she know? Oh no, I bet Rush said something.

Rylan cleared his throat, but when he opened his mouth, he wasn't sure what to say. He had no idea what his mother would think about him and Everly being together. If that's what was happening. Everly hadn't told anybody else about the Coruscare soul bond.

What Lian would think of *that* detail was another mystery. Everything was so complicated, so tenuous.

It didn't really matter what Lian thought of any of it. Rylan was an adult now and would do what he wanted. And she hadn't been in the position to be a mother to him for so many years anyway, since he left her for the Darkfreys. It felt weird to expect her to take that role now.

But somehow, since returning to Howell House and learning about the person Lian was, he found himself wanting her approval. Not only because she was his mother, but because she was a good person who he looked up to.

Rylan titled his head. "Mom—"

"We need a pickup for Tammy!" Callan came sprinting over.

"What happened?" Lian snapped.

Callan rubbed a hand on the back of his head. "She just, umm, got emotional, I guess?"

Lian fixed him with a piercing stare. "Rush has my car out on a grocery run. Hers is only a two-seater, and I'm not keen on anyone going anywhere alone right now."

Everly pushed the screen door open and stepped out onto the porch, chewing a corner of toast.

Her gaze caught Rylan's briefly and she smiled bashfully before looking away. "Want me to go? I can drive Harper's van. I'm sure the couple staying in it won't mind as long as we're back with it soon."

Rylan regarded the large front yard and field. There were a few other cars and vans that had been liberated from the Darkfreys, but they were being lived in too, and had lean-to-style tarps attached that wouldn't be easy to move. Harper's camper at least wasn't pegged down.

"I'll come, too," Rylan and Callan said at the same time.

Lian shook her head and pointed at Rylan. "Annabeth wants you for something, sounded important." Her fingertip swung over to Callan. "And don't you have some training to be running right now?"

"But, I, um ..." Callan winced.

Everly reached back inside and grabbed the keys off a hook in the hall, then sat on the steps to pull her boots on. "It's okay, we'll be fine. I think it's my turn to do a Dark Corner pickup anyway, like a rite of passage."

Lian strode over to where Harper's campervan was parked and flagged down its residents to let them know.

Callan pulled his hair back tight then let it go, mumbling something under his breath before wincing again and heading to where they held the training classes.

Rylan crouched beside Everly. She hadn't braided her hair today and the pale gray waves sparkled around her face. "Annabeth can wait."

She smiled back at him. "I won't be long. We'll talk when I get back, okay? No interruptions."

Rylan stared at the worn and weathered timber of the steps. He still felt the desire to be beside her, keep her safe, but he also knew now how strong she was.

And how if he expressed his yearning to protect her, she'd worry it was coming from the influence of the Coruscare. He chewed his bottom lip.

"Hey." Everly's eyes turned to Lian's back, then checked the house behind them before coming back to Rylan.

She placed the whisper of a kiss on his cheek. "I miss you, too."

Rylan almost pulled her into his arms then and there, but Lian called to Everly, and she jogged away, waving back to him.

Does that mean she feels the same about me? Rylan's heart felt full to overflowing, as though it expanded, pressing against the inside of his ribcage. He already longed for her

return. He wanted to talk with her, no interruptions, just time spent alone, the two of them together. He wanted to feel her lips again, he wanted more. He wanted all of her.

The campervan vanished down the driveway between the long morning shadows of the trees. He'd have to wait. Every moment until Everly got back to him was going to feel like forever. But he'd already waited this long.

The skin on his cheek still tingled as he headed into the house to find Annabeth.

"Oh good, hi, come in." Annabeth barely turned her head from where she sat on one of the mattresses on the floor of her shared room.

She had some very ancient-looking tomes spread out around her, lying open. In her hands she held the notes that Jasper had taken from the Mesmans.

"Are these the books you stole? I thought you meant textbooks or something, not priceless relics." Rylan stepped carefully between them and took a seat on the bed nearby.

Annabeth looked at him properly then, smiling sweetly. "Well, when Jasper told me what was going on, with the recruiting and the Mesmans trying to open a shroudpool, I figured I needed books that actually had info about shadyr magic in them. None of our modern textbooks have that."

"Fair enough. What did you want me for?"

"I've been going over and over these, but I can't work out how Kole is doing it. Getting old shadyr magic to work, that is." She pointed to some of the man's handwriting on the notes.

"This here? This is written in the old shadyr language, or at least a phonetic representation of that spoken-only language, and I think it's literally a spell. Seems to be about activating the lures from what I can translate. And this here too, one for improving vision. I can read it, and I can say it, but nothing happens."

"Because we don't have magic like the pureblood shadyrs anymore." Rylan frowned, still unsure why she needed him.

Annabeth got to her feet and hopscotched through the laid-out tomes to come and sit beside him. "Right. I mean, we have some artifacts that behave magically, but actually casting spells doesn't work. So how are *they* doing it? I was hoping you'd tell me about what you saw that got them trying to kill you in the first place. Maybe it will answer the question."

"I didn't see much, really. Some bones, which they must have been using to make lures. I tied that to the missing bodies that I was looking into, but honestly never had any idea of the scale of what they were doing, or how. Sorry."

"Oh. That's okay. Would have been nice to get a lead though. I'm going nuts trying to work it out." Annabeth sighed in a way that slumped her whole body.

She had only been part of his brace at the Darkfreys since Callan left, but she'd always been diligent and took failure very personally.

"Hey, it's okay. Maybe even with what magic they have, they still can't open a shroudpool anyway. I mean, with their secret out in the open, you'd think they'd get it done as soon as possible. But it's been weeks, and nothing has changed. Maybe there's something they're still missing. You don't have to stress so much."

Her blue eyes glossy, she half-smiled, then looked back at the books.

"Everly's really nice," she said out of nowhere.

"Uh, yeah?"

Annabeth sighed and tucked her red hair behind one ear. "As soon as I saw you two together, it was obvious that she was the one, that it was her who had your heart this whole time."

Oh. Rylan had wondered at times whether Annabeth's feelings for him were more than normal brace companionship, although never thought much of it. He'd been cluelessly lost in his own emotions, but it seemed she had him clocked.

Even now, he was only crossing the threshold of understanding, of being honest with himself, and others.

He laughed wryly and shook his head as he tried to form that understanding into words. "No. I never really gave her my heart. I was always too busy trying to protect it, by pushing her away. I was so scared of losing someone I loved again that I denied how I felt and focused only on protecting her, to protect myself."

How much of that was the Coruscare's influence, he didn't know. Without it, would the desire to love and be loved have won over the desire to protect? Without its influence, would he and Everly even have become friends in the first place? He only knew that he was free now, and everything he thought and felt was his own.

"I think that's changing now though. I think I can finally give her my heart, freely."

Annabeth nodded once. "You should. You deserve to be happy."

Rylan bumped his shoulder against hers. "Hey, you too."

Her freckled nose scrunched and she looked away.

Rylan stood up slowly, the mattress rising with him. "Let me know if you need any more help going through these. My ancient shadyr is rusty, but you don't have to do this alone."

"Your ancient shadyr is *non-existent*." Annabeth laughed. "Although I don't know how good mine is either, honestly."

She reached down and pulled one of the books onto her lap. "Like this passage here about when the shadyrs first created the portals to this dimension. It uses the term 'the Beast of Teeth and Stars.' Like those are words that make any sense together."

A chill ran along Rylan's body, so cold it seemed to stick his feet to the floor with ice. "It says what?"

"I mean, there was an artifact with a similar name that went missing from Darkfrey

Estate some years back, but it was a Bane, not a Beast. So, I'm thinking I'm just translating it wrong. I'm probably getting the whole thing wrong, but every way I look at it, it says beast, monster, abomination—"

Rylan's voice was rough. "You don't know about the Bane?"

"Not really? Just its name?"

Rubbing his hands across his close-cropped hair, Rylan paced in the small patch of bare floor. "It's the artifact that freed me from Everly. It affects her in that way because of the Coruscare. That's another name for it—the Beast of Teeth and Stars. An eidolghast called Everly that—she could understand it—that's how we made the connection."

His words tumbled out, his thoughts churned around by fear of the other connection that was being made.

"The Coruscare *is* the Beast of Teeth and Stars?" Annabeth sought confirmation as her face grew pale.

Rylan stopped pacing. "What does the passage say?"

Annabeth's jaw worked but it took a moment for words to come out. She turned back to the book, reading along with a finger. "That—that the shadyrs used ... used pieces of the Beast of Teeth and Stars, used its magic to break through the shield between dimensions to flee from the eidolghasts to a new world."

Rylan's fingers shook as he whipped his phone from his pocket. Every second felt too slow as he brought up Everly's number.

The call rang, rang, and rang out.

"No answer? It could just be bad reception." Annabeth had gone white, and she hovered beside Rylan, checking on his phone screen as the second call timed out.

Rylan shook his head and tried Lian's number. It rang, and rang, and—

"Hey, what's up?"

Rylan exhaled in relief. "Where are you now?"

"On our way b—" static crackled. "Got Tammy, but there's a tree d— SSHHHKKKK—on the road. We won't be lo— Mmff MMFF!"

"Lian? Mom?"

A loud pop and crunching sound came through the line, and the call disconnected.

Lian's heart only felt at ease once she got Tammy in the car with them.

After the attack on Everly's home the night before, and every attack on her loved ones leading to that night, her emotions were tightly strung.

She knew the world could be cruel and loss happened, even to those who were

most protected, but this wasn't chaos and chance.

This was the cruelty of a few power-mad individuals targeting her and her family.

A humming fury had grown in her, like she'd swallowed a live wasp every time someone she cared for was put at risk.

Tammy had vanished from their home of her own accord, even if she hadn't meant to, but Lian didn't want her out on her own a moment longer than she had to be.

The drive on the way to Dark Corner with Everly was quiet. And given the red, sullen expression on Tammy's face when she climbed into the van, Lian expected the drive back to be equally so. Tammy folded her arms and glared at the wall of the campervan in front of her, occasionally shaking her head as though disagreeing with some internal argument.

I wonder what set her off.

The dirt laneway leading back from Dark Corner was rough, and Everly took it carefully in the rattly vintage vehicle.

"When did you learn how to drive?" Lian asked, curious.

Years back, she had imagined teaching Everly when she taught her boys, but since she lost them all when they were barely teenagers, the time never came. And Lian highly doubted that Everly's own mother would have taught her.

"I had a job at a pizza place when I first moved out. They needed more delivery drivers, so I learned as quick as I could."

Lian did the math in her head. "You wouldn't have been old enough to drive alone."

Everly cleared her throat. "I may have been working off a fake ID."

Lian stared out the windscreen into the dark woods around them. Even at mid-morning the forest was black as the depths of the sea.

She'd been so worried when Everly left home, but also proud. Striking out on her own at such a young age had a lot of risks but staying in that awful home probably had just as many. Lian had meant many times to go to Everly, and offer her support, to let her know that she hadn't been abandoned by the whole family, but she'd been so lost in her own grief during that time.

Before she knew it, Everly had moved away.

"I think your time away from Shroudhaven was good for you, but I'm glad you're back," Lian said, keeping her eyes forward.

"I think I'm glad I'm back too, now," Everly replied. "Although, part of me wonders whether continuing to live my life without knowing monsters are real might have been better."

"I'm glad you brought my son back too. In more ways than one."

"How do you mean?" Everly glanced over quickly before refocusing on the road.

"It's as though your presence softens him. That first night after he woke up, all

I saw was a Darkfrey soldier. But the more time he spends time with you, it's like he's becoming the person he used to be. He's becoming my son again."

A buzzing sound came from the pocket of Everly's red jacket. She pulled out the phone and glanced at the screen. "Speak of the devil."

The phone went back into her pocket, still ringing, and she returned her hand to the steering wheel.

"You don't want to get that?"

"Not while I'm driving. We'll be back soon anyway, and I'll talk to him—WOAH." Everly hit the brakes as they came out of a turn.

The van lurched on the unsealed gravel and shuddered to a stop, inches from a large tree lying across the road.

"Lucky you weren't on the phone," Lian muttered, her hands braced on the dashboard.

"Sorry." Everly winced.

"Not your fault."

"What is it?" Tammy leaned over from the back, shaken from her sulk.

Everly unbuckled her seatbelt and clicked her door open. "There's a tree on the road."

"I can see that *now*," Tammy mumbled.

Everly called back to them from in front of the van. "It's not too big, I think the three of us will be able to drag it out of the way."

The sliding door grumbled as Tammy rolled it open, almost as much as Tammy did. Lian climbed from the passenger seat, adjusting the sword sheathed on her belt. It was an instinct, a security blanket. Up ahead, Everly had paled and placed a hand on her stomach.

Down by her thigh, Lian's phone vibrated in her long cardigan's pocket. She frowned when she saw who was calling. "Hey, what's up?"

It was hard to tell whether the sigh she heard over the line was him or the normal static. "Where are you—SSHHHKKKK?"

Lian walked over to the trunk, eyeing it as though she could gauge its weight. "On our way back. We've got Tammy, but there's a tree down on the road. We won't be lo— Mmff MMFF!"

Heavy fabric went over her head, blocking her vision. Her phone was knocked from her hand. It clattered onto the road, followed by a stomping, crunching sound. Beside her, Tammy shrieked.

Footsteps moved around behind Lian. Two people—no, three.

The roar of an engine approached rapidly, and gravel crunched. Car doors slammed.

"The info was good. We've got the two of them, and the old lady."

"Load them up, quick."

Lian didn't know the first voice, but that one was Vonny.

Lian tensed, still as a statue as she took in all she could of her blacked-out surroundings. Tammy grunted and there was a *thwump* of a punch or kick. Only a soft groan came from Everly's direction.

Hands grabbed the back of Lian's cardigan, forcing her forward. "Vonny? What are you doing?"

"Just picking up some things we need. Took long enough for that cursed kid to show up here, but we figured she would at some point."

Everly groaned louder, her words forced and clipped. "They've got ... Bane."

The two of them ... They're after Tammy and Everly then.

Not a chance in the Everdark was Lian letting them be taken. She hinged at the waist, bending at a ninety-degree angle and ducking away from the hands that guided her to Vonny's vehicle.

Rolling to the side, she drew her sword in the same moment. The few pinpricks of light that sparkled through the bag over her head vanished.

A shoe scuffed in the dirt behind her. She struck out, feeling the air around her blade, the catch of it on fabric. Heard her target stumble as they dodged. To the right. She struck again lightning fast and met flesh, slicing along in a liquid motion.

A woman cried out, the voice unfamiliar.

"Shit, how's she seeing us?" a man called.

"I don't need to see you to kill you," Lian hissed, charging at the voice.

The ground was uneven, and she wished for good footing. The man crashed across the gravel in his attempts to escape her blade, making him an easy mark. Only a car door slamming saved his life, as Lian whirled toward it, refocusing.

"Leave her, we've got what we came for," Vonny yelled as the engine revved.

The man hurried past her and Lian struck. The blade sliced lightly along his skin. He grunted and ran faster. She tried to follow, dashing to where she heard the car door open and slam.

Her shin smacked hard into the rough bark of the downed tree. She went face-first over it, chin smashing into the hard-packed ground. Her teeth rattled and her sword slid out of reach. Car wheels skidded and flying gravel pelted Lian as she scrambled to her feet and wrestled the bag off her head.

The black jeep sped away from her, vanishing down the winding road, taking Tammy and Everly with it.

12

Rylan gripped the wheel with choking strength as he raced along the dirt road to Dark Corner.

"It could just have been bad reception," Callan said from the passenger seat, trying again to call Tammy, Everly, or Lian.

They'd had to wait until Rushelle got back with Lian's SUV. Rylan had been ready to go on his own, either take Rushelle's tiny yellow sports car or simply *run* his way there if he had to, but by the time he'd explained the urgency and argued it out with the others, Rushelle returned.

They didn't even unload the produce. Rylan swung himself into the driver's seat, and Callan, Harper, Cherry, Jasper, Denny, and Annabeth filed in. There was a moment of drama with separating Harper and Neri, but Rushelle stayed back to calm the young woman down.

Shadowed by the mammoth, twisted trees on either side, a slim, gray figure jogged along the road toward them.

Rylan brought the car skidding to a stop beside Lian.

He flung himself out of his seat, looking between his mother and the empty road that continued on to Dark Corner. "What happened? Where are the others?"

Lian bent over, hands on her knees, dragging in deep breaths. "Darkfreys. Vonny. Took them."

She straightened, and her face was as grim and gray as her cardigan. A vivid streak of red under her chin contrasted with her pallid skin.

Callan and the others were halfway out of the car.

"Get back in, we're going!" Rylan barked.

"Going where?" Callan stood on the edge of the car on his side, looking over the roof. "They could be taking them anywhere."

"My bet's on the estate," Rylan said.

"Bets aren't going to be worth anything if we end up in the wrong place." Lian pushed Denny back into the car and climbed in after him.

Harper's face was pale, and her lips pursed as she tapped away on her phone, still standing by the car door. Rylan's face turned hot. What was she doing? Posting a damn selfie?

"Ugh!" she grunted. "Not enough reception!"

"Get in!" Rylan roared at her.

Harper's head snapped up and she climbed in fast. "Ev and I set up tracking for each other, ages back. You know, two girls living in the city."

Rylan nodded, tightening his grip on the wheel. "Keep checking. But we have to move."

The wheels were spinning as Harper shut the door.

Jasper's voice was quiet. "If the purpose of kidnapping Tammy and Everly is to use them to open the shroudpool, it is likely they would take them to the place where they were building that structure I saw."

"Maybe that's not what they are doing? They could just want, I don't know, leverage or revenge or something?" Denny put in.

"I wouldn't be surprised it if was all of the above," Lian muttered.

Tense silence filled the car, the only sound the tapping of Harper's fingernails on the phone screen. They were off the dirt road and back on the highway when Harper gasped.

"They are at the estate," she exhaled the words in a rush, and held up her phone screen where a blue dot pinged on a map.

Rylan pressed the accelerator harder.

"At least we know where they are, but what do we do with that?" Cherry asked, desperation cracking his voice. "What are we going to do, frontal assault the whole damn Darkfrey army?"

"If I have to," Rylan growled.

"I know another way in," Denny sang out.

Annabeth shook her head. "All the gates are guarded and watched lately, even if we didn't take the main drive."

"Nah ah. Not this one. It's a secret way in."

Rylan stared at him in the rearview mirror, and Denny leered back smugly.

"It's down around the bottom of the falls, back where the estate looks over the river. A special little entry only those of Darkfrey blood know about. And how do I know about it then, you ask?" Denny paused dramatically, but nobody asked. "Alexis showed it to me. Made a nice little place for our rendezvous."

Harper groaned, and Cherry muttered under his breath.

Denny raised his voice. "And by rendezvous, I mean hot monkey sex."

"We're going in the front gate," Rylan grunted.

They were near the main street of Shroudhaven, and he swung the car around a

corner to avoid an oncoming bus. Speeding down an alleyway, he scraped one side of Lian's SUV against a dumpster.

"Aw, come on man, don't be like that. This is legit!" Denny whined.

"It could be worth a shot," Callan added. "If we can get in without having to fight our way in, we'll get in faster, and also not dead."

The turn to go either up the hill to the estate or around to the falls bore down on them.

"I know you guys don't believe that Alexis and I are in a deep, meaningful, and hot-as flaming-monster-trucks relationship, but trust me for once. I am what I am, but I'm not a liar."

Rylan gritted his teeth and slammed his hands on the dash. "Fuck!"

He spun the steering wheel, veering off toward the falls.

He spoke through clenched teeth. "This had better be real."

Denny leaned back in his seat. "If anything, I'm too honest, which is why people can't handle me."

He called out directions as they drove along the side of the river. He sent them off to the left, then as the road went from sealed, to dirt, he climbed over the middle seat, and pushed through to lean over into the front.

He waved his finger in front of Rylan's face. "It's coming up here, here! HERE!"

"Where?"

"Turn right!"

Rylan swerved fast. The road they ended up on was more like a goat track, rough and overgrown. Branches smashed against the windscreen as they hurtled along.

"You'll have to stop now before—"

Rylan ground the car to a halt, inches from the edge of a rocky cliff that plummeted down beside a waterfall.

Gasping deep breaths, Rylan peeled his hands from the steering wheel. He glared back at Denny.

Denny slapped him on the back. "Come on, entry's just up ahead."

Drawing a machete from his bag, he slung the pack over his shoulder and was first out of the vehicle.

Rylan climbed out of the driver's seat, his body aflame with raw nerves. The rocks under his feet were slick with spray from the falls and verdant with moss. He backed up, taking in the steep, cascading tiers of cliff and running water. Right at the top, he could see the high walls of the back end of Darkfrey Estate.

Denny had already set off, following what could barely be considered a trail. He hacked at ferns and twigs that crossed the path, even though they would barely have tickled to pass by. Lian and Harper were close behind and the others fell into line.

Callan moved by Rylan's side as they marched after them. His brows were low over his eyes, and his lips fallen from their usual smile.

"Did the stuff you and Annabeth were reading say anything about why they want Tammy?"

"No."

"They definitely wanted both of them," Lian called back, pushing a dripping branch out of the way.

"Doesn't mean they wanted them both for the shroudpool ritual though." Callan's voice cracked and he marched a bit faster.

"You think being part of the ritual is going to be a better outcome than straight-up revenge?" Rylan snapped a tree limb out of his way. "We have no idea what the Mesmans are going to do with Everly, whether or not she'll survive the process. You've seen what their favorite ingredient in their dark magic is."

Nobody said it out loud, but the word screamed through Rylan's mind.

Bones.

He couldn't lose her. Not now. Not like this.

"Tada!" Denny sang from up front. He stood before a sheer cliff face that Darkfrey Estate sat above.

"What? We can't climb that! Even if we had gear." Rylan stalked toward Denny, ready to smack the dumb grin off his face.

Denny was the only one to have any supplies with him, having grabbed his Shit Hit The Fan bag on his way out, but there couldn't be enough in there to help them scale a cliff.

"Ta. Da." Denny enunciated again slowly and pressed a chipped-out section of stone.

With a dull, echoing scrape, a narrow door-shaped section of rock opened before them.

"Well how about that." Lian gazed into the dark tunnel ahead. "Even I had no idea this was here."

Denny folded his arms and his face split in a wide grin. "You can all thank me now."

Rylan pushed past him, striding along the rough incline of the tunnel.

"Or later, later is good too."

"Do you guys mind if I put a light on? I realize I'm the only human here right now, I don't want to mess with your dark vision," Harper said from somewhere down the line.

"Do whatever you want, just keep up," Rylan shot back.

"Hey! You're not the only one worried about Everly. *And* Tammy," she snapped, shouldering him out of the way as she took the lead.

Light shone from her phone, illuminating neatly cut-stone walls marked with worn carvings.

Rylan rolled his neck and twitched his nose. He spoke softly but wouldn't have been surprised if it echoed to everybody around him.

"I'm sorry. I know you love her every bit as much as I do."

Harper caught his eye for a moment, but never slowed her pace. "You'd better."

The pitch turned steeper, with steps cut into the dark rock. Veins of quartz sparkled around them, and Annabeth gasped, running her hands over some of the carvings before Cherry and Jasper pushed her on.

Rylan's heart hammered and sweat beaded on the back of his neck.

When what appeared to be a dead end loomed before him, Denny yelled out, "There it is! Just find the switch. No, over on the side, no, the other side! Little knobbly bit."

The tunnel was narrow, and everyone shuffled around as Denny pushed to the front beside Rylan. It took him a moment of feeling around before he found the right spot and the mechanism clicked, setting off a sequence of clockwork sounds.

Harper smiled thinly at Denny. "Thank you. I still don't like you, but thank you."

"You'll learn to love me, babe." Denny grinned, preening his beard.

"And I'm already regretting opening my mouth."

Cherry scoffed, "I bet Denny hears that a lot."

"Can we focus?" Rylan grunted.

This wasn't the time. Every second counted. He tried to imagine that Everly was okay, just held captive but unhurt, that they still had time. But dread pooled molten metal in his throat.

The tall section of wall slid to the side with the sound of a small earthquake, revealing an interior secret passage within Darkfrey Estate.

And at least twenty Darkfrey shadyrs standing guard.

13

V omit dripped down Everly's chin and her head churned like it was filled with an ocean storm.

She'd been dragged, shoved, lifted, kicked, and through the roaring nausea of having the Bane so close to her, she barely noticed. She could feel it, strapped to her chest now, unwrapped and bleeding. Her shirt was soaked through with the thick, slippery soup of eidolghast blood.

The memory of how that blood came to fill the Bane, of the expanding and contracting orb, sacrificing thousands of creatures in its ravenous motion, filled her mind and her throat burned as she gagged again.

Her body flushed with heat then shivered into an icy sweat.

Something sharp jarred into her back and her hands were pulled behind her and roughly bound together. The bag was ripped off her head, and she blinked, trying to see through her sickness, which blinded her nearly as thoroughly.

Everything was in black and white, formless blobs of light and shadow.

"*Tammy?*" she tried to say, but only a scratchy cough emerged.

"Everly!" The call came back from the blurry, dark blob straight across from her.

It hurt to open her eyes wider, but Everly pushed, lifting them to take in her surroundings. Slowly, her vision wavered back into color. Edges cleared.

Tammy was right in front of her, out of arm's reach, even if her arms were free to reach out.

They were both tied to a large, twisted contraption. Their placement mirrored each other, bound on lower rings of multiple concentric circles formed from bones and sinew, and things Everly couldn't name even if she could see with perfect clarity.

She knew what she was looking at. She'd seen sketches of it. She heard Jasper's description of seeing it half built.

Her mouth felt numb and tasted of bile and blood. She forced it to form the words, hoping Tammy understood.

"Go. *Go.*" She had to go.

If the Mesmans wanted both of them, needed both of them for their ritual ... they

couldn't. They couldn't have them both.

Tammy sobbed and shook her head.

"She's not going anywhere."

Everly flinched. She hadn't noticed Vonny was right beside her. She'd put all her effort into focusing on Tammy.

Vonny raised her voice. "You're not going anywhere, are you? Because if you do, you'll never see your friend here alive again."

"Please, I can't control it! Especially when I'm—You can't, don't do it, please!" Tammy flickered, then with a sob of effort, solidified herself.

Kole Mesman moved into Everly's narrow field of view. His bulky, bestial muscles blocked sight of Tammy entirely as he stood in front of the girl. "It's fascinating, these powers you've been cursed with."

"But are they going to work? Are they going to take us to Blaise?" Vonny checked Everly's bonds, tightening them until Everly couldn't feel her fingers.

"Of course!" Kole roared, his voice wildly uneven. "I've worked it all out. The spell has been adjusted. Her link to the Dark Corner shroudpool will take us where we need to go."

Kole moved around in front of Tammy.

She loosed a series of panting shrieks. When he stepped away, she slumped in her bonds.

A river of red streamed down her face.

Tammy. The word caught in Everly's throat. *What did he do to her?*

Her continuing whimpers were both heartbreaking and comforting. At least she was still alive. Kole turned on Everly, stalking forward, a bloody knife clutched in his ham-hock fist.

"And our other ingredient. The Coruscare itself." His eyes were round and bloodshot.

He clutched Everly's chin roughly. With his other hand he brought the sharp blade to her forehead, tracing it lightly over her skin. Everly shuddered but couldn't pull away. She cast her gaze around, seeking aid, anyone who could help her or Tammy. There had been other shadyrs there when they were ambushed near the dormant Dark Corner shroudpool, but it seemed to be just the Mesmans now.

I must be at the estate. Jasper had said the structure was in an old ballroom, but there wasn't much of a ballroom that remained.

The space they were in was huge, and only thin beams of light pierced through arched windows that had been papered over. The remains of hardwood boards were stacked to one end of the hall, and the structure Everly was attached to stood on a level beneath the demolished flooring, built on what seemed to be an ancient ruin.

Dusty, chipped flagstone paved the ground beneath her feet, and low, crumbled walls surrounded them, tumbled down to knee-height lifetimes ago.

The excavated room echoed strangely, but if Tammy's screams hadn't brought attention to them, Everly doubted any help would come.

There has to be something, some way out of this.

Everly tried to draw on her own strength, to bring the light of her dragon out and fight back, but the Coruscare had fled to the deepest place within her, cowering from the Bane that was bound to her skin.

It was hard to even summon enough energy and clarity to keep her eyes open, to speak. She opened her mouth to argue with Kole, to plead for him not to do something so dangerous. He pressed his hand and the knife slid into the skin of her forehead.

Everly screamed but only a harsh whisper emerged.

Kole cut and carved, squeezing her jaw so hard to keep her still that her cheeks split against her teeth. Tears streamed down Everly's face—not enough to clear the blood that ran into her eyes.

She couldn't stop the Mesmans. Whatever they were going to do to her, to Tammy, to the world, she couldn't stop them.

It felt like the end, and all she could think was she never got the chance to tell Rylan that she loved him too. That she loved him from the moment they had met and every dream of romance and passion she'd had her entire life had been about him and only him.

And that dream was just breaking through into reality like a rainbow cutting across a stormy sky and it was already *over*, and it wasn't *fair*.

Kole finished cutting into her skin and let her go. Her chin flopped weakly against her collarbones.

Agony pounded through her head, and the new healing powers she had didn't kick in.

Turning from her, Kole stripped off the white shirt that was stretched over his misshapen skin, flexing his oversized muscles as he did.

The world was stained scarlet through Everly's vision but still his body looked *wrong*.

Dark blotches embedded in his flesh formed complex patterns across his back and chest, revealed as he turned on the spot and raised his hands. Crooked objects jutted from his forearms.

Everly worked to blink her eyes clear, fighting off a wave of panic. They were bones. He had opalescent bones embedded all over his torso and arms. They weren't quite human, not the usual shapes of rib or femur or fingerbone. They spiraled and branched strangely and seemed to ripple with their own motion.

"What have you done to yourself? You're crazy," Tammy blurted from across the room, her voice high and strained.

Kole kept his arms raised above his head. "This isn't madness, this is power. You're seeing the source of my magic. I've made myself one with the ancient shadyrs, so I could bring all shadyrs into a new era of victory."

Tammy thrashed against her bonds. "With your lures? You have no idea what you've done. It was your fault. All along it was your fault!"

Kole turned away from her as though she hadn't even spoken. His deep voice boomed as he spoke in a language Everly had never heard. One that made her vision waver and her stomach heave with the dark power that oozed from each syllable.

The ritual structure moved.

The outermost ring of bone lifted from the ground and spun in slow circles. White light and black shadows swirled along with it, crackling and wailing.

Then the inner section, where Everly and Tammy were bound, shifted. Everly's boots left the ground as the bones she was tied to screeched and screamed like a chorus of human souls in purgatory.

Tammy yelled, panic jittering through her words. "Blaise wanted to close the shroudpool to save you!"

The structure took Tammy off the ground too, leaning her in toward Everly, bringing the two of them closer and closer in the center of the spinning rings. Energy sparked between the two of them.

Kole kept chanting, but Vonny stepped in front of the ritual, her blond bob flying around her face. "It was your fault. You took him out there. What would he think we needed saving from?"

"He was scared you would be killed, like the parents of so many other kids were getting killed by eidolghasts. But it was you doing the killing!"

Vonny took a step backward, her eyes wide. "No. He ..."

Was Tammy getting through to her?

Keep talking Tammy. Make her see.

"Let him go. He's gone. He's gone and we can't get him back," Tammy scream-sobbed.

Vonny's face went rigid, her eyes glittering. "He's not dead! We're going to get him back. You'll see! If you survive. And if you don't, then that's two birds with one stone."

Tammy turned to Everly, open-mouthed and shaking. Everly gazed back, her own body shuddering in waves of sickness and the pull of shadowy magic.

I'm sorry, Everly wanted to say, and she could see those words on Tammy's lips too. The infernal ritual shifted them ever closer to each other.

"What's going on in here?" a voice rang out into the acoustics of the hall.

Mordan Darkfrey stepped out from the shadows, flanked by three braces of shadyrs.

Grasping for strength, Everly cried out, "Stop them, please!"

Mordan ignored her, stalking over to address Vonny. "I heard you had the Kyrstelle

and Boderleth women brought in. What are you doing with them?"

"It's time. They are what we need to open the shroudpool, to get our boy back." Vonny stood at attention, her chin raised and voice strong.

Mordan glanced toward the swirling ritual. "I didn't think you'd pull it off. Still can't be sure you will."

"Don't let them! You can't let them open a shroudpool here at the estate! Look how big it is!" Tammy cringed back, trying to separate herself from Everly as they drew close to touching.

The shadyrs at Mordan's back exchanged concerned glances, but not one of them broke rank or spoke up.

Mordan stared for a long moment at the spinning rings and streaks of white and black magic curling around them.

Then he smiled. "Hrm. Maybe this could be a good thing. A shroudpool under our control? We could foray into the Everdark ourselves, strike at the source of evil directly. Our army, although depleted, is still strong enough."

"No," Everly breathed the word harshly, lost under the thunderous magic growing ever louder. "No! I've seen it, I've seen the Everdark. You can't."

"You have no idea what we're capable of," he shot back. "We are the strongest, the best of what shadyrs can be."

Everly and Tammy shared wide-eyed, terrified looks.

Blood still oozed from Tammy's forehead. They were nearly nose to nose, and Everly could see it was some ancient glyph carved there. The blood now dripped upward, flying and spinning into the tornado of the spell. Everly could feel the tickle of the same effect on her own throbbing forehead, clearing her vision from the tint of red.

"Go ahead," Mordan told Kole, although Kole had not once hesitated or paused in his chanting. "There will be great victories ahead for our kind, and the good of all our world."

Everly's mind flashed with visions from her dreams with the Coruscare. Endless plains of shadow, swarmed so thickly with eidolghasts that it was as though the ground itself was one impossibly large creature.

Mordan thought himself unstoppable, but Everly knew in her bones, if the portal opened, they wouldn't stand a chance.

14

R ylan swung the first punch. "I thought you said this wouldn't be guarded!" Denny swerved his body under a roundhouse kick by a Darkfrey, then brought up his machete to block something hard. A sharp clang echoed through the passage. "Alexis said it would be all clear!"

Callan pushed in beside Rylan. "What the ghast do you mean, 'Alexis said'?"

The hallway was narrow, and the Darkfreys had them closed in on two sides. In the low light, knives flashed, and the spark of electricity glowed at the end of military-style stun batons.

"I texted her on the way in." Denny took down the Darkfrey in front of him with an uppercut. "Thought we could hook up."

"You did what?"

"You absolute idiot!"

"Were you trying to get us all killed?"

"Could you be any more selfish?"

Rylan, Cherry, Lian, and Harper yelled into the fray.

Whatever was going on with Denny and Alexis, whether it was all in his mind or not, the ghast-blighted asshole had ruined their chances of getting to Everly unnoticed.

Rylan had to hold back from aiming his next right-hook at Denny.

Callan groaned, then raised his voice in a commanding yell. "We can rip the asshole a new one later. Let's beat the Everdark out of this lot first."

They had left Howell House in a rush, almost entirely unprepared. Harper and Lian both wielded their swords, and Denny had his machete. Whatever else Denny had in his pack, he wasn't sharing. None of them had their body armor on. They were outnumbered, and outmatched.

But also ready for some payback.

Rylan's knuckles cracked against the cheekbone of one Darkfrey. He yanked the baton-shaped taser from the man's hands as he reeled backward.

That was for the Darkfreys abandoning the search for my missing body.

Electricity popped and zapped as he jabbed it under the man's chin.

That's for lying to me and killing my father.

An elbow caught his cheek and flung his head sideways. He spat blood. Growled. He shouldered the woman into the wall, cracking the long taser across her knees.

That's for trying to kill us at The Crow's Nest.

He pressed forward, breaking away from the line held by Callan, Annabeth, and Denny beside him, and Lian, Harper, Cherry, and Jasper at their backs. He smashed his forehead into the bridge of another man's nose.

That's for sending an eidolghast to Everly's home.

He barreled into the crowd of Darkfreys, arms burning as he struck out with all his strength. He grabbed a head and smashed it into the wall beside them. He thrust the taser deep into a belly. He kicked out the feet of another, bringing the end of the weapon down over their neck as they crumpled.

That's for taking Everly. And that. And that.

Trembling with rage, breath scorching in his throat, Rylan sought another target. Only a litter of bodies lay before him. Back down the hall, the others had stilled, panting and resting against the wall.

Callan swore. "More coming! We've got to move!"

"This way! I know where we are now." Lian slipped past Rylan and took the lead, speeding ahead like a gray ghost in the shadows.

Rylan wasn't sure where they were. He'd never screwed around in the secret passages and ancient tunnels that riddled the estate like some shadyrs did.

But he knew the old ballroom that Jasper had said was their target. It was in the east wing of an older building. He just hoped Lian could lead them there, and fast.

Footsteps thundered after them as they bolted along the narrow passageway. Rylan's shoulders scraped against the rough-cut stone, ripping his long-sleeved T-shirt.

Lian led them without hesitation through three intersections. Their pursuers faded out of earshot, but Lian didn't slow her pace.

A buzz of energy built within Rylan. A bare tingle at first, but quickly becoming a swell of recognizable power.

"I can feel her, she's close!"

They burst out from behind a faded tapestry and Rylan quickly got his bearings in the long hallway of the abandoned wing. They were right across from the arched double doors of the ballroom, which stood ajar.

Rylan was the first one through, slamming the doors open wide.

He only had half a heartbeat to take in what he saw.

"Everly!" he bellowed.

She was bound and suspended in the center of a massive, dark structure that stood from an excavated basement through to high ballroom ceiling. Her face was as

red as her jacket.

Magic streamed and spun like black and white lightning between her and Tammy, who was tied opposite to her. They cringed away from each other but were pushed ever closer.

Kole and Vonny stood at their feet, chanting as bones and darkness wove circles before them. At the door near Rylan stood Mordan Darkfrey and a crowd of other shadyrs.

And then Everly and Tammy's cheeks touched.

Time slowed and *thwumped*. A shockwave of light and dark energy smashed across the room, knocking down everything in its path. Rylan flew off his feet and skidded along the floor on his back, tangling with other bodies. A column of energy shot upward, blasting through the roof of the ballroom. Sunlight streamed in from the midday sky above.

Then everything sucked backward in a rush, timber and plaster flying through the air like bullets.

The world turned dark.

Everly dragged in a sharp breath that scraped into her lungs. Darkness engulfed her, smothering and thick.

She didn't know where she was, whether she was asleep or awake, alive or dead. But she could breathe. That was a good sign. The air she took in was gritty and bitter, leaving a rancid tang in her mouth. The ground beneath her was sharp, and viscous liquid washed against her in a choppy tide, oozing into her clothing.

Her forehead throbbed, but clarity returned to her thoughts. She moved a hand and found it freed. She clasped it to her chest. The Bane was gone.

What happened? Where am I?

"Everly?" Tammy cried out from nearby.

"I'm here." Groaning into a sitting position, Everly fought away the panic and swell of acid in her stomach.

Nothing but utter, inescapable blackness filled her sight.

Need light. Come on.

She concentrated all her effort on controlling the Coruscare's powers, forcing them out from the depths they had cowered into. She flickered like a faulty fluorescent tube.

"Come on!" she grunted, trying again as though turning over the engine of an old car.

A low illumination spread across her fingertips, up her arms. It hardly dinted the darkness, still a solid wall of black encircling her.

"Everly!" Tammy stepped into the light, then crumpled onto her knees.

She reached her stained hands to Everly, but pulled back before they touched, shivering. Dried blood caked around her eyebrows and down the sides of her nose.

A flurry of tentacles rushed past them, and Everly pushed herself back along the puddled ground, out of its way.

Oh no. No no.

"We're in the Everdark?" she whispered, but she already knew the answer.

"Watch out!" Tammy leaped to her feet and tugged Everly up behind her.

She could clearly see farther into the midnight world than Everly.

A moment later, a weroth three times larger than the one from the theater strode through the edges of her vision.

Everly scrunched her eyes closed with effort, trying to bring more of the Coruscare out. They needed more light. She needed a way to defend them.

But the dragon was weak.

The prolonged contact with the Bane kept it subdued, and she only managed to create a larger dome of light. The usual levitation effect didn't emerge with it, her feet still firmly set on the slick ground, ankle deep in slime. But the light was large enough to see the shroudpool before them, the stream of eidolghasts flowing toward it, and Vonny and Kole standing at the fringes of day and night.

"They're going through to our world. Oh my ghast, there are so many of them," Tammy whispered, her eyes glittering with stars brighter than Everly had ever seen.

The eidolghasts hissed and howled at Everly's glow as they passed, but the massive shroudpool was too alluring to them, their chance to move from this blighted, used up, and overcrowded world to a new one where they could spread their darkness again.

Some tried to advance on Everly and Tammy in their small bubble of light. Everly struck out a hand, and light crackled across her fingertips. No tendrils emerged, but it was enough to ward the creatures back.

"I can't stop them going through. The Bane really knocked the Coruscare around."

Tammy threw her jacket on the ground, and power surged around her, a swirl of shadows and bright-red sparks transforming her into a red winged demon. "We need to get through, too. Maybe we can help hold them back on the other side."

"Blaise? Blaise?" Vonny and Kole yelled out into the world of monsters and darkness.

Everly's head swung to the Mesmans with a sneer. Couldn't they see what was around them? There was no way their son was here, or anywhere. There was no way he survived this realm for years on his own. She wasn't sure *they* were going to survive it for much longer.

Clearly they couldn't see, because they broke into a run away from her.

"Come back here! Stay in the light!" she yelled after them.

Part of her didn't care. Part of her still stung, red raw and bleeding from their cruelty. Part of her wanted them to die as *revenge*.

But as she felt the Coruscare growing stronger, its voice curling around her conscience, she refused to listen. She would hold onto what made her human, to what she thought being a good human looked like.

"They're going to die," Tammy said, her voice flat and aching.

"Come on." Everly jogged cautiously after them and Tammy kept by her side. She swore a string of curses but didn't argue their course.

The Mesmans moved out of Everly's field of light, ignoring her pleas to come back. She strained, her head pounding, making the size of her illumination grow.

The Coruscare had recovered more now, and it pulled her to a stop for a long few seconds as it shot out a glittering tendril. She gasped at the unexpected action as the soul eater made its namesake known, drawing in a feed from a nearby ghast to help it grow stronger. The open wound on her forehead tingled as it knit together.

Then the light expanded to encompass the area ahead, in time to see the Mesmans being crunched in the five different mouths of an eidolghast that dwarfed the weroth they saw before. The hydra-like beast fought over their torn bodies, tearing free hipbones in an explosion of viscera, chewing thighs with teeth like chainsaws.

Everly's blood filled with ice, and a nausea unrelated to the Bane washed over her. Tammy sobbed a wordless wail.

"We've got to go, we've got to get out of here," Everly said, choking the words out around acid.

The multiheaded behemoth slithered away toward the shroudpool. Everly watched it, terrified for a moment it would turn on them. She dulled her light as much as she dared, hoping not to draw its attention.

Tammy's gaze remained fixed on where the Mesmans had fallen. She moved again, but in the wrong direction. Toward them, instead of their escape.

"Tammy!" Everly dashed after her, growing the light again.

Her feet skimmed the ground, lifting from the sludgy layer of what she imagined was a millennia's worth of blood. Fissures cracked the ground around them, burbling the clotted fluid, and burning with black flames.

"There's something there, something ..." Tammy ran past the Mesmans' corpses without giving them a second glance, to a bundle beside a tumble of broken smoky crystals.

Her bat-like wings fluttered behind her, speeding her steps. Everly worked hard to keep up, fending off eidolghast that approached on each side, her light tendrils under

control again.

Tammy landed on her knees with a crack.

"It's him. It's Blaise." Tammy clutched at the ragged bundle, lifting a scrap of fabric with a Darkfrey logo embroidered onto the side.

"How do you know? It could be ... I don't know, has anyone else ever been lost through a shroudpool before?" Everly offered.

She shot short glances at Tammy while keeping her eyes on their surroundings. An auerdax stared at them from the edges of her light for a long moment before turning away.

Tammy shook her head, plunging her hands into the slime and bones before her, her shoulders slumped in a curved arch. "Their spell worked. It brought us to him."

The Mesmans found their son after all, but died seconds before discovering him dead. Everly wasn't sure what the better outcome would have been.

Whether their death was a mercy compared to what would have happened if they had lived for a few moments longer. If they had seen that it was all for nothing. Their son was gone, all along.

"Tammy, we've got to go." Everly lashed out her light whip to fend off a herrelspurn that dove at them from above.

A gust of fire singed the heavy air.

Tammy didn't respond, her hands working in the blood-soaked ground.

The air tremored, shivering across Everly's sphere of light. A sharp blade of fear stabbed her ribcage, making her heart pump double time. Her dragon squirmed inside her as though trying to free itself from the cage of her body.

Something was coming. Something *big*.

Everly floated down beside Tammy. "I'm sorry, I'm sorry you lost him, Tammy, but we have to get out of here, right now!"

"I'm sorry too. But I've already grieved for him all I can." Tammy turned around.

Her face was marked where tears washed lines down her red-tinted skin, but her expression was still, solid. She lifted her hands to show a basketball-sized orb, covered in slick, dark fluid. Her shadyr galaxy eyes glittered.

"This is what Blaise wanted to close the Dark Corner shroudpool with. Even if we didn't close it entirely, this thing at least made it dormant. We could use it to do something about the shroudpool the Mesmans made."

Tammy wiped away some of the blood covering the orb with her sleeve, and Everly gasped.

It's the thing that created the Bane.

That sacrificial machine of mass destruction. She couldn't even think straight. She just wanted to be home, with family, with Rylan. Eidolghasts still threatened their circle. A force that made her skin want to turn inside out on itself approached at a rapid speed.

The thing Tammy held could be their salvation or their destruction. She didn't know what to do, but Tammy looked at her with such hope in her eyes that she nodded and rose back up.

Tammy stood as well, then the needle point of a weroth arm speared right through her shoulder.

15

Rylan jumped to his feet. Where Everly had been, now stood a two-story-high rippling pool of pure darkness.

No. No, we were too late.

Debris covered the ground all around the shroudpool, roof tiles, bones, and timber beams lying thick. There was no sign of Everly.

Or Tammy. Or the Mesmans. But Rylan could only seek Everly, could only scream her name. He could only hope she was in there, somewhere under the shattered ceiling, hope that she was okay.

"They actually did it." Mordan dusted himself off beside Rylan, staring wide-eyed at the portal to another dimension.

His mouth gaped, opening fish-like a few times as he took in the devastation. Then his eyebrows dropped and eyes gleamed.

In a commanding voice, he addressed the Darkfrey shadyrs scattered around him, "To me. You—go and rally reinforcements. We have the Everdark to defeat today."

"What have they done?" Lian hissed.

She helped Harper to her feet, the rest of their team nearby equally horrified at what lay before them.

"Everly," Rylan gasped out her name, and broke into a run toward where he last saw her.

Footsteps clamored through the rubble behind him, but he didn't know or care who they belonged to.

Then the shroudpool bulged.

Like an octopus pushing its way free from a tar pit, a vasmire emerged, almost gingerly, testing its surroundings with twisting tentacles.

That was fast. Rylan's blood chilled. There were a few active shroudpools in the region, kept as well-patrolled and monitored as they could be. Maybe one or two eidolghasts a day came through them and were dealt with as quickly as possible by the Darkfrey shadyrs.

But they were nowhere near the scale of this portal. Most weren't even as big as a regular doorway. This ... this shroudpool was large enough to drive a mining truck through. Rylan shuddered.

Does the size of the shroudpool affect the size of the eidolghast that can come through?

A cry like booming horn and nails on a chalkboard pierced the air. Rylan ducked as a herrelspurn flew out from the shroudpool above the vasmire. Then a weroth bigger than he'd ever seen stepped through, spearing the vasmire under a needle-like leg.

Ghast dammit. He had to find Everly before they were overrun.

The massive shroudpool must be like a beacon to the beasts.

Rylan allowed his body to change. He could no longer sense Everly's presence, the essences the Coruscare held inside her.

He tried not to think about what that could mean. But with three eidolghasts and counting in the vicinity, he had plenty to draw from, and experience enough to shift with it however he wanted. The strength of a werewolf. The regeneration of a vampire. The wings of a demon.

The shadowy mist of his change cleared as the shroudpool bulged again, and a horde of ghasts burst through. Dozens of them. They squabbled and clawed at each other as they stampeded around him. Some took to the air, flying off into an unnaturally darkened sky.

There was a scream beside him, quickly muffled as a Darkfrey shadyr was bitten clean in half by the mammoth-sized weroth. Her legs fell to the ground, still twitching. More screams echoed in the distance across the estate.

Rylan growled, rolling under the gelatinous limbs of some creature he'd never seen before in person or in theory.

One massive eye swiveled in the sickly-pink gel that formed a rough, constantly morphing body. His shadyr nerves twitched, trying to pull his change into ghast-knew-what that bizarre beast would shift him into.

It was all he could do to dodge the mass of eidolghasts clamoring through the space, rushing to break free and wreak havoc on his world and tear apart anything that stood in their way.

He caught a glimpse of Lian, Harper, and Denny, backed against the entryway, which had been smashed through and crumbled beside them. Jasper, Cherry, and Annabeth had gotten mixed up in the braces of shadyrs with Mordan, fighting side by side.

No one noticed or cared that the Howell team had joined the mix. It was shadyr versus the darkness and that was all any of them could focus on. Not Rylan, though. It was him versus anyone or anything that got between him and Everly.

Callan appeared at his side, clawed werewolf hands dripping in green ichor.

"Can you see them?" He howled over the sound of smashing walls and cries of war.

A sharp weroth limb lanced down from above and Rylan pulled Callan to the side. "Not since the pool opened."

He could barely see three feet in front of him, constantly moving to dodge the lashing of tentacles, teeth, and talons. They were overwhelmed, flooded with monsters.

A great cry came from the end of the hall. At the elevated edges of the ballroom, hundreds of Darkfrey shadyrs poured into the space. A surge of hope flamed through Rylan.

One squad took off flying, bat wings pushing them into the gloomy sky to hunt down the herrelspurn and other airborne eidolghasts. Others swarmed in groups of four over the monsters that matched the change they'd taken. The numbers were on their side, but still more beasts clambered through the massive shroudpool.

"Push forward!" Mordan commanded, shifting into pallid skin and pointy teeth.

The Darkfrey braces caught up to Rylan and Callan, bringing down eidolghasts as they went. Mordan fought beside them, eyes sparkling.

Rylan turned back toward where Everly had vanished. Callan pressed in at one shoulder, and more shadyrs came in at his other side. And they pushed.

A wall of shadyrs met the throng of eidolghasts. Fur and acid flew, flashes of flesh, blood, and darkness streaked through Rylan's sight as he charged into the thick of the battle. A teeth-lined tentacle ripped across his back, tearing from shoulder blade to bicep.

He pitched backward to pin the slithering limb between himself and the stone floor. Latching a clawed hand around the tentacle, he tore it free from the body that owned it.

His left arm hung limp but would heal quickly enough. He couldn't let it slow him down. A Darkfrey offered him a hand to help him to his feet. He nodded his thanks, and they pressed forward again.

They were almost there, had almost pushed the horde back to the shroudpool. It felt good, fighting side by side with those he'd lived with, trained with for so long, instead of fighting against them. They'd betrayed him, in so many ways, but they were still a kind of family to him.

They were all dedicated soldiers and fought together like a seamless engine of eidolghast destruction.

Callan caught his eye, a grim smile pressing his lips together. They were close, the shroudpool almost within reach. It loomed over them, a wavering black hole that seemed to absorb all light around it. Wriggling, wormy strands squirmed across the surface.

"Push on!" Mordan yelled from their backs. "Into the Everdark! We will hold them on the other side, then purge their evil for good!"

A war cry of approval sounded from a few of the shadyrs around them, but many others only gawked from Mordan to the portal of nightmares before them.

"Don't listen to him! He'll get you all killed." Lian's voice rose strong over the

cacophony of battle. "Do what you can to hold off the ghasts, but don't step through that shroudpool. It's suicide."

The path to the shroudpool was cleared. Mordan stepped in front of it with a brace by his side. But none stepped through.

Rylan clawed into the tiles and timber around the edges, calling Everly's name and searching for any glimpse of her red jacket or pale, ashy hair. Callan mirrored him, yelling for Tammy.

"Go through, I said! That's an order!" Mordan bellowed.

One shadyr took a small step forward, then quickly retracted. Mordan growled, stalking toward her.

"Cowards!" His hands thrust against her chest, throwing her across the room.

She landed beside a vasmire, which rolled its tooth-covered tentacles over the top of her before she could get back to her feet. Her screams were muffled, disappearing beneath sickening chewing sounds.

Mordan's sharp teeth bared as he snapped at the remains of her brace. "I've ordered you to go through and fight the Everdark, and I will not suffer disloyalty."

"He's mad, can't you see? He doesn't care about any of you!" Lian yelled from across the battlefield, working with the other Howell and Darkfrey shadyrs to hold back the scattered eidolghasts.

Rylan took in what he could of his periphery as he clawed through the rubble.

"I can't find her," he cried to Callan.

Callan's werewolf snout wrinkled, and he shook his head. "You think ... you think they ended up on the other side?"

Mordan swung his attention to them, grin widening. "Didn't you see? Them and the Mesmans, they were all sucked through when the pool formed."

Rylan's heart compressed with a pressure that could form a diamond. "No ..."

"Go after them," Mordan goaded with a sharp-toothed smile. "Go. Be my first soldiers to set foot in enemy territory. Show these other cowards what bravery looks like."

Rylan stood from his crouched position. He crunched across the debris, the shroudpool in his sights. If Everly was in there, he was going. Mordan could be lying ... but Rylan couldn't sense Everly's presence.

Either way, she's not here anymore.

If there was even the slightest chance she was still alive on the other side, Rylan had to go to her.

Then he noticed Callan matching his trajectory. Rylan stopped and grabbed his brother's arm.

"What are you thinking? You aren't going through."

"I have to. If Tammy is in there ... I have to."

Rylan froze, hand clenched around Callan's skin. He had every intention of going through himself. He was going after Everly, had only thought of Everly. But he didn't want his brother stepping through to a place no one had ever returned from.

He shook his head at Callan. "If I find Tammy, I'll bring her back too. But you're staying here."

The massive weroth came crashing to the ground across the room, taking out half a wall as it was felled. Skirmishes still raged all around them and flowed out into the grounds. Mordan screamed at the shadyrs, but none approached the shroudpool.

"Are you kidding me? If you're not letting me through, I'm not letting you. You think I want to lose you, too? That's what will happen if you go alone. At least if we're together ... we're together."

Rylan's jaw twitched. When Callan had left the Darkfreys before him, it felt like a betrayal, but the loss of his brother then would be nothing to losing him to the hellscape of the Everdark.

"I don't want you to get hurt. There's basically no chance we come back from this. Not without a miracle."

Callan nodded slowly, never breaking eye contact with Rylan. It was clear in his firm gaze that he understood the risks entirely.

"Then let's keep our fingers crossed for one."

Shoulder to shoulder they marched toward the shroudpool.

"Rylan!" Harper's voice screamed from behind. "Lian! What are they doing! Where's Everly? RYLAN WHERE'S EVERLY?"

Rylan looked back but kept walking. He saw Lian physically restraining Harper, who screamed and strained toward him. He saw Annabeth and Cherry, fighting back-to-back, turn to catch his eye, mouths dropping open in shock.

And then a churning slick of shadows washed over him.

Everly swooped forward, catching Tammy with one arm as she hung skewered by the weroths leg. She thrust her other arm out, lashing the weroth with a strand of light.

It squealed, rearing back. Its long, spidery limb slurped out of Tammy's chest as it pulled free. The orb Tammy had collected smacked onto the ground. Her full weight fell onto Everly, pressing her down onto the slippery stones. Energy crackled where Everly and Tammy's flesh met, and Everly shifted her weight so her jacket created a barrier between them.

The weroth roared and snapped at them, and Everly directed her light toward it again. The tendril shot out in a flash, trying to capture the creature, to consume it. The weroth moved faster, skittering away into the surrounding dark.

"Tammy?" Everly cried, high-pitched.

Tammy's head lolled. "Mmf."

"Hey, hang on, okay?" Everly readjusted Tammy's weight so she could hold her more comfortably.

Eidolghasts surged around them, pressing into the edges of Everly's light, as though driven to a frenzy by the scent of Tammy's blood. Everly loosed a second tendril, then a third, swatting and striking at the creatures. She was hyperaware of Tammy's closeness, her body, her soul, pressed against Everly's chest.

Right there, like a snack for the Coruscare.

Beads of sweat flushed her face and neck as she directed its wrath and hunger outward. She found it easier to do with the motions of her arms, but needed one to keep Tammy held up. It would have been even better if she could get two arms around Tammy, lift her properly so she could make her way back to the shroudpool and escape this nightmare.

But the ghasts kept up their threat, and Tammy remained slumped against her, and Everly could barely take a step forward while splitting her focus on both.

"Tammy? Hey, can you teleport yourself out? Can you get back to Dark Corner?" Everly urged.

If Tammy could go, Everly could put all her energy into fighting through to the portal, get back to their world, and hopefully get someone to Dark Corner in time to give Tammy the medical care she needed.

"Try for me. Don't you dare even argue, just try!"

"Mmf," she said again, her mouth muffled against Everly's shoulder.

She moaned a low, long note that juddered out into a sob.

Her words were a rough breath. "Can't. Not working."

Her head flopped backward. The red skin and wings of her demon form seemed to grow dull and retract, as though her body was failing to hold the form. Everly had seen similar in Rylan, the night he almost died on the street in front of her house.

He had looked like a vampire, but when his body had taken more damage than it could handle, he faded back to something more human. He was lucky that there was enough regeneration power left even in that form to help him hang on.

"Change!" Everly cried out. "Change into vampire form, so you can heal. Come on, Tammy, please!"

There had to be a vasmire out there in the storm of monsters.

Tammy's head wobbled limply; her face turned up to the endless black sky.

Everly's mind raced. Could she try to take Tammy's soul into her, like she did with Rylan? Keep it safe until they could return her to her body? But what if her body didn't survive? She could feel the urging of the Coruscare to let it do it, let it consume her, but with that urging came no reassurance that it would be saving her.

She tried to rouse Tammy, to feel for her pulse, but had to return her attention to a new weroth stabbing its saber legs at them. It opened its huge maw, the internal glow eerie in the dark world, like a deep-sea predator, luring its prey.

Behind it, outside of the reach of her light, came the sounds of another scuffle. Everly lassoed the weroth with two tendrils together, and flung it away, just as a dismembered head of a herrelspurn bounced onto the ground before her. A few other eidolghasts that had been testing Everly's defenses scattered.

"Everly!" came a voice that made her heart backflip.

"Rylan?" she replied in a squeal.

Two massive, humanoid forms strode into the light. If it hadn't been for his voice, Everly wasn't sure she'd have been able to recognize Rylan as he stood before her.

Monstrous, three times his normal mass, armor plated and ridged with spines. His skin glittered a metallic blue where it showed through his torn clothing.

Rylan lunged toward her, stopped short by the view of the lifeless girl in her arms.

"What happened to Tammy?" The second voice was Callan's, in a form matching his brother.

"A weroth got her, her shoulder. I don't know ..." Everly stuttered, eyes stuck on Rylan.

"I'll take her," Callan said, reaching out arms almost as thick as Tammy's torso.

He lifted her and cradled her against his chest. She'd faded back almost entirely to human form. Her head rolled to the side, and she let out a low moan. Alive. For now.

With her arms free, Everly stepped into Rylan's. His skin was hard as steel, like embracing a knight in full armor. "What are you doing here? How?"

"We came after you," he whispered into her hair, bringing a hand up to brush the back of her head.

"You're crazy," she whispered back, flushing from a gratitude and relief she had no idea how to express.

"Watch your six!" Callan growled, and Everly pushed away, shooting her strands of light at a vasmire's tentacles that slithered and whipped around them.

"We need to move. What happened to the Mesmans?" Rylan's voice growled over their name.

"Gone. Dead. We found Blaise though. His remains. And this." Everly bent to collect the intricately carved orb.

She felt sick handling it so she passed it to Rylan. "Tammy thinks it might be able to close the shroudpool the Mesmans made. Or at least make it dormant. Just ... be careful with it. I'll explain if we get out of here."

Rylan looped an arm around her, bringing her close to his steel-plate chest, and placed a firm kiss to her cheek.

The heat of his lips left a tingling mark behind. "Let's get out of here then."

Without Tammy's weight, and with the Coruscare near fully recovered, Everly blazed bright, launching off the ground until her feet floated near the brothers' heads.

"I don't even know what you two are at the moment, but I hope it's fast."

Rylan nodded. "You set the pace and we'll keep up."

"Faster than I've ever been. Yay for my first time in super-multiform." Callan grinned wryly, but it didn't meet his eyes.

He checked Tammy, then set his sights forward to the shroudpool.

Everly took off, her light spreading around the brothers below her. Shooting-star tendrils stepped around them, stilt-like, forming a protective cage as they ran.

"On your right," Rylan yelled, and Everly struck out.

A thick chain of light sliced deep into a surreal creature of crystalline daddy-longlegs limbs and clockwork eyes.

"What in the Everdark was that?" Everly asked.

"I'll explain if we get out of here." Rylan smirked back, keeping his eyes on guard. "Up front!"

Everly attacked and Rylan spotted, again and again, pushing their way into the flow of monsters all trying to get to the same destination.

The Coruscare's powers renewed with a vengeance, followed by the odd sensation of fullness, satiation, glee, as Everly smashed their way through the monsters.

She hadn't intended the powers to consume any ghasts, hadn't allowed it, hadn't even noticed it happen. But somewhere in the mad melee of whipping light and nightmarish beasts, the Coruscare had fed again.

The thought unsettled her, but not as much as the understanding deep in her core that destruction was coming for them, like a tsunami on the horizon.

She cleared their path to the shroudpool with a burst of light and Rylan stared at her in awe. "Maybe with you on our side, we could take on the whole Everdark."

Sweat drenched Everly's chest and she shook her head firmly. "We need to get out, and we need to close the door. Eidolghasts aren't the only thing here that's a threat."

"Something worse?" Rylan's eyebrows furrowed, wrinkling his shining blue skin.

"You remember the dream we shared that time? With the being of darkness that obliterated everything it touched?"

"Oh," Rylan said flatly.

"WHAT?" Callan said.

They reached the shroudpool, and Everly formed a fence of light to hold off the eidolghasts trying to press through around them. "Big. Bad. The Coruscare's dark twin. And I think we've attracted its attention."

Callan turned wide eyes from her and carried Tammy through the dark portal. Rylan hesitated.

"I'll be right behind you." Everly drew herself down to his level.

"No, together," he said.

Everly bit her lip and nodded. They stepped into the wriggling slick of magic.

And came out together on the other side.

Everly gasped fresh earth air into her lungs, and it tasted of blood. There were bodies scattered around what was left of the room. Fights still raged between Darkfreys and ghasts, spilling out into the now visible grounds. Mordan Darkfrey stood before her, teeth bared and eyebrows high as he took in their sudden appearance.

Harper called out, and Everly turned to find her friend.

Then every hair on the back of her neck rose so high her skin twinged painfully. The Coruscare shuddered within her.

And from the shroudpool behind her, a mass of infinitely black nothingness burst through.

16

Like a nightmare made real, a maddening brume of darkness swirled above the shroudpool. Everly gazed up at it, her and the Coruscare's shared panic short-circuiting her brain.

It's here. It followed us.

"What is that?" Mordan spat at her.

Dark twin. Infuscur. Void. Destruction. The end. The Coruscare answered from within, its light flickering. Everly couldn't speak.

The *Infuscur* spun like an empty galaxy, filling the sky. And then it rushed down at them.

Rylan caught Everly with one arm. He pulled her to the side in a tumbling leap. Callan took Tammy, dodging in the other direction.

Darkness fell over Mordan like black ink poured into water, obscuring him entirely. As the midnight cloud contracted, Everly was sure she'd find Mordan gone, erased from the world.

Instead, the dark being rushed into him, pouring into his eyes, ears, nostrils, mouth. His body twitched and jerked, joints turning at wrong angles as he hovered over an ebony-stained crater.

He stilled. An aura of juddering darkness ran like ribbons around his body. His fully black eyes turned to Everly, and he smiled.

"Oh shit." Everly brought up a shield of light with less than a second to spare.

Darkness lashed at her, clashing against the glittering strands with sizzling energy. Her defense held, but the force of the attack threw her backward. The soles of her boots clattered across debris as she steadied herself.

The Infuscur's tendrils were similar to the Coruscare's but inverse. Long ribbons of blackness that seemed to suck in the light rather than sparkle. It whipped out again, striking three Darkfrey shadyrs who stood closest to what had been Mordan.

It passed right through them, and in its wake, the shadyrs crumbled, falling into powdery pieces, then faded into nothing.

It made them nothing at all.

Everly's mouth hung open but she couldn't breathe. She'd had this nightmare, too many times. It had scared the life out of her even in her dreams, and now it was here, real, in front of her.

Rylan attempted to drag her away. Callan ran to Lian, Harper, and the other Howell House shadyrs at the end of the hall. Tammy remained cradled in Callan's arms, her life ebbing away with every jostle, every second her wound was untended. Cherry, Jasper, Annabeth, even fucking Denny—she couldn't see any of them turned to *nothing*.

And I'm the only one with a chance of facing the Infuscur.

"Get to the others and get out of here. Now." Everly didn't give Rylan a chance to argue.

She sped forward, burning like a comet toward the Infuscur.

Mordan raised himself off the ground, shooting back at her with glee in his dark eyes. But Everly was sure there was nothing left of Mordan in that expression.

Their energy smashed into each other's, and the buildings around them shook.

Everly struck with everything she had. Her glowing tendrils were caught easily in dark ribbons, wrenched, and swung. It flipped Everly around it and flung her to the rubble-strewn ground.

Everly hit hard, even with trying to cushion the fall with her light. Her skin burst on her temple, shoulder, hip. Bones crunched. She was still shaking off a view full of stars and spots when the Infuscur struck at her again. She dragged herself backward, onto her feet, and the black ribbons struck where she'd been. Fallen walls and roof tiles crumbled and vanished under their touch.

One ribbon looped around her boot. She screamed as she shot every bit of power out around her. She forced the darkness off her in the miniscule gap of time between her shoe disintegrating and that same destructive force touching her flesh.

It's too strong. We're no match for it.

The Coruscare and Infuscur may have been some twisted kind of twins, paired entities of light and dark, but Everly only held two-thirds of the Coruscare.

Mordan held the Infuscur at full power. And it was throwing her around like a ragdoll. She couldn't beat it. Not like this.

Everly burst upward, pushing as high as her powers could lift her, breaching the broken roof of the ballroom.

She had only a moment before the Infuscur chased after her. Long enough to see her friends checking back with worried glances as they made a dash away from the battle of opposing energies.

Good. She just needed to buy enough time for them to escape, then try to get herself clear. She hardly finished the thought before darkness lashed in front of her nose and she reeled backward, hitting the edge of the broken roof and sliding out across the tiles.

The Infuscur kept close pursuit, harpooning the roof around her. Beams and shingles evaporated, and a car-sized section fell out from underneath Everly. She took the opportunity to go down with it. Dust exploded around her, filling the room.

Shutting off every bit of her light, Everly scrambled over the fallen roofing. She could barely see, her eyes and lungs stinging with grit.

She aimed on instinct for the gap in the wall she'd seen from above. The sound of lashing ribbons came from behind her. The Infuscur sought her with the reach of its void-touch tendrils, stabbing them through the obscuring cloud.

Everly's hand landed on the edges of broken bricks, and the dust cleared. She stared out into the training yards of the estate.

It couldn't be much past midday, but the world had become dark as an eclipse. The screams and blows of skirmishes echoed from every direction, and shadyrs, herrelspurn, and other flying eidolghasts clashed in the sky.

And still more eidolghasts emerged through the shroudpool. The Darkfrey line there was scattered, and she couldn't do anything more while the Infuscur sought her destruction.

Everly took off, sprinting toward the shadows of a nearby covered walkway, hoping it would conceal her.

Her heartbeat pounded in her throat and her face burned as she ducked between a thick pillar and hedge. She took a chance to glance back.

The Infuscur raised itself high over the shattered ballroom, lashing at the building as though it could find her by obliterating everything around it. With its attention remaining there, Everly fled.

She headed in the direction she'd last seen Rylan and her friends running.

She went left up a side path and almost smacked face-first into a weroth that chewed on the body of a Darkfrey shadyr. It took a significant effort to keep her light inside. She couldn't risk attracting the Infuscur again.

She skidded the other way, across a garden bed, her one bare foot punctured by woodchips. Bounding up entry steps to the main building, she spotted the Howell team down the hall, filing into a secret passage she and Lian had used once before. They fretted and argued, Rylan's growling voice echoing down the corridor.

Harper spotted Everly first and ran to meet her halfway. She threw her arms around her, squeezing tight. Everly squeezed back, panting hard.

"Did you beat it? Is it gone?" Harper questioned with fierce eyes.

Everly could only shake her head. She had no breath left for words.

Harper chewed a lip for a moment, then took Everly's hand and dragged her to join the others. There was a pat on the arm from Lian, and a nod from Callan, still holding Tammy close to his now more werewolf-shaped form.

Rylan reached for the fresh blood near Everly's temple. The torn skin there had already closed, but his fingertips came away glossy and red.

A rumble from the other end of the building heralded a rout of Darkfreys coming their way, something large on their tail.

"Out, quick!" Lian hissed through fanged teeth, waving them into the passageway. They bolted in, running together in a tight group.

It was bizarre seeing the team in all different shadyr shifts. Normally they all changed together, all vampires, or all werewolves. But with so many eidolghasts around, each shadyr had their own type, or mix of types.

Cherry had ghosted out, while Annabeth and Jasper seemed to be varying mixes of vampire and demon. Denny and Lian stuck to straight-up vampire.

Rylan had held his mammoth, armored form, but their escape tunnel required something smaller, and shadows obscured him momentarily as he shifted to a combination of vampire and nyevmer.

Pale skin and fangs, with the hint of sparkling blue scales forming a smooth protection across his shoulders and down to clawed hands. Everly doubted a nyevmer had swum free of the shroudpool. He must have been drawing its essence from within her, within the pool of eidolghast energies that the Coruscare had absorbed over eons.

Everly wished the shadyrs could take on some kind of Coruscare form, or that all of them had the power to use the essences within her to change into whatever they wanted, like Rylan had been imbued with since his soul was freed.

Anything to give them an advantage over what felt like frightening odds. For now, Everly would be happy if they could just get out of there alive.

Their escape tunnel didn't last long. They tumbled out through the shattered passageway where half the building had been torn away, opening them to the outside world. Lian searched about wildly, then pointed across the devastation to a hole showing beneath splintered floorboards.

The spine-scraping screech of a herrelspurn cut through the air and they dived into that dark hollow as a gust of fire caught the air behind them.

Everly skidded down a slope of loose bricks, hips and knuckles grazing as she tried to slow her descent. Her feet hit flat ground, and she wobbled upright in time to catch Harper tumbling after her. Rylan came through last, keeping his eyes on the gap above them, teeth flashing as he watched for any pursuers.

"I've never been down here before," Lian spoke into the dusty darkness. "But the garages are that general direction. I say we help ourselves to a vehicle and get the Everdark out of here."

Everly's entire body screamed with over-tired muscles, and her lungs burned. Harper kept her phone held up for both of them, and the light trembled as they ran.

"I've been here before." Rylan's pushed through to the lead and took a right when they hit an intersection. "This was where I first saw evidence of the Mesmans' work, in a small room up ahead. But they blindsided me and cleared everything out before I worked out who it was or could do anything about it."

Rylan passed a doorway, did a double take, then jogged back to it. Everyone stopped beside him, crowding to see what caught his attention.

Through the ancient cut-stone doorway lay a room too dark for Everly to see what made the others gasp. Harper shined her light in, and Everly glared at the array of skeletal figures standing before them. The carved-out room was so filled with bones it was like an ossuary. An army of misshapen undead standing at attention.

"Looks like they decided this space was safe to use again," Rylan muttered.

Denny stabbed at one of the bone effigies with his machete. "A ghast-blighted storeroom for all their dark magic shitfuckery."

"Those are the lures?" Annabeth said, her words trembling.

"Yeah, but I don't think they are activated, or whatever. They aren't doing that horrible wiggly thing they do when they are," Everly said.

"Come on," Callan snapped, eyes locked on Tammy's marble white skin. "We have to keep moving. We don't have much time."

Everly's body groaned, but she drew every resource she had to keep up. The tunnel hit some stairs, which took them to an exit in an old brick toolshed.

Once outside again, Everly looked around, trying to get her bearings and track where the Infuscur was, but she'd never been in this part of the estate before. The sky was so dark now, she worried the Infuscur could be right above them, camouflaged by its aura of black around Mordan's body, and they wouldn't even see it.

Denny smacked the flat of his machete in his hand then pointed across a section of smaller cottages and training courts. "Garage is down that way. No more tunnels to take out here. Ya'll ready to hoof it?"

He didn't wait for a reply, just took off across the shadowed lawn.

Bursting from their cover, they ran fast after him, keeping as close together as possible without elbows and feet clashing.

The manicured grass muffled the sound of their boots, and it felt unnaturally cold under Everly's bare foot. Down the hill, she could see where a long, low building met with a laneway that snaked around and joined the main drive.

They might actually make it. Get in, get a car or two, and get out.

But then what? How long could they hide from this? How far would this hellscape spread, as eidolghasts kept spilling through the enormous, unchecked shroudpool?

How much of the world would the Infuscur dissolve into nothingness?

Everly knew they had to get away, they had to regroup, save Tammy. But after that

... after that might come nothing anyway. It felt like the end of the world.

Without warning, Denny veered off to the left, away from their target.

"Denny!" Rylan scream-whispered.

"What stupid thing is he doing to get us killed this time?" Harper rasped out. "He is going to be on the receiving end of some open palm cheek music if we survive this."

"I can't wait for him this time. I'm moving on." Callan slowed only enough to give them all a view of Tammy, her huddled mass a painting of black, white, and red.

Rylan nodded. "Anna, Jas, Cherry, stick with him, get some engines running. We'll go and get this jerk back in line."

With nods to acknowledge the order, they split off, leaving Rylan, Everly, Harper, and Lian to chase down Denny. Everly wondered how Rylan made the call on the split, but was grateful he didn't send her on without him.

She didn't want to leave his side, or Harper's, or Lian's. When apocalyptic sounds crashed and cried from every direction, all she wanted was her family close.

If this was the end, they were what would keep her fighting.

Denny kept ahead of them all the way to where one of the cottages had been split in half, one side standing nearly pristine, and the other lying in a jumble of red brick and torn upholstery.

By the time they reached him, he was lifting a slab of ceiling plaster with a grunt. A woman dragged her legs out from beneath, then moaned up onto her feet.

"Alexis?" Rylan gaped.

She didn't answer. She was too busy thanking Denny with a tongue-filled kiss.

"Okay," mumbled Harper, staring at the couple with more horror in her eyes than she'd shown before. "So this really is the end of the world."

"Alexis *Darkfrey*?" Everly blinked, struggling to take in what she was seeing.

The woman's hourglass figure fit snuggly into a high-tech-looking black catsuit, and a fall of silky blond hair tumbled down her back.

Everly choked. "You mean ... it really was real?"

Denny lifted his head to the sky and crowed, "Told you so!"

"Keep it down!" Rylan said.

"Real enough maybe, but she still ratted us out on our way in, cost us the time we needed to stop all of this." Lian's top lip curled, revealing pointed teeth.

Alexis gasped, throwing a hand to her chest and pleading to Denny, "It wasn't me, I swear! Father was monitoring my phone. I didn't know until today."

"I believe you, babe," Denny crooned and leaned in for another kiss.

Rylan pushed them apart with a shove on Denny's shoulder. "You think that's where the Mesmans got their other info, about where Tammy and Everly were this morning? What else have you been texting?"

"Dick pics, mostly." He shrugged.

"Oh for ghast's sake." Harper dropped her face into her hands. "Can we just get out of here now?"

Alexis wrapped a hand tightly around one of Denny's. "I'm coming too. I should have gone with you sooner, I'm sorry."

Lian's eyes narrowed, shooting between the woman and the devastation of the estate behind them. "Don't you have kids out here somewhere?"

Alexis's pretty red lips twisted up. "Those clingy brats? Who cares? They're Darkfreys. Someone else will look after them."

"She's as awful as he is," Everly mumbled, finally seeing where the chemistry came from.

Alexis leaned into Denny, fawning. "They're not my family anymore. I'm done with it all. Everything is sorted. Screw that arranged marriage and the ugly little spawn it produced. It's just you and me now."

"I don't want to hear *anything else*," Rylan grunted, rubbing between his eyebrows. "Just ... get to the garage."

Everly and Harper silently communicated through woeful expressions of withheld bile, and then they were moving again. Their path passed the ruined cottage and brought them coming around to the garage from the lane leading in.

As they sprinted along the loose gravel, two cars whizzed past them, unfamiliar faces in the drivers' seats. At least some of the Darkfreys had enough sense to get themselves out of there, but so many more were staying, loyal to the end.

Everly wondered how many were dying. Whether the squads of younger, barely trained kids were rushing into battle, and being slaughtered.

Whether Alexis's kids were among them.

Another car raced toward them then peeled to a stop, skidding on the loose surface. The electric window rolled down and an older man with bulging eyes stuck his head out.

"Denny, boy! Whatcha doing here in all this mess?"

Denny reached out a hand, fist-bumping the man. "Uncle Teddy! We're here to save the world, of course. Might have been a little late though."

"Well come on then, jump in! I'm off to the bunker. Got a little bit of room for you if you want in." Teddy's eyes bulged even further, then squinted unevenly. "Only you though."

Oh, that *Uncle Teddy*, Everly remembered. Wait, wasn't that Tammy's Uncle Teddy with the bunker? Were they related?

Everly didn't care at this point. She held her breath, partly hoping Denny would go, partly wishing she had a bunker to hide out the end of the world in too.

"Aw, nah, that's all right, Teddy. I'm not going to go hide. Going to fight this thing

out, 'cause I'm a damn good shadyr and I gotta show all these losers up."

Alexis leaned into him. "You are so fucking hot right now, I would do you in a chillifest portapotty."

Teddy's shoulders lifted and dropped, and he accelerated away.

Rylan muttered a string of unintelligible curses, then took Everly's hand in the last dash to the open garage doors. "Almost there."

They hit the entrance as a large van pulled up from the shadows of the building, Cherry at the wheel. He called back, and Jasper slid the side door open. Inside, Callan and Annabeth squeezed around where Tammy lay on the end bench seat. They'd obtained a first aid kit from somewhere on the way and were focused on stemming blood loss.

About to climb in, Everly checked back for Harper and Lian, and — "Ugh, where's Denny?"

"Are you kidding me?" Rylan's teeth grinding were almost louder than his words.

Down in the middle of the lane where they had just been, Denny and Alexis stood together, making out with all the passion of love-sick teenagers.

And behind them, the void-black silhouette of the biggest weroth Everly had ever seen needled its way toward them. Its mouth opened in a jagged green grin.

17

"Look out!" Everly screamed.

Denny and Alexis split apart, in time to not have the weroth's mouth close around both of their heads.

Instead, it just closed around Alexis's. The slurping crunch echoed across the air and turned Everly's guts to ice water. A range of curse words flew from the van behind her.

Alexis's body rag-dolled onto the gravel, spurts of blood arcing from her neck like a sick fountain.

Denny loosed a roar, already swinging at the creature with his machete.

Rylan and Lian were a few steps into a run when one of the weroth's pointed feet stabbed right through Denny's stomach from behind, and he froze statue-still with his machete mid-swing.

Everly tensed. If she glowed up now, she could get in and get the monster off him, kill it before the Infuscur noticed, if she was lucky. It was worth the try, even for Denny.

But everything happened so quickly, she didn't have a chance.

Denny surged into motion again, writhing and swearing, as the weroth lifted him like a skewered hors d'oeuvre toward its gaping maw. Lian, Harper, Everly, and Rylan charged forward again.

The pack on Denny's back swung loosely over one arm, and he dug a hand in, pulling out a long, gray brick.

Rylan skidded to a stop. "Is that C-4?"

"I thought I took it all off him!" Lian stared, wide-eyed.

The weroth swallowed Denny whole. There was a faint click.

Rylan screamed, "Get down!"

The four of them dropped onto the rough ground.

The force of the blast rushed through Everly's hair and over her back, and she was hit with a sound like lightning directly striking her eardrum.

Sharp pieces of gravel and chunks of acidic flesh flew over her head.

One hit Everly's bare foot, sizzling and stinging her skin. She gasped and kicked it off. Rylan maneuvered his body over hers as the bloody rain pattered over them.

A short moment that felt like an eternity later, the sound stopped, and Rylan rolled off to her side. "You okay?"

She nodded. Her ears rang and her vision blurred as she got onto all fours, checking the others.

Harper stared up at her, wide-eyed. "I died an hour ago, didn't I? None of this is even real anymore. That absolute, idiotic, jerk! He can't … can't be *gone*?"

Everly's stomach clenched, and she swallowed back vomit.

He was gone? Of course he was, but her brain didn't want to comprehend the loss.

That anyone she knew could *be dead* was something she didn't want to face. That there was no body to look at and confirm made it harder to grasp the fact. Or maybe there was something left of him. Everly didn't want to examine the pieces of gore that had spattered all around them too closely.

She pulled Harper to her feet and then right into her arms. They broke away a second later, still wide-eyed and pale, but both knew they couldn't linger. The blast would attract attention.

Cherry brought the van to a halt right beside them, side door still open. Jasper grabbed Everly's arm and yanked her in, followed by Harper, Lian, and Rylan.

They burned out of the estate as fast as Cherry dared drive.

C herry brought the Darkfrey van to a screaming stop at the steps to Howell House. Everly opened the sliding door and moved back so Callan could take Tammy out first.

Their arrival was met with a crowd of concerned faces and shouted questions. What was happening at the estate? Why had the sky gone dark?

"What happened to Lian's car and all my groceries?" Rushelle cried.

Then she took in their blood-stained, torn clothing and the bundle that was Tammy. She puffed up and cleared a path through the crowd of shadyrs awaiting answers.

Everly only knew Tammy was still alive by how fast Callan moved.

Lian climbed onto the porch and yelled to the expectant faces. "Everyone get inside. Get clear of the yard, and shelter in the house, lights off. Danger is coming."

"But what happened?" Lucas pushed to the front, his brace right behind him.

Molly stared at the darkened sky, her face pale and trembling.

"We told you the Mesmans wanted to open a shroudpool. Well, they did." Lian's shoulders slumped, and she pushed her way inside.

The crowd muttered among itself, then split off in a hurry, running to tents and

makeshift homes to gather supplies before filing into the homestead.

Everly followed in after Lian, with Harper and Rylan close behind her.

"Neri?" Callan's voice cracked around her name.

She came galloping down the stairs, Birdie cuddled tight in one hand. She pushed straight through to Harper, throwing her free arm around her. Birdie yapped in the small gap between them.

"I was so worried! So worried! You were away so long, and the sky went black and I thought a sea storm was coming and you would be washed away from me!"

Harper's brown eyes filled with tears. Her un-made face was blood-spattered and worn.

She pressed her cheek to Neri's forehead for a moment then whispered, "Tammy needs you."

Neri broke away and looked around for her, finally realizing that she was what Callan carried. "Oh no. Oh no!"

Callan moved through to the living room. He lay Tammy onto a couch, turned a small side lamp on and the ceiling lights off, pulling curtains closed for good measure.

Neri dashed in after him, and a second later, her voice filled the house. The strength of it echoed through Everly's own aching bones. The Coruscare had healed the cuts and bruises she'd sustained already, but it didn't touch the deep, dull pain inside. She wasn't sure it was the sort of injury that Neri could repair, either.

It was loss, despair, hopelessness.

Still, the mermaid girl sang her mixed-up, yearning tune, and the beauty of it reminded Everly that she was still alive. And while ever she was still alive, she'd keep fighting for those she loved.

She could keep trying to fix things.

With a nod to Harper and Callan, who remained with Tammy and Neri, Everly continued to the kitchen, turned the lights off, and took a seat at the dining table. She placed her phone beside her, so that a little light remained for her to see by.

She wasn't sure whether keeping the house blacked out would keep them safe, but it might at least buy them some time before more eidolghasts or the Infuscur came barreling up to their door. Rylan sat close beside her, his shoulder pressed against hers. Cherry, Jasper, and Annabeth took seats across from them and stared down at the worn wood of the table.

Over in the kitchen, Rushelle clicked on the kettle then looked them over. "Where's Denny?"

Lian shook her head. She opened the pantry and rummaged around on a low shelf. Standing back up, she had an armful of beer cans, which she shared out around the table.

"They're warm, sorry, but I can't keep them in the fridge 'cause Denny steals them.

Or did. But still. We have to toast the dumbass."

Rushelle took hers while her red lips wobbled and her head shook.

Everly accepted one, cracking the tab with a sigh. Around the table cans popped and hissed.

It was Cherry who stood up, raising his beer. "To Denny. He died the way he lived, doing something stupid."

Everly half-smiled, but her eyes drooped, heavy and sore. They all lifted their drinks in return. "To Denny."

"And to every shadyr who fought and died today, and will fight and die today." Rylan's eyes were hard and sparkled in the low light. "The dark must fall."

The three across the table nodded firmly, and Everly wondered how many of them saw bodies of people they knew back there. Friends they had grown up with, teachers they'd trained with. Family.

The shadyrs around the room murmured together, "So the sun may rise again."

Everly took a token sip of warm beer, the fizz sharp up the back of her nose. She put the can back on the table and tried not to cry.

The front door creaked and closed, creaked and closed, as the house filled up around them. Lucas and his brace joined them at the table, and more shadyrs stood throughout the room until they were shoulder to shoulder.

Hushed murmurs filled the space.

"They really opened a shroudpool? Impossible."

"I got a call from a friend up the hill. Things sound bad out there."

"But one shroudpool couldn't do all of this, could it?"

"My brother is still at the estate. I told him to get out of there, but he wouldn't listen."

Lian moved to the head of the table, taking a big swig of her beer then thumping it down.

"This is how things are," she said, her voice cutting across the whispers. "The Mesmans opened a shroudpool. A bloody massive one. Eidolghasts are coming through at a faster rate than I've ever seen. More than I've ever seen. Bigger than I've ever seen. The estate is a war zone. And to top that off, some other big nasty has come through and possessed Mordan."

"The Infuscur," Everly offered. "The Coruscare knows it."

Rylan's eyebrows furrowed. "Looks like it knew the Coruscare, too. What can you tell us about it?"

Everly nodded and opened her mouth, but Lian cut in. "Someone here at Howell House was passing info to the Darkfreys. That's how the Mesmans grabbed Everly and Tammy, how they knew where they'd be. None of this would be happening otherwise. Maybe we need to keep what we know in a tighter circle."

She glared around the room, catching the eye of every shadyr.

"It wasn't Jasper, if that's what you're thinking." Cherry kept his eyes forward on his beer, missing the split-second puppy dog look Jasper gave him.

"It could be anyone," Rylan said, casting his gaze over the crowd with a look of spite. "How many of you have we brought in, fed, shared this home with? All it took was one of you betraying us for the Darkfreys. For what? Did you think you were going to go back to them? To the ones who killed our families to make us better soldiers? They turned us against each other, when now more than ever it's clear we should all have been on the same side. One where we don't kill or betray our own kind."

Grumbles of agreement spread across the space.

"Whoever it was, what does it matter now?" Everly offered.

She didn't like the idea that someone there was the reason the Mesmans caught her and Tammy, almost killed them both, and started all of this. But there were bigger things to worry about. Neri still sang in the living room, and the tune raised hairs on Everly's neck the longer it went on.

Please pull through, Tammy.

"The Mesmans are gone. Mordan is gone. Half the estate is gone. Who is anyone going to pass info on to now anyway?"

Lian dropped onto her chair with a huff. "That's a point."

Neri stopped singing, and the room went silent.

No more singing meant one of two outcomes. Everly held her breath.

Shadyrs shuffled over, bunching up tighter to clear a path. Callan walked in, with Tammy at his side. He had an arm around her waist, and she looked woozy, but alive.

Lian pressed her hands to her chest and sniffed.

"You made it." With no spare seats at the table, Lian shot up fast and offered hers to Tammy.

With a weak smile, Tammy flopped down into it.

She muttered, "Yup, you managed to drag me away from death's sweet embrace yet again. I mean, thanks. I guess."

Everly sniffled out a cross between a giggle and a sob. She reached across to place her hand close to Tammy's, but not quite touching.

"I know you're happier here with us, and we're all happy you're here too."

"Maybe. Whatever. Shut up."

Behind them, Neri beamed. Harper's dusty cheeks had tracks cleared by tears. Callan leaned on the wall behind Tammy, breathing like he'd run a marathon.

Tammy's eyes widened. She sat straighter and leaned toward Everly. "Did you get it? What happened to the orb?"

"We got it," Rylan said, bringing the green crystalline sphere up and placing it on

the table in front of him. "What is it?"

Tammy sighed. "It's, ugh, I can't say its proper name, but it translates roughly to Swallower."

Harper rubbed a hand down her face. "Aw man, Denny would have loved that."

Tammy's face fell, but she continued, "The Mesmans had it, and Blaise, he snuck peeks at their work, and he thought ... He thought he could close shroudpools with it. It was supposed to somehow absorb the shroudpool."

Timid before the crowd of shadyrs hanging on her words, she licked her lips. "It didn't work. At least not for us. We mucked around with it for a while out at Dark Corner and got no results. But then, his parents showed up, caught us out. And then, then that thing activated. It pulsed, just a bit—"

Visions from the dream of the Coruscare's past, with the orb pulsing, expanding and contracting and crushing the lives of thousands of eidolghasts into tiny drops of blood, flooded over Everly. The Coruscare stirred within her, riled up. She could hear its thoughts overlaying into hers.

We can beat our dark twin. We need to beat it. We just need to be stronger. She didn't sip any more beer, but she squeezed the can tight in her hand, dinting the metal.

Everly refocused on Tammy's voice. "The orb ripped through the shroudpool and knocked Blaise down with it. I used to think it was all ... I don't know. Bad timing. My fault. My curse."

Around the table, everyone shook their heads.

Tammy shook hers too. "It wasn't. We saw today how Kole is using old shadyr magic. He's got bones, ancient shadyr bones, embedded all through his skin. It was Blaise and me trying to say the old spell words, but the Swallower reacted to Kole. And despite everything terrible that happened, we did sort of close that shroudpool. It's not gone, but it's dormant. And if we could use this thing again to close the one at the estate, we might have a chance."

Everly could almost feel the threads of hope spreading across the room. Backs straightened. Eyes widened.

She exhaled softly then lifted her voice. "I've seen that before too. In the Coruscare's memories. It was used by the Infuscur to make the Bane, or at least, fill the Bane with energy, the condensed blood of thousands of eidolghasts. It looks ... Dangerous is an understatement. And we don't even know if we can activate it without Kole's magic."

"It's still something." Standing behind Tammy, Lian folded her arms. "A chance to close the portal. Maybe you've got the power to use the orb? If the Coruscare was powerful enough to open a portal, maybe it can close one too?"

We could. We could close it. Everly frowned at the sickening sphere. "Maybe? I could try."

Lian pointed to Everly. "Okay. Everly keeps the orb with her."

Then she jabbed her finger to their close group around the table. "And we get Everly to the shroudpool safely."

"How do we do that, with that Infuscur thing zooming around, turning people into nothing?" Cherry asked.

"And especially hunting the Coruscare," Rylan added.

"Don't suppose you saw a weak spot on it with that fancy sword of yours?" Lian asked Harper with a lift of her chin.

"No, sorry. Same as with Everly. No result on them for an easy kill point."

We can beat it. We can ... if we were whole.

The final word echoed down into Everly's toes, tingling and cold. Whole.

Then we beat the Infuscur. Then we close the shroudpool.

Everly squeezed her temple, trying to block out her dragon's voice. It had never spoken so much while she was awake before, never so clearly. Never so loudly. What it was saying gave her hope, but also terrified her.

Could she really trust the thing inside her? Could she continue keeping it under control if it were stronger? Did she have a choice not to try when this could be the end of Shroudhaven, maybe the end of the world?

"What do you know about this Infuscur being?" Lian asked her.

Everly blinked, trying to gather her thoughts. "It ... it's the yin to the Coruscare's yang. It possessed Mordan because it and the Coruscare are more energy-based creatures. They can't exist in this dimension for long without a host. The Coruscare is power and light and essence ..."

A few shadyrs around the room, including Annabeth, looked at her with awe-filled eyes.

"*Not* to be confused with goodness though. It exists to consume. The Infuscur exists to destroy. It is null, void, nothingness. The Coruscare can't beat it by taking its soul because it has none. These two beings, they've spent forever fighting each other. But when they're both at full power they are basically equals and cancel each other out. The Infuscur only broke apart the Coruscare last time by using the Bane."

Rylan slammed his hands on the table. "Shit, where is the Bane now?"

A swell of sickness rose in Everly's mouth, and she choked it back. "I don't know, it was on me before the portal opened, but I didn't see it after that."

Or feel it.

Rylan held her gaze with eyes darkened by heavy brows. "We need to make sure the Infuscur doesn't get it and use it against you."

"It doesn't need it, not really." Everly looked away from him. "I'm only holding two-thirds of the Coruscare in me. It's not at full power. The Infuscur thrashed us

out there."

She was leading her friends down the line of reasoning to a conclusion she wasn't sure she wanted. As though it would be easier if they made the decision for her.

"So we power you up again!" Harper clapped her hands, hope glittering in her eyes. "And we already know where the third piece is. Then you'll be safe and could even kick the Mordanfuscur's butt."

And there it was. The idea. The hope. Laid out like a noose around her throat. *Yes. We will win.*

Everly tried to smile in a reassuring way, but her lips twisted and curled. The Coruscare was being so loud, and she didn't understand why it had such confidence. If both it and the Infuscur were at full power, they would just be back to their endless, futile clash of equal opposites.

Rylan grabbed Everly's hand where it trembled under the table. "That doesn't sound safe. Look what happened to Mordan. The thing in him has total control. It was like it burned Mordan out of his own body."

"It is a lot of power for a human body to contain," Lian murmured.

"Ev's got this." Harper put her hands on hips lost under the old shirt of Everly's she still wore. "Mordan had no idea what hit him, but Everly's been keeping a crazy extradimensional deity locked down almost her whole life. She's got the experience and the strength. If anything, she's been more in control since getting the second piece."

Everly turned her face to her friend, drinking in the words. She almost made it sound possible. *Maybe I can do it. We can do it.*

Lian paced, moving closer to Everly. "Do you agree?"

Everly's words scratched out over a dry throat. "Making the Coruscare whole would give us a fighting chance, and I'll do my best to keep it under control."

Lian assessed each of the team for a long moment with narrowed eyes.

She closed them briefly, then let her words out in a long breath. "Okay then. We go for the third piece of the Coruscare, then head to the shroudpool fully powered and try to shut it down."

Bringing her gaze to the other shadyrs who stood around the room, she added, "And you lot, get ready. We'll gather up as many of the scattered Darkfreys as we can, and let you know when it's time to move."

The room started to clear out, hushed murmurs following the crowd. They couldn't go very far with every room and hallway packed, so word of the plan spread like a game of whispers out to those farthest away.

Neri thumped one fist on the table, startling Everly. "I'm coming too this time. I'm not going to sit on my own all scared and waiting. If you're all going out and getting hurt, I want to be there and sing to you then, not when you come back almost dead."

She wrapped a hand tightly around Harper's wrist, in a way that suggested she wasn't going to let go without a fight, and stared at the others with eyes rimmed in red.

"I'm in, too," Rushelle said.

"Neither of you have to. You don't have to be fighters. No one would mind if you stayed here," Lian told them.

"Ma'am, you've let me sit out plenty." Rushelle pressed a blond curl back into her high do. "And I'm more than grateful for that. You've let me be me. But today, I want to do more."

"You do enough. More than enough. You all do." Lian tugged her gray cardigan tight around her beanpole body. "I don't want to lose any of you. Even Denny, that stupid, stupid man ... was a loss I don't want to bear. But right now, I'm not sure we have any other options but to fight."

Callan peeled himself off the wall and stood tall beside his mother. "And we'll all fight together."

Everyone moved then, going to find supplies or to do whatever they felt they needed before what was likely a suicide mission. Only Everly stayed at the table, alone among a crowd of strangers, staring blindly into the space that had so long been her truest home.

Rylan returned to her side. He'd swapped his torn shirt for body armor, and he placed a pair of replacement boots in Everly's size in front of her, then drew his chair so close to hers that she was straddled between his thighs.

He whispered, "You don't have to do this. If you don't want to."

She half-turned her face, and found it nose to nose with his. "It might be our only chance to save the world."

"I'm not sure that's worth losing you. You are my world. I'm done with being the loyal soldier, giving away my life and everything *I* want for the cause. For a war we didn't start. Why does that have to be your responsibility? Why does it have to be your risk, your sacrifice? It's your choice, and you don't have to if you don't want to."

Everly shifted away, catching her breath. She didn't want to risk losing herself. She didn't want this to be the end. And a sharp feeling in her gut still didn't trust the Coruscare, no matter how pliantly it behaved. But what else could they do?

"We'll go and get the third crystal, but we won't use it unless we absolutely have to, okay?"

Rylan bent down and pressed his forehead against hers, exhaling a sigh. "I've been doing my best to be okay with you being in danger, but I can't lose you now. I would fight every beast from the Everdark with my bare human hands if it meant keeping you safe. I would die for you. *YOU.* Not the thing inside you. I'm just scared that what I do isn't going to make a difference."

Everly closed her eyes to the warmth of his touch, bringing a hand to his cheek.

He leaned into her palm. Everly wondered whether she was the only one who *could* make a difference, and the thought left her shivering.

The creature inside her had enslaved part of Rylan, had killed her dad, had killed and consumed so many.

Deep in her bones she knew it was a threat to everyone she loved, but now, the only way to save them was to make that creature *stronger*.

18

A lone siren wailed in the distance, blending with faraway thundering crashes and the wind that howled down the main street.

At midafternoon, Shroudhaven gave the distinct impression that it was the early hours of the morning. The streets were dark, their emptiness broken by teams of shadyrs rushing by, chasing, or being chased by creatures of the Everdark.

The building beside Everly had a long, jagged gash carved into the side. Granite blocks had crumbled away as though slicing through a sandcastle.

She turned her face up, and found the Infuscur, high in the ashen sky above the town. Its black-hole silhouette hovered and stalked over the streets, long dark ribbons dragging behind it like a jellyfish, tangling and obliterating all in its wake.

At times, it would lash out, attention drawn by movement, and there would be screams that silenced too quickly.

It was looking for her. Hunting the Coruscare.

"Cover," hissed Rylan from the front.

Everly, Harper, Neri, Rushelle, Callan, Tammy, Lucas, Molly, Benson, and Parker pressed themselves into the shadows of the wall at their backs as a herrelspurn swooped through the street.

Everly glanced over those with her, those who volunteered to go with her to get the third Coruscare piece. There had been others, but Lian needed assistance as well, and they figured a smaller group would be more likely to go unnoticed.

Everly was both glad and terrified to have her friends there with her. Harper had a battle-ready gleam in her eyes and moved with almost the same military precision as Rylan and Callan.

Everly didn't know Lucas's brace very well, but having their extra support was appreciated. Even from the youngest of their group, Molly, whose attempt at a brave face was ruined by trembles and twitches.

The poor thing looked terrified. Tammy had pulled up well from her brush with death, now suited in body armor like the rest of the shadyrs. They even found a spare suit for Neri, although it was too large for her boney chest, and hung crookedly.

With her being the least experienced of them all in situations of mortal peril, it was good she had something. She still clung to Harper's wrist, her hand like a shackle, but she kept up and kept quiet. Rushelle held the back of the line, bright-eyed and alert.

Rylan leaned to the side, checking the glass door behind him.

With a quick crack of his elbow, he split the glass, reached in, and flicked the lock. "Let's go through. We can get to the next block under cover, then look for Barry again from there."

Everly pressed her lips together tightly. Finding the third piece wasn't proving as easy as they'd hoped. They knew Cardboard Box Barry had it, but they still had to find him.

They'd circled around five blocks of Shroudhaven main streets already without any sign of him or his underground cardboard world.

With Rylan at the lead, they shuffled through the lawyer's office, heads down and silent. Inside, the sounds of wind and wailing beasts dulled, and a different sound drifted through the space. A lilting tune came from an old-fashioned radio on the reception desk.

There's a mermaid in my lighthouse, and her heart belongs to me.

There's a mermaid in my lighthouse, to her I own—

A crash of shattered plastic and static fizzle burst from the radio, which now had the pointy end of Harper's whip sword lodged into it. The length of it hung between the radio and her hand, then with a tug and a click, she reeled it back into a rigid blade.

Rylan put his finger to his lips and glared, but no one said anything. They crept through to the back corridor past private offices. Within one, a couple of people huddled together, tucked under a desk.

Lucas patted the doorframe and flashed them a smile. "We're with emergency services. Nothing to worry about. Just having some issues with, a, um—"

"Town-wide gas leak," Callan offered.

"Escaped dangerous animals," Rylan said at the same time.

"Both?" Lucas shrugged. It was pretty clear their excuses were only going to cover so much this time. "Please stay inside and keep quiet as best you can."

The older woman and man nodded and ducked down farther. Everly wondered how much they knew of what really went on in this town.

In Shroudhaven, everyone had at least one strange story that others pretended not to believe. Everyone had someone they'd lost to unexplained circumstances. Gone missing in the woods. Drowned in the lake. Mauled by wild animals.

Everyone knew that when the sun went down, when the lights were out, you stayed inside, or you might never make it home. People joked that the estate on the hill was run by vampires.

Maybe nobody said the word 'monster.' Maybe they didn't know about shadyrs,

or understand that despite their vampire, werewolf, or ghost forms, they were the ones fighting to protect the world. But Everly was sure that people knew.

Deep in their gut, they knew. Shroudhaven wasn't a normal town.

They reached the end of the building, and Rylan pulled the floor bolt and flicked the lock of the back door. It opened to a narrow alleyway around the corner from where they'd started.

At the mouth of the lane, a group in Darkfrey uniforms had the remains of a vasmire under their boots, wrenching the last of its life from its tentacles. It flopped wetly to the ground, and they dashed off toward another target.

All except for one, who glared down the alley.

Everly knew that square-edged, action-figure silhouette. His blond crew cut was gray and gritty in the low light.

"You runts. This is all your fault!" Nilson Darkfrey bellowed at them, approaching in heavy strides.

"How is this our fault? You think we asked to be kidnapped and tortured by the Mesmans?" Tammy stepped to the front.

The top of her head barely reached the man's shoulders, and she was a third his weight, but she held her ground as he approached. "And it was your dumbass daddy who gave them the go-ahead! He could have stopped this!"

Rylan spoke softly. "Come on, Nils. We've all lost a lot already. We don't need to be against each other. Come with us, help us, we might be able to stop things getting worse."

Nilson spat on the filthy pavement in front of them. "I'd never fight beside traitors. Only one of you remained loyal."

He lifted his chin, offering Molly a nod.

Her face froze in a look of horror.

"What does he mean, Molly?" Lucas asked in a deep, low tone.

Her head snapped toward him, and she gaped, her young eyes round as a full moon. Her feet worked their way slowly backward. Then she ran, bolting off around the corner.

"Ghast dammit," Lucas hissed, slamming a fist against the wall.

He took a step as though about to make chase but swung his attention back to the Darkfrey looming over them.

Nilson's meaty face split in a humorless grin, glaring between Tammy and Everly. "You, and her, that bliv, running around full of cursed magic like it's not a problem, not a threat to all of us. I should have put you down out in the woods with the other animals when I had the chance."

His hand shot out, wrapping around Everly's neck and crushing hard.

Everly's eyes bulged, and she swatted at his tree trunk arm. She could free herself with the dragon's light, but it would call the Infuscur that stalked the skies above right

to them.

Shouts went up around her as Rylan and Harper lunged onto Nilson, dragging at his arms. He stumbled sideways with their weight but didn't loosen his grip around Everly's throat.

Panic swelled in her as her lungs screamed, and with it, the dragon rose too. If she lost enough control of her own body, it would take over for self-preservation and the Infuscur would come for her and her friends.

Through the pounding in her eardrums, Everly heard a spitting growl from above. She turned her gaze to the roof's edge, and saw two gleaming blue eyes staring back.

Rylan jabbed punches into Nilson's ribcage. Harper pressed the edge of her sword to Nilson's throat. They were both thrown back by the sleek, furred body that smashed down onto Nilson's face.

Nilson screamed, letting go of Everly. She reeled back, gasping for air through her crushed windpipe. Her vision wavered over Nilson, who stumbled backward, swatting at the creature that clung to him with deeply buried claws, hissing and yowling.

"Zozo?" Everly croaked.

The cougar's paw slid from where it had dug in to Nilson's scalp, down the full length of his face, carving four lines of ruby gore in their wake.

Nilson swore and thrashed, but Zozo readjusted around his swinging body, climbing him like a tree, puncturing his flesh with every step. The undead cat snapped its wide muzzle around Nilson's throat, sharp teeth glinting in the low light as they sunk into his flesh.

Nilson's screams turned to gurgles.

He stared at the sky, arms hanging limp and feet marching on the spot as though of their own accord. Then he toppled flat onto his back.

Zozo went down with him, never loosening the vise grip of his jaws.

Everly and the others remained still as Zozo kept his teeth in Nilson's neck for a long moment after the man had stopped twitching. When he finally detached, the white fur around his muzzle dripped red, and the low growl rumbling from his throat sounded satisfied.

This was the man who had killed the old lady that tended Zozo back to life. The one who slaughtered so many other animals that Nell had rescued. Zozo had taken his revenge.

Everly expected the big cat to turn tail and run, but instead, he padded silently up the alleyway toward her.

Harper and Rylan shot her concerned glances as she took a step forward herself, then crouched down to Zozo's level.

The tan fur across his forehead sat unevenly between thick scarring, and his eyes glowed an eerie, milky blue. When Everly reached out a hand, Zozo bumped his forehead into her palm. She brushed over his fur and rubbed behind one ear.

"What are you doing here? You're not tied to me anymore."

Zozo snuffled, then vaulted himself up the wall and onto the roof, taking a guarding position like a gargoyle on the edge.

"Was that … *a cat*?" Neri gasped out the words, her eyes locked onto Zozo.

Everly figured it must have been her first time seeing a cat of any kind, and she looked *very* impressed.

"That was Zozo. I … don't know why he came back."

"Of course he came to help you." Harper stepped forward, lifting Everly's chin so she could inspect the rapidly fading bruises around her neck. "It's because of who *you* are, how *you* were kind to him. Not because of the Coruscare's soul bond. I mean, how many people would see a zombie cougar stalking around their home and think, 'I'd better put some food out for it'?"

"You've been *feeding a zombie cougar*?" Rushelle scolded.

Tammy shook her head, pinching the bridge of her nose. "How you've stayed alive this long, I have no idea."

Everly's cheeks burned hot.

Callan tilted his head, grinning. "Maybe we should all be following her lead. I mean, zombie cougar feeding paid off."

Lucas and his remaining brace shuffled at the edges of their group, muttering between each other, then Lucas spoke up. "We're going after Molly. I'm sorry to be cutting out on you guys, but …"

"Molly's one of your brace," Callan said softly.

Lucas winced and nodded. "I'm sorry she screwed up, hurt you guys. But she's just a kid. We all know how Darkfrey indoctrination messes with your priorities."

Rylan grunted.

Rushelle patted Lucas on the back. "Go get the little duck. No one should be out there alone. We'll be just fine."

With one last look back at them, Lucas, Benson, and Parker split off, running the way Molly had gone.

"Come on," Rushelle said. "In amongst all the animal attack excitement, I think I saw something box-shaped down thataway."

She took off, and the others followed. Everly avoided Nilson's body as they jogged by.

Rylan moved up beside her. "Harper's right. It's who you are that drew me to you. It's always been that. Your kindness, your caring. Even after everything you've been through, you still reach out to comfort others. You make the world brighter than all the Coruscare's light."

Breath caught in Everly's hard-working lungs. She found hard to keep her eyes on where her feet fell rather than only on him. She wanted to be everything that he seemed to see in her. To be her best and do everything she could for those she loved. They deserved that and more.

Her backpack, which held the Swallower orb, thumped as she ran, and soon that bag would also hold the third piece of the Coruscare, waiting on the moment they needed to fight back and end this. "I wouldn't be who I am without you, Lian, your family. Your love. I wouldn't have even known love without you."

"I'm sorry I took that away from you for so long." Rylan's eyes narrowed as he looked ahead. "It's him, Barry. Up on the corner!"

The older couple from the law office hadn't taken their advice. Barry had them in tow, ushering them toward his blanket-draped cardboard box as a herrelspurn circled above.

They nodded to him with familiarity then crawled in and didn't reemerge.

"Barry," Callan called out as the old man moved to follow them in.

Barry straightened, arching his back in a way that exaggerated his pot belly, and he tugged on his braided beard. "Ah, it's you lot. You need somewhere to lay low?"

"We actually need something more," Harper said. "We need the crystal heart of your maze."

Barry grinned crookedly, guffawing at the joke. But as nobody else joined in the laughter, his face fell.

He gave a swift shake of his head. "Oh no. No, you can't have that. I mean, my house is yours, but without the heart, there is no house. I got people in there I'm keeping safe from all this."

He waved his hands, pointing in every direction.

"All of this isn't going to end any time soon unless we have the crystal," Everly said, her voice lacking confidence even to her own ears.

Barry was out here saving people. Maybe that was what they should be doing. Helping him get everyone into shelter to wait it out. Come up with some other solution. There were too many 'what ifs' circling in Everly's head and getting tangled on each other.

No. We have a plan, and we should stick to it.

Barry's head swung side to side, his beard following it like a pendulum. "What do you think you're going to do with it, anyway?"

Harper said, "We need to break it to release the thir—"

"BREAK IT?" Barry howled into the empty street.

Less human howls echoed back.

Everly held up her hands in a gesture of peace. "We won't break it yet. Only if we need to. We've got a plan to make everybody safe again, to close the portal that's flooding the town with monsters. I can stop all of this chaos. But I need to get that piece of crystal."

"She's right." Rushelle quirked her red lips, out of place on the dim street in her sunny yellow halter top. "None of us have more of a chance than Everly here to bring an end to this destruction. I know we're asking a real big sacrifice from you, but we're all going to lose everything anyway if we don't do something. She can do it. The kid seems about able to do anything."

Barry pressed a hand to his chest as though he was having a heart attack. "Oh child. I hope you're right. I hope you are. If you think you can stop all of this, I'll give you the heart of my world. 'Cause someone has to stop this."

He didn't say the other part, but Everly felt it. That if she destroyed his sanctuary and couldn't stop the Infuscur or close the shroudpool, there'd be nowhere left to hide.

"Come on then, let's get to it," Barry said, his voice clogged with grief.

Harper, Neri, Tammy, and Callan followed him into the box maze. The hairs on Everly's neck rose, as she bent down to crawl in after Rylan.

Rushelle held back the blanket doorway for them, waving them along like herding sheep.

"Thanks," Everly smiled at her.

"No problem, duck." Rushelle's last word caught, and she stilled.

Pieces of skin peeled and floated from her pretty pinup face. A black ribbon whipped away as her body crumbled into nothing before Everly's eyes.

19

Rushelle's typewriter-shaped necklace hung in midair for a moment, miraculously untouched as the rest of her faded away. It jangled to the ground. Then all Everly could hear were her own screams.

Hands grabbed at her, dragging her along the smooth cardboard tunnel. Everly stared at where Rushelle had been. Where she had smiled back with friendly eyes an instant before she was erased from existence.

Blackness rushed at her, diving from the sky and swooping like a wave of shadows toward the cardboard box entrance. As the Infuscur shot more dark strands out from Mordan's body, the corrugated boards folded closed by themselves, shutting the flaps like a barricade.

Everly's screams cut out, and she held her breath, waiting for the box to crumble and fade away like Rushelle had. Nothing happened.

The magic that ran the strange cardboard maze had closed them off and removed them entirely from the outside world.

The hands around her waist and shoulders pulled her through to where the tunnel was tall enough to stand. She met Rylan's eyes as he pulled her to her feet.

A hot sting punched her nose and her tears spilled freely.

He pulled her in close, pressing her face to his chest. "I know. I'm sorry."

Neri let out a harsh wail, muffled quickly to a stark silence by the cardboard walls. There were no echoes, except for Rushelle's last words, looping nonstop in Everly's head.

No problem, duck.

She couldn't be gone. It didn't make any sense that someone so full of life and love could be there one moment then wiped clean from the world the next.

Tammy muttered strings of denial and sobbed out curses against Callan's shoulder. Harper pulled Neri close and whispered comforts into her tangle of curls. Barry stared at the ground, whispering something that sounded like his own version of last rites.

Everly watched them all as Rylan stroked her hair, and her insides seemed to fill with cement. Which of them would be next? Which loss would crush her world to pieces next? Would she be able to endure it?

Make me whole. Then we can save them all.

Everly nodded to the voice in her head, her cheek moving against the firm material of Rylan's chest armor. *I have to be strong enough to save them. And I'll do whatever I have to do to make that happen.*

"We need to get to the final piece of the Coruscare." Everly's words feeling sticky and heavy.

We need to make it all worth it.

Barry shuffled to the lead. His hand gestures suggested he was following some strange process of navigation along the straight tunnel. Everly took in the bizarre space. She'd never seen inside Barry's kraft-colored world herself, but Harper had described it to her.

Being inside it was different though. She felt like a child, playing in a massive box fort, like the time Lian had bought a new fridge and she and Rylan made a cubby of the leftover packaging, staying in it all day.

Rushelle would have loved this. Everly imagined her buddying up to Barry, telling him about her books.

How many of her stories will now remain unwritten? Everly's eyes felt flayed raw, and she struggled to keep them open. They followed along without speaking, footsteps scuffing against the soft cardboard. Shoulders slumped, but they all kept a fast pace toward their last hope for salvation against further loss.

When Barry pushed through into the central hub space, he called out, "Okay folks, plans have changed and you can't stay here."

At least a dozen heads popped up from around the room where they had clustered together in small groups beside the makeshift beds and mismatched lampshades, gossiping and sharing stories of what they couldn't possibly have seen outside.

"I don't want to go back out there!" one man cried.

"S'all right, I'm going to send you out a special way." Barry strode over to a sidewall, gave it a bump with his hip, and then dug his fingernails into the cardboard. With a tug, he peeled open a door-sized flap.

"Head straight through, don't take any turns, and you'll end up down by the river at the far end of town. Should keep you out of reach of the danger, at least for a little while. And here's hoping this lot will have everything fixed up before then."

There were grumbles and whimpers of shock, but the civilians gathered their bags and coats and shuffled their way over to him. As they did, the view through to the middle of the room cleared, and Everly caught her first sight of the Coruscare crystal hanging there like a twisted modern art chandelier.

It glowed, calling to her. And she glowed in return.

Her heart was wrapped in chains, dragging her forward.

"Evie, what are you doing?" Rylan growled.

Everly stared at her shining hands, then cried out as her feet lifted from the ground. "I'm not! I'm not doing this."

Stop it. STOP IT. I'm in control! she roared into her own mind.

The Coruscare remained silent, apart from a rising sense of victory.

Glittery tendrils appeared and stepped her across the large space, floating her over stacks of canned food, furniture pulled from trash collections, and crates of water bottles, then over cardboard dividers that screened the wide hall into smaller rooms.

Everly turned back to the others, gaping. The civilians had paused in their exit to see why the lighting had just brightened, and stared at her in wonder.

"Get them out of here!" she screamed, and Barry pushed them out through the doorway.

"What's happening? Ev?" Harper yelled.

She chased after her, running zigzag through the maze of cardboard screens and supplies. The others were right behind her, trying to keep up.

"I'm not in control. The Coruscare is doing this."

Her body turned icy, as though she'd had her major arteries cut and the blood drained from her.

She had never been in control.

The Coruscare seemed to chuckle from within her, rattling her chest.

What were you doing? Playing dead? Telling me what I wanted to hear? Pretending I had you leashed?

Everly clenched her teeth and tensed her whole body with effort. She must have *some* power over the dragon still, or it wouldn't have bothered with games.

She focused all her being onto taking the reins. Her eyes ached and her fingers tingled. The movements of the scintillating tendrils slowed, becoming a grating mechanical motion. But she continued moving forward.

Everly cried out. It was strong, so much stronger than she'd ever realized.

I've been feeding. Sneaking. Building energy to defy you.

What? When? She had noticed it take in souls during the chaos of fleeing the Everdark, but also ... also bodies kept being found in the morning.

Shadyr, human, and eidolghast bodies, all around Shroudhaven. Lian's old friend, Candace. So many others. Dead in their sleep. No wounds. No explanations ... No soul left after it had been consumed.

Her dreams had been so strange, with a sensation of movement she'd never experienced before, because she *had* been moving.

The Coruscare had been hijacking her body and taking it out to feed every night. That's why she was never overcome by its hunger. It had taken over when she was weakest against it, when she hadn't known what it was doing, until it could take over entirely.

"Fight back!" Rylan broke free of the others and plowed straight as an arrow toward her, crashing through low cardboard walls and vaulting over beds.

"I'm trying!" With a roar of strength, she pulled back on the Coruscare again, dragging it to a complete stop.

But it already had one tendril around the hanging piece of crystal.

Glittering light around shining glass, the Coruscare squeezed. The crystal cracked.

"Run! Get out of here! All of you, now!" Everly screamed.

The room filled with light. It swirled across Everly's flesh, rushing like a blast of molten metal up her nose and down her throat.

We.

Are.

Whole.

The words thrummed through her.

We will take back our realm. Take this realm too, maybe. But first, first we take revenge.

Everly wanted to whimper like an infant, to thrash and whine. It said it would help them, that it would close the shroudpool, but it was clear that the Coruscare didn't intend in any way to do so.

It used her, and now she could feel it using her up.

She couldn't see where anyone else was in the blinding glow, but she worked her jaw, trying to push out words through an uncooperative mouth. She could feel herself fading and needed the others to know the creature's plans.

"It's going ... revenge on Infuscur ... but doesn't ... won't close shroudpool. Wants ... Everdark back."

Did she even speak? Existence felt like a dream that slipped away so fast she couldn't be sure she'd ever held it.

She was light. She was power. *We are whole.*

Creatures moved around beneath them.

Nothing but motes of dust, specks of life beneath her attention.

Everly grunted at the thought, trying to steal back focus to her own eyes.

Not specks. Friends. Family. Love.

So much she hadn't said. So much she hadn't done. So much she wanted to do to save them. She wanted to reach for them, but her body was so numb she might as well not have had a body at all. Her head felt like it filled with tepid water, drowning her from within.

She tried to hold onto her vision, her consciousness, but it washed away like a sandcastle in a storm.

With her final scrap of self, she cried, "Rylan! Rylan, I love—"

20

Light streamed from Everly's mouth and eyes like a beam from a lighthouse, cutting off her words. Rylan smashed right through a low wall of cardboard, fingertips reaching for her as though his touch could pull her back, could wrench that creature of light right out of her body. But as his hand grasped out, there was nothing left in the space where Everly had been.

Rylan blinked, the brightness burning globs of color into his vision. He whirled around to track her.

Pieces of broken crystal crunched under his feet, and through partial blindness he glimpsed Everly, disappearing through an exit like a shooting star.

If it was still Everly at all.

If she hadn't been forced out of herself entirely by the Coruscare's full might.

No. I can't think like that. She's strong. She's still in there, fighting.

"Ev! Everly!" Harper screamed.

A piece of cardboard the size of a flap from a box floated from the ceiling. Rylan swatted it away, heaved in a deep breath, and ran. He had to catch up, if he could just *reach* her, maybe he could get her back.

"Oh no, oh no, oh no. It's all falling apart!" Barry cried from behind him.

Rylan glanced back for a fraction of a second but didn't slow his pace. Barry had moved over with the others, running with Harper and Neri.

Callan and Tammy were ahead of them, trying to catch up with Rylan. All of them were yelling. Rylan's name, Everly's name, other things—Rylan couldn't hear exactly what over the roar in his ears, and the smashing, scrunching sounds around them, and his desperate mind screaming *get her back*.

A sheet of ragged cardboard as big as Rylan flopped down in his path. He dodged to the side and leaped over a stack of water bottles. Unable to control his frantic momentum, he collided with the corner of the exit passage. The cardboard tore like wet tissue against his shoulder. A howling sound pushed through the hole left behind, echoing from a vortex of darkness.

"This place is coming down around us!" Harper yelled.

A high-pitched scream that was probably Neri followed.

"Rylan!" Callan called. "We have to stick together!"

Rylan kept going, pounding his feet against the tunnel floor that grew uneven and soft beneath his boots. He just had to reach her. She was already out of sight.

The exit came up quickly. The passageway lurched, shifting sideways. The walls crumpled and compressed, crushing in on him. Dark gaps split between the cardboard and a nightmarish cacophony of yowling wind sounded through them, though the air remained still, stifling.

The scratchy cry of an old man's voice came from behind him. The strained voices of Harper and Neri followed. Rylan burst out through the ratty floral sheets into fresh air, his gaze shooting left and right.

Where is she?

Callan and Tammy appeared at his shoulders, bumping into him in their haste. They breathed hard, gasping breaths.

"No, no!" Callan bellowed, dropping down out of Rylan's field of view.

There was no sign of Everly, no glow or flash of light in the streets around them. Every nerve in his body itched to keep running, keep chasing after Everly, but he didn't know which way to go.

Rylan tore himself away from his search to check on his brother.

Tammy joined Callan with a cry, landing on her knees. The box they had just emerged from lay flat on the ground. "Harper, Neri?"

Callan dragged back the crumpled tarp, flinging it away.

Rylan crouched beside him, grabbing at the loose sheets of cardboard. They came away freely, revealing nothing but dirty pavement beneath.

A muffled squeal came from Tammy as she scraped at the concrete with her black fingertips, as though she could dig through. "Where are they? *Where are they?*"

"They were right behind us, but they stopped to help Barry ..." Callan reached over and put a hand onto Tammy's, stilling her as she fingerpainted the ground red.

She gulped, then flung herself into his arms, pressing her face into his shoulder to muffle her sobs.

Rylan stared at the concrete, disbelief clouding his eyes. He squeezed the cardboard in his grip, flipping it over, checking both sides as though there could be a magic portal hidden under one of the moldering scraps.

They had been right behind him. And he'd lost them. He lost Everly's best friend.

"What do we do now?" Tammy's words wheezed out through harsh breaths.

Callan caught Rylan's gaze and his usually bright, smiling eyes were so dull that it made Rylan's chest convulse.

Brightness flashed in the distance. Rylan turned his face upward, seeking Everly.

High in the sky, above the estate, light and darkness clashed. Living lightning and sentient shadow tangled together and blasted apart, as dueling gods waged war.

"No, keep going!" Barry grumbled and reeled back from Harper's outstretched hand. One of his feet had plunged straight through the decaying cardboard, suctioned into the void beyond.

Harper shook her head and reached for him again. Neri whimpered at her side, wide-eyed, and reached out as well. They both clasped their hands around one of Barry's arms. His wrist felt like soft crepe paper wrapped around bone.

"Don't worry about me, there's no time," he pleaded with round eyes under bushy brows.

"No way. You're coming with us." Harper tightened her grip and pulled.

There wasn't a chance she was leaving him behind. Not this kind man who had come to see if she needed help when she was having an argument with Everly on the street. Who had helped them run from the police. Who had saved potentially countless citizens of Shroudhaven from the things that prowled in the dark.

With the sound of a vacuum coming unclogged, Barry's foot slid free, and the three of them tumbled onto the worryingly soft floor.

When Harper turned around, the exit closed over with a patchwork of card and brown paper. Everly had sped out through there before them.

Not Everly, the Coruscare. It seemed to have taken control entirely. At least for now. Harper still hoped Everly could regain control. She'd pushed her friend to this, and if she'd pressed Everly into something that destroyed her, how could she ever forgive herself?

She may not have to feel the heavy lump of guilt in her throat for long though. Harper swung around and she scrunched her face when she saw the other end of the tunnel collapsing in toward them.

"No, there has to be another way out." Hers and Neri's hands were still grasped tight around Barry's.

He shook his head and pulled away, groaning as he brought up his foot. His shoe was gone, and the top layer of skin had been scraped clean, as though someone had hit him with a sandblaster.

Barry's wide eyes watered. "I'm sorry. You shouldn't have stopped for me."

"It's okay, I can heal you so you can run again, then you can tell us which way to go." Neri raised her voice in song, and it sounded strangely muffled, interrupted by the

howling and crumpling board sounds.

Barry's skin smoothed over, and he stared open-mouthed at Neri. "Just when I thought I'd seen everything in this wild town."

Harper had her eyes on the tunnel they'd run through, where the cardboard warped and folded like twisted origami toward them. Harsh, ripping sounds followed. She stood and pressed her hands against the closed exit.

"Barry, how can we get out?"

"I can't see any other exits, no other routes. Normally the direction is clear to me but it's like it's all gone, the whole cardboard system just isn't there. This is all that's left." Barry shook his head and brushed his fingers over the healed skin of his foot, as though only touch could make him believe his eyes.

Harper put a long, shining fingernail between her teeth, chewing it roughly in a sudden return of a habit she'd kicked before she'd hit puberty.

"Neri, she got her powers from being close to a piece of that crystal for so long. You've been near your crystal heart of the maze for ages, right? Maybe you have something too, some special power of your own, even without the crystal."

Barry's wrinkled face creased into heavier lines across his forehead. "Like healing?"

"I don't know, hopefully something that gets us out of here. Like finding the right way ... like you normally do." Harper's voice grew quiet as she went on.

She was clutching onto a hope that didn't make sense. That probably *was* Barry's power. His ability of navigating the strange cardboard tunnel system. But the tunnels were gone, and he'd already said he couldn't sense any other directions to go.

That was it. There were no other options, and their single remaining passageway was contracting upon them fast. The cardboard pressed against the top of Harper's head, and she ducked.

Barry's eyes tilted downward, heartbreakingly. "I'm sorry. I'll try ... if there's anything I can do, but ..."

But they were trapped. They'd run out of time. The world was closing in on them, becoming nothing, and they were about to be crushed or shredded or lost into that howling void.

Not Neri. Harper couldn't bear to imagine Neri's life ending there. Not Neri, so full of wonder and enthusiasm for a world she'd been locked away from. So kind, despite all she'd suffered. Not Neri, who filled Harper's heart with warmth and longing in a way she'd never felt.

Why did she have to come along? And why did I have to be so arrogant, thinking I could keep her safe?

Harper threw her arms around Neri. "I didn't want this for you. I wanted you to have a good, long life to make up for everything you missed out on so far. I don't want

this to be the end for you."

The scrunching, tearing, yowling sounds grew louder, and the ceiling bowed in above them. They dropped onto their knees, still holding each other.

"I'm okay," Neri replied, her voice trembling. "I'm okay because I'm with you."

"But I don't know how to save you from this!" Harper's whip sword hung heavy from her belt, but not it, nor any skill she'd pushed herself to be the best at during her life, could stop a magical dimension from crushing them within its implosion.

"You don't have to save me from everything. I just wanted to be with you."

Harper tangled her fingers into Neri's thick, curled hair and pressed it to her face as though it could stem her tears. "I didn't want to say anything, because I didn't want you to feel any sort of pressure ... but if this is the end, I want you to know that I like you, more than as friends. I like you in a romantic way, in the way that I want to be beside you every moment."

Neri pulled away enough to look into Harper's eyes. "I feel like that about you too. Like, you're my Prince Charming."

Harper scoffed gently. She had introduced Neri to fairy tales in a subtle attempt to explain some of the hazards of the world, including the risks of 'love at first sight,' or anyone who would lock a princess away in a tower.

Neri shook her head fiercely. "But in a good way! You saved me, and looked after me, but never asked or expected anything from me. You've let me have time to learn who *I* am. And *I* like you."

A hysterical laugh shuddered from Harper.

There she was, in one of Everly's old T-shirts, makeup undone, hair untamed, eyes untinted, and Neri looked at her as though she was *everything*.

In careful, tentative, questioning motions, Harper moved her mouth closer to Neri's. Neri met her in the middle, her lips plump and soft and tasting of the sea.

The cardboard moved beneath them like they were on a waterbed. They clung to each other for stability as pieces of shredded board rained around them. The roof caved in lower, and they had to lie down, curled on their sides to stay face-to-face.

Neri stared wide-eyed at a hole above them, then turned back to Harper, offering a wobbly smile. "Having the time I've had with you, it almost makes me forget everything else before. I wish we could have had more, but it's been enough."

Of all the ways Harper thought she might go out—even with adding a slew of new and terrifying options since coming to Shroudhaven—she never thought it would be in a collapsing dimension made from cardboard, clinging to a mermaid she loved.

She wouldn't be able to help her best friend, if there was any chance of still saving Everly. She hoped Rylan would do that for her. The guy was okay. She could almost see what Everly saw in him these days, and she was certain he would do anything to save her.

She had to hold onto that thought, hoping for everyone else out in the world to go on without her, Neri, and Barry.

Harper looked at him through the small gap between sheets of pressed cardboard, tearing apart before her eyes. He had tears filling his smile lines, and he rubbed his forehead, muttering to himself as though still trying to muster up some magical way to save them all. She released one hand from Neri and reached to hold onto Barry's.

His fingers felt leathery in hers, and he gave her a tight-lipped smile. "I'm sorry you got stuck here for me. You two, you're some of the good ones. You thought about me before yourselves. You know love in the most selfless way. It's always been how I've tried to be. I always tried to act out of love, trying to save people. I think that's why I always thought of the crystal as a heart, too."

Harper's body was pressed and pulled between strange, opposing forces, crushed and suctioned as their tiny pocket of space closed even farther and tore apart at the same time.

She squeezed Barry's hand. "I think it was you who was the true heart of this place all along."

One of her legs slipped through a hole, and she cried out as her skin peeled and flayed. Barry lurched sideways, falling into the same hole.

Neri sung to them, as the last scrap of cardboard life raft fell away.

21

Rylan's entire body was a raging tornado of sensations as he ran with Callan and Tammy to the arranged meeting point.

His eyes burned from unshed tears. The icy chill of beshadowed mist stung as it swirled around his feet. The screams of dying humans and unearthly shrieks of hunting monsters echoing through the unnaturally dark streets would haunt him for the rest of his life, no matter how short that might be.

But all he could think about was Everly. Everly, gone, taken over by the being inside her. Rushelle, Harper, Neri, Barry, all lost. *Everly* ...

The Boutique All came into view as they rounded a corner. It had seemed like a good place to regroup, back when they'd had the audacity to make plans, the naivety to think they could take some action against the overwhelming hellscape that was engulfing the town.

Seeing the ridiculous name and aging facade of the budget store now, Rylan swallowed back sickness in his throat.

We should have been here, regrouping before making our move to win this. But now ... Now what can we do?

The front windows had blown out at some point and glass glittered across the ground like scattered diamonds, reflecting the blasts of light that flashed from above. The three of them checked the street was clear, then dashed across and vaulted in through the open frontage.

In the darkness of the store, scores of shadyr eyes stared back at them.

When he saw Lian's face, Rylan thought his heart might stop completely, that his body would simply give up and shut down. She stared at the three of them, open mouth shaking as her eyes counted over them, again and again, as though their missing numbers would magically reappear.

"What happened?" Her normally stoic tone was absent, her words strained and cracking. "Where are the others?"

It was Tammy who answered, but not in words. A sob escaped from her, and she ran into Lian's arms, clinging tight as her body heaved with sorrow.

Tears filled Rylan's eyes with a suddenness that made him inhale sharply. He clenched his jaw and wiped quickly with the heel of his hand.

There was a not-small part of him that wanted to run into his mother's arms and weep, too. He wanted to hold her for all of the years he grew up without being able to, for all the pains and the lies and the times he'd tried to be so strong, all for nothing.

He was lost, untethered, his whole world flipped upside down then dropped from an immense height so that it shattered on a hard, unyielding ground.

And he didn't know how to put himself back together. Not without Everly. Not if she was gone.

The hope that she still existed was the only thing that kept Rylan on his feet.

Lian's eyes were wide and panicked as she looked over Tammy's shoulder to Rylan. She repeated in a whisper, "What happened?"

"The Coruscare took over." Rylan's husky voice scraped to a rattly whisper. "As soon as it got near its final piece, it ... took over. It's gone to fight the Infuscur, but from what Everly said, it's not going to close the shroudpool."

She'd said more, with her last words before the light overwhelmed her.

Rylan, I love—

Her voice still echoed inside him to the beat of his heart. "Everly tried to fight it ..."

"I'm sure she's still trying," Lian said vehemently.

"Rush? Harper? Neri?" Cherry stepped forward, and Rylan blinked at him as though he'd appeared in a puff of smoke.

Cherry, Annabeth, and Jasper stood beside Lian in front of the crowd of other shadyrs they'd gathered from Howell House and anywhere else they could find them. They all listened in, soft mutters of conversation passing between them as they made sense of news that to them wasn't personal. To them, wasn't a hole in the chest the size of a cannon ball.

"The Infuscur got Rushelle," Callan said softly. "She's gone."

Lian put a hand over her mouth as though stifling a scream.

Rylan swiped the wet from his eyes again. He had to hold it together. "Harper and Neri—and Barry—they didn't make it out of the cardboard tunnels. I ... don't know what that means for them."

"FUCK!" Cherry hollered.

A chorus of shushes replied.

He repeated himself in a softer whisper. Running his hands into his red hair, he leaned face-first against a nearby shelf of greeting cards. Jasper moved closer to him, putting a hand on his back and murmuring in his ear.

"Lucas's brace?" Lian asked with a small shake of her head, as though she couldn't bear another answer.

Rylan shared a knowing glance with Callan then said, "Got separated out on the streets. They might be okay."

Lian's shoulders slumped, and she kept turning her face left and right in small, repetitive denials.

Annabeth rolled her head around and stared at the ceiling, fidgeting with the piece of bone on her necklace. "So, what now? We've lost the Coruscare. Did Everly still have the Swallower, too?"

Rylan had forgotten about it, but for all he knew it was still with Everly. He nodded.

Annabeth grunted in frustration. "With what we learned about how Kole was using magic, I thought maybe I had an idea for closing the shroudpool at the estate. But I need the Swallower."

Rylan stared blindly for a moment at Annabeth, and out over the crowd of shadyrs behind her who waited to be told the plan, now that Plan A had crumbled out from under them.

The shroudpool still needed to be closed. The shadyrs trapped by eidolghasts and dueling gods at the estate needed to be rescued. That was what everyone else was there for, what they were all prepared to risk their lives for.

But Rylan could only think of Everly, and her last words, and whether she would ever forgive him for losing Harper and Neri if he could even get her back. He'd gone colder inside than when he held Everly's body in icy seawater as she cracked apart from the Bane.

Rylan clenched his fists. *The Bane.*

He locked his gaze with Annabeth. "If you think we can close the shroudpool, we will get the Swallower back. The Bane is still out there, somewhere. If I can find it, maybe it can subdue the Coruscare enough to help Everly take over again. We get her back, and get the Coruscare under control, and finish this."

And if finishing this means using the Bane to break the Coruscare apart again, break Everly apart, could I do that?

Rylan didn't want to consider that outcome.

Tammy turned within Lian's embrace, her face red and splotchy. "The Bane was on Everly right up until the shroudpool opened. But I didn't see it in the Everdark. It must still be somewhere near the shroudpool. There was a lot of rubble, it's probably buried under there."

Lian nodded in slow motion, her voice flat. "That's something. If we could get it, it might turn the tide in our favor again."

Lian raised her voice to the watching crowd. "We've lost a lot, too much. But we have to keep going. They would want us to see this through. We've got our mission."

She caught Rylan's gaze and nodded to him. "The rest of you, split into groups

and work on extracting any shadyrs or civilians trapped at the estate or nearby, then fall back. Do not engage with either Mordan or Everly—or the things controlling them."

A man in the crowd called out, "What about the estate? How do we get it back?"

Rylan knew many of the shadyrs there, most of them recent defectors from the Darkfreys. But through the blur in his eyes, he couldn't work out who the man was. It didn't really matter. There was a rise of murmurings in support of his question and Rylan understood why, because he felt the same. The estate itself was their home, or had been, for so long.

Lian rubbed her eyes. "Look, I'm not your leader or your boss. You're welcome to do whatever the Everdark you want to do. I'm just telling you that there are two gods of destruction laying each other out near a massive shroudpool that's spilling eidolghasts like a gushing wound."

Low whispers reverberated in the space as her words sank in.

Lian raised her chin, her gaze hard. "I think it's best that you keep things to a strictly 'save who you can and get out alive' plan. Because we're all shadyrs, which means in a way we're all family, and I don't want to lose any more family."

The man stared them down silently for a long moment, then nodded. The crowd broke up into smaller groups, conversing, sometimes arguing, before leaving the cover of the store. Rylan trusted that they would do some good. That's what they'd been trained to do.

The problem was, they'd been trained to put the good of the world and the fight against the darkness above everything, even their own lives. What was the point of winning if they lost everything they were fighting for along the way? The touch of Lian's hand against his arm made Rylan twitch, his whole body tense and on edge.

"We'll do anything we have to do to get her back." Her brown eyes were hard and sparkling, and she had her other hand on Callan's shoulder. "But please be careful with yourselves. For me."

Rylan gave a thin-lipped smile and nodded numbly. He wasn't sure any amount of care could save them from what they were about to face.

The crowd cleared, leaving just them, Tammy, Cherry, Jasper, and Annabeth.

"Since we barely got out of that Everdark-blighted place alive last time, how are we supposed to get ourselves right back up to that shroudpool again?" Cherry asked, his voice flat despite the sardonic tone of his words.

"Could we find some kind of distraction?" Annabeth asked.

"Oh no ..." Lian's eyes widened.

Rylan tensed, ready for danger. "What?"

His mother's mouth twisted wryly. "I have a terrible, terrible idea."

Despite their efforts to sneak their way back into the estate and avoid the worst of the fighting, Rylan's arms were already covered in eidolghast blood.

"Pin its wings! I'll go for the weak spot," Rylan yelled over the herrelspurn's roar.

The eidolghast ambushed them as they crept around the corner of a dorm building, trying to get inside. It lashed out a leathery wing, catching the hooked claw around the shoulder strap of Rylan's body armor.

Ripping back, it pulled Rylan tumbling toward it, until the straps gave, tearing through.

He came to a rolling stop directly beneath the creatures hideous face, and the glow of flame rose up its neck.

Woah no. He wasn't prepared for fire, not shifted into the heat proof form being near a herrelspurn provided. With so many creatures around, he'd stayed shifted into a more manageable mix of vampire and werewolf form.

A figure body-slammed the monster's long, twisting mass of necks from the side, redirecting the jet of fire away from Rylan.

"Thanks."

Callan smiled as he gave him a hand up. "Do I look like the kind of guy who lets his brother get cooked?"

Rylan tugged on Callan's hand, pulling him away as the monster swung a wing at them again.

Jasper and Annabeth leapt in unison, landing on top of that wing and holding it still beneath them.

Rylan grinned viciously. Having Callan, Jasper, and Annabeth fighting by his side made Rylan feel at home, as though he had a solid brace at his back that could overcome anything together.

"We've got the other one," Cherry called out.

He and Tammy were the least experienced of the lot. Rylan was worried they'd hold the team back when hit with the influx of eidolghast energy, considering how Tammy hadn't been able to control her mermaid form not long ago.

He'd even whispered to Lian that they should be left out of this mission, but Lian wanted them kept close by.

In the thick of it, Rylan noted that they were handling the influx of eidolghast energy well. They both managed to hold a stable form, and both chose vampire. The easiest and one of the earliest forms shadyrs learned, but with its regeneration powers, a good pick.

They launched themselves together at the herrelspurn's other wing, catching it less elegantly and efficiently as the others had with theirs, but still effective.

Callan and Rylan grappled the creature from each side. They each ripped into the tangle of flesh that formed its multi-strand neck, but it kept moving, lifting them from the ground as it thrashed, shaking them like ragdolls and throwing them off.

"Where's this weakspot?" Lian appeared beside the two boys, legs wide in a martial stance and hand on her sword in its hilt.

Rylan had never known the warrior side of his mom. Seeing her so brave and at ease in front of a roaring, flame-breathing monster gave him a newfound respect for her.

"I don't know exactly. Harper and her sword aren't here ..." Rylan pushed down his guilt and grief, they wouldn't serve him now. "But it's one of the necks."

"Right." Lian nodded once, and as the creature thrashed around against those pinning its wings, she drew her sword.

With feet placed firmly, and head turned away, Lian stilled, waited, and then slashed the black shadyr sword through the air in front of her. The screeching eidolghast stilled, its masklike face and needle filled mouth hanging limp for one moment, before dropping away clean from its tangle of spaghetti-like necks.

With a *sshckt* Lian sheathed the sword again and inspected her work. "Beheading pretty much always does the job too."

"That it does," Rylan replied, eyes wide and grin growing. Turns out his mom was kind of amazing.

Mixing with the turmoil of all his other emotions was the sadness that he hadn't known that sooner, that he'd abandoned her for so long. He had no time for that now though. They had a mission.

The herrelspurn was dead, its body twitching slightly but no longer a threat.

"Everyone good?" he checked around the team as they came back together.

They nodded silently in reply. Each of them carried a heavy pack they'd loaded up back at Howell House, and even with shadyr powers, Rylan's body rebelled with fatigue. He'd been fighting so hard, so long. They all had.

But nobody complained.

Then Tammy's face turned upwards and pulled long in horror. She let loose a whimpering scream.

22

Rylan followed Tammy's terrified stare, expecting to see another herrelspurn flying down towards them. But something darker moved, crawling along the side of the building.

A weroth, bigger than any he'd ever seen before clambered like a spider along the wall their way, its pointed legs stabbing through the stonework with each step, crumbling debris down upon them.

How did that thing even fit through the shroudpool?

"No, no, no." Tammy shook her head, backing toward the building entrance.

Still breathing hard from the previous fight, Rylan didn't particularly want to try to take that giant down either.

"Go, get inside, quick!" He herded the others before him, racing towards the main doors as the weroth raced down the walls to block their path.

Rylan pushed through the doors last, tumbling across the marble floors as the weroth jabbed limbs like rapiers toward them. One caught the back of Rylan's arm, leaving a thin puncture wound. He hissed at the sting and rolled further away.

The weroth roared through the doorway, too large to fit. The ancient wooden beams of the doorframe splintered and cracked.

"Keep moving, fast!"

Back on their feet, they dashed down the hall as the building shook, plaster raining over them from the cracking ceiling. Lian led them down into the system of tunnels and they ran single file through darkness.

Close to their destination, they had to leave the shelter of the underground tunnel and make a break across clear ground, giving a view of the battlefield in the sky. The clash between Coruscare and Infuscur above was a spectacle that unwillingly drew the eye like a gory car crash.

Light tangled and tore into darkness against the backdrop of gloomy gray. They would part, circling far out across the town, then rocket back toward each other with an impact that made the earth shake.

At times, they would swoop low enough that the tiny human bodies suspended within those massive energies were visible, then they'd shoot back into the sky, so fast and far that Rylan worried they would leave the planet entirely.

Can Everly's body survive this?

He had to hope that the Coruscare would make sure of that. He knew it had done what it could to protect her in the past. If she died, it seemed to fear it would, too.

The Infuscur caught the Coruscare's glow tightly in a wrap of void-dark tendrils. The light flickered, faded, then burst free. Diminished, the Coruscare dipped and bobbed away, shooting long, glittering strands downward.

Rylan saw where they hit—a group of shadyrs mid-combat with a weroth. The Coruscare latched onto every one of them, shadyr and ghast, consuming their souls to renew itself. Their bodies dropped, empty and used up, and the Coruscare returned to the fray, glowing as bright as ever.

It will just keep eating souls to keep going. It could keep fighting the Infuscur like that forever. It has to be stopped.

The Infuscur too seemed to draw some kind of negative sustenance from what it destroyed, as though annihilation renewed it.

Rylan reached the entry to the next building and ushered the team in ahead of him. He caught their glances of concern as they passed, having seen the same as he had.

They all knew the Coruscare had to be stopped. But could it? And what about the Infuscur?

Even if they got the Bane, brought the Coruscare down, closed the shroudpool, they'd still have a god of void and annihilation to deal with and no idea how. Part of Rylan hoped that Everly—the Coruscare—would defeat it and take the revenge it clearly wanted, but for all Rylan could tell as he looked back one last time, they seemed at a stalemate.

Turning away, Rylan ran after the others through the building and into the deep, older tunnels. They reached the room they'd found on their way out before, which held the Mesman's collection of inactive lures.

A corner of the ceiling had broken through since they'd last been in there. The gaping hole revealed the sky above. The room that had been on top of them was mostly gone, vanished to nothing as if it never existed.

Flashes of light from the warring gods flickered through. The intricately combined black bones stood like an ominous army in the dim illumination.

Lian and the others already had their packs off, unloading blocks of C-4 and rolls of fuse. Rylan joined them, wondering again at how Denny had ever managed to accumulate such a massive stash of explosives. Lian supposedly confiscated it all from him, but even then, he'd still kept enough to go out in a spectacularly messy way.

"Just how big is this explosion going to be?" Tammy asked, eyeing the stacks of

pale putty and blasting caps.

Lian pulled a crumpled wad of papers out of her pack and unfolded them, grunting at the printed diagrams and notes. "Do I look like a munitions expert? I'm just hoping they go off at all."

"I almost wish Denny was here. Almost." Cherry leaned over Lian, squinting at the instructions.

Tammy sighed. "Yeah, the dumb bastard would have loved this."

Rylan knew as much about rigging C-4 as the rest of them, which wasn't much, so he left them working on it and checked on Annabeth. She had moved closer to the boney effigies and shifted back into human form.

"You good?" Rylan eyed the sharp blade she held to the back of her forearm.

She gave him a trembly smile. "Give me a weroth bite any day. Somehow cutting myself is so much worse."

"Want me to do it?"

She jerked away as though he'd snatch the knife. "I've got it. Just need to get my head together. This is, well, if it works, this is kind of huge."

"Don't go getting those horrible things activated until we've worked this out!" Lian called over, her hands busy laying out a length of fuse.

Rylan squeezed past a couple of lures then climbed the wall near the hole. Sticking his head out, he saw half-crumbled walls and remaining building standing on one side, and an open view over a large section of the grounds on the other.

Splintered timber chairs lay pushed up against one wall and a large painting of Mordan Darkfrey had fallen on top of them. It was once a classroom Rylan had studied in.

"Can we get the fuse up through here?" he called to the others. "We've got a good vantage to watch incoming ghasts, and some walls to take cover behind."

Lian eyed the roll of fuse. "Looks like it's pretty long. I think we're done setting these. Let's get this unrolled and see how far we get."

Cherry nodded and took a step away from the stacked C-4. "I don't know what's scarier. Thinking that we got it wrong, and it won't work, or that we did it right and it's ready to blow."

Jasper moved closer to him. "I believe we have followed the diagrams accurately. But there's no indication as to the explosion size."

"Death by a swarm of eidolghasts, death by explosion, death by disintegration, or death by having our souls eaten. We have so many exciting options now," Tammy replied.

"How about we aim for not dying?" Callan took the detonator, pulling it across the room as Lian stayed to help unroll the fuse.

"I mean, I suppose that's an option, too," Tammy grumbled as she followed behind him.

Rylan gave Callan a boost through the hole and watched him disappear around the corner of a crumbled brick wall. He helped Tammy up as well, and Cherry and Jasper lined up to join them.

"How's it going, Anna? You're on."

"Okay, okay!" With a deep breath and set face, Annabeth plunged the knife into her skin.

Her lips twitched and twisted but she made no sound. She cut a straight, one-inch gash, nice and deep, then dropped the knife. Reaching to her throat, she grabbed her necklace and tore it free. She took the small piece of bone from it—ancient, original shadyr bone—and closed her eyes as she pushed it into the bloody wound she'd made.

Lian appeared by her side with gauze and a bandage and wrapped the injury. With her other hand, Annabeth extracted from her jacket pocket the spell notes Jasper had stolen.

"Okay, let's see if this shadyr bone does what it's supposed to do." Annabeth stared at the page, her eyes moving over the text a few times before she opened her mouth again.

She nodded as though to herself, then spoke. Her words were incomprehensible, guttural, and eerie in a way that made Rylan's bones shiver and his eyesight blur. He could hear a pattern in her words, a melody, as she repeated a verse over and over.

When she stopped, his heart was pounding, and a sheen of sweat prickled all over his skin. Annabeth looked about the same, the color drained from her face.

She leaned weakly against Lian. "Did it work? How do we know if it worked?"

In the gloomy room, the bones of the effigies seemed to wriggle.

Above Rylan, Cherry called out. "It worked! It definitely worked!"

Rylan pounced up the corner of the room again to look out through the hole. Across the estate grounds, there was movement. Eidolghasts, dozens of them, prowling their way.

"Come on, out of there, quick!"

He dropped back onto the stone floor with a thud and gestured Lian and Annabeth to him, then got into position to boost them up. Annabeth grabbed his shoulders and stepped onto his entwined hands, and with a push, he threw her up and out. He bent down again for Lian.

"Hurry!" Annabeth called back.

With a strain of his muscles, Lian too disappeared up through the hole.

Rylan stretched his wolf-like arms and used his long claws to scrabble out of the hole himself. He rolled onto the floor of the room above to see flames gusting in the air over his face. Two herrelspurn swooped low, wrestling with each other midair as they rushed for the lures.

Getting to his feet, Rylan bolted after Lian and Annabeth, following the line of

the fuse across the long classroom toward the still-standing walls.

A glance over his shoulder as he ducked beside Callan wasn't enough for him to count the approaching beasts. Easily a dozen, two dozen, maybe more. They squabbled and fought among themselves, driven into a frenzy by the mass of activated lures in the underground room.

The herrelspurn were already there, clawing at the hole in the ground.

Rylan frowned at the detonator in his brother's hands. They were a decent distance away from the explosives, but if the blast was going to be big enough to take out that many ghasts, were they really far enough away?

"Did you use all the bricks?" he asked.

"Yup," Callan replied. "I mean, what were we going to save them for?"

Tammy popped her head over the wall then ducked down again. "That's a fuckton of ghasts. I hope this is going to be enough to take them out."

"Even if we just get a bit of a boom, it should be enough to draw more attention over here while we go and get the Bane. That's what we're after, right?" Cherry said with a shrug.

Rylan checked over the wall again. The area above the underground room was now a writhing mass of creatures. "Either way, I think it's boom time now."

Callan's eyes were on Tammy as he nodded and held up the detonator. With a push of his thumb, it clicked.

The shockwave hit the wall at their backs, blasting right through. It cracked against Rylan's bones, smashing through him like a ghost train as bricks and mortar flew.

He didn't even hear it, his head drowning in a numb, pounding hum of its own.

The force of the explosion left him flat on his back, and the sky above him was filled with a hailstorm of black bones, flooring timber, and bloody chunks of eidolghasts. He groaned, his lungs too flattened to cry out in the pain that hit his every muscle.

Blinking eyes that were filled with patches of darkness and floating spots, Rylan was sure that the regeneration from the part-vampire form was the only thing keeping him alive. He could only hope through a pain-deadened mind that the others were still alive too.

Fucking Denny and his fucking C-4. We should have known he'd have way, way too much.

At least it had cleared out a lot of eidolghasts, but it had knocked him down too, for too long. Rylan could barely drag air into his chest, let alone make a dash for the Bane as planned.

He could only lie, paralyzed, staring at the sky as his head spun in dizzy nausea.

At the edges of his vision, silhouettes of more eidolghasts lumbered their way, drawn by the explosion. Above them, the Infuscur had the Coruscare grappled again, held tight in a web of darkness.

The Coruscare faded fast, and twisted around, moving strangely. It seemed to be folding on itself, reaching for something at its core.

Something small fell from it. The bag that Everly had carried. It drifted, empty, to the ground.

Even from the great distance, Rylan could hear what seemed to be Everly laughing, but a twisted version of it, tainted with the sound of a being not from this reality.

The Coruscare held the small orb shaped artifact above it with glowing tendrils.

The Infuscur writhed, letting go of the Coruscare and backing away, but too slow.

The Swallower expanded, exploding out to a massive green sphere across the space where the Infuscur had been. The Coruscare reared back, trying to keep clear, but strands of its light were sucked inward, caught in the web-like orb as well. The world shuddered as the Swallower crushed back down again into a tiny ball. The darkness was gone. The light went out.

Two bodies tumbled from the sky.

Rylan wheezed, pushing himself onto his elbows. His eyes locked on the falling figures.

No, no, no. If the Coruscare is gone, Everly can't take that fall.

It was a moment of both relief and heartbreak when a dim glow sputtered back to life around Everly before she hit the ground nearby.

With a grunt of effort, Rylan rolled to the side and onto all fours.

He had to move. This might be his only chance. Ghasts were still heading their way, the Infuscur might be down, and the Coruscare too, at least for now.

He had no doubt it would be finding its next meal to repower itself as quickly as it could. If he could get to the Bane and back to Everly before then, they might have a chance to take control.

He lifted his head, ears still ringing, and cast a gaze across the bloodied rubble.

He counted out his team. Lian and Annabeth, Callan and Tammy, Jasper and Cherry, lay sprawled throughout the debris. Groans and sobs came from twisted and reddened bodies, but they all moved.

They were all alive.

Rylan gritted his teeth. He didn't have time to do more for them. If he was going to help anyone, he had to get to the Bane.

As he stood up, his ankles threatened to crumple beneath him. His body stitched itself back together, but not fast enough. In a swirl of black mist and red sparks, he let go of the partial werewolf form he'd been holding and drew entirely on vampire essence to increase his healing.

Before the magical smoke had faded away, he broke into a staggering run down

the rubble-strewn corridor.

He wasn't far from the old ballroom that housed the shroudpool, just the next building along.

Struggling to run in a straight line, he ricocheted from wall to wall along the corridor, then barged open the door at the end. He almost lost his footing down the few steps outside and staggered drunkenly onto the lawn.

Light flashed in the distance. The Coruscare, gaining strength. Rylan paused for a single moment to catch his breath and the sharp leg of a weroth pierced down beside him. He snatched it in two strong hands. Wrenching in opposite directions, he tore the pointed end free.

The weroth's glowing maw snapped at him as it tripped over its amputated limb and fell flat onto the ground. Rylan leaped onto it, driving its own sharp leg into the soft spot at the top of its head.

Without the fur of werewolf form, the weroth's acid burned his pale, vampire-like flesh. He cried out, eyes stinging, as he rolled back onto the grass and pushed forward to the shroudpool. His whole body was racked with more pain than he'd ever known.

His bones stabbed him from within. His skin sizzled. His heart was squeezed in a vise. It would all be worth it if he could get to the Bane, save Everly. He just had to push forward. A light flashed again at his back, casting his shadow in front of him, driving him faster.

He climbed in over the broken wall of the ballroom and half-ran, half-crawled across the tangle of timbers and bricks toward the shroudpool.

As he drew closer, another herrelspurn burst through the massive portal, swooping out and into the sky. Rylan ducked low, rolling toward the base of the shroudpool.

In among the rubble there were pieces of bone in all shapes and sizes, smashed from the blast of the spell coming into being. Wishing he still had his werewolf claws, but not daring to take the time to shift again, Rylan plunged his hands into the sharp mess, digging down through the knee-deep wreckage.

Splinters pricked deep into his fingers and when his hands came away wet in a red so dark it edged on black, at first, he stared, confused. With a blink of understanding, he dug faster. It was the blood of the Bane.

A large sheet of roof plaster, drowned in blood, lay in the space he cleared. He lifted it with both hands, tossing it aside.

Beneath it lay the Bane. Crushed, torn into two battered pieces by a sharp edge of stone beneath it, floating in a deep pool of blood.

A wild, animal-like sound burst from Rylan's throat, and he fell onto his hands and knees.

It was gone. His last hope to save Everly was gone.

23

The blast still rung in Lian's ears as she dashed across grass stained with blood. She'd seen Rylan head off toward the Bane.

Hopefully he would have it soon and be able to save Everly—or at least stop the Coruscare. Lian didn't want to think that way, but her reserves of hope were running perilously low.

Each flicker of light that came from behind the main building where Everly had fallen, growing in strength each time, scared her more. She almost turned that way, to try to get Everly back herself, but figured she'd be nothing more than another snack to rebuild the Coruscare's strength if she did.

She had decided on a different mission for herself. She'd tracked where Mordan's body had tumbled from the sky—somewhere around the back of the palatial main building.

Around the corner, the manicured gardens were roughed up. Neat hedges were bent and torn through, and a couple of statues toppled onto the marble paths. A white-eyed stone head lay decapitated at Lian's feet as she searched with her gaze. More bodies scattered the ground than she wanted to see, eidolghast and shadyr.

Things were calmer now, with many of the shadyrs having fled and eidolghasts taken out in the explosion. Some of the bodies around the estate were probably still alive, or could be saved, if they got medical attention soon enough.

But that couldn't happen until the omnipotent creatures inside Mordan and Everly were stopped, and the shroudpool closed.

The twilight dimness confused Lian. She couldn't comprehend what the time was, how much time had passed since the shroudpool's opening blocked out the sun that should be shining above.

Maybe it was nighttime already. Maybe years had passed as they battled. Her body sure hurt like it had been that long. Even with full-vampire form regeneration going, it was barely keeping up with her injuries and strain.

A deeper darkness caught her eye, and she scurried down the pathway as silently as she could, one hand on the hilt of her slim sword that hung from her belt.

Mordan lay against the round rim of a grand fountain. His body was twisted at an odd angle, with his head on the ground and legs up over the edge, dangling in the water. His chest heaved with sharp breaths.

"Mordan?" Lian could see it was his body, but that didn't mean it was him.

He groaned as he tilted his head back to see her. "You? Where is everyone else? What happened?"

It certainly seemed to be Mordan in control. Did that mean the Infuscur was gone?

Lian stepped forward cautiously. "You've been under the control of something real nasty. I guess that's what you get for opening a portal to the Everdark in your backyard."

With a grunt and stomach-curdling crack of bones, Mordan lurched to the side, bringing his legs down onto the ground with his torso and rolling onto his front. "If my shadyrs followed my orders, this wouldn't ... you put doubt into them. You turned them ... mutinous."

"Oh, so this is all my fault, is it? See, here's the thing you never understood. They aren't *your* shadyrs. Using them as you pleased for your war. If you ever understood that, maybe half of them would still be alive." Lian crouched to his level, scrutinizing his broken body.

A haze of darkness surged outwards from him. A black ribbon shot toward Lian, and she rolled backward. On instinct, she unsheathed her sword and swiped it blindly in front of her as she got back onto her feet.

There was a hiss and a crack as she quickly sheathed the blade again, desperate to have the use of her eyes in case she had to dodge more of the destructive strands.

The Infuscur withdrew, the ribbon jittering and broken.

Well, that's interesting.

Mordan let out a gurgling roar, and the darkness slurped back into him. Obsidian eyes cleared into a sparkling shadyr gaze.

"The thing ... it's trying to take control again. Getting stronger ..." He coughed, and a thick ichor dripped from his mouth.

He shuffled into a sitting position, leaning against the rim of the fountain. Lifting his hands in front of him, he stared as though trying to make sense of his own body parts. A couple of fingers hung limp the wrong way.

"So much power ..."

"Oh no, don't you even think about it."

Lian half drew her sword from its sheath. It would only blind her once fully drawn, but halfway was enough to send Mordan a message.

Mordan glared at it, then her, and spat a wad of clumpy blood from his mouth. "Thief."

Lian nodded. "It's quite the bounty, too. You never knew what its power was. Just thought it was cursed to blind its user."

"Enlighten me then, what does it—" darkness shimmered around Mordan, and he clenched his teeth as his eyes blackened again, then cleared— "do?"

Lian couldn't be sure it had made contact with the Infuscur before. She hadn't seen exactly what happened. But if it didn't cut the ribbon of darkness, why did it withdraw?

She found a final glimmer of hope to hold onto. "It can cut into creatures that aren't there. It can cut into nothingness, and destroy it."

Mordan's reddened lips twisted into a mocking grin, but when Lian kept her expression firm, his smile dropped, and fear flashed across his eyes.

"You wouldn't. You couldn't. No, Lian, don't do this. Help me. I ... I can control it."

Lian shook her head and pulled her sword an inch higher from its sheath.

Mordan tried to back up, blocked by the marble fountain edge behind him. "Come now, you're not a murderer."

"Aren't I? Isn't that what the Darkfreys create? Isn't that what we shadyrs do? We kill monsters. I tried to be different. I tried to live a life without being a killer, but you dragged me back into it. You dragged my sons into it. I have lost so much to this world of death and darkness."

The sharp tip of the blade traced the lip of the sheath, steady in Lian's grip. Her words blew out through clenched teeth.

"But maybe, maybe if I kill just a couple more monsters, my sons and all the rest of my family can live a better life, without being killers. Without becoming monsters themselves. I can do that for them."

Mordan bared his blood-stained teeth at her, and the darkness of the Infuscur surged out from him again.

Lian adjusted her stance. "I don't like having to kill you, Mordan. But luckily, I don't even have to see it happen."

Her vision went dark as she whipped her sword out, then down.

She aimed right for where she knew Mordan's chest to be. It struck, meeting the resistance of flesh, ribcage. Lian leaned into the hilt, pushing through.

Mordan's cry of pain was short, cutting out into a sputter as she twisted the blade. The hilt tingled beneath her palms.

A shudder of disgust rattled her bones as she wrenched the sword back and sheathed it.

But she kept her eyes closed a few moments longer.

Taking in a shaky breath, she opened them.

Mordan sat deathly-still before her, facing up to the sky, his mouth hanging open. His chest around the wound was black rather than red, spidering out in cracks. The cracks spread rapidly, running over his flesh and clothing alike, turning them gray and

ashy as they went.

Before Lian's eyes, Mordan's body crumbled away into dust. It spread over the path in the light wind.

"What in the Everdark …?" Lian whispered, staring at what was left behind.

Where Mordan's chest had been lay a twisted crystal of matte black. As large as her arm, it was so dark it looked more like a hole in space than a real object.

Despite every instinct inside her screaming not to, she reached out to touch it. She couldn't leave the thing there, unguarded. If it was what she thought it was, she worried what would happen if it broke.

The crystal was smooth as room-temperature oil under her fingers, and when she touched it, she heard a crackle of energy from her side.

Putting a hand on the hilt of her sword, it zinged with the same tingle she'd noticed before. It flickered with the opposite of sparkling—shimmers of blackness, imbued with dark power.

"Okay then," Lian muttered.

She took a deep breath, then drew the sword briefly, but it didn't react in a way out of the ordinary. She'd have to work out what that meant later.

She hmphed as she crouched down and picked up the dark crystal carefully with two hands.

Bringing it near her face, she tapped on the glassy surface with a broken fingernail. "Got you."

One god-like monster down.

Lian drew a long breath, filling her lungs with air that tasted like hope. As long as Rylan got the Bane, maybe, just maybe, they would be okay.

Rylan knelt in the thick blood, hunched over, staring blankly at his hands. In a moment of panic, he tried to put the Bane back together.

The ornately etched metallic material that formed the artifact was thin and had torn right down the middle. A messy, twisted tear. Each half was crushed and bent in on itself, so it didn't even line up cleanly.

He tried reshaping them, his fingers sliced by the jagged edges. He tried holding the pieces back together, but it didn't miraculously reform. Not that he thought it had any reason too, but he needed something to happen. He needed something to work.

The warped pieces didn't even bleed anymore. Once the residual blood had dripped off, there was no constant oozing as the Bane used to do when not wrapped

in its parchment. All power had ebbed from it, spilled onto the floor.

What do I do? What do I do now?

He firmed his jaw and brought his shoulders back. He'd do whatever he could. He would never stop fighting for Everly.

The beams of light in the distance were slowly moving his way. What had Everly said? The Coruscare wanted revenge, and it wanted the Everdark back. The realm it once ruled before it was broken.

If the Infuscur was down, then the Coruscare would be headed to the shroudpool next. If it went through, if it took Everly with it, he might lose her forever.

He wouldn't let that happen. No matter what.

But how? The defeated voice in his head asked. *The Bane is gone.*

Rylan wouldn't let himself think that Everly was gone though. She was still in there, even if the Coruscare was at the wheel, she must still exist. And as long as she did, she'd still be fighting. So he would too.

"Did you find it?" Lian's voice reached him, followed by footsteps crunching through the rubble.

Rylan turned from the pool of blood to her. He stood up, and almost threw himself into Lian's arms as Tammy had done before, needing that comfort that only his mother could provide, a comfort he'd been missing most of this life. It was only the sight of the thing she cradled like a baby in her arms that stopped him.

Rylan blinked a few times to clear away the tears that washed over his vision. "Is that ...?"

Lian nodded, readjusting her hold to give him a clearer view of the matte-black crystal. It twisted around on itself, creating hollows and overlapping threads of intricate, delicate patterns.

"The Infuscur, trapped in whatever stasis this is. Must have the same near-death defenses as the Coruscare."

A wave of relief buoyed Rylan. He'd seen it and Mordan's body fall, and the Coruscare had given up its chase too, but it was good to know for certain the destructive creature was gone. One less threat to worry about, locked in that crystal prison.

"It was down, and Mordan is gone, too," Lian continued.

She stared at the pool of blood, a frown exaggerating the wrinkles across her forehead. "The Bane?"

Rylan shook his head, his teeth and mouth clamping shut as though trying to hold back his voice, as though saying it made it reality.

He forced the word out. "Broken."

Lian's eyes met his with the full comprehension of that word and it almost broke him too.

Light glowed from over the other side of the shattered ballroom wall. So close now.

Rylan spoke desperately, "It's going to go back into the Everdark. The Coruscare is going to take Everly away with it."

Lian glowered at the crystal in her arms as though she were about to smash it in anger. "If the Infuscur was still out there, at least it would keep the Coruscare busy, keep it here."

They could free the creature again, let it infect someone else. But at what cost? The battle between the opposites of light and dark was destroying all around it. Without additional weapons to take advantage of, the two of them just canceled each other out in an endless war.

If only they could cancel each other out for good, without obliterating and consuming everything between them ...

A thought formed in Rylan's mind, too scary to put into words. But he tried anyway.

"What if ... we release the Infuscur again, but into Everly? Put it in there *with* the Coruscare. No two separate bodies for them to fight with. The two of them might battle it out inside her rather than across our world."

"That's ..." Lian blew out a long breath. "That's an idea, but it has to be a huge risk. What if Everly isn't strong enough to withstand that?"

Rylan had an answer for that, and it was the part of his idea that didn't scare him. He'd considered the huge strain it would have on Everly, on her body and psyche.

"She'll be strong enough. Because I'm going to let her know what is happening. I'm going to be there for her, to help her."

Lian's nose wrinkled. "How?"

The light of the Coruscare crested the broken wall of the ballroom, lifting over the open roof like a sunrise. Everly's body hung within that bright glow, the Swallower held between her hands.

Rylan stared, burning trails into his eyesight. "I'm going to get it to consume me."

Lian put the black crystal down in a nest of broken roof tiles, then snatched his shoulder in one hand, shaking him until he looked back to her. "What good will having your soul eaten do?"

Rylan grew calm as the light drifted closer. "She's going to catch me, like she did before. She did it last time on instinct, and she understands so much more now. I trust her."

"We don't have the Bane! There'll be no way to get you back, even if—"

"It doesn't matter. I'll be with her, and we'll do what needs to be done." Rylan brought his arms around Lian, holding her tightly. "Break the Infuscur crystal over Everly as soon as I'm gone. If it works, hopefully it will lessen the Coruscare's control. Try to get the Swallower off her then. We'll do what we can from the inside."

He stepped back out of their embrace. Lian stared at him for a breathless second. Her voice was small and scratchy. "It's a good plan."

Rylan wasn't sure he'd call it good. There were so many ifs, so many ways it could go wrong.

But it was something, and that was more than he had a moment ago. If having the Infuscur and Coruscare housed together in the same physical form worked how he hoped, with the two of them destroying each other from the inside, then the powers that let Everly hold onto souls might not last long.

He would only be with her for the end, one way or another. But if that meant she pulled through on the other side without those ghast-blighted deities possessing her, he'd do that for her, and so there'd be a world for her to live in afterward.

And if the Infuscur couldn't inhabit Everly too, if the Coruscare kept control, and took itself back into the Everdark, at least he'd still be with Everly, in her dreams. At least the others might be able to close the shroudpool behind them and save this world.

The Coruscare floated lazily, triumphantly toward the shroudpool, dragging the tips of Everly's feet over the rubble. Rylan faced it, blocking its path.

"You're not leaving here without me," he yelled at it.

Everly's eyes turned to him, burning white as stars.

"Come on, damn you! You remember me, right?" He put his arms out to the sides, palms turned upward. "I know you want to eat me again. Do it!"

Scintillating threads shot out from the Coruscare at him.

This is it.

"Rylan, I love you. I never stopped," Lian said from beside him. "Callan too. All the rest. Just ... hold this for me?"

Lian pressed something cold into Rylan's open palm.

On instinct, he closed his hand around it, and the world vanished.

24

Confused ghosts surrounded Everly.

The space around her was like a shimmering cage of crystal, as though she'd been trapped inside a massive, pure white geode. She knew she was annoying the Coruscare. A thorn in its side that refused to blink out of existence and let it have its way.

At times, it would try again to assert its influence over her, like a heavy pressure squeezing her from all sides, making her want to disappear and become nothing. But she would push back. And remain.

She was still there, still herself, and still trying to regain control.

Then the first of the souls hurtled past.

She could sense their essence, and then the crunch and slurp of the Coruscare's ethereal consumption. The satisfaction. The boost to the soul eater's power.

That was when Everly knew she had to change tack.

She might never gain control of her body again. Even with two pieces of the Coruscare in her, it had only lulled her into thinking she had control. It was always too powerful for her, and now it was whole.

But somewhere, out in the real world, there was the Bane. The others could get it back, use it against her. Break her, if they had to. She knew it would be hard for them. Harper would fight it, Rylan too. But maybe Lian would be strong enough to do what had to be done.

If it was between her life and stopping the Beast of Teeth and Stars from ruling over two dimensions, Everly knew what she'd choose.

And if she could save as many souls as possible in the process, maybe they would be spilled back into their bodies when the Bane broke the Coruscare. Even if there was a chance that could be the outcome, Everly wanted to try for it.

The spirits now surrounded her. She didn't know any of them. Darkfrey shadyrs mostly. Eidolghasts had been consumed, too. Everly could sense the difference between their energy and shadyr energy.

She let the ghasts go through. The idea that they were also keeping the Coruscare fed wasn't something she liked, but she had no idea what having spirits of those monsters

roaming around in this space would mean.

The shadyr spirits wandered, shocked and distraught. Many seemed to think they were dead, that they were now trapped in some kind of purgatory. Some cried.

Everly tried to explain but had to keep most of her attention on task.

Sometimes souls would fly so fast and thick, she'd miss one, and feel a surge of guilt as someone's essence was consumed and lost for good.

Everly had no idea what was happening outside, or how much time had passed. It felt like an eternity.

Maybe this was purgatory, after all. If she could control the world with the sheer need of her wishes, she'd be back in control of her body, with her friends and family. With Rylan.

She missed them all so much, and despite being surrounded by a crowd of bewildered ghosts, she felt utterly alone.

Then a new essence streamed inward. And it felt different to the others. It felt familiar.

Straining her will, whatever part of her power she held in this unearthly space, she reached out and caught them before the Coruscare could devour their soul.

A figure materialized in her outstretched hands.

"Lian?" Everly choked out her name.

Oh no.

Lian's shoulders dropped, and she smiled wanly back. She didn't seem confused at all about where she was or finding herself there with Everly.

Reaching out a hand, she patted Everly's cheek. "Good catch, kid. Looks like you've been busy."

"I ... I've been trying. But ... it got you. No, it got you ..." Stifled sobs interrupted Everly.

She stood frozen, gaping at Lian, not wanting to believe it.

Lian waved a hand as though it were nothing. "Shh, it's okay. We have to be quick now, so listen. The Infuscur has been subdued, and we have its crystal. We're going to break it, on you, okay? It's going to be happening any moment now."

"What? Why?"

"We're hoping the two bloody beasts take each other out while trapped together in you. Maybe they will at least keep each other busy enough that you can take control again. Or something that helps."

Everly shook her head, lips twisting. "If the Infuscur is down, you should have used the Bane on me. Take out the Coruscare too. Who knows what having the two of them together will do?"

Lian's eyes glittered, and she cupped Everly's cheek in her palm. "We ... didn't

want to do that to you. We're hoping you'll survive this. That's why I'm here. To help you, any way that I can."

"You came here on purpose?" Everly winced at the high whine of her voice. Her bottom lip trembled.

"Of course. You know I'd do anything for my kids."

Everly pulled Lian close and squeezed her in a crushing embrace. "I'll get you out again, okay? When this works, and I'm in control, I'll use the Bane to put you back into your body. I'd do anything for you, too."

Lian sniffed and patted the back of Everly's white hair. "I know."

With a heavy sigh, Lian pulled back, but kept Everly's hands in hers.

There were so many other questions Everly needed to ask.

Had anyone else been lost? How was the Infuscur beaten? What was happening with the shroudpool?

But the glimmering crystal ball around them dimmed suddenly as shadows spilled over the world. Ghosts of shadyrs cried out.

Lian squeezed Everly's fingers. "Get ready. Things are about to get crazy. But you can do this."

Everly centered herself, drawing strength from the love in Lian's eyes, the reassurance of her touch.

Lian, who had never been bonded to her by the Coruscare, but had been there for her as much as Rylan had. Who showed Everly kindness and caring where her own mother had failed.

Any strength she had, she owed to Lian.

"*We* can do this."

A prickle of energy zapped through Rylan's hand, and the blindness confused him for a moment too long. Then the rush of denial and grief came with realization.

No, no! It wasn't meant to be this way.

He roared a painful howl and dropped the sword. Vision returned with a brightness that blinded in its own way.

His mother stood in front of him, wrapped in pulsating strings of light.

Rylan's breath caught in his throat as he stared through watering eyes. His knees wobbled, thighs ached, body wanting to fold in on itself.

You can't stop. You can't grieve. You have to do what has to be done.

The Coruscare was distracted. He had to act now, or Lian's sacrifice would be for nothing.

He spun wildly, searching for where Lian had put the Infuscur crystal. There, a couple of steps away, hidden behind a tumble of roof tiles, nested in a puff of torn insulation.

She didn't have to do this. It should have been me.

Lian's body went limp. The tendrils unwound themselves, and she flopped loosely to the ground, lying on her side as though asleep. Rylan picked up the obsidian-like stone.

I only just got my family back.

The Infuscur was disturbing to touch. Slick and smooth, yet matte and sharp. It was transparent emptiness and solid blackness at the same time, making him dizzy to look into it.

He clenched his teeth, fighting back the rattle of sobs that trembled up his spine. His face burned with the effort to hold back tears enough to see.

The blood from the Bane, the broken, useless Bane that couldn't get his mother back, oozed into his boots.

Keep moving. Follow the plan.

The Coruscare had stilled, hovering where it had paused to lash out at them. It reeled its tendrils back in, and through the eye-stinging glow, it seemed as though Everly's face twitched.

Something was happening inside her. He had to act now.

Mom ... please save Everly.

Rylan hefted the heavy crystal up, and with a howl of effort, threw it, javelin like, at Everly's feet.

It shattered spectacularly. Thousands of dark shards burst from the point of impact like a swarm of insects, and a cloud of darkness exploded out.

The force knocked Rylan onto his back.

It engulfed the light of the Coruscare entirely. Inky swirls spun like a miniature tornado, then rushed into Everly's body.

The darkness disappeared. The light went out. Everly floated down into a kneeling position, staring blankly through her own clear blue eyes.

"Evie?" Rylan rolled forward off his back and scrambled on hands and feet across the rubble to her.

She sat upright, expression empty, hands hanging limp at her sides.

Lying beside her was the spherical artifact.

Rylan's chest contracted when he got close. There were dark and light cracks running like veins across her chest, up her neck, over her cheeks, splitting her skin. Flickering energy shone and shadowed from within.

But the gods of the Everdark weren't showing themselves.

Is that it? Did it work?

Rylan put a hand against her cheek with a feather touch. "Evie, are you there?"

With a gasp, she blinked and looked right at him. "Rylan?"

Her mouth trembled and a single tear spilled down her cheek, tracing the lines that marred her flesh. A swirl of darkness moved across one eye as though someone had splashed a drop of ink into it, then it was burned away with a flash of light.

Everly pitched forward and cried out painfully.

It wasn't over.

He gathered her hands into his, squeezing them gently. "Is ... is Lian with you? Do you know what's happening?"

Her face crumpled, and she nodded.

"I'm sorry. I'm so sorry." Rylan choked out the words, for Everly, and for Lian, if there was any chance she could hear them.

Everly's chest heaved, and she screwed her eyes shut. "I can feel them. Fighting."

"Let them. Keep them stuck inside so they can't renew themselves by eating or destroying. Let them use each other up until they are gone. Just stay strong so we don't lose you, too."

Everly's head tilted. "I'm trying. Lian ... she's helping. Her strength is helping me stay aware. But it's too much. It feels like the universe is being ripped apart inside of me."

She shook her head in a tumble of messy, white hair.

Through the corners of his eyes, Rylan saw movement. A quick glance confirmed it wasn't a threat, but Callan and the others joining them.

His brother moved closer. "What's—"

"Keep back. It's not over," Rylan called out.

He didn't have time to communicate to them everything that had happened, was still happening, but they accepted his order and took positions around the ballroom and in front of the shroudpool, guarding them.

Rylan returned his attention to Everly. "You have to stay strong, okay? You always were the strongest of us all. No matter what happened, you'd always keep going, keep trying. I know you can get through this. You have to, because I'm not strong enough to lose you."

"I—" Everly's eyes went entirely round, and she reeled back in a panic.

She threw one hand out as though reaching for Rylan, but at the same time she scrambled away.

She cried, raggedly, "Lian said ... if you have to stop this, stop us ... use her sword. It might ..."

Her back arched so forcefully it threw her off her feet, and she hovered there,

tipped backward in midair. Arms and legs jerked and twitched, bones cracking with the unnatural bends. Her hands balled into fists and her teeth bared.

"Fight it, Evie. Fight it!"

Shafts of light and darkness shot out from the cracks in her skin, and she bellowed. Jet black painted the lengths of her flying hair, streaking between the white.

Her cries pitched low then high, moans of pain that made Rylan want to throw himself forward into that maelstrom and hold her.

Then ribbons of night and day struck out. The owner of each reached for sustenance, any power that could give them an advantage.

Rylan flipped backward, splashing into the pool of Bane blood. Something sharp scraped his leg—a long blade, crackling with energy.

Lian's sword.

The tendrils were almost on him. He snatched the blade out of the pool in a stream of flying red droplets, and his vision blanked out.

Rylan swung the sword blindly, body thrumming with adrenaline. It made contact, passing slower for a moment, as though cutting through a stream of sand.

There was a glassy tinkling of small objects smashing near his feet.

What? He threw the sword high into the air, gaining brief seconds of clarity.

The tendrils of the Infuscur and Coruscare had backed off but approached again. Two small crystals in opposite shades lay smashed at his feet, and a tiny swirl of each energy clung around his legs. He tried to stumble back from the broken essences of the creatures, but they slid in through his pores in a sensation that rattled his spine.

The sword arched and came back down, and he caught it. His heart raced, and blacked-out vision turned gray, streaked through with dark and light streamers, rushing toward him.

With a cry, he lashed the sword out again, swinging it like a bat. It hit those streams, slicing through again.

Sparkles of light and shadow spun across his grayed-out sight, landed a long distance away, smashed again.

Rylan screamed through gritted teeth. The Infuscur and Coruscare kept reaching for him, relentless in their efforts to strengthen themselves.

He could see them now. That's all he could see, with the sword hilt clenched in his fist. And every time he cut them, he was spreading them farther. Some had already absorbed into him.

Is that what's letting me see them?

He didn't know what the other consequences might be. The pieces were tiny. Much smaller fragments than the pieces that Everly had taken in one at a time.

The attacks kept coming, and Rylan swiped and slashed, chipping away. More

pieces fell at his feet. Some lay unbroken. Others flew far out of his field of view.

He had no idea this sword had the power to cut through those tendrils. He wondered how Lian seemed to know.

Sweat poured down Rylan's neck and chest. His arms burned, shoulders aching from fighting back the never-ending assault. He went onto one knee, unable to stand as he put all his strength into keeping the creature's whipping strikes at bay.

And then, the light and dark that filled his vision withdrew.

The strands were so much thinner now, and tangled in on each other, wrenching and wrestling. They zoomed away, and Rylan dared to let the sword's hilt roll out of his hand onto the ground.

The tendrils of the beings slurped back into Everly's body, fighting each other all the way. A burst of solid darkness expanded around her, then shrunk away. Then a glow of pure white, in and out, like a heartbeat.

Thu-thump. Darkness.

Thu-thump. Light.

Between each, the cracks on Everly's skin split wider. She raised higher and higher into the air.

Darkness. Light. Darkness. Light.

Then nothing. And she fell.

On stiff, aching legs, Rylan pushed into a run. Ankles twisted over the uneven ground. He stumbled, righted himself, and reached out. Everly slammed into his arms.

The weight from the fall brought Rylan cracking down onto his knees, but he held her up.

He wouldn't let her fall. He wouldn't let her hit the ground.

Sparkling pieces of the opposing gods littered the rubble, and he couldn't let her body break the shards and absorb them again.

She let out a soft, breathy grunt.

Rylan shifted his hold on her to tilt her head toward him, resting it against his chest. "Hey, hey, you still with me?"

"Uh-hm." Her eyelids fluttered, and strained open.

The cracks across her skin that flickered with white and black changed before Rylan's eyes. The glow of energies faded, stuttered out. But the cracks remained. A flush of red tinged their edges, and blood oozed in to fill the space.

"I can't ... can't feel anything," Everly said, sounding like she spoke around a swollen tongue. "Does it mean they're gone?"

Rylan nodded, even though he didn't know. He had no way of knowing for sure, but he wanted to comfort her. There was no sign of the beings in her, and he hoped with every goosebump that spread over his skin that they were gone.

They are *gone.*

And Everly had been strong enough to pull through on the other side without them.

"You're amazing. You did it," he whispered and placed a soft kiss against her forehead. She turned away from him.

He pulled back to see why, but her head wobbled limply to the side, eyes blank and mouth parted.

"Evie?" He shook her gently, but she didn't respond. "Everly? Please, come on, wake up. Wake up!"

The cracks that dripped blood over her skin ... what if they were inside, too? He pulled her closer to his chest, holding her tight.

"Help! She needs help!"

She'd pulled through in spirit. She'd kept her *self*, her consciousness intact as gods warred within her, but now her body was giving in.

They had beaten two otherworldly deities of destruction only to have her die from mundane injuries. It wasn't fair. It wasn't right. If they only had Neri, something ... They had all given everything they had.

And now there was nothing left.

25

E verly was alone.

She opened her eyes to an endless field of flowers that changed from roses to daisies to tulips as she observed them.

I'm dreaming, she thought. Rain fell around her, but she remained dry. No clouds filled the sky, which shone a startling bright cyan.

The crowd of confused ghosts she'd gathered were gone.

"Lian?" Everly called, turning her eyes to every horizon. She narrowed her gaze to scan for signs of her dragon, or its dark twin.

No reply. No sign of the creatures.

They were gone, all of them. She'd finally rid herself of the soul eater, and that made her feel as though she could float as effortlessly as its powers had allowed her to do.

They had beaten it. The Coruscare, the Infuscur, were defeated. She trusted the others to find a way to close the shroudpool. And it would be over.

The flowers around Everly were velvety and warm. Comforting. She wanted to curl up among them and sleep. Even in this bodyless existence inside her mind, she felt tired. As though falling asleep in a dream was all she wanted to do.

I'm fading away. That thought should have panicked her, but it only drifted slowly to her awareness, with a tinge of sadness. Rylan, Harper, Neri, Callan, Tammy, Cherry, and all the others, they would live, and go on without her. Out there, in the real world.

The very edges of her world, her self, seemed to be turning off. It wasn't light, or darkness that swallowed those places, but a sense of peace, gentle and cozy.

This is the end.

Part of her wished she could turn around and find Rylan there, or Lian, or even Zozo. That some fragment of their beings was still with her. She wanted to be with someone, have their support, as her life shut down around her. But also, in being so starkly alone, she felt a lightness she'd never known.

Still, she knew she wasn't *truly* alone. She knew out in the real world, Rylan was right there with her, holding her. That if he could hold her body together with the sheer strength of his will, he would.

So that's what she had to do for him. She had to hold on.

But Everly could feel that her body was too far gone.

Maybe, maybe she could be healed.

Where was Neri? Everly hadn't seen her among the group of shadyrs who had guarded around her and Rylan. Maybe she was safe back at Howell House, or somewhere with Harper. A cold worry wormed through Everly. She hoped they were okay.

All she could do now was try to stay okay herself, and hold onto life for a second longer, then another second, and another. As long as she could.

Ripping of flesh, sharp cries, an inhuman wail—the sounds of fighting came from behind Rylan.

Another eidolghast had emerged from the shroudpool. His friends worked to keep it away.

Rylan could barely lift his head to acknowledge the battle.

Everly lay deathly still in his arms.

That was all he could understand and couldn't understand at the same time. His whole life he'd just wanted to keep her safe. Whether that desire came from him or the Coruscare's bond with him, he wasn't sure. He didn't care. But even if she was far away, as long as she was safe, he could survive.

He'd only just allowed himself to want more. He still wanted her to be safe, but he also wanted *her*. To be near her, to love her.

He would have done anything to save her, but it wasn't enough.

The others yelled nearby. He couldn't make out their words. An anger stirred that they were doing anything other than mourning. He knew it wasn't logical. He knew they were protecting him as he was paralyzed by grief. He knew there wasn't anything any of them could do to change the outcome.

Callan, Tammy, Cherry, Jasper, and Annabeth were among the voices he heard.

There are so few of us now ...

Had Callan noticed Lian's body lying crumpled nearby? What about Tammy, who had already suffered so much? Would this break her? Rylan squeezed Everly into him, pressing his forehead to hers as his tears dripped between them.

The ground shook in sympathy with his anguish, as though the very earth sobbed for those lost. Then a louder rumble caused the broken roof beams in front of Rylan to slide around on top of each other.

What's happening?

Rylan looked up, checking the horizon in case some gigantic eidolghast was about to crush them underfoot.

But the source of the shaking and grumbling earth seemed to come from across the room. A pile of broken bricks bulged from beneath. Like a lava bubble it grew, grew, and then burst in a spray of torn paper and cardboard. It rained across the destroyed ballroom like confetti.

A hole appeared, and from it, Rylan heard a voice.

"They're here! This is it!"

Harper? It couldn't be, could it? Rylan swallowed hard and his hands shook with a fresh flush of adrenaline.

The hole was large enough to drive a small car into. It angled at a smooth decline into the earth, lined with layers of brown corrugated board.

Bent low, Harper jogged out, with Neri and Barry right behind.

Rylan's throat closed up in disbelief.

Then he dragged in a breath and bellowed, "Here! Over here. We need you, now!"

Standing back up to full height, Harper saw him and Everly first. "Oh no!"

She crashed across the debris at a perilous pace, sliding and scrambling on her hands and knees when loose rubble knocked her feet out from under her. She reached them in seconds and turned her head between where Lian lay nearby, and where Rylan held Everly. Then she knelt close, casting her eyes over the bleeding cracks on Everly's skin.

Running her hand over Everly's forehead, then down to a pulse point on her neck, she said, "I think she's still holding on. That's my girl. Neri? Please, we need—"

Neri was already there. She didn't even wait for Harper to finish the request.

She started to sing. Her face furrowed in a frown that her wide-open mouth exaggerated as low, mourning notes emerged. The force of her voice vibrated through Rylan's body, right to his bones with a frisson that left him renewed.

Barry stepped up behind them, offering an awkward half-smile under worried eyes.

Rylan gaped at them in awe. "How? I thought we'd lost you."

Harper shuffled across the ground to Lian. "I thought so too. But we worked out that Barry has powers, like Neri, from being so close to the Coruscare crystal for so long."

She checked over Lian's crumpled body, moving the lifeless arms and head into a more comfortable position, frowning deeply all the while. She caught Rylan's eye for a second but didn't say anything more.

Barry shrugged bashfully, tilting his head to Harper. "T'was this lady here who helped me work it out, saying I was the heart of the maze and all. Figured I'd have a go making a new maze on my own. I couldn't do exactly that, but we got enough space to keep ourselves safe, then started working out how to make an exit."

Harper crawled back. Deep lines were etched into her forehead and her eyes shone,

glossy with tears.

"Is it working?"

Rylan checked the cracks in Everly's skin, but they didn't seem to be closing. He imagined them running deep into Everly's body, down through her organs, into her bones.

The reverberation of Neri's song ran through Rylan, and he only hoped it worked the same for Everly, that those healing notes hummed through her, finding every break, every pain, and knitted her back together.

"They're back?" Tammy cried as she stumbled over to them. Callan followed, both of them with clothing shredded and spattered in gore. Tammy gasped at the sight of Everly and Lian, and Callan pulled her into a hug which she didn't fight.

Callan gave Rylan a smile that seemed confident. "Neri fixed me up when I was cut down the middle. She's got this. It's going to be okay."

Rylan wasn't sure it was exactly the same, but he nodded in thanks. He was also far too aware of how Harper chewed her lips and sniffled away tears at regular intervals ever since checking on Lian.

She wrapped a hand around one of Everly's and leaned her head onto Neri's shoulder, humming in harmony to her tune.

Barry watched over the scene, running his hands down his long beard. "Sorry it was a while getting back to you all. Took me a bit to get the hang of how to go where we wanted to go, and even after that, took us a while to find where you were. Harper here was clear that was where we needed to be."

"I knew you guys would be getting into all kinds of danger without us." Harper half-smiled, then her body shook in a silent sob. "If only ..."

Neri's voice lilted and lifted, strumming notes in Rylan's heart as the fractures in Everly's flesh sealed.

He huffed a laugh of relief. "It's working, she's healing."

As though zipping closed, the bleeding gashes turned into fine, cobweb-like scars across her skin. Her pupils moved beneath closed eyelids, then peeled open in a burst of light.

Her whole body glowed a warm, golden glow of a sunny day, and she lifted weightlessly from Rylan's cradling arms.

Gasping a deep breath, she turned upright, black-and-white-streaked hair hovering around her face as she took them all in with wide-awake eyes. Then she lowered back to the ground beside Rylan and the light dulled away again.

"Are you ...? Was that ...?" Rylan reached for Everly, wanting to know with his hands that she was real, back together, that she was herself.

Had he missed one of the crystals? Had the Coruscare survived and taken over

again? Why was she still glowing?

She caught his hands in hers and smiled, though her eyes remained sad. "I'm okay. I'm me, just me. Everything ... everyone else is gone."

Her voice cracked over the word 'everyone.' "I guess not all the powers went with them though."

Rylan's voice was barely a whisper, as though his question could break the illusion of a reality he could barely believe. "How do we know it's really you?"

Everly smirked. "On a scale from one to smuggling me your uneaten lunch in third grade because you were too scared to let your mom know you didn't like her sandwiches, how embarrassing of an anecdote do you want?"

Rylan laughed as relief and wonder burst from his lungs. "I'd forgotten that. But that wasn't really why I did it. I just wanted to make sure you were eating properly."

Everly's eyebrows lifted. She pouted and squeezed his fingers in hers.

"Of course you did."

"You probably still have powers like Neri and Barry still have powers." Harper pushed in over their clasped hands, throwing her arms around Everly's shoulders.

"Seriously though, you've got to stop scaring me like this. I missed a bunch, so I have no idea what you've just gone through, but as long as you're here, and whole, and still my goddess of a best friend, we'll work it out."

"I'm good," Everly murmured through Harper's hair. "It's like, for the first time in my life I'm not carrying the weight of that monster. I feel ... light."

"Told you all she'd be all right," Callan said.

Tammy play-punched him in the side. "Insufferable optimist."

"Adorable pessimist," he countered.

Behind them, Neri still sang. Her voice grew ragged and racked with sobs.

She paused to draw in a long breath, and whispered, "Why isn't Lian waking up? She should have woken up too."

Then she returned right back to her song, louder again.

Harper pulled away from Everly, her bronze skin paling, lips moving but words not coming through.

Rylan knew what she was trying to say but couldn't.

There was no coming back for Lian.

Harper had no way of knowing why, what Lian had done, why her body lay prone. Yet when Harper had checked her for life, it was clear she'd found none.

Everly understand too. Her face crumpled as she looked to him.

Rylan shook his head. "The Bane was destroyed. I'm sorry."

Everly stuttered in a breath. "The Coruscare is gone. Even if we had the Bane, I don't think she's ... I don't think there's any way to get her back, if she even still exists at all."

Harper frowned at their conversation, then moved closer to Neri, wrapping her arms around her and shushing her softly.

"What happened? What do you mean?" Callan asked, his voice hard.

"Lian's gone," Harper said gently.

Tammy's eyes widened. "*Gone* gone? There's got to be something we can do, she can do."

She pointed at the still singing mermaid girl.

Harper shook her head, pulling Neri in tight. "It's too late. I'm sorry."

Neri's song cut off with a guttural sob.

Callan ran his hands back through his hair then folded over, crouched down with his head on his knees. Tammy stood stock-still, but her body flickered, phasing in and out.

Rylan and Everly's hands were still wrapped around each other, and Everly squeezed tight. He should offer some words of comfort, for her, for the others, but he didn't have the strength left in him.

Would it have been better if it had been him instead of Lian? It should have been that way. Everyone else here would mourn him less than her. She had been a protector and mentor to so many who had no one else.

Rylan had missed too many years of her courage and care due to his stubbornness, blaming her for something that was never her fault. And even still, when it came to it, Lian had put his life before hers. Even when he had abandoned her, she had remained his mother to the very end.

Getting Everly back, and Harper and Neri, was a win greater than he'd dared hope, but loosing Lian was a loss he couldn't fathom, one full of shame and regret.

Rylan wasn't sure how such conflicting feelings could exist within him at the same time. Relief and joy clashed against sorrow, and he wondered if this was how Everly had felt when gods of light and darkness fought within her. As though the riot of emotions swirling at his core could eat him away from the inside out.

"I'm so sorry. This is my fault," he murmured.

"No. I'm done with that. This isn't your fault, or mine, or anyone here. You can't pick through a sequence of events full of moments out of your control to find the one time your action might have changed things *if* you had known the future." Everly sat back, snorting a breath.

"You can't think like that. You can't live like that. It's not that moment that matters, it's your intentions in every other moment. You *try*. Isn't that what you told me once? You try to fix things. You try to make things better. You are the light in this world." Everly held his gaze with the intensity of eternity before addressing the others. "All of you are."

Harper nodded firmly, smiling through streaming tears.

At a distance, Annabeth stepped closer, awkwardly. She was breathing heavily and

wiped sweat from her temples. "Um. I know this isn't a good time, I'm sorry. But we still have a massive shroudpool over here, and there are still ghasts spilling through."

She gestured behind her, where Cherry and Jasper, along with a dozen other shadyrs, finished off a vasmire.

Rylan nodded slowly. He had to keep moving. They had to finish this. For Lian, for everyone they had lost. He had to try.

He got to his feet, pulling Everly up with him as though their hands were fused together. Annabeth watched them, then scuttled closer over the debris.

"Is that? It is!" She reached down near Everly's feet and pulled the Swallower out from a hole between splintered timber.

Everly shook her head. "The Coruscare is gone. I don't know if the power I still have will get that to work."

Rylan squeezed her hands. "You can try."

Everly bit her lip and nodded.

Annabeth examined the orb, rolling it like a basketball between her palms. "I've got a little something to put into it now too. If Tammy remembers enough of the ritual, if she can guide us, we might have a chance."

Tammy remained where she'd been standing before, unmoving, but solid. She blinked at them as though just taking in the conversation.

Then her expression firmed into a snarl. "Let's shut this ghast-forsaken portal down."

26

Every moment of the day when Blaise had fallen into the shroudpool was burned into Tammy's memory.

Like a hot brand on her consciousness, she remembered every word, every action, from having relived the moments over and over internally for years. As though that could somehow have changed the outcome. She never thought those painful visages would be good for anything other than fueling the guilt she thought she deserved.

As she crouched beside Annabeth, sounding out the words of the spell Blaise had tried, her heart beat strong and fierce with purpose. They *would* close this shroudpool.

She only wished Blaise could be there to see it.

Annabeth translated the words Tammy only knew by sound into words she knew from her studies of ancient shadyr linguistics. She scrawled them down with a pen and scrap of paper she'd scrounged from somewhere, while the rest of the team fought back monsters around them.

Clothing and armor hung shredded from the shadyrs and the range of forms they took. All were spattered with blood in dark reds, greens, and black. Neri sat with Tammy and Annabeth too, safe within the ring of shadyrs.

Neri's singing had attracted some eidolghasts back to where they'd entered this world, and still more came through the portal.

Neri's singing didn't bring back Lian.

Lian had been such a solid, ever-present support for Tammy in recent years that she couldn't believe she was gone. She couldn't imagine going back to a home without her, without Rush, even damned Denny.

Would Birdie miss them all too? The thought of the old pup searching the house for them in confusion almost toppled Tammy into a pit of despair.

Was Callan hurting as much as her? Or more? Tammy screwed her eyes closed, pushing the grief away. There would be time to grieve later. Lian's wasn't the only body on that battlefield, and there would only be more if they didn't get the damned shroudpool closed.

With the piece of true shadyr bone embedded into her arm, Annabeth thought

she'd be able to make the ritual work. Tammy's heart ached to know that even if things hadn't gone terribly wrong, the spell would never have worked for her and Blaise.

They just didn't have the magic. They had repeated the spell and ritual over and over and over that day to no effect. It was only when Blaise's parents arrived that anything happened.

It was Kole's presence that activated the Swallower, knocked Blaise into the portal, and left that shroudpool dormant from the half-completed ritual. Tammy knew why now—Kole's dark magic, which had caused so much pain and loss.

At least they could use what they'd learned to try to end this.

The smashing, scrabbling sounds of fighting eased. The current wave of eidolghasts were defeated. More shadyrs had joined them around the shroudpool.

Many had ignored Lian's orders to clear out to somewhere safe. Now that the gods of the Everdark were no longer clashing in the sky, the shadyrs were coming together with a glint of hope in their eyes.

Everly glowed, unwrapping a tendril from a defeated weroth.

Harper yanked her sword free. "Really glad you got to keep some powers."

Everly snorted softly. "Feels like a decent consolation prize for having to host a soul eating deity most of my life."

Callan stretched out his back, wolfish snout wrinkling. "If this isn't over soon, I think my bones are going to grind themselves to dust with overuse."

Everly floated back to the ground, and they came over to Tammy, Annabeth, and Neri.

"Watch out," Rylan said, pulling Everly to the side by her arm.

Tammy followed his gaze to see a piece of unbroken crystal there.

Callan watched with a funny expression on his face. "Sooo, aah, if some of those bits of crystal did break on or near you, should that be a concern? Asking for a friend."

Tammy eyed him with a frown. Did he get hit, too? A bright, sparkling chunk had smashed against her shoulder earlier. It was a worry, but on the scale of all the current worries, she'd ranked it fairly low for now.

"Yeah, I have a friend who'd like to know too," Cherry said.

"Is that me? Am I the friend?" Jasper said.

Annabeth put her hand up without looking away from the words she had written. "I got done as well."

Rylan sighed and rubbed his forehead. "So, everyone then? At least a few of each kind broke near me. I don't know what it means, but so far I'm not feeling the urge to either eat or obliterate any souls."

Still catching her breath, Harper put her hands on her hips. "Are you guys telling me that magic powers were raining from the sky and I missed out?"

Everly looked to her feet as she stepped over another piece. "Personally, I don't want even a little bit of those things in me again. But they're small. The Coruscare and Infuscur are so broken up and spread out, hopefully they won't have any influence over you. Be careful though, just in case."

"Aw, I was kind of hoping I'd get some of those cool light whips." Cherry flung his hands out as though slinging a rope. He flicked one, then the other, then a bright spark glittered across his fingertips.

"Holy shit." He plunged his hands into his pockets and froze in place.

"What didn't you understand about being careful?" Everly scolded.

"All right, I think I'm ready to try this," Annabeth said, standing up, her eyes still going over the words of the spell. "Swallower in the middle, right at the base of the Shroudpool. Then get clear, I guess."

"Want me to try anything? I'm not sure whether the powers I have left will work now they aren't from the Coruscare itself," Everly offered.

Annabeth shrugged. "Let me try the spell first and we'll see how we go."

Rylan scooped up the orb and put it into place. They all moved back and watched as Annabeth began chanting the words.

The hairs up the back of Tammy's neck stood on end and a warm hum filled the air as though the words lay thick throughout it.

Tammy mouthed along to the spell silently. The Swallower wobbled on the ground, shuddering on its own. Shadows danced across the surface of the portal. Annabeth reached the end of the incantation, and nothing else happened.

"Ugh. I can feel it. I can feel it almost working, but I don't have enough power. That one little bone from my necklace isn't cutting it." She rubbed a hand over the bandage on her arm, frowning. "It also feels like, I don't know, the spell is trying to draw from something else inside me. But it's still not enough."

"The Coruscare," Rylan said, his eyes on Everly. "It managed to activate the Swallower, to use it against the Infuscur."

She nodded. "And it was the Infuscur that made it in the first place. I'd guess either of them would have the power for this. They're gone now though, at least from me."

Everly chewed her lips for a moment. "But maybe all the smaller bits combined could be enough to give the spell the boost it needs."

"Okay, anyone that got hit with a crystal, gather in," Rylan hollered and waved them together, close to Annabeth. Callan moved beside Tammy.

With questioning eyes, he laced his fingers into hers. She squeezed back in reply. Cherry and Jasper moved in as well. A few other shadyrs from around the ruined ballroom joined them, confusion twisting their faces, but willing to follow orders.

Everly, Harper, and Neri stood at their backs, keeping guard.

The group linked hands, and Annabeth spoke the words again. This time, when Tammy mouthed along, she did so with a loud, strong voice.

The ground trembled, and the air grew stifling, heavy in Tammy's throat. Her vision wavered and something inside her ignited. A hot spark of power, flaring into flame.

The Swallower shifted, rolled, righted itself, and flew into the air.

It hovered there for a moment, right in the middle of the shroudpool.

With a cacophony of booms, the small orb exploded outward. It grew larger and larger, engulfing the shroudpool entirely in a green web. Pressure sent air blasting around them. Tammy and Annabeth shouted the words over the deafening rush of wind and flying debris. And the Swallower grew larger.

It expanded out, right toward where Tammy and the others stood, rushing toward her face.

On instinct, Tammy thrust her hands forward as though to hold it back. Her blackened fingers met the intricate webbing of the artifact. Reality flickered in and out. With a thunderous crack, the crystalline web stopped.

The beats of a million broken hearts pulsed beneath Tammy's touch. A throbbing, slurping sensation. The inky blackness that stained her skin flowed into the orb, absorbing into it, and darkening its surface.

Tammy cried out the final words of the incantation. The Swallower shuddered, rippled, and rushed back in on itself. The implosion pulled Tammy forward, onto her hands and knees, and the others fell around her.

As the sphere grew smaller, the place where the shroudpool had been became clear again. And it was gone.

We did it. We did it! Oh, Blaise ... Tammy huffed a soundless, teary laugh as she stared at her pale, normal hands.

The Swallower retracted back to its original size, warping and twisting crookedly where black lines marred it. A howl of screaming monsters emerged as it split down the middle and fell, cracking into two halves.

Callan flopped over on his back across the rubble and gazed up at Tammy with tired eyes and a laughing mouth. "I thought for a second we were going to be taken out along with the shroudpool. You ... you are so fucking amazing."

Tammy huffed, and wiped her eyes with pale, peachy fingers. She couldn't stop staring at them. Her tainted, Everdark-cursed hands were gone.

She was no longer cursed. Maybe she never had been. Maybe she could finally accept that. She broke her gaze away from her fingers to smile back at Callan.

At those lips that had *kissed* her. *He had kissed her.* Maybe she could even start accepting *more.*

Above them, the sky seemed to melt. The unnatural darkness that clung there dripped down like rain, revealing bright beams of a flaming sunset.

"It's done. It's over. It's really over." Everly sat sprawled on the ground, arms wrapped around Harper and Neri on either side.

"And we won. Can you even believe it?" Cherry laughed.

Tammy giggled along with him, and sobbed, and smiled, and sniffed. Callan reached up and pulled her down beside him.

She stared at the lightening sky that showed off all its best colors in defiance of the nearing night.

They had won, and yet they'd lost so much. The surviving victors sat, tangled and wrapped together in a messy bundle of laughter and tears, amid the broken pieces of those who didn't last to see victory.

Tammy scrapped a handful of crumbled brick into her hands. This place that had once been her home lay in ruins. "For a win, there's not much left."

Callan's chest rose and fell in a sigh. "As bad as the Darkfreys could be, they were a large part of what protected the world from darkness overtaking it. A lot of that protection is now gone."

"Looks like that Swallower thingy is busted too," Cherry sighed.

"But we're still here," Tammy said.

"We are still here," Everly replied.

Her face was smeared with dust and streaked with tears, and her now black and white hair hung in a tangle. Her smile spoke of a deep inner peace that sent a surge of longing through Tammy. She wanted that peace, too. She could almost taste it, on the horizon.

Everly turned her face to the sky, and orange light set her aglow. "And you don't have to be a Darkfrey, to fight against the darkness. You just have to try."

27

"Neri's lost her voice," Harper called out over the makeshift triage field. The moon hung full and bright, stalked by the shadows of clouds across the night sky.

Everly straightened, cracking her back, strained from hours bent over carrying stretchers. Hours spent sorting the bodies of those who could be saved from those who couldn't. Their faces would haunt her nightmares, but the work had to be done.

Neri's song lilting across the blood-spattered lawns of the estate grounds was all that had kept Everly going, all that had revived so many of the shadyrs who were too close to joining the list of couldn't-be-saved.

The silence snuck up on Everly. She'd noticed Neri's voice growing hoarse, quieter, as the night went on, but she'd had so much to focus on herself that she missed the moment the singing stopped.

Beside her, Rylan shifted from the strong, werewolf-cross-dragon form he'd been using to free survivors from under fallen rubble back to his normal self.

There weren't many eidolghasts around anymore. Any surviving ghasts had fled the battle to terrorize another day. Although a few monstrous corpses lay scattered nearby, Rylan said it was as though the small pieces of Coruscare energy in him let him still choose his forms as he pleased. That was going to be interesting for the other shadyrs who got a dose of the soul eater as well.

"Come on, let's go check in with the others," he said to Everly, pushing a strand of hair back from her face.

She nodded numbly. If Neri was out of action, that was going to slow things down. They needed to work out what was next.

Sitting on a low garden wall, Neri took small sips from a water bottle as Harper knelt beside her and rubbed her back.

"You did so, so well. It's okay," Harper cooed.

"I ... I want to ..." Neri's voice was like the soft scratch of fingernails over bark.

Harper leaned in and pressed her forehead to Neri's. "I know. You've done so much already. You've saved so many lives."

To the side, a team of shadyrs had already begun taking over the triage and treatment. One looked up from his patient. He wore a Darkfrey hoodie and had the all-boney-joints appearance of a boy in his late teens.

"We can take over from here. I mean, we don't exactly have musical healing magic, but if that option isn't available anymore, we'll make do with sutures if we have to."

An older woman frowned at Everly and Rylan. "You guys are still here? Go and take a break. Consider that doctor's orders. You're relieved."

With a grunt of frustration, she returned to flashing a light into the eyes of a boy that was way too young to have been involved in the fight.

With another huff she said, "Thank you, for everything. But also get the Everdark out of here."

Everly stared at their surroundings. There was still so much to be done, but she knew she couldn't push on any longer without her body giving in entirely.

With a nod to Rylan, they followed Harper and Neri away. Somewhere along the path through the grounds, Callan and Tammy joined them, then Cherry, Jasper, and Annabeth.

Getting from the estate to Crowea's bar went by in a blur.

Exhaustion made the edges of Everly's sight hazy, and often when she blinked, she was surprised she had the energy to open her eyes again.

She wanted to find a bed and sleep for a million years, to dream dreams unhaunted by any other soul.

She wanted to find a place to sleep beside Rylan, holding him in the real world instead of her sleeping mine.

But Rylan told her they had to go and toast those they'd lost.

"It's shadyr tradition. It's what we do. Even after the longest of nights."

On the way, they saw shadyrs busy trying to put the Humpty-Dumptyed town back together. News had gotten out of the shroudpool closing. Now everyone was working together on damage control.

The cleaning crews had done a surprisingly efficient job of clearing the broken monster bodies off sidewalks. Everly didn't think there was much they could do about the townsfolk though. For many, it would have been confirmation of what they always suspected. Others would continue to live on in denial.

It was a strange weather event, escaped dangerous animals, gas leak, anything to avoid knowing that monsters truly crept in the shadows of their home.

When they reached The Crow's Nest, Everly was glad to see the establishment still standing, although there were streaks of blood marring the heavy door. As they stumbled into that warm space filled with jangly clutter, eyes turned to them, and a silence fell.

Almost every table and seat was filled. Battle-bloodied and bent, shadyrs clung to their drinks and watched as Everly, Rylan, Harper, Neri, Callan, Tammy, Cherry, Jasper, and Annabeth stepped inside. The Howell team. The runts. The outcasts. The blivs and freaks.

A chair scraped the floor as a man lunged to his feet, raising his glass. Then an avalanche of sound hit them as the rest of the room followed.

At the bar, Crowea beat her fist on the bar twice.

Her voice boomed out, "The dark must fall!"

Thump thump, feet and hands across the room beat a reply.

"So the sun may rise again," all chorused.

Only Everly, Harper, and Neri didn't answer the call. She'd heard those words before, when they toasted Denny with warm beer a lifetime ago.

Rylan bowed his head to Everly. "This is what we say when a brace loses someone in battle. We will fight to hold back the darkness, in hope of a better day."

Tammy sniffled and pressed a hand to her chest. "Both outside, and in."

Everly nodded, and echoed the reply, "So the sun may rise again."

They approached the bar as the other patrons returned to their seats.

Crowea had a row of shot glasses lined up, filled with clear alcohol. She pulled another bottle and dripped a single drop of thick, black liquid into each. With a swipe of a lighter she caught them all aflame.

"Drink your sorrows, babies. Take them in and know them well. They will grow lighter with time."

Rylan took one and blew out the flame. "To Lian. The best mother and leader any of us could have asked for, even if it took me too long to realize it."

Everly reached hesitantly for a shot, and Crowea slid a glass with all clear contents her way with a wink. Everly took it, and when she tipped it back, found it to be water.

She returned a confused, thankful smile to Crowea, unsure when the barkeeper learned she wasn't much of an alcohol fan. The old witch smiled back knowingly, beneath wrinkled skin and the ghast-tooth embedded in her eye.

The others tipped their drinks back too, then placed the glasses on the counter for a refill. Crowea repoured them again as before.

Tammy lifted hers, staring at her pale fingers holding that glass.

"To Rush. She had more love, joy, and kindness in her than anyone in this world. She ... she ..." Tammy choked up.

"She wrote one heck of a spicey story," Harper added.

A man with a Viking's stature and well-groomed red beard appeared next to them. His eyes were as red as his hair, tears streaming from them.

"She was too perfect for this world." He took a long mouthful from a pint-glass as they all drank.

"You knew her too?" Cherry asked.

His shoulders slumped forward as he nodded, then he walked away, sobbing into his cup.

Crowea moved along the bar to pour the same darkness-tinted shots for a group of three shadyrs who had just stumbled in. Everly squinted, and recognized Lucas. Him, Molly, and Benson. No Parker. Their faces were gray and drawn, especially Molly's, as she shook with silent tears under Lucas's arm.

Everly's sympathy swelled for the girl. She must have been a few years younger than Everly, trained her whole life as a Darkfrey.

She'd passed info back to them, info that kicked all of this off, but she no doubt thought she was doing the right thing. Told she was doing the right thing, along with all the other lies the Darkfreys had fed her through her entire life.

Everly couldn't find it in her to place blame. Punishing mistakes, casting people out, that was the Darkfrey way. If they wanted the sun to rise bright again tomorrow, things had to change. Everly's shot glass of water was empty, but when she caught Lucas's eye, she raised it to him as they drank their sorrows. He nodded solemnly in return.

A table cleared and Cherry shooed them toward it. "Go grab some seats, I'll get some more drinks."

Everly dropped into the low lounge. Her muscles ached from scalp to heels. Harper sank in beside her with a dramatic sigh. Her shirt—Everly's shirt—was pockmarked with tears and spotted in blood.

"I let you wear my clothes for one day and you've gone and ruined them," Everly said, half-smiling.

Harper's eyelashes fluttered in confusion as she looked at herself. "I put this on today? How was that this morning? Also, that's the last time I'm going to let you guys dress me."

She put on a mocking voice. "What's the worst that can happen if you don't put on your makeup? The end of the world?"

"I mean, technically it didn't end," Callan said.

Harper dismissed him with a wave. "Only 'cause we saved it. Still, every time I get dressed now, I have to consider, are these the clothes I'm going to be facing apocalyptic disaster in?"

The lounge was a two-seater, but Neri squeezed in next to Harper, bringing them all close together. Rylan took an ottoman to Everly's other side, and Callan and Tammy took armchairs across from them. Annabeth pulled over a couple more chairs for herself, Cherry, and Jasper, who were still at the bar. Groans of relief sounded all around.

"Let's not have any more end of the world situations any time soon, okay?" Callan sighed.

Tammy tsked. "Spoilsport."

There was a life, a smile in Tammy's eyes that Everly hadn't seen before. Like a sun rising strong from the darkness within the girl. Everly desperately wished Lian could have been there to see it. To see that they were okay, and would be okay.

Her voice sounded quiet against the clinking glasses and mournful toasts around the room. "I wish I could have kept Lian with me. That I didn't lose her along with the Coruscare. It would have been nice to have her there in my dreams, to be able to tell her that everything turned out, that we're all here. Thanks to her."

Rylan leaned with his elbows on his knees, head hanging, bouncing in small nods.

Then he looked up, mouth twisted in the barest of smiles. "Maybe she is still out there. A little piece of her in everybody who now has a piece of the Coruscare in them."

Tammy lifted her hands to cover her mouth as tears flushed her eyes. "Do you think so?"

Callan held Rylan's gaze, jaw clenched. "I like the sound of that. I'll look for her, in my dreams."

Tammy nodded enthusiastically. "Me too. Even if she's just a feeling. Even the smallest essence, I'd be honored to carry her. She carried all of us, gave us so much, and accepted us when no one else did."

Everly reached for Rylan's hand and squeezed it hard. He tangled his fingers in hers and didn't let go.

Cherry and Jasper stood by the table, carrying glasses and two jugs filled with colorful liquid, leaves, and flowers.

Cherry stood solemnly, staring at Tammy.

"I like the sound of that, too. That Lian is still with us. It's a comfort," he said softly as he shared out cups. "I found my parents tonight."

Callan sat up straight. "Found them, how?"

Cherry shook his head. "They didn't make it."

"Oh no, I'm so sorry," Harper said, reaching out to him as he took a seat.

He held her hand for a moment, then shrugged. "Yeah, it's ... rough. But it also made me realize how long I'd been hung up on hoping for their approval. Even after I'd scolded Jasper for seeking approval from the wrong people."

He twisted a wry smile at Jasper as he took the seat beside him, still somehow looking neater than all the rest of them in his beige cardigan. "All the love and acceptance I needed was here already, and damned if I ever needed anyone's approval to be myself anyway."

Jasper side-eyed him. "The audacity of fitting so much wisdom into such a handsome body."

"Like you can talk." Cherry leaned in until their shoulders pressed together.

"Here, cheers to love and acceptance," Harper said, pouring a drink and handing

it to Cherry.

"The pinker one is a mocktail. For the kids," Cherry said, passing the cup along to Tammy.

"How very dare," she hissed, and passed it along to Everly.

Everly chuckled and sniffled as she took the drink happily. Harper poured from the other jug for everyone else except Neri, who chose non-alcoholic as well.

Mostly through short whispers, pointing, and meaningful looks, since her voice still hadn't returned. Harper handed Neri the glass with a smile, and their fingers entwined for a moment, causing a blush across Harper's cheeks that Everly didn't miss.

Everly raised her eyebrows when Harper turned her way.

Harper bit her lip and leaned in close to whisper to Everly. "She likes me. Like, *likes* me."

Everly put an arm around Harper and pressed her head against hers, cheek to cheek, whispering back, "Of course she does. Who wouldn't?"

A slim man in an expensive business suit approached their table. "Um, hi, I'm not sure if I'm in the right place. I'm here for Rushelle. I'm her partner, and was told this was where to be, since ..."

He pulled a silk handkerchief from a pocket and dabbed his nose.

Cherry's eyes grew wide, and he looked across the room then back at the man. "Aah ..."

The man followed his gaze. With a nod of recognition, he walked over to where the red-bearded man sat.

"Oookay, so while we were at the bar, this other dude said he was Rush's partner too," Cherry said, pointing across at a big guy in a leather biker's jacket, sitting beside the Viking man.

They both stood up to their imposing heights as the businessman approached them.

"Are we about to have a situation here?" Rylan asked.

The three men moved closer together, then arms went out and wrapped around each other in a sobbing huddle.

"Holy shit," Harper hissed, staring shamelessly.

"You don't think ..." Tammy said.

Harper nodded. "That our Rush was living her own real-life reverse harem? I am definitely thinking that right now."

"Complete with all the spicey scenes," Tammy laughed.

"Can I imagine you imagining all those spicy scenes?" Callan asked from behind his drink.

Tammy gave him a withering look. "Someone call an exorcist, because I think Callan's channeling Denny."

"Dick pics!" Harper exclaimed suddenly and broke down into hysterics.

She laughed so hard the couch shook.

"Um, are you okay?" Everly asked.

Harper gasped in breaths between her laughter. "Denny said … that's what he sent … Alexis … and Mordan was monitoring … Can you imagine?"

She wheezed, tears of mirth pooling under her eyes.

Everly put a hand over her mouth, frozen as she tried to process that thought and the various levels of disgust, absurdity, and tragedy that came with it.

"I really *don't* want to imagine," Tammy groaned.

"I'm with you. Team 'Let's not imagine things more horrifying than the Everdark'." Everly snorted and leaned forward from the lounge with her hand up to high-five Tammy.

Tammy hesitated for a moment, then lifted a pale hand to slap against Everly. As their palms met, a flash of light glowed around them.

Tammy gasped back, folding her hands against her chest.

Everly snorted again. "Kidding. Sorry. Couldn't resist."

"Oh my ghast! My hands mightn't be cursed anymore but they can still strangle people just fine!" Tammy huffed, but a smile broke across her lips. "You're lucky I can't teleport away anymore, or I would have made you do pickup."

Callan leaned across onto the arm of his chair, smiling at Tammy. "I'm happy you don't vanish anymore. I like it much better when you're right here with me."

"Gross," Tammy grumbled, rolling her eyes, but she leaned across onto the arm of her chair too and planted a kiss on his cheek.

"I knew it!" Harper let out a hoot so loud someone across the bar dropped their drink. Cherry and Everly joined in, whistling and cheering.

Tammy sank back into her armchair, pulling her hood over her head. "Kill me now."

Laughter spilled across every lip as free as the tears from their eyes.

A round of drinks came over with thanks from Lucas, and then another round came from a group of Darkfreys at the bar, and then another.

Callan threw back a shot, then slumped, giggling hysterically. "I'm not sure if they are thanking us or trying to murder us with alcohol."

Everly went to pour herself another glass from the mocktail jug and found it empty. "And that's my cue to call it. I'm so exhausted."

"How exhausted are you?" Cherry hollered back like it was a pantomime.

Everly twisted her lips and put on an old-timey comic accent. "I'm so exhausted I feel like I've been to the Everdark and back and all I got for it was a lousy dark twin to the soul-eating god that possessed me."

Callan pointed a finger at her enthusiastically. "Oh! That happened! We did that! We went to the Everdark and back again!"

"To the Everdark and back again!" Tammy echoed, raising her drink.

Everly groaned melodramatically, resting her head on the lounge. "We're never getting out of here. I just want to go home."

Rylan scooched closer until they were sharing an armrest. He stared at the drink in his hands—one from earlier in the night, mostly untouched. "Where is home going to be for you now?"

Everly gaped at the question. She hadn't even started to think about what would be next.

She was free. Free of the Coruscare, and any obligations that came from hosting a dangerous supernatural creature from shadyr mythology. She could go home to her and Harper's apartment in the city. But *home* didn't feel like the right word for it anymore.

In Rylan's low-cast gaze, with long lashes lying over his high cheekbones, she could see so much of the boy she'd spent her whole life loving. His feelings were his own now, and so were hers, and she still loved him. With a yearning that she'd cross the Everdark again to satisfy.

"Home is wherever my family is. It's with the people I love," she said.

He looked at her from the side of his eyes.

"It's with you." She reached over the armrest, grabbing the torn body armor on his chest and turning him to face her.

Rylan's Darkfrey crest tattoo that lay over his heart was visible where the ripped armor hung loose, spattered with dust and blood. When Everly had first seen that tattoo in her dreams, she worried that Rylan had become nothing but a Darkfrey soldier.

Now, she could see it was a symbol of the best parts of him. His loyalty, his devotion to helping others, and his desire to make the world safer for those he loved.

"All the world is filled with monsters, of one kind or another. It's the good people you surround yourself with, the people you love that make it bright. That's you. It's always been you. I love you."

Rylan closed the gap between them, wrapping his hands into her black-and-white-streaked hair as their lips met.

They kissed each other with a hunger even the soul eater couldn't match. With a love that had held on, unrequited, all their lives.

And Everly glowed.

EPILOGUE

Nails slipped satisfyingly into the timber, and Everly smiled. Her new nail gun was making short work of framing up the replacement wall and window for her kitchen.

It also felt good being able to buy the new things she needed, knowing that she wasn't going to be moving them all again somewhere else. This was home. For good.

And although she did break down crying when they gave her the 'family discount' at Pimey's Hardware, it was as much happiness as sorrow.

The rebuild was a big job, but she had the tools, and could do the work. Building supplies were in high demand for a while after *the incident*, as most Shroudhaven residents vaguely referred to it as.

Everly, Neri, and Harper had lived for a few weeks with the gaping hole tarped over, surviving on takeaway alone without a functioning kitchen. Everly loved every moment of it, sharing that home with them, even if the walls were broken.

They had cleared enough of the antiques store by then to create a living area in there, and the upstairs loungeroom she'd been camping on the couch in became a real bedroom for her. She'd even splurged on a brand-new king-sized bed, which she and Rylan had been putting to a lot of use.

She blushed at her own thoughts. If younger Everly could ever have known ...

A movement in the corner of her eye brought a low rise of anxiety washing over her. She inhaled slowly as she turned to see what it was.

Even under the sparkling light of a rare, sunny day, Shroudhaven could still be dangerous. Not that her anxiety needed true danger to set it off.

The caramel flanks of the cougar she knew so well slunk around the corner of the fence and down the side path to the back of Everly's home.

"In broad daylight? You're getting bold." Everly returned to her work, punching in a couple more nails.

Zozo would find the food where she'd left it for him. Not that he needed it. He was looking noticeably rounder, and Everly knew that Neri—utterly obsessed with the cat—had been putting out extra food on top of his regular feedings.

Everly exhaled deeply as the spike in her anxiety settled. Stepping back to check her build, she smiled. Anxiety was still a constant for her, but for now, she had it under control. Now that it wasn't tangled in the spirit of what she used to think of as her dragon.

Now she never had to worry about consuming souls again. Now she had a better understanding of events around and inside her. It would never be gone, but she had the tools, and could do the work.

Some days were harder than others as she healed through her trauma, but she found that she loved herself regardless. And she knew that the family she'd found accepted her too.

Her phone pinged, and Everly pulled it from the back pocket of her jeans.

Rylan: *I know you wanted to get lots done on the house today, but can you come up to the estate early? Got big news. Real big.*

Checking the time, she saw it was a couple of hours until she was expected there for training. She still struggled to get her head around the concept of being a teacher.

There wasn't a whole lot she felt she could teach, but then again, there wasn't exactly anyone more qualified.

No one else had hosted the Coruscare except for her.

Now that a few dozen shadyrs found themselves with at least a fragment of that being inside them, Everly had agreed to do what she could to share her experience with them.

Days had been spent combing the area around the final showdown to gather any unbroken pieces of the Coruscare and Infuscur.

One particularly large piece went to Barry, in hopes he could get his tunnel system back together again.

Another was sent to the Crybel's Cove shadyrs for the lighthouse rebuild.

The rest were locked away for safety.

The full implications of hosting even small parts weren't known yet. Especially for the Infuscur.

Everly tapped out a reply: *OMW, <3 U*

Everly wondered what the big news could be, but it wasn't curiosity that had her downing her tools for the day. Any excuse to spend more time with Rylan was a good excuse.

Everly poked her head into the living room-slash-antiques-store area. "Hey, can I take the van for a bit?"

Harper emerged from the side room, dressed in a lacey Lolita dress, skin deathly pale, with a perfectly placed line of blood dripping from her mouth. "Sure, we'll be busy here for a while."

Some antiques Everly's dad had left her turned out to be surprisingly valuable, but nobody wanted anything from the 'room of cursed toys,' as Harper had dubbed it.

She and Neri decided to work on her haunted doll photoshoot she'd imagined when they first explored the untouched old rooms. Then they'd hire a skip bin and send the creepy playthings off for good.

Neri stepped out, camera hanging from a strap around her neck, brown curls bundled on her head. She wore the long cotton dress Lian had given her the night they'd brought her home from the lighthouse.

She wore it at least once a week. When Everly speculated that it was going to fall apart at the seams soon, Neri proclaimed she was going to learn how to sew. She had taken to learning new skills with a near-Harper-level of enthusiasm and dedication.

Taking on being the photographer for Harper's shoots was her current mission.

"Do you think the lighting is working on these?"

Harper leaned in close to look at the camera screen and gasped.

"You have such a good eye." She pecked a kiss to Neri's cheek, and Neri's nose wrinkled happily as she turned and kissed Harper back.

"I'm going to get tooth decay around you two with these high sweetness levels."

Harper blew Everly a kiss. "Bye-eeeee! Don't get kidnapped and kick off an apocalypse again, kay?"

Everly chuckled. "I'll do my best."

Harper waved over her shoulder as she returned to looking at the camera. The tips of her fingers seemed to sparkle for a moment.

Everly did a double take and Neri let off another flash from the camera, testing the reflections. Laughing at herself, Everly grabbed the campervan keys and headed out.

Managing to not get kidnapped and kick off an apocalypse, Everly drove in through the Darkfrey gates and up to the main building.

Only half the structures at the estate remained standing after the incident. A few more were so damaged they had been cordoned off, deemed unstable and requiring demolition at a later stage, but much of the other debris had been cleared.

All activities and dorms had been scaled back into the buildings that remained largely untouched. The shadyr community worked together to keep essential functions running. Things like patrols, cleaning crews, training, and schooling for the younger, far too frequently orphaned shadyrs.

All those who had defected to Howell House returned, including Annabeth, Cherry, and Jasper. Only Rylan, Callan, and Tammy remained at Howell House now, although they spent a large amount of time at the broken estate.

Callan had told Everly that Lian managed to start again from a broken place, to become something more when she'd lost almost everything, and he and Rylan intended to try to do the same. They took on leading roles in getting the estate and shadyr community back on track.

Everly knew Lian would be proud. Maybe she was, somewhere in her sons' dreams.

Although with Mordan gone and legalities a mess, there wasn't much they could do on a larger scale until questions of funding were answered.

Alexis Darkfrey's children, the only line surviving from Mordan, weren't even in their teens yet.

Only a few hardcore Darkfrey fanatics treated them as heirs to the shadyr throne. Most others had been either directly or indirectly hurt by the Mesmans' dark magics and Mordan's choices, and were happy to work toward a new way of life for the shadyrs of Shroudhaven.

As Everly strode the long hall, she could feel the eyes of the portraits of famous shadyrs watching her.

It didn't surprise her to see their gaze shifting, actually following her with eerie accuracy as she passed by.

The estate wasn't the place it used to be, in more ways than one.

When the Bane had broken, it spilled tons of mixed, ancient eidolghast blood that had flowed, soaking into the ground and setting off a permanent, low-level beshadowing throughout the estate.

There were some early calls for evacuation, but the side effects seemed to have limited themselves to mild haunted house vibes.

It still sent a shiver down Everly's back.

Callan walked the hall toward her, shaking his head and laughing to himself.

"This is going to set off some risen hackles, big time," he said, chuckling some more. "You're not going to believe it. I can barely believe it myself."

"Should my hackles be rising? Are you going to clue me in or what?"

Callan smirked and shook his head. "I'll let Rylan have the honors. He's up in the meeting room to the right. I've got to go tell Tammy."

Everly found the room mostly from the stream of flustered men and women in suits filing out of it, sorting papers and gossiping between themselves. She waited for them to pass, then stuck her head through the doorway.

Rylan stood near a polished boardroom table, sorting a thick wad of papers into sections. He wore a similar bemused smile to his brother's.

"What in the Everdark is going on?" Everly moved forward, trying to catch a glimpse of meaning from the documents.

Rylan scooped them out of her view.

He came around to the front of the desk, leaning against it and patting the spot beside him for Everly to join him.

Everly rested her hip against the table and Rylan handed her a collection of clipped together papers off the top of the stack.

A wall of legalese met her eyes. "What is this?"

"A copy of the last will and testament of Mordan Darkfrey," Rylan explained. "Leaving his estate to his children Nilson and Alexis."

Everly nodded. That's what had been expected all along.

"So Nilson," Rylan handed her the next sheets, "he didn't have any kids, so they had a setup where his portion of the estate would go to Alexis and her children, to keep things in the Darkfrey line, of course."

"Okay, so Alexis's kids are the sole beneficiaries, we figured that already."

Rylan sighed and chuckled with the same breath. "Except then we get hit with the kind of chaos that only one special person was able to bring to the party. Denny."

Everly's face scrunched back in shock. "What?"

Rylan handed her another document, pointing at a date and entry down the page.

His body shook with contained laughter. "Alexis had her will changed in secret. She left everything to Denny."

"Nooo, what? I mean, she had that real ride-or-die thing going on with him in the end ... but *Denny*?" Everly stared at the name on the page as though the fleet of lawyers had somehow made a mistake.

She flipped the pages back and forth, but they were clear. "What ... what does that mean though, with Denny gone?"

Rylan's bemused mirth eased, and his chest stilled. A softer smile curled his lips as he handed her the next document.

"I was worried at first they were going to say it went back to Alexis. But as big of a jerk as the guy could be, he clearly knew who had his back at the end of the day. Not that he had much to leave, as far as he knew. I reckon he thought he'd only be leaving his RV ..."

Rylan pointed at the papers, and Everly gasped.

"Lian? But then—" Everly snatched the final document from Rylan's hands, leafing through for confirmation.

Rylan grew solemn and nodded. "Callan and me. She only added us on once we'd come home. Once she trusted us enough to continue the home she created at Howell House and not clear her family out in some twisted service to the Darkfreys. If all of this had happened a few weeks earlier, Callan would have got the lot."

Rylan huffed a bewildered laugh.

"The lot, as in, *the lot*?" Everly jumped to her feet and waved the papers at their surroundings.

"Yup."

Everly froze, hands still midair and papers crinkling.

Rylan winced. "Yeah. It's ... a lot. There you go. That's the big news. Honestly?

Still in shock myself."

Everly lowered slowly back onto the desk and put the wills down.

That *was* big news.

Plunging her hands into the pockets of her red bomber jacket, Everly tried to comprehend what it would all mean.

She couldn't imagine either Rylan or Callan ruling from on high as Mordan had, from his gilded office, commanding the army of shadyrs he thought he owned.

Just because the brothers owned the estate now, didn't mean they ruled it.

And that could make all the difference.

Looking up at Rylan, she smiled. "I think you are going to do wonders for the estate and all the shadyrs here."

Rylan shrugged. "I don't know. I mean, I know I want to help rebuild a home for shadyrs. There's so much work to do. And I want to help keep fighting back the darkness. That's such a huge part of me. But also, maybe I want to take a break from being a full-time soldier for a while. Find out what other parts of me there are."

"I am so on board for exploring your parts." Everly smirked. "But seriously, I think that sounds like a really good idea, finding yourself."

Rylan swept an arm around her waist and dragged her over in front of him, between his legs. "As long as I can find myself with you. Because I have a feeling that the me I find just wants to focus on making the most beautiful woman in at least two realms happy."

"Not being my protector?" Everly wrapped her arms around his shoulders.

"Like you need one," Rylan scoffed then leaned in close. "I'm happy just soaking in every bit of your light that I can, for every moment that I can."

Rylan buried his face into her neck, pressing warm lips into the dip of her collarbone and then running a trail of kisses to her ear.

A thrill of goosebumps chased after his touch, and Everly melted under his warm hands.

Before she lost all sense to his touch, she said, "You know I used to wish that we were soul mates, fated to be together. I'm glad that wasn't the case."

Rylan pulled back. "Ouch. Thanks?"

"Because it means we could *choose* each other. We didn't get here because of some unfightable destiny, but we're here because we fought *for* each other. Because we wanted it." Everly ran her fingers down Rylan's cheeks, staring into his warm, olive-green eyes that looked like home. "And I want you, more than anything."

Rylan's gaze sparkled.

He picked her up around the waist, carrying her over to kick the door closed, then kissed her in a way that made her head spin with a rush of pleasure.

Of all the monsters and mysteries that had bombarded Everly since returning to

Shroudhaven, nothing surprised her more than how she'd been able to find herself a home in that place.

That a house of tormented memories could grow warm again.

That abandoned fantasies of love could blossom into something better than she ever dreamed.

That with so much darkness, so too came a glorious light.

THE END

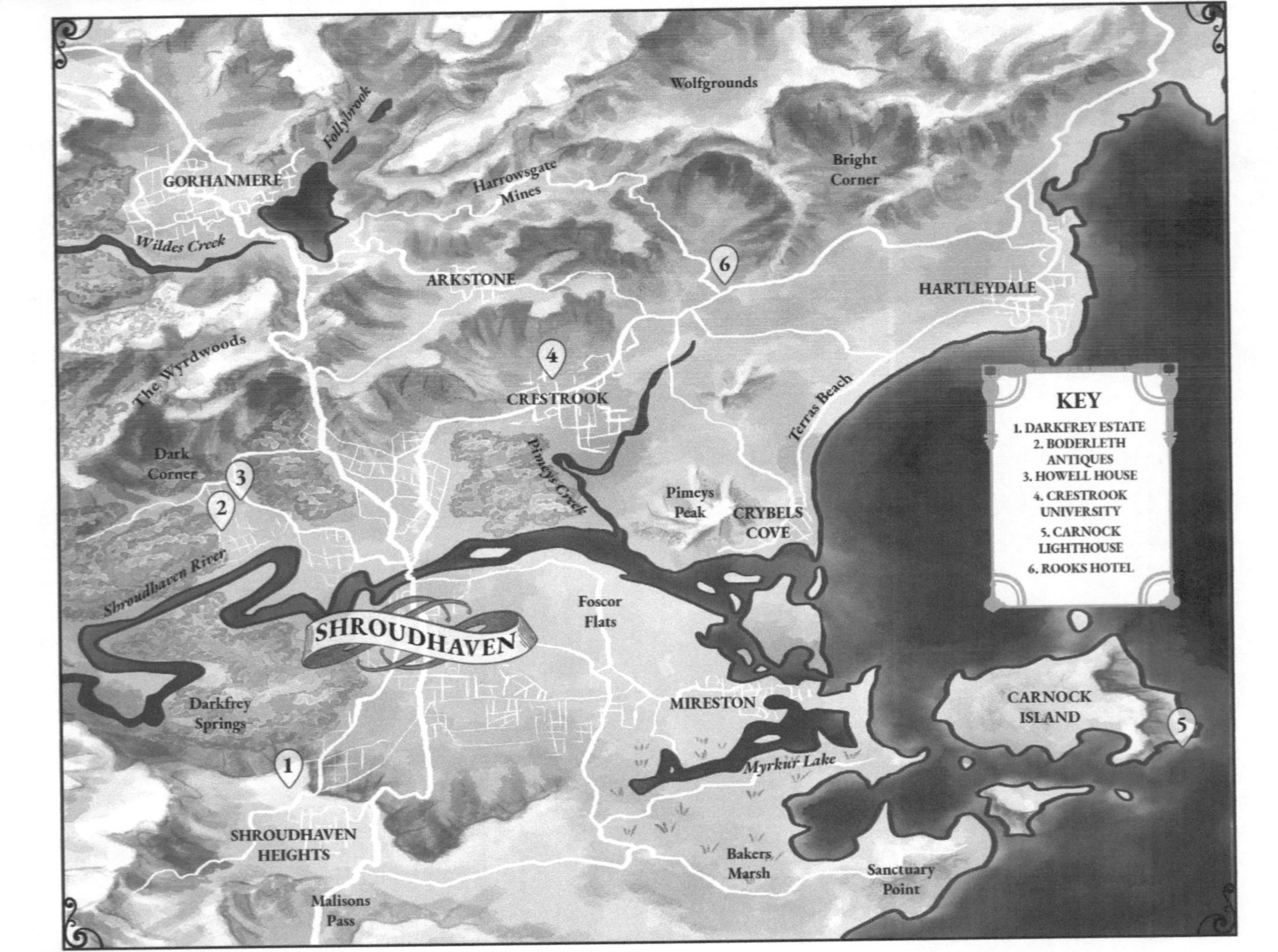

Wolfgrounds
Follybrook
GORHANMERE
Harrowsgate Mines
Bright Corner
Wildes Creek
ARKSTONE
HARTLEYDALE
6
The Wyrdwoods
4
CRESTROOK
Terras Beach
KEY
1. DARKFREY ESTATE
2. BODERLETH ANTIQUES
3. HOWELL HOUSE
4. CRESTROOK UNIVERSITY
5. CARNOCK LIGHTHOUSE
6. ROOKS HOTEL
Dark Corner
3
2
Pimeys Creek
Pimeys Peak
CRYBELS COVE
Shroudhaven River
Foscor Flats
SHROUDHAVEN
Darkfrey Springs
MIRESTON
CARNOCK ISLAND
5
1
Myrkur Lake
SHROUDHAVEN HEIGHTS
Bakers Marsh
Sanctuary Point
Malisons Pass

ABOUT THE AUTHOR

Whether it's painting artworks or writing novels, creating fantasy works is Selina's biggest passion. She lives in Australia with her husband and daughter and loves food, gardening, geekery, and all things fantasy.

FIND OUT MORE ABOUT SELINA

Official Website www.selinafenech.com

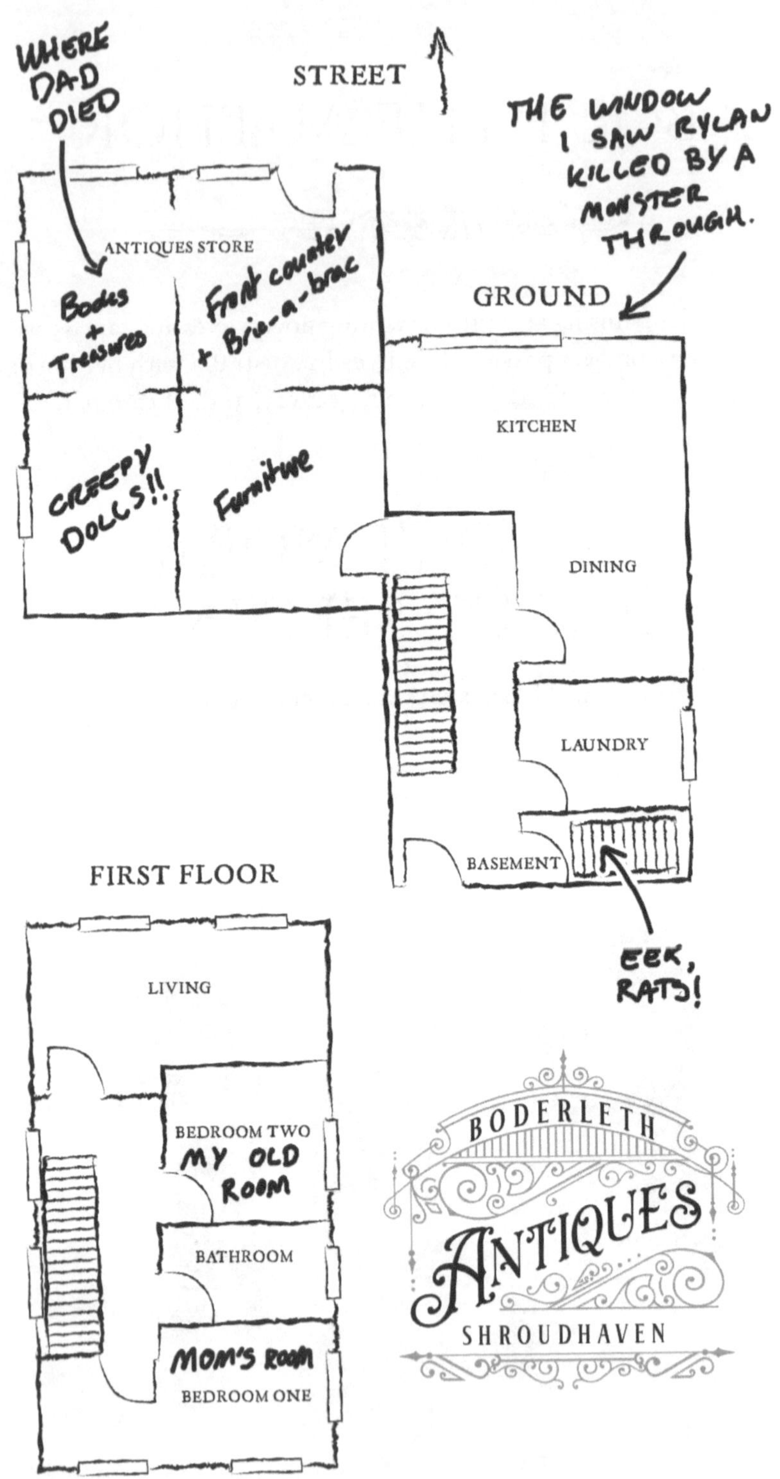

WHERE DAD DIED
STREET
THE WINDOW I SAW RYLAN KILLED BY A MONSTER THROUGH.
GROUND
ANTIQUES STORE
Bodies + Treasures
Front counter + Bric-a-brac
CREEPY DOLLS!!
Furniture
KITCHEN
DINING
LAUNDRY
BASEMENT
EEK, RATS!
FIRST FLOOR
LIVING
BEDROOM TWO
MY OLD ROOM
BATHROOM
MOM'S ROOM
BEDROOM ONE
BODERLETH
ANTIQUES
SHROUDHAVEN

THERE'S A
MERMAID
IN MY
LIGHTHOUSE

THERE'S A MERMAID IN MY LIGHTHOUSE,
AND HER HEART BELONGS TO ME.
THERE'S A MERMAID IN MY LIGHTHOUSE,
SHE KEEPS STARING OUT TO SEA.

PLUCKED FROM UNTAMED TIDES,
MY SWEET PEARL SHE SHINES,
FOR ME, HER EYES BURN,
FOR ME, HER EYES BURN.

HUNGRY LIGHT SHINES OVER THE WAVES
AND MY MERMAID SHE YEARNS,
WHEN WILL I RETURN,
WHEN WILL I RETURN.

THERE'S A MERMAID IN MY LIGHTHOUSE,
AND HER HEART BELONGS TO ME.
THERE'S A MERMAID IN MY LIGHTHOUSE,
TO HER I OWN THE KEY.

MY LOVE FLOWS AS DEEP
AS THE OCEAN'S BLACK HEART,
IT BEATS IN THE NIGHT,
IT BEATS IN THE NIGHT.

FOREVER I WILL GUARD MY TREASURE,
MY PRIZE LOCKED UP SAFE.
MY STAR SHINING BRIGHT,
IN LOVE UNDER THE LIGHT.

MORE BOOKS BY SELINA A. FENECH

Fairy Tale Retellings

Enchanting fairy tale retellings with unconventional romances and twists. Young adult standalone stories.

Empath Chronicles

Teenagers with superpowers fueled by emotions … what could go wrong? A young adult superhero romance.

MORE BOOKS BY SELINA A. FENECH

Memory's Wake Trilogy

A modern girl lost in and hunted in a fairy tale world. An illustrated young adult portal fantasy with Arthurian and Victorian themes.

Shadow Dragon Saga

Into a haunted realm, an impossible creature is born and must be protected. A young adult epic fantasy with dragons.

www.ingramcontent.com/pod-product-compliance
Lightning Source LLC
Chambersburg PA
CBHW060720190726
48285CB00001B/2